M. TOPPING

Heiyah!
The journey begins.
Happy reading,
M. Topping

PARAMERION

outskirtspress
DENVER, COLORADO

Outskirts Press, Inc.
http://www.outskirtspress.com

ISBN: 978-1-4787-5941-6

Outskirts Press and the "OP" logo are trademarks belonging to Outskirts Press, Inc.

PRINTED IN THE UNITED STATES OF AMERICA

Chapter One

"We will not suffer the weak to walk amongst us. You have disobeyed your commanding officer, gone against your Emperor, and dishonored your family. We hereby strip you of your title and condemn you to exile. Go forth friendless, penniless, and nameless. If you ever return here, we will put an end to you; even if you are flesh of mine own flesh. No child of mine will balk at what must be done. Be but a vagabond without home or name," proclaimed the Emperor.

The Emperor looked forbidding as he stood as still as a statue in his straight-lined, amaranthine, floor-length robes. His eyes could have been obsidian, as they were as brumal and cimmerian. He stared at Andraste without compassion. His distinguished brow was set in firm disapproval, while his thin lips pursed in agitation.

"You may disclaim me. You may label me a traitor. However, I would see myself as a traitor towards our Empire were I to step aside," proclaimed Andraste. Despite her Imperial armor, she looked slight and delicate opposing the great form of the Emperor.

"My Emperor, let us not be too hasty. Andraste is young, she has much to learn," pacified the Emperor's eldest son, Brion.

Brion besought his father earnestly. He did not move his sandy hair out of his steel-colored eyes as the wind began to blow. Brion wore the grey robes of a scholar and his ruby, Imperial cape, which swept about him as he approached from the far side of the courtyard. The Emperor's dark eyes did not acknowledge his son's presence at all. The Emperor glowered only at Andraste. She did not yield. The Emperor withdrew his great sword and placed the point on the ground before him. The sound echoed across the silent courtyard. His wide sleeves only revealed his charcoal, leather, gloved hands on the ornate hilt. The blade gleamed red in the afternoon sunlight.

"One last chance, Andraste, execute this man for his crime. You are a Commander of the Imperial Army. If you disobey, you will no longer be of my service or of my family. Either way, he will die," stated the Emperor.

"I shall never kill a man for so little an offense. Is not life more valuable?" Andraste asked as she thrust herself between the kneeling man and the Emperor.

The Emperor pushed one fist into the chest plate of her Imperial Armor. The force of the blow knocked her helmet off, but still Andraste stood before the condemned. Her long, hazel hair fell around her shoulders and she stared determinedly at the Emperor with her sea-green eyes. Her crimson cheeks against her porcelain skin were the only sign of her discomposure.

"Ideals will forever be more valuable than life. If not for our ideals, then what are we to strive for? What else to live by? In order for this Empire to be strong, there will be no exceptions. There will be no mercy. I am ashamed of you. Get out of my sight, Andraste, go now!" bellowed the Emperor.

"Have you forgotten, my Emperor? You are but an earthly sovereign--a ruler of life on this earth. The gods know all and stand witness. Please, do not do this, I beseech you, my Emperor," said Andraste. She bowed to the Emperor and remained in her pose.

The Emperor raised his sword without hesitation and stepped forward.

"Andraste, move!" yelled Brion.

"If you interfere, your punishment will be the same as hers," declared the Emperor.

Brion was already moving across the courtyard to stand by the prostrate warrior, but he was too slow.

The Emperor brought down his great sword down on Andraste and the condemned, so powerful was he that he could take many lives with one blow. However, too many years of grueling training had her blocking the attack before she was conscious of her actions. It was a move for survival that she found her own sword in her hands. With a fluid movement she had disarmed her father. His great sword was flying through the air as if in slow motion. The sound of it hitting the stone of the courtyard echoed menacingly. The silence that followed was even more chilling.

"You dare raise your blade against me? I, who have raised you, taught you everything you know, and groomed you to be my heir?" roared the Emperor. There was not an ounce of forgiveness in his glacial, aphotic eyes.

"Father-" Andraste started, lowering her sword.

She felt mortal fear as her father raised his hand towards her. The strongest sorcerer of the age stood before her without a look of remorse.

"You were forewarned. Death would be too quick a punishment for you. Let all know, any who raise a hand against me or the Empire, shall meet a painful death. I curse you. Let this curse consume you prior to the year's end, and may you wallow in your pain and insignificance," sentenced the Emperor.

As he spoke a violent, swirling orb of shadowy, violaceous smoke gathered around his out-stretched palm. The Emperor did not hesitate for even the briefest of moments. As he stared at Andraste it was if he did not even see her.

"Father-" Andraste began in horror.

She did not finish. A bolt of resplendent, violet lightning shot forth from her father's hand and hit her directly in her shoulder. Not only did it burn, but it felt as though it cut into her soul. Her chest plate fell off useless, and, by its disconnection, the rest of her shoulder armor, sleeve armor and hand guard. The force threw her across the courtyard into the opposite wall, where she lay motionless. It was unlike any pain she had ever known. The mark burned. It was the continuous sensation of being too close to a fire, but unable to move away from it.

She was unable to move as the Emperor beheaded the man that she had tried to save. The Emperor turned on his son.

"As for you, who dared interfere, may you suffer, unable to save the one you tried to protect. No magic or healing power in these lands will save her. May you watch for the next year as she slowly dies. May you be voiceless, so that you may learn the benefits of being silent. Leave now, never again will I ever utter Brion or Andraste," spoke the Emperor, and he turned his back on his children.

Brion felt the cold touch of magic sweep over him like the caress of a dissatisfied lover that had turned sharply into murderous intent. His scarlet, Imperial cape cascaded to the stones beneath his feet in an undignified heap, leaving him only in the grey robes of a scholar.

The power of the second curse had already taken effect. However, even if Brion could have responded, he had no words to say. He examined the dark bruise across Andraste's shoulder. The guards, many they had known for all of their lives, gave them a large breadth as if fearing they too would be cursed by association. No one dared to help them.

"Emperor Ricimer, what about the other prisoners?" asked a guard.

"Kill them all," ordered the Emperor.

Brion picked up his motionless sister and began walking out of the stone courtyard. He looked down at his sister and was grateful that she had lost consciousness. For many years to come, he would never forget those screams.

Brion started to descend the great staircase that led to the next level of the Citadel. He felt eyes upon them from the sandalwood latticed windows of the red painted structures. It was as if the ornate, tiled golden roofs that dipped and magnificent red columns had eyes themselves. The golden and scarlet lanterns that once looked so welcoming, now appeared to him as a warning. The candles within the hanging lanterns burned with contempt.

Brion crossed the bridge over the moat. The sea-green waters lapped tranquilly against the enclosure. Even as the cold winds of the North blew the last of the leaves from the trees, a few starlight-colored water lilies still bloomed. He headed down yet another level and reached the stables. Still he did not see a soul. Not one person that he had known since infancy dared to help them. His heart grew cold and unforgiving.

Brion gently laid his sister in a pile of hay. He had so recently arrived at the Citadel that his own horse has not yet been unpacked. He was lucky, as he needed everything that was in his saddlebags now that he was an exile. However, he had nothing for Andraste.

"Lord Brion," whispered a voice from the shadows. A plump dark-haired woman thrust two saddlebags at him and Andraste's bow and quiver.

"For my lady," whispered the woman. Her name was Paulina. She was wife to a great warrior, Laelius, who was Andraste's mentor. Brion wondered why Laelius had not come himself. Paulina risked her own life to aid them.

Paulina's sepia-colored eyes glistened with tears as she put a well-used hand to examine the pulse of the unconscious Andraste. Brion hesitated in his actions as he watched Paulina tend to his sister. He wondered why Andraste had come alone, and not brought her unit or squadrons. However, he lacked the ability to voice his questions.

Brion took Paulina's offerings and bowed low to the woman. Paulina had hurried back into the shadows and out of the stables before he had even raised his head. Brion saw that Andraste's own horse had already been saddled. Someone had secured an ancient sword to her saddle and two bedrolls. A thick, charcoal cloak had also been thrown over the saddle. Brion secured the saddlebags and rucksack to Andraste's horse. He then picked up Andraste and lifted her on to his own horse. He mounted behind her, and took the reins of Andraste's horse. It followed obediently.

As they rode out of the Citadel, Brion surveyed the magnificent red columns, scarlet painted structures, ornate, tiled golden roofs that dipped, and temples. He committed them to memory. He wondered if he would ever lay eyes upon his homeland ever again. Before he rode out of the Citadel, he stopped briefly at a stone statue of a Luduan. The statue had the body of lion, but the head of a dragon with a long mane and the claws of a dragon. It had a single horn protruding from its head. Its gray stone eyes surveyed Brion with compassion. The statue had stood on those grounds millennia before the Citadel had been constructed. Brion placed a hand on the statue's broad chest. He prayed for justice and truth to be restored to the Empire once more.

Brion looked down at his unconscious sister. He knew that the fate of the Empire relied on the reversal of the spell and her full recovery. He prayed with all of his heart and soul. He took one last look of the stone Luduan. He urged his horse onto the open road, and left his homeland without a backward glance.

It was three days before Andraste woke.

She felt as though she was being rocked in a hammock. Her eyes adjusted. She was inside a tiny, wooden room that smelled strongly of salt and the sea. The wooden walls had not been treated in decades. It had no windows. Due to the darkness of the room, she was unsure of the hour, which left her feeling more disoriented. The only furniture it possessed was a bed. The sheets were both thin and coarse. She could hear seagulls calling and the sound of waves. She could smell brackish water.

Brion leaned over her as he realized she was awake.

"Where do we go?" she asked. Her voice was hoarse and unattractive.

He did not answer her. Andraste noticed he no longer wore the robes of a scholar. He was dressed in the attire of a mercenary. Her own attire had been changed into the same trade. She felt naked without her Imperial armor and cloak that had so long protected her.

"Why do you not answer me?" inquired Andraste.

Brion slowly poured her a glass of water and fixed her with a pointed gaze. His steel-gray eyes were not unkind.

The memories came rushing back to her like a spring flood after substantial snows. Her bruise seared with pain as she thought of the bolt of lightning striking and penetrating her shoulder. She dropped the glass of water and it hit the floor. Water poured forth in all directions. Brion picked it up, poured her another glass, and offered it to her.

"You must hate me," she stated.

Brion pushed the glass towards her. She took it gingerly and looked to Brion. He gestured for her to proceed. She drank it greedily as if she had never tasted water before.

"What is our destination?" she asked. He stared at her as if willing for her to say the answer.

"We travel by sea. You are taking me to my uncle's lands? To the Island Kingdoms?" she asked.

He gave the slightest inclination of his head in confirmation.

"The land across the sea is known for their healers, but they cannot fix this. Not dark magic, you know that," she said, and looked at her brother, "You are taking us there for sanctuary? So I can live out of the rest of my days in relative peace?"

His eyes narrowed. He already knew what she was going to say.

"This is no time for sanctuary. I refuse to yield. We must thwart the Emperor. He no longer hears reason. I must become more powerful. We must find a way-" she was stopped as Brion picked up the pitcher and threw the contents in her face.

She stared at him speechless. She blinked a few times, and then used a coarse, thin blanket to dry her face.

"I may have little time left, but in that time I will follow my heart. Will you give away to tyranny, brother? Will you step aside to complacency? It is now that we must fight. Today is all we have. We must right the wrongs of our father for our homeland, for our people, for our family, and for ourselves," besought Andraste.

Brion was unmoved.

"I will journey forth to the Darklands," announced Andraste.

Brion shook his head.

"It is our only chance, our one and only opportunity to prevail," she said. He pointed at her.

"We disguise ourselves. I know the perils. But we are nameless. We are without country. We can prove our values as warriors. Before I was born you were a warrior of some renown, even as a boy. Our path leads to swords, not books. Your mother's people were a fierce mountain clan. Your mother fought herself against the Emperor-" Andraste stopped as Brion smoldered at her.

She had never mentioned his mother before. Her father's first wife had not been a love match, hardly the case. Brion's mother had been executed for plotting against the Emperor. The Emperor had not taken long to take a second wife, her own mother, and oddly, enough her mother had loved her father. Her own birth had secured her place as the heir to the Empire, and Brion and his two brothers had been swept aside. Brion had been sent to the Imperial University. He was no longer permitted to be taught swordplay or magic as it may have endangered her claim. It had been a rare act of mercy on behalf of the Emperor. It was only two of such actions that she knew of. The other act was the sparing of her life, even if by a year.

"I am not bloodthirsty. I do not yearn for battle, but if we do not act, who will?" she asked.

Brion's eyes narrowed even further. He glowered at her. He crossed his muscular arms in front of his chest.

"I am no child. You do not have to follow me, Brion. I do not ask that of you. Each of us must follow our own path. I recognize that as the way of the world," Andraste said gently.

Brion glared at her in betrayal. She knew what he had sacrificed for her, and it cut her deeply. Her shoulder throbbed, and involuntarily, she put a hand to it. The bruise seemed darker than before. It was a painful reminder of everything that she had lost.

Brion was tapping the table to get her attention. He looked at her with concern.

"Do not trouble yourself. I am well," she lied.

She stretched out her arm and moved each of her fingers. Brion reached for her outreached hand, and grasped her slender fingers in his large ones. Sea-green and storm-gray eyes met. By his unwavering look of love and determination, she knew that Brion had decided to come with her.

The siblings departed the boat two stops before her uncle's lands. They got off at a small fishing town that Andraste had never even heard of. She doubted it was even on a map. The boarded windows of the houses, taverns and shops betrayed no sign of their inhabitants. Not a single door was open. She did not see a single person walking around the village. Nonetheless, she felt as though they were being watched closely. What troubled Andraste the most was the unearthly silence. There was not a familiar sound from the bustling village, not a sound of the village's inhabitants.

There was only one other traveler from their boat, who departed at the same village. He wore no distinguishing colors or insignia. He was uncommonly tall, even taller than Brion. He had broad shoulders and carried a broadsword across his back. His long hair was tied back in a ponytail and was a deep red shade, which was unusual for those parts. As if sensing her study, he turned to look at her. His eyes were a startling blue, deep like sapphires.

Andraste was glad that she had fully secured her hair and hood in order to obscure her appearance. Brion wrapped his cloak tightly around him as he took their horses from the deck hand. He led them towards the road out of town and Andraste wordlessly followed. When they were away from the docks, Andraste turned to Brion.

"If we were followed, then it is a wise choice that we did not head straight to my uncle's. We would have only brought him pain," surmised Andraste.

Brion stood surveying the horizon behind her. He had also noticed the ship hoisting the colors of the Empire coming into port. The Imperial ship bore the red irregular sails that resembled dragon wings. The red sails were stunning against the warm glow of the setting sun over the deep blue seas.

Andraste picked a closed alabaster bloom from the verdigris hedgerow. It smelled of the last of summer. It smelled of memories of peace from long ago.

She would have liked a night at an Inn before they started on the road, but she knew they did not have the time or the luxury at they once did. They could at least find somewhere to camp off the road. The fewer people that saw them or they talked to the better.

"Good morrow," a deep voice called to her. She was struck by the voice. Although he spoke only two common words, he conveyed confidence and authority. It was a voice that was distinguished and could not be ignored.

Andraste turned to face the speaker, lowering the bloom in her hand as she did so. Brion was immediately between her and the approaching traveler. The traveler led a fine white stallion by its lead. Andraste realized he was the same auburn-haired traveler from the boat.

"Show some fortitude, man! All I issued was a greeting. See, I am but one traveler. Forgive me. I did not mean to frighten you," apologized the traveler. He bowed eloquently.

His accent was warm. He spoke slowly and deliberately as if every word had profound significance, which was typical of those from the Southern lands. He was overly polite, yet another indicator of the Southern lands. The traveler slowly raised himself from his bowed position, awaiting their response. Brion did not move, lower his guard or step aside from Andraste.

He even put his hand to his hilt.

"Our courage is resolute. We do not fear one man," stated Andraste.

She still continued to survey the traveler. As he approached, she realized he was younger then she had first thought. However, his eyes made him seem older. They possessed a sadness and intelligence that intrigued her.

"And what flower have you gleaned from the hedgerow?" asked the traveler as he reached Brion's side.

"It is a Northern stargazer. They only bloom at night," replied Andraste. She threw it to the traveler and he caught it with his left hand. He examined the blossom. He raised his sapphire eyes to her.

"My name is Aldrich. Might I travel with you so long as we share the same road? The bandits and thieves in these parts are a menace," asserted the traveler.

Brion looked at Andraste and shook his head adamantly.

"Where does your journey take you?" she asked.

"Down this road a way. And you?" queried Aldrich.

"The same direction. If you mean us no harm, then I will allow it. However, if you try anything, you should know my comrade is a fierce warrior, and he will cut you down without a thought," warned Andraste.

"And, you, my nameless friend, are you also a warrior?" catechized Aldrich.

"Yes," replied Andraste.

"Are Northerners always so unfriendly?" inquired Aldrich.

"Yes," Andraste surmised unflinchingly. To her surprise, the traveler laughed.

"Are Northerners always so honest?" questioned Aldrich with a bemused smile.

"Yes," concluded Andraste.

"That may or may not be true. What is the saying? Yes, a Northerner may never lie to you, but they may not tell you the truth either," said Aldrich.

"Probably has as much merit as the saying, 'A Southerner always speaks the truth regardless of cost, detriment, or sense'," replied Andraste.

Aldrich smiled in response and looked towards Brion, who was trying to catch Andraste's eye. Brion gestured towards the road. His side glance to the harbor did not escape her.

"We should not tarry. The sun will not accompany us for long," settled Andraste.

Not seeing if the traveler followed, she spurred her horse down the road. Brion quickly joined her side.

It was lonely country. The land was flat, made of tall grasses and offered little cover. Its only advantage was that they could see for miles in all directions. The tall grasses were golden and rustled by a western wind. Andraste saw bison grazing in the east. The animals paid them little heed. Due to the flatness of the land, the sky seemed infinite. The clouds were like silent giants padding overhead.

They rode on and did not take a single rest. Twilight came and went, and they rode by the light of the moon. The grasses appeared almost silver in the moonlight. The stars shined brightly overhead and pointed their direction. However, they were obliged to stop as clouds obscured the light of the moon and their starry compass.

"Do you always make such haste?" probed Aldrich as she dismounted. She was impressed that he had kept pace with them.

"Do you always ask so many questions?" she retaliated.

"Touché," responded Aldrich. He dismounted and turned to Brion.

"Does your comrade do all of the talking?" he asked Brion, who was taking a brush out of his saddlebag.

"My comrade is mute," said Andraste, wincing as she did. She was glad that her horse was between them so the traveler could not see her reaction.

"I meant no offense," apologized Aldrich.

Brion shrugged in response and continued to brush his horse.

"Have you traveled together long?" asked Aldrich.

Andraste was starting to be irritated by all of his questions. A Northerner would never be so presumptuous.

"He is my brother," answered Andraste.

"It must be wonderful to have a constant companion. All of my brothers are dead," disclosed Aldrich softly.

Brion stopped grooming his horse and looked pointedly at Andraste. He was trying to tell her something, but she was not sure what it was. He nodded his head towards Aldrich, whose back was turned. Brion waved his hand to her as if to continue.

"That is most unfortunate," she said.

Brion continued to motion with his hand. He stopped as Aldrich turned back towards them.

"They must have been young to succumb to such an early demise. Many youths pass so early these days. What was the cause?" she asked.

"The Black War," divulged Aldrich.

Seldom people spoke of such things. As a Commander for the Imperial Army, she normally would have had her hand on her hilt ready to draw her blade: a Southern traveler traveling by moonlight in Northern lands talking about losing family in the Black War. It did not add up. As a Southerner, he would have been fighting against her people. What was he doing in the North? Travel visas from the South were extremely rare.

"So many died on both sides," lamented Andraste, trying to defuse the tension. She did not know how the mood had changed so quickly.

"Did you lose anyone?" inquired Aldrich.

"My mother," admitted Andraste. She wondered why she acknowledged such a thing. She never spoke of it. No one ever spoke of the loss that drove the Emperor mad.

"I am sorry for your loss," responded Aldrich.

Aldrich was watching Brion carefully. Andraste was positive Brion was trying to tell her something now. Brion was looking increasingly frustrated.

"How fares your brother?" inquired Aldrich.

Andraste realized at that moment what Brion was trying to tell her. He had become more insistent. This time it was not regarding Aldrich.

She heard the hissing of a blade through the air. Effortlessly, she put a hand to her sleeve and withdrew the concealed dagger. She lunged at Aldrich. Aldrich cried out in alarm, but side-stepped her, reaching for his own blade. Andraste struck Aldrich's attacker in one blow and the attacker fell lifeless before he even hit the ground. A second attacker was already upon her, but Brion struck him down with an arrow.

As the moon came out from behind the clouds, Andraste lunged at a warrior barreling out of the darkness. He was wearing full Imperial armor. These were not mere thieves and bandits. The attacker wore heliotrope robes, and he brandished an Imperial sword. Andraste knew it instantly as the sound of her blade hit his, and the ringing resounded through the crisp, night air. The Imperial blade's design was that of one made for an officer. The swordsman was not one that she recognized, signifying he was one of the Emperor's personal guards. The Emperor's personal troops and officers were only known to the Emperor. However, this officer was no match for Andraste. She quickly dispatched him.

Andraste turned and found Aldrich fighting three warriors. With a mighty blow, Aldrich struck two down at once. The resemblance to her father at that moment was uncanny. She remembered the Emperor coming towards her and the prisoner, raising his great sword. Her heart rate quickened.

She felt the feathers of an arrow scrape by her cheek and she dodged the sword coming for her side. The arrow met its mark and her assailant fell to the ground.

"That makes seven. There should be one more," Andraste announced to Brion. It did not escape her that the men at her feet were her countrymen.

It was Aldrich, who took down the remaining man. Andraste winced. However, she could not keep her eyes off Aldrich. He would be a match for her, if she had to fight him.

Silence once again enveloped them. The moon hid behind clouds once more. Andraste debated whether she and Brion should escape under the cover of darkness. The bruise on her arm was burning. She found it hard to concentrate.

"I apologize. I am the reason for this attack. I truly regret that I put you both in danger," confessed Aldrich.

He bowed to them in the darkness. Brion had already found his way to her side. Brion looked to her. She wished that Brion could speak for them.

"Why were they after you?" she interrogated.

"I fight for the Resistance," answered Aldrich, "I wrongly thought that I had lost all of my pursuers in the Midlands."

Aldrich dropped to one knee.

"Are you injured?" asked Andraste. She was already reaching into her saddle bag.

"It is but a scratch," speculated Aldrich.

"They use poisoned blades," informed Andraste. Brion took her horse by the reins and led it forward.

"How do you know that?" asked Aldrich.

Andraste ignored him. Brion had already mounted his horse and was leading her horse to her by the reins.

"We cannot leave him to die," she hissed.

Brion leaned from his horse and used one finger to push directly into her cursed shoulder.

"I know, we need to go, but I shall not leave him to die," she repeated.

Brion's shoulders slumped and he took a deep breath. He looked to the stars for patience, but they were hidden again behind shadowy clouds.

Andraste took a bottle and a bandage out of her bag. She hurried to Aldrich's side. She took off her gloves and dropped some of the liquid onto a bandage and carefully applied the bandage without touching the infected area herself. Aldrich let out a hiss of pain. He gritted his teeth as to not make a sound. Andraste had seen battle-tried men scream in agony at the application of this ointment.

She felt something soft hit her face. Brion had thrown her an additional roll of bandages, but had no way to warn her in the darkness.

"Thank you, Brion," she uttered softly. She proceeded to wrap the cloth around Aldrich's arm.

"That is an unusual name," commented Aldrich, and then he passed out.

Brion wacked her on her head as he passed.

"It might be unusual in the South, but in the North it is fairly common!" defended Andraste.

Brion dismounted in order to help Andraste throw Aldrich over his horse. They had no way to secure him. Aldrich made no indication of realizing his predicament. Once more, Brion tried to convey her hence.

"He will fall," cautioned Andraste.

Brion impatiently boosted her onto the horse behind Aldrich. Aldrich's stallion snorted in displeasure. Andraste soothed the stallion. Brion had already mounted and taken her horse by the reins. Making sure that Aldrich was secure, she then proceeded into the night.

They rode until the horses could go no farther. Luckily they were out of the plains and were well into the forest. The trees were ancient and ranged from eighty to one-hundred feet. There were oak, beech, maple, linden and sweet gums. Brion had led them off the main road and deep into the shelter of the woods. An owl called out to them as they passed, letting them know that he was watching.

Andraste felt Aldrich stir.

"Easy," chided Andraste. She placed a hand on his back to make sure he settled. He did not fight her.

She gestured to Brion to make camp. Brion dismounted and then came to help her put Aldrich on the ground. Andraste surveyed Aldrich's wound. Brion took first watch, while Andraste changed Aldrich's bandages and forced him to take some water. She found a spot on the opposite side of the clearing. She fell asleep almost as soon as her head hit the ground.

She woke and felt that someone was watching her. Brion had placed blankets on her, and secured her hood. Making sure it was still in place, she sat up slowly.

Aldrich was watching her carefully.

"Thank you for your aid. Where did you learn such healing arts?" asked Aldrich. Although his sapphire eyes were lowered, she knew he was calculating her with every second.

"It is a soldier's knowledge," stated Andraste. She rose deliberately and stretched.

"Uh-huh," murmured Aldrich.

"May I see?" asked Andraste. He looked at her with mistrust, and drew his arm away.

"If I wanted you dead, between those warriors and that wound, you would be," reasoned Andraste.

Gingerly he let her look at his wound. The potion seemed to have worked to its fullest potential. It looked like a regular wound. It would take a few days to heal, and he would need help in the meantime.

"It needs to be cleaned," said Andraste. She saw that Brion had already started boiling water, but he was nowhere to be seen.

"He went to hunt," remarked Aldrich. An awkward silence fell between them.

"If we are to be traveling together, I should be able to call you something. It does not have to be real your name," offered Aldrich.

Andraste was relieved. Aldrich had forgotten that she had called her brother by his true name. Aldrich was still waiting for her response. His mouth was set in a firm frown as the silence lengthened. She began to tend to Aldrich's wound.

"I have no name," confided Andraste.

"No name?" asked Aldrich incredulously, and he raised an eyebrow.

"It was taken from me," confessed Andraste.

"Where are you from? I could call you after your county," suggested Aldrich.

"I have no country," replied Andraste. She felt as though her heart had shrunk to the size of a walnut.

"No name and no country. I at least have a name, even if my country no longer exists," mentioned Aldrich softly. His sapphire eyes locked on Andraste. He asked, "Who took them from you?"

"The Emperor," stated Andraste, but her heart was saying my father. It repeated it over and over again in her mind.

Brion had entered the clearing, carrying two rabbits, but Andraste knew he had been watching them for some time.

"I see you fight with a Paramerion. That is a curious weapon to use for this age. However, what is a warrior known by but by his fighting style? If you have no objection, I will call you Paramerion," said Aldrich.

"That is a mouthful," objected Andraste. Brion seemed to like the sound of it.

"And what should I call you?" asked Aldrich. Brion held up his bow.

"Well is it not obvious? Call him Loudmouth," she stated. Brion opened his mouth and laughed soundlessly.

"You Northerners are a strange bunch," observed Aldrich.

"While if we were not laughing, we would be weeping and what good would that do us?" proposed Andraste.

Aldrich moved to help Brion skin the rabbits, but Brion pointed to Aldrich's corner. Andraste stood to do the same and Brion flourished the same motion.

"Are you injured as well?" inquired Aldrich. He seemed very concerned despite just meeting her twelve hours before.

"It is an old wound. It is healing, but my brother is oversensitive. He is older, and accordingly, perceives himself as the she bear and me as his cub," reprimanded Andraste.

Brion did not respond in any way. He continued to prepare the rabbits. Aldrich produced a loaf of pumpernickel bread from his pack and threw her a third.

"Now that we have fought and bled together, will you tell me where you are headed?" questioned Aldrich.

"The Darklands," replied Andraste.

Aldrich lowered the piece of bread he was about to consume.

"Whatever for?" asked Aldrich.

"I search for a weapon powerful enough to defeat the Emperor," reported Andraste.

"You would state such a purpose to a stranger?" questioned Aldrich.

"Did you not state you fought for the Resistance?" retorted Andraste. Aldrich smiled and showed pearly white teeth.

"You mean to enter the Ruins?" inquired Aldrich.

Andraste put down her meal. Aldrich must have received a noble education to realize her intentions so quickly. Brion was watching Aldrich with new found curiosity. Under different circumstance, Andraste could picture the two in a tavern discussing obscure footnotes over a pint. The image tickled her.

"Yes," replied Andraste.

"No one has ever returned," cautioned Aldrich.

"You must have seen warriors with Ruin blades in your travels. If it cannot be done, then where did the warriors obtain the blades?" countered Andraste.

"I just wanted to verify you were as crazy as I am," remarked Aldrich.

"You mean to enter the Ruins as well?" questioned Andraste.

Aldrich nodded in confirmation. Brion looked from Andraste to Aldrich and back again.

"Your brother does not approve your plan," commented Aldrich.

"No," conceded Andraste.

"But he is going with you anyway?" asked Aldrich.

"Yes," answered Andraste.

"Loudmouth that makes you more deranged than either of us," rejoined Aldrich.

Brion scowled at him, while Andraste laughed. She could not remember the last time she had laughed. Brion seemed startled by the sound.

"You two must be in serious trouble," said Aldrich softly. He peered at Andraste with his sapphire eyes. Andraste's merriment faded immediately. She shrugged and stood.

"Eat quickly. We need to get moving," she ordered.

"But the rabbit," protested Aldrich. Andraste looked unconvinced.

"Loudmouth, do you want to eat it raw?" asked Aldrich. Brion shook his head.

"You are outvoted," declared Aldrich.

Brion proceeded to roast the rabbits over the fire. Andraste refused to admit defeat. Instead she turned on Aldrich.

"What takes you to the Darklands?" asked Andraste.

"I also seek a weapon to defeat the Emperor," replied Aldrich.

"For what offense?" questioned Andraste, "Or is it just retribution for the Black Wars?"

"I would not fight for so low a cause as revenge," growled Aldrich.

"Then for what cause?" inquired Andraste.

"For equality and freedom," stated Aldrich.

"The Empire's laws are the same in every part of the Empire," replied Andraste.

"It would seem so to a Northerner," rejoined Aldrich, "What is the penalty for a Southerner to enter Northern lands without a visa?"

"Death," answered Andraste.

"Is the penalty the same if a Northerner enters Southern lands without a visa?" asked Aldrich.

"No, but travel is restricted in the North for Northerners as well. It is dangerous country. Additionally, the movement of individuals is monitored by the government in all areas of the Empire," replied Andraste.

"Should not a man be able to travel without the tallying of a bureaucrat?" asked Aldrich.

"It is for all of our security that travelers are surveyed. There have been many acts of terrorism. Do you think inconvenience is parallel to death?" asked Andraste.

"But if a man calculates the risk and chooses to proceed, why should he not?" retaliated Aldrich.

"You would choose freedom over security?" questioned Andraste.

"If only I had the choice to decide," responded Aldrich.

"Do not blame the North. You have already decided. You are here are you not?" retaliated Andraste.

"I have entered the Northern lands on my own volition. However, if I am caught by Northern troops, I will be executed. Is life so worthless that it can be forfeited for merely crossing an imaginary line drawn by men?" asked Aldrich.

"Laws are instituted to protect the people. Laws are formed to create order. To disobey our laws is to undermine the order that governs our society," replied Andraste.

"And if the people have no say in those laws? Are they to succumb to the will of one man?" questioned Aldrich.

"The Emperor is not to be questioned," responded Andraste. However, she did not convince even herself with her response.

"And what are you taxed in the North?" questioned Aldrich. Brion shot him a murderous look.

"Taxes are high across the Empire for all, even in the North. The penalties for not paying are high," retorted Andraste. She did not look at Aldrich.

"Under Southern rule, taxes were never so high that citizens could not pay. They were never sent to work camps. We cannot afford to buy the goods provided by the North. We have no way to protest. We have no voice. We have no representation," argued Aldrich.

"One does not protest the Emperor. Even those who were born in the North," admonished Andraste.

"The punishment for dissent is death. Never in our combined histories has rule been so absolute and totalitarian. Those who have fought in the Resistance or led rebellions have been executed. Yet, they have no way to voice their grievances without fighting. There is suffering in all of the lands that I have traveled. There is anger and discontent," stated Aldrich.

"I have traveled the lands as well, and seen what you have seen. However, it is not solely the fault of the North. I have seen corruption. I have seen greed. You cannot throw all of the problems of the Empire as the fault of the North," insisted Andraste.

"Yes, but who leads the Empire? Which realm has all of the seats of power? Which realm produces the most Commanders for the Imperial Army?" inquired Aldrich.

"The Imperial Army is drafted from all of the Empire," stated Andraste.

"One should choose if he should fight or not. One should not have to fight rebellions in his homeland, fight his own countrymen," replied Aldrich.

"I have dealt with the Resistance, with rebellions. I have seen honor, courage and mercy performed by the Northerners you so despise. It is true the Emperor needs to be disposed, but I will not hear all of the North so criticized," said Andraste.

"You are from the North then?" questioned Aldrich.

"I spent my youth enlisted in the Imperial Army, so I have traveled extensively throughout the Empire," answered Andraste.

"Perhaps your travels have been more instructive then mine," said Aldrich.

"Perhaps we see things differently," rejoined Andraste.

"Did I anger you?" asked Aldrich.

"It was only conversation for the road," replied Andraste.

"If I offended you, I apologize," responded Aldrich.

"I am not offended," returned Andraste, "I hope that I am able to reverse your opinion of the North."

"I may never agree with you, but I will not oppose your right to speak," said Aldrich.

"I look forward to many more discussions," returned Andraste. She turned to Brion who was watching them carefully. He seemed amused.

"What?" asked Andraste. Brion shrugged and returned to cooking the rabbits.

"Your brother likes a good fight?" asked Aldrich to Brion.

Aldrich bent to try to get something out of his pack. Andraste stopped in her tracks. Brion shot her a look over his shoulder. Aldrich raised his head to determine why there had been no response from either. Brion just nodded at Aldrich in agreement. If the Empire was looking for a man and a woman traveling together, it would be better for her to be travelling disguised as a man. She continued to wear her cloak. It was all for the better if she had no face.

Due to his wounds and exhaustion from the road, Aldrich slept whenever they made camp, which kept him from asking too many questions. He seemed to understand her intentions, but he let it pass unquestioned. He was a cheerful traveling companion and excellent hunter, even injured. She had seen few who could match him. Brion grudgingly admired him as well.

Andraste had hoped that the aching in her shoulder would lessen as time passed, but to no avail. Despite fortified meals and adequate rest, her shoulder continued to ache. She also thought that the bruise was getting bigger, but she hoped it was just paranoia. Brion fussed over her like a mother hen. She also knew her suffering was nothing compared to Brion's losses and his anxiety over the curse.

Brion drove them at a fierce pace towards the Darklands. The road was lonely and the countryside nearly silent. It felt as though winter had come too early. The air was pregnant with pause as if waiting for a winter storm. A fierce wind plagued them from the North. It howled at her back as if trying to pull her back towards her homeland. The trees danced to a melody only they could hear, but the storm never came.

Andraste saw movement ahead in the distance and saw a camp of vultures either seated on the ground or circling lazily overhead. The vultures watched them approach, with calculating, hungry eyes. The fowl squawked amongst themselves as if predicting the days the trio of travelers had yet to live. One even seemed to smile at her and open its beak in expectation as if tasting the aroma of an upcoming appetizer.

"The vultures here are rebarbative," commented Aldrich.

"Have no fear, traveler. Look at how distended and potbellied they are. They have dined recently, frequently, and well," responded Andraste.

"You are also rebarbative," replied Aldrich. Brion smiled as he looked to Andraste for her response.

As they rode their horses closer, the vultures did not take to the sky. The fowl were watching them with beady, expectant eyes. Andraste slowed to study them, but Brion quickened his horse's pace to a gallop and Aldrich followed. Andraste did not want to be left behind, so she urged her horse ahead.

Andraste was relieved when they came upon a small village. However, not one person greeted them. The trees around the village had been cleared in order to make room for farmland. However, they did not see anyone in the fields despite it being the end of harvest season, nor did the fields look like they had been tended for some time.

"This is the second village we have encountered that is uninhabited," said Andraste. She surveyed the fields wearily, and then looked to Aldrich.

"Those who cannot pay their taxes are rounded up to work in the mines," stated Aldrich.

"Commander Matthias is responsible for the Southern and Midlands. He allows this?" asked Andraste.

"I have no qualms regarding Commander Matthias except that he has not visited the Southern lands in some time as he has been fighting slavers in the Southwest. His minions do not adhere to the Northern laws," replied Aldrich.

They rode throughout the village, and came across rows of fresh dug graves. Andraste stopped her horse.

"What happened here?" asked Andraste.

Aldrich shook his head. Brion continued riding on ahead.

"Your brother is unbothered," said Aldrich.

"He is anxious to reach the Darklands. We can do nothing for the dead," replied Andraste. She pushed her horse to catch up with Brion.

They had not ridden long before they came upon a wagon that had seen better days, being pulled by two, gangling, undernourished and graying oxen. The people they ferried seemed in slightly better condition, but only slightly.

"Good morrow," called Aldrich as they rode into hearing distance.

"Good morrow," responded a man wearily. He eyed the three riders with distrust. A small boy and girl were seated next to him. He pulled his wagon to the side of the road to allow the riders to pass. Brion rode ahead and waited agitatedly as Andraste and Aldrich stopped to speak to the wagoner.

"You are the first soul we have seen in days," said Aldrich.

"There are many souls about, but most likely buried," replied the wagoner.

"How do you mean?" asked Aldrich.

"There is trouble in the North. Rogue military bands have left the North and are taking whatever they please. We left our village to attend the fair in the Midlands to sell my wares. When we returned, our village was destroyed and everyone we knew dead," replied the wagoner.

"What will you do?" inquired Aldrich.

"We will return to the Midlands. I have a brother who lives there. Perhaps the cities will be safer in these troubled times," replied the wagoner.

Andraste watched the children. They were silent and watched their father carefully. They were fragile and underweight. Their young eyes watched their every movement with terror.

"You look hungry," said Andraste. She reached slowly into her saddle bags and pulled out three apples.

"Can you catch?" asked Andraste.

The little boy nodded. She threw the apples to the boy. He caught each one and passed two to his sister. She held them in her lap.

"Many thanks," said the wagoner. He nodded to his children, and they bit hungrily into the apples. He did not take the third.

"I wish you luck on your journey," replied Andraste.

"And to you. Where are you headed?" asked the wagoner.

"We head towards the Shadow Mountains," answered Aldrich.

"A dangerous place, I would not go there. Keep your luck, you will need it more than I," responded the wagoner. Andraste passed the wagon and joined Brion. Aldrich slowly followed her.

"Hardly amiable," commented Aldrich as they rode out of hearing distance.

"That was practically a blessing for a Northerner," responded Andraste, "Our reality is harsh. We have not the time for the pleasantries of the South."

"They will most likely encounter trouble on this road. We could ride with them a ways," suggested Aldrich.

"We will encounter many more with tragic tales and desperate situations. We will aid them and many more by reaching the Darklands," maintained Andraste.

Aldrich looked over his shoulder to the wagon. The little boy waved at him, and Aldrich returned the gesture. The boy's father rested his free hand on the boy's head.

"We will only bring them more trouble if we remain with them," cautioned Andraste.

Aldrich rode on in silent agreement, but he was not pleased. Brion urged his horse into a gentle trot, and Andraste followed. They did not speak further on their journey.

Near midday they reached a decrepit, stone bridge crossing an overflowing river. Brion slowed and waited for Andraste to reach his side. The bridge was guarded by a group of warriors in various states of disheveled, lousy and mismatched Imperial uniforms, furs, and armor. Brion looked at her and then slowly urged his horse forward.

A scrawny warrior left the group and barred their path. He was covered in filth and missing several teeth. The stench of him nearly made Andraste topple from her horse. However, she showed no signs of discomfort. She watched the warrior approach.

"By order of the Emperor, you must pay our toll if you wish to pass," announced the warrior. He was average height and build. He raised a spear towards Brion. It was evident he had little experience with such a weapon.

"You are a bunch of lying scavengers. Northern troops would not be in such disarray. Besides there is no toll on this road. Move aside and I will let you live," replied Andraste.

"We outnumber you: five to one. The odds are in our favor. Pay the toll, and we will allow you to live," rejoined the warrior. He raised his spear higher.

"You are a coward and a thief. This is your last chance to step aside," warned Andraste.

The warrior pushed his spear threateningly towards Brion. It caught on Brion's hood and was pulled down. The warrior stepped back in alarm, and then threw himself to the ground prostrate at Brion's feet.

"My apologies, my lord. I did not recognize you," said the man. The warriors behind him knelt to one knee as well.

Brion glared at the man and then urged his horse to jump over the man's prostrate form. He continued onto the bridge. Andraste's eyes were still locked on the would-be highwayman. She heard the hoof beats of Brion's horse fade into the distance. Aldrich's horse stomped uneasily at her side.

"You are lucky, knave. My lord has decided to spare your life," decreed Andraste. She followed after Brion and beckoned for Aldrich to follow.

"I know your voice," stated one of the highwaymen. He tentatively raised his eyes to Andraste.

"Where are your men, Commander?" asked the highwaymen.

"They follow behind. As will a wagoner with our supplies, let them pass without any trouble. If I hear you have troubled them, I will return, and your lives will be forfeit," announced Andraste.

"Yes, Commander," replied the warrior. He returned his eyes to the ground.

Andraste glanced to Aldrich. She could not see his reaction because he also wore his hood. She urged her horse forward and Aldrich followed. They rejoined Brion on the other side of the bridge.

"Who are you to instill such fear?" asked Aldrich.

"I was once a soldier of some renown," replied Andraste.

"So well-known and feared as for a score of men to lay prostrate at your feet without even seeing your face? You turn thieves and cutthroats into obedient lambs? Who are you?" questioned Aldrich.

"I am Paramerion. I am first and foremost a soldier. I am your travel companion and ally. Do not ask me again. If you cannot abide by our arrangement, then you are welcome to go your own way," replied Andraste.

Aldrich followed behind her in silence. Brion shot him a calculating look.

"Are your men really following us?" asked Aldrich.

"No. It is just Brion and myself," responded Andraste. Andraste caught a glimpse of Brion's smile before he raised his hood.

"If you have such power, why not order the stragglers to return to their homes?" asked Aldrich.

"They may have not obeyed. We would have defeated them, but we need to make haste. We cannot challenge every band that we encounter. We have not the time or the manpower. We must reach the Darklands," said Andraste.

"Why such haste?" asked Aldrich.

"There is something I must do before the year is out," replied Andraste. She urged her horse forward before Aldrich could ask any more questions.

Chapter Two

"We will stop at the refuge. They will offer us shelter," informed Andraste.

"The refuge? I thought the next city was Andrastia," said Aldrich.

"It is a refuge for women and children. The city dwellers named the city after its founder," explained Andraste.

"Andraste Valerianus?" asked Aldrich. Andraste looked at Aldrich sharply.

"The founder of the city was Andraste Valerianus?" questioned Aldrich.

"Indeed," replied Andraste.

Andraste urged her horse out of the forest and onto the Northern road. She hesitated at the sight before her. Emerald flames engulfed the building and voluminous clouds of violet and black smoke billowed towards the heavens. It was as though all of the buildings had lights on within as the windows glowed with unearthly emerald light. From every direction there was the stench of burning and the sound of destruction.

"Militant sorcerers," concluded Aldrich, "But why attack a refuge?"

Brion took Andraste's reins and shook his head. Andraste's fingers still rested on her hilt. Her eyes rested on the city in flames. A group of soot-covered women was desperately forming a chain to throw water from the moat onto the emerald flames. However, they were being attacked by a mismatched band of warriors on foot, similar to the one Andraste had encountered on the bridge.

"Vultures," hissed Andraste.

A band of female warriors was keeping the attackers at bay with spears and swords. Brion felt Andraste's tension and released her reins. Andraste urged her horse forward, unsheathing her sword as she rode towards the battle. She struck the first attacker down before he even knew she was beside him. She pushed her way through to the female warriors. Brion was starting to drive the attackers back with his arrows, while Aldrich fought at her side. He moved without hesitation. Over and over again he raised his great sword, protecting her exposed side as she cleared a path to the women. They finally reached the front line. Aldrich protected her back as she approached the leader of the women.

"You must abandon the city. There is no hope to extinguish those flames," commanded Andraste.

"We are just trying to buy time," replied a blonde woman. She turned to study Andraste with pale blue eyes.

"Tacita," greeted Andraste.

"Commander?" asked the woman in surprise, "You are not dead?"

"Not yet," answered Andraste, "We will have to talk later. You must start evacuating the city."

"My sister leads a party on the Southern road. We are but a distraction," replied Tacita.

"Head towards my brother, Titus's lands, he will give you shelter," said Andraste.

"Yes, Commander, that was the plan," replied Tacita, "But he is already here."

Andraste turned to follow Tacita's eyes to the Northern road. She saw a party of Imperial troops riding towards the city. They were in their full Imperial battle armor. Andraste saw her brother, Titus, at its front. He paused to survey the emerald flames engulfing the city, and then his eyes landed on her. He gave orders to his men and then urged his horse forward.

"Retreat, Tacita," commanded Andraste.

Tacita gave a signal and the women hastily began to head towards the Southern road, while the attackers fled towards the tree line as they saw the approaching Imperial troops. Aldrich made to pursue the retreating warriors.

"Aldrich," called Andraste. Aldrich brought his horse alongside hers.

"You must ride. Titus Valerianus follows the law exactly. He will execute you without question. Ride towards the Eastern road and wait in the
tree line. If we do not reach you within an hour, go ahead without us as we
will not be coming," said Andraste.

"I would fight with you," avowed Aldrich.

"I know, but one of us must reach the Darklands. Go! Titus comes,"
reasoned Andraste.

She slapped the rump of Aldrich's horse with the flat of her blade. It
bolted towards the Eastern road. Brion was too far away from her to reach
her in time. Titus struck at her with all of his might.

"My men will be here quick enough, speak quickly, traitor," ordered
Titus, "Are the rumors true? Are you exiled?"

"Yes," responded Andraste as she shielded the blow. Titus's gray blue
eyes were calculating her words.

"So the Emperor's sorcerers are destroying your lands?" asked Titus. He
frowned as he looked to the women escaping towards the Southern road.

"As you see," replied Andraste. She charged at Titus, but he deflected her.

"Did the Emperor execute your cousins?" asked Titus. He came at
her again.

"Yes," answered Andraste as she deflected the bow. Titus took time to
turn his horse around and come again.

"For what offense?" inquired Titus.

"I still do not know," replied Andraste, "Did you know the Emperor is
executing citizens for not paying taxes?"

"No, I had not heard," replied Titus. He came at her again, but he surveyed the attackers heading into the woods.

"We have encountered many deserters and rogue bands," said Andraste.

"They are hungry. The Empire is coming apart at the seams," replied
Titus. He surveyed his sister and said, "Blood of mine, I will let you go this
time, but if I catch you again within the Empire, I will execute you."

"Will you help my people?" asked Andraste as she watched the departing women.

"Yes, it is our oath to protect the weak," replied Titus, "Now strike me so it looks believable. I will be relieved from command if it is suspected that I helped you."

"More than that, you will lose your life," said Andraste.

"Make haste!" growled Titus.

Seeing an opening, she struck Titus but did not cut through his armor. The power of her blow knocked Titus off his horse. He swore at her from the ground. Andraste grabbed Titus's horse's reins and pulled it along with her as she urged her horse towards the Eastern road. Brion joined her side and they rode hard towards the forest. Andraste glanced behind her and saw Titus slowing rising to his feet. He watched them ride into the distance. She left his horse at the tree line.

It had not been long before they came across another band of warriors. However, they were better organized and disciplined. Andraste reared her horse before their road block. Brion knocked an arrow to his bow. Andraste surveyed the warriors in front of her. This band knew how to carry themselves and wield their weapons.

"Easy. These are the travelers I told you about. They are with me," asserted Aldrich. Aldrich rode his horse onto the road.

"Yes, my lord," replied one of the warriors. He surveyed Andraste and Brion with intelligent, brown eyes. He had long, straight dark brown hair that was tied back in a ponytail. He had fine pointed features and a mouth that was designed for sneering.

"May I introduce the Resistance. This is Lord Kasimir," acknowledged Aldrich.

"Now is not the time for introductions," replied Andraste.

"Does Titus follow?" asked Kasimir.

"He will escort the refugees to his lands," answered Andraste. She looked to Aldrich and added, "But I cannot linger here."

"Why would he let you escape?" questioned Kasimir.

"Obviously, he has bigger problems," answered Andraste.

"I have never seen Titus bested before," stated Aldrich. He surveyed Andraste curiously. His sapphire eyes sparkled at the thought of a Northern Commander defeated.

"What do you do here?" asked Andraste as she surveyed the

Resistance warriors.

"We have been disrupting the Northern food trains for the Imperial Army," replied Kasimir. He exchanged grins with the long-limbed, golden-haired lord to his right. Both lords turned to Aldrich for approval, but he was watching Andraste's reaction.

"Titus is not your greatest enemy. He will provide order and security in the days to come for the common folk. Do not hinder his efforts," stated Andraste.

"Spoken as a command. Are you used to having your orders followed?" asked Kasimir.

"I am stating the obvious," replied Andraste.

She hastily turned her horse as she heard crashing through the trees. A female warrior leapt out of the tree line. She was fully-dressed in Imperial armor and her scarlet cape flew behind her along with her long, dark-brown tresses. The look in the woman's eyes was madness. Andraste drew her sword and met the warrior's blow.

"Varinia!" hissed Andraste.

"Traitor," growled Varinia.

"You are outnumbered. Retreat!" commanded Andraste.

"Frightened for once? You have finally lost the Emperor's favor," smiled Varinia.

"I do not wish to fight you, but I will if you impede my progress. Return to the Imperial Army. Titus will be angry with you for disobeying his orders. Your duty is to the refugees," said Andraste.

"You, traitor, can no longer command me. My duty is to the Emperor, who will reward me well for disposing of you. The price on your head is higher than for all of the Resistance Commanders combined. What did you do for the Emperor to lose his favorite? You could always do no wrong in his eyes," replied Varinia, "You had best taken your chances with me. The Arisen hunt you."

Varinia raised her sword at Andraste, but was struck in her right shoulder by an arrow. Varinia dropped her sword to the ground, but she reached for a crossbow and aimed it at the Resistance warriors. Her steel-gray eyes showed no fear. Varinia tried to fixate an arrow with her wounded arm, but she could not complete the movement. She scanned the direction of the arrow and her eyes registered on Brion.

"Your watchdog still barks," stated Varinia. She glowered at Brion.

"Retreat," urged Andraste. Varinia calculated Andraste and then the warriors behind her.

"I will come for you, turncoat," swore Varinia. She turned her horse around and rode back towards the Imperial Army.

"That is the second Valerianus you have made retreat," stated Aldrich.

Andraste did not respond. She approached Brion instead.

"Was shooting her necessary?" asked Andraste. Brion nodded his head once. Andraste said, "She will not forget. She will come for you as well."

Brion snorted to demonstrate the notion caused him no concern and turned his horse towards the East.

"The Resistance force is camping not far from here," said Aldrich. Andraste surveyed the Resistance warriors, but sheathed her sword.

"Lead on," said Andraste.

Kasimir turned his horse onto the Eastern road and rode ahead. The golden-haired lord rode at Kasimir's side and Brion joined him. Aldrich waited for Andraste to join him before proceeding.

"Loudmouth, at your side is Lord Eadbehrt," introduced Aldrich.

"Southerners?" questioned Andraste as she surveyed the lords' armor and weapons. The two lords were the best equipped out of the assembled men and wore a fashion Andraste was not familiar with.

"Yes, but the Resistance is composed of warriors from across the Empire," replied Aldrich.

"Only Southern men sport such long locks," commented Andraste.

Andraste scanned the Resistance troops for familiar faces. She did not recognize a single warrior. She turned her attention to Brion, who was still watching the way that they had come. She looked back as well and Aldrich fell silent. Kasimir and Eadbehrt were studying Andraste and Brion intently. She moved her hand to check her bow and Kasimir and Eadbehrt's hands both went to their blades. She laughed softly and Brion turned at the sound. Brion gestured for her to stop. She removed her hand from her bow.

They rode into the remnants of an ancient city and joining a company of Resistance warriors. They all eyed Andraste and Brion with distrust. However, Aldrich was greeted warmly by whoever he encountered. The other warriors would bow low to him in the Southern style and ask him questions.

Andraste rode near the end of the encampment and dismounted. Brion set about cleaning their weapons and Andraste tended to their horses. Andraste's shoulder was aching to the point of distraction. It still felt like it burned. She rubbed her cursed shoulder. She saw that Aldrich was watching her intently and she moved her hand away. Aldrich freed himself from his well-wishers and approached from across the clearing.

"Sleep a while, the others will watch over us," said Aldrich.

"Only dead men let their guard down," returned Andraste.

"Suit yourself," replied Aldrich. He moved to rejoin his men.

"We should move to higher ground," stated Andraste.

Aldrich paused but he continued on his way. Brion rose and followed Andraste to the highest point of the ruins. Andraste let their horses graze and then she climbed onto the wall. She could see for miles around in all directions. She sat cross-legged and placed her sword across her lap. Brion joined her and sat with his back against her own. She heard the laughter of the Resistance troops below, but she ignored them. She closed her eyes in order to get some rest. She fell asleep almost instantly.

She was awoken by a rowdy song. She smelled burning wood and leaves. She opened her eyes and saw a large bonfire sweltering below. The forest was uncommonly silent. A distinctive, foul odor drifted on the Northern wind.

"Put out your fire!" cried Andraste. She felt Brion start at the sound of her voice.

"Why?" asked one of the Resistance troops. In the distance they heard a blood-chilling horn.

"What is that?" cried Kasimir.

Brion pulled Andraste's arm and she looked towards the North. She could hear the sound of troops moving through the trees. She heard the screaming of a dying man.

"Our sentry on the Northern road," called Eadbehrt. The Resistance troops were mobilizing slowly.

Andraste took up Brion's sword as well as her own and ran down the length of the wall. She heard another scream. It was closer than before. She jumped into the thick of the Resistance troops and ran forward with both swords raised. A stench of decay and death approached from the tree line, and Andraste ran straight for it.

The night's sky was hidden by a veil of ominous clouds, so there was no starlight to guide her. She ran only towards the reek of corpses. The wind changed and the smoke of the bonfire blew towards her. It further blinded her progress, but still she charged. In the darkness, she saw two, amaranthine spheres gazing at her from the distance. Andraste ran straight towards the violet orbs and struck with both of her swords simultaneously. The head was swiped cleanly from her victim's shoulders, but still the amethyst orbs illuminated brilliantly. She did not hesitate. She severed the limbs from the body as well, and then combatted her second attacker. The third and fourth attackers were struck down from Brion's arrows and Andraste sped forward to cut off their heads.

"Do any of you use magic?" yelled Andraste.

"Not one," replied Aldrich. He seemed to materialize out of the darkness.

Andraste's blade was at his throat before she recognized him. She quickly turned towards the darkness and listened. She put herself between Aldrich and the fifth attacker.

"Do not let them touch you," warned Andraste.

She struck down their assailant and then removed her charcoal cloak. Her cowl stood firmly secured. She took up a torch from the bonfire and lit her cloak on fire. She threw it up into the air.

"Ignite!" commanded Andraste.

The charcoal-colored cloak expanded into red flames and hesitated in the air. Andraste gestured towards the corpses and the cloak hastened to develop all five corpses. Whatever it touched was engulfed by ruby flames.

"What are you-" started Aldrich. Once again the horn sounded in the distance.

"Ride. Get your men to ride. Your lives depend on it!" commanded Andraste. She whistled for her own horse.

Aldrich gave the order and his men hastened to do his bidding. Andraste mounted her own horse and waited only for Brion to join her before she sped from the ruined city. She did not slow her pace until the sun had begun to rise over the Northern Mountains. She stopped to let her horse rest at a mountain stream. Brion reached her first and offered her his own charcoal cloak. She wrapped it around her shoulders and concealed her form.

"Who attacked us?" asked Aldrich as he rode to her side.

"The Arisen," replied Andraste.

"The rumors are true?" questioned Kasimir as he joined them. Andraste did not respond.

"Who are the Arisen?" asked Aldrich.

"It is said there is a legion of undead soldiers in the North that under the cover of darkness fulfill the desires of the Emperor," answered Kasimir.

"Those are stories to scare children," alleged Aldrich, but he was silenced as Andraste did not contradict Kasimir.

"The North is a dangerous place," surmised Andraste.

"So you have said before. Are there not any further details you wish to share?" demanded Aldrich, "We lost comrades tonight."

"I gave three warnings. You heeded only one. Let that may be a lesson to you if we continue onwards together. I do not speak for my own amusement," answered Andraste.

"Why must they not touch us?" asked Aldrich ignoring her hostility.

"Their scratches and blood are formidable as any poison. You will die, and you will join the ranks of the Arisen. You will become a soulless corpse that only hungers for death and destruction," answered Andraste.

"Your other warnings were to head to higher ground and no fires?" verified Eadbehrt. He surveyed her with deep blue eyes. He stroked his golden beard absently as he considered her words.

"Yes," replied Andraste.

"Why?" asked Aldrich.

"The Arisen are drawn by fire. They fear it as fire can vanquish them.

They will come to extinguish any fire in their proximity. Higher ground is just common sense. You will have a higher advantage point and better be able to protect yourself if you are hunted," replied Andraste.

"Only fire can kill them?" asked Eadbehrt.

"And magic, but we had little at hand," answered Andraste.

"But you are a magic user, you used an enchantment to spread the flames," said Kasimir.

"No, you did not utter a spell or use an enchantment. You commanded the flames with one word. How is that possible?" asked Aldrich.

"My magic is limited. When I was young, I was schooled by Ice Palace warriors," replied Andraste. She surveyed the men that had joined them.

"Varinia Valerianus said the Arisen hunt you. Why?" demanded Kasimir.

"I seriously displeased the Emperor," replied Andraste.

"What? Were you late for a banquet?" scoffed Kasimir, "What offense could be so great as to justify the release of undead soldiers?"

"Steady, Kasimir. Paramerion is our ally. And if the Emperor pursues him so badly, then it will aid the Resistance to hinder the Emperor's desires," stated Aldrich.

"Yes, my lord," grumbled Kasimir, but the look he shot Andraste was murderous.

"You have lost four," stated Andraste, "We must ride or your will lose more comrades. We must leave the Northern lands by nightfall."

"Have you no compassion?" asked Eadbehrt.

"My duty is to the living," answered Andraste.

"The horses will need rest," advised Aldrich.

Andraste turned her attention to the men and horses and evaluated their condition. Brion nudged her shoulder and pointed towards the East.

"We may not find welcome there," said Andraste. Brion looked pointedly towards the men.

"Where does he want to go?" inquired Aldrich.

"The Summit," answered Andraste, "It is out of our way, but it would shield us from the Arisen for the night if we are permitted to enter the city. However, if they recognize Loudmouth or myself, we all may die. You will have to speak for us."

"The penalty for a Southerner caught in the Northern lands is just as high. Why would you want a Southerner to speak for you? What did you do?" pushed Kasimir.

"It is what I did not do," replied Andraste.

Even though Brion wore his hood, she could sense him glowering at Kasimir. Kasimir did as well because he looked away and fell silent. Kasimir and Eadbehrt awaited Aldrich's orders.

"Lead on," bade Aldrich. Andraste turned her horse southeast and rode towards the Summit.

The Summit was the oldest city in the North. It was the last city before leaving the Northern lands and was a gateway to trade for the East, West, and South. It was a mixture of buildings in the state of opulence and shacks. Many structures were just built on top of old structures, so they looked half-hazard and dangerous. The city was bustling with noises and smells that drifted over the city wall.

"State your business," ordered the city watch.

Aldrich signaled for their company to stop and he approached the watchman that spoke to them through an octagonal opening in the wall. It was barred and the tip of a crossbow bolt glinted in the afternoon light. Aldrich stopped and raised his face upwards towards the window.

"We encountered Arisen on our journey. We wish only shelter for the night," answered Aldrich.

"How far off?" asked the guard.

"Half a day's ride behind, may be less," responded Aldrich.

"So two nights," stated the guard, "You are not from around these parts, are you? Arisen only travel on foot by night."

Aldrich fell silent. He glanced uncertainly towards his men. Andraste saw Kasimir and Eadbehrt tense, which made the men grow uneasy.

"Lady Moira has decreed that no strangers are permitted within the city, not at times like these," said the guard.

"Northern hospitality has always extended to travelers. Would she turn her back on those in need and go against her pledge?" asked Andraste.

"You will not criticize, my lady. She acts to protect us all. Two cities have fallen into chaos-" started the guard.

"That is enough, Fulvius. I will see the face of the one who reminds me of my duty," interrupted a woman's voice. Brion raised his head at the sound and shot a cautionary look to Andraste.

Andraste dismounted and handed her reins to Brion. She left her bow and quiver on her horse and waited. The great doors of the Summit opened and a woman dressed in black silk robes appeared before them. She was heavily jeweled, and held her head proudly. Her brown tresses were braided innately in the Northern style. The lady studied Andraste with more curiosity then contempt. The woman was guarded by twenty guards and twenty more aimed crossbows at their party from the battlements.

"Approach," ordered the lady.

Andraste handed her sword to Brion before doing so. She approached the lady slowly and stopped six paces away.

"Bow to my lady-" started Fulvius.

"Wait," commanded the lady. She approached Andraste cautiously. Andraste slowly lifted her hand and removed the cowl from her face. As the lady recognized Andraste, she fell to her knees and bowed her head. Her guards quickly knelt to one knee and bowed their heads as well.

"Do not give me away," warned Andraste. She quickly helped the lady to her feet.

"Come in at once, quickly," bade the lady.

The guards stepped aside and the bows overhead were lowered. Andraste gestured for Aldrich and his men to approach. Brion was the first to proceed into the Summit.

"Is this all? Where are your squadrons? Where are the Victorious?" asked the lady.

"They will not be coming," answered Andraste.

"Did they fall in your rebellion?" inquired the lady.

"I cannot take them where I am headed. The way is too dangerous," responded Andraste.

"Too dangerous for the Victorious?" questioned the lady.

Brion had reached them. He bowed to the lady and took her hand. A look passed between them and the lady smiled.

"I see that you already know my brother, Loudmouth. I am Paramerion," stated Andraste.

The lady studied Andraste with large nutmeg colored eyes and then glanced to the approaching warriors.

"I attended the University with your brother. I am glad that you are well. I hear he shares your fate, whatever that may be," said the lady. She gestured for them to follow her.

Andraste felt uneasy as the gates closed behind them. Aldrich approached them. Kasimir and Eadbehrt flanked his sides. All three Southerners bowed eloquently to the Northern lady.

"Let us make our introductions indoors. We do not know who watches," said the lady, "My guards will show your men to quarters. With so many refugees, we are short rooms at the moment."

"We are honored by your hospitality," returned Aldrich. Andraste ignored him, although the lady studied Aldrich under lowered lashes.

"Have many have come?" asked Andraste.

"Your Northern lands have been obliterated by the Emperor. However, many are fleeing from the North as well due to the Arisen and the Emperor's experiments. Other houses are rising against the Emperor due to the chaos," answered the lady, "Refugees are being housed here, as well as in Titus's lands, and in your lands in the Far East."

They followed her into a ruby painted palace. It resembled the Citadel, but on a much smaller scale. It still had a golden dipped roof and violet lanterns hung along the covered passageways. There were extensive gardens and a large pond filled with water lilies.

"Rumors of your death at the hands of the Emperor have caused many of the Imperial Army to defect. Others are waiting for more solid news, but I fear it will be too late for them to flee," informed the lady.

"I ask that you do not speak of me or that you have seen me," said Andraste.

"Is that a command?" asked the lady.

"Yes," answered Andraste.

"I will abide," replied the lady. Aldrich listened to their exchange intently.

A servant girl pushed back a screened door and the lady gestured for them to proceed. They were seated on full cushions around a low mahogany table. The room was dark, but lit by candles that dangled from the walls in silver holders. A second servant brought in vases of rice wine and small glasses. She set it before her lady and bowed before leaving the room. The lady poured them each a glass and offered them platters of food.

"While you are under my roof, let us remain friends," said the lady. She raised her glass towards Andraste.

"While we are under your roof, let us offer our protection," returned Andraste.

Andraste raised her glass to the lady and then took a sip. Brion made the same gesture, and Andraste motioned for the Southerners to do the same.

"I am Moira Icilius, Lady of the Summit," announced their hostess. She pulled out an elegant fan from her robe and began to fan herself.

"I am Aldrich. May I introduce Kasimir and Eadbehrt," introduced Aldrich. The lady turned her eyes to survey Aldrich. Her brown eyes were congenial, but astute.

"My Southern lords, you are a long way from home," stated Moira.

"They fight for the Resistance," commented Andraste.

Aldrich glared at Andraste, but was surprised as Moira laughed heartedly. It was a musical sound full of mirth.

"She already knew. It was a redundant statement," stated Andraste as she observed the three hostile stares at her back.

"Why do you find this humorous?" glowered Kasimir.

"Paramerion's industrious military career and service to the Emperor makes this exceedingly facetious. Particularly, considering-" started Moira. She lowered her fan as Brion silenced her with a wave of his hand.

"As you wish, my lord," said Moira. She turned her brown eyes to Andraste, "I am surprised that you of all people would align yourself with the South."

"These men are too young to pay for the faults of their elders or those of the Southern Crown," replied Andraste.

"For what offense?" asked Aldrich.

"The Southern crown executed my mother," replied Andraste.

"The death penalty in the South is extremely rare. I have no recollection of it being used in my lifetime," said Aldrich. He frowned as he studied Andraste.

"But it did happen. It was a catalyst for the Black War," responded Moira.

"How do you know so much?" inquired Kasimir.

Aldrich shook his head at Kasimir and frowned at the rudeness and delivery of the inquiry. However, Moira was not offended. She poured Kasimir more rice wine.

"I hold my lands through the accumulation of intelligence," replied Moira.

"You peddle in secrets?" questioned Aldrich.

Moira poured Andraste another glass of rice wine. She only smiled at Aldrich but admitted nothing.

"There was one such execution. It was kept very secret. I do not know the particulars. My lord, you were being fostered in the Shadow Mountains at the time," admitted Kasimir.

"We have no reason to lie to you," stated Moira. She poured Aldrich a second glass of rice wine.

"Then why not tell me your true name?" asked Aldrich. He raised his sapphire eyes to Andraste over his glass.

"Because I will never be that person again," answered Andraste.

"Yet, even though you lost your name, title, and lands, you still command respect," alleged Aldrich.

"You mistake yourself, it is fear," answered Andraste.

"Forgive me, Commander, you are mistaken. You are and will always be honored in the North despite the edict of the Emperor. That is why I risk my own lands and people to shelter you," interjected Moira. She bowed her head to Andraste.

"I will not forget this kindness," replied Andraste.

"My lord, why are you so silent? At court or in company, you usually speak for Paramerion. These are the most words I have ever heard the

Commander speak," smiled Moira. Brion did not meet her eyes. Aldrich looked in surprise from Andraste to Brion.

"My brother was injured during my duel with the Emperor," said Andraste.

"Sorcery? That always was your weakness," said Moira. She frowned as she looked to Brion, "How could both of you not inherit your parents' formidable powers. It stands against reason."

"We are just unlucky," said Andraste.

"Twice cursed," replied Moira. She looked to Aldrich who was following the conversation with interest.

"You do not know, do you?" asked Moira. Once again Brion gestured her for silence.

"A second command, you are both uneasy. Born to command and yet rarely do so," stated Moira, "As you are my friend, my lord, I will keep your secrets."

"For what price?" asked Andraste. Aldrich raised his eyebrows.

"None, your brother helped me when I was most in need," answered Moira.

Andraste turned her eyes to Brion, but he communicated nothing. He raised his glass to his lips and surveyed Moira. His eyes narrowed.

"You must be exhausted from the road. My servants will show you to your rooms. Commander, if you will follow me, you will be safest in my rooms," said Moira.

Andraste rose and saw the startled faces from the Southern lords. Moira surveyed them in surprise.

"How do you keep such a secret?" asked Moira. She giggled behind her fan.

"You have an understanding?" asked Aldrich.

"Hardly," barked Andraste. She followed Moira out into the corridor and shut the screen behind them.

"If they, if anyone knew who I was, I would be pursued across the Empire especially if civil war is coming," said Andraste.

"So you travel as a man and allow the rumors of your death to spread. It is a sound move," said Moira, "However, you just mortified your traveling companions. Southern propriety does not allow an unmarried man to enter the chambers of a maiden."

"I apologize for any slight to your reputation," said Andraste.

"In the North it does not matter so," replied Moira. She glanced to Andraste, "You are not how I pictured you at all."

"What did you expect?" asked Andraste.

"They call you the Demon of the North, and yet you are so civilized, so composed," stated Moira, "I expected Varinia, but instead it is like I am speaking with Brion."

"Varinia is no example for any of my family. I do not know why she carries on so," sighed Andraste, "It is shameful."

"She is very much like the Emperor," agreed Moira.

They had reached Moira's chambers. Moira sent the servants away and showed Andraste to her bath chambers, which were filled from the waters of a hot spring. Andraste removed her cloak and cowl. Moira studied her once more.

"No, you do not look like Brion or any of your siblings. You are the image of the late Empress," said Moira, "I see none of your father in you."

Andraste did not respond. Moira left her alone and Andraste removed the rest of her clothing. She climbed into the pool and closed her eyes. It was the first time that she had been alone since she was cursed. Andraste took a deep breath and relaxed in the waters. The bruise had doubled in size. It was spreading. Andraste submerged her head under the water so that she would not see it.

After relaxing for a time in the waters, she wrapped herself in an oversized towel and used another to dry off the excess water from her hazel tresses. She used one of Moira's combs to detangle her long hair. She emerged some time later.

"Are you injured?" asked Moira as Andraste entered into the chamber. Her bruise was not fully covered by her towel.

"It is nothing," replied Andraste. She turned away to examine her saddlebags, which must have been delivered by a servant.

"Your things are being laundered. I have set robes out for you," said Moira.

"Many thanks," replied Andraste. She dressed behind the screens in black silk robes. Her sash was also black. Moira came behind her to secure the sash. Moira wrapped thick furs around Andraste's shoulders.

"I would see Brion," remarked Andraste.

"He is using my laboratory. He is making some sort of salve," informed Moira. Once again her eyes went to Andraste's shoulder.

"I have asked my people not to enter this part of the palace for the remainder of the evening. You will not be seen," said Moira.

Moira gave her directions and Andraste headed towards the laboratory. She could hear the vigorous grinding of a mortar and pestle. She entered the room and came face to face with Aldrich. He paused as he studied her. Andraste realized that he had not recognized her in the slightest.

"My apologies," said Aldrich. He stepped away from the door so that she could pass.

"It is nothing," replied Andraste.

Aldrich bowed to her as she passed, but his sapphire eyes followed her. Brion hesitated in his task and studied Aldrich. Kasimir and Eadbehrt also joined him in the chamber. She approached Brion, who resumed grinding the mortar and pestle. Andraste began to remove the leaves off the stems of the herbs Brion had gathered.

"Despite your Northern apparel, you have the look of the East about you," commented Kasimir.

"If you imagine me Eastern, then you would know that I may not speak to you without being properly introduced," replied Andraste. She did not raise her eyes from her work.

"You do look familiar as if we met long ago," said Eadbehrt. He studied her intently. She felt Kasimir and Aldrich studying her as well.

"You must have been on the road a long time to say such a thing to a stranger," commented Andraste.

"I truly meant it. I thought the Northern customs permitted more frankness," stammered Eadbehrt. Brion snorted but continued his work. Andraste turned her attention to Aldrich.

"And you, my lord, have you nothing to say?" asked Andraste.

"As you said, my lady, we have not been properly introduced," replied

Aldrich. He took Andraste's hand in his and raised it to his lips. Her hand smelled of lavender. Brion raised his sword point to Aldrich's neck and his eyes offered no quarter.

"That is not a Northern custom," said Andraste. She blushed as Aldrich let go of her hand and she stepped behind Brion. Brion glanced down at her. She shook her head and he lowered his sword.

"My apologies again," said Aldrich. He bowed to her. Andraste turned her attention to Brion.

"Do you have what I came for?" asked Andraste. Brion produced a container from his saddlebags and handed it to her.

"You attend the Commander as well? Lucky devil," said Eadbehrt.

"Can you tell us why the Commander receives such courtesy?" asked Kasimir.

"It is Northern hospitality," replied Andraste.

"Then you could stay a while with us? After we have been introduced?" inquired Eadbehrt. Andraste laughed in response.

"I will accept that as consent. I am Eadbehrt, Lord of the Pearl Coves. To my left is Lord Kasimir of the Southern Marshlands, and to my right is Aldrich Caelius," said Eadbehrt. However, his smile fell as he saw Andraste's expression. Her own smiles had been replaced by the firm set of her jaw. Her sea-green eyes flashed. She froze Aldrich with her scrutiny.

"I see I have offended you more, my apologies," said Aldrich.

"Thrice you have apologized. Furthermore, you are lost for words this evening. Are you mesmerized by the lady's beauty as well?" teased Kasimir. Aldrich did not return his friend's smile.

"You are the crowned prince of the Southern lands," stated Andraste.

"Guilty as charged," answered Aldrich. He folded his arms across his chest.

Andraste looked up at Brion and found him watching her reaction. She realized that Brion had known all along. Andraste tightened her fingers around the container.

"He cannot help it," alleged Kasimir.

"Why are you angry, my lady?" asked Eadbehrt.

"A Southerner could not possibly understand," replied Andraste. She left the laboratory without a further word. She heard the sound of Brion returning to his work and the low voices of the Southern lords.

"My lady," called Aldrich.

Andraste halted at the sound of his voice but she did not turn around. Aldrich shut the door to the laboratory behind him as he approached. He bowed to her and remained bowed as he said, "Whatever the offense, I do beg your forgiveness."

"You are a prince, you should not beg," reproached Andraste.

"Regardless, I entreat your forgiveness," replied Aldrich. He remained bowed.

Andraste was moved by his action despite her anger. She partially turned and reached her fingertips to rest on his head for but an instant. She turned to leave and her black robes swept across the stone floor.

"May I ask your name?" asked Aldrich as he rose.

"The only name I can leave you with is Eldgrimson," replied Andraste.

"Eldgrimson? Are you one of King Aelius's daughters?" inquired Aldrich.

"King Aelius's daughters are both dead. They were executed by the Emperor," answered Andraste. She looked down to the floor. Due to Aldrich's silence, she glanced back up. His sapphire eyes burned with rage.

"That is unforgiveable," said Aldrich.

"There are many actions that are unforgiveable," replied Andraste. She turned to proceed down the hall once more. She heard Aldrich follow her. He pursued a different tactic.

"Do you stay long in the North?" asked Aldrich.

"No, anyone with any sense will leave as soon as possible," answered Andraste.

"Will you return to the East?" inquired Aldrich. He had caught up to her and walked by her side.

"Someday," replied Andraste.

"Are you always so mysterious?" asked Aldrich.

"Not mysterious, I am only cautious. A Caelius is not to be trusted," responded Andraste.

They had reached Lady Moira's compartment. The door was wide open and she heard laughter from within. Moira came to the door and surveyed Andraste, "Lady Eldgrimson are you really the one to be lecturing the prince on trust?"

"I am not to be trusted either," acknowledged Andraste. She bowed to Aldrich in the Northern style. As he returned the gesture, she quickly entered Moira's compartment.

"May I speak to Paramerion?" asked Aldrich.

"Paramerion is not available. But you may take tea with Lady Eldgrimson and me," replied Moira.

"I would be honored," said Aldrich.

Aldrich followed Moira into the compartment, who was unbothered by the hostile glare from Andraste. Moira gestured for them both to be seated. Andraste sat on the ground nearest the fire and arranged her skirts about her before taking up a shamisen that lay by the sofa. As she began to play a Northern ballad, her hazel tresses fell down her shoulder. Aldrich stopped in his tracks as he watched her in the firelight.

"Please be seated," said Moira.

Aldrich quickly seated himself on the opposite sofa from Moira, who set a cup of tea on the table between them. Aldrich reached for it.

"Thank you," said Aldrich.

"If you travel to the Darklands, you must be planning an attempt on the Ruins," said Moira.

"You are excellent at intelligence gathering," stated Aldrich. He took a sip of his tea and raised his eyes to Moira. The look in his eyes was discerning.

"Have you studied the Ruins?" asked Moira. Aldrich inclined his head but said nothing.

"I imagine you would not need to since you travel with the Commander," said Moira.

"How do you mean?" inquired Aldrich. He set his tea down.

"The Commander has conquered two Ruins already," answered Moira, "Do not look so alarmed. A Northern warrior would not boast of such feats."

"But it is said that it cannot be done," stated Aldrich.

"The Commander comes from a long line of warriors. They have tackled the impossible for generations with varying degrees of success," said Moira, "As does Lady Eldgrimson's line. Aelius Eldgrimson is also a Ruin conqueror. Have you not seen his sword?"

"The ruby blade?" asked Aldrich, "I thought it but one of the East's secret forging techniques."

"No, that blade came from the Eastern Ruin. When he obtained it, he united and became King of the Island Kingdoms," replied Moira.

"That is not true. The Island Kingdoms have been united for millennia unlike the mainland. However, the strongest warrior is elected to lead," corrected Andraste.

"Not hereditary?" asked Aldrich.

"That is a Southern tradition," answered Moira.

"So you did not inherit your lands from your father?" asked Aldrich.

"No, I claimed the Summit as my own," replied Moira.

"Lady Moira is a great sorceress," stated Andraste. Aldrich eyes narrowed as he studied Moira.

"You do not trust sorcerers, Prince Aldrich?" asked Moira.

"It is nothing personal, but you must understand how a non-magic user feels," replied Aldrich.

"Yes, but I do not dislike you though you are a great warrior, and I carry no weapons," stated Moira. Andraste glanced up from her playing, but quickly feigned disinterest.

"Yes, he is a great warrior. Prince Aldrich has never been defeated at tournament in the swordfights or jousting," informed Moira.

"Do you enjoy the tournaments?" asked Aldrich. He raised his sapphire eyes above the rim of his tea cup.

"Only if I may partake; it is forbidden for women to fight in the Southern tournaments," responded Andraste. Aldrich quickly hid his surprise.

"Lady Eldgrimson is also a tournament champion in both the East and the North. Were you permitted to fight in the West?" asked Moira.

"They do not have tournaments in the West, just duels to the death," answered Andraste.

"Where did you train?" asked Aldrich.

"I was schooled at the Ice Palace," replied Andraste.

"As was the Commander; I know very little of the Ice Palace," stated Aldrich.

"That is strange. Was not your Queen Mother schooled there?" asked Moira.

"My mother does not speak of her childhood," replied Aldrich.

"It is forbidden to speak of the Ice Palace training," acknowledged Andraste.

"Northern secrets?" asked Aldrich.

"Northern education," replied Andraste.

"Do I need to intervene? Such hostility while we drink tea is unseemly," commented Moira. Andraste smiled slightly at Moira and resumed playing the shamisen. Moira poured another cup of tea for Aldrich.

"The guard said that two other cities had fallen," said Aldrich.

"That is true," said Moira. Her merriment faded, "Although Titus has assembled his troops and is now regaining order despite no orders from the Emperor."

"No orders from the Emperor?" asked Andraste. She frowned and a glimpse of regret showed in her eyes for a moment.

"You have reached the conclusion," replied Moira.

"He will have to defect or face execution," stated Andraste.

"I am sorry," said Moira. She set down her tea cup on its saucer on the table and folded her hands in her lap.

"You are a friend to Titus Valerianus?" asked Aldrich as he saw Andraste's concern.

"Many of the Valerianus heirs are our allies. They had no more choice of parents then you did," stated Moira.

"And the heir, Andraste Valerianus, what is she like?" asked Aldrich.

"It is rumored that she is dead. She confronted the Emperor over the deaths of her cousins and his injustice," replied Moira. She contemplated the contents of her tea cup.

"When did this occur?" inquired Aldrich.

"Near a month ago," responded Moira.

"That is right. Andraste Valerianus is also an Eldgrimson. I am sorry for your losses," said Aldrich. His eyes went to Andraste but she paid him no heed.

"It is as if the Eldgrimsons are cursed. They all die so young," pondered Moira.

"I do not believe in curses," stated Aldrich.

Andraste smiled in spite of herself. The pain in her shoulder began to burn more intensely as if to disprove the prince.

"They are real," cautioned Moira, "Do not tempt fate."

"Our fates are already decided. How could I tempt fate?" asked Aldrich.

"For a moment I forgot you were a Southerner," replied Moira, "Ask the Commander about curses."

"Do no such thing," said Andraste. She frowned and set the shamisen against the sofa.

"The Commander is not one for discussion," commented Aldrich.

"I am sure the Commander is still analyzing whether or not you are a threat. It is the way of the North," proposed Moira.

"But we have traveled together for weeks. We have fought and bled together," said Aldrich.

"That is true, and the Commander did not leave you to die despite the inconvenience. This is a promising beginning," alleged Moira. Her eyes laughed as she looked to Andraste.

"Do you think the Commander would have left me to die?" asked Aldrich.

"The Commander's goal must be accomplished or we will all fail," stated Moira, "Give the Commander time."

Aldrich considered Moira's words and looked to Andraste. She offered no advice.

"I thank you for the tea. I should return to my comrades or they may believe I have been taken hostage," said Aldrich. He rose and bowed to the ladies.

"Do they treat hostages to tea with ladies in the South?" asked Andraste.

"We do not keep hostages in the South," replied Aldrich.

"I may not see you in the morning. Come again any time, Prince Aldrich. You are always welcome at the Summit," said Moira.

Aldrich bowed to her once more and left the compartment. Moira waited for his footsteps to fade down the hall before she spoke.

"The Southern prince is intriguing. How is he as a travel companion?" inquired Moira.

"If he was not a Caelius, I could befriend him," admitted Andraste.

"You do not have friends, so that is quite a compliment," stated Moira.

"My reputation precedes me," said Andraste.

"I think the prince had more than friendship on his mind. Take care," cautioned Moira playfully. She smiled at Andraste and her nutmeg eyes were mischievous.

"Once he learns my name of birth, he will only contemplate my death," stated Andraste.

"It is a shame the Valerianus and Caelius family feud began. The Caelius family and the Eldgrimson family have always been allies," lamented Moira.

"It is a shame the Caelius family executed my Eldgrimson mother," retorted Andraste dryly.

"It is also said that the Empress promised your hand to the Caelius family," stated Moira.

"The dead cannot fulfill promises," replied Andraste, "If such a treaty existed, it would have been nullified by the Black War."

"Your anger may not be justified. Emperor Valerianus decimated the Southern lands for the execution for the Empress. The prince lost most of his family in the Black War. You are both victims of your parents' choices," said Moira.

"I am aware," responded Andraste, "But we are speaking too much of the past. It is the future that I must focus on."

"When do you depart?" asked Moira.

"First light. We will only endanger you by remaining longer," replied Andraste.

Moira poured Andraste the last of the tea. They sat together in companionable silence as Andraste played softly on the shamisen.

Chapter Three

Andraste was ready at dawn. She found that all of her clothes had been freshly laundered and mended, as well as her travel-worn boots. She secured her cowl and cloak and headed towards the stable. Brion was already waiting for her with their horses.

"Let us go," said Andraste. Brion gestured his head towards the stables. Andraste turned to see what he was watching. The Resistance troops were mobilizing.

"So they come?" asked Andraste.

Brion nodded once and watched Aldrich approach. Andraste mounted her horse and rode towards the city gate. The gate opened for her and she did not wait to see if the Resistance troops followed. She did not speak to any of the troops until they made camp that evening.

"You seem invigorated from your time at the Summit," commented Kasimir from across the clearing. She heard snickering from the Resistance troops. She eyed Kasimir coolly until he looked away.

"I did not get to thank our lovely hostess," frowned Eadbehrt.

"Nor did we see the Lady Eldgrimson," said Kasimir.

"She was also staying in Lady Moira's chambers. You must have seen each other. It must have been crowded," said Eadbehrt. His comments warranted laughter from the nearest men.

"You are confused with Northern customs. I stayed in Lady Moira's compartment, which is made of many rooms, including a salon and different bedrooms. It is a complete residence within itself," corrected Andraste.

"How unfortunate, she was an exceedingly agreeable lady,"

commented Kasimir.

"But not as beautiful as Lady Eldgrimson," stated Eadbehrt, "And those eyes! By my soul, the color of the Southern seas, I have never seen their equal."

Andraste bit into a loaf of bread so that she did not have to respond. She turned her back on the Southern lords and surveyed their situation. It was the best they could do. They would soon be reaching the Shadow Mountains. She began searching through her bag and Brion looked at her questioningly.

"I feel as though I have forgotten something very important, but I do not know what it was," sighed Andraste. Brion watched her as she completed her search. She did not find anything missing. She put everything back in the bag and then looked up at Brion.

"Do you think it will be a month by land to the Darklands once we have crossed the Shadow Mountains?" asked Andraste. Brion nodded once and gestured a rolling motion with his hand.

"We do not have a boat," replied Andraste. Brion made a crown motion with his hands and placed it on Andraste's head.

"We will not trouble my uncle. We have time. If we ask for his help, we will only endanger his people," said Andraste. Brion's eyes went to her shoulder.

"Surely you must know something about the Lady Eldgrimson? No one at the palace could tell us anything," called Kasimir.

"We are discussing an attempt on the Ruins and you are still discussing a lady? You need to focus or you will die," chided Andraste.

"It will take over a month to reach the Darklands. Are we only to discuss the mission on the journey? It will make it seem more like a year," stated Kasimir.

"Your brother seemed to know her," commented Aldrich.

"Then ask Loudmouth," rejoined Andraste. Brion lowered his hood and surveyed the Southern lords.

"She is related to King Aelius?" asked Aldrich. Brion nodded once.

"Does she have lands in the East?" asked Kasimir. Brion nodded again.

"Your first question is regarding property?" disapproved Andraste.

Kasimir smiled and looked to Brion.

"Is she spoken for?" inquired Aldrich. Brion shook his head.

"Someone who interests the Southern prince! What on earth did she say to you?" asked Kasimir.

"Her words were succinct and not welcoming," replied Aldrich.

"There is the attraction," snorted Eadbehrt.

"Perhaps you should find a lady that enjoys your company, my lord," suggested Kasimir, "There are many Southern ladies that would satisfy that requirement."

"Why was she in the North?" asked Aldrich, ignoring his comrades. Brion huffed and looked to Andraste.

"You think Brion can explain that in a nod?" asked Andraste.

"You could answer," stated Kasimir.

"As you said it will be along ride to the Darklands," responded Andraste.

"Will she be safe when she leaves the North?" asked Aldrich. Brion shook his head.

"You should worry about yourself. Our way is equally dangerous," cautioned Andraste.

"Why does she hate the Caelius family?" asked Aldrich.

Brion looked once more to Andraste, but she had walked away from the discussion. Brion drew a finger across his throat.

"Death?" inquired Kasimir and Brion nodded.

"She lost family in the Black War?" questioned Eadbehrt. Brion nodded again.

Aldrich's shoulders sagged. He also turned away from the discussion. Brion looked for Andraste but could not find her in the clearing. He went to their horses and found that her bow and quiver were gone. Brion took up his own bow and quiver and hastened into the forest. He had not gone far before he saw a group of wild turkeys. He scanned the forest ahead of him and paused.

An arrow flew towards the largest of the turkeys but it missed its mark. It bounced off a tree into the forest. The turkeys sprang into the air. Brion knocked an arrow to his bow and shot the nearest one. He quickly shot a second. He scanned the trees again to the direction of the other hunter's arrow. The other hunter did not fire a second shot.

Brion approached cautiously to a thicket. Andraste sat with her back against an ancient oak. Her breath was labored. Brion knelt by her side and loosened her cloak. Andraste straightened hurriedly.

"I am fine. I just missed," said Andraste. Brion shook his head.

"I do miss at times," stated Andraste.

Brion looked at her skeptically, before putting a hand to her tunic. Andraste nodded and Brion pulled back the edge of her collar. He surveyed the bruise. It had doubled in size once more. It now covered her entire shoulder and towards her chest. Brion frowned and produced a container of salve from his pouch. Andraste applied it to her own shoulder and Brion looked away. When she was done, he produced a jar of pills from his pouch.

"No," swore Andraste.

Brion ignored her and took two from the jar. He offered them to her.

"The way is too dangerous," decreed Andraste.

Brion put the pills in her hand and closed her fingers. He produced a canteen from his pouch and offered it to her. The look in his eyes was determined. Andraste sighed and accepted the canteen. She took a swig and then the two pills. They had a distinctly bitter taste. She grimaced and pushed the canteen back towards Brion.

Brion rose and went to gather his turkeys. When he came back, he offered a hand to Andraste and pulled her to her feet. He took her bow and quiver and put them over his shoulder. Andraste did not object. They slowly made their way back to camp. Brion took her bedroll from her horse and laid it on a soft bit of earth. Andraste approached the bedroll and lay down.

"Wake me for our watch," said Andraste. Brion covered her with his own blankets. Andraste had already fallen into a deep sleep.

"Is your brother alright?" asked Aldrich as he approached Brion. Brion nodded once.

"Is it the old injury?" questioned Aldrich. Brion nodded once more. Aldrich surveyed Brion and then looked to Andraste.

"Lady Moira said I should ask the Commander about curses," said

Aldrich. Brion glared at Aldrich and put a hand to his hilt. Aldrich looked once more to Andraste.

"How are you going to cook those turkeys without using fire?" asked Kasimir.

Brion pointed to the sun. He seated himself on the ground and started deplucking the turkeys. Aldrich aided him in his task.

"Fires are permitted during daylight?" asked Aldrich. Brion nodded.

Andraste dreamt of an all-encompassing fog. She raised a hand before her face and could scarcely make out her fingertips. The scent was of sulfur and brimstone. The fog was dense, hot and composed of purple and black mists. No matter which direction she traveled, the fog did not dissipate. She was trapped. The fog seemed to usurp all of her energy. She felt her life force being drained away.

"Danger," warned a woman's voice. The voice was both welcoming and familiar, but Andraste did not recognize it.

A bolt of ruby lightning struck the ground before Andraste's feet and the fog dissipated in a five foot circle around her. Andraste was able to make her way through the fog.

"Danger," repeated the voice.

A red flaming star encircled in a red sphere emerged before Andraste. Red flames shot from the star and highlighted a path for her. Andraste ran down the ruby path and emerged out of the fog. She turned to thank her rescuer. She was face to face with an emerald dragon with sea-green eyes.

Andraste woke with a start and sat straight up from her bedroll. Brion approached and put a hand to her forehead. She was soaked in sweat. He offered her a plate of roasted turkey. Andraste knocked it away and picked up her sword. Brion turned his attention to follow her eyesight. He froze as he listened to the wind. Andraste waited only an instant before running into the night.

"What is it?" called Eadbehrt.

Andraste did not heed him. She ran past the sentry and into the forest.

"I see nothing," yelled the sentry.

"We have reached the Midlands. We should not have been pursued," said Kasimir.

Andraste hesitated. She could hear the sound of movement through the trees. The Resistance troops could also hear it. Andraste paused and surveyed the forest. They were being surrounded. Brion and Aldrich had reached her side. Aldrich took a step forward, but Andraste blocked his progress with her sword. He froze beside her and looked down to her. Andraste did not respond. Brion pulled her arm back towards the Resistance troops, but Andraste shook her head.

"Arisen?" asked Aldrich.

Brion nodded his head. Aldrich was unnerved by the look of fear in Brion's eyes. Brion pulled once more on Andraste's arm. She shoved him behind her. She did not know why she acted but she drew a circle in the air before her. Once she reached the top of the circle, she made a star. Red flames grew in the pattern she drew in the air.

"Perimeter," commanded Andraste.

Red flames shot around them and grew from the ground forming a barricade between them and the approaching Arisen. An Arisen soldier threw himself at the barricade and he was engulfed in the flames.

"What is this?" asked Aldrich.

Brion shook his head and looked at Andraste in wonder. Andraste dropped to one knee. Brion knelt at her side.

"It will hold until dawn," said Andraste. Brion looked at her in concern.

"We have no other option," stated Andraste. Her breath was labored.

Aldrich remained standing, guarding them both and watching the attempts of the Arisen. It was a long night as they heard the sounds of the Arisen scratching and attempting to get through the barrier. More and more approached, but could not get through. The barrier would propel ruby bolts of lightning at any Arisen that approached too close.

Andraste struggled to remain conscious near the end of the night. The sun slowly began to make its way over the horizon and the Arisen retreated into the darkness. As soon as the radiant, golden disc was ascending the horizon, the barrier fell and Andraste collapsed onto the earth. Brion picked her up in his arms and carried her back to the camp.

"Aldrich-" started Kasimir.

Aldrich silenced Kasimir by shaking his head. Brion knelt over

Andraste and examined her bruise. It had spread even farther.

"The Commander?" questioned Aldrich from ten paces away.

Brion shook his head. He began to gather up their belonging and load his horse. Aldrich had his men do the same. Once they were all ready, Brion knelt by Andraste's side. Andraste awoke and surveyed Brion curiously.

"I had the strangest dreams," said Andraste.

"Are you ready? Do you need assistance?" asked Aldrich.

"We are fine," stated Andraste. She rose and wondered why Brion looked at her with such concern.

"It was an impressive display of sorcery. You must be exhausted," said Aldrich.

"I do not use magic," replied Andraste. Aldrich looked to Brion, who looked at Andraste in confusion.

"You just did," said Aldrich.

"I am sure I would remember if I used sorcery," stated Andraste. She looked to Brion for affirmation. Brion drew a circle in the air with a star in the middle. Andraste looked at him.

"It is not time for games. Get a move on," ordered Andraste.

Brion and Aldrich exchanged looks. Andraste mounted her horse as if she had a full night's sleep. Brion cautiously proceeded after her. Aldrich looked to Brion for explanation, but Brion only shrugged. Andraste urged her horse through the forest and road like the Northern wind. The warriors followed behind her like leaves caught in the wind, caught and transfixed in her wake with no other alternate path to follow.

They took a long break at midday to rest the horses. Andraste watched in amusement as the men trained amongst themselves. However, her smile faded as she saw Aldrich enter the ring. He unsheathed his broad sword and advanced on Kasimir. The level of each swordsman's expertise was apparent within minutes. Aldrich was by far the superior. Not one of his men was able to get close enough to land a blow.

Brion joined Andraste's side and they watched the duels. Brion nudged Andraste in the ribs.

"He is quite good," admitted Andraste. Brion smiled down at his sister and then returned his attention to the duels.

"Are you up for a challenge?" asked Eadbehrt.

Aldrich turned at his comrade's words and surveyed the pair. Brion shook his head. By the time he looked to Andraste, she was already at Aldrich's side. Aldrich took a few steps back in order to avoid the reach of her blade. She dodged the quick sweep of Aldrich's broad sword, which landed heavily in the mud. Andraste ran up the length of the broad sword and brought her sword down towards Aldrich head. He dropped his own sword and she was sent careening forwards. She turned herself in the air and used her own sword to support her landing. She raised her head to survey Aldrich and paused. He was watching her next move intently. She heard the call of a Northern swallow and she stood perfectly still. She met Brion's eyes and he drew his bow.

"What is it?" asked Aldrich.

"The swallows have all flown south for winter," said Andraste.

Aldrich turned so that his back was to Andraste's and he surveyed the clearing.

"At the ready," ordered Aldrich. His men instantly took positions and stood with their weapons raised.

"If you give us the traitor, we will allow the rest of you to live," said a voice from the wood line. An officer in the amaranthine robes of the Emperor's personal guards rode into the clearing. He had his crossbow raised pointedly at Andraste.

"Traitor?" asked Aldrich, "What is the offense?"

"The offenses include dishonorable conduct, disobeying a commanding officer, and attempting to assassinate the Emperor. Are those enough charges for you?" asked the officer.

The officer was joined by near two score horsemen around the perimeter of the clearing. They all raised crossbows towards Aldrich and his men. Andraste put a hand on Aldrich's hand and lowered his sword. She slowly began to approach the officer.

"Where is your brother?" asked the officer.

"He did not stay with me for long," replied Andraste, "Besides all you asked for was me."

"He is also a traitor," replied the officer. His eyes scanned the Resistance troops before him.

"What harm could a scholar do?" inquired Andraste.

The officer never got to make a reply as an arrow pierced him through the throat. More arrows came streaming towards the Emperor's guards from the wood line. The officer fell from his horse to the ground. Andraste stole his horse and rode towards the nearest guard, raising her sword as she did so. She disrupted the order of the formation of the Emperor's guards. The nearest man could not shoot her without risking shooting his own men.

The Emperor's guards tried to regroup, but they were outnumbered by the Resistance troops. They quickly had their bows wrestled from them. Instead the Emperor's guardsmen drew their swords and charged recklessly towards the Resistance troops. Not one of the Emperor's guards survived as each man refused to surrender.

"We need to treat your wounded quickly," advised Andraste.

"Poisoned blades?" asked Aldrich.

"Yes. Loudmouth will help those he can with the supplies he has. I will go into the woods to find more herbs," replied Andraste.

"It is your fault that they were wounded. Why did you not surrender?" asked Kasimir.

"Regardless of my surrender, the guards would have killed you anyway; since I acted, the majority gets to live," answered Andraste. She continued her progress towards the wood line.

"Never trust a promise from a Northerner," advised Eadbehrt.

"No. Never trust a promise from an Emperor's guardsman. If they returned to the Emperor without their target, or showed mercy, the Emperor would have their heads," replied Andraste. She entered into the woods.

"What do you search for?" asked Aldrich. He had lost her in the wood line.

"If we are lucky, we will find silver bells," replied Andraste.

"Silver bells?" inquired Aldrich.

"It is a small, delicate flower with tiny, gray petals. It can cure most poisons," answered Andraste, "However, Husband Keeper or Healer's Lace would also suffice."

"Where did you learn such things?" questioned Aldrich.

"It is a soldier's knowledge," responded Andraste.

Aldrich headed towards the sound of her voice and found her crouched by a fallen tree. She was picking flowers from underneath the debris.

"We are fortunate," said Andraste. She held up a handful of delicate, silver flowers that looked like bells.

"Some would call it luck," replied Aldrich.

"There is no such thing as luck. Take these to Brion immediately. I will head on to see what else I can gather," ordered Andraste.

She handed the flowers towards Aldrich and headed further into the woods. Aldrich returned to camp and found Brion tending a wounded man. Aldrich offered the flowers to Brion.

"From Paramerion," said Aldrich.

Brion accepted the offering but looked at the flowers critically. He looked questioningly to Aldrich.

"I have no instructions. Paramerion seemed to think you would know what to do," said Aldrich.

Brion sighed and took the flowers in his hands. He smelled them first and then rubbed a petal between his thumb and index finger. He smelled it and began to cough. He placed the flowers gently on a blanket and then turned back to the wounded. Aldrich saw that the men had been laid out in a line from lesser to serious injuries. Brion began to tend those who had not received a poisoned injury first. Aldrich walked among his men and spoke to those who were conscious. He hesitated as he came to the side of Kasimir. He was the last in the line. He was feverish and did not recognize Aldrich when he spoke to them.

"Step aside," said Andraste gently.

Aldrich turned and saw that her arms were full of herbs and moss. She whistled and Brion came to her side immediately with the silver bells. He offered them to her. She looked at Brion judgmentally for a moment as she removed her gloves, but then turned her full attention to Kasimir.

"Bandages," commanded Andraste.

She looked up to survey the wounded as she did so. Brion spread his cloak on the ground for her while Eadbehrt brought her the requested item. She spread out the bandages and then began mixing herbs, petals and moss on top of the cloth. When she was content with the poultices, she nodded to Brion. They began moving among the wounded soldiers. Andraste instructed the nearest guardsmen and they began to help as well. Aldrich watched for a moment and then followed their example. She tended to Kasimir herself.

"You!" said Kasimir. Andraste realized that her cowl had come undone.

"Sleep," urged Andraste.

She touched her hand to Kasimir's forehead and he quieted. She quickly fastened her cowl and finished her work. She looked up and saw that Aldrich had seen the exchange, but not her face as her back was to him. She moved onto the next patient. However, she kept glancing uncertainly to Kasimir's sleeping form. The pain in her shoulder was intensifying, but still she moved down the line of wounded soldiers. She did not take a break until all been attended to. She stepped forward to start at the beginning again, but Brion pushed her gently towards their blankets.

"I will rest, but only for a little while," promised Andraste.

"You have done enough. I thank you for your pains," said Aldrich.

"Have you better positioned sentries then before?" asked Andraste.

"Yes," answered Aldrich. He was becoming used to her frankness. He did not even offer a rebuke, even though Andraste waited. He moved towards the wounded men, and she returned to her blankets.

They had no choice but to ride out the following morning. They could not risk lingering in one place for too long despite their wounded. However, due to her care, none were in critical condition. They were also irritatingly cheerful. Andraste imagined it due to their Southern heritage.

"They do not complain," commented Andraste to Brion as they rode ahead.

"What would be the point?" asked Kasimir. He rode to her side and glanced over his shoulder. The nearest rider was still some ways in the distance. Andraste tensed as she felt Kasimir studying her.

"I will not out you. I owe you my life, and it is not our way to reveal a lady's secrets. But, why? Why keep your identity a secret from my lord?" asked Kasimir.

"You know what pursues me. They have found me again and again despite my disguise. How quickly do you think they would trace me if they could follow my name or face?" retaliated Andraste.

"My lord would keep you safe," said Kasimir.

"I can keep myself safe," replied Andraste, "I do not need a man's protection."

"We all need allies, my lady," retorted Kasimir.

"Do not call me so again," warned Andraste.

"As you wish," said Kasimir, "But know that there is not a man in the Empire, who could equal my lord in honor. He would keep your secret and he would protect you."

Kasimir turned his horse and rode back to the Resistance troops before Andraste could respond. She turned her eyes to Brion.

"What do you think?" asked Andraste.

Brion only looked at her in response and made no indication of his opinions. Andraste sighed and returned her eyes to the road.

"We will reach the fort at the Shadow Mountains momentarily. I possess friends there, but they may be quarrelsome to strangers," warned Aldrich.

"You have friends in the Shadow Mountains?" inquired Andraste.

It was not a land that was welcome to strangers. She had been denied entry on many occasions, while traveling with the Imperial Army.

They reached the end of the paved Imperial road. They looked down from the mountain and across the valley. The valley was covered in the amethyst shadows of the mountains. The golden and scarlet leaves of the trees were obscured by the shadow colors. They rode for hours until they reached the fort, which was built into the North side of the mountain.

Aldrich bid them stop in front of the gates. He took the lead and lowered his hood.

"Aldrich? Is that really you?" bellowed a voice from the guard post.

"Gregor, you simpleton, I stand before your eyes and still you ask?" yelled Aldrich. There was grumbling and laughing from the guard post.

"Password?" asked Gregor.

"Well knowing you, it is probably the name of a woman. Leah? Lyla? Azalea?" asked Aldrich. The Resistance troops laughed behind him.

"How could you forget the name of your own niece?" questioned a little voice in outrage.

"That is right. Aaliyah!" called Aldrich with a booming laugh.

The doors to the fort were opened. They rode into the courtyard. Guards surrounded them on all sides. They seemed relieved to see Aldrich, but they did not approach; although, a few did exchange greetings with him.

A little girl ran down the stairs to meet them, but she was swept up in the arms of a giant of a man. The giant had no hair, warm brown eyes, biceps the size of tree trunks, and a jolly disposition.

"I apologize, Aldrich, but you know the protocol," apologized the giant.

The giant was more eyeing Andraste and Brion then his friend. The little girl was fighting to get out of the giant's grasp. Aldrich laughed at her, but kindly. At the sound, the child laughed as well. Aldrich dismounted and motioned for them to do the same.

"You will have to meet the sorceress," said Aldrich to Andraste.

His eyes narrowed as he saw her tense. She felt the bruise in her arm began to burn.

A beautiful woman in an indigo, velvet gown came sweeping down the stairs. She also had deep red hair like Aldrich's and the same sapphire eyes. She pierced Andraste with a gaze and seemed to see into her soul. Andraste looked to Brion. The woman stared at Brion, but he met her gaze unflinching.

"I will pass a crystal over you," informed the woman.

"You will not greet your brother first?" asked Aldrich. The woman glared at Aldrich.

"You may not even be my brother," retaliated the woman icily.

"Have you had trouble here?" inquired Aldrich with deep concern, but the woman did not answer him. She only passed a large crystal over him. It did not respond. However, she seemed moderately relieved.

"Who are you?" she asked, turning her sapphire eyes towards Andraste and Brion.

"These are my companions, who saved my life from the Emperor's personal guards. This is Paramerion and this is Loudmouth. They are exiles from the North," introduced Aldrich.

The woman raised the clear crystal towards Brion and it did not respond. She then turned towards Andraste. The crystal first turned a blinding light, and the woman opened her mouth in surprise. Suddenly, however, the crystal began to turn the color of a smoky-topaz. The pure light emanating from the crystal turned purple and then black. The crystal began to hiss and shattered into a thousand shards.

The friendly demeanor of the guards turned and they pointed their spears directly at Andraste. Brion drew his bow quickly and fastened arrows to his quiver. Aldrich stepped in front of Andraste and put his arms out. The guardsmen still held their position. They looked to the sorceress for guidance.

"The crystal says you will be a great friend to us, but you are cursed," interpreted the sorceress.

"That is true," confirmed Andraste. She surveyed the sorceress. Aldrich did not move from his position.

"How were you cursed?" asked the sorceress.

Brion pointed his bow directly at the sorceress. The guards moved forward. Andraste put a hand on Brion's bow. Brion looked at her, and slowly lowered his weapons.

"I was cursed by the Emperor," stated Andraste.

"Why?" asked the sorceress.

"I betrayed him," answered Andraste. She felt the bruise in her should begin to burn.

"How?" questioned the sorceress.

"I refused to kill a prisoner," replied Andraste.

"What was the prisoner's offense?" queried the sorceress.

"He did not pay his taxes. None of them had paid their taxes," said Andraste softly.

"The punishment for that offense is death?" asked Aldrich.

Andraste refused to answer.

"You said them?" probed Gregor.

"What happened to them?" asked Aldrich.

Andraste refused to answer yet again. Brion looked increasingly menacing.

"You have also been cursed," commented the sorceress as she looked at Brion a second time. She smiled, "You used magic to conceal it from the crystal. Were you also cursed by the Emperor?"

Brion refused to give her any inclination of an answer.

"What was his offense?" asked the sorceress.

"He protected me," whispered Andraste in shame.

The pain in her arm was almost more then she could bear. The sorceress seemed to sense it. She raised a hand towards Andraste. She instinctively raised her sword. Aldrich put a cautionary hand on Andraste's wrist.

"My sister will not hurt you," Aldrich promised, "She is trying to help."

"There is no cure. You will be hurt if you interfere," cried Andraste in warning.

"Who told you that? The Emperor?" laughed the sorceress.

Andraste blushed crimson underneath her cloak. She had trusted her father completely, and never doubted that his word was anything but an ultimatum. Andraste hesitated but she lowered her sword. Aldrich slowly stepped aside.

"The Northerners tell us that we are weak. The Northerners say that we will never cope with the formidable powers of the North. Let us see how the Caelius family magic compares to the Valerianus!" the sorceress proclaimed with pride.

Brion tried to stop the sorceress, but the guards raised their spears to his throat. Still Brion tried to get forward, a drop of blood splattered from where the spear tip grazed his throat. He opened his mouth in a silent, "No!!!"

As soon as white, radiating light burst from the sorceress's hand, Andraste's entire arm was enveloped in amethyst light. The intense pain in her arm tripled. The amaranthine light expanded and attacked the sorceress, throwing the two women to opposite sides of the courtyard.

In the confusion, Brion fought off the spears and bounded towards her side. He put her behind him and picked up her sword in one hand. He held one of the guardsmen's spears in his other hand. He stood poised to fight in any direction. The look in his eyes was ominous. To her amazement Aldrich was also with them, guarding her exposed side.

"Everyone calm down," bellowed Aldrich.

The burning subsided in her shoulder, she moved back her cloak to look at her arm, the bruise had grown, and it was no longer the color of a normal bruise. The color had transformed from the violet bruise into an unforgiving charcoal hue.

The sorceress was also on the ground, shaken but unharmed; although, she had lost all of her color.

"Brother, that is a powerful, dark, ancient magic that you are protecting so valiantly," the sorceress cautioned. Gregor gently raised the sorceress to her feet with great tenderness.

"And they told you not to interfere, Marcella," quipped Aldrich. He was incensed. He still stood between Andraste and the approaching guardsmen.

Marcella motioned with her hand for the guards to stand down. She slowly approached Andraste, and Gregor followed at her side. Gregor's eyes were locked on Brion, who had not dropped his weapons.

"I atone for my rash behavior. It was my intent to aid you. I beseech you to forgive my pride. I should not have meddled. That is no normal curse," opined the sorceress sadly. The sorceress turned her sapphire eyes to Andraste, "You will die in less than a year."

"That is true," confessed Andraste.

Aldrich's eyes widened in shock as he looked from Andraste to Brion. Brion shook his head defiantly. He threw the spear to the ground and put a hand on Andraste's uninjured shoulder.

"Time is not something we have in abundance. Our aim is to enter and return from the Darklands," said Andraste. The sorceress turned scowling to Aldrich and asked, "Is this your insanity? Is it finally catching?"

Aldrich said nothing. Brion sheathed his sword. He looked to Andraste.

"We only shared the same road. Our ideologies are polar opposites. To defeat a curse such as this, you must destroy the caster. My only hope is to obtain a weapon from the Darklands that can defeat the Emperor. My life depends on it," asserted Andraste.

There was a murmur throughout the assembled.

Aaliyah had finally broken free from the hold of the guardsmen and she tackled Aldrich. Aldrich swept her up in his arms, and swung her around in a large circle. Aaliyah giggled with pleasure.

"We have kept you outside long enough," said Marcella with a forced smile, "Please come in and be welcome. As magic did not heal your wound, perhaps we can find a potion or ointment for relief?"

"You are too kind," replied Andraste. She bowed to Marcella in the Northern fashion as did Brion.

Andraste and Brion were led away to separate corridors. Andraste's room looked like a soldier's barracks. It was so sparse that at first she thought it a cell. The impression was mainly bestowed by the cold and darkness of the cave walls. The room contained a small wooden bed, but it was outfitted with handsome linens and warm furs. A thick blue rug lined the floor. In the back of the room there was also a small cherry table, outfitted with candles, and a chair with a leather cushion.

Fresh clothing had been provided on the bed and a bath had been drawn, although the water was beginning to cool. Andraste bathed quickly. She surveyed the bruise on her arm. It had spread all the way down her left arm and to her fingertips. Although the bath washed away the dirt and grime of her journey, Andraste still felt tainted. She dressed quickly in the new clothing, and covered herself with her charcoal cloak, securing her hair and hiding her face.

Someone knocked at her door. She found Brion waiting for her. He too was dressed in clothing provided by the Shadow Mountain warriors. They turned down the corridor and found their way to the dining room. They passed an office and Andraste heard raised voices. She paused.

"I beseech you, brother, something is not right. The crystal test was necessary because we encountered a shape-shifter. Then you happen to meet these two on your way here? Paramerion fought the Emperor and won in a swordfight, but lost to magic. Who could get that close to the Emperor? Almost defeat the Emperor and yet be spared? The Emperor is not known for mercy. It is obvious they have both suffered. But if the brother could ward off my crystal, why did he not ward off that curse? He is powerful enough. He may be more powerful than me," warned Marcella.

"You may be the sorceress in the family, but I trust my instincts. They will be our allies. I am not one to trust lightly," said Aldrich coolly, "Tell me more about the shape-shifter."

"He passed as one of the guardsmen. We did not know the shape-shifter was here until the body of the guardsman was found. Poor soul, he had been dead for weeks, and the shape-shifter still passed amongst us," expounded Marcella.

"Was anything taken?" asked Aldrich.

"Some books and maps regarding the lands beyond the sea. That is all," replied Marcella.

"So not someone from the North?" proposed Aldrich.

"I suppose not," answered Marcella.

"Did they discover any of the Resistance plans?" inquired Aldrich.

"As per our protocol, we do not keep such things in writing," rejoined Marcella. She sounded deeply offended.

"You have done well in my absence," replied Aldrich.

Andraste heard the sound of a chair scraping against a floor. Aldrich must have stood. Brion pushed the small of her back and they hurried down the corridor into the great hall.

"You have been studying magic?" Andraste hissed at Brion. Marcella's question echoed in her mind: why did he not ward off the curse?

Brion grabbed her by the shoulders and turned her to look at him. He was speaking to her, but of course there was no sound. She tried to read his lips. His storm-colored eyes were full of sadness.

"I do not follow," Andraste said, "but I believe you would never hurt me, and if you could have helped me, you would have."

Brion pulled her to him in a big hug, and then awkwardly shoved her aside.

"We should go," said Andraste softly.

Brother and sister found their way to the dining hall. A servant showed them to their seats. The hall was illuminated by fireplaces around the room. Mirrors hung from the walls to reflect the light from the fires. The hall was lined with long wooden tables and benches.

Aldrich had reached the dining hall and sat beside Andraste. She found his presence comforting. Aldrich did not seem to mind that she was cursed; although, everyone else in the hall was giving her wide room and eyeing her with distrust. Aldrich was dressed in elegant clothing. He had removed his armor. She realized that all of the men were without their armor or weapons. She was glad that her cloak concealed her sword and daggers.

She felt a small hand tug at her cloak.

"Why do you wear a cloak?" asked the red-haired child.

"That is a rude question, Aaliyah, and you have not introduced yourself," reprimanded Aldrich over his stein.

Aaliyah blushed to the roots of her hair at her uncle's rebuke.

"I am Aaliyah, daughter of Marcella and Gregor Tarquinius," she said quickly. She curtsied awkwardly.

"I am Paramerion. I wear my cloak because I am cold," replied Andraste.

It was cold in the hall, but she felt like a fool eating with her hood on. However, there was the chance that she battled some of the assembled warriors before. If someone recognized them, she had no doubt of their fate. She and her brother would both be killed.

Aaliyah was called over to her mother. Andraste saw that there were two other red-haired children at Marcella's table.

"Prince Aldrich-," started Andraste.

"As I have no kingdom, I am no prince," reminded Aldrich.

"It is true that the Southern lands were incorporated into the Empire, but its people are left to rule itself," stated Andraste.

"A puppet government overseen by the Emperor. The royal family is left to live at the palace for appearances and Imperial events," responded Aldrich. He had lost his normal cheer and good will. Andraste decided to change the subject.

"If the late Empress had lived, and the Black War had been prevented, you would have been betrothed to Andraste Valerianus," commented Andraste.

Brion spit out his beer.

"Yes," said Aldrich, "Lucky for me I guess? I hear she was fierce. The men who fought her say that she was a demon."

"That is about true," agreed Andraste.

Brion kicked her underneath the table.

"But rumored to be the beauty of the Empire. I am sure many men would have put up with a demon for beauty like hers," said Aldrich.

"You spoke in past tense," mentioned Andraste.

"It appears that while we were on our travels, she was killed in a skirmish. One less Valerianus to worry about," asserted Aldrich.

He saw the look exchanged between Andraste and Brion.

"I apologize. Was she a friend of yours?" asked Aldrich.

"The Valerianus family is no friends of ours," replied Andraste.

"You never really answer my questions, do you?" questioned Aldrich.

Music started to play and a woman with long black hair stole Aldrich away for the first dance. Marcella approached and seated herself at their table.

"Who is the lady dancing with Aldrich?" asked Andraste.

"Decima, Lady of the Shadow Mountains, our foster sister. Before the peace treaty, when our kingdom fell to the Empire, the Lord of the Shadow Mountains welcomed us and raised us as his own. Even after our home was restored to us and our protection assured, our Mother, the Queen, had us remain here for years," explained Marcella.

The Lady of the Shadow Mountains was beautiful with her long raven hair and dark eyes. She was tall and slender. As she danced her bangles clinked pleasantly. Aldrich seemed to be enjoying himself immensely. He was an excellent dancer. Aldrich and Decima were talking rapidly.

"Do you dance, Paramerion?" asked Marcella. Brion laughed soundlessly.

"I will interpret that as no," said Marcella. She took a sip of her wine, "When you do plan to journey to the Ruins?"

"We will take a day to rest and then we will ride on," said Andraste, and she looked to Brion for confirmation.

"If you would heed my warning, I believe your brother could be instructed to fully use his powers. We would need two months, preferably three," said Marcella. She spoke to Andraste, but her eyes were locked on Brion.

"Time is something we do not have," admonished Andraste.

"If you go now as you are, Paramerion will die," foretold Marcella.

Andraste looked to her brother. He showed no emotion or opinion. He stared directly at Andraste as if he to say: you choose.

"What sort of power?" asked Andraste reluctantly.

"I assume then you come from a noble, powerful family within the Empire and must have been entitled to the inestimable powers of the Citadel. I assume due to your injury that you were close to the Emperor, and that is why he chose to spare your life. However, the nature of the injury is so cruel, that you must have been very close, indeed, for him to make you so suffer. I will not press you for details. You are our allies, and we currently have the same goal," said Marcella. She said this as if she was discussing the weather, but it still gave Andraste chills.

"My brother has never shown any development of those powers to which we are genetically disposed," Andraste finally said.

"But that is not true is it?" asked Marcella. She looked at Brion. He colored underneath her sapphire gaze and would not meet Andraste's eyes.

"At the University then? You fulfilled more than your scholarly studies?" asked Andraste. Brion squirmed in his seat and would still not meet her eyes. He could offer no explanation.

"It will take time to reach the Ruins," said Andraste softly.

"So three months from now, you could reach the Ruins more powerful than before, and return to dispatch the Emperor," suggested Marcella.

Marcella offered Andraste her hand in the Southern style as if to be kissed. Brion nodded his consent. Andraste took the offered hand but only grasped it in the Northern style. Marcella offered her hand to Brion and he kissed her hand.

"Our real battle will be delaying my brother. He is all ambition. We will not bring it up after he has been drinking. Tomorrow at breakfast, we will inform him of our decision. Tonight may you both rest even if it is only for a few hours," said Marcella. She rose and took her leave.

Brion watched her with admiration.

"Married with children, Brion," Andraste said softly.

Brion blushed crimson. He shook his head at her.

"I wish you could tell me about this sorcery," said Andraste.

She knew from his eyes that Brion wished so to. Andraste sighed. She rose and also took her leave. She saw Aldrich still dancing, now with a lady with soft blonde hair and hazel eyes. She wondered what it would be like to not have a care in the world, and be able to dance with a handsome prince in the moonlight.

Andraste shook her head. She took her leave and returned to her chambers, where she collapsed, fully-dressed on her bed and fell fast asleep.

"Absolutely not! We leave at this instant. We do not have two months to twiddle our thumbs. Our position is always precarious here. The longer we stay, the longer we put the people of the Shadow Mountains at risk!" declared Aldrich over breakfast as his sister informed him of their consent.

"You are not strong enough. You will need combined magic and swords to return from the Ruins," insisted Marcella.

"Paramerion does not have two months to sit around, while you and Loudmouth study ancient scrolls and whisper incantations," stated Aldrich. His sapphire eyes flashed.

Andraste felt useless. She tensed and grasped her hands into fists.

"I have foreseen it. Paramerion will die at the Ruins," said Marcella softly.

"Is that true? Or are you just saying that to get your way?" queried Aldrich.

"We are not children any more. I would not make such a prediction lightly, not when everything is on the line," swore Marcella. Brother and sister scowled at each other in the early light.

"Sorceress, I will trust your judgment as have Paramerion and Loudmouth. As we go together, I give way to their choice," conceded Aldrich through gritted teeth.

He swept out of the hall angrily, his blue cape tossing behind him.

"Forgive my brother, he is still very much a child," said Marcella. She turned on Andraste, "If you will excuse us, we will start our lessons immediately."

Andraste paused awkwardly, not knowing what to do.

Brion smiled at her confidently and made a shooing motion with his hand. Feeling like she was a five-year-old child once more, she left the hall. She roamed the grounds. All of the halls and rooms looked very similar as they were carved out of the mountain wall. The halls were caliginous due to the stone and scarce torches. There was very little artwork or tapestries. People eyed her with distrust wherever she went, but they did not interfere.

There was a commotion at the gate, and Andraste hurried towards the sound.

A group of fourteen warriors on fine Imperial horses stood in a row in front of the gate. However, they did not wear the colors or insignia of the Empire, only their Imperial armor. Their faces were concealed by cloaks. She went to Aldrich's side at the top of the wall.

"More of the Emperor's personal guards?" asked Aldrich.

"Not exactly," Andraste stated as she recognized their charcoal cloaks.

"We seek no trouble with you. We seek only the Commander of the Victorious, recent exile of the Empire. There may have been two travelers. Did they pass this way?" called one of the warriors.

The warrior's voice was gruff and Andraste would know it anywhere. The man lowered his hood, revealing dark eyes and a scar across his face. He had a face of a man that had multiple encounters with death. His bearing was equally balanced between confidence and caution. His name was Laelius, and Andraste had known him all of her life.

"Let me handle this," admonished Andraste.

Aldrich gritted his teeth for the second time that morning. He moved to speak, but stopped as Andraste jumped onto the top of the battlement, and then down to the ground below.

"That is a twenty-foot drop!" swore a guard.

She landed in a crouch, and slowly arose, her hand on her hilt.

"You will have to name yourselves a new Commander. I am Paramerion. I want no trouble with men of the Empire," asserted Andraste.

Laelius handed his spear to one of the warriors. He then dismounted.

"You think disguised, I would not know you? I would know you anywhere. I care not what name you use," said Laelius brusquely.

He saluted her. All of the men on their horses saluted her. Andraste surveyed the men before her. This was her unit. These were men that she had chosen personally, fought with, bled with, traveled with and lived with. They had seen friends die and buried them together. She knew their stories. She knew their families.

Andraste felt sick as she realized the cruelty of her father. The Emperor sent her own comrades after her, since she had not completely left the realm of the Empire. She felt her heart break even more. Her scar began to throb unmercifully.

"You know why we have come," stated Laelius.

Her hand tightened on her hilt.

"I assume I know your orders," she answered.

Andraste stood posed like a lioness waiting to fight. She felt someone jump down beside her. Aldrich rose from a crouched position, his great sword in hand.

"This is not your fight, Aldrich," Andraste said, not taking her eyes from the men.

"Fight?" questioned Laelius. He slowly knelt at Andraste's feet.

"We will follow you to death and beyond as our oaths foretold," vowed Laelius.

"Have you not also made the same oath to the Emperor?" asked Andraste.

"You and I both know he is mad. We cannot keep our honor intact and follow such a man," said Laelius. He had not moved from his kneeling position. The warrior hung his head in shame.

"Laelius, my friend, I cannot consent. You know the penalty for desertion," said Andraste sadly.

"What is the penalty for desertion?" asked Aldrich.

"They will kill their entire families," replied Andraste.

Aldrich looked at her in horror. She heard the men above the gate talking amongst themselves.

"Your first thought was correct. The Emperor ordered us to hunt you within our lands and kill you both should we find you. We left as ordered in order to give our families time to flee. They should have reached the Island Kingdoms by now and joined the Resistance. The Emperor will have also realized our betrayal," alleged Laelius.

"Turn back while you can, say you never found me. Rumors of the curse must have reached you. I have at most a year to live. Return to your families while there is still time," plead Andraste.

"The time to fight is now. We must fight for the fate of our families. Many years from now, when we are old and nodding by the fire, reveling in the days of our youth, will I think of time spent hiding behind the power and security of the North? No, I will remember the days that I spent beside my battle brothers, fighting the good fight. I have no regrets at this time. But, at this moment, wore I to turn away, I would forever more consider myself a coward. I might as well throw down my spear and return to my wife and be her kitchen maid. Are we not warriors? Do we not hear the call of battle and charge? You have a plan do you not?" asked Laelius, and his eyes shone with faith as he stared at Andraste.

"I have an idea, but it may not work, and those who join me may die," admitted Andraste.

"Where have I heard that before?" asked one of the warriors.

"Gardenia," said a second warrior.

"Thoran," said a third.

"Alexius," chimed a fourth.

"You know we are no rookies. We did not make this decision lightly, and would not have come without consensus. Here we stand, united, and ready to serve," proclaimed Laelius.

Andraste looked at one face to the next and was honored by their determination.

"I am a guest here. I cannot vouch your safety. This land is under control of the Caelius family. But that being said, I will camp with you in the mountains as I always have," swore Andraste.

She offered her hand to her second-in-command. He grasped it, rose and clasped her with his other arm in the Northern style. Aldrich stepped forward to address the newcomers.

"I am Aldrich Caelius and you are welcome. We will always welcome men of honor," declared Aldrich.

Laelius stepped back in surprise and the men on horseback looked uncomfortable.

"We thank you for your words and for your hospitality," said Laelius.

The gates opened behind Aldrich. He moved to talk to Gregor and the men. Marcella had appeared to perform the crystal test. Each of Andraste's warriors dismounted, grasped Andraste's hand, and moved to be tested. She stood outside with Laelius.

"The Southern prince does not know who you are," stated Laelius when he was sure they would not be overheard.

"He does not know who I once was. My fate has changed. I will never be who I was. He knows me as Paramerion and we are allies. You will like him, Laelius. He is a man of honor," informed Andraste.

"Friendship and allegiance must be built on a foundation of trust. You must tell him," urged Laelius, "He may never forgive you, if he discovers your true identity."

"I no longer have that name or country. We share the same principles and mission. That is all that is needed," Andraste declared and indicated that the conversation was over by turning towards the gate. All of the warriors had passed the crystal test.

"We are honored to have the Victorious amongst us," stated Marcella. There was a sound of disbelief amongst the Shadow Mountains guardsmen.

"The Victorious?" asked Aldrich. He was now concerned.

"You did not realize?" inquired Marcella as she looked at her brother in disbelief.

"Who are the Victorious?" questioned Aaliyah appearing at her mother's side. She peaked behind her mother's skirts at the warriors.

"The Victorious are the most elite fighting force of the Empire. They only answer to their Commander. The Emperor gave them free reign to travel where they were most needed and act as they saw fit. Only fifteen are chosen, and only replaced upon death. They are warriors of nearly unmatchable power from across the Empire," replied Marcella and her voice carried across the courtyard.

"They took the flagship at Thoran with but fifteen warriors," said one of the guardsmen to Gregor.

"You let the Victorious inside the fort?" asked Gregor cautiously to his wife.

"Their intentions are clear," said Marcella lifting her crystal to her husband's face.

"You lead the Victorious?" asked Aldrich. He was staring at Andraste with a mixture of unease and admiration.

"I led the Victorious. My countrymen, however, like me, no longer serve the Emperor. May I introduce Laelius, Valens, Thracius, Priscus, Otho, Laurentius, Hadrian, Glaucio, Gnaeus, Felix, Cato, Avitus, Nero and Maximianus," replied Andraste.

The courtyard was silent as the Victorious and guardsmen surveyed each other. The tension escalated as Laelius reclaimed his spear from his comrade.

"You are awfully short compared to your men," said Aldrich finally.

Andraste looked at her men surrounding her. She had to look up to do so. It was true, they were all at least a foot taller than her.

"Aldrich!" sighed Marcella. However, Andraste and her men laughed.

"How does one become the leader of the Victorious?" asked Gregor.

"The strongest of us is elected to lead us," answered Otho.

Aldrich looked to Andraste. She knew despite his forced cheer that he was measuring her with those sapphire eyes.

"Your brother, did he make it?" asked Laelius and the merriment of the Victorious faded.

"Yes, we are both well," responded Andraste.

She wondered where Brion was. Marcella winked at her mischievously.

"Lady Aurelia and Lady Caecilia?" asked Felix. His normally merry, dark eyes watched her earnestly as she approached. His well-muscled shoulders tensed as he saw her expression.

"Both dead, as are your cousins, Brádach, Eachann, and Fionbharr, charged with the duty of protecting them. I arrived too late to be of service," said Andraste. She put a hand on Felix's shoulder. Felix grasped her free hand. All of the Victorious fell silent. Felix turned so that he faced his brethren. Pure, simmering hate burned in his eyes like coals. He brushed a calloused hand through his wavy, raven hair.

"For what reason?" asked Felix.

"The Emperor would not respond in kind," replied Andraste. She released her hand from Felix and turned to survey the guardsmen.

"I am sorry for your loss. They were two of the sweetest ladies I have ever encountered," said Felix.

"And I for yours," said Andraste softly.

"Gregor, show the Northerners to their quarters. I am sure they will need some rest after their journey. We will all meet again at dinner," ordered Marcella.

Andraste felt Aldrich watching her as she left with the men to see where they would be settled. Once they were behind closed doors, her men seemed relieved.

"The custom here is to not bring your weapons to the dining hall. Join me in a little while and leave your arms," ordered Andraste.

"Commander-" started Thracius. His steel-gray eyes darted to Laelius as he shifted uncomfortably from foot to foot.

"We will bring our war fans, as we have done in similar situations," said Laelius, "Unless you object?"

Andraste did not object. She too carried a metal fan from her belt. She nodded her consent before she left the room. She made her way to the dining. She sat at an empty table and was shortly joined by Brion.

"How go your lessons?" asked Andraste.

Brion shrugged. He broke into a wide smile as her men entered the hall. He rose and grasped each of their hands in the Northern style. They were asking too many questions at once and it was an awkward silence when they realized he could not speak. He looked ashamed at his plate.

"So it is true, your brother also shares in your fate of the curse," stated Nero. His blue eyes flashed angrily as he put a scar-covered arm on the table. His small frame was tense with anger.

"How could you be so reckless? Look at what it has cost you!" Laelius swore at her heatedly.

"It had to be done. After the deaths of Aurelia and Caecilia, I had to investigate. Would you serve an Emperor that would murder his own defenseless nieces? Murder his people for minor offenses?" cried Andraste.

"Why did you not wait for us?" challenged Laurentius.

The eyes of the Victorious turned to her and she had a feeling that other eyes as well as their voices carried across the cavern.

"I thought he would hear reason from me," Andraste said softly.

"Then he is too far gone," declared Laelius.

"The curse. Does it hurt?" asked Gnaeus. He was the youngest and slightest of the Victorious. He had a boyish-face which made him seem younger then he was.

Andraste said nothing.

"Our Commander would not tell if you it did," commented Avitus. Gnaeus looked abashed and lowered his wide dark eyes to the table.

"Tell me of your journey," interrupted Andraste.

Aldrich had entered the dining hall with his niece following behind him. The child was chatting away without taking time to breathe. He nodded at Andraste as he saw her gaze. He continued to Marcella's table. Decima rose and curtsied to him prettily.

"How are you going to get anywhere if he thinks you are a man?" inquired Laelius. All of the men at her table guffawed. Brion shook with soundless laughter.

"I was starting to think you really were a demon," remarked Otho.

"That is enough," said Andraste and her tone was deadly.

Silence fell on the table, but her men exchanged meaningful glances. They were served platters of roasted fowl with carrots and potatoes, grilled bass and trout, a rich venison stew, loaves of fresh made bread, and platter of fruits and cheese.

Marcella saved Aldrich from her daughter's intentions. Decima joined Aldrich and he offered her his arm. The pair then proceeded to the Victorious's table. Aldrich seated Decima across from Andraste and then walked around the table to sit by Andraste's side. The warriors tried to feign their amusement.

"What is so funny?" asked Aldrich.

"Do Southern lords not sit by their ladies?" asked Otho.

"No, the custom is that a lady sits opposite a lord, if they are not blood related," said Aldrich, "Is it not the same in the North?"

"Ladies sit by their lords in the North," replied Maximianus. He glanced to Andraste at Aldrich's side.

"Seriously! Victorious sitting around discussing seating charts. This can hardly be interesting for Lady Decima," snapped Andraste.

"I find our differences fascinating," said Decima. Her voice was more of a purr.

"Why do you all carry fans? Is that not a woman's accessory?" asked Aldrich.

"They can be most useful," replied Laelius.

"Do you not carry war fans in the South?" inquired Andraste. Aldrich shook his head. He eyed the fans with distrust.

"They are mostly use in defense. War fans are used to block blades and disarm opponents. Commanders will use them to issue orders to troops," stated Laelius.

"What does the lady wish to discuss?" interjected Gnaeus gallantly.

"Tell me about your homeland," suggested Decima.

"Which homeland?" inquired Otho.

"What do you mean?" asked Decima.

"It is true seven of us hail from the Northern lands, but all from different territories. There are three men from the Island Kingdoms, one Midlander, one Westerner, and two Southerners," explained Maximianus.

"I would have assumed the Emperor's elite force would have been composed of all Northern men," replied Decima.

"Is the Imperial Army not made of warriors from across the Empire?" rejoined Andraste, "As our mission was to protect the Empire, I enlisted warriors from all territories."

"But the North still dominates," commented Decima.

"The North had the most volunteers," replied Andraste.

"Your numbers only added up to fourteen," said Aldrich.

"I spent my youth divided between the North and the Island Kingdoms. I served in the Imperial Army for eight years. As I have fought and bled for the Empire, I consider myself a citizen of the Empire, not one territory," replied Andraste.

"The Resistance fights to establish lands to their boundaries before the institution of the Empire. What will do you when the Emperor falls?" questioned Aldrich.

"The Emperor will have to fall before we continue this discussion. I do not deal in hypotheticals," answered Andraste. Aldrich and Andraste studied each other.

"And you did not answer my question. I would hear about your homelands. Let us start with the Island Kingdoms," pacified Decima.

"Bunch of inebriated sailors and bloody pirates," commented Nero.

"We prefer swashbuckling adventurers, dauntless explorers, or privateers," corrected Felix.

"So you are from the Island Kingdoms?" asked Aldrich.

"Yes, I hail from the Salt Islands. Valens is from the Spice Islands, and Hadrian from some tiny island that it is yet to be named," answered Felix.

"The Island Kingdoms are a loose federation of all of the eastern islands, which are ruled by King Aelius," commented Valens.

"And you?" asked Decima turning her lovely eyes to Andraste.

"My time there was spent in the capitol of the Island Kingdoms. My mother's homeland is the most Eastern Island on our maps," said Andraste.

"The beautiful Island of Fortune," interjected Felix.

"You share the same birthplace as the former Empress?" asked Aldrich.

"Yes," answered Andraste.

"But why did you call them pirates?" asked Decima to Nero.

"Because they are known to take ships when it suits them," responded Nero.

"It is true. Southern ships have been attacked by the Island Kingdoms," stated Aldrich.

"The Island Kingdoms are heavily populated. They do not possess the land or the resources like the mainland. They survive by fishing, trading, and protecting their coasts from ships from other rival Empires, such as Lionden or Parnesian. Wrongful attacks have only occurred on Imperial ships when the ship did not hoist its colors. Once a mistake is made, the Island Kingdom ships usually escort the ship to their destination. King Aelius is severe in punishing captains that take Imperial ships," defended Valens.

"No wonder relations are so poor with the other Empires," commented Aldrich.

"Why so bothered? Are you trying to forge allegiance?" inquired Felix.

"Indeed," replied Aldrich.

"Any success?" asked Andraste curiously.

"We have opened communications with the Parnesian Empire. However, all they want is sand," answered Aldrich.

"Sand?" repeated Andraste. She looked to the Victorious.

"Whatever for?" asked Valens.

"I could not say," stated Aldrich, "But we are shipping it by boatloads."

"And in return?" asked Felix.

"Charcoal," replied Aldrich.

"The Island Kingdom ships are also known for liberating slave ships from Lionden. With your love of freedom, I am surprised you would so despise freedom fighters," said Andraste.

"The slave ships are not permitted to sail in Southern waters or make port in our cities," responded Aldrich.

"It is evident that Aldrich Caelius has not spent time on a slave ship. If you had, you would hunt them as we do," said Hadrian. He returned his gaze back to his stew.

"Is that a problem? Does Lionden take people from the Island Kingdoms?" asked Aldrich.

"It has been known to happen, but under the watch of the Empire, the attacks have become rarer," responded Felix, "However, we are not so quick to forget."

"Have your people been recovered?" asked Decima. Hadrian did not respond.

"Hadrian released himself and the people on his ship from captivity. However, by the time I and the Imperial Army reached them, the Lionden slavers had slain all of the captives on the other ships in retribution," said Andraste, "We burned the slave ships. The Emperor did not permit us to proceed to the Lionden Empire."

"And that is when you were chosen to join the Victorious?" asked Decima.

Hadrian rose, bowed to Decima stiffly, and left the table.

"The slavers pillaged and burned all of the villages of his homeland.

There was nothing to return to. Our Commander offered him a home with us," responded Valens.

As the dishes were cleared away, music began for dancing.

"Is there dancing every night?" asked Andraste.

"Yes," said Aldrich.

"We only dance on feast days," explained Laurentius.

"Why is that?" asked Decima.

"To give the warriors time to recover," responded Maximianus.

"Your warriors need two months to recover from dancing?" asked Aldrich.

"Well there is the Dance of Swords, which is a competition of sword-play between warriors. The victor is allowed to kiss the Queen of the Feast," explained Gnaeus.

"Did you partake in the competition?" Decima asked Andraste.

"Our Commander is always the victor," said Laelius.

Aldrich and Decima were confused at why the warriors found this so funny.

"Would it be rude to ask for a display?" asked Decima.

Andraste rose herself, "Which of you, ingrates, is ready?"

Brion rose and pointed to her seat. Andraste knew he still worried about her injury.

"So long as I live, I will fight. I will not sit in a corner resting until my time comes. Fortune favors the brave," declared Andraste. She was saluted by the clinking steins of the Victorious.

Brion sat down defeated.

"I will fight, Commander," vowed Otho.

"We will need two swords," said Andraste. Aldrich had two swords brought to the hall.

"You are in for a treat," said Laelius to Decima. He did not join the dance.

"It will be over soon if our Commander starts," alleged Cato. Otho glared at him.

"The Victorious will entertain us with a dance from their homeland," Aldrich announced to the hall.

"What music?" Marcella started to ask. However, the other thirteen warriors had already formed a circle around the duelist.

Usually the circling warriors would have used swords, but they had left their swords in their rooms as Andraste requested. However, each warrior had at least a dagger concealed in his boot or hidden under a sleeve. Andraste shook at her in head in disapproval at her men. The men began to stomp and then raise both daggers. The dagger in the left hand was held still, so that the dagger in the right hand of the warrior beside could next hit with the dagger in his neighbor's left hand. It was an eerie melody that filled the hall.

Otho was tall, slender and muscular. He had short dark hair, dark eyes and a hooked nose. He came from the Midlands. He was lethal with a blade. As was tradition, the two warriors in the center of the circle bowed to each other. Otho charged without hesitation.

"So fast," commented Aldrich to Laelius.

In the time that Aldrich had turned to speak to Laelius, Andraste had unarmed Otho. Gnaeus caught the hurled sword and entered the circle. He lunged at Andraste, but her sword met his blade with a clash.

"Has Paramerion ever lost?" asked Aldrich in admiration as Gnaeus was defeated.

"Rhinauld, Paramerion's foster brother, is the closet I have ever seen. Paramerion has lost duels to him, but that was after nights of heavy drinking," admitted Laelius.

Brion looked embarrassed.

"Rhinauld?" asked Aldrich.

"Lord of the Salt Islands," verified Laelius.

"And where is their foster brother, now?" asked Decima.

"He is on a quest of sorts. The Emperor promised him the hand of Andraste Valerianus, if he retrieved relics from three Ruins," responded Laelius.

"That is extreme, is it not?" questioned Aldrich, "It is rare for anyone to return from the Ruins."

"Rhinauld is doing fairly well, I imagine from pure dumb luck. Paramerion and Rhinauld have retrieved two relics already. However, they parted ways after the executions of Lady Aurelia and Lady Caecilia. Rhinauld went for the third Ruin, and Paramerion to confront the Emperor," answered Laelius.

Aldrich turned his gaze back to the sword dance. Paramerion had defeated all of the opponents and was taunting with gusto for them to come again, but to no avail. Laelius watched his pupil with pride. Andraste rejoined their table, smug. Her cursed shoulder had not stopped her. It throbbed unpleasantly, but it had not thwarted her fighting.

"Perhaps, some more genteel dancing for the evening?" suggested Marcella.

She seemed unsure of how to proceed. The guardsmen and Lords were discussing the show of swordsmanship.

"Of course," said Aldrich rising, offering his arm to Decima. He looked to Andraste, "Shall I introduce you to-"

"I do not care to dance," interrupted Andraste.

"As you wish," replied Aldrich. He and Decima proceeded to the dance floor.

The Victorious had retaken their seats as the musicians started playing music.

"You will not stay, Commander?" asked Laelius.

"You do not care to watch the dancers?" asked Otho.

"Or dance yourself?" asked Marcella, making her way to their table.

"You would have a better partner in Avitus or Cato. They hail from the Southern lands and are more familiar with your dances," said Andraste, "There are scrolls I wish to study in the library, if it would not displease you."

"Please, help yourself," said Marcella. She looked to Brion, who also rose to follow Andraste. They headed to the library.

"Show me what you have been reading," ordered Andraste.

Brion unrolled a large scroll. It was in a dead language. It was very faded.

"How do they have this?" asked Andraste. Brion gestured to the Caelius crest on the wall.

"I know, but-" started Andraste. She sat down and stared at the scroll.

She was not going to be able to translate this scroll. It was beyond her.

"Can you read it?" Andraste inquired to her brother. He handed her his notes.

"You wrote your notes in the ancient language of my mother's country?" Andraste asked exasperated. Her head swam just looking at the tiny characters. Brion looked at her pointedly.

"Yes, I can read it, but it will take me some time," said Andraste. She yawned and rose, "But not tonight. I am proud of your progress. I had no idea you had become such a scholar. Truly, Brion, it is an accomplishment."

Chapter Four

The morning brought ill tidings. A messenger brought the news that Empire forces were moving towards the Shadow Mountains. The full force would reach the fort within the week. It was decided that they would journey further south to the City of Sorcery. Even the Emperor would think twice before committing his troops to such an engagement. The City of Sorcery was on neutral territory and the University opened to any who had the ability. An untrained sorcerer was a liability to everyone.

"I am sorry we have put you to such trouble," Andraste apologized to Decima and Marcella. Andraste bowed to them.

"We fight the same battle. There is no need for apology," said Decima. The lady turned and left.

"Decima was betrothed to my eldest brother, Marius, who was slain in the Black War," said Marcella, "She has never been the same."

"I thought she was interested in your younger brother," admitted Andraste.

"No. She has sworn to never marry," replied Marcella.

Their conversation was cut short as Aldrich joined them himself.

"Do you come with us, or will you stay with Decima?" asked Aldrich.

"I stay in the Shadow Mountains with our foster sister," declared Marcella.

"I am sorry that I cannot stay with you," said Aldrich.

"Our best hope is for you to head towards the Ruins. I have sent word to the City of Sorcerers. My teacher will be waiting to continue Brion's training. His power needs to be unlocked. Someone has sealed it a way.

Brion already knows more than I do," acknowledged Marcella. She did not look pleased by the admission.

"It that common in the North?" asked Aldrich.

"No. It is unmentionable," responded Andraste.

She looked for her brother. He was listening intently to Felix tell a story. His shoulders shook with silent laughter.

"Who would have done such a thing?" questioned Marcella.

Andraste did not answer. If the Emperor had known his son had such power, he would have had him executed. Brion would have been a danger to their father and her claim to the Empire. Brion, who had loved her and taken care of her since her mother's death, could have posed her greatest threat.

"The horses are ready, Commander," informed Laelius.

Andraste grasped hands with Marcella.

"Until we meet again," said Andraste.

"Once you conquer the Ruins, we will meet you in our homeland at the Southern palace," said Marcella, who smiled, but it faded as she turned to her brother.

Andraste turned her back on them so the pair could depart in privacy. Andraste mounted her horse. Nero and Valens left to ride ahead as scouts. They were quickly joined by two Southern guardsmen, who met them speed for speed. Andraste watched them as they faded into the distance. It was only Aldrich, Kasimir and Eadbehrt, who joined their party.

"There were volunteers, but I will not deplete Decima's forces when the Shadow Mountains could be attacked," explained Aldrich.

"You need no explanation," said Andraste. However, she was pleased by his words, and knew he would earn her men's respect as well.

"May I introduce Lord Eadbehrt of the Pearl Coves, and Lord Kasimir of the Southern Marshlands. The guardsmen that rode ahead are Detlef and Falk," said Aldrich to the remaining Victorious.

"You volunteered?" asked Felix incredulously.

"Did not you?" questioned Andraste, "Ride on, Felix."

"Yes, Commander," answered Felix. He saluted before riding past.

"I am surprised that you allow such jesting amongst your men," commented Eadbehrt.

"Do you think that no one can speak in the North? Think for themselves? That we go about our missions in silence?" asked Andraste.

"Of course not. He was referring to that fact that the Imperial Army is known for its order and discipline," interjected Aldrich.

"None of us remained in the Imperial Army for long," answered Maximianus.

"The Victorious are known for their courage, but I would classify it as insanity," said Laelius. He surveyed the Victorious.

"That is why it is such a band of misfits," commented Otho, "The other Commanders did not know what to do with us, and so, we were allowed to join the Victorious."

"That is revisionist history," stated Maximianus. Andraste laughed.

"To be continued, my fine historian. We ride," ordered Andraste. Seeing that they were all assembled, Andraste spurred her horse onto the road.

Andraste looked out across the vista. They were in Midland mountain country and the view was breathtaking. The mountains were near blue in the morning light. The mountains rolled into the distance infinitely. Bold, warm clouds flirted with the blue sky, and the sun peaked through like a hesitant chaperone. The trees nearest them sported gold and burnt orange leaves. A few leaves were beginning to fall and were carried on the wind.

"Do you think it odd that we have not seen a soul for three days?" asked Aldrich.

"Is it usually so unpopulated," replied Andraste.

"It is lonely country. However, we have not seen any Imperial troops that we know are coming. Nor have we received word from the Shadow Mountains," said Aldrich.

"Should we send a messenger?" asked Andraste.

She would usually not sacrifice one of her troops on such an errand, but knew Aldrich worried for his family and his people.

"No. When we reach the City, there will be news either way," responded Aldrich.

They stood looking down to the valley below.

"You have retrieved relics from two Ruins already," Aldrich said finally.

"Yes, but it was mostly Rhinauld," replied Andraste. Aldrich looked as though he did not believe the statement but he let it pass.

"What will we encounter?" asked Aldrich.

"I was surprised by how different the two Ruins were. There are traps, spirits, and monsters. One was controlled by fire, the other was dominated by ice," answered Andraste.

"And yet you still returned," stated Aldrich.

"Not all of us returned," contradicted Andraste.

"I did not know-" started Aldrich.

Andraste put a hand up to stop him.

"Why is it that so few know that two relics have been found?" inquired Aldrich.

"The Emperor and his secrets. He is using Rhinauld for his goals," replied Andraste.

"You do not think the Emperor would have let him marry his daughter, if she had lived?" questioned Aldrich.

"No. The Emperor would not care over such an insignificant detail. All but one of my sisters are already married and have children, or promised to-" Andraste stopped abruptly realizing that she had said too much.

"The Emperor is your father?" asked Aldrich.

Andraste could see him struggling with the information. His hand slid to his hilt.

"Yes," answered Andraste.

"You want to kill your own father?" questioned Aldrich.

"He cursed my brother. He has killed two of my relatives and his people for no reason. There are worse things occurring in the Citadel. My father or a stranger, he must be stopped," responded Andraste.

"Who are you?" inquired Aldrich.

He removed his hand from his hilt, but he seized her roughly by her arm to turn her to him.

"Paramerion," responded Andraste.

He studied her intently, and released her arm.

"You do not wear that hood due to disfigurement," stated Aldrich.

"No, but the curse is spreading," said Andraste.

It had consumed her entire left side. She took off her glove and lifted a shadowed hand for Aldrich's inspection.

"Your own father cursed you?" asked Aldrich incredulously.

"Yes," answered Andraste. They stood glaring at each other on the overlook.

Andraste turned as she heard the crunch of tree branches behind them. Brion lifted his bow and gestured towards the valley.

"I will hunt with you," agreed Andraste.

"So you brother is also a Valerianus?" asked Aldrich. He kept his eyes locked on Brion.

"We both once bore than name," replied Andraste, "Come, Loudmouth. We want to return before dark."

Aldrich did not follow them. Once they were out of sight, Brion looked at her questioningly.

"I know who he is, but I trust him," asserted Andraste.

Brion raised his eyebrows. She did not speak for the rest of their hunt. Brion caught two rabbits and a score of doves. Andraste felt exhausted just by walking beside him. She did not lift her bow once. As they approached their camp, they could hear the distinct sounds of yelling and fighting. Andraste and Brion both ran towards the sound.

Brion braced his arm in front of her, so she would not charge into the clearing. She surveyed the scene. A family of trolls was wreaking havoc on their campsite. The Southerners were already on the ground, many unconscious. One troll had Aldrich upside down by his ankle. He had dropped his great sword, but Andraste saw several slashes on the troll's chest and face.

"Put him down at once!" Andraste yelled at the troll. The troll sniffed the air.

"Valerianus?" the troll asked. Brion joined her side.

"Two," answered a second troll.

The troll slowly put down Aldrich on the earth. Aldrich struggled to regain his dignity.

"What on earth are you doing?" asked Andraste.

"They attacked us," replied the troll.

"Not you," said Andraste. She glared at Aldrich.

"They are trolls!" protested Aldrich.

"Most Midland trolls are peaceful. Do you not know anything?" she yelled. Aldrich stood and glared at her.

"It said it was going to eat us," replied Aldrich.

Andraste looked up at the troll.

"Are your people still vegetarians?" asked Andraste. The troll nodded once. She glared pointedly at Aldrich.

"Why are you here?" questioned Andraste. The troll shifted uncomfortably.

"We were ordered to seek and find a party of Southerners, Victorious, and two Valerianus," replied the troll.

"How big is the unit that comes?" inquired Andraste.

"Score of men, maybe more," replied the troll.

"Go, now! Tell them we went in another direction," ordered Andraste. The troll stood unsure and looked to its family.

"That is an order from the Valerianus house," confirmed Andraste.

The troll bowed awkwardly. The trolls headed back the way they had come. The ground shook with their steps.

"You can order trolls?" asked Aldrich.

"The Midland troll territory fell to the Empire long ago. Trolls are uncommonly stupid and bound by family units. They will not understand that I am exiled and that they should not accept my orders. They will always see me as Valerianus," said Andraste, "That is something you have in common."

She turned her back on Aldrich before he could respond. She surveyed the injured Southerners. She inspected their wounds. They were bruised and shaken, but had no serious injuries.

"Laelius!" yelled Andraste.

"Yes, Commander," said Laelius. He came from out of the night.

"You allowed this to happen? You watched them get beaten?" questioned Andraste angrily.

"I told them not to engage, and that we could reason with the trolls. They ignored my warning. I refuse to be beaten for their ignorance and pride," responded Laelius.

"Assemble!" Andraste yelled at her men. She was surrounded by the Victorious on one side and the Southerners on the other.

"We are in this together. Victorious, you will protect these men as if they were me. They are in unfamiliar country and do not know the ways of the North. You must keep them from pointless errors and unnecessary harm. Do not forget the true enemy," Andraste said. She turned on her men, "I will perceive any similar actions on your part as mutiny, and you will be punished accordingly."

"Yes, Commander," said her men.

"We need to ride. The Northern unit will be on our heels, and they will not be as stupid as the trolls," ordered Andraste.

"Debatable," alleged Otho.

They packed up their camp quickly and readied their horses. When all were assembled, they rode hard into the night. When Andraste felt that they were a safe enough distance away, she had them make camp in order to rest the horses. Her shoulder was aching. She was certain the pain was getting worse.

She took care of her horse, and then spread her bedroll underneath the branches of an oak tree. She fell asleep instantly. She was woken later by Brion. He had prepared a quick rabbit and dove stew. He forced a bowl into her hands. Andraste took it. She could hear the Southerners talking in the night. The Victorious had camped on the opposite side of the clearing.

"Heiyoh!" called Priscus as he entered the clearing with Thracius.

"Nothing to report," said Thracius to Laelius.

"Nero and Laurentius relieved you?" asked Laelius.

"Yes, sir," replied Priscus.

Laelius gestured for them to take some stew. Priscus and Thracius took their places on the Victorious side of the clearing. The Southerners watched the exchange and then resumed their conversation.

"Kasimir, did you not see Paramerion's face when he tended your wounds after the attack of the Emperor's guards?" asked Eadbehrt.

"I was feverish, my lord. The only face I dreamed of was that of Lady Eldgrimson," replied Kasimir.

"She did have face out of dreams," agreed Eadbehrt.

"Truly? It sounds as though she would rival the beauty of Andraste Valerianus, the way you two carry on," commented Detlef.

"I never saw the princess, so I could not make a comparison," replied Kasimir.

"It is said that Andraste Valerianus rebelled after the executions of her young cousins. The Resistance says that she was not killed in a skirmish. She was executed by the hands of the Emperor himself. Brion was the sworn protector of Andraste. What man could stay with the Emperor after that?" asked Eadbehrt.

"It is a shame. She was said to be the best of the Valerianus heirs. She was most likely to be Empress. She was a Commander in the Imperial Army as well. One of the four Commanders referred to as the Northern pillars. She led the Imperial Army at Alexius and Gardenia," said Falk.

"I thought that was Titus?" inquired Aldrich.

"No. He led the Army at Thoran. She led the attack on the Flagship there," replied Falk.

"A fearful task, indeed. To think her own brother had her assigned to the front," commented Detlef.

"The lady volunteered," replied Kasimir.

"Remarkable courage," admired Eadbehrt.

"She was also the only Valerianus to solve problems instead of just executions. Remember the incident in the Midland capitol?" asked Falk.

"What happened?" questioned Aldrich.

"The Midland government was divided into two sides on almost every issue. It led to a complete halt of all production. There were strikes, fights, and a political shut down. The situation almost escalated into civil war. The princess was sent to resolve the situation with the Imperial Army, but not one drop of blood was shed," answered Kasimir.

"What was her solution?" asked Aldrich.

"She gave one party the control of the city on the first, third, and fifth days of the week. The second party had control on the second, fourth and sixth days of the week. They both had to rest on the seventh. Each party would institute its policies on its designated days, but they could not implement great change because the rival side would reverse the policies on their days," responded Kasimir.

"That is both ridiculous and inefficient," replied Aldrich.

"No, it was genius," returned Kasimir, "The struggle was confined to the bickering of the politicians, while a balance was made. Even with the inefficiency of the new system, they still produced more goods than before."

"And no one died," stated Falk, "Can you think of Valerianus interference without at least one person dying?"

"Any man would mourn the loss of such a lady. It must be Brion," suggested Eadbehrt.

"Paramerion did once call Loudmouth, Brion," agreed Aldrich. Brion glared at Andraste.

"The princess did order executions," interjected Falk.

"Of corrupt Northern lords," said Kasimir. Aldrich raised his eyebrows.

"Do you not know the details?" asked Kasimir. Aldrich shook his head.

"There was a Northern lord that was gouging his people for gold. When his subjects could no longer provide, he would force them to labor in his mines," explained Kasimir.

"What was his punishment?" asked Aldrich.

"She had him buried alive underneath the weight of the collected gold," answered Kasimir.

"But all Northern lords and officials collect unseemly taxes. Why only punish one?" asked Aldrich.

"He was the only lord in her jurisdiction that did so," said Falk.

"Each of the Northern Pillars was assigned a territory. The princess watched over the East, Tobias the West, Matthias the South, and Titus the North," answered Kasimir.

"If Loudmouth is Brion, then do you think Paramerion is Titus?" proposed Detlef.

"No, we saw Paramerion fight Titus in the North," answered Aldrich.

"Then who is Paramerion?" asked Falk.

"Matthias? The third brother? Brion, Titus and Matthias share the same mother. Their mother fought against the Emperor before and was executed for her actions," suggested Eadbehrt.

"No, it cannot be Matthias. He still leads the Imperial Army," contradicted Kasimir.

"Perhaps it is Tobias, Lord of the Mystic Caverns," suggested Detlef.

"Mystic Caverns?" asked Aldrich.

"It is a territory in the far West. It is said that Tobias, once the Commander of the Victorious, was engaged to Andraste Valerianus. Perhaps he joined the Resistance after her execution?" asked Detlef.

"I would not call it an engagement," said Otho from across the clearing. The Southerners fell silent.

"What would you call it?" asked Falk.

"The Emperor wanted to arrange a marriage between the princess and a Western Lord, who was a murdering, back-stabbing lecher. Needless to say, the princess objected. The Emperor said he would stop the marriage if there was a Northern lord that she would accept. She named Tobias, who spoke for her then and there," explained Otho.

"It was awkward at the time," said Maximianus.

"Why?" asked Detlef.

"He was her commanding officer," answered Otho.

"The princess was a member of the Victorious?" asked Aldrich.

"She was one of the founding members," answered Laelius.

"Was she so great a warrior?" questioned Eadbehrt.

"She is crazier beyond all reason like many of the Ice Palace warriors. She is near undefeatable with a sword, lethal with daggers, and uncanny with a bow. Her hand to hand combat is passable. She acts more on instinct then foresight. A bear would have more accuracy with a lance or spear. She is proud and never listens. That being said, I have never met a warrior, who I would more blindly follow into battle," said Laelius. He shot Andraste a look from across the clearing.

"Was," corrected Valens. He did not look at Andraste.

"You must miss her. I am sorry for your loss," said Aldrich.

"I feel that she is always with us," responded Otho. Maximianus shot Otho a look of warning.

"You most of all, Felix. What are you going to tell Rhinauld when he hears of his lady's death?" asked Valens.

"I will let our Commander tell him. My Commander ordered me to remain behind when Andraste went to confront the Emperor. It was only luck that Brion returned to the Citadel at the same time," stated Felix.

"Your Commander witnessed the execution of the princess?" asked Aldrich. He looked puzzled.

"Loudmouth and Paramerion were both present during sentencing," answered Laelius.

"Why would you miss her most of all?" asked Detlef.

"It was not Brion, who was her protector. They went separate ways near two years ago as he went to return to his University studies. The duty, which I swore to the Lord of the Salt Islands, and which I have failed, was to protect her. I should have been there, as Valens loves to remind me," replied Felix. He stared at the ground.

"We all failed," stated Maximianus.

"The Emperor would not have spared you or any of us. My princess had faith in people. She believed that they would do the right thing, including the Emperor," said Laelius.

"She was wrong," said Otho. Laelius turned his back on the Southerners. Otho remained where he was.

"Is your Commander the Lord of the Mystic Caverns?" asked Kasimir.

"Our Commander is not Tobias. When the Lord of the Mystic Caverns realized that the princess did not return his feelings, he left the Victorious. He returned to his lands, married a local woman, and never looked back," stated Nero.

"So then who is your Commander?" asked Aldrich.

"Paramerion," answered Andraste clearly, so that they could all hear her.

The Southern lords ended their conversation. Brion raised his eyebrows. Andraste lowered her voice so only Brion could hear her.

"I like being Paramerion," Andraste whispered, "You know what would happen if it was rumored I was still alive? My hand would be sought to booster claims for the Empire after the Emperor has fallen."

Brion glanced at Aldrich and then back to Andraste.

"He hates our family and by extension me," replied Andraste, "He wants nothing, but to be rid of the Empire. Once we defeat the Emperor, we will go our separate ways."

Brion put a hand on her arm. She had heard it too. They were being approached from the North. They both picked up their bows silently. Andraste nodded to Brion. They both released arrows into the night. They heard screams as their arrows met their mark. The Southern lords were on their feet. Andraste was already deep in the woods, following her arrow.

"Scouts," confirmed Andraste as she examined the body. The scout wore the heliotrope-colored robes of the Emperor's personal guard.

"They are close," said Laelius.

"They will have heard the sound," added Glaucio.

"We will stand our ground. We should be evenly matched," said Andraste. She turned towards the Victorious, "Tree formation and bows. I want absolute silence. They will not see it coming."

"And us?" asked Aldrich.

"Get out of sight," ordered Andraste.

"We will fight," defended Aldrich, "We do not hide."

"I said get out of sight. Do you want to be caught in the crossfire?" snapped Andraste.

Her men were already climbing trees and being concealed behind branches. Aldrich nodded to his men. They did not have time to grab their bows. They hastily climbed trees as well. Brion extended his hand from the tree and pulled Andraste up. She climbed higher into the tree.

They waited. The sun was beginning to rise and cover the clearing in gentle light. Andraste heard the sound of a man yell as he found the body of one of the scouts. Horses were galloping in their direction. The horsemen wore the amaranthine uniforms of the Emperor's personal guards. Andraste waited for the last horse to pass through. The unit had stopped and was surveying their camp. She released her arrow and made her mark. There was a volley of arrows from the trees.

The Imperial guards fell from their horses to the ground. Andraste knocked another arrow to her bow and released it. She took down the commanding officer. There was another wave of arrows, followed by a third. The guards had nowhere to escape. Andraste watched the men on the ground. She waited. There was silence once more in the clearing. She dropped out of the tree and approached. Avitus also left his position and examined the bodies of the fallen.

"See. Just about as smart as trolls," commented Otho. He dropped to her side. Andraste drew her sword.

"No survivors," confirmed Avitus.

"Not an arrow that missed its mark. All kill shots," Kasimir said to Aldrich.

"My lords, if you hunt the Victorious, you will find that you are the hunted," warned Laelius. He stared at Aldrich without remorse. Aldrich met the gaze without hesitation.

"Nero, Laurentius," called Laelius. They waited a few minutes for the men to approach the clearing. The rest of the men busied with packing up their belongings and extinguishing the fire.

"Heiyoh!" called Nero before he entered the clearing. He spoke to Laelius as he gathered his horse, "Nothing from the West."

"Heiyoh! Nothing from the East," confirmed Laurentius as he entered the clearing.

"Heiyoh?" asked Kasimir.

"Short for hey, do not shoot me, I am on your side, etc.," said Otho.

"Has that happened before?" inquired Aldrich.

"During the Forest Wars, after a particularly hellish skirmish, we were all separated. Our Commander, just a member at the time, green as could be, rounded up the majority of the Victorious and we held our position. However, a blood, mud-covered creature crawled into our camp. Our Commander shot the creature in the shoulder. Unfortunately, it ended up being Tobias. His only response sounded like 'Heiyoh.' Henceforth, whenever we return or enter our camp, we yell 'Heiyoh'," explained Felix.

"You shot your commanding officer?" questioned Aldrich. Andraste ignored the question.

"Tobias should have announced himself. That night we encountered many demons, monsters, and things that were classified as unknown. We could not tell friend from foe," interjected Laelius.

"But, in the North, is not the penalty death for wounding an officer?" asked Kasimir.

"Tobias took the punishment himself. He said he had not properly instructed his troops and the fault was his. The penalty for incompetence in an officer is forty lashes," answered Nero.

"He sounds like a noble lord," stated Eadbehrt.

"We should move on," said Andraste.

She did not wait for a response. She rolled up her bedroll and saddled her horse. It looked at her with weary eyes. She stroked its neck. She mounted her horse and rode out of the clearing.

Andraste made camp early. She knew the horses and her men were tired from days of hard riding and fighting. She saw her Victorious fashion rods for fishing by the mountain stream.

"Is the fishing good here?" inquired Aldrich.

"Yes, rainbow trout," replied Andraste.

Aldrich looked uncertain. He glanced towards the Victorious, who were watching him closely.

"Are your men always so protective?" questioned Aldrich.

"They worry about the curse," responded Andraste.

She turned her eyes to her men. As they saw her gaze, they resumed their tasks. Aldrich stood still. He raised his sapphire eyes to her.

"We should have listened to Laelius about the trolls. I am sorry for the trouble," said Aldrich.

"There are no trolls in the South?" asked Andraste.

"I hear your men tell tales of trolls, monsters, and mythical beasts. In the South, they would just be tales. I thought they were teasing us at first, but, now I know they are true," said Aldrich.

"The North is dangerous to all who enter. Some of the bans, the travel visas are for your safety," replied Andraste.

"And yet you ride in the wilderness," responded Aldrich.

"We are the strongest warriors of the Empire. We go where we are needed. My men answer to me, and I answer only to the Emperor," stated Andraste.

"It must be nice to enjoy such freedom," replied Aldrich. Andraste turned on him.

"Do not mock me, Aldrich Caelius. We have suffered greatly, as have our people. The South is not the only region with claims against the Emperor," asserted Andraste.

"I did not mock you-" started Aldrich.

Andraste punched Aldrich in the ribs. He did not flinch.

"Ouch!" Andraste cried. She dropped to her knee.

"You are the one who hit me," reminded Aldrich.

"The curse is burning," said Andraste.

The burning sensation consumed her whole arm. She sensed an ominous presence, as if someone was looking for her. Brion was at her side instantly. He carried a crystal in his hand and it bathed her in radiant, pure light. She felt the sound of the Victorious surrounding them, as well as the Southerners.

"Sorcery," declared Thracius.

"The Emperor is targeting Paramerion. He is following the curse," said Gnaeus watching Brion's movements.

"Is that why the curse is spreading?" asked Aldrich.

Brion looked at Aldrich in surprise, but nodded.

"What does that mean?" inquired Laelius.

"It means that the Emperor has rejected his offer of a year. It means that our Commander is running out of time," responded Gnaeus.

"Is it true?" asked Aldrich. Brion nodded.

"How do you know such things?" interrogated Kasimir.

"My grandfather, Gaius, is the Grand Sorcerer of the Empire," said Gnaeus, not looking at the Southern lord.

"Are you a sorcerer?" demanded Aldrich. His eyes narrowed.

"I can do simple divination, some healing potions, but that is the extent of my abilities," said Gnaeus.

"Lady Gaia, however-" started Nero.

Gnaeus silenced his comrade with a blow. The Southern warriors looked at the Northern warriors in confusion.

"You will not speak of my sister," stated Gnaeus. Laelius put a controlling hand on Gnaeus's arm.

"I am fine. It is stopped for now," said Andraste.

Brion directed her towards their blankets. He took a bottle of ointment and two pills from his saddlebags and turned to her, holding it in his hand. His intentions were clear.

"I will do it myself," protested Andraste.

She took the two pills and swallowed them while he watched. The effect was instantaneous. She was a sleep before her head hit the ground. The ointment rolled out of her hand.

"How long do we have before the curse is complete?" asked Aldrich.

Brion held up two fingers.

"Two months? Down from ten months to two months in a week?" asked Aldrich.

Brion shook his head. His eyes glistened with angry tears.

"Two weeks?" cried Aldrich. Brion shushed him.

"We are not going to make it to the City of Sorcery. That is why you have been taking us east and not south," commented Aldrich.

Brion looked abashed. He gestured towards the South.

"No, I will not let you go to the Ruins alone. Marcella said Paramerion would die if you went now. You will need our combined strength," announced Aldrich.

The two men glared at each other. The silence lengthened. Brion extended his arm in truce. Aldrich grasped it.

"But how did Paramerion not realize it?" inquired Aldrich.

Brion held up the jar of pills.

"You have been drugging him since the Shadow Mountains? When he fought the sword dance was he drugged? The skirmishes with the Arisen?" asked Aldrich. Brion nodded.

"So his full strength is even greater?" inquired Aldrich in disbelief. Brion nodded once more.

"Be that as it may, we will not reach the nearest Ruins on foot in two weeks' time," stated Aldrich. Brion nodded, but he smiled.

"We would have to take a boat," determined Aldrich. Brion nodded again.

"We do not have time to camp. I say we ride," said Aldrich. Brion agreed.

Aldrich rallied their comrades. Brion mounted his stallion. Laelius lifted Andraste to Brion. After making sure she was secure, Brion urged his horse onward.

It took two days to reach the Eastern Ocean. The men and horses were exhausted, as they had only made camp when absolutely necessary. The ocean was a steely gray, and the waves were rough. The sky was dark and full of promise. There were no seagulls flying in the sky. They had already taken cover in the roofs of the port town. The wind that smelled of salt and seaweed was beginning to pick up and howl.

"We have reached the ocean, but now what? Can your Northern horses fly?" drowled Kasimir.

Brion only smiled. On the horizon appeared a large flagship with emerald sails detailed with golden dragons. The ship was headed towards the port town.

"The King of the Island Kingdoms? Why would he help us?" asked Eadbehrt.

"Because everyone hates the Empire," returned Otho and all of the Victorious laughed. The Southerners laughed as well.

Brion urged his exhausted horse forward.

"Loudmouth is right," confirmed Aldrich. He urged his stallion on as well, "Let us make haste!"

Brion had not expected Andraste's uncle to meet them in person, yet there he was.

King Aelius of the Island Kingdoms paced back and forth on the deck of his flagship. For the first time, Brion felt anxious. Brion wondered how far the Southern prince would aid him if this King chose to avenge the death of his own daughters at the hands of the Emperor.

"Brion!" hailed the King. His booming voice echoed across the bay. Aldrich locked his eyes on Brion. The Southern lords exchanged looks. Brion undid his hood so that he could meet the King's eyes.

Heads from the townspeople turned as the armor clad King came on to the shore. The King of the Island Kingdoms was a special specimen of his man with his great frame. He had wild, unkempt golden curling hair and a full golden beard that framed his thick lips. His eyes were the same sea-green color as Andraste's.

Brion bowed his head from his horse. The King offered his arms to take Andraste. Brion hesitated.

"You think I would harm my sister's child?" The King bellowed as he turned from red to scarlet to crimson.

"I would never harm my niece. Now stop being a fool. We have no time to waste," ordered the King. He had decades of authority and command to aid him.

Brion looked into the older man's eyes and relented. Ever so carefully he lowered his sister to the King's awaiting arms.

"Niece?" asked Aldrich as he blushed to the roots of his red hair.

Laelius ignored Aldrich, dismounted and gestured for the rest of their company to do the same. They led their horses onto the ship and let the ship hands take them below. The King and Brion had disappeared into the King's own cabin.

"Niece?" repeated Aldrich.

"Did you not find it odd you have never seen Paramerion bathe or relieve-" started Gnaeus to Aldrich.

"That is enough!" snapped Laelius reprimanding the younger warrior, "Show some respect for the princess."

"Princess?" breathed Aldrich and then he remembered his last conversation with his comrade. It seemed so long ago.

"So you mean all of those stories and talk on the road were witnessed by a princess of the Empire?" asked Detlef.

Laelius shrugged in response at the indignant guardsman.

"You should have told us we traveled with a lady!" stuttered Falk.

"Are your standards so different in the South to have to be advised on how to behave in the presence of a lady?" asked Maximianus.

"Is it so common for women to be warriors?" questioned Eadbehrt.

"Yes, many of our comrades are female. There is one whole squadron composed of female warriors. They are responsible for guarding the Ice Palace," answered Gnaeus.

"Is it not so in the South?" asked Nero.

"No!" said all of the Southerners at once. All five men were more embarrassed then they could say.

"Cato, Avitus, you are also from the South. Has our Commander's gender bothered you as much?" asked Laelius.

Avitus laughed in his face, while Cato shrugged. Laelius turned and faced Aldrich and his men. They looked abashed. The ship had started to leave the port.

"So, if she is the niece of the King of the Island Kingdoms-" started Eadbehrt.

"Lady Eldgrimson," said Aldrich. He exchanged glances with Eadbehrt, but Kasimir would not meet his eyes. Aldrich was flushed with anger.

"My princess is Andraste Eldgrimson Valerianus, heiress to the Empire," stated Laelius. He watched Aldrich's reaction carefully.

"Was," commented Otho softly and Laelius flinched.

"She would have been the next Empress," restated Laelius.

"All this time, after all of our talks, no one admitted she was Andraste Valerianus. No one said that your Commander should be addressed as she," said Aelius. He surveyed the Victorious with distrust.

Laelius turned to face the Southerners, "If you have changed your mind, now is the time to leave. If you cannot fight with a woman, if you cannot fight with the daughter of the Emperor, then now is your chance to go. But I will tell you, you will never find any warrior as strong, as noble, or as valiant. We, the Victorious, gave our vows to fight, not for the Emperor, but to Andraste Valerianus. It was she who spared our lands and our people from the Emperor's cruelty and wrath. It was for she whom we will live and die."

"I have heard stories of Princess Andraste and her mercy. I will be honored fight by her side but I will not abide being lied to," alleged Aldrich.

His men bowed their heads in acknowledgement, but they all looked uneasy.

"Your words sound as they should, but I doubt their sincerity," said Laelius. Aldrich and Laelius approached each other, each looking as he would do the other in.

"You mean you have traveled all this way, and not known who you traveled with?" boomed a voice behind Aldrich.

Aldrich turned to see the King of the Island Kingdoms approaching from the cabin and laughing heartily. The Island men followed suit. Aldrich felt like a fool. He noted that Brion and Laelius did not laugh.

"How is your patient?" Aldrich asked Brion, and the King's laughter faded.

"The best we can do is to keep her sleeping until we reach the Ruins. I hear that you, Prince of the Southern lands, have been much aid to my niece. I will not forget it. I thank you and welcome you to my ship," said the King gravely.

Aldrich bowed his head in acknowledgement.

"Brion, show our guests to their quarters. I have things to do," said the King as he entered the Captain's cabin.

"The King is not good with people," said Otho once the King was out of earshot.

"He is well, considering," commented Gnaeus.

"Considering?" asked Falk.

"The Emperor did execute King Aelius's daughters. They were not yet sixteen and seventeen," answered Gnaeus sadly.

The men grew silent. Brion motioned them to follow him below deck. He saw that the men were properly quartered and then returned to his sister's side.

The curse was spreading at a rapid rate. The ointment was no longer stopping its progression. It had consumed Andraste's entire left side. Her forehead burned with fever. Her hair was soaked with sweat and her cheeks were rosy with heat. Brion clasped her hands in his and prayed. He was joined by four of the King's sorcerers. Brion watched them cautiously. They did not speak to him. They each drew a chair to a corner of the bed and began to sing.

Brion heard the door open and the King entered the room. He put a hand on Brion's shoulder, "We cannot stop the curse, but we can delay it. There is a chance that within the Ruin there is a relic that can heal any illness or counteract any curse."

Brion nodded. He clasped the King's hand. The sorcerers' singing became louder and the sleeping princess was involved in a gentle green light. She seemed to relax and drift to an easier slumber.

Fortune favored them with a strong wind that allowed them to sail to the Darklands in record time. They reached the black sands and all talk on the deck seized as the black island came into view.

"Should we wake her?" Laelius asked the King. Brion shook his head in protest. Aldrich's eyes rested on the King.

"You will not succeed without her," the King spoke directly to Aldrich.

"Brion, you will stay here with the sorcerers and aid in their protection spell. You are not strong enough for offensive magic. You will perish if you follow her. She will be well protected by the Prince of the Southern lands," said the King.

Aldrich did not know what he had done to earn the King's liking. They had spoken over the course of the journey. At one point the King had tried to instruct Aldrich and play some sort of game with dominos, but the King could not remember the rules. Accordingly, the King won every game.

"Wake her," the King ordered Brion.

Brion reluctantly turned towards the cabin.

The curse had started to creep up her neck and onto her face. It had started to reach across her right shoulder and down her arm. Brion sat on her bed and took her hand in his. With his free hand he placed it on his sister's forehead. Andraste's eyes fluttered open.

"Brion?" asked Andraste. She looked around at her surroundings.

"You drugged me," she stated.

She sat up slowly and looked at the four sorcerers. As was befitting their trade they were heavily cloaked, so she could not see their faces.

"Many thanks," Andraste said softly. She put a hand to her hair and realized her own cloak was missing. At the same time she realized the progress of the shadow that had enveloped her. She gasped.

"My sweet one, do not worry. We have reached the Darklands. Do not lose hope. We still have a chance," said the King as he took the place on her other side.

"Uncle!" she cried. She threw herself at the burly man and he wrapped his arms around her. She thought of her young cousins.

"I was too late. I had no idea. I am so sorry!" she cried into her uncle's shoulder.

"Now is not that time for mourning, Andraste. We must fight in order to honor those we loved. You must enter the Darklands. You must go now," the King advised gently. He dried her tears with his cloak. He was struck by how much she resembled his beloved sister.

"Yes, Uncle," said Andraste. She tried not to look at the progression of the curse. Brion covered her with her cloak. She secured her hair and concealed her face.

"I have asked Brion to stay behind. The Southern prince will accompany you on shore," said the King.

Andraste was startled and turned on her uncle. Her unwavering faith in him diminished.

"The reason my daughters died was that Aurelia told a prophecy. You and the Southern prince were destined to meet, which you have. You found your way to the Darklands and you must enter together," ordered the King.

Andraste offered her hands to her uncle and her brother. Brion kissed her hand. Her uncle met her gaze, squeezed her hand, and then let go. Brion offered the crystal Marcella had given him. He put it in her cloak pocket.

"Thank you, Brion," whispered Andraste.

She walked out onto the deck. The limited sunshine still nearly blinded her after the week of darkness that she had spent in slumber.

"P-" started Aldrich. He was unsure of how to address her.

There was some snickering from the Victorious and the deck hands.

"What ails you?" asked Andraste puzzled.

"Nothing!" snapped Aldrich looking abashed.

"This is not going to end well," commented Kasimir.

Aldrich held out his hand to Andraste to help her to the boat. Instinctively Andraste reached for the offered hand and faltered.

"You know," she stated softly. Aldrich did not meet her eyes.

"Are you angry with me?" asked Andraste.

"Yes," answered Aldrich.

"I am as I always was. I am still your ally," replied Andraste.

He still held out his hand to her, but he lowered his eyes. Andraste took his hand and stepped in to the waiting boat. Aldrich leapt in behind her. The boat was lowered into the water. Felix and Laelius rowed them to the black shore. Before he could aid her, Andraste jumped out of the boat and into the surf. Aldrich was only two steps behind her. She lifted her pack out of the boat and he followed her example. He offered to take her pack, but she brushed past him.

Silently they walked onto the black sand. Aldrich was surprised by its coldness. It was so different from the warm, pearly sands of his homeland. The wind did not offer any relief. It was also cold and the whole area was silent. There was nothing living within eyesight. Not even a weed grew. Aldrich watched Andraste moving along the beach. She did not wait for him. She did not look over her shoulder at the ship. She moved on steadfastly and without fear.

Aldrich hurried after her. They walked for a good while along the cold sands. They did not seem to be making any progress. There was a circle of stones in the distance, but the more they walked, the farther away it seemed to be.

"We are getting nowhere," commented Aldrich.

"But we can no longer see the ship," retorted Andraste. Aldrich wondered when she had looked.

"You have no reason to be angry with me. Everything I have said to you has been true," stated Andraste. She glanced quickly at Aldrich to see his reaction. His eyes flashed angrily, and his face was sent in firm disapproval.

"But nor did you disclose: I am Andraste Valerianus, future Empress, and you owe me your allegiance," retorted Aldrich.

"I was exiled. I no longer bear that name or privilege. Besides did you introduce yourself as Aldrich Caelius, future King of the Southern lands?" inquired Andraste.

"No, but for near a month that has been clear, and you never mentioned-" started Aldrich angrily. He composed himself.

"How could you not have guessed? For weeks you have been discussing my identity with your men. For all of your talk of equality, you never once supposed I was a woman or that a woman could be equal to you!" cried Andraste.

"It is not a question of equality. The customs and traditions of the South are vastly different from the North-" began Aldrich.

"So genders can be held unequal if it is due to customs and traditions?" asked Andraste.

"That is not what I was saying and beside the point!" rejoined Aldrich.

"You have the power to make all people, regardless of gender, equal in your lands, but instead you wage guerrilla war against the North in the name of equality," rebuked Andraste.

"The North holds all Southerners as unequal, but we are discussing your deception, my lady, not equality in the South," stated Aldrich.

"From the beginning, I told you my name and my country have been taken from me. I have been dishonored. I am no longer Andraste Valerianus. I am Paramerion. If it appeared deception to you know that it was for my own protection," said Andraste.

"My lady, I do not accept such an excuse. I have seen you in battle. You are more than capable of protecting yourself," rejoined Aldrich.

"Do you know what it is like to be pursued across the Empire? Not for yourself, but for your name, your title, your birthright?" asked Andraste.

"Actually, I do," replied Aldrich. Andraste stopped and turned to study Aldrich.

"I thought at times that you did know my former name," said Andraste softly.

"My lady, you forget- you are supposed to be dead," responded Aldrich. Andraste proceeded forward.

"I am sorry to disappoint you," said Andraste.

"That is not what I meant!" exclaimed Aldrich. Andraste ignored him and quickened her pace. Aldrich followed after her.

"You were playing games with me at the Summit. You and Lady Moira must think yourselves very clever," alleged Aldrich.

"I did not trust you then as I do now," replied Andraste.

"Trust? How dare you speak of trust," reproached Aldrich angrily.

Andraste pushed him roughly. They were both on the ground before he could blink. He saw a bolt of lightning pass through the spot where he had stood only moments before. Andraste shielded him from the aftershock with her body. She collapsed to one knee. Her breath was labored. They staggered to their feet. Bolts of purple lightning reached out for them, but they dodged them and ran out of reach. They took shelter behind large black rocks and waited. There was nothing but silence.

"Paramerion?" asked Aldrich.

"I am unscathed," answered Andraste. She dropped a handful of white sand.

"Brion's crystal," said Aldrich.

"I should not have brought up that topic under our current situation. We should continue this conversation later," stated Andraste.

"You care more about me being angry with you then being shot at by lightning?" asked Aldrich incredulously.

"Do you not as well?" questioned Andraste. She rose cautiously, and then, seeing that it was safe, she held out her hand to him. However, Aldrich hoisted himself to his feet, ignoring her offered hand. He studied her intently.

"I thought you said there would be monsters and spirits?" asked Aldrich.

"We also have the sorcerers sending protective spells from the ship. Each of the Ruins is different. The spirit guarding the realm has the ability to choose its form and its obstacles," answered Andraste.

"Is this typical Northern education?" inquired Aldrich.

Andraste turned to glare at him, but realized he was joking.

"Is it me or are we a lot closer to the rock formation?" asked Andraste.

"Careful," cautioned Aldrich.

He pushed her behind him with one hand and headed forward.

There were twelve black marble pillars in a circle. In the middle of the circle on either side were two marble arches. They approached the marble arch nearest them cautiously. They looked inside the arch and saw inside the arch a room full of treasure, scrolls, armor, tapestries, and artwork.

Andraste looked to the side of the arch and once again only saw black sand. She saw Aldrich lean to look on the other side as well.

"It is a magical dimension. It will take us somewhere else," alleged Andraste.

"I am the spirit of the Darklands. As you have gotten this far, I will grant one of you a wish," stated a voice.

From the opposite arch, they saw a form began to materialize. It appeared to be a woman in long robes that trailed after her, but they could not see her face. She seemed to float towards the middle of the circle.

"Tell me why each of you have come," instructed the Shade.

"I wish to find a power that will allow me to defeat the Emperor and restore my homeland," said the prince.

"And you?" asked the Shade.

"I strive to find the power to defeat the Emperor and rebuild the Empire," said the princess.

"Both of you wish to defeat the Emperor?" repeated the Shade. She seemed amused. She approached closer to them.

"I can allow but one to pass. Those are the rules that were given to me. You must duel to the death," decreed the Shade.

Aldrich stepped back. Andraste stepped closer to the Shade and stared at her with a calculated gaze.

"No harm will come to the one who enters?" asked Andraste.

"You have my word," vowed the Shade.

Andraste unsheathed her sword. Aldrich stepped away from her. His look of distrust intensified. With a fluid movement she swung her sword.

"Wait-" started Aldrich.

He jumped back, but then realized her true intention. He lunged to grab her wrist, but he was too late. She had plunged her own sword through her chest.

"Paramerion," said Aldrich. He caught her in his arms as she fell. Her blood was warm as it hit his bare hands.

"I will die anyway. Protect the Empire," she whispered.

"I will ask you one more time," said the Shade. She was standing next to the nearest pillar, "What do you wish for, oh, prince?"

"I wish for the power to heal any injury, illness, spell or curse," yelled Aldrich.

"No!" protested Andraste.

It was too late. Aldrich felt a great power seize hold of him. He seemed to glow with unearthly light. It was not like the sorcerer's magic that was brilliant and fast. It seemed to radiate from his very being. Aldrich removed the sword from Andraste's chest and placed a hand on her wound. Andraste felt the warmth of his power spread across her. Her wound healed instantly.

She opened her eyes and saw a golden spirit phoenix above Aldrich. The phoenix shot towards her and enveloped her in flames. She felt the curse retaliate. Her shoulder ached with excruciating pain. She could not raise herself from the ground.

From the source of her original bruise raged amaranthine fire. The violet flames rose from her body and turned into smoke in the form of a cobra. As the end of its tail left her shoulder, she felt a great weight lifted from her body. The phoenix dived at the cobra breathing fire. The cobra struck at the phoenix and missed. The phoenix came again and decimated the cobra. The phoenix let out a sharp call and then disappeared.

Andraste felt the remnants of her cloak fall from her shoulders. The phoenix's fire had burned away not only the curse but part of her shirt as well. She saw her color had returned to normal and the original bruise that had marked her arm had turned into an image of a phoenix. Aldrich turned his back on her and handed her his own cloak. Andraste concealed her bare shoulder and out of habit raised the hood.

"Such sacrifice," mocked the Shade.

Aldrich glowered at the Shade.

"But such sacrifice will not accomplish your goals," criticized the Shade.

Andraste rose to her feet weakly. She felt drained of all her energy. However, she stood strong and stared with determination at the Shade.

"We will succeed," declared Andraste. Aldrich stood by her side.

"I do covet loyalty. In the millennia that I have stood at my post, I have never seen such commitment. Usually the warriors that hear this request battle to the death amongst themselves. One warrior may survive and obtain his wish but he is forever scarred by the betrayal. If your comrade had not relinquished his true wish, you would have perished. As I see you reborn, and come again to stand before me, I will grant you your one wish. I wish to see what you make of your fate," said the Shade, "Slayer of Emperors and Destroyer of Empires, what is your wish?"

"I wish for the power to defeat the enemies of the Empire," declared Andraste fiercely.

The Shade formed an image of a long, thin, gently curved sword in her hands.

"Go into the tower and retrieve this sword. However, if you take anything else, you will never be able to leave. You may not climb the stairs. You, my fine prince, may not follow her. Only one may enter," warned the Shade.

Aldrich made no move to follow Andraste. Andraste cast one last look at him and then entered into the room between the arches.

The room was at the base of a tower. It had a long stairway leading up. Up above her there was a glass ceiling that looked up to gray skies. It was snowing.

Around her were heaps of gold coins, jewels, statues, scrolls, rich clothing, books, and other treasures. She glanced down at a scroll and realized it was in an ancient language that she could not read. Brion would have given his life for that scroll. She scanned the piles of treasure, looking for the sword. There was an axe with dried blood on its edge. There was a whole suit of golden armor. There were shields decorated with crests that she did not recognize on the floor. Then she saw it. The long sword was leaning against the far wall, partially concealed by the tapestry.

Andraste went for it. An emerald scaled tail flicked against the pile of gold. Andraste hesitated.

Of course, it would not be that easy.

As silently as she could, Andraste made her way across the tower floor. She picked up the edge of the cape to make sure she would not knock over piles of gold. She stepped gently on the floor and felt something under her foot. The tail flickered again. Perhaps, so long as she did not disturb, break or take anything, the dragon would continue to sleep.

Andraste had reached the far wall. Her hand grasped the hilt. Andraste allowed herself to take a deep breath and then she ran like hell. She felt a cascade of gold coins and jewels rain down on her. She felt the tail nearly miss her head. Her ankle was grazed by a pointy talon. The blow knocked her off her feet. It pierced through her boot and left a gash. She could feel blood trickling down her ankle. She stood unsteadily, but quickly. She came to face to face with an emerald head. The tanzanite eyes were as large as her entire head. Andraste froze motionless.

"I played by your rules. All I have taken is the sword!" she yelled at the dragon angrily.

It blinked at her. She could see herself reflecting in its large eye. She shook out her cloak so it could see that she had nothing else. It breathed steam out of its nostrils. Andraste could feel the heat against her skin.

"Victoria?" asked the Dragon. The Dragon blinked at her again and moved its eye closer to her face. Andraste's fear overwhelmed her bewilderment. Seeing an opening, she ran towards the arch.

"Wait!" the Dragon commanded.

Every bone in Andraste's body rattled with fear. She paused terrified. She was so close to the opening. She could see a shadowy figure approaching the entrance on the other side. It paused. The figure was unable to enter.

"Paramerion!" entreated Aldrich. However, his voice came to her like a whisper. Even so, it broke the force that held her.

Andraste dove through the opening. Dragon fire singed her cloak, and the heels of her boots. She felt arms encircle her and pull her through the rest of the way. The cold wind of the black sands blew out the flames from her cloak and boots as she was drawn through the portal. She trembled uncontrollably. The sword fell from her hands onto the black sands.

"You are safe. I have you. You are okay," Aldrich told her. She regained her composure and pushed herself away.

"Dragon," she whispered.

If she had not been so shaken, and if the end of the cloak had not been in flames, he might not have believed her. Andraste sat on the sand to remove her now useless boots. She tore a piece of her pants to wrap around each of her feet.

"That is not the oddest part," she said. Aldrich raised an eyebrow.

"It called me by my mother's name," said Andraste.

"Why would a dragon, if it could talk, call you by your mother's name?" asked Aldrich.

The Shade laughed coldly.

"Perhaps not brave enough. You will regret not listening to the Dragon's wisdom. Sometimes those we assume are our enemies are not. Take care. You asked for the power to heal any injury, illness or curse, which is what you were granted. However, no power on this earth can bring back the dead. If you try to undo the order of the universe, then you will be claimed by the shadow powers," hissed the Shade.

"Shadow powers?" questioned Aldrich.

The Shade faded and the earth began to tremble.

"Run!" yelled Andraste.

She limped towards the beach. Aldrich saw the pillars began to shake and fall. They ran as fast as they could until the last pillar had fallen. Andraste ignored the pain in her ankle. She slowed as they seemed to be out of range.

"Are you bleeding?" asked Aldrich.

"It is nothing," replied Andraste.

Aldrich grabbed her ankle and she cried out. She balanced precariously on one foot. His grasp was firm. He supported her as he examined her ankle. The cloth around her ankle was soaked in blood.

"You should have told me," ordered Aldrich, "Take a seat."

Andraste sat on the sand, and Aldrich took her ankle again in his hand. Amber light enveloped around his grasp on her ankle. Immediately the pain ceased. Andraste flexed her leg and rotated her ankle. Realizing that she was no longer bleeding or in need of his assistance, Aldrich gently placed her foot on the sand and released her.

"Many thanks," said Andraste, not looking at him.

"It is nothing," said Aldrich as he studied the stars.

"You could have had the sword. You could have wasted our opportunity to defeat the Emperor! Why did you save me?" asked Andraste.

"I saw my brothers and father killed before my eyes during the Black War. I could do nothing to stop it. If I had been older or stronger, I still would have died. I will never let anyone die before my eyes again, not if I have the power to stop it. You chose death over defeating me, which we both know you could have done easily. That is three times you have saved my life. I would never trade a life for power," swore Aldrich.

He pulled her to her feet. He seemed to radiate anger.

"Aldrich?" she asked softly, looking up to him. Her eyes reminded him of the seas around the Southern palace.

"Yes?" replied Aldrich after he remembered he had the ability to speak.

"I regret that I did not tell you. I thought you would not understand. I was wrong," atoned Andraste.

There was unspeakable sadness in her eyes. It was remorse that could not be put into words. They were interrupted as they heard approaching footsteps in the darkness. Aldrich released her and withdrew his sword. He put himself between her and the approaching men.

"Aldrich?" asked Kasimir from the darkness.

"Commander?" asked Laelius.

"We are here," responded Aldrich.

They were surrounded by their comrades.

"We heard raised voices across the sand, so we came to investigate," said Laelius. He was surveying Andraste from head to toe, particularly at how she had covered herself in the prince's cloak.

"We are fine," affirmed Andraste.

"Let us return to the ship," said Aldrich authoritatively.

Aldrich swept in front of her and was followed by his lords. Andraste followed silently behind him. Her eyes locked on Aldrich's form. The Victorious asked her question after question.

"Our Commander is tired. No more inquiries," ordered Laelius.

They reached the row boats. It was a silent boat ride to the ship. When they reached it, the row boats were hoisted onto the ship. It seemed to take a lot less time than before. It was Brion who helped her over the railing. She threw herself into her brother's arms.

"The curse is gone," she professed. Tears fell from Brion's eyes.

"But you still cannot speak?" probed Andraste. Brion shook his head.

"Then one of you asked for the power to heal?" inquired the King. He had emerged from his cabin at the sound of voices on deck.

"I did," admitted Aldrich. He did not look at his men.

"Then I am twice in your debt. I owe you my niece's life. I will not forget," avowed the King.

Aldrich did not respond. He rejoined his men. However, he turned as Andraste approached him.

"I have no right to ask anything from you. But please, will you help my brother? He was cursed by the Emperor because he pleaded for my life. Please help us," beseeched Andraste.

She bowed to Aldrich and waited for his response.

"I would never refuse the request of a lady," said Aldrich curtly.

She raised her eyes to the prince. Aldrich reached out his hand towards Brion, who took one step back to brace himself. The golden spirit phoenix reappeared and blazed above Aldrich's head. The phoenix soared several circles overhead and then dove straight at Brion. It went straight through him and then disappeared. A phoenix mark appeared on Brion's throat. He coughed several times. One of the Victorious handed him a flask. Brion took it and drank deeply.

"My sister and I are also in your debt," croaked Brion. He also bowed to Aldrich. However, it did not escape him that Aldrich only looked to Andraste.

"That is all well and good. However, how are we going to defeat the Emperor?" asked Otho.

"With this," said Andraste, "Between his power to heal and my power in battle, we are now invincible."

She pulled the long sword from beneath her cloak. The Southerners, the Northerners, and the men of the Island Kingdoms all roared. Aldrich smiled briefly, but it soon faded. Aldrich was led below decks with his men and the Victorious, while Andraste was led to her uncle's cabin. The door had no more than closed behind Brion that Andraste turned on him.

"Who sealed away your powers?" asked Andraste.

"The Empress," replied Brion. Andraste looked at him in shock.

"You know what would have happened to my two brothers and me if the Emperor had known. The Empress begged for him to spare us. When she realized my power, she sealed it way to protect us," said Brion.

"Can it be undone?" inquired Andraste.

"I thought it would have been reversed with her death, but it was not so. I will have to speak with the sorcerers in the South that Marcella recommended," responded Brion.

"Why did you not tell me?" inquired Andraste.

"It had to be a secret. You must see that," replied Brion. Andraste did not look at him.

"I am tired," said Andraste.

Brion bowed to her and left the cabin. Andraste curled up on the bed and fell into an exhausted sleep.

Chapter Five

"So you are still with us," observed Aldrich as she walked onto the deck. She joined him at the railing. She moved slowly and with great care. Although she had been released from the curse, she felt weak. Aldrich offered her his arm. Andraste ignored the gesture.

"Can a warrior not lean on another warrior?" asked Aldrich.

Andraste studied him carefully before accepting his offered arm. She leaned into him for support.

"You still wear your cloak?" asked Aldrich.

"It is cold and windy," stated Andraste.

She tightened her own cloak about her. Aldrich smiled and moved a hand to his own cape. Andraste stepped aside quickly as he moved. He removed his own cape slowly and offered it to her. Andraste accepted it and draped it about her shoulders. Aldrich reoffered her his arm for support.

"Where are we headed?" asked Andraste.

"You do not know?" laughed Aldrich.

"Unless I am on the battlefield, I am treated as no more than an ornament," said Andraste.

"We are sailing to my palace in the Southern lands," informed Aldrich.

"Then we shall see Marcella," smiled Andraste. She looked up at him.

"Yes," confirmed Aldrich.

"That may be the first lord I have ever seen you allow touch you—other than that rascal from the Salt Islands," commented the King as he approached them. Andraste dropped her hand on Aldrich's arm and took several steps away from Aldrich.

"Is my lady so shy?" asked Aldrich.

"Shy?" laughed the King, "You mistake my meaning. She has either beat up or verbally abused so many suitors that none of the Northern or Eastern lords either have the courage or willingness to approach her. The Demon of the North they call her for good reason."

"That is cruel, King Aelius," admonished Brion briskly.

"I am tired. I am going to lie down," replied Andraste. Andraste handed Aldrich his cape and turned towards her cabin.

"Retreating? So unlike you, Andraste. It was just a little fun," her uncle yelled after her.

She felt Aldrich's eyes follow her. She paused by the door by her cabin, but she heard the voices of her men below. She slowly went below deck, putting her hands on the ropes to guide her. She paused on the stairs to let her eyes adjust to the dark.

"For the last time, we are not pirates! We are able-bodied seamen, adventurers and explorers! The subjects of the Lionden Empire have ofttimes and methodically tried to conquer and ruin my country. Henceforth, I will try to ruin those in the attempt of such action," declared Felix, "However, we the men of the Island Kingdoms, do not rape or pillage. We drink more beer than grog. I have and will never say argh matey or yo ho!"

"You just did, Felix," admonished Andraste. The men laughed. Laelius moved over so that she could sit beside him on the bench.

"Besides the men of the Island Kingdoms abide by the Code," asserted Valens.

"Code?" inquired Kasimir. Andraste answered in a clear, measured tone:

"Every person shall abide by the Command. At all times shall a man keep himself and his weapons fit for service. Any who act in a manner unbefitting a man, as to tarnish his own honor will be released from service and banished from the Island Kingdoms.

The Capitan shall have two shares and a half in all of the prizes. The First Mate, Doctor, Carpenter and Boatswain shall receive one share and a quarter. The rest of the Company will be rewarded proportionally to their deeds. Any man, who suffers loss of limb while in service, shall be compensated accordingly from the obtained prizes.

Any who are guilty of cowardice shall be marooned on an island. Any who is convicted guilty of mutiny or keeping secrets shall be marooned on an island. Any who steal from the Company shall be marooned on an island.

Any who meddle with a woman without her consent shall suffer present death.

Every man's quarrels shall be settled on shore. However, any who attack another member of the crew, while at sea, shall receive forty lashes. Any who do not properly attend a flame on board shall receive forty lashes.

Anyone who is convicted of gaming or defrauding shall suffer the punishment as rendered by the Captain and the Company. Any who withhold a prize from the Company shall suffer the punishment as rendered by the Captain and the Company."

"Can all ladies recite the Code?" asked Kasimir.

"Any man, woman or child of the Island Kingdoms could tell you as much," replied Valens, "It is our way of life. We have few laws besides the Code."

"Such is the freedom of the Island Kingdoms," stated Andraste.

"No laws regarding property?" asked Aldrich as he came down the stairs.

"It is yours if you can keep it," replied Valens.

"And family law?" asked Eadbehrt.

"She is yours if she consents, and the children are yours if she says so," said Valens.

"So you do not have marriage?" asked Eadbehrt.

"We do not partake in elaborate ceremonies like you Southerners. We have no high priests or temples. It is true the nobility follow the standards of the Northern court, but for the common folk, an exchanging of pledges is adequate," answered Felix.

"What sort of pledge?" questioned Falk.

"Do not worry, if you hear words from an Island woman, you will know exactly what she means," replied Valens. He winked at Falk.

"Well, Commander, for purposes of this discussion, what was the pledge you made to my lord?" asked Felix mischievously.

"It was not that sort of pledge. I pledged that I would never poison him or slit his throat while he was sleeping, and he pledged to never lay a hand on me or let any other," said Andraste. Brion sighed and shook his head.

"Not exactly words of love," agreed Felix.

"And this is the man who has entered three Ruins for your hand?" asked Kasimir incredulously. He looked to Aldrich, but his eyes were locked on Andraste.

"Rhinauld and my sister entered two Ruins to win her freedom," replied Brion. Andraste glared at Aldrich and the Southern lords.

"Freedom?" asked Eadbehrt.

"Despite her military service, the Emperor has tried to marry her off several times to less than satisfactory lords," replied Brion.

"When you find a lord that is satisfactory, I will sheathe my sword and never leave my hearth again," said Laelius. He was applauded by the Victorious. Andraste turned her glare on Laelius.

"By their emphasis, you must set a great deal in satisfactory," said Aldrich.

"Not at all. I will marry the man who can defeat me in a swordfight and best my bow," answered Andraste, "Why would I marry a weakling?"

"Those criteria hardly seem the best qualifications for a husband," stated Aldrich.

"Have you put much thought into qualifications for a husband?" inquired Andraste.

"It is more that my lord is an advocate for love matches," replied Kasimir.

"Why? Who are you to be shackled to?" questioned Felix.

"I am not attached," replied Aldrich. He sent a glowering look to the Southern lords.

"That look is scarier than yours," commented Maximianus.

"As it should be! Such matters are private and should not be spoken of so lightly. Words carry significance," admonished Andraste.

"As you are not engaged to the Lord of the Salt Islands, we can suppose that he has not been able to defeat you?" asked Eadbehrt.

"Andraste was taught by the best archer in the North. Rhinauld has no chance," replied Laelius.

"Were you her teacher?" asked Aldrich.

"No, Brion," replied Laelius.

"So you have no intention of marrying the Lord of the Salt Islands?" inquired Kasimir.

"The woman that marries Rhinauld will never be happy," replied Andraste. She rose from the bench.

"We will change the subject, please do not leave on our account," pacified Eadbehrt.

"Perhaps you would rather hear of Aldrich's potential brides instead? As he is not engaged-" started Kasimir.

"We should be discussing our next move," interjected Aldrich. He took a seat across from Andraste at the table. Andraste slowly reseated herself.

"Nothing can be decided until we hear news from the North," stated Brion.

"It will also take time to carry messages across the lands and ready the Resistance troops," interjected Kasimir.

"We will need only a small group, even just the Victorious and myself, to enter the Citadel," said Andraste.

"You do not mean to wage war?" asked Eadbehrt.

"Your forces would be no match for the full might of the Imperial Army. The most detrimental damage to the Empire resulted from small guerilla attacks. I know a hidden passage into the Citadel that will be the fastest and most direct way to the Emperor," asserted Andraste.

"Assuming he is at the Citadel," stated Laelius.

"You know the Emperor has not left the Citadel in years. Where else would he be?" asked Andraste. Laelius ignored her question.

"You think we should wage war?" asked Aldrich.

"My Commander has left the Imperial Army, which will leave a vacancy in the East. I know that you are modest, but you led and united the Northern Pillars. Tobias, Mathias, and Titus will not fight against you unless they are blackmailed," alleged Laelius.

"So the time to attack the North is now, before they have had time to reestablish their forces," proposed Kasimir.

"Varinia will have already taken my place," informed Andraste.

"Do all of your sisters serve in the Imperial Army?" asked Eadbehrt.

"Only Varinia and I," answered Andraste.

"And Mavourneen," added Laurentius.

"She is one of the Emperor's personal guards, an assassin by trade. Technically, she does not serve in the Imperial Army," corrected Laelius.

"She still serves the Empire with honor," defended Laurentius.

"She does not pursue her trade by choice," said Andraste sadly.

"None of us served the Emperor by choice, not for some time. Varinia has the ambition, but not the ability to lead. She is no replacement," stated Brion.

"With Northern leadership in disarray, it appears the best time to advance," alleged Eadbehrt.

Kasimir and Eadbehrt both turned to Aldrich, but he only surveyed the faces of the warriors at the table and judged their words.

"It troubles me that you are so eager to attack the North," said Maximianus quietly. The men grew silent.

"Maximianus raises a crucial point. Our mission is to defeat the Emperor. There are many realms in the North that may aid us, or at least let us pass unnoticed, but if you turn this into a Southern purge against the North, then there will be no hope for us. We will be thwarted and attacked at every turn. You will start a second Black War," cautioned Andraste.

"You believe that the defeat of the Emperor will solve all of our problems?" asked Aldrich.

"Of course not, but by working together for our future, instead of warring amongst ourselves, we will pave way for a more reasonable and just Empire for us all," said Andraste.

"The Empire will fall," stated Aldrich.

"The Empire will rise," retaliated Andraste. They glared at each other across the table.

"We will not survive without the unification of our Empire. The Lionden Empire is too strong," said Laelius.

"For eight years my men and I have fought the Lionden Empire. The

Lionden will tear us apart limb by limb if we do not stand together. Aldrich, you may believe you can form an allegiance with the Lionden Empire, but it will only be for as long as it benefits them. You must be careful who you take as bed fellows," said Andraste.

"You cannot say such things to a Southerner," admonished Brion.

"Why not? It is a common expression," stated Andraste. She glanced to Aldrich, who crimsoned further underneath her stare.

"Do you not understand my point?" asked Andraste.

"I understand your meaning," replied Aldrich. He did not look at her.

"What aid can we expect for our cause?" inquired Kasimir.

"On our behalf, obviously, we can expect aid from the Island Kingdoms. There will also be those who defect from the North, who will come to fight behind Andraste," said Brion.

"Any forces from the West?" asked Kasimir.

"Not likely," answered Andraste.

"We have few friends there," said Brion.

"I thought Titus had strong ties with the West?" questioned Eadbehrt.

"True, but they despise my sister," replied Brion.

"What did you do?" asked Aldrich.

"My sister spent a short time as Commander of the West. Due to her overturning of Western laws and traditions, our relationship with the West has been less than amiable," stated Brion. The Southern lords looked to Andraste for explanation.

"As the penalty for meddling with a woman without her consent in the North and the East is death, I applied the same law to the West. I also applied the same penalty to domestic abuse," amended Andraste. The Southern lords looked at her in shock.

"The Westerners treat dogs better than they do women," alleged Laelius.

"What is the penalty in the South?" asked Andraste.

"For both offenses, the perpetrator would surrender all of his possessions, lands, and, if applicable, titles. There would also be a mandatory prison sentence," replied Aldrich.

"Do such penalties discourage such acts?" questioned Andraste.

"Probably more than the death penalty," answered Aldrich.

"Death after all is so final," said Kasimir.

"If you had seen what I have seen, you would not be so flippant. The West is full of barbarians. I have seen women beaten in the street for looking at their lord. I have seen women meddled with by multiple men with no recourse at their disposal. I have seen women beheaded for learning how to read. I have seen children used as target practice. There is no humanity left in the West. There are only monsters that reside there," said Andraste.

"The more moderate punishments did not deter the barbarity," stated Brion.

"Andra!" called the King above deck. Andraste rose and all of the men followed suit.

"I beg your pardon, my lords, my uncle calls," said Andraste as she headed towards the stairs.

"Land ho!" a crew member called.

"That must be record timing," commented Eadbehrt.

"The King of the Island Kingdoms possesses a unique magic. His people believe he is the god of the sea himself," replied Brion.

She paused as the ship crested a large wave. She lost her balance and grasped onto the ropes. She felt a hand steady her. She looked down the stairs to find Aldrich on the step behind her.

"Andra!" the King bellowed. She hurried up the stairs and onto the deck.

She gazed off across the horizon. The ship was rapidly approaching a golden city. She joined her uncle at the helm. Aldrich went to the opposite side of the ship and was shortly joined by his men. The Victorious were also coming up from below.

"The Southern capitol," said the King, "I brought you and your mother here once before. You were very young."

"I do not remember," admitted Andraste sadly.

"It was right before the start of the Black War," said the King.

"You mean before she died," stated Andraste.

"Yes," replied the King. He did not take his eyes from the port.

"Will you be joining us, Uncle?" asked Andraste.

"No, my dear one, I will be returning to the Island Kingdoms. I will be raising my navy and gathering our allies for your prince. He was your mother's choice for you. He is a good man, Andraste, you could do far worse," suggested the King.

"Uncle!" swore Andraste.

Her uncle lowered her hood, so that he could look into her sea-green eyes. Her long, hazel hair escaped and blew in the wind. He kissed the top of her head. Without another word, he turned around and issued orders to his men.

Andraste blushed a pretty shade of pink and turned around. She saw the Southern lords staring at her at the opposite end of the ship. Aldrich's back was turned to her. However, as he saw the reaction of his comrades, he turned to face her. Laelius stepped in front of her. She was blocked by his large shoulders.

"Have you never seen a woman before?" barked Laelius to the Southerners.

Andraste was immediately shielded by the Victorious. She secured her hair and raised her hood.

The ship gave a lurch as the platform was connected from the ship to the moor. There was already a crowd assembled. News of their adventures had already spread throughout the South. Aldrich braved the wrath of the Victorious to approach her. He shouldered his way through and offered his hand, "My lady?"

Andraste hesitated and she looked to Laelius, who stepped aside. Andraste took Aldrich's offered hand. Aldrich led her across the gangway, and then wrapped her arm in his. He was all smiles and laughter. He greeted people he knew. He grasped offered hands in his free hand, but also carefully protected Andraste on his arm.

The architecture was magnificent. The buildings were all four or five stories tall. From each level, there were lush gardens with vines, flowers, and greenery hanging over the sides. The buildings were constructed from a simple mudbrick with stone arches incorporated into the structures. The buildings looked as though they had endured a thousand years and would endure a thousand more. There were tall palm trees blooming throughout the landscape and ponds filled with water lilies. The breeze blew gently and the scent of lilies and jasmine filled the air.

"There are carriages waiting," said Aldrich.

Andraste's attention was drawn back to the prince. She saw the carriages waiting in the distance. They were placed upon ornately decorated elephants.

"Is it far?" asked Andraste.

"The palace sits on top of the hill," responded Aldrich. He pointed in the direction of the palace. The city was built around its base. The palace seemed to shine on top of the hill.

"May we walk? I have never seen the Southern capitol. I can go myself if you wish. I do not mean to keep you," said Andraste.

"It pleases me that you wish to see it," replied Aldrich.

The other Southern lords and guardsmen, Brion and some of the Victorious departed in the waiting carriages. Six of the Victorious followed ten steps behind the prince and princess. Andraste blushed as she heard the voices from the crowd.

"So it is true then?"

"Yes. Look at the Northern armor. The Victorious and the princess have joined our prince."

"Which one do you think is Paramerion?"

"The big one."

Aldrich realized that she was not listening to his tour and fell silent. Aldrich led her away from the city onto a deserted path that wound its way up the hill towards the palace. The fuchsia was in full bloom along the path, perfuming the air with a sweet, welcoming fragrance. She picked one stem to examine it and then lifted her offering hesitantly to Aldrich. He took it and put it in a button hole of his shirt. She picked a small bouquet as they progressed up the hill.

"What are the glass buildings nearest the palace?" asked Andraste.

"Those are greenhouses. They grow nearly all of the food for the city. We need to be self-sustaining thanks to the policies of the Empire," stated Aldrich.

Andraste winced.

"I meant no offense," said Aldrich.

He looked down at her but could not see her reaction underneath her hood.

"Is the fishing good here?" asked Andraste.

"You really do not know how to make small talk do you?" rejoined Aldrich.

He laughed at her and Andraste tried to pull away, but he had her arm firmly secure.

"Yes. The fishing is extraordinary. Does my lady care for seafood?" inquired Aldrich.

"After my mother's death, I was sent to live in the Salt Islands. I have not had seafood since that time. In my youth, most of my time was spent in the North, which is landlocked. The common fare is mostly game birds, venison, and the like," said Andraste.

"Do you miss the North?" asked Aldrich.

"It is a cruel but beautiful place. You must be strong to survive in the North," said Andraste softly. Aldrich felt her shiver underneath her cloak.

"Do you have other family there?" inquired Aldrich.

"Other than Brion, I have fifteen half-brothers and half-sisters," said Andraste.

"Fifteen?" repeated Aldrich.

"Well there was Brion's mother, my mother, and the Emperor currently has four Muses," said Andraste.

"Do many Northerners have multiple wives?" questioned Aldrich aghast.

"Yes. Is it not so in the South?" retorted Andraste.

"No, we marry once," said Aldrich. He blushed, "Do Northern women take multiple husbands?"

"No," said Andraste, "Have I said something wrong? Why are you so embarrassed?"

"Such things are not talked about," responded Aldrich.

Andraste glanced back to Laelius in confusion. He shrugged. Andraste returned her attention to Aldrich.

"Have you ever noticed how much the prince blushes around our

Commander?" asked Felix.

"Well, she is a savage beast," replied Otho.

Andraste heard them both soundly thonked on the head by Laelius. She hoped Aldrich had not heard their discussion.

"May I ask you a question?" asked Andraste.

Aldrich stopped and looked at her.

"If your father has passed, why are you not King?" questioned Andraste.

"It is seen in our way, that a man is not a man until he marries, for it takes two people to master life together. An unmarried man would be unfit to rule because he does not have a partner," responded Aldrich, "You could say we are not equal until we find our life partner."

"In the case of widows and widowers?" queried Andraste.

"Regents until the heir comes of age and marries," responded Aldrich.

"Why is Marcella not Queen? She is married," questioned Andraste.

"Property passes to the eldest son," answered Aldrich.

"And if there are only daughters?" asked Andraste.

"Then property would pass to the closet male relative," replied Aldrich.

"For all of your talk of freedom and equality, do you not find that hypocritical?" asked Andraste.

"It is the way it has always been," replied Aldrich.

They had reached an overlook. They stopped to look down on the golden city. The sea-green waters lapped lazily on pearly sands.

"While we are on the subject of unions, I have thought of a way to pay you back," said Andraste. She handed the bouquet that she had picked to Laelius.

"You owe me nothing-" started Aldrich.

However, he stopped speaking as Andraste undid her cloak and let it drop at her feet. She turned to look at the prince. The wind gently blew the folds of her deep blue dress. Aldrich was speechless as he looked down at her sea-green eyes that seemed to mirror the waters of his homeland. He colored as she put a hand to his face.

"I would be dead if you had not asked for the power to save me due to my mortal injury, and secondly due to the curse. You have returned my future to me. I vow to spend the rest of my life to repay you for my life.

Your worries are my worries. Your battles are my battles. I will stand by you for all of my days. I will witness your life. I will look to you and follow. You will never be alone, for I will be at your side. Together we will forever be.

I would have no sanctuary if you had not let me into the Shadow Mountains, and, now, your kingdom. For this freedom, I agree to be your Muse."

The Victorious stopped dead in their tracks. Aldrich became increasingly aware that every blade, spear, and axe was slowly being aimed in his direction.

"My lady, I feel you do me great honor, but I do not know what a Muse is," admitted Aldrich.

Andraste removed her hand from his face and blushed deeply. Aldrich was enchanted by how pretty the color suited her.

"In the North for feats of great valor or victory, a lady may choose to live with the Victor for as long as she chooses as his lady if he consents," communicated Andraste.

"But I have already offered you sanctuary, I do not understand," sputtered Aldrich.

"Any children that come from the union would be mine and take my name," purported Andraste blushing even deeper crimson.

"You wish to have my children?" asked Aldrich. The Victorious tensed.

"Children could result from such a union," replied Andraste.

"If it is marriage you want, I could propose in a more suitable away fitting for your stature and birth-" started Aldrich.

He bent down to kiss her and was amazed as the lady slapped him squarely across his face.

"I am not speaking of marriage," declared Andraste. She turned her back on him glowering.

"You are proposing to be my mistress?" inquired Aldrich in alarm.

"You will need to marry a lady of great fortune and consequence in order to survive. For your people and your kingdom, you need to marry well. I am dishonored. I have no lands, no name, and no fortune. All I have to offer is myself," stated Andraste.

"My lady-" started Aldrich.

He reached for her, but she stepped aside. She would not look at him.

"Andraste," Aldrich said clearly.

He winced as the trumpets blew behind him.

Laelius approached Andraste. The warrior reached down and picked her fallen cloak and folded it over his arm. He offered her his arm and Andraste took it. He also returned the bouquet to her. She surveyed the sea.

"Shall we continue, Aldrich Caelius?" asked Laelius. His voice was cold and deadly.

Aldrich glanced over his shoulder and saw all of the goodwill he had won with the Victorious was now gone. He was met with looks of pure hatred.

Aldrich turned on his heel, not sure exactly what had transpired. By trying to gauge her feelings, he had somehow ended up in insulting her publically and before her people. He glanced over his shoulder. Andraste seemed to have retreated inside of herself. Her beautiful face seemed set in stone. Her skin was like porcelain. Sensing that he was watching her, her blush intensified. Aldrich looked straight ahead.

Aldrich was relieved to see his mother, Marcella, and Decima waiting for him on the steps of the palace. He was less relieved that his mother had brought the entire court with them in a full processional. He walked up the steps half-way and realized that Andraste had waited at the bottom of the steps. Aldrich turned and offered his hand to her. Laelius withdrew his arm from the princess leaving her unescorted between them.

Andraste slowly walked up the stairs and took Aldrich's offered arm. She still would not meet his eyes. She kept her eyes focused on the steps beneath her feet. Aldrich approached his mother, Marcella, and Decima.

"Your Majesty, may I present Andraste Eldgrimson Valerianus. You may have also heard of her as Paramerion, Commander of the Victorious, my savior and friend," introduced Aldrich.

There was a murmur of excited interest among the courtiers behind them.

Andraste stood straight, but would not raise her eyes to the Queen.

"Do not fear child. You will find no rebuke here. You were too little to remember, but your mother was my greatest friend. I miss her every day. There was a time when she and I had hoped our two families would be united- but this is an old woman's ramblings. Come, princess, and be welcome," said the Queen.

She reached for Andraste's hands and leaned forward to kiss her on both cheeks. Like her children, the Queen was tall and slender. Her graying auburn hair was pulled off her neck in a bun, and she gazed at Andraste with sapphire eyes like her son's. The Queen was all poise and dignity, but she waited patiently and smiled kindly as she waited Andraste's response.

"I am touched by your Majesty's words to such an exile as myself," said Andraste.

"My son introduced you under two names, by which do you prefer?" asked the Queen.

"I am Paramerion," answered Andraste.

"Good," affirmed the Queen.

"I picked these for you on our walk," said Andraste. She offered the humble bouquet to the Queen.

"A thoughtful gesture, indeed. Wild flowers have always been my favorite," remarked the Queen. She took Andraste's bouquet in one arm and smiled in approval to Aldrich.

The Queen and Marcella both wrapped an arm around her and led her into the palace. Andraste felt uncomfortable despite their words of welcome and kindness. Even if the King had ordered her mother's execution, the Queen had not intervened in the murder of her greatest friend. It seemed as though the Queen felt no guilt for her actions. Andraste felt her anger igniting inside her like the rekindling of a fire.

Aldrich was swept the opposite direction to greet his own friends and courtiers. However, Andraste could feel him watching her. She blushed to think of what the Queen and Marcella would think of her when he told them about her offer.

"You will forgive me. I had not realized that Paramerion and you were the same person. I have prepared two sets of rooms," started the Queen.

"If it were up to me, I would choose the rooms for Paramerion. I have spent most of my life as a warrior and I wish to be nearest my men," said Andraste and she wondered where her Victorious had been swept off to.

"As you wish," said the Queen, but the choice seemed to puzzle her exceedingly.

The rooms Andraste was led to were painted deep red. There was a bedroom, wash room, study and meeting room that led out onto a balcony out looking the sea.

"It is beautiful," said Andraste.

"I hope everything will be to your liking. Now rest. You must be exhausted from your journey. Marcella, Decima, you will attend me," ordered the Queen.

Andraste bowed to the Queen. Marcella patted her arm comfortingly in passing, and Decima brushed by quickly without comment. Andraste was left alone on the balcony to gaze at the sea. She stood for nearly an hour until a knock on her door awakened her from her contemplations. She opened the door to find Aldrich royally dressed.

"I would not disturb you, but as my duty as your host, I have come to see you have everything you need," said Aldrich. He bowed to her as he came into the room.

"I require nothing," stated Andraste.

"Are you not dressed for dinner? Do you need an attendant? Are you alone?" asked Aldrich. His eyes darted to the room behind her.

"I am not. I do not. Yes, I am," replied Andraste.

"I would not have been so forward, but your brother or guards are always with you. I will find someone at once," said Aldrich.

"We have been alone many times before," reminded Andraste.

"Yes, but I thought you were a man," retorted Aldrich.

Andraste winced as Aldrich fled the room in confusion. He did not even shut the door. Andraste heard him talk to someone briefly in the hall. Marcella poked her head in the door.

"I have brought you some things," said Marcella. She saw the look of confusion on Andraste's face.

"Our customs are very different. While you are here, you should know that a lady may never have a man in her room without another lady or family member present, preferably both," said Marcella, "I do apologize. It was very bad form for my brother to come in before you were properly settled and acquainted with our ways."

Andraste sat down on a sofa.

"Are you sure you want these rooms? They are so masculine," questioned Decima.

She had entered behind Marcella, who was directing servants to unload some dresses and boxes in the bedroom.

"Yes, I like them very much. They remind me of the Citadel," replied Andraste.

Decima waived the servants away.

"Did my brother upset you?" asked Marcella.

"No, I am fine," affirmed Andraste.

"Let us get you ready for dinner," intervened Decima.

"Why did you slap him?" asked Marcella, unable to be deferred.

"I will slap you if you do not leave her alone," countered Decima.

"It might start a new fashion. You should know the whole palace is discussing it. As my brother never has actually been slapped by a woman before, and generally thought to be a lady's man, everyone is, of course, intrigued," gossiped Marcella.

Decima raised her hand towards Marcella, who laughed. The two women glared at each other.

"Fine, I give in. I think the light green would be fitting for tonight. It is one of Aldrich's favorite colors," said Marcella wickedly. Decima sighed.

Andraste felt utterly exposed due to the thin fabric and low neckline. In the North she would have been shrouded in layers or robes and furs, but the Southern fashion seemed much more restrictive. Andraste instinctively searched the new clothing for a cloak. Marcella knocked her hand way, "It will be much too warm. You will not need it."

When they entered the dining room, Andraste was overwhelmed by the luxury. Marcella was also correct: it was very warm. Additionally, giant oil lamps hung from the ceiling and produced an outstanding amount of light.

"Where are my Victorious?" Andraste asked as she scanned the tables.

"They are sitting with Aldrich's men," assured Decima. She gestured to the far side.

"But you are with us," said Marcella.

"May I say hello?" asked Andraste. She was already stepping towards their direction.

"Two months by sea is not enough time with them?" asked Decima.

Andraste looked to Decima sharply, but saw the ghost of a smile on Decima's face. Decima and Marcella flanked her sides. The Victorious rose at the sight of her and Aldrich's men followed suit.

"My lords, is everything to your liking?" Andraste asked as she approached their table.

"Did you hear?" asked Glaucio. Andraste shook her head.

"Aldrich had our families sent for from the Island Kingdoms before we left for the Darklands. They are all settled in the city," said Gnaeus. His eyes twinkled.

"Gnaeus is going to cry," remarked Otho.

"You would too, if, you had a wife as lovely as Iovita," remarked Avitus.

"You should not say such things about your own sister," commented Nero.

There was a loud wave of laughter from Northern and Southern lords.

"Are they here tonight?" asked Andraste searching the crowd. She was astounded by the number of tables and guests.

"Yes," confirmed Laelius as he rose.

"If it please you, I will join you later," said Andraste sweetly to Marcella and Decima. Her whole face shone with joy. Marcella seemed unsure, but relented as she saw Andraste's face.

Laelius led her to the far corner. The ladies and children rose to greet her. Laelius's youngest children were nearest and ran to embrace her. They did not come up to her waist. Andraste picked up the youngest, Laelius, named after his father, and swung him around.

"Do not bother her ladyship, Lae," clucked Paulina.

"Lae would never bother me," insisted Andraste.

She kissed the boy all over his face and he giggled. Paulina also embraced her. Andraste felt the scrutinizing gaze of the Southern lords and ladies upon her.

"Lae, you have gotten so big! You will be lifting your father's spear soon!" praised Andraste. Lae beamed at her. He showed her his tiny arm muscle with great pride.

"Did you have everything you needed on your journey? I grabbed as much as I could. It all happened so fast," said Paulina.

"It was you?" asked Andraste. Her eyes welled with tears. She leaned to rest her forehead against Paulina's. They stood in silence for a moment.

"I would have done more, but the children were with me. I could not risk it," said Paulina.

"When I am able, I will repay you for this kindness. We would not have survived without your generosity," alleged Andraste.

"It is nothing," replied Paulina.

"You are a brave woman, Paulina. I miss having you amongst the Victorious," said Andraste.

"Thank you, my lady," replied Paulina.

"I would not intrude, but my mother wishes you to be seated," interrupted Aldrich at her side. He was all dignity and poise. The prince was well suited by the Southern fashion. He smiled at the child in her arms, but the smile did not extend to Andraste.

"I apologize. I would never cause you trouble intentionally," replied Andraste.

She regretfully handed Lae back to his mother. Paulina winked at her as she took her son in her arms. Andraste had spent many afternoons in Paulina's kitchen and ate most of her meals around Laelius's table when she returned to the Citadel. Lae reached for her again. Andraste squeezed Lae's hand and patted the other two children on their heads.

"My lady," said Aldrich coolly. He offered her his arm.

"Can Southern ladies not walk on their own?" Andraste inquired as she stepped before the offered arm.

"It is custom. It will be a slight, if you do not accept," advised Aldrich.

Andraste took his arm immediately, and he seemed less angry.

"I thank you for what you have done for my people. It means the world to me," said Andraste softly. Aldrich's features softened.

"No one should have to be parted from their families a day longer than necessary," responded Aldrich.

They did not speak again as he conveyed her up the hall. Aldrich seated her next to his mother. Aldrich sat across from her. He had to walk all the way around the table to get back to his spot, so she was at the mercy of the Queen. Aldrich would not look at or speak to her when he regained his seat.

The Queen gave words of welcome and then invited Brion to tell the hall their adventures. Brion used magic so that his words created pictures on the wall. Andraste was pleased that he brushed over many of the arguments and embarrassing moments, which left the adventure seeming rather glorious indeed. Aldrich looked at her bemused expression and laughed.

"What is so funny?" inquired the Queen.

"My recollection of events and my brother's differ greatly," answered Andraste.

"My lady is too modest," said Aldrich.

This comment made Andraste blush as she remembered their earlier conversation.

"Is the food not to your liking? Would you prefer something else?" inquired Aldrich.

"It is fine. I was listening to Brion," answered Andraste.

Brion had rejoined the table and resumed his place at her side.

"But you have not eaten a thing," said the Queen.

"I taste all of the dishes before my sister partakes. We mean no disrespect, but we have had poison related incidents in the past," said Brion. He surveyed the platters and made a quick gesture with his hand.

"A divining spell," explained Brion, "In the North, the militant sorcerers are known for their knowledge of poison and assassination, as well as their knowledge of dark magic."

"There is trouble in the North?" inquired Decima.

"Yes. I would not be surprised if there was civil war soon," replied Brion.

The music started to play. Aldrich rose from the table but turned as his mother struck him lightly with her fan.

"Perhaps, princess, you would care to dance?" asked the Queen.

"I do not know these dances, your Majesty," responded Andraste quickly.

"My son can teach you," pushed the Queen with a frown.

"Lady Decima dances so well," protested Andraste.

Decima put down her wine goblet and came to Andraste's aid.

"I will dance this one, but the dance of swords is next, so you are next," warned Decima.

"My men are too drunk and happy for such a dance," replied Andraste.

The Queen colored slightly.

"Let me guess, such things are not spoken of?" asked Andraste.

Decima laughed as she headed to the dance floor on Aldrich's arm. They made a beautiful couple. Aldrich seemed perfectly at ease. He and Decima were deep in discussion. Decima's eyes darted to Andraste, who looked away quickly.

"If you do not enjoy dancing, do you play an instrument?" asked the Queen.

"I do not, your Majesty," answered Andraste.

"Do you draw or paint?" inquired the Queen.

"Not at all, your Majesty," replied Andraste.

"Is this common for a lady of the Northern court?" inquired the Queen.

"No, but I spent most of my time on the battlefield, not at court," responded Andraste.

"So what are your talents?" asked the Queen.

Andraste took a sip from her goblet and took a moment before replying. She said thoughtfully, "I know 120 ways to kill a man."

The Queen nearly choked on her wine.

"My sister is joking," intervened Brion. He shot Andraste a look of warning and mouthed, "Penniless vagabond."

"Your Majesty, please forgive me. I am overwhelmed by the events of the last few months. I am ever so grateful for your hospitality. I know so little of your customs that I fear that I may do something to offend you. Please give me some time to become acquainted with your ways before I embarrass us all," apologized Andraste. She tried to sound sincere.

"Have no qualms, my dear. I am but Queen as a formality. My son, although not crowned, is regarded as king. You are welcome because he wants you here. He has told me much about your adventures, so I can see why," said the Queen.

Andraste was inwardly horrified as she thought of what Aldrich could have said about her. However, her face remained neutral.

"But go to bed, if you must. I see, like my son, you find no joy in large gatherings," said the Queen.

The leave being granted, Andraste was out of the great hall and finding her way to her chamber as rapidly as her feet could carry her.

Andraste had a hard time falling asleep, and when she did, her dreams were troubled.

She dreamed that she was once again in the Darklands. She was in the Tower. The Dragon spoke to her, but she could not understand. This angered the Dragon. The Dragon's tanzanite eyes seemed to become swirling galaxies. Once more the Dragon called her Victoria. The Dragon was confused. It needed her help. Andraste approached the Dragon and held up a hand to its face. The Dragon's eyes no longer seemed to recognize her. It spouted a large wave of red-hot fire from its snout that consumed her offered hand.

Andraste screamed as she sat up in bed. She felt disoriented and confused. She heard running. Aldrich was the first one through her door, followed by two Victorious.

Aldrich was at her side asking, "Are you hurt?"

"Dragon! Fire-- so much fire," she whispered. Her eyes were pure panic.

"It is okay. You are okay," comforted Aldrich. He reached for her hand, but withdrew as the two Victorious watched him with a deadly glint in their eyes.

"The Dragon-- it called me Victoria," said Andraste. Her sea-green eyes looked up at Aldrich in confusion.

"I know. Do you know where you are?" asked Aldrich.

"The Darklands," replied Andraste.

She felt confused again. Her head spun. She felt the silk sheets against her body. She looked at her surroundings and shook her head, "No, the Southern palace."

Andraste blushed as she brought the blankets up around her night gown. Aldrich tried valiantly not to look at her.

"I will take my leave. My chambers are across the hall if you need me," said Aldrich. He bowed to her. It was as if they were in the ball room, and he was simply taking his leave.

"Your chambers?" repeated Andraste. She blushed crimson.

"Across the hall," reiterated Aldrich.

Aldrich still did not look at her. He bowed again and left her bed-chamber. The Victorious shut the door behind him, but she could still hear him talking to Brion and Laelius in the library.

"Does she always have nightmares?" inquired Aldrich.

"They started on the boat, but they are getting worse," admitted Brion.

"When you have seen all of the things that we have seen . . ." Laelius trailed off.

"But why the Dragon? Why is the fire so terrifying?" questioned Aldrich.

"You know how the Empress Victoria died?" Brion finally asked. Aldrich made no comment.

"She was burned at the stake for dark sorcery. Andraste is terrified of fire," said Laelius, "She has been since she was a child."

Andraste drew the covers over her head, feeling ashamed. She did not want to hear any more of the conversation. When she fell asleep again, she did not dream.

Andraste slept later than normal. She woke and examined the books and maps in her library. She was intrigued by the maps that had been pro-vided for her. The latest placement of troops had been mapped out for her. The Emperor was massing troops at the Shadow Mountains and from the West. The Island Kingdoms had the East and the South well protected. Any attack from the Emperor would have to come by land.

She was joined by all of the Victorious, except Brion, who was studying with the Southern sorcerers. Laelius made no comment about her nightmare.

"I am glad you all reunited with your families. But the holiday is over. We must focus," commanded Andraste.

Laelius looked at the troop movements in deep thought.

"One evening and the holiday is over?" asked Maximianus.

"Too much holiday for our Commander," commented Otho.

"Saddle the horses, we are going on patrol. Ask Aldrich's men for a guide," ordered Andraste.

"You could ask me yourself," suggested Aldrich. A knock followed belatedly as he walked into her library.

"I assumed you would have other duties," said Andraste hastily.

"Other than protecting my people? I would hear what you have to say," declared Aldrich.

"My brother, you have forgotten, you are needed in the Chambers of Justice this morning. You have been gone for quite a while," appeased Marcella appearing at his elbow.

"It can wait," alleged Aldrich.

"I would be happy to escort the princess," said a decadently dressed man at his elbow.

The obese man was dressed in all velvet. He reminded Andraste of a sofa. She imagined the rings on his hand alone could have bought a small country. The man was much shorter then Aldrich, who towered over him.

Aldrich was thinking desperately of a way to get out of the Chambers of Justice.

"There is no need, Lord Arnold. I will ride with the Commander. We would not take you away from your business," intervened Decima.

The lords all bowed to her as she swept into the room.

"Then it is decided. The ladies will ride together. Additionally, I will send one of our patrols with you as escorts," said Aldrich quickly.

"We will be fine. I am sure Lady Decima is an excellent guide," advised Andraste.

"I have no doubt. I hear you know 120 ways to kill a man?" inquired Aldrich. His sapphire eyes laughed at her, although his face remained serious. Andraste was lost for words.

"It is just a precaution. As you are my guest, and my foster-sister is attending, I will send a patrol. It is also important that we are seen as working together, not apart," affirmed Aldrich.

"As you wish," replied Andraste.

Aldrich excused himself and went to carry out his business. Marcella trailed behind.

"Who was the little man?" asked Laelius.

"Arnold is perhaps the wealthiest man in the City. He has bought his title. He is a known womanizer and slave trader in the Lionden Empire. The prince cannot stand him," explained Decima, "Shall we go?"

Decima eyed Andraste's clothes in moderate alarm as Andraste came from behind the table.

"It will be quite scandalous if you wear men's clothing while you are here. I mean no insult if that is the way of the North," said Decima.

"I am here as a warrior, and as such, I will dress as befits my duties," replied Andraste.

"The Queen will not be happy," stated Decima as she led the way to the stables.

"How was your ride?" hailed Marcella as she walked down the steps of the palace. She was followed by three beautifully attired Southern ladies in luxurious gowns and precious jewels. Andraste estimated it had taken three hours just for the ladies to have their hair done. The Southern ladies scrutinized Andraste as thoroughly as any opponent Andraste had ever encountered.

"No complaints," replied Decima.

"Would you care to join us? Gerlinde, Ziska, Sonje, and I are on our way to the sewing room," invited Marcella.

"I will join you," said Decima. She turned her attention to Andraste.

"Thank you, but no. I have arranged to see the wives of my men," replied Andraste.

"What are they doing?" asked Gerlinde.

Andraste looked over her shoulder and saw that the families of the Victorious were busy making arrows. Paulina was leading the older children in combat training. Paulina swept her spear in a wide arc and knocked an older boy onto his knees. He dropped his spear.

"Northern sewing circle," replied Andraste.

"Do all children learn combat?" asked Sonje.

"Indeed. Every man, woman and child," answered Laelius. He surveyed his wife fondly.

The Southern ladies scrutinized Andraste once more.

"The North is a dangerous place," said Andraste.

"Lady Paulina is fierce," admired Decima.

"She was trained at the Ice Palace," said Laelius proudly. He watched Paulina's lesson progress.

"She was a member of the Victorious before her children were born," said Andraste.

"Gaia and Gnaeus were born long before then. They were about twelve and ten," amended Laelius.

"Who cared for them while you were at war?" asked Ziska.

"Paulina's mother," answered Laelius.

"Is it common for women with children to fight?" asked Marcella.

"Most women who enter the Imperial Army do not marry and become career soldiers. Many lands are held by women when the warriors go to war," answered Laelius.

"How masculine," said Gerlinde. She surveyed Paulina with a look of disapproval.

"How necessary," replied Andraste, "Do you think that warlords, demons, and thieves will not attack because only gentle creatures are at home?"

"Warlords and demons?" asked Ziska. The ladies exchanged glances.

"Surely you jest?" asked Gerlinde.

"Hardly," replied Laelius.

"Their hands must be coarse from such work," stated Gerlinde.

"Coarse hands are not as harsh a fate as death," remarked Marcella. She shot Gerlinde a look of warning.

"We should continue to the sewing room," said Ziska.

"I doubt embroidered cushions will be of much use to their husbands, when they are fighting for our freedom," said Andraste. Her tone was light, but her gaze sinister.

"The arrows are for you?" asked Sonje. She turned her kind, brown eyes towards the Victorious.

"They do not make them for their amusement," replied Andraste. Her attention was turned back to the training games as Avitus brushed past her.

"Ennius, your guard is too low," Avitus scolded his young son.

"If I want your opinion, I will ask for it," replied Paulina.

Laelius chuckled, and the rest of the Victorious laughed. Paulina shot Laelius a look and he quieted. Avitus still approached his son and took the spear. Ennius looked to Paulina.

"Look here," commanded Avitus. He demonstrated the proper stance. Paulina took a step towards Avitus.

"Heiyoh!" called Iovita. Paulina threw Iovita her spear, which Iovita brandished with ease.

"Who is that?" inquired Marcella.

"Lady Iovita, my daughter-in-law and Avitus's sister. You should know each other; Avitus and Iovita hail from the South, although their father's lands were confiscated after a rebellion," replied Laelius.

"Which lands?" questioned Marcella.

"The Silent Sound," answered Andraste.

"However, Avitus has won lands in the North for his service," replied Laelius.

"Like that makes a difference," replied Gerlinde angrily.

"Why were his family's lands not returned to him?" asked Marcella.

"That power belongs only to the Emperor," replied Andraste.

Iovita quickly knocked Avitus off his feet and had the spear point at his throat. The Victorious and their families laughed. Gnaeus approached to pull Avitus to his feet. He clamped his comrade on the back.

"Perhaps I will have Iovita take your place," called Andraste. Avitus looked progressively more displeased.

"I would rather take my husband's," replied Iovita.

"A duel then?" asked Laelius. As Andraste nodded her consent, Gnaeus sighed. He picked up the fallen spear.

"Gentlemen dueling ladies?" asked Marcella. She did not look pleased.

"It is good exercise," stated Andraste. She did not take her eyes from the field. The combatants were moving faster and faster.

"It is like a dance," said Decima. Andraste smiled at her.

"So close!" sighed Sonje as Gnaeus knocked the spear from Iovita's hand. Iovita laughed as Gnaeus took her hand and kissed it.

"There are children present," commented Maximianus. Gnaeus laughed as he swept his wife into his arms.

"Iovita may challenge you once more when we return from the North," said Andraste.

"Hopefully we will have a grandchild by then," commented Laelius. Iovita blushed into Gnaeus's shoulder.

"Do you think you will be away that long?" asked Marcella.

"Who can tell?" asked Andraste.

"I hope Aldrich is not gone so long this time," said Gerlinde. She pouted prettily.

"You think he will go with the Victorious?" asked Decima.

"He said as much last night," replied Gerlinde. She lowered her eyes to survey the field.

"At the social hour, we were all there. Although he would have preferred the princess," said Sonje. She smiled kindly at Andraste, but it faded as Gerlinde's eyes flashed and her lips pursed. Sonje fell silent.

"It is his duty to attend you. He does not do it by choice," sniffed Gerlinde.

Marcella scowled at Gerlinde, but before she could speak they were approached by a Southern lord. He was dressed in the uniform of the Southern guardsmen. His keen, brown eyes were set on Laelius. He approached with purpose. He bowed eloquently when he reached Laelius.

"Lord Laelius, the new volunteers are practicing now if you wish to see them as we discussed last night," said the man.

"This is Egnatius, the Captain of the Caelius Guardsmen," introduced Laelius. The man bowed to Andraste. Laelius continued his introduction, "Egnatius has fought in several wars, including the late Forest War. He saw us all fight on that day and has still chosen to befriend us."

"Well met. I will see these volunteers as well," said Andraste.

"Yes, Commander," acknowledged Laelius.

"How droll," said Gerlinde.

Gerlinde nudged Ziska and they headed towards the sewing room.

Sonje followed reluctantly behind, while Decima remained where she was. Egnatius looked uncertainly to Marcella.

"Report to Aldrich of their progress at dinner," commanded Marcella.

Egnatius bowed to Marcella as she passed and then looked to Laelius, who shrugged. Egnatius led the way to the training ground.

"They are a sorry bunch," observed Laelius as they approached.

Not one of the recruits had hit their targets. Andraste watched another group that she assumed was attempting to wrestle.

"So were this lot when we started," responded Andraste. There were several snide remarks and disgruntled comments behind her back.

"I can hear you," stated Andraste. She smiled mischievously as she turned on her Victorious.

"I bet you cannot hit all of those targets. Not after your injury," claimed Otho.

"I bet you two stars that I can," said Andraste. The Victorious laughed.

"Stars?" asked Egnatius.

"We are granted stars as a demonstration of our rank. Four is the highest number, which is carried only by Laelius. Otho is at three. If he obtains a star, he will share the same rank as Laelius. However, if he loses he will be demoted to one star and have to do all of the grunt work," explained Gnaeus.

"Should you bet over such things?" questioned Egnatius nervously.

"It is good for Otho to lose," answered Laelius.

All of the Victorious but Otho laughed.

"I accept," declared Otho. He handed a star from his tunic to Laelius.

"How many stars does the princess have?" inquired Egnatius.

"Probably fifty, but she does not wear them," responded Laelius.

Maximianus procured a bow for his Commander. He bowed ceremoniously and backed away. She hit him lightly with the feather end of her arrow. There were eight targets. She hit them all within three minutes. She turned to Otho.

"Now what did you say about a warrior of the Ice Palace?" asked Andraste.

"That they are crazier beyond all reason," affirmed Otho, and Andraste laughed. Laelius handed her the star.

"What do you do with all of the stars, my lady?" questioned Egnatius.

"Please call me Paramerion. I sew them on to a quilt," replied Andraste. She moved to speak with the rest of the Victorious.

"She is joking," said Laelius, "She gives them to our children for jobs well done or things well said. Once a child comes of age, and if he or she has obtained four stars, he or she is given the opportunity to train with us."

"Have any succeeded?" asked Egnatius.

"My eldest son, Gnaeus, is the first," stated Laelius proudly.

Andraste's smile faded as she saw Aldrich watching her from the balcony. He did not look pleased. He was dressed for dinner. She was reminded of her attire, which was coated in dirt and sweat from the road. Her hair was starting to come undone from her braids. She turned towards the Victorious as Aldrich came down the stairs. Aldrich addressed her before she could address her men.

"Is my lady ready to come in for dinner?" Aldrich asked politely.

He bowed over her hand and kissed it in the Southern fashion.

"We are planning a war-" started Andraste.

"Leave us," said Aldrich. His tone left no room for questions.

The courtyard cleared in minutes of the Southern recruits and guardsmen. Andraste nodded to her men to follow suit. Decima waited at the stairs, but she turned to examine the flowers growing out of the wall. Andraste remembered Marcella's warning about not being left alone with an unrelated gentleman. She took a step back from Aldrich. He studied her for a moment before speaking.

"I know our state, our mission, and our troubles. But I will remind you, my lady, that as a guest in my kingdom, you will observe our customs. I want you to win my people's hearts so-" started Aldrich.

"I am a soldier. There is no place for me at dances," protested Andraste.

She took a step forward. Aldrich also took a step forward. They stood glaring at each other.

"I am here to help you. Use me in ways that will benefit you," said Andraste, and she blushed deeply. She started, "I meant-"

"My lady, please do not enlighten me," interrupted Aldrich. He was at the end of being civil and truly worried by what she might say.

"We are not going to win the war tonight. Come in to dinner," finished Aldrich. He frowned as he realized that she was not going to relent.

"Then I will deal in terms you do understand. If you beat me in a swordfight, you will not have to enter, but if I win, you will have to come to dinner, dressed like a lady, your best behavior, and sit at my table for two hours every evening," proposed Aldrich.

"Agreed," snapped Andraste.

Andraste took off her cloak and dropped it on to the ground. Aldrich walked a few paces withdrawing his great sword as he turned. Andraste realized at that moment that she had underestimated him.

Aldrich came at her with such speed that he nearly had her with the first lunge. She ducked out of the way. She withdrew her own sword and countered his next attack. He drove at her hard. The look of determination in his eyes chilled her. This was not her companion from the road. This was an angry, leader of men, who meant business. However, Andraste did not want to accept orders from anyone any longer.

She drove the prince back. Aldrich swung at her head and she dropped to the ground. He swung at the ground and she jumped over the blade. Instinctively she dove at his heart and panicked, fearing she may actually hit him. She veered to the side. He sensed the same danger, but saw her beginning to take the fall as a result. He dropped his own sword as she threw hers to the side, and he caught her in his arms. They both fell to the ground panting.

"Tie?" compromised Aldrich.

"One hour," relented Andraste. She stood and made her way to Decima.

"If you were not so stubborn, you would realize that was probably the best and most unusual sword fight these walls had ever seen. Besides I think you have done the prince in," declared Decima.

Andraste turned. The prince had not moved from the grass. Andraste smiled in spite of herself.

Andraste returned to her chambers, bathed and dressed in a silvery, white gown. Decima only braided back a few pieces of Andraste's hair, so that the remainder was loose in the back in the Southern fashion, unlike the braids that Andraste usually wore. Decima handed Andraste a delicate wooden fan. Tiny jasmine flowers were painted on its edges. The fan smelled of sandalwood.

"A gift from my foster brother," said Decima. Andraste froze and did not take it from Decima's outstretched hand. Decima's smile faded.

"In the North, the exchanging of fans can symbolize an understanding," informed Andraste.

"I am sure my brother knows nothing of such a tradition. He would not be so bold. Is it so different from accepting the gown you wear? Accept the fan as a gift of kindness. Surely you must have noticed that all of the ladies in court carry such a fan?" asked Decima.

"My people will know the significance," said Andraste.

"But they will not know who it is from. Marcella or I could have given it to you. Would that mean that we have an understanding?" teased Decima.

Andraste gingerly reached for the offered fan. It was extremely light. She undid her belt and left her war fan on the table. She felt a feeling of misgiving as her eyes rested on it. She picked up and opened the lady's fan.

"We have missed dinner, but we must go down for the social hour as promised," said Decima.

Upon their entrance to the main hall, Andraste searched the room for Aldrich. She spotted his blue cape across the room.

"If he does not even acknowledge you tonight, he would be in the right. You behaved so badly, Andraste," censured Decima with disapproval.

However, Egnatius said something to the prince, and Aldrich turned immediately. His eyes were locked on her, and he headed to her side. Whispers began to circulate throughout the ballroom. However, Aldrich was not the first to reach her.

"Lord Arnold," said Decima, not bothering to hide her displeasure.

"Princess, may I have the honor of this dance?" asked the Lord.

He bowed over Andraste's hand and kissed it. However, it did not look as gallant as when Aldrich made the same gesture. The way Arnold watched her also made her feel as though he was undressing her with his eyes.

"Sir, I do not mean to dance tonight," replied Andraste tersely.

The Lord looked as though he would insist, but Andraste offered her hand to Aldrich immediately as he approached. She did not see any signs of grass or dust on him. He must have bathed before reentering the ballroom. Aldrich took her arm and wrapped it in his protectively. He did not acknowledge Lord Arnold. Decima took her leave.

"I wish to introduce you to my friends," said Aldrich.

"I would be enchanted," replied Andraste. She snapped her fan open and gracefully fanned herself.

"I must say the Southern fashion truly suits you," praised Aldrich.

"Are you mocking me?" asked Andraste. Aldrich stopped and looked down on her.

"No, you are truly lovely this evening," said Aldrich, "I mean you are always lovely. Well except for the cloak part. I prefer when you are uncloaked. I mean-"

"Please do not enlighten me," Andraste purred.

She lifted her sea-green eyes to him above her fan. Aldrich was lost for words when he reunited with his group. Egnatius made the introductions.

"I hear you are not such a rarity. All women are trained to fight in the North?" asked Kasimir.

"Not many men or women are as talented as my sister," replied Brion.

"Or can so fluster our prince," stated Eadbehrt.

Andraste hid her face behind her fan. Aldrich glanced down at her and quickly changed the subject. It was a pleasant enough evening. Andraste heard the clock chime the hour, and she removed her arm from Aldrich's. His smile fell as he turned to her.

"It would please me, if you would stay longer, if you wish," said Aldrich softly.

Andraste hesitated. She felt that she should leave to make her point, but as he spoke so gently to her, she felt as though she could not refuse.

"I was going for lemonade," responded Andraste.

"Allow me," said Aldrich. He released her arm to retrieve the requested beverage.

"Lemonade?" inquired Brion.

"I liked it better when you could not speak," snapped Andraste behind her fan, but she smiled prettily towards the Southern lords.

"That fan is lovely. Where did it come from?" asked Brion. He glanced over her shoulder towards Aldrich. Andraste glowered at her brother.

"We need to talk about court decorum as soon as possible. Is it true? Did you actually ask to be-" Brion started, but he stopped as Aldrich had returned.

"A thousand thanks," said Andraste.

"I am moderating the deal to standard behavior and not best," responded Aldrich, but his eyes laughed as he reclaimed her arm.

"Well in that case," began Andraste. She turned to say something wicked to her brother, but Aldrich caught her firmly by his hold on her arm.

"That is why you have this insufferable custom, to trap maidens!" Andraste whispered behind her fan to Aldrich. He stifled a smile.

Andraste turned suddenly as she heard a blade whisper through the air. She caught the knife in her fan, and quickly closed it. The dagger stood inches from Aldrich's face. She had not spilt a single drop of the lemonade in her other hand, which was still intertwined with Aldrich's.

Andraste handed the glass to Aldrich, and released herself from his hold. She removed the dagger from the delicate fan, which splintered in the process. She aimed to throw the dagger in the direction that it had come. She paused as her eyes registered on the target. Aldrich tensed by her side. Andraste lowered the dagger and approached her intended target. She glowered at him. The smiles from the Victorious and the Southern lords faded. Glaucio went to his knees. He bowed his head.

"Did you throw this dagger at me?" asked Andraste. Her tone was cold and deadly.

"No, Commander, at Aldrich Caelius," responded Glaucio.

"For what reason?" interrogated Andraste. She looked even angrier.

"To prove a point. The Southern lords bet that the Northerners did not have skill equal to their own with daggers. They bet you would not deflect it, and I bet you would," replied Glaucio.

"You willingly threw a dagger at our host?" questioned Andraste.

"Yes, Commander," responded Glaucio.

"You know the penalty for such an action by our laws?" asked Andraste.

"It would be death, Commander, but we are not in the North," replied Glaucio.

"I do not care where we happen to be. You are always subject to the laws of the Empire," Andraste glowered, "What if you had missed? What if I had not caught the dagger?"

"And yet you did, Commander. I had no doubt," answered Glaucio.

"In the South there is no offense that is punishable by death," admonished Aldrich behind her.

Andraste stood surveying the man before her. She took a few minutes to weigh the verdict. Glaucio stayed on his knees surveying the floor.

"Your stars," ordered Andraste.

Glaucio winced and would not meet her eyes. However, he took the two stars from his tunic and placed them in Andraste's out-stretched hand.

"I will remind you that we are guests in these halls, and I will behead the next one of you who so blatantly disrespects the hospitality and good-will of our host," avowed Andraste. She pierced each of her men with her gaze of disapproval.

"It was just a show of skill-" started Otho. Laelius silenced him with a look.

"Glaucio, return to your quarters," ordered Andraste.

Glaucio rose. He bowed to Andraste and quickly left the hall.

"You are angry," said Aldrich.

"He could have hurt you. He could have hurt a bystander," replied Andraste, "There are better ways to show our Northern skill."

"Such as?" asked Aldrich.

Andraste was distracted by the sound of a fly buzzing by her ear. It flew upwards to the ceiling beams. Andraste flipped the knife in her hand. She threw it. It nailed the fly to the support beam. She turned her eyes to Aldrich.

"I see your point," admitted Aldrich.

"It does not bother you that he threw a dagger at you?" inquired Andraste.

"Your interception was remarkable," said Aldrich, "I can understand why he would want to prove his Commander's skill and that of his home-land. You are so fond of bets. I would have thought his actions would have pleased you?"

"The breaking of Imperial law never pleases me," answered Andraste. She looked down at the splintered fan in her hand.

"I will find you another tomorrow," said Aldrich.

"Thank you, but no. I will carry my war fan," declined Andraste. She did not meet the prince's eyes. Brion approached them.

"That would be wise," said Brion, "Do you not know the significance of such a gift in the North?"

"Significance?" asked Aldrich.

"The exchanging of fans is a symbol of an understanding," replied Brion.

"We did not exchange fans," stated Andraste quickly.

"I gifted the princess a fan as is a common present in my lands," said Aldrich. He glanced at Andraste. Brion was studying his sister carefully.

"It looks as though the ladies are retiring," commented Brion, "You must go, Andraste."

"So when the Queen departs, the ladies do as well?" asked Andraste.

"Yes, they retire to the Music Room or Sewing Chambers based on the Queen's preference," confirmed Brion.

Andraste glanced towards the Queen. She did not look pleased.

"Until tomorrow," said Aldrich.

As he kissed the top of her hand, he raised his sapphire eyes to hers but she did not meet his eyes. He released her hand. Andraste bowed to Aldrich in the Northern fashion, but her thoughts were on Glaucio and his behavior.

She made her way quickly to her chambers. She found that Marcella had sent her a sleeping draft. She drank it quickly and climbed into her bed. She fell asleep almost immediately. She did not dream that night.

Chapter Six

There were three knocks on her door. Andraste opened her eyes. Not even the sun had yet risen.

"Commander?" called Laelius.

"Yes," Andraste replied.

"A Northern force approaches the city from the West. Aldrich and his Commanders are riding out to meet them," reported Laelius.

"I am coming," said Andraste.

She threw on her clothes, hastily tied her hair back, and tugged on her boots. She picked up her sword and hurried out of her room.

"How many?" asked Andraste.

"Five squadrons," stated Laelius.

"Our men?" inquired Andraste.

"Readying the horses," replied Laelius.

They ran down the halls to the stables. There was a flurry of activity as horses were being readied and palace guards were taking their positions. She saw that her men were assembled. She scanned the crowd for Aldrich.

"He just left," confirmed Brion as he came to her side.

Andraste mounted her horse and scanned her men to make sure all were ready. She urged her horse west out of the city.

The Resistance forces were stopped on an open plain. Andraste made her way to Aldrich. Brion and Laelius followed her. The rest of the Victorious kept their distance.

"Only five squadrons? We can take them easily. What are you waiting for?" one of the Southern lords was asking. Aldrich's eyes were locked on the opposite field.

"They have not yet attacked. It is a small force. Perhaps they are delivering a message?" suggested another lord.

"Five squadrons to deliver a message?" asked Kasimir incredulously.

"Commander," cautioned Laelius.

Andraste turned her attention to Laelius, whose eyes were locked on the opposite side of the plain on the waiting Northern forces.

"Go back to the city," urged Brion to Andraste. She turned her eyes to the opposite side of the field.

"Do you know them?" asked Aldrich. The Southern lords stopped their conversation and all eyes turned on them.

"The cobra banner is that of my sister, Varinia. I assume she is in charge," answered Andraste.

"Look again," stated Brion.

"The falcon. It must be our brother, Matthias. He is responsible for the Southern territories," said Andraste. She frowned and glanced to Brion. His eyes were fixed on the opposite field.

In the distance, she saw the banners of her own troops, a red dragon on black banners. Her breath caught in her throat.

"They sent her own troops to fight us," Laelius explained to the Lords. Aldrich was watching her carefully.

"But where are my other two squadrons? There lines are mixed. Where is Mikhael? Something is not right," said Andraste as she scanned the Northern formation.

"Return to the city," said Aldrich, "You should not have to fight your own men or siblings. I will not ask that of you. We will not judge you any less."

"It is civil war. If I step aside for this battle then should I step aside for every battle that follows?" Andraste retorted angrily. She was still scanning the troops.

"Who is my replacement?" Andraste asked to Laelius.

"It is Tobias," replied Brion.

Brion had his eyes locked on Andraste. Laelius snatched her reins before she could charge forward. Andraste glared at him.

"Who?" asked Egnatius.

"The former leader of the Victorious," replied Brion.

"I thought you served until death," said Kasimir.

"Tobias lost a duel to my Commander, and so he was replaced by the victor," replied Laelius.

"He was permitted to resign after he broke off his engagement to my sister," said Brion softly.

Andraste felt all Southern eyes upon her. She kept her face emotionless. She did not look at Aldrich.

"But only five squadrons?" asked Eadbehrt as he surveyed the field.

"I rely on quality, not quantity," replied Andraste.

"Still, it is a suicide mission," stated Laelius.

"To punish me," concluded Andraste.

"Yes," confirmed Laelius.

"Varinia probably volunteered," stated Brion, "She will kill her own flesh and blood to become the next Empress."

"The others?" asked Aldrich.

"The desertion penalty," replied Laelius.

"There are three riders approaching the center of the field," announced Egnatius.

"It is their leaders. They will want to speak," said Brion.

Andraste reclaimed her reins from Laelius. She urged her horse forward. She silenced Aldrich with a look. He said nothing and rode after her. Egnatius rode on Aldrich's open side.

All three Northern Commanders were dressed in their full armor. They also wore the red capes of the Empire. Matthias looked like a younger version of Brion. It pained Andraste to look at him, but not half as much as when she looked to Tobias. His brown eyes widened in surprise as he saw her. He quickly looked away. Varinia saw his response and turned her eyes to Andraste.

"You?" cried Varinia and her steel-blue eyes flashed. She tossed her dark brown hair. Her anger turned into a disappointed smile, "Still alive?"

"Silence!" Tobias bellowed, "Remember your place, Captain."

Tobias still did not look at Andraste.

"To allow a traitor and an exile to approach us? You would so insult the Valerianus house?" Varinia snapped at Aldrich, who had taken the lead.

Andraste saw Matthias scan the troops behind her for Brion. She inclined her head in Brion's direction. Matthias followed the movement and his eyes locked on Brion. Tobias shot a look of warning to Varinia. She held her tongue.

"And you would so insult the South? To ride in full force, without invitation, into Southern lands?" replied Aldrich.

"Imperial lands," corrected Matthias.

"You would house a traitor? Such an offense is punishable by death," retaliated Varinia.

"That is not why we came," said Matthias, "Do not take me for a fool, Aldrich Caelius. The amount of troops and supplies being gathered here is against the Imperial Rules and Regulations. You know this."

"The South plans on removing itself from the Empire. We will not submit to a mad sovereign who executes his people for imaginary offenses," stated Aldrich calmly.

Varinia colored deeply.

"I have written terms for the Emperor regarding a peaceful division," continued Aldrich.

Egnatius held out a scroll in his right hand. Slowly he rode forward and extended it to Matthias.

"The Emperor will not accept this," replied Matthias. He did not move to take it.

"Brother, deliver the message to the Emperor. There is nothing in our Code that says you cannot take the message. This is a senseless battle," pleaded Andraste.

Matthias surveyed her and his eyes softened. He took the message from Egnatius.

"Coward!" yelled Varinia.

Varinia took a dagger from her sleeve and stabbed Matthias through the vulnerable link in his armor. Matthias fell from his horse. Andraste dismounted immediately and went to Matthias's side. She rolled him over in her arms. His steel-gray eyes were opened wide in shock.

Andraste heard angry shouts and the sound of blades being drawn on the Northern side. Matthias's men were turning on Varinia's squadron.

"He is dead," confirmed Andraste. She removed her glove and gently shut her brother's eyes. She did not move from his side.

"My father would have acted the same," stated Varinia.

"That does not make it right," responded Tobias.

"If you take that message, you will face the same fate by my sword," swore Varinia.

Tobias did not move.

"How many more must die, Varinia?" Andraste asked. She looked up to her sister, "Solve this with a duel; one of your warriors versus one of ours. If you fight, all of your forces will be wiped out. Are you so eager to die?"

"Silence!" commanded Varinia. She spat on Andraste. Andraste did not move from her place. However, Andraste did not remove her gaze from Varinia.

"We accept," answered Tobias. He addressed Aldrich.

"It will be a fight to the death. The traitor will fight for the South. If she loses, the South must surrender," glowered Varinia.

"Agreed," said Andraste.

"No-" started Aldrich.

"I will not lose," stated Andraste, "And if I lose, then my life will be forfeited, and not one of your men."

"We are honored by your courage," said Egnatius to Andraste. He bowed his head to her. Aldrich did not respond.

"How noble," Varinia snarled. Her cold eyes turned on Tobias, "You will fight for the North. The Emperor still doubts your loyalty."

Andraste kept her eyes on Matthias. She heard Tobias dismount. She gently placed her brother's head down on the grass. She undid her cloak and threw it over her horse's saddle. She heard Tobias remove his armor.

"Fool," hissed Varinia.

"It will be a fair fight," said Tobias.

"Her armor was removed for her lack of honor. That is no reason to endanger yourself," said Varinia.

"Honor? You dare speak of honor? Murdering your own brother?

Attacking an opponent when his back was turned to you? There is only one true Valerianus on this field with honor. There is only one Valerianus capable of ruling this Empire. You divide people, Varinia, while Andraste unites and leads. You need to recognize this before the Empire destroys itself," commanded Tobias.

Varinia smoldered in speechless rage.

Andraste moved away from the horses. Tobias let her precede twenty paces before following. She stopped and lifted her sea-green eyes to Tobias. He stopped as well. Now that his face was turned only towards her, she could see the pain and regret in his eyes. A gentle breeze blew the tall grasses across the plain, as the sun began to rise behind the Southern troops.

"One of you will have to move sometime," ordered Varinia.

Tobias did not move.

Andraste scanned the Southern troops and then the Northern troops. Her eyes rested on her three squadrons. She unsheathed her Ruin sword. Tobias's eyes landed on the red blade in recognition and then admiration. He unsheathed his own sword. They saluted each other with their swords, and then Tobias charged. They exchanged blow after blow, neither one giving an inch. The sun progressed across the sky. Andraste saw an opening, she weighed her options. She decided to risk potential injury. Tobias's sword grazed across her sword arm. Andraste grinded her teeth as she felt the tearing of her skin. However, the tip of Andraste's sword landed on Tobias's heart. She hesitated.

"You win, do it," ordered Tobias, "Varinia will accept nothing but one of our deaths."

Andraste looked into his eyes and could not move.

"I would have followed you anywhere," said Tobias. He threw his weight forward into her sword. The sword went into his heart.

"NO!" Andraste yelled.

She caught him in her arms and fell to the ground from his weight. His breath was shallow. He raised a hand to her. She grasped it tightly in her own hand. She felt his grasp weaken. He breathed his last breath. The pain from her wound was nothing compared to the agony in her heart.

"Tobias," Andraste whispered.

His hand fell limp in her own. She gently lowered his arm to the ground. There was silence on the field. Slowly Andraste heard the sound of horses approaching Varinia.

"We will take our lord's body," said a soldier dressed in Andraste's colors.

"There was no honor in his death. Leave it! That goes for the traitorous prince as well," ordered Varinia.

The soldier's face tightened.

"I will see to them. Go!" commanded Andraste.

The soldier saluted her. She lifted up Tobias's fallen sword to the soldier.

"Take it to his wife, for his son," ordered Andraste.

The soldier did so. Varinia made as if to speak but she was silenced by the looks of loathing from the Northern soldiers.

"Now leave," ordered Andraste to Varinia, "Or is your word so easily broken?"

Varinia stared at Andraste with hatred. Wordlessly, Varinia turned her horse and as she did so, the Northern forces retreated. Andraste felt the attention of the Southern forces shift to the retreating Imperial Army. She hastily bound her wound from a scrap of her tunic.

Andraste removed her blade with great care from Tobias' chest, and then threw it across the plain angrily. Andraste's eyes registered on Matthias's body and the scroll now covered in his blood. Brion and the Victorious approached. Brion's face was agony. He knelt by his brother's side. Andraste left Tobias to Laelius' care and approached Brion. Her arm and tunic were covered in blood. Andraste wrapped her arms around Brion's neck. He buried his face in her shoulder.

"Shovels?" Laurentius asked the approaching Southern guardsmen.

Aldrich nodded to one of the Southern guardsmen, who went to retrieve some.

"Aldrich Caelius, you should return to your city and booster your defenses. The Emperor will send the Imperial Army next," informed Laelius.

"I will help you bury your dead," responded Aldrich.

Aldrich looked to Egnatius and inclined his head towards the Southern troops. Egnatius bowed to Aldrich and rode back to the Southern forces. Egnatius gave the order and the Southern forces returned to the city. A handful of the Southern lords remained with Aldrich. Two southern guardsmen returned with shovels. Brion rose and the Victorious took them and started digging. Andraste returned and sat by Tobias's body. Andraste kept her face set in stone. She saw Aldrich take a shovel and help Brion with their brother's grave. Her lip trembled. Laelius put a hand on her shoulder and stood by her side. Andraste looked away.

The graves being dug, the Victorious lowered each body into its resting place. Andraste rose and dropped the first handful of dirt into Tobias's grave. Brion made the same gesture on Matthias's grave. The Victorious took over filling the graves. Brion took Andraste's hand in his. They watched silently as the graves were filled. Once they were done, there were ten minutes of silence.

Andraste took a deep breath and sang the required words:

"I will forever feel your absence.
I wish you were here once more.
But rest and no longer dwell on earthly affairs.
Your time is won, so sleep my friend.
Go to the halls of our fathers.
We will remember your deeds forever more.
There is no cause to linger.
Go to everlasting peace and rest.
I will see you once more as fate decrees.
My heart, that aches, will find peace,
When we are once more reunited.
But that time is not for us to decide.
Sleep, my friend, and remember,
All is one forevermore.
You are one with the earth.
Someday I will return to the earth,
And we will be united again."

Brion kissed Andraste's forehead gently.

"It is not your fault," comforted Brion. Andraste took a deep breath.

"We must not linger in the open. We need to return to the city," cautioned Laelius.

Andraste took one last look at the graves and then mounted her horse. Aldrich wordlessly lifted her sword to her. He had cleaned it while she was not looking. Andraste wordlessly accepted it and returned it to her sheath. She did not meet Aldrich's eyes. She turned her horse and followed the Victorious back towards the city.

She left her horse at the stables and retired to her chambers for the rest of the day. She tended to her own wound. It was a long and laborious process. Afterwards, she could not sleep. The pain in her arm was excruciating and she feared her dreams. However, she did not attend the feast. She did not want company.

Aldrich sat with the Victorious for dinner. They did not jest and laugh as they usually did.

"How is your Commander?" asked Aldrich. Brion did not respond.

"You must be wondering about the engagement," said Laelius. Aldrich did not respond.

"Tobias loved my princess. This is true, but she never loved him," said Laelius, "When Tobias realized that she did not love him in return, he released her from their engagement. He left the Victorious and returned to his lands. She and Tobias had not spoken in years."

"Then how do you explain the child?" asked Nero.

"The child?" repeated Aldrich.

"There are rumors that a child, being fostered by the Lord of the Salt Islands, is the child of Andraste and Tobias. This is a blatant falsehood," said Laelius. He glared at Nero.

"But you have seen the boy. He looks just like Andraste," said Nero.

"The child looks more like Rhinauld," responded Felix.

"Her foster brother?" inquired Aldrich.

"It cannot be Rhinauld's," commented Valens. He exchanged looks with Felix.

"Rhinauld nor Tobias is the father of the child in question. My sister and Rhinauld were in the North when the child was born, so obviously, she is not the mother," defended Brion.

It was the first thing he had said since the battle. The Victorious grew silent.

"I would not mention the child to the Lord of the Salt Islands or to either of his sisters. It is a tender subject," ordered Brion. He looked to each of the Victorious.

"So it is true? They come?" asked Gnaeus.

"They will be arriving with the King of the Island Kingdoms and their combined forces in a few days," said Brion. The men looked to Aldrich for confirmation.

"My Queen confirmed this upon our return," said Aldrich. He took a long drink from his stein.

As the first rays of sun crept through her window, Andraste rose. Despite an extensive search, she could not find any of her travel clothes. She dressed in a sea-green linen gown and pulled on her boots. She picked roses from her balcony. The thorns pricked at her hands and made her fingertips bleed but she kept at her task. The action also caused her wound from the previous day to ache; however, she continued picking roses. She wrapped her bounty in her cloak. She strapped her Ruin sword around her hip and threw her bow and quiver across her shoulder.

The doors to Aldrich's room were shut, but she could hear him moving about his own chamber. It sounded as if he was pacing. Andraste soundlessly closed the door to her own chambers and made her way towards the stables. She set her load on the floor so that she could saddle her horse. She laid her head against her horse's neck and then loaded her gear. She mounted and rode out of the palace.

She rode to Tobias's and Mathias's graves. She dismounted and let her horse graze. She divided the roses among the two graves and then sat between them on the grass. She admired the stillness and tranquility of the plain. A gentle mist hovered over the plain, while an Eastern wind blew across the plain and the tall grasses danced merrily. The sun had risen over head but it was accompanied by thick, pearly clouds that were tinged with shadow.

"Do you even know I am here?" asked Andraste aloud. She rose hurriedly before her tears could begin to fall.

Andraste whistled for her horse and mounted. She turned her horse back towards the palace but she hesitated. The Eastern wind brought with it the smell of the seashore. Andraste urged her horse forward following the scent of the sea. She rode until she reached a sleepy little fishing village. She could see fishermen in the distance on the ocean unwinding their nets. She rode to the beach and stopped by an elderly fisherman who was mending a net.

"Good morrow," called the fisherman.

"Good morrow," replied Andraste.

"You must have ridden far this morning," said the fishermen.

"Why do you say that?" asked Andraste.

"It is near three hours to the palace," replied the fishermen. Andraste surveyed the fishermen and he continued, "You must be from the castle. We do not have many fine ladies hereabouts."

"Did you catch anything?" inquired Andraste.

"Not for years. My injury keeps me from going back to sea, but I keep myself busy mending the nets," replied the fishermen, "You should head back to the palace, Lady Eldgrimson. A fierce storm is brewing from the North."

"How do you know my name?" asked Andraste.

"Beryl eyes, hazel hair, flawless, alabaster complexion, you could be no other. When I first saw you riding out of the mists, I thought you were the ghost of the Empress herself," said the fishermen. He smiled kindly at Andraste.

"May your nets ensnare a magnificent catch," said Andraste.

"May your road be without peril," replied the fishermen.

Andraste turned her horse about and headed back the way she came. As she reached the graves, she saw that hundreds of other flowers had joined her own, but she saw not a soul in the distance. The first drops of rain began to fall. It was a gentle rain, a warm, forgiving rain unlike the icy, tormenting rains of the North. The sun still peeked in and out through the clouds, temporarily halting the progress of the showers.

Andraste strayed from the road to the palace and traversed the beaches. The rain began to intensify and the wind to augment. She rode inland and found a sheltered cove. She saw torches lit from a cave in the side of the cliff. Andraste hesitated and turned her horse back towards the road.

"Commander," called a voice.

Andraste looked over her shoulder and saw Egnatius standing at the foot of path. He approached her cautiously, and bowed eloquently when he reached her.

"The storm will be brief, but it will worsen. There is shelter in the cave. My lord is present," said Egnatius.

"I should return. My men will be looking for me," said Andraste.

"They cannot leave the palace with this storm. It will pass shortly. Come in and dry yourself by our fire," invited Egnatius.

Egnatius slowly turned back down the path. When he was near twenty paces away, he turned to look over his shoulder. Andraste rode cautiously after him. Her horse climbed up stone steps that had been carved into the side of the cliff. They reached a cave and Andraste dismounted and left her horse with the Southerners' horses.

"It may take a while for your eyes to adjust to the dark," said Egnatius. He offered his hand to her in the Northern fashion. Andraste took it and he led her carefully up the stone steps.

"What is this place?" asked Andraste.

"It is the base of the Southern Ruin," explained Egnatius, "You would have to go much further in order to enter the challenges. However, it shelters those in need. You do not need to fear."

"The Commander knows no fear," commented Aldrich.

Egnatius dropped Andraste's hand and stepped to the side. He bowed to Aldrich.

"I had come to see what kept you," said Aldrich.

"I seem to have found the Commander by chance," replied Egnatius.

"Were you looking for me?" asked Andraste.

"Yes. I was worried you had left for the North," replied Aldrich.

She brushed past him and headed cautiously after Egnatius. The stairs were becoming more steep and narrow. Andraste picked up her skirts in one hand and lifted them slightly so she would not trip on the stairs.

"You are soaked through," stated Aldrich.

"I am not cold. It feels like a Northern summer," replied Andraste. Aldrich draped his cape about her shoulders as he passed.

"You will catch a cold," remarked Aldrich.

"That is nonsense," stated Andraste. However, she fastened the broach on the cape. When she glanced upwards she could see Aldrich smiling in the torchlight. Andraste stepped away quickly as she heard footsteps on the stairs.

"I thought I heard your voice," said Marcella. She took Andraste's arm in her own and led her up the stairs. They emerged into a second larger cave. The cave was illuminated by torches secured in brackets from the walls. There was a fireplace carved into the far wall. As Marcella and Andraste approached, the Southern ladies moved out of the way.

"Do not move on my account," said Andraste. She freed herself from Marcella's arm and crept towards the shadows. Marcella examined her hand in the torchlight.

"Are you bleeding?" asked Marcella.

"It is nothing. Only from thorns," said Andraste. She hastily hid her hands underneath the folds of the cape. She could feel Aldrich's eyes on her from across the room. He busied himself with pouring a glass of wine.

"You left the roses on the graves?" asked Sonje. Andraste did not respond.

"I am sorry for your losses. We left our offerings as well," said Marcella.

"They were beautiful," conceded Andraste.

"Did you see us?" asked Gerlinde.

"No. I saw the flowers on my return," replied Andraste.

"How far did you ride?" questioned Egnatius.

"A small fishing village to the East," answered Andraste.

"That is no small distance. You made good time," stated Egnatius.

"I told you the wind would be easier to catch then the Commander," said Kasimir.

Aldrich had silently reached her side and offered her the goblet. As she reached to take it, a gold light grew between them. Where the light touched her fingers, the scratches and cuts from the thorns instantly healed.

"It is not necessary," said Andraste. She moved away, but Aldrich held her hand.

"You are much trouble for the prince," stated Gerlinde. Aldrich glared at Gerlinde from across the room. Gerlinde continued, "It is true. You have ridden all across the countryside this morning looking for her, and it is evident she does not want or need your aid."

"That is enough," admonished Kasimir. He stepped between Gerlinde and Andraste.

"You too?" asked Gerlinde.

"The princess is grieving," said Marcella.

"Forgive me. You lost one of your fiancés yesterday did you not?" asked Gerlinde.

"You show your ignorance most when you speak of things of which you know nothing," responded Andraste.

Gerlinde's mouth opened in shock, but she could not think of a rejoinder. Gerlinde closed her mouth and turned to face Kasimir. Andraste moved closer to the fire and turned her back on the Southern nobles. After a few minutes, the nobles started a conversation, but Andraste only half-listened. She sipped on her wine and watched the flames. Andraste set her goblet on the ledge above the fire when she was done. Andraste moved nearer the opening of the cave and undid the fastening on Aldrich's cape. She left it on a peg built into the cave wall. Aldrich joined her side and spoke softly to her so the others could not hear.

"You intend to ride?" asked Aldrich.

"The storm is already dissipating," answered Andraste.

"Do not ride in the storm," advised Aldrich. He studied the storm raging outside.

"I have ridden in worse," stated Andraste.

"I cannot fight with Northern logic," remarked Aldrich. He moved to follow her.

"You should remain with your people," said Andraste.

"If a Northerner can ride in a Southern storm, then so can I," alleged Aldrich.

"That is a fine example of faulty Southern logic," replied Andraste, "Besides, I have already had to ferry you across the Empire on my horse when you were wounded. I would prefer not to do it again."

"You are prone to injury. Who is going to heal you if I am not with you?" inquired Aldrich.

"I have managed for decades without your healing powers," stated Andraste.

"I cannot fathom how," replied Aldrich, "But I have duties I must attend to at the palace."

"I will not stand in the way of your duty," said Andraste.

She stepped aside so that he could lead the way down the stairs. Aldrich proceeded before her and Andraste grabbed his cape from the peg before heading after him. She wrapped it back around her shoulders. As they entered the first cave, she whistled for her horse.

"Northerners do have a way with horses," admitted Aldrich grudgingly as her horse sauntered over to her. He had to retrieve his own stallion by the reins in order to get him to budge.

"I prefer horses to people," conceded Andraste.

Aldrich led his horse by the reins down the stairs and Andraste followed his example. By the time they had reached the beach, the storm had regressed to a few rain drops.

"See," said Andraste.

"It could have also raged for an hour," rejoined Aldrich.

"But it did not," replied Andraste. She mounted and turned her horse towards the palace. She stopped as she did not hear Aldrich's horse pursuing her. She turned and saw that Aldrich was studying her.

"Why do you stare?" asked Andraste.

"You are so capable," replied Aldrich. He mounted quickly.

"Are Southern ladies not?" inquired Andraste.

"That is not what I meant," answered Aldrich.

He rode after her and took the lead. Aldrich galloped ahead of her and Andraste paused to watch him before urging her horse to follow. They reached the palace at a rapid gallop. Aldrich did not slow as he reached the city. The path cleared for him as he approached. Aldrich had already led his stallion to his stall as Andraste rode in. Aldrich faltered in his instructions to the stableboy as Andraste surveyed him. He left his conversation and approached Andraste.

"Yes, my lady?" questioned Aldrich.

He took the reins of her horse. Andraste dismounted in a fluid, graceful movement on the opposite side from Aldrich. The horse stood between them and raised its head to Andraste. She stroked its neck absently.

"I would not have left without you," said Andraste, "Earlier you said that you thought I had left for the North. I will not leave without you."

"You have been thinking about that all this while?" asked Aldrich.

"It will take both of us to defeat the Emperor," replied Andraste. She turned as she heard footsteps. She saw Paulina making her way cautiously towards them.

"Approach," said Andraste. Her features softened and she smiled at Paulina.

"My lady, I have come to offer you a dinner invitation. Will you honor us with your presence at our cottage this evening?" asked Paulina.

"Why so formal?" inquired Andraste. Paulina glanced to Aldrich.

"I am required to attend the social hour, so I must decline," said Andraste. She turned her eyes to Aldrich, "I apologize for missing yesterday."

"You are forgiven. Please attend the dinner with your people, I would not stand in your way," said Aldrich.

"Prince Aldrich, it will be a humble meal, but what we have, would you share with us?" asked Paulina.

"I would be honored," replied Aldrich.

"We are honoring the lives of two great Northern warriors," said Paulina. She bowed to Aldrich in the Northern style and then to Andraste. Andraste's smile faded and she looked away.

"What may I bring?" asked Aldrich.

"You have provided us accommodation and security. You need bring nothing," said Paulina. She smiled mischievously at Andraste, "And you bring nothing because we do not want to mourn more than two this evening."

Paulina turned and headed back towards the Victorious accommodations. Andraste glanced to Aldrich, "For the record, my cooking never actually has killed anyone."

"You have other talents, my lady," said Aldrich. Her look was murderous so Aldrich said, "I did not ask. What hour do you think?"

"Before the sun sets, but I do not know where the Victorious are housed," replied Andraste.

"I will come for you in two hours and we will walk together, if this arrangement pleases you?" inquired Aldrich.

"It pleases me," responded Andraste.

"Forgive me, I have business to attend to until then," said Aldrich. He bowed low to Andraste. She curtsied low and held her position so that she could meet his eyes.

"I thank you again for your kindness towards my people. It means the world to me. I will find a way to repay you," promised Andraste.

She rose quickly before he could respond. She turned to see Kasimir and Eadbehrt riding into the courtyard. Aldrich straightened and followed her gaze.

"Until this evening," said Andraste. She turned and hurried from the courtyard.

"Heiyoh," called Felix from the shadows.

"So you have decided to show yourself?" asked Andraste as he reached her side, "You have been following me since dawn."

"The Southerners did not notice," replied Felix.

"What do you want?" asked Andraste.

"Our King comes tomorrow. He will see you at the banquet," answered Felix.

"How many warriors does my uncle bring?" questioned Andraste.

"Unspecified," replied Felix.

"Will he fight with us?" questioned Andraste.

"Not verified," answered Felix.

"Any news from Rhinauld?" inquired Andraste.

"He is returned from the Ruins. It is unknown whether he obtained the third relic," replied Felix, "There is no news from the North."

"And the Victorious, what do they do with their free time?" asked Andraste.

"Most spent the day with their families," replied Felix.

"Except for you?" questioned Andraste.

"As did I. You wound me. Have you forgotten we were fostered together in the Island Kingdoms?" asked Felix.

"Of course not! It is the only reason that I allow your insolence, and why I permitted you to shadow me today even though I desired to be alone," said Andraste.

"I know. That is why I left you alone," responded Felix.

"Oh, Felix. We need to find you a wife so that you may bother her in your free time," sighed Andraste. They had reached her chambers.

"There is no reason to guard me. Prepare yourself for this evening. We honor Tobias and Matthias," said Andraste.

"I will wait at my post until the prince comes to fetch you. I swore your protection to my lord and my King," said Felix.

"You think the prince will protect me if the need arises?" asked Andraste.

"I know he will," replied Felix.

"So he has won one vote out of fourteen," stated Andraste.

"Do you mean to make him a member of the Victorious?" questioned Felix.

"You know that is not for me to propose. The vote must be unanimous," responded Andraste.

"He still has time to prove himself. He will earn your trust yet," said Felix.

"I do not trust anyone," stated Andraste.

"Yes, Commander. I know," said Felix as Andraste entered her chambers and closed the behind her.

Andraste had no more than bathed, dressed in a robe, and began brushing the tangles out of her hair when she heard a knock on her door. Iovita entered before Andraste could answer. She was dressed in scarlet and charcoal Northern robes, depicting her status as the wife of a member of the Victorious. She had scarlet Northern robes folded in her arms.

"I cannot wear the Valerianus colors," said Andraste.

"You are still our Commander. You are still our leader despite the edict of the Emperor. You are still recognized as Andraste Valerianus in these halls and by the Southern people. You must follow protocol, princess. Paulina would have come herself, as your friend, but she is busy preparing for the dinner. Forgive my words, but we have always been frank," said Iovita. She bowed to Andraste and held the robes to her.

"You need make no apology. I expect honesty from my Victorious," said Andraste. Andraste took them from her but eyed them uncertainly.

"But I am not-" started Iovita.

"You know better, Iovita. Our circle is family. Look what disaster my actions have caused for all of you," said Andraste sadly.

"It was our choice to come. How could we have remained in the North while you suffered alone? My brother and my husband do not hesitate from the necessary. They do not fear the impossible," stated Iovita.

"That is why they are Victorious," approved Andraste. Iovita hesitated by the door.

"Speak," said Andraste.

"Shall I help you dress your hair in the Northern fashion?" asked Iovita. Andraste nodded her consent and Iovita sat behind Andraste on the bed. Andraste passed Iovita the comb.

"My lady, are you bleeding?" asked Iovita.

"I was wounded yesterday in my duel with Tobias. It is nothing," said Andraste.

"But no one said-" started Iovita.

"It is nothing. No one needs to be bothered," said Andraste. She picked a roll of bandages from her saddlebag and then sat back on the bed. She began to bandage her arm. Iovita took it from her and began to tend the wound.

"The prince-" began Iovita.

"I cannot depend on him to heal me for every wound. I will become careless. Our wounds are reminders of our flaws. We must remember to correct our mistakes," said Andraste.

"He would not see it as weakness. I have never seen a lord who was so gentle, generous or kind. It would please him to be of assistance," alleged Iovita.

"I will tell your husband you have spoken so kindly of a Southern lord," teased Andraste.

"It is not kindness. It is truth. You may need stitches since it is still bleeding," said Iovita.

"It is nothing. I reopened it riding," said Andraste.

"You stitched this yourself?" asked Iovita, "You have fourteen sworn brothers, all trained in field medicine."

"I am capable," said Andraste.

"Begging your pardon, Commander, but you are insane," said Iovita.

Andraste laughed and Iovita smiled weakly, but she still eyed the wound with concern. The new bandage seemed to hold.

Iovita picked up the comb and dressed Andraste's hair in silence. She helped dress Andraste in the scarlet Northern robes, and tied the charcoal sash around her waist.

"We could not get your dress uniform or imperial cape from your chambers. We had too little time," stated Iovita.

"You risked so much for apparel. I am honored by your dedication and your friendship," reassured Andraste.

Iovita bowed to Andraste and turned to leave the room.

"Do not worry anyone about this injury. Tell no one," commanded Andraste.

"You are punishing yourself needlessly," replied Iovita.

"That was a command," insisted Andraste.

"Yes, Commander," answered Iovita. She left without a further word and Andraste heard the door close behind her. Iovita did not stop to talk to Felix.

Andraste walked onto her veranda and stood at the balcony watching the sea.

There was a knock on her door and then Felix entered. Andraste turned to face him from the veranda.

"Commander, Aldrich Caelius waits," announced Felix. He opened the second door so that Aldrich could enter, but Aldrich did not move from his position.

"You may go," responded Andraste. Felix bowed to Andraste as he departed.

"I had already forgotten. You may not enter my chambers without another lady or family member present," said Andraste.

She left the veranda and approached the doorway. Aldrich's eyes did not leave her for a moment. Andraste hesitated and Aldrich diverted his gaze. He stepped further into the hallway so that she could proceed.

"I do not know the way," admitted Andraste.

Aldrich proceeded down the hallway, but he kept glancing down at her. She maintained her silence and held her hands behind her back.

"You are armed," stated Aldrich as he looked to her Ruin sword.

"It is our way," said Andraste.

"Should I be armed?" asked Aldrich.

"I will protect you, and by doing so, my Victorious will protect you should the need arise," said Andraste, "But that is not what you were asking. You think this is a trap?"

"No! Is it a point of decorum? Should I-" started Aldrich. He was startled as Andraste laughed gently.

"You are fine as you are," said Andraste. Aldrich folded his arms across his chest.

"Keep your eyes on your path, Aldrich Caelius. You are bound to trip if you keep staring at me," reproved Andraste.

Aldrich blushed and lowered his eyes to the ground. He did not speak as they continued on their path. As they reached the steps leading down to the city, they met the Queen.

"What a transformation," praised the Queen. She surveyed Andraste from head to toe, "This is the daughter worthy of Victoria Eldgrimson and Ricimer Valerianus."

"You put such faith in appearances?" asked Andraste.

"Such things matter," replied the Queen.

"We should be going," said Aldrich quickly. He offered Andraste his arm.

"My condolences, princess," said the Queen. Andraste tensed at the title.

"Thank you," said Andraste. She raised her head proudly and took Aldrich's arm. He guided her down the stairs. When they were out of sight of the palace, she released his arm.

"The Victorious are not accommodated at the palace?" asked Andraste.

"My commanders thought it a peril to my security. But this is not the reason I had them housed elsewhere. I thought they and their families would be more comfortable in the cottages near the guardsmen, actually where the Southern guardsmen live. Egnatius lives there as do many of the Southern commanders. I thought it would be good for them and their families to become acquainted with the Victorious," said Aldrich.

"You always think of everything," commented Andraste, "But do your commanders not see me as a threat? Why am I housed across the hall from you?"

"They were worried for other reasons. However, when they saw you duel, you earned their respect. They saw you as the Commander of the Victorious," replied Aldrich.

"What were the other reasons?" inquired Andraste. Aldrich only blushed and cleared his throat.

"Oh, I see," said Andraste.

"It is not like the North. Single lords and ladies are housed in separate floors and wings of the palace. But as you are my personal guest and under my protection, I want you near me at all times," said Aldrich.

"Am I your ward?" asked Andraste. She laughed and Aldrich shifted uncomfortably.

"For Southern purposes, yes," replied Aldrich.

"You once accused me of being fully capable of protecting myself," alleged Andraste.

"I know this to be true, but you are also a Valerianus in Southern lands. No harm will come to you so long as you are under my roof and under my protection," swore Aldrich.

"You are truly concerned," stated Andraste. She raised her eyes to Aldrich.

"Yes," said Aldrich.

"I am sorry that I cause you so much trouble," said Andraste sadly.

"It is no trouble," stated Aldrich, "You have made my life so much more interesting."

"Interesting," repeated Andraste, "I have always loathed that word. It covers all manners of turpitude."

They had reached a level that housed quaint cottages. The streets were narrow and the cottages leaned over the road. Andraste saw that her Victorious and their families were entering one of the cottages nearest them. She saw Laelius at the door of the cottage. She proceeded ahead of Aldrich.

"Please come in and be welcome," said Laelius. He was dressed in ceremonial Northern robes. Without his full armor and all of his weapons, Laelius was much more approachable. He appeared to be a respectable host and not the deadly assassin Andraste knew him to be. By Aldrich's expression, she noted that he had drawn the same conclusion. They passed through the quarters and into the backyard. All of the cottages opened into a shared common area. Northern lanterns danced among the branches of dogwood trees.

Aldrich surveyed the common area and noted all of the Victorious and their families were attired in ceremonial Northern apparel. He also noted that all of the Victorious were armed. The Victorious surveyed Aldrich with equal interest as did their families.

"You are fine," said Andraste softly. She could sense his tension without even looking at him. She offered her hand to him in the Northern style. Aldrich took it and she led him towards Paulina, who was dressed in beautiful charcoal-colored robes.

"Her robes are different from the other ladies' since she was once a member of the Victorious," explained Andraste.

"But some of your men are not from the North. Why do they wear Northern robes?" asked Aldrich.

"We have a flare for drama," replied Maximianus as he offered Aldrich a stein, "And truth be told, they are quite comfortable."

Iovita offered Andraste a glass of rice wine from a porcelain tray. However, she kept her distance so that Andraste had to reach for it.

"Commander has a taste for Northern rice wine. However, it is not as good as the Southern ales," said Maximianus. He clinked his stein against Aldrich's who smiled in response. However, Aldrich's smile faded as Andraste reached for the glass. Her robe pulled back and he saw the blood-spotted bandage around her arm. Andraste followed his gaze.

"Saucy minx," swore Andraste. She nearly dropped her wine glass in her haste to conceal her arm.

"I told no one as commanded, Commander," replied Iovita. She smiled mischievously and headed towards Paulina's house.

"Did you just call my daughter-in-law a saucy minx?" asked Laelius. He laughed whole-heartedly.

"So Tobias did injure you in the duel," said Maximianus. Otho swore across the courtyard and threw a pouch of coins to Maximianus.

"I bet you would win but you would be injured. Otho bet you would win outright," said Maximianus.

"But when were you injured?" asked Aldrich.

"Near the end, right before her sword rested on his heart. She sacrificed her forearm in order to get close," stated Maximianus.

"So that is why you did not attend dinner," said Laelius, "You tended the wound yourself?"

"Who bet Tobias would win?" asked Andraste. She ignored Laelius' prior question. Laelius and Aldrich exchanged looks.

"Glaucio," replied Maximianus, "It is like he trying to lose your favor."

"Glaucio is the only one who has seen Tobias and I duel before. It was a sound bet. Tobias could have won," stated Andraste.

She put her arms behind her back, but Aldrich reached for her arm. He removed the bandage and studied the wound. The golden light grew between them. The conversation across the courtyard faded as the assembled surveyed the prince's actions. Aldrich's discomfort intensified.

"They are surprised because I am permitting you to touch me. They do not resent your healing. You are doing nothing wrong," mollified Andraste.

"Why did you not tell me? Earlier, you said it was from roses-" started Aldrich.

"I did cut myself on roses," said Andraste.

"So clumsy," stated Otho, "Even flowers injure you."

"I believe the word you are looking for is delicate," said Felix.

"You all worry too much. I can tend-" started Andraste.

"Commander," interrupted Laelius. Andraste stopped her protest and bowed to Aldrich and the Victorious.

"Thank you for your concern," said Andraste, "Let us proceed with the events of the evening."

"As we have already committed the bodies to earth, we thought a reverse sequence of events would be proper," informed Paulina.

"In Northern ceremonies, first there is a wake, second there is a funeral, and third there is the burial," explained Andraste to Aldrich, "In this case, we will have the funeral next and then the wake. The families will sit closest to the reader of the sutras, followed by closest friends, and then other guests. As our host and honored guest, you will sit by me."

"As you wish," replied Aldrich.

Andraste led the way to a makeshift altar that Paulina had constructed. It was covered with flowers and candles. Andraste sat on her knees in the Northern style of prayer. Brion joined her left side and sat in the same style. Aldrich followed their example and sat by Andraste's right side. Laelius approached the altar as the rest of the guests knelt.

"He will not read from a text?" asked Aldrich.

"As our people were first nomads all of our rituals are passed in the oral tradition," answered Andraste.

"And why do you not recite?" asked Aldrich.

"Usually reciting is performed by men, and the songs performed by women. In this case the women of the family of the deceased would sing the song that I sang yesterday," said Andraste.

They fell silent as Laelius began to light the candles on the altar. Andraste reached for Brion's clenched fist. Brion took a deep breath and released his hand so that she could hold it. Laelius began to recite the burial sutra and his booming voice carried across the courtyard.

"I speak in the old tongue for how will the gods hear, if we do not speak their language," translated Andraste. Brion's hand tightened in her own. Andraste raised her voice so it would carry across the courtyard to translate for Aldrich.

"In the beginning, before the time of man, the heavens and the earth were not yet separated. The gods roamed and did as they pleased. However, they grew bored and lonely. The powers of creation and imagination abounded and from this our world was created. However, after the gods created rivers, mountains, oceans, and deserts, in fact all of the lands that now exist, their loneliness intensified. There existed beauty and limitless potential that longed to be shared.

Accordingly, the leader of the gods decided to create a people in her own image, and thus the first man and woman were created. This disrupted the balance of nature. For where ever a power of creation arises, a power of destruction develops in order to maintain equilibrium. Additionally, the other gods grew jealous of man.

"You will love him better than us," they cried.

The leader of the gods denied this allegation, for her heart possessed infinite love, but the other gods were not deterred, and so in order to protect man, the leader of the gods thus separated the heavens from the earth; gifting the heavens to the gods and bestowing the earth to man.

The other gods were not pacified, and so the leader of the gods took away everlasting life from man in order to temper and humble him. The leader of the gods, however, saw this not as a punishment but rather as a gift to man, so that he would always try to better himself and enjoy life to the fullest for however long that life may be. She gave to man not only life, but the importance and significance."

Laelius had finished his recital, but he waited for Andraste to finish her translation. When she was done, he lit the incense on the altar. Brion and Andraste rose to approach the incense urns in front of the altar. Three times they offered incense to the urn. The other assembled guests performed the same ritual at other urns located throughout the courtyard. As the guests continued the ritual, Andraste spoke:

"Tobias and Matthias recognized the importance and significance of life. This is why they gave their lives to preserve and protect the Empire. It is for the value of life that they fought so valiantly for so long. The leader of gods gifted man life, so that we may live so that we may fight, so that we may strive for improvement. Tobias and Matthias lived.

Tobias was the best man I have ever known. I followed him. We followed him across the Empire, attempting the impossible because he did so. He was a man of men. He was a leader, not only by birthright, but through his actions. Varinia questioned his honor and resolution, but I never saw him waiver. His loss is one that we will feel for decades to come.

Matthias, my brother, was also a man of honor. He often faced impossible decisions from the Emperor with no room for failure. And yet, Matthias saved lives where he could and dealt justice by our code. In the North, compassion is often scorned, but Matthias was a man of compassion. He did what he thought was right even at great personal cost. The Southerners may not see him in such a light, but they do not have to deal with the punishment of the Emperor. We all bear scars from the Emperor's justice.

We have lost many comrades due to the Emperor's causes and justice but we bear the task of remembering why they died. It was rarely for the Emperor. It was for our people, our families, our battle brothers, and ourselves. We honor them through our swords, our bows, and our spears. We honor them through battle. We will honor them by following their example. We will not waiver from right. We will not stray from our ideals, no matter the cost. Our path is the hardest because we strive for honor. It is through battle that our comrades will never be forgotten, and through the telling of their deeds that they will always be remembered in our hearts."

"Heiyoh," cried the Victorious as they rose.

Andraste met the eyes of each of her fourteen men, and then rested her eyes on Brion. Brion shook his head, indicating that he did not wish to speak. Laelius knelt beside Brion's right side. Andraste moved to join them and returned to her kneeling position. There were ten minutes of silence before the assembled began to sing.

"Although we stand together, one by one we go,
You heard the call of our lands, and that was all you needed to know.
You aided those in need, never turned your back on the weary,
You always fought bravely, not by words, or by theory.

Someday there will be peace; someday there will be no more sorrow,
Your deeds of yesterday are not forgotten, not today or tomorrow."

Andraste waited for the last words to fade into the evening air. She took a deep breath before rising. The rest of the assembled rose as well, except Brion who remained kneeling before the altar. Andraste placed her hand on his head. Her eyes met Laelius's and she nodded once. Laelius found Paulina and took her arm in his in the Northern style. Together they led the way to the buffet tables. Andraste left Brion's side and approached Aldrich.

"Questions would not offend me," said Andraste as Aldrich looked at her inquisitorially.

"Is there a reason why you did not want to use our temple or priest?" asked Aldrich.

"As I stated earlier, our people are originally nomads. There was rarely a temple or priest at hand when needed. Our traditions have been passed down through the ages by word of mouth, taught to us by our parents and village," answered Andraste.

"The words are altered from our texts, but the core is still the same," commented Aldrich, "Usually only the priest speaks and sings. The Northern way is more inclusive."

"High praise indeed," said Andraste.

"I did not mean-" started Aldrich. He stopped as Andraste smiled at him.

"Some of your Southern lords and ladies have attended," praised Andraste. Aldrich followed her gaze behind him.

"Paulina invited each of them personally. She would make quite a diplomat," approved Aldrich.

"She is something," agreed Andraste, "Their whole family is an example of the North. Have you met their children?"

"I have only met Gnaeus. I have met some of the children of your Victorious. I do confess, I have never seen such well-behaved children," answered Aldrich.

"We will be leaving for our mission soon, and the Commander is contemplating children," said Otho. Maximianus laughed at his side.

"We are praising children already in existence," amended Andraste.

"It is time for you to have a family of your own. You are running out of excuses," chided Paulina. Andraste blushed and looked to Laelius.

"Leave her alone, Paulina. She still has not found someone who can best her sword or her bow," said Laelius.

"She does not need a warrior. She needs a healer. Injured again were you?" questioned Paulina.

"Paulina," ordered Andraste. Paulina laughed and headed to greet the other Southerners. Laelius proceeded at her side.

"After you left me, what did you do this afternoon?" asked Andraste.

"I had to make an appearance in the Chambers of Justice," answered Aldrich.

"Does the court meet every day?" inquired Andraste.

"Not usually, but my absence this time was extensive. I have much to attend to," replied Aldrich. His eyes turned to the center of the courtyard.

"During meals it is common for Northern ladies to entertain the assembled with dances or songs," said Andraste.

"Will you perform?" asked Aldrich.

"It would not be proper for me to do so due to the occasion," answered Andraste.

"Not dancing because it is not proper?" scoffed Maximianus, "Dance for our host. Consider it a challenge."

"Not tonight," said Andraste.

"That is a shame. My lady is known for the Northern fan dances," praised Paulina. She approached with the Southern lords and ladies.

"It is true. At Alexius, one of her dances near halted the siege in its tracks. Tobias was exceedingly distracted," laughed Laelius.

"Dancing during a siege?" asked Kasimir dubiously.

"It was a near a year we were at Alexius. The troops grew restless. During the day, we started having duels, dance and song competitions in order to while away the time," answered Laelius.

"The Alexius warriors did not attack these exhibitions?" asked Aldrich.

"No, they were as bored as we were," answered Andraste.

"When the Commander danced, both sides halted in their efforts.

Those were the first fifteen minutes of peace we had seen in over a year," said Laelius.

"And yet you told the Queen you had no talents," mentioned Aldrich.

Andraste's attention was diverted across the field as she saw Felix take up a fiddle and speak conspiratorially with Otho and Maximianus.

"Otho, do not sing that song you are concocting. I have heard some of the verses and it is not appropriate for children," ordered Andraste.

"Yes, Commander," said Otho. He and Maximianus exchanged mischievous looks.

"Song?" asked Eadbehrt.

"120 Ways to Kill a Man," answered Paulina.

"Rhinauld will find that highly amusing," said Laelius.

"Your intended?" asked Gerlinde.

"He is not my intended," answered Andraste.

"And if he returns with the third relic?" inquired Kasimir.

"Then our houses will be united," said Andraste.

"Any lady would be honored to have champion of three Ruins as her husband," admired Sonje.

"Unless the lady is also a champion of three Ruins. Will you demand he conquers a fourth?" teased Paulina.

"He will want to best me. Perhaps we will see who can conquer the Southern Ruin," answered Andraste.

"You would toy with a man's life?" asked Gerlinde.

"When you meet Rhinauld, you will see. He and my lady are made from the same cloth. They have no fear. They live for adventure, and never turn from a challenge," said Paulina.

"You think he is your lady's match?" questioned Gerlinde.

"No. Their love is fraternal. They bicker worse than any brother and sister," said Paulina.

"Really, I am right here," stated Andraste.

"Perhaps it will remind you to behave- that and your uncle's presence," said Laelius.

"Have you heard if any were injured? Is Henry with him?" asked Andraste.

"So the feud continues?" questioned Paulina. Aldrich looked to Laelius for explanation.

"Sir Henry is a Knight of the Salt Islands. He was also fostered with Andraste and Rhinauld. When my Commander and Henry are in the same room, insults fly about like barbed arrows," explained Laelius.

"Verbal abuse? No duels?" asked Kasimir.

"I beat Henry long ago. He has not challenged me again," said Andraste. She smiled wickedly and Paulina laughed.

"He should have picked jousting. He would have won. Sir Henry is the best jouster from all of the Island Kingdoms," stated Laelius.

"Your memory escapes you, husband. My lady beat him in the last tournament," said Paulina proudly.

"I was not present, dear one," rejoined Laelius.

"It is said the Lord of the Salt Islands is the most handsome man in all the Empire," interjected Gerlinde.

"Indeed, he is," said Paulina.

"And he knows it," commented Andraste.

"He is not to your liking?" asked Gerlinde.

"I like him well enough," answered Andraste.

"High praise," commented Aldrich. He exchanged looks with Kasimir.

"Will Lady Rhiannon come? If Henry comes, then her ladyship must be near," said Paulina.

"Sir Henry is the lady's protector," explained Laelius.

"Rhinauld should not bring her to the mainland. It is too dangerous. He should leave her at my castle on the Island of Fortune," said Andraste. She frowned as she considered Paulina's question.

"You forget, Commander, that your lands will no longer be safe," said Laelius.

"You forget that the islands are guarded by the Eldgrimsons. The Emperor cannot match the power of the Silent Guard. Titus has also sent troops. They are protecting the refugees," replied Andraste.

"Silent Guard? I thought that was just a legend," commented Kasimir.

"The Empress was a Silent Guard before she married the Emperor. They are very real," confirmed Andraste.

"Then is it true due that they guard a barrier that incases demons of legend?" laughed Kasimir.

"We do not speak of the evil in the East," answered Andraste. Aldrich turned to face Andraste.

"You are not joking," stated Aldrich.

"No," said Andraste, "I am serious as a summer's drought."

"How is it that the Northerners and Easterners seem to live in some sort of fairytale?" asked Gerlinde, "We have no such creatures or adventures in the South."

"I imagine you to be blessed," said Andraste. She turned her attention to the altar and saw that Brion still knelt in prayer.

"What does he chant?" asked Sonje.

"The Northern sutra," replied Laelius, "It normally would have been recited when the bodies were being prepared for burial. There would have been a vigil. There are 500 verses."

"And Brion knows them all by heart?" asked Aldrich.

"My brother is an impressive scholar," replied Andraste.

"You should eat, my lady," said Paulina.

"I will eat when Brion does," replied Andraste, "I will join him in his task."

Andraste turned towards Brion. Laelius fell into step beside her. They resumed their kneeling positions. Laelius began to join in the chant as well. Andraste listened silently and kept her eyes on the flickering candles on the altar. As twilight fell, Thracius and Priscus walked around the courtyard and lit torches, while Laurentius and Cato lit lanterns.

An icy wind blew from the North and Andraste felt the hairs on her neck rise. She put her hand to her Ruin sword. Brion paused in his chanting and rose.

"Commander?" asked Laelius.

"Guard Aldrich," commanded Andraste. Her voice carried across the courtyard.

Aldrich found himself immediately encircled by fourteen Victorious. Kasimir, Eadbehrt, and Egnatius started to make their way to Aldrich's side. Their family members hastily retreated into the cottages. Iovita and

Paulina herded the Southern ladies into their cottage. Laelius handed Aldrich one of his daggers.

"What is it?" asked Kasimir.

"Sorcery," answered Gnaeus.

"What form?" questioned Aldrich.

"It is both strange and powerful. I cannot sense its intent," replied Gnaeus.

"Secrecy be damned. You are authorized to use any power at your disposal. Your mission is to protect Aldrich Caelius," ordered Laelius. Even he, a non-magic user, could sense the growing power approaching them.

The wind picked up and thick, nebulous clouds covered the stars. The darkness enveloped them and made them feel much colder. Crackles of thin purple lightning began to flash by the altar. Brion put a hand to Andraste's shoulder but she blocked him. The altar cracked in two and crashed to the courtyard.

"Commander?" questioned Maximianus.

"You have your orders," barked Laelius. The Victorious tensed as they watched a violet haze begin to form from the remnants of the altar.

A shade appeared before Andraste and Brion. Brion went to his knees.

"It is a trick," cautioned Andraste, "Their souls have parted."

"What do they see?" asked Kasimir.

"It is Matthias or meant to resemble Matthias. She is right. I sense no soul," said Gnaeus.

"You would choose the Southerners over your own flesh and blood?" asked the shade.

A second shade materialized beside the first. Tobias stood before Andraste and only gazed at her with smoldering anger.

"You would choose the Southerners over your sworn brethren? Do you forget the vows you made? Once more, exile, do you desecrate the honor that binds us? Have you no shame?" asked the first shade. Tobias still gazed at Andraste with undisguised fury.

"Look at her eyes," said Nero, "We may have a problem."

Andraste's eyes had turned into two brilliant rubies that blazed with anger.

"She grows stronger," mentioned Gnaeus.

"Should we evacuate?" asked Laelius to his son.

"Her power has never hurt any of us before," answered Gnaeus.

"She says that she has not magic," said Aldrich.

"Perhaps it is the Ruin sword?" proposed Laelius.

"I saw her use magic before she had the sword. She had no recollection of the events," said Aldrich.

More shades were beginning to materialize in the courtyard. The Victorious and the Southerners tensed as they recognized faces of fallen comrades and brethren. The shades began to berate them. The torches and the lanterns were all extinguished. However, the shades recoiled as Andraste rose.

The shade of Tobias stepped towards her. Thracius and Priscus sent bolts of white lightning at the shade from their position, but it was unaffected.

"Our magic will do nothing," stated Gnaeus.

Ruby light began to radiate from Andraste. Brion took a step back from her. However, she did not notice his retreat.

"Be gone unearthly foe. You do not belong here," commanded Andraste. She removed her Ruin sword and placed both hands on the hilt as she placed it on the ground.

"Tell your Emperor, I come for him," ordered Andraste.

A cyclone of ruby light swept from Andraste and purged the area within five-hundred feet in every direction. The shades dematerialized before their eyes, the storm clouds evaporated, and the icy Northern wind retreated. Andraste waved her hand and the torches and lanterns ignited. She waved her hand once more and the altar rebuilt itself. Andraste slowly resumed her kneeling position before the altar. Her eyes still blazed with ruby fire.

"Anima," whispered Eadbehrt as he studied her ruby eyes.

"She cannot be," stated Kasimir.

"It is the only explanation," rejoined Eadbehrt.

"It seems as though we are living a fairytale," commented Kasimir.

"What is she?" asked Aldrich.

"She is an Anima. She was born with the powers of the ancients. However, due to her lineage she possesses Northern and Eastern magic. Her powers only awaken in times of great need," admitted Laelius.

"Does she know?" questioned Aldrich.

"No, nor did Brion," replied Laelius. "She will not remember using magic. Do not question her. It confuses her."

"She is dangerous," said Kasimir. He held Aldrich's gaze.

"She has the power of the gods. She can defeat the Emperor!" cried Eadbehrt, "For an Anima to appear, there must be more than just the conflicts of man abounding."

"What are you not telling us?" asked Aldrich.

"Now you know as much as I. I feel that Aelius Eldgrimson knows more, but he would not discuss the matter with me," responded Laelius.

"Secrets will get us killed," said Aldrich.

"I agree," replied Laelius.

Andraste opened her eyes, which had resumed their normal sea-green hue. She looked up at Brion, who was still standing and watching her carefully.

"Are you done reciting the sutra?" asked Andraste.

Brion nodded once. Andraste rose to her feet. She turned and surveyed the Victorious behind her. They still encircled Aldrich.

"No dueling at wakes," ordered Andraste.

"Yes, Commander," said Laelius.

The Victorious immediately spread out across the common area. Andraste took a step forward and faltered. She raised a hand to her head. Laelius was at her side instantly and offered her his arm.

"I feel a bit light-headed," admitted Andraste.

"You should eat something," said Brion. He still kept his distance, but he watched her with concern.

"Yes, you are right," agreed Andraste, "But you should eat as well."

Laelius led Andraste to the buffet table.

"Where is everyone?" asked Andraste.

"The children needed to be put to bed," replied Laelius, "The ladies will return shortly."

"I will go to bed shortly. I am more exhausted then I anticipated," said Andraste. She accepted the plate and her eyes turned to the Victorious. The Southern lords were watching her closely.

"Am I always to be studied?" sighed Andraste.

"Your beauty intrigues them," said Felix. He offered her a glass of water. Andraste glared at him and Felix laughed in response. However, he stood before her so that his broad shoulders blocked her from the Southerners' scrutiny.

"It is so quiet," commented Andraste. She frowned as she listened to the night.

"You are right. We should be telling tales of Matthias's and Tobias's deeds," said Laelius.

"It is hard to be merry when the loss is so painful," said Felix. However, he picked up his fiddle and began to play songs from his homeland.

Chapter Seven

"Are you sure you do not want to rest-" started Brion.

"I heard speak of a Ruin not too far from here. I just want to speak to the Spirit," said Andraste.

"It will still be difficult, and after the last battle, you may not be at your best," cautioned Brion.

"It has been two days since I fought Tobias. Aldrich healed my wound. What will sitting in my room or weeping in the temple accomplish? I will honor their memories through acting, not through tears," responded Andraste.

"My lessons continue with the Southern sorcerers. I will not attend you," informed Brion.

"I understand," replied Andraste.

"We may want to stay within the city in case the Empire attacks," advised Laelius.

"No force could reach us from the North in two day," said Andraste.

"As you wish. We are always at the ready, Commander," stated Laelius.

"Address our host before you leave," reminded Brion.

"I will," smoldered Andraste.

Andraste put her quiver across her back and picked up her bow. Laelius opened the door for her. Andraste heard laughter from Aldrich's chambers. She knocked on the door before entering. She found several Southern ladies seated on Aldrich's sofas. They were scrutinizing her from head to toe.

"I am delighted to see you again," said Gerlinde. However, she looked as though she had not been delighted by anything in years.

"Is he available?" asked Andraste.

"He is busy," replied Gerlinde. She eyed the shut doors to the bedchamber.

"Will you relay a message?" questioned Andraste.

"I am no messenger," responded Gerlinde. Andraste and Gerlinde studied each other.

"Is this the fashion in the North?" inquired Gerlinde.

"Actually, we usually go about only in furs and our daggers," replied Andraste.

Laelius laughed behind her. Andraste turned on her heel.

"We should wait for Aldrich," advised Laelius.

"He is indisposed," returned Andraste.

She quickened her pace down the hallway. Laelius followed reluctantly. The Victorious were already assembled in the courtyard. Egnatius approached her. He bowed deeply.

"May I assist you, princess?" asked Egnatius.

"Thank you, but no. I will see the Southern Ruin," said Andraste.

"Will my lord attend you?" questioned Egnatius.

"He was indisposed with his harem," replied Andraste.

"Harem?" repeated Egnatius. He colored. He lowered his eyes from Andraste.

"We will return shortly," said Andraste.

She turned her horse out of the courtyard. She raced out of the city and took the southern road. The Victorious thundered behind her.

It was a remarkable day. There was not a cloud in the sky, which was a brilliant blue. The waters of the ocean were cerulean and clear. The sands were pearly white. She took them down to the beach and they rode on the sands. A gentle breeze blew from the East. She kept them at a brisk pace. After an hour they approached the ruins of a white castle.

"No resistance?" asked Otho.

"This is not like the other Ruins," agreed Maximianus.

"I do not like it," said Laelius.

"Hadrian, Valens, Felix to me," ordered Andraste, "The rest of you wait here."

"Commander?" asked Laelius.

"We do not know what lies ahead of us. I will not risk you all," responded Andraste.

"But you will risk the men from the Island Kingdoms?" inquired Felix.

Andraste silenced him with a look. She dismounted her horse and handed the reins to Laelius. Hadrian, Valens and Felix were quick to join her on foot. She headed towards the white castle. They approached a great, green, fertile maze, but a light, no larger than a star, shimmered in front of them.

"What is that light? Should we follow it?" inquired Valens.

She glanced towards her men and then proceeded into the maze. She followed the light blindly, and did not hesitate when faced with choices. She followed the light. Her men followed her in silence. They moved quickly to keep up with it.

They reached, what must have once been, the throne room of the white palace. A great white stag grazed from the tall grasses growing from between the white tiles. Felix reached for his bow. Andraste put a hand on his bow and shook her head. Felix lowered his hand. The stag seemed to glow and then turned into the shade of a king. They could not see his face for the light was so blinding.

"Why do you come, Empress? You have conquered three Ruins. I can read your hearts. You come without a wish or without a quest for treasure. What do you want of me?" asked the king.

"I wish to know why Aurelia and Caecilia died. I wish to know the prophecy," responded Andraste. Felix winced at the names, as did Hadrian and Valens.

"Are you certain? To know a prophecy is to know your fate. If you try to change fate, you will disrupt the balance of nature. Balance is your purpose: that is what you were born to do and why you are graced," responded the king.

"Fortune favors the brave," replied Andraste, "I will hear this prophecy."

The king studied Andraste and then each of her men. He granted her request. He foretold:

"The Northern lady falls,
The Southern lord rises,
When they meet, evil stalls,
And victory disguises.
The balance that was lost
Will once again restore
But at the greatest cost
As war takes lives once more.
Evil comes to destroy
All the life in these lands
Powers must the two employ
Together as fate demands.
The dead will not yet sleep
Lord and Lady must fight
Evil returned to the deep
Before all is yet right."

"What is this evil?" asked Andraste.

"It is an evil you already know, have known, and will know again," responded the king.

The light faded and they were alone in the courtyard.

"Well that was vague," stated Valens.

"One thing is clear," concluded Felix.

Andraste turned to look at him.

"We are stuck with Aldrich Caelius until this is over," announced Felix.

The maze before them opened back on two sides like a curtain. Andraste headed towards the opening. She looked out and saw the beach. Laelius and her men were still waiting for them on foot. They stepped out of the Ruins and rejoined their comrades.

"What did you obtain?" asked Avitus. Valens shook his head.

"Knowledge," answered Felix.

"Never ask a Spirit questions," replied Hadrian. Andraste sighed.

She mounted her horse.

"Do you see that dust cloud?" inquired Laurentius. His eyes were on the western road.

"Sand storm?" proposed Cato.

"Riders?" asked Laelius.

"A great many," confirmed Andraste, "Bows."

Her men quickly mounted their horses and readied their bows. As the sand storm approached, they saw two squadrons from the Imperial Army. One was dressed in the amaranthine robes of the Emperor's personal guard, and the other in the ruby Imperial Army uniforms. The ruby-dressed troops bore the banner of a cobra.

"So soon?" asked Maximianus.

"Ambitious," replied Felix.

"Varinia never retreated," alleged Laelius.

"As we will not," stated Andraste.

Andraste pulled an arrow from her quiver. She pulled it taught against her bowstring. She surveyed the approaching force. They had slowed down to a halt. She saw two riders approach them. Andraste lowered her bow. Her men followed her example.

"I bare a message," snarled Varinia from her horse, "Our Emperor says that if you surrender, and grant him the Ruin sword as a gift, he will let you return to the North and resume your position as a Commander of the Imperial Army."

"And the curse?" asked Andraste.

"He will remove it," responded Varinia.

"I reject his offer," replied Andraste.

"Good," hissed Varinia.

Varinia had scarcely uttered the word before she charged her horse ahead. The second rider followed her. He was dressed in purple robes and wore the cape of an officer. Andraste could not see his face due to his helmet. The other Imperial riders charged ahead.

"Great," said Otho.

Andraste released her first arrow. It was joined in flight by the other arrows of the Victorious. They let out as many arrows as they could before the first riders were upon them. Andraste raised her sword and warded off the first attacker. Laelius hurled his spear across the field and knocked a guard from his horse. He took the second guard's head off with one sweep of his blade. The wind began to howl and spin sand about, making it nearly impossible to see.

"The Ruin?" called Laelius.

The ground underneath her Victorious was firm, but she saw the Imperial soldiers begin to sink into the sand before her. Varinia leapt out of the danger with a handful of her soldiers and rode towards safety. The Emperor's guards that were between the sinkhole and the castle charged ahead towards the Victorious. The Victorious fought off the wave of attackers. Andraste pierced her attacker with her Ruin sword and he went down. She bent to remove her blade. She felt a piercing pain in her back, as an arrow pierced her shoulder. She looked to see the officer sinking into the sand with a crossbow in his hand. Otho pierced the officer's throat with an arrow.

Andraste saw that three of her men had also been struck by arrows. She signaled for the Victorious to move to higher ground towards the Ruins. She kept her eyes on the battlefield. The corpses of their foes were sinking into the sands. The survivors had already retreated and proceeded out of sight.

The arrow in her back was burning. She could feel blood escaping from the wound and soaking her tunic. She fished out a jar from her saddlebag and threw it to Laelius. Her aim was off, but he scooped it from the sands.

"Poisoned arrows," concluded Andraste. Laelius approached her. She shook her head, "Our men."

Laelius poured a bit of the bottle of each of Laurentius's, Glaucio's and Cato's wounds. They howled in pain as the liquid was administered. Laelius then approached Andraste. He cut off the shaft of the arrow, and poured the liquid on her wound.

"We need Brion," Andraste said through gritted teeth.

"More?" asked Laelius as he looked at the empty bottle.

"It is not working. The poison has evolved," responded Andraste, "Ride for the city as fast as you can."

Andraste turned towards the road to the Capitol. Her back burned. She urged her horse as fast as she could. She slumped in her saddle and held onto her horse's neck. She looked back and saw her men riding behind her.

Cato fell from his horse. Laelius waved her on as he and Avitus stopped to return Cato to his saddle. Felix charged forward to ride beside her. They rode on. They passed the sentry tower. The sentries started yelling and asking questions as they saw Andraste's blood soaked tunic.

"The Victorious quarters- closest," ordered Andraste. Felix took her reins and led her horse through the crowded streets.

"Make way!" bellowed Felix.

The crowd parted in confusion. Felix drove their horses forward. Andraste tried to focus. She nearly fell into Paulina's arms as she ran out to greet them. Felix jumped off his horse and came to Andraste's side. She half-walked and was half-carried into Paulina's house. She heard the sound of the other Victorious approaching.

"Poison?" questioned Paulina as she surveyed Andraste's wound.

"Yes," confirmed Laelius as he entered the house.

"The others?" asked Andraste.

"Fine, they had more of the potion. It will give them time," responded Laelius.

Paulina took a knife and cut off Andraste's tunic. Her corset was soaked in blood.

"We must get the arrowhead out while we wait for Brion," said Paulina. She took out a tool bag from her cabinet.

"I am sorry, my lady," started Paulina.

"Do it," ordered Andraste.

Laelius took her hand in his and grasped it. Andraste squeezed it with all her might as Paulina used her tools to remove the arrowhead. Andraste breathed deeply as she heard the arrowhead pulled out of her upper back. She buried her head into Laelius' arm so that she would not scream. She closed her eyes. Andraste let out a stream of curses that made even Laelius blush.

"Where the hell is Brion?" yelled Andraste. She could no longer focus on the room before her.

"My lady!" censored Paulina. Laelius rose and addressed someone who entered the room.

"Get Brion now!" ordered Andraste.

Andraste felt a warm light envelop her. It took away her pain. She felt a tingling sensation in her back, but it was not painful. It tickled. She felt her head begin to clear.

"My men?" asked Andraste.

"I saw them first," replied Aldrich, "If I had known you were injured, I would have come immediately."

"I am fine," replied Andraste. She rotated her shoulder and stretched her arms.

Aldrich surveyed the wound with concern but did not approach closer. Laelius stepped between Andraste and the Southern lords. He folded his arms across his chest. Paulina approached with a bowl of clean water and cleaned Andraste's blood covered back. Egnatius shifted uncomfortably.

"What happened?" asked Aldrich. He turned his eyes to Laelius.

"Two Imperial squadrons," answered Laelius.

"So soon?" inquired Egnatius.

"They offered us amnesty but my Commander refused," stated Laelius.

"So they attacked?" questioned Egnatius. Laelius nodded in confirmation.

"It was reckless to leave with only fifteen warriors. You should have told me your plans. Why did you not wait for me?" demanded Aldrich.

"Your harem does not take messages," replied Andraste.

"The Commander ran into the wives of your commanders while you were meeting on the veranda," mediated Egnatius hastily.

"Empress," interrupted Paulina.

She offered Andraste a clean tunic. Andraste was reminded of her appearance. She turned her back on the Southern lords. She went behind the screens and removed her corset. She pulled the tunic over her head. Even with the clean tunic all she could smell was blood. She remerged from behind the screen.

"I am forever in your debt, Paulina," said Andraste. She bowed to Paulina, who returned the gesture. Andraste headed out of Laelius's quarters and into the street. Laelius followed her.

"Laurentius, Glaucio, Cato," called Andraste.

"They are fine, Commander," pacified Laelius.

Nevertheless, Andraste proceeded into the deserted street. She felt her head spinning, she slowed her movements, but she continued her path. She stumbled into Brion as he charged towards the house.

"Where have you been?" asked Andraste.

"As we discussed this morning, I was in the sorcerer's tower," replied Brion, "Are you well?"

"You should have been with us," responded Andraste. Brion said nothing.

"They have developed a new poison. Obtain the arrowhead so that we can develop an anecdote for the troops," ordered Andraste.

"Where are you going?" asked Brion.

"To see Laurentius, Glaucio and Cato," replied Andraste.

"Aldrich treated them. I gave them a sleeping draft. They are recovering and sleeping as you should be," said Brion gently.

"What? Are you going to drug me again?" asked Andraste. Her hand went to her hilt as she turned on Brion.

"Andraste," said Brion. He paused. She heard footsteps behind him on the path.

"I have kept your secrets. But these days, you keep you secrets from me. You have more secrets then the Emperor, Brion," growled Andraste.

"She is feverish," Brion said to Laelius, "She does not know what she says."

"Get the sword," ordered Laelius.

"Andraste," said Brion gently, "I have been by your side since you were born. In twenty-four summers there have been only five summers that we were parted. Do you remember? Four of those summers you were at the Ice Palace and the last two years, you left on your own accord."

"Why did she seal your powers? Why would she do that if you were not to be trusted?" asked Andraste.

"Do not talk about her now. We will talk later, when we are alone," said Brion. His voice rose.

"Do not agitate her," warned Laelius.

Andraste was stuck between them on the path. Brion reached for her. Andraste hit him soundly in the chest with her palm and he went down. Laelius dove at her and she knocked him to the ground with a swift kick.

Nero bounded out of the darkness towards her and she met his side with another kick. He went flying backwards, but he repositioned himself and came again. Andraste countered and struck him in the face. He went down. Maximianus approached her from one of the houses. Andraste began to draw her sword.

"That is not necessary," said Aldrich in her ear.

He placed a hand on her own. He applied the slightest bit of pressure on her hand. Her sword went back in its sheath. She saw a golden light appear between their hands. She held his gaze. The light grew between them. She felt her head begin to clear. Aldrich wrapped her arm in his and led the way down the street. Andraste did not protest.

"You lost a lot of blood. Can you walk to the palace?" asked Aldrich.

"I am fine," stated Andraste.

"I could carry you," suggested Aldrich. He was watching her carefully.

"I am fine," reiterated Andraste. She pulled her arm free from Aldrich, but she felt woozy. She hesitated.

"You are injured," said Aldrich.

"You healed me," replied Andraste. She stepped forward uncertain. She could not remember which way to return to the palace. Her vision was blurry.

"Forgive me," said Aldrich. He swept her up in his arms. He asked, "Can a soldier not help a wounded comrade?"

"When was the last time you carried Eadbehrt or Kasimir?" rejoined Andraste. Aldrich laughed softly as he headed down the path.

"I imagine I could if they were light as you. You think I am strong enough to carry those gluttonous specimens of mankind?" inquired Aldrich. To his surprise Andraste giggled, but she quickly suppressed it. He smiled down at Andraste in his arms.

"How is your shoulder?" asked Aldrich.

"I am fine," answered Andraste.

"I know, but how is your shoulder?" inquired Aldrich. He caught a glimpse of a smile as she hid her face in his chest.

"Just another scar," replied Andraste. Aldrich did not pursue the subject further.

"Do you really plan on carrying me the whole way back?" asked Andraste, "I feel better. I can walk."

"We are almost there. You and your men fought off two squadrons of Imperial guards and protected my city. You received wounds in the battle. Not two days have been completed since you lost a comrade and a brother in the defense of my lands. The least I can do is carry you back to the palace," said Aldrich.

"You are not like the other lords I have known," replied Andraste sleepily.

"What?" asked Aldrich. However, he received no response. Andraste had fallen asleep.

Andraste woke and felt disoriented. She looked around the room and recognized it as her room in the Southern palace. She did not recall how she had gotten there. She did not remember returning to the city at all.

She took a hot shower. She stood under the hot water for what seemed like hours. It was marvelous. Once she was clean, she dressed in a charcoal colored gown. Her Ruin sword was nowhere to be seen. She found Brion sitting on her sofa. He eyed her wearily.

"Are you going to strike me?" asked Brion.

"Why would I strike you?" inquired Andraste.

"You do not recall?" questioned Brion.

Andraste looked at him confused. Brion sighed and decided to let it go.

"Where are you going?" asked Brion.

"The temple," replied Andraste.

"Do you want me to go with you?" inquired Brion.

"No, look into the new poison," responded Andraste.

"So you remember that?" questioned Brion.

"The last thing I remember is riding towards the city for the anecdote. Cato, shame of the Victorious, fell from his horse. What do you want me to remember?" asked Andraste.

"Nothing. I will look into the poison," sighed Brion. He rose and left the room.

Andraste waited a moment before following after him. When she entered the hallway, Brion was already out of sight. She walked quickly past Aldrich's rooms. She could hear voices from within.

She found her way to the temple. It was deserted. She lit two candles and knelt before the altar. She closed her eyes and took a deep breath. She heard someone walking down the aisle. She glanced behind her and saw Aldrich. He stood behind her and did not move. Andraste rose and turned to him.

"What can I do for you?" asked Aldrich.

"Nothing," responded Andraste. Her eyes went to the Ruin sword in his hand.

"Are you well?" inquired Aldrich.

"I am fine," replied Andraste. She stood before him.

"Not going to go on any more rampages?" questioned Aldrich.

"What do you mean?" asked Andraste.

"So you really do not remember?" asked Aldrich.

Andraste looked up at him. He studied her. His gaze was only broken by the sound of the temple door opening.

"Will you return my sword?" requested Andraste.

"Would you fight me for it in a temple?" returned Aldrich.

"No, not in a temple. What about a trade? What do you want?" asked Andraste. She raised her sea-green eyes to him again. Aldrich did not respond.

"A kiss?" asked Andraste. Aldrich started.

"Are you still feverish?" inquired Aldrich. He did not look amused.

"I will give you one kiss for my sword," offered Andraste.

She reached for him. She wrapped an arm around his waist and stepped forward. She could feel him tense beside her, but he did not object. She raised her lips towards his. She heard the temple door close and she released him. She walked past him and rested her hand on the hilt of the Ruin sword. He released it to her grasp.

"Bad time, Commander?" asked Otho. Aldrich shot the approaching warrior a murderous look.

"What is it?" returned Andraste as she walked towards the exit. She strapped the sword around her hip as she progressed.

"I was sent to inform you that Laurentius, Glaucio and Cato are all well, as are Nero and Laelius," replied Otho.

"What happened to Nero and Laelius?" asked Andraste.

Otho glanced at Aldrich, who shook his head in response.

"Nothing, Commander. I just thought you might be wondering," replied Otho.

"Laelius and Nero are fierce warriors. Nothing could bother them," said Andraste, "If there is nothing else, I am going to return to my chambers."

"No, there is nothing else," responded Otho. He bowed to Andraste as she passed.

Andraste did not leave her chambers for the remainder of the morning. She read over reports that had been forwarded to her from Aldrich. She adjusted the troops on her map accordingly. Brion and the Victorious left her alone. However, she knew that she could not hide in her room forever despite her heartache. She roamed the palace halls and was drawn to the sound of chatter from the assembly rooms.

Andraste viewed the ceiling and observed a large mural painted on the ceiling. It depicted all of the gods and goddess. The god of justice was depicted in the center of the mural, in the act of balancing a scale. Andraste noted that the god was depicted with auburn air and sapphire eyes. She smiled in spite of herself. The discussion in the front of the room had been halted. She saw that Aldrich had risen from his seat.

"Paramerion, do you have a request?" asked Aldrich.

"No. I wish to observe the Southern judicial proceedings," replied Andraste.

"You will hear better from up front. Please join us," said Aldrich.

Whispers circulated across the Chamber of Justice. Andraste approached the steps leading up to the dais. There was a long sapphire velvet-cushioned bench at the top of the stairs. Marcella was seated on Aldrich's far left. She was embroidering a golden rose. She smiled warmly as Andraste approached. Aldrich met her at the stairs and offered her his hand. He led her gently to the bench and seated her on his right.

"I did not mean to interrupt," protested Andraste.

"Your interest in our justice system pleases me," returned Aldrich. He retook his seat and his sapphire eyes turned to the parties before him.

"Proceed," ordered Aldrich.

"I am Fritz, the potter. I bring this cause on to be heard before this court as the lower courts were unable to reach a verdict upon my first filed complaint," said a large man with brown curly hair. He had a full beard and mustache. His eyes were hazel and merry.

"State your complaint and your requests for relief," directed Aldrich.

"This wretch ran before my cart, which caused my horses to rear, and the whole cart toppled over, wrecking a near a year's worth of work. I estimate the losses to be over one-thousand gold pieces. I request all of my expenses to be reimbursed, and any other relief deemed necessary and proper by this Court," entreated Fritz.

"Fritz, I have seen your wares. I doubt that is a just estimate," countered Aldrich. There was laughter in the chamber.

"It is still my livelihood, my prince," said Fritz. He shifted uncomfortably.

"And who responds to these charges?" asked Aldrich.

"I do, Prince Aldrich," replied a youth, "My name is Mose."

"What is your defense?" inquired Aldrich.

"I admit, my lord, I did run in front of Fritz's cart, but he was unable to control his horses because he took to the bottle at near midmorning and continued until the incident, which was later that afternoon. Furthermore, his cart has been in disrepair for sometime. I refuse to reimburse his losses due to his negligence," replied Mose.

Andraste looked to Aldrich for his response.

"Yes, my lady?" asked Aldrich.

"Mose speaks eloquently on his own behalf, but he is still a child. Is there not an adult to speak for him?" inquired Andraste.

"He is an orphan. He has no one to speak for him. It is also his fifth time before this Court," replied Aldrich. He surveyed Mose, who met his eyes without hesitation. Fritz still would not meet Aldrich's eyes.

"Were there any witnesses?" asked Aldrich.

"The tavern owner can attest to Fritz's intoxication, and the other vendors to the state of his cart," replied Mose.

"The vendors can also attest to my loss of property," added Fritz.

"I have heard enough. Mose you will work for Fritz as his apprentice for one year to pay the debt. Fritz will house and feed you, but you will receive no wages. If you break this arrangement, you will go to prison to work off your debt from there," decreed Aldrich.

"I have no need for an apprentice," protested Fritz.

"This is my verdict," replied Aldrich, "Mose, I do not wish to see you before this Court again."

"Yes, Prince Aldrich," said Mose. He bowed low to Aldrich, and Fritz hastily did the same.

"Next case," called Aldrich. He glanced to Andraste, but she kept her face neutral.

"I have a matter of property to discuss," said Lord Arnold. He was dressed in flamboyant magenta velvets. He seemed to have doubled-size overnight.

Two of his guards pulled a tall muscled man by chains towards the dais. The prisoner was dressed only in breeches. His olive-colored back was heavily scarred by lashes. Aldrich rose angrily and addressed Lord Arnold.

"Your case was already ruled on in the lower court," said Aldrich, "You must respect its verdict."

"I must protest. It is an affront to the Lionden Empire!" swore Lord Arnold.

"In my lands, your property is a human being with rights. You were ordered to release him. Why have you not done so?" asked Aldrich. Aldrich glowered at Lord Arnold. However, the slaver was not deterred.

"Were a horse to escape from one of the ships and swim to shore, would you not return him to his master?" inquired Lord Arnold.

"Slavery has never and will never be accepted in my lands. You will release the Parnesian at once," bellowed Aldrich. His words echoed throughout the chambers. Andraste had never seen Aldrich lose his composure before. The chambers had fallen to complete silence. Lord Arnold bowed to Aldrich. His beady eyes went to Andraste.

"Princess, surely Imperial law overrules Southern law in this matter. Lost or stolen property must be returned to its owner," stated Lord Arnold.

"If it was an object, yes, you would be correct. However, this is a person we are discussing. Lord Arnold, do you know the penalty for slave trading under Imperial law?" asked Andraste.

"No, princess," replied Lord Arnold.

"It is death. Do you want to reconsider beseeching my guidance in this matter?" inquired Andraste.

"Yes, thank you, princess," mumbled Lord Arnold. He hastily retreated from the room. His soldiers dropped the chains and the Parnesian stood studying Andraste not Aldrich.

"You are far from home," stated Aldrich. He gestured for one of his guards to release the Parnesian from his chains. However, the Parnesian broke free of his own chains. Still his dark gaze was only on Andraste.

"I am an ambassador for the Parnesian Empire. I was sent with a message for Andraste Eldgrimson, daughter of Victoria Eldgrimson," said the Parnesian.

"Not many address me by such a name," replied Andraste, "May I inquire for your name?"

"Mine is a matriarchal culture. I am Abhay, son of Aditi, Empress of the Parnesian Empire. She apologizes that she could not come herself as we are at war," said the Parnesian.

"With whom?" asked Andraste.

"The Lionden Empire," replied Abhay. Andraste exchanged glances with Aldrich.

"Why would you seek an audience with me? I can offer you nothing. You would be better seeking an allegiance with Aldrich Caelius," said Andraste.

"We follow the web of time. It says I must speak with you," responded Abhay.

"You are an Anima," stated Andraste.

"Yes," stated Abhay. Andraste surveyed the man before her with new curiosity.

"You could have freed yourself easily," said Aldrich.

"I wanted to know what sort of people you were," replied Abhay, "If I may, I will make myself presentable and speak to you both later."

"We would be honored," replied Andraste.

"Please stay in the palace as our guest," said Aldrich.

The Parnesian bowed to them both and Marcella rose to follow him. She spoke to Aldrich as she passed, "You two are speaking as one. The chamber is divided. The people are both strengthened and uneasy by this union. Tread carefully."

Marcella was gone quickly. Andraste and Aldrich exchanged looks. Aldrich frowned as a golden-haired lord approached the dais. The lord scarcely concealed his hostility towards Andraste. She surveyed the lord without expression.

"Lord Jared, what brings you to this Court?" asked Aldrich.

"As you know, I am responsible in my district for collecting the Imperial taxes and bringing them to the Capitol for submission to the Imperial Tax Collector," replied Lord Jared.

"I am aware," stated Aldrich.

"The taxes were increased two-hundred percent, and my district cannot pay. The Imperial Tax Collector says I must round up those who cannot pay and send them to the North to pay off their debt," said Lord Jared.

"Is the Imperial Tax Collector present?" asked Aldrich.

"I am here, Prince Aldrich," responded a well-dressed Northern lord.

"When did this increase occur?" inquired Aldrich.

"Just this cycle, Prince Aldrich," replied the Northern lord.

"There was no such law passed. The Emperor only made one decree this year and I was present," said Andraste. She rose and surveyed the Northern lord, "You are a liar and a disgrace to your office."

The Imperial Tax Collector shifted uncomfortably underneath her gaze.

"We have lost so much due to the Resistance attacks. I cannot return to the Emperor empty-handed," besought the Imperial Tax Collector to Andraste, "You above all others know the penalty."

"That does not give you the right to increase the taxes without an Imperial decree nor to enslave Imperial citizens. Yes, Southerners are citizens of the Empire. You will remember your duty, Lord Tax Collector," admonished Andraste. She retook her seat and looked to Aldrich.

"Andraste Valerianus has spoken. Lord Jared you will pay only the annual amount, which is reasonable and just, to the Imperial Tax Collector. Lord Tax Collector, I will not sit by and watch my people be enslaved for any reason. This is your first and only warning," said Aldrich.

"Andraste Valerianus no longer has the right to speak," insisted the Tax Collector.

"I respect her wisdom and justice. I will heed her advice. The North has lost its greatest asset," replied Aldrich.

"It is Varinia Valerianus that you should fear and heed. She is now responsible for these lands and she will come for Northern justice," declared the Tax Collector. He bowed to Aldrich and left the room without leave.

There was murmuring throughout the chamber and Aldrich raised his hand for silence. He looked to Andraste and then back to the crowd.

"That is enough for today," said Aldrich. He rose and offered Andraste his arm.

"Yes, it is a valid threat. You should prepare your forces," said Andraste.

"We are always prepared," returned Aldrich, "We will join the War Council. The arrival of the Parnesian affects all of us."

"The arrival of the Parnesian troubles me. I do not want you out of my sight until he leaves," said Andraste. When she looked up at Aldrich, he was smiling. Aldrich was still smiling when they joined the War Council. Marcella had also joined the council and was addressing a captivated audience.

"I hear the Chambers of Justice were most interesting," commented Kasimir.

"Your spirits are very high," stated Eadbehrt. Both Southern lords looked to Andraste.

"He is oddly pleased with my concern for his safety," admitted Andraste.

"What did you say?" asked Brion.

"It does not matter. We must discuss the Parnesian," answered Andraste.

"Do you think the Parnesians will join our allegiance? It would turn the odds in our favor," said Kasimir.

"No, why would they join our civil war when they are already at war with a foreign power?" rejoined Andraste, "They must want something, and I fear we will not be able to provide it."

"Fear?" repeated Laelius. He exchanged looks with Maximianus.

"Yes. This is our chance to make them our allies, and if we cannot aid them, we will lose the chance forever," said Andraste, "It is important we become allies for the future. Something is seriously wrong for them to approach us, and to send their prince. It is my understanding their dynasty does not leave their palace for any reason."

"It is rare for any Parnesian to leave their Empire," agreed Aldrich, "Our ambassador went to their palace for all of our trade negotiations."

"Sand. Why would they want sand?" asked Andraste, "I see no reason."

"And to send us charcoal that we do not need in return," said Aldrich.

"Should we leave? Are you going to have this conversation between yourselves?" asked Kasimir.

"Two would hardly make a council," replied Andraste. However, she turned her attention to the warriors. She hesitated as the Parnesian appeared in the doorway.

"I am not familiar with your ways. In mine it would be rude for me to appear without being summoned. However, our need is great. I beg your apologies," said Abhay from the doorway. He was fully-clothed in Southern apparel. He addressed only Andraste.

"Prince Abhay, please join us and be welcome," invited Marcella.

"We do not use such titles. Please call me Abhay," said the Parnesian.

"Why have you come?" asked Andraste.

"Surely greetings are acceptable first," reproved Marcella.

"The Valerianus are as frank as my own people. We value this," said Abhay, "There are things we wish to discuss, but we could not through ambassadors. Surely by our trade exchange, you have guessed our dilemma. Rumors from the North suggest that you have a similar problem."

"Honestly, we are baffled," replied Andraste. The Parnesian looked taken aback. He quickly composed himself.

"The undead soldiers that cannot be defeated except by sorcery," stated Abhay.

"They have spread to the Parnesian Empire?" asked Andraste.

"Our foe came from the Lionden Empire. They are similar to your Arisen. When I said we were at war with the Lionden Empire, this is perhaps a mistruth. The evil was created by the Lionden dynasty, but we do not fight the Lionden citizens. In fact, we shelter many refugees in our city," said Abhay, "Why are you so puzzled?"

"I believed it was only our Emperor who created the Arisen, but if the Lionden have also done the same, then great evil is coming," answered Andraste.

"The evil has been here for decades. When I was a child, all three Empires met together. Lionden and Valerianus wanted to form an expedition to the Far East to investigate the Old World and determine our origins. We, Parnesians, did not join in. Our scriptures foretell of a great evil in the East that should never be approached," said Abhay.

"However, the Lionden and Valerianus did not heed your warning," stated Brion. Abhay nodded in confirmation.

"When they returned, the first Arisen appeared in the Lionden and Valerianus Empires. We besought aid from the Lionden Emperor, but he was not moved, nor Emperor Valerianus, so we retreated behind our walls. This was a fatal mistake. The Arisen are growing exponentially. Our own dead join their ranks," said Abhay.

"We have a similar problem in the North," admitted Andraste.

"We have been lucky they have not made it to the South," commented Kasimir.

"You will find that the Arisen will not travel over sand," said Abhay. Andraste and Aldrich exchanged glances.

"So that explains your desire for sand, but why did you send charcoal?" asked Aldrich.

"In order to burn the bodies of the Arisen- it is the only way to keep them from reanimating," replied Abhay.

"What do you want from me?" asked Andraste.

"I know I have come at a bad time. In many ways your Empire faces a graver danger then our own. Emperor Valerianus has fallen. What are you going to do?" asked Abhay.

"Fallen? Do you mean he has been defeated?" questioned Kasimir.

"He means the Emperor has been consumed by the shadow powers," replied Andraste, "It is a Valerianus problem. I will deal with it."

"You say that so calmly, but are you capable of patricide?" questioned Abhay.

"I do not balk at what must be done," replied Andraste. She raised her head proudly.

"If you fail, this Empire will fall like the Lionden. If my people are attacked by both sides, we will also fall. There will be no hope for life on this continent," warned Abhay.

"How can the Lionden Emperor not do anything?" asked Aldrich.

"He has also fallen," returned Abhay.

"You came such a long way for so little information," said Andraste.

"Yes, but your answer was essential. It has determined my next action. I must return to my Empire. You should keep Aldrich Caelius close, something targets him. As your paths are tied together, you will need each other to defeat the Emperor," said Abhay, "Your children will also be important in the future for these lands."

"We have no children," said Andraste.

"You will," said Abhay. Andraste looked skeptical, while Aldrich studied the ceiling.

"They say predications made by Animas are never wrong," commented Eadbehrt.

"Then I will keep Aldrich close. I sense an evil presence. I thought at first it was you, but now I feel it is Northern aggression," said Andraste. She studied Abhay intently. He surveyed her with equal curiosity.

"I have spent too much time already. I must return to my ship," said Abhay.

"I thought your ship was taken by slavers," said Kasimir.

"Yes, but my crew will have taken the Lionden ship by now," rejoined Abhay. He smiled for the first time since he had arrived in the Southern palace.

"You do not wish to stay the night? You have earned rest. We would welcome your crew in our halls," invited Marcella.

"My duty is to my people. Do not trouble yourself, I will find my own way to the port," said Abhay. He bowed to Andraste. Aldrich looked to Marcella and nodded. She followed Abhay out of the room.

"The Parnesians just took a Lionden ship on our waters," said Kasimir.

"That sounds like a Lionden problem. I will not interfere," rejoined Aldrich. He flashed a grin to Kasimir, but it faded as he noticed Andraste's expression.

"Commander?" asked Laelius.

"Laelius, I want you to watch over the Queen personally. The rest of you will watch over Marcella and her children. I never want any of them alone. Laelius and four of you go now. Aldrich you will be with me at all times until I determine the source," said Andraste.

"All times?" questioned Kasimir. He cast a rakish grin to Aldrich.

"You spent months on the road with me. It is no different," said Andraste.

"Slightly different," commented Otho.

"I will not yield on this issue," said Andraste.

"Apparently this issue will yield children," commented Kasimir.

"We are about to embark on an assassination attempt of the most powerful sorcerer this Empire has produced in our history. A prophecy and an Anima have stated that Aldrich and I must go together or we will fail. Our survival depends on Aldrich's life. Do you still think my intentions are romantic?" asked Andraste. Kasimir would not meet her eyes.

"Why do you protect my family? Do you think they are in immediate danger?" asked Aldrich.

"The Emperor is cruel. He will use whatever tools he has at his disposal. He will harm them to get to or to harm you," alleged Andraste.

"Coward," hissed Kasimir. His dark eyes flashed.

"Shall we discuss our route to the Citadel?" asked Aldrich.

"No. I will tell no one the route we plan to take. Not even you," said Andraste.

"We cannot make further Resistance plans until the King of the Island Kingdom arrives. This council is concluded. I-we will be in my study if you need us," informed Aldrich.

"Needless to say, the Queen will not approve of this arrangement," stated Kasimir.

"Leave the Queen to me," sighed Aldrich.

He swept out of the room and Andraste followed after him. Aldrich did not offer her his arm. She quickened her pace to reach his side. She took one look at his scowl and decided not to ask questions. Aldrich stormed into his chambers and Andraste followed. Aldrich shut the doors behind her before proceeding to his study. He poured two glasses of wine and set one on the far corner of his desk. The other he took in his hand and proceeded to his leather chair. Before him was a pile of reports, he seated himself and began to read.

Andraste rounded his library, examining the titles. Her skirts rustled against the floor as she moved. She reached for an old volume, but it was just out of her reach. She stretched further but she still could not reach it. Aldrich's hand grazed her side as he reached to pick the book for her. He held a report in his other hand. His eyes were still on the page.

"Any news?" asked Andraste. His sapphire eyes went to her face and he realized their proximity. He froze with book and report in both of his hands. He handed the book to Andraste and returned to his desk.

"Most of these reports are from Southern lords responsible for bringing their district's taxes to the Capitol. They were all ordered to pay the tax increase we discussed at court earlier," said Aldrich. He began writing a reply.

Andraste leaned her Ruin sword against the wall before sitting in one of the chairs across from Aldrich's desk. She sat cross-legged in the chair and made sure her skirts were seemly. She opened her book and began to read. She turned to the second page and reached for her wine glass. As she glanced up, she saw that Aldrich was studying her.

"I have never seen you look so domestic," said Aldrich.

"Would you prefer I did something else?" asked Andraste.

"No, as you were," said Aldrich. He returned to his work.

Andraste adjusted to a more formal poise. Aldrich hid his smile behind a report. A breeze blew in from the veranda and rattled the doors. Andraste shivered as the breeze brushed over her shoulder.

"Are you cold?" asked Aldrich.

"No," replied Andraste. Aldrich set down the report on the desk.

"I need nothing," said Andraste. Aldrich still rose and went to his bedchamber.

"Ouch!" said Aldrich.

"What is it?" asked Andraste.

"I think something bit me," replied Aldrich.

Andraste practically flew to his bedchamber. She overturned her chair in the process.

"Something bit me again," said Aldrich. He scanned the room.

Andraste took his wrist between her fingers. There were two purple puncture wounds on his wrist. They were already starting to ooze, and the surrounding flesh to swell.

"Snake bite?" asked Andraste. She surveyed the room in alarm.

"We do not have poisonous snakes in the South. I just picked up my cape from the bed-" started Aldrich.

Andraste threw the coverlet off Aldrich's bed. They both froze as they heard a thud against the wall. Andraste unsheathed her Ruin sword and dove towards the sound, swinging her blade as she did so. A furious snake pounced at her wrist. Andraste sliced it all the way along its body. Blood spattered on the wall.

"It is a Northern viper. Heal yourself immediately," ordered Andraste.

Aldrich summoned his spirit phoenix but nothing happened. Andraste turned in alarm. Aldrich fell to his knees. Andraste dove for him and wrapped him in her arms.

"I cannot save you," said Andraste.

Aldrich had never seen fear in Andraste's eyes before that moment, not even when she faced her own death. Tears poured from her eyes. She rested her forehead against his. He noticed that her eyes had flecks of gold. Her lips were the color of a Southern rose. She moved her lips to his full lips and kissed him gently. She closed her eyes. Aldrich lifted a hand to her face and returned her kiss. He took her breath away with his kiss.

"Aldrich, I-" started Andraste.

Aldrich silenced her with another kiss. He pulled her to him. Andraste opened her eyes in surprise. She saw a golden light growing between them where her hand rested on his wound.

"Of course, we conquered the Ruin together so I gained part of your power," said Andraste.

"What do-" started Aldrich.

"Take off your clothes," ordered Andraste.

"No," said Aldrich firmly.

"We need to find the other snake bite quickly. You could still die," stated Andraste. She released herself from his grasp and rose. Aldrich stood as well.

"I will summon-" started Aldrich. He froze as Andraste pointed her Ruin sword at him. With a flick of her wrist, she cut through his tunic and it fell to the ground. She circled him searching intently for puncture wounds.

"Do not-" began Aldrich.

Andraste had already raised her sword and cut off his breeches. Aldrich lowered his hands to cover himself. Andraste knelt by his side and put her hands behind his knee. The gold light intensified. She kept her eyes on the wound. She did not move until the light faded away completely.

"This is humiliating," said Aldrich finally. Andraste rose and raised her eyes to his own. She blushed prettily and looked way quickly, but then looked back up just as quickly.

"Maybe you should check me as well," suggested Andraste.

Aldrich froze. Andraste pulled the sheet from the bed so that he could cover himself. When he turned back around, she had removed her gown and stood before him only in her undergarments. He raised his hand to her forearm and stopped short of touching her skin. He slowly moved his hand to her shoulder. No light grew between them. He used his other hand to do the same to her other arm. He continued his near caress down her sides with both hands.

"Aldrich," warned Andraste.

"I am being thorough," said Aldrich. He moved even more slowly down her hips and down her legs. His thumbs barely brushed her inner thighs. Andraste tensed and Aldrich laughed softly as he rose. His face was near touching hers as he looked into her eyes. Andraste raised her lips to his own, but Aldrich did not move.

"Surrender," said Andraste. Her lips brushed Aldrich's as she said the word.

Aldrich's resolve and principles waivered, before she knew it Aldrich had her pinned to his bed. He hesitated only for a moment. His mouth locked with hers in a question. Andraste unsecured the sheet from around his hips in response.

Andraste was awoken by the sound of knocking. She stirred sleepily and found herself entangled in Aldrich's legs. His hand caressed her bare skin. Realizing that she was awake, he gently lifted her face to his so that he could kiss her.

"Caelius," said Kasimir. Andraste was wide awake instantly. Aldrich did not release her from his grasp.

"What?" called Aldrich. He ran his fingers down her side.

"It is a good thing your princess stationed the Victorious with your family. Thankfully, no one was injured, but we seem to have a snake infestation," replied Kasimir through the door.

"I am aware," answered Aldrich.

"Where is your fierce protector?" asked Kasimir.

"Around," replied Aldrich.

"Are we going to continue this conversation through the door?" inquired Kasimir.

"No. I am going back to sleep," answered Aldrich. He nuzzled Andraste's neck. She did not relax until she heard Kasimir's footsteps fade down the hall.

"Why are you so tense? I am the one to lose everything if you were found here," stated Aldrich. He continued his trail of kisses down her neck. Andraste gently pushed him away. Aldrich kissed the inside of her wrist instead. Andraste bent over the side of the bed to pick her gown from the floor.

"Stay," said Aldrich. He kissed the phoenix on her shoulder, "It is just dawn."

"I cannot be found here. You said it yourself," replied Andraste.

"I would relinquish my kingdom if it meant I could have one more hour with you," said Aldrich. He brushed away her hair so that he could kiss her neck. He felt her pulse quicken.

"I should go," said Andraste. She once again removed herself from his grasp. Aldrich frowned as he watched her dress. She picked up her Ruin sword from the ground and moved towards the door.

"Andraste," said Aldrich. She hesitated at the door but did not look at him. She heard him get out of bed and she quickly left the room. As she was exiting into the hall, she came face to face with Egnatius.

"Good morning, Commander," said Egnatius. He bowed to her.

"Snake," said Andraste, "Northern viper."

"We have had four others since last night," replied Egnatius, "My lord?"

"He is unharmed," replied Andraste.

"As you see," said Aldrich from behind them.

Andraste glanced behind her and saw that Aldrich had pulled on a shirt and breeches, although his long auburn hair was not pulled back nor did he have shoes.

Andraste took a step towards her own chambers.

"I should check-" started Aldrich.

"Who saved you from the Northern viper?" asked Andraste.

"Paramerion," cautioned Aldrich.

"I can take care of myself," said Andraste.

She proceeded to her own chamber and shut the doors. She jumped as she found four Victorious seated in her meeting room. The door rattled behind her. She heard the sounds of Aldrich and Egnatius heading towards her door. She stepped aside as she felt the door handle move and Aldrich came through the door with Egnatius at his heels.

"They startled me that is all," sighed Andraste.

"You? Startled?" scoffed Laelius. He glanced to Aldrich.

"Why are you not with the Queen as ordered?" rejoined Andraste.

"Gnaeus, Avitus and Cato are with her in my place, so that I could make my report," replied Laelius, "I did not imagine having to wait so long."

"We had a bit of a snake problem" replied Andraste. Laelius's eyes went to Aldrich. Otho and Felix passed pouches of coins to Maximianus.

"Have you found their source?" asked Andraste.

"It is taken care of," responded Laelius. He glanced towards Aldrich and Egnatius.

"I still want the Caelius family guarded at all times," said Andraste.

"Yes, Commander," replied Laelius.

"Where is Brion?" asked Andraste.

"The Southern tower. He still continues his studies," answered Laelius, "I will leave these three with you in the meantime. You could also be targeted."

"We already checked your chambers. We know how much you fear snakes," said Felix.

"I am not afraid of snakes. I just do not like how they move," replied Andraste. Laelius stifled a laugh as he proceeded out of her chambers.

"The only time I ever heard you scream was after an encounter with a garden snake. It was not half a foot," said Felix. He smiled mischievously at Aldrich.

"I was twelve," replied Andraste defensively.

"Did you check the covers?" asked Aldrich.

"Northern vipers are not known for snuggling," commented Maximianus.

"Hand over the pouch. You just lost one for saying that word," said Otho.

"There was one in the prince's bed," said Andraste. She continued to pour herself a glass of water. Maximianus threw one of the pouches of money to Felix.

"What were the bets?" asked Egnatius.

"Do not answer," replied Andraste. Her tone was deadly, and her eyes murderous as she looked to the three Victorious.

"Yes, Commander," said Felix, Otho and Maximianus in unison.

"Felix, as my foster brother, you can remain inside. Go guard the veranda if you must be here. Max, Otho, you can both take sentry positions at the door," said Andraste. The three warriors rose to fulfill her commands. Andraste turned to survey the Southern lords, "You see I am well protected. Please carry on with your duties."

"Go on ahead. I will meet you in my study," said Aldrich.

Egnatius bowed to them both before returning to Aldrich's chambers. Andraste heard him stop to converse with Maximianus and Otho in the hall.

"Are you okay?" asked Aldrich. Andraste nodded once before draining her glass of water.

"Will you attend the Chambers of Justice with me this morning?" asked Aldrich.

"No. My curiosity should not distract you from your duties," replied Andraste.

"Will you be at the training yard this afternoon?" inquired Aldrich.

"No. My horse will need exercise," answered Andraste.

"I expect to have you on my arm at the social hour as specified by our duel," said Aldrich.

"As you wish," said Andraste.

Aldrich bowed to her, and when he raised his sapphire eyes, they were hurt. He closed the doors after him as he left. Andraste heard Felix approaching from the veranda.

"I do not wish to speak," stated Andraste.

"Are you wounded?" asked Felix.

"No," replied Andraste in surprise.

"You are usually only short with us when you are injured," said Felix. He turned on his heel and headed back to the veranda.

Andraste considered Felix's words as she bathed. She took great care in dressing and preparing her hair. When she was finished, she tried to read the reports that Aldrich had sent her, but she could not focus.

"Are we going for a stroll?" asked Felix as he saw her rise.

"Yes," replied Andraste. She made her way towards the Chambers of Justice, her three Victorious flanking her sides. The Southern lords and ladies swept to the side as she passed and bowed or curtsied. The Chambers of Justice were empty.

"Perhaps the training yard?" suggested Felix.

They made their way down to the training yard. They found the off-duty Victorious training with Egnatius's men, or rather soundly defeating them in the dust of the training yard.

"Where is your lord?" inquired Felix. Egnatius turned around to face them as he heard the question. He bowed to Andraste before answering.

"He is not here, Commander. He went to receive guests at the port," answered Egnatius.

"Anyone of interest?" asked Maximianus.

"The King of the Island Kingdoms has arrived. I am not familiar with the others," replied Egnatius.

"We should go pay our respects to your uncle," said Felix.

"The Eldgrimson will summon us when he wants to see us," replied Andraste.

"The Eldgrimson?" asked Egnatius. He smiled before asking, "Like the demon of legend?"

"Yes, that is what his people call him behind his back. Mind you, never to his face," answered Felix.

"You also encountered a Northern Viper? The prince would tell us nothing of the encounter," asked Kasimir from across the training yard.

"We found it and disposed of it. There is not much to tell," answered Andraste.

"I hear they are uncommonly fast," said Egnatius.

"That is true. You were lucky neither of you were bitten," said Maximianus.

"Aldrich was bitten. That is how we found it," replied Andraste.

"Your guard was low," criticized Felix, "It is not so easy being a protector? Now is it?"

"No, Felix, it is not. I can now fully appreciate your agony for the last year," replied Andraste.

"Sounds like you are about to be rewarded," said Maximianus. He elbowed Felix it in the ribs.

"No, I have just decided to not tell Shannon that you have been flirting and dancing with Southern ladies," said Andraste. Maximianus and Otho both laughed heartedly.

"Do not speak to Shannon," said Felix, "She should not be angry as we do not have an understanding."

"You do not have an understanding. The rest of us all understand that you should marry her and as soon as you can," said Maximianus, "She is a good lass."

"Do you think she will come with the court?" asked Otho. He exchanged looks with Maximianus.

"Do not be so cruel!" cried Felix.

"We should go see. Put him out of his misery," purported Maximianus.

"If I have a few hours of freedom left, then let me spend it here with my brothers," cried Felix.

"Has Shannon come?" asked Valens across the courtyard as he heard Felix's distress.

"Here is for hoping," replied Maximianus.

"It is always good entertainment," explained Otho to Egnatius.

"Ten coppers says she beats him soundly for not writing," said Thracius.

"No one will take that bet. It is inevitable," replied Priscus.

"What should I do, Commander?" asked Felix.

"Ask someone else for romance advice. Maximianus?" asked Andraste. The Victorious laughed from across the field.

"Beats me. Ask one of our married comrades," replied Maximianus.

"Ten coppers says she up and married Cuàn," said Otho.

"Do you think so?" asked Felix.

"That is not a good sign, Felix. You do not know whether to be relieved or devastated. You should make your mind up before the lady comes," advised Maximianus.

"No one deserves mixed signals," said Otho. Maximianus and Otho both looked pointedly to Andraste.

"Mind your own business, my hens," chided Andraste.

"Are you going to duel today?" asked Nero. The Victorious paused to study Andraste's attire.

"No," replied Andraste. She shifted uncomfortably underneath their scrutiny.

"When your lord returns, where do you think he will go first?" asked Felix.

"It will most likely be near the banquet. The feast will start early tonight. I imagine you will find him there. If I see him before then shall I tell him you were looking for him?" asked Egnatius.

"No," said Andraste quickly, "We were worried about the snake bites. That is all."

"Worried enough to search the palace, but not worried enough to go to the port?" asked Otho.

"She does not want to see her uncle," said Maximianus.

"I will see my uncle later. If Aldrich went without me, then he must have things he wishes to discuss with the King of the Island Kingdoms alone," reasoned Andraste.

"Such as?" asked Felix. He exchanged looks with Maximianus and Otho.

"Sailing," replied Andraste.

"Sailing?" inquired Felix. Maximianus and Otho laughed.

"What did you were think they were discussing?" asked Andraste.

"Marriage proposals?" suggested Felix.

"He would be better off discussing that with me. That is not for my uncle to decide," said Andraste briskly.

"Not an outright denial or refusal," commented Maximianus. He held out his hand to Otho. Otho put coins in Maximianus's hand.

"You knaves will bet on anything," sighed Andraste.

"As will you, Commander," said Otho.

"I would bet against that," said Eadbehrt, "Lady Gerlinde's father has been petitioning the Queen all morning for a union between their heirs. Gerlinde is the favorite Southern lady for a potential bride for my prince. Not only is she beautiful, but she comes from the richest Southern province. Her father has an army at his disposal. It would be a beneficial match for them both."

"Except that they do not love each other," stated Kasimir. He bristled at his comrade.

Egnatius and Eadbehrt both monitored Andraste's reaction closely. She kept her face neutral and looked instead to Felix.

"Perhaps we should petition the Queen as well," suggested Felix.

"I am not concerned," said Andraste, "It is no business of ours."

"It looks as though Caelius has returned. You can ask him yourself," said Kasimir.

Andraste's face brightened and she smiled as she turned towards the direction that Kasimir was looking. Her men turned to survey the prince storming across the field from the stables. Andraste's smile faded as she saw two furious, sapphire eyes bearing down on her. She took a step backwards. Felix and Maximianus stepped in front of her protectively, both of their hands with to their hilts. Her other Victorious stopped their training and turned to watch Aldrich approach.

"A word, my lady," said Aldrich. He stopped five paces away from Maximianus and Felix.

"Proceed," said Andraste from behind the protection of Maximianus and Felix.

"Are you or are you not engaged to the Lord of the Salt Islands?" asked Aldrich.

"She is not," answered Felix.

"I will hear my lady's answer," said Aldrich.

"I am not, nor have I ever been," replied Andraste. She put her hands on Maximianus's and Felix's arms. They let her pass, but they still kept their hands on their swords.

"You swear on your honor?" asked Aldrich.

"Yes," replied Andraste.

"Your uncle seems to think otherwise," said Aldrich.

"He does not know the true nature of my agreement with Rhinauld. That is between Rhinauld and myself," said Andraste.

"What is-" started Aldrich.

"That is none of your business," said Andraste sharply, "It affects a lady that is dear to my heart, and it is not to be spoken of lightly. It is a matter of honor and the hopes of many."

Aldrich stood watching Andraste intently. He relaxed his poise, Maximianus and Felix both retreated a few paces. Andraste approached Aldrich cautiously.

"And you, my lord, are you lately engaged to Lady Gerlinde?" asked Andraste.

"What?" asked Aldrich.

Andraste did not hesitate for an instant. She punched Aldrich squarely in the face. Aldrich stood for a moment stunned and then turned back to look at Andraste, but she had already turned to face her men. Maximianus and Felix stared at her in disbelief. She flexed her hand before folding her hands behind her back.

"My response was appropriate," said Andraste.

She swept past them and headed towards her chambers. Maximianus and Felix fell into step behind her. She saw the remaining Victorious leave their positions and come join them.

"Paramerion," called Aldrich. Andraste did not slow her pace for an instant.

"What on earth was that about?" asked Felix.

"Do not ask me questions," ordered Andraste.

Chapter Eight

Andraste was on time and dressed when Marcella and Decima came to call for her. She said very little to either of them. They gave her space. Whispers followed her down the hall. However, the Southern lords and ladies made way for her and bowed or curtsied as she passed.

Neither Aldrich nor the Queen was in the dining hall.

"I hear we are to have visitors tonight," informed Marcella.

"Who do you mean?" asked Andraste.

"Three flagships have entered the harbor. Earlier today my brother went to greet your uncle personally. I do not have information about the others," explained Marcella.

"What were the crests?" inquired Decima.

"A black raven-" started Marcella.

Andraste was on her feet and running around the table before Marcella had even closed her mouth. She had just started briskly down the center of the aisle, when the great doors opened. Her uncle entered first. He was followed by two well-dressed knights in their full armor. Behind the knights were two guard units, followed by a lady and her attendants.

Brion, Aldrich, and the Queen had arrived behind her at the end of the aisle nearest the raised dining table. Andraste was equidistant from both sides.

"Rhinauld, Lord of the Salt Islands," said Brion to Aldrich.

"We met earlier," replied Aldrich dryly.

The Lord of the Salt Islands would be poorly described as gorgeous. All of the ladies in the hall were already discussing his charms behind their fans: his curly dark locks, his emerald eyes, his bearing, his perfect form, etc. Aldrich was not the only warrior in the hall to grimace.

"Who?" questioned the Queen.

"The princess's foster brother," replied Brion.

Andraste briskly approached her uncle. She stopped momentarily to bow. The King of the Island Kingdoms acknowledged her and proceeded to the Queen. Andraste hastened to the dark-haired lord. The lord handed his helmet to his fellow knight and met her with almost as great speed. Effortlessly, he picked her up by her waist and twirled her around in his arms. Andraste's troubles seemed to melt away. She looked happier then Aldrich had ever seen her.

"Remember, we have not seen our foster brother in some time. When Andraste was told that she was to die, she did not go to him or Rhiannon, although, that was my intention. She chose instead to fight," cautioned Brion.

"It is no concern of mine," stated Aldrich. His face was expressionless.

Rhinauld had placed Andraste gently on her feet.

"Sir Henry," Andraste greeted the other knight. The knight in silver armor inclined his head in the slightest of acknowledgments. His light-brown hair fell into his eyes as he did so. He reached a slender hand to brush his bangs out of his gentle brown eyes. He was just barely taller than Andraste and slight of build. He stepped aside so that Andraste could proceed, knowing that it was the lady behind the guards that was Andraste's end result. The guards parted for her, and the petite dark haired lady that emerged was the image of Rhinauld.

"The Lady Rhiannon of the Salt Islands, Andraste's foster-sister," breathed Brion. He was unable to conceal his admiration. The dark haired beauty was the object of many a lord's attention.

Both ladies embraced and dissolved into a puddle of skirts and tears.

The King of the Island Kingdoms had reached the Queen of the Southern lands. As he kissed the Queen's hand, he entreated, "It has been a hard year for my charges. We have lost many. Please forgive them on my behalf."

"There is nothing to forgive, Aelius," replied the Queen.

The dark knight scooped Andraste from the floor as the brown-haired knight gallantly lent an arm to Rhiannon. He produced a handkerchief for Rhiannon. Rhinauld said something into Andraste's ear and she laughed. He raised her hand to his lips and kissed it. They proceeded down the aisle.

"Before the evening commences. We have some announcements that may interest you. Particularly, you Brion, as I hear your house and the Salt Islands are to be united. But, Andraste will want to tell you herself," informed the King of the Island Kingdoms.

Aldrich's face was set as cool as stone; although, his eyes burned as he watched Andraste reach for the dark knight's arm. Rhinauld wrapped his arm around her waist as they walked. Her second hand touched the dark knight's side as she asked him a question. When she looked up to Rhinauld, her face shone and she listened intently to every word of his response. Rhinauld released her as they had reached the Queen and prince.

"Your Majesty, Prince Aldrich, we are delighted to be your guests," said Rhinauld. He bowed low to Aldrich and the Queen.

"You are welcome, lords and ladies," said the Queen, assuming no such words would be delivered from her son.

"My Empress," declared Rhinauld proudly, and he bent down to one knee before Andraste. He withdrew three pieces of gold from a hidden pocket in his cape. He continued, "I bring to you three relics from the Ruins as promised."

There were gasps all along the hall.

"Three relics from the Ruins," the dark knight repeated. He hoisted them into the air so all could see.

Andraste did not take the offered relics from his hand. She felt an evil presence lurking underneath the shiny surface of the metal. It called to her.

"You have done well, brother," she said, and bent to kiss him lightly on the forehead.

"Be that as it may, do you remember our deal, my Empress?" asked the knight seriously. His emerald eyes upturned to Andraste expectantly.

"Brion Valerianus and Rhiannon of the Salt Islands step forth. Lady Rhiannon, your guardian has consented to this union. Brion, as my vassal and servant, do you acknowledge my right to marry you to who I see fit?"

asked Andraste.

"Yes, my lady," said Brion in totally shock. He could not keep his eyes off Lady Rhiannon.

"Then it is our great pleasure to announce the betrothal of my brother, Brion, to Lady Rhiannon," said Andraste. There was a great cheer from Northerners and Easterners.

"I do not understand," said Aldrich to the Queen.

"The Emperor had forbidden the match, but under the ruse that Andraste would marry the Lord of the Salt Islands, the Emperor agreed to the combining of their houses with the obtainment of three relics," said the Queen, "I understand that Brion and Rhiannon are childhood sweethearts, but when the Emperor learned of their affection, he banned Brion from any contact with her."

Aldrich did not comment. He watched Andraste go back in forth, like a hummingbird, between Brion, Rhiannon, and Rhinauld.

"Do you know the second part of the arrangement?" inquired the Queen, glancing at her son.

"No," admitted Aldrich.

"The princess is free to marry who ever she chooses," stated the Queen.

"Does she not have that right already, since she was exiled?" asked Aldrich.

"To the North it is a matter of honor. It was agreed upon and now it is fulfilled. I am sure the princess views it the same way," responded the Queen.

The Queen of the Southern lands and the King of the Island Kingdoms took their places at the head of the lead table. Brion offered his arm to Rhiannon and followed after them. Rhinauld first offered his arm to Andraste and saw Aldrich watching them. Instead he nudged Andraste in the ribs. Andraste looked up, blushed prettily, and led Rhinauld to Aldrich.

"My sister wishes us to be friends," stated Rhinauld.

He held his hand to Aldrich, who had no choice but to accept it. Felix, whose homeland was also the Salt Islands, had joined them and wrapped an arm around Rhinauld's neck.

"You will not after you hear what our *Empress* suggested," said Felix,

"She offered to be his Muse."

The hand that was offered in friendship had turned into a death grip. Rhinauld's eyes flashed as he locked grips with the prince. Aldrich's grip also tightened in response. They stood glaring at each other.

"Have you touched her?" Rhinauld asked in undisguised fury. The look in his eye was murderous. Aldrich held Rhinauld's gaze without wavering.

"That is the best part! The prince refused her. No, this is the best part. He proposed and she refused," laughed Felix.

"Oh, Andra, you are so infuriating," sighed Rhinauld.

Rhinauld released Aldrich's arm and bowed deeply saying, "I apologize on behalf of my sister. Please forgive her, Prince Aldrich. She meant to show great honor, but being herself, she messed it up completely."

"Rhinauld!" gasped Andraste in horror.

"You realize in this kingdom you could not have proposed a more serious insult to the prince?" asked Rhinauld, "The penalty for adultery is total disgrace: loss of property, loss of title, loss of honor. Their entire system is built upon the sanctity of marriage, and the union produced between husband and wife. It is the basis for the rest of their society and culture."

Andraste stared at a tapestry on the far wall and raised herself to her full height.

"It is not so in the North," said Andraste. She did not remove her eyes from the tapestry; although, she blushed deeply.

"It has been explained to me, and I recognize it to be a misunderstanding. Our customs are so different," offered Aldrich. He turned his eyes to Andraste and waited her response.

"But it is still a matter of honor," said Rhinauld. He glared at Andraste and turned back to the prince, "I challenge you to three contests."

"No. It was my mistake. He has nothing to prove. He is a Ruin conqueror, a fierce warrior, and a future king," declared Andraste.

"I want my intentions towards this lady to be open and honorable. I accept your challenges," said Aldrich, ignoring Andraste's outburst completely.

Rhinauld and Aldrich stood judging each other. Andraste was speechless for a moment. Her mind began to race with all of the things Rhinauld could propose.

"Rhinauld, if you say Ruins, I swear by the gods that I will kill you with my own hands. You would not have survived the first two without me-" started Andraste.

"So scary," said Rhinauld at the glowering princess. Aldrich's mouth twitched into a suppressed smile.

"The first challenge will be-"started Rhinauld dramatically,"Drinking!" Henry and Andraste both flinched.

"Drinking?" repeated Aldrich. He blinked.

"Yes, a real man must hold his own, now come!" said Rhinauld.

Rhinauld clamped a hand on Aldrich's back and they went off towards the Victorious table. The men of the Island Kingdoms followed them. They were greeted by the Victorious. Felix explained the challenge and all of the men laughed.

"Henry, please," begged Andraste.

"This once," conceded Henry as he stroked his goatee. He bowed to her and followed after them.

"You look daft standing there by yourself,"commented the King of the Island Kingdoms. He offered her his arm.

"I think my honor is about to be determined by the stupidest challenges ever proposed," said Andraste.

"That is a good reason to stand here looking daft, but come eat," ordered her uncle. Andraste returned to their table, but her eyes were on Aldrich and Rhinauld.

"What are the other challenges to be? Is this a Northern custom?" asked Marcella with concern.

"I will object if there are any grounds on loss of limb or possible maiming," appeased her uncle. The King rose and went to join the crowd watching the drinking contest.

"So that is Aldrich Caelius," said Rhiannon as Andraste sat by her foster sister's side. She looked mischievously at Andraste, "Who do you want to win?"

"I fight my own battles. I will enter the contest myself," said Andraste. She started to rise but Rhiannon pushed her playfully back to her seat.

"You are concerned for the Southern prince?" asked Rhiannon.

"I am concerned Rhinauld will embarrass us both," replied Andraste.

"He is Lord of the Salt Islands. He will remember his dignity," said Rhiannon.

"You have not traveled with him as much as I," rejoined Andraste. Rhiannon and Andraste exchanged concerned looks.

"This will be interesting. Felix is approaching Shannon," said Rhiannon.

"How is she?" asked Andraste. Rhiannon shook her head and sighed.

"Lady Shannon," addressed Felix. He bowed eloquently before the dark-haired beauty.

"Do I know you? You look so familiar," said Shannon. She studied Felix curiously.

"My lady, you know, we have known each other these twenty summers at least," replied Felix.

"So long? And are we friendly?" asked Shannon.

"Indeed. I regard you as one of the most treasured of my acquaintances," responded Felix.

"Truly? You astonish me: I am so treasured, and yet you supposed to not write one single solitary letter these eleven months?" asked Shannon.

"Uh-oh," said Andraste. Rhiannon giggled beside her.

"I was on the road, my lady," replied Felix. He retreated as she stepped forward.

"And I was home guarding your lands and mine," responded Shannon.

She drove Felix back another pace. Felix tried to hold his ground. He looked to the Victorious for support. Maximianus pantomimed a hanging. Laelius shook his head and did not look pleased.

"You are right. I am a worthless knave. You deserve much better," said Felix. He tried to grab her hand and kiss it, but she would not let him.

"I agree," replied Shannon. She turned on her heel and joined Rhiannon and Andraste at her table. Felix watched her progress in despair. He was summoned by the Victorious.

"Nicely done," said Rhiannon as Shannon took her seat. Andraste raised her glass to Felix and shook her head.

"I hope we become great friends. I am Decima," said the Lady of the Shadow Mountains as she extended Shannon her hand. Shannon took it.

"This is Shannon, Lady of the Gray Sands," introduced Andraste.

"It looks like they are on their next round," approved Marcella. Andraste turned her attention back towards the challenge.

"What is it?" asked Andraste.

"Dirty jokes?" asked the Queen as she strained to listen. There was a loud bellow of laughter from the men's table.

"The drinking round has not stopped," commented Decima.

"I have not heard a good dirty joke in years. People just stop telling you the good stuff after you are Queen," said the Queen.

All of the women started laughing hard and the contest paused in its tracks. The Queen was telling a joke in Marcella's ear and all she exclaimed was, "Mother!"

"Tell the gentleman that they have both lost. This round has gone to the Queen," said Decima to a lord, who was walking by.

The lord delivered her message and the men's table guffawed. Rhinauld threw back his head and laughed. He then winked at Andraste mischievously. Andraste's smile faded.

"Fine, then for the third challenge, I challenge you to the dance of swords," dared Rhinauld. The laughter in the hall died completely.

"Your Majesty, you did say no maiming," reminded Marcella loudly.

"Oh, let the boys have their fun," retorted the King from his position, "Besides your brother has not accepted yet."

"But Uncle, he does not know that Rhinauld is the greatest swordsman from the Island Kingdoms," said Andraste.

"So little faith in Aldrich already?" asked the King.

"My son is no squire. He will hold his own," stated the Queen with pride.

"I accept," avowed Aldrich and he rose. His men rose cheering him.

Henry returned to Andraste's side. He bowed and said, "My lord would not hear reason, Empress, but they have both been drinking heavily, so I do not think they will actually come to blows."

Aldrich did not spare even a glance at her as he met Rhinauld in the center of the aisle. The two duelists did not even wait for the circle of swordsmen. Aldrich attacked first with his great sword.

Andraste held her breath as she watched. She rose from her seat as those around her also stood. The two swordsmen were so fast it was hard for her even to follow. Someone stepped in front of her and she missed the final blow. She heard a large wave of cheering and the two combatants laughed and grasped hands. She could not see who was making their way towards her.

The crowd parted and Aldrich stood before her.

"I am not familiar with this custom, but I imagine you will now have to dance with me. I name you the Queen of the Dance, and then we dance?" asked Aldrich.

"It is the Queen of the Festival, and the custom is a kiss," amended Andraste.

The prince took a step back as his men laughed. Andraste stepped forward and stood on her tip toes. She placed a hand on Aldrich's shoulder. She hesitated. Her sea-green eyes gazed into Aldrich's sapphire eyes. He put a hand to her waist to steady her. She leaned into him. She raised her lips to Aldrich's bruised cheek that she had punched earlier, and chastely kissed him.

"Is that all?" asked Kasimir. The men laughed.

Aldrich silenced them with a glare. He slowly released his hold on Andraste.

"Are you engaged to Lady Gerlinde?" asked Andraste.

"No, my lady, I am not," replied Aldrich quickly.

Expecting another blow, he stepped out of her reach, but Andraste caught him by the side. She stepped into him and kissed him passionately before he could protest. Catcalling ensued from the Victorious and the Southern lords. Andraste withdrew first and blushed prettily. She lowered her eyes to the floor. Aldrich kissed her hand gently before returning to his table.

"I like him," Rhinauld whispered in her ear as he came to her side.

Andraste blushed. Her eyes flashed to Aldrich's table. The prince was watching them closely. She returned her eyes to Rhinauld.

"Are you going to tell me about your adventures?" asked Andraste.

"Not tonight," replied Rhinauld.

Music had started for the first dance of the evening. Brion rose and offered his arm to Rhiannon. Rhinauld claimed Andraste for the first dance. Andraste danced with each of Rhinauld's knights, all of who she had known since childhood. Aldrich did not dance at all, even when Decima approached him. Aldrich watched the couples from the Island Kingdoms dance.

Andraste retired from the dance floor and began speaking to Rhinauld at great length. Brion, Rhiannon and Henry joined them. Rhinauld waved away any of his knights that approached. He asked few questions and listened intently. Near the end, Brion took over as Andraste could not retell the deaths of Matthias and Tobias. Rhinauld pulled Andraste to him and she laid her head on his shoulder.

Aldrich rose and swept from the hall quickly. He retired to his chambers. He left the doors to his chambers open. He was shortly joined by Marcella, Gregor and Decima, who saw him leave the ballroom.

"Such an interesting lady," Marcella commented, watching her brother's reaction under lowered eyelids.

"Is your shoulder hurt?" asked Decima, "Rhinauld did strike you hard."

Aldrich did not admit it, but his right-back shoulder blade hurt exceedingly. Aldrich permitted Decima to rub an ointment on to it. He heard her intake her breath as she surveyed the bruise.

"That is an eyesore. The things we do for women," said Gregor. He laughed at Aldrich.

"Are we not even going to discuss the Northern vipers?" asked Marcella.

They heard voices coming down the hall. It sounded like some sort of song.

"120 Ways to Kill a Man? Again? Otho makes up more verses every day," sighed Andraste.

"You must mind your tongue, Andra. Saying such things to the Queen! And you wonder why they call you Demon of the North," scolded Rhinauld.

Aldrich turned to see Andraste on Rhinauld's arm. She paused in the doorway. Her eyes narrowed as she saw Decima's hand on the prince's shoulder. Andraste did not stop to speak. Rhinauld pulled her on to her chambers. Rhiannon and Brion followed arm in arm, deep in conversation, and Henry brought up the rear. He bowed as he passed their doorway in acknowledgement.

Aldrich rose and shut the door to his chambers angrily. He poured himself a drink.

"You are king of these lands," commented Decima, "If you want to join them, go join them."

"Let me see the relics," said Andraste. Her voice carried across the hall.

"That is something I must see," said Marcella and she shoved past her brother. Gregor followed after his wife. Decima waited in the doorway. Aldrich put on his tunic and trailed behind.

"May we join you?" asked Marcella gaily as she entered Andraste's chambers.

"Of course, my lady," said Rhinauld gallantly. He bowed, but not as elegantly as before. The dark knight was three sheets to the wind. Henry stood between Rhinauld and the ladies.

"Hopeless," commented Andraste with a hiccup.

"We were going to examine the relics," explained Brion. Rhinauld tossed the relic onto the table with all of the maps.

"When you put them together, they look as though they are part of a shield," commented Marcella. She picked up the pieces and then put them down on the table.

"Go ahead, Andra, it will not hurt you. I have been carrying them for years," commented Rhinauld.

"I do not want to touch them," protested Andraste.

She retreated from Rhinauld. She backed into Aldrich. She was forced to take a step forward.

"Come on," dared Rhinauld.

Marcella's eyes narrowed.

"Do not-" Marcella started.

Rhinauld forced the partially assembled shield into Andraste's hand. It was enveloped into a purple haze of smoke that turned into radiating dark energy.

Aldrich put his hand out and the golden spirit phoenix appeared between Andraste and the shield. The shield lifted in the air by itself. Aldrich pulled Andraste behind him. The phoenix dove down at it and drove the purple glowing back into the shield. The shield fell to the floor with a resounding clang. Andraste fainted. Aldrich caught her in his arms. A glowing light consumed her as he lifted her.

"I have been carrying them and nothing like this has ever happened," remonstrated Rhinauld.

"The curse may be gone, but she will always be marked by the dark magic," Marcella said quietly.

Aldrich placed Andraste in her bed. He moved a strand of hair from her face.

"Paramerion?" questioned Aldrich. Her hand fell from his. She looked deathly pale.

Aldrich sat on her bed. She leaned into him, as she did so golden light developed where their hands touched. Her color seemed to improve. Aldrich gently moved her further into bed, so that he could sit against the headboard. He had one leg stretched out on the bed, touching her form and the other leg on the ground. The golden light spread between them wherever they touched.

"I must protest-" started Rhinauld.

"You did this! You have no right to protest!" bellowed Brion darkly, "Leave! And take that thing with you!"

"I will also stay with the princess," said Marcella, "She is very weak."

Rhiannon also sat on the edge of Andraste's bed. Brion settled down on the sofa and stared daggers at Rhinauld, who was dragged from the room by Henry.

Aldrich spoke to no one. He adjusted to give Andraste more space, but her grip on his hand tightened. He closed his eyes.

Aldrich dreamt of the Darklands. He felt the cold black sands between his toes. The icy wind that blew from the North kissed his neck. He was enveloped in a mist. It warmed his skin unpleasantly. He turned and found himself face to face with the emerald Dragon. It was enormous. The malachite scales glinted in the sunlight like gemstones. The Dragon put its face close to his own and stared at him with deep tanzanite eyes. He heard a woman's voice. As he looked into the Dragon's eyes, he saw a face of a woman staring back at him. She was uncannily familiar.

"Will you protect her?" asked the Dragon.

"The woman in your eyes?" asked Aldrich.

"Not me," corrected the Dragon, "Andraste."

"Yes," swore Aldrich.

"She must live. You must protect her or all is lost. Not just this Empire. All will suffer," declared the Dragon.

The Dragon's head moved and he saw Andraste cradled in the Dragon's arms. Aldrich stepped forward.

"She will not heed my warnings. Evil comes. You must be ready," warned the Dragon. The Dragon allowed Aldrich pick up Andraste in his arms.

"She has two sides. You must protect her from her strength, but you must also protect her from her weakness. She could follow the path of the Emperor still. You must keep her with you. You must not be parted. It takes two to master life," presaged the Dragon.

"But why?" asked Aldrich.

"We are out of time," confirmed the Dragon.

The Dragon was dissolved in deep amethyst smoke. The woman's voice faded. Aldrich saw the Dragon blow billows of smoke and red fire. The red fire enveloped him and Andraste. The Dragon was protecting them from the amaranthine flames.

"Go!" ordered the Dragon.

Aldrich's eyes opened. His heart was racing. Andraste still lay perfectly still, but her head rested gently on his chest. Aldrich glanced to Marcella. She and Rhiannon were both soundly asleep in their chairs.

Andraste's eyes opened. Her beryl eyes were alarmed as she looked up to Aldrich. He could feel her heart race.

"Shhh," he mouthed silently and glanced meaningfully towards the inert ladies.

Andraste became aware of their surroundings and their proximity. She withdrew immediately and adjusted her clothing. Aldrich rose and left the room hastily.

Andraste woke Marcella and Rhiannon, assured them of her wellbeing and sent them on their way. By the time she was bathed and dressed, Rhinauld was waiting for her in her antechambers. She also saw new reports had been dropped off on her table.

"Are you well?" inquired Rhinauld.

"I am fine," responded Andraste.

"I did not know. I would never-" Rhinauld started.

"I know," interrupted Andraste. She moved to exit the room, "Come to the gardens with me. I want to hear of your and Henry's adventures."

"Yes, Empress," said Rhinauld.

She wrapped her arm in his as he joined her side. He seemed to rally.

Andraste noticed that Aldrich's doors were wide open, but the chambers were deserted. They made their way to the gardens. The view took Andraste's breath away. The walkways were supported by stone pillars and arches, which were wrapped in vines. Trees had been planted throughout the garden, transporting it from a sunny paradise into beautiful woodland. Once in the shade of the trees, the most beautiful flowers grew on the ground. There were fountains that were filled with water lilies. The air was filled with their aroma and birdsong.

"It is said these gardens were built by a Southern king for his Northern bride because she yearned for the lands of her homeland," said Rhinauld.

"I have never seen the North look like this," replied Andraste.

Andraste released Rhinauld's arm, so that she could go towards the sound of children's laughter. She found that many of the Victorious children were playing with Southern children. They did not possess the qualms that divided their parents. She saw that Aaliyah and her siblings were playing with Laelius's children.

"What are you doing?" Lae yelled to them.

"My brother is going to tell me his latest adventure," responded Andraste.

Rhinauld threw his cape on the ground, so that Andraste could sit. Lae approached them and climbed into Andraste's lap. Some of the other children followed and took places around Andraste. Andraste looked up expectantly at Rhinauld.

"A proper audience. I am honored," said Rhinauld to the children. He bowed to them. The girls giggled.

"I suppose we should start when we last parted. We both left the Island Kingdoms. You returned to the North, and I sailed southeast to the uncharted islands," said Rhinauld.

"How long did you sail?" asked one of the children.

"We sailed two months in the fiercest seas that I have ever encountered. And that is saying something, as I am a man from the Island Kingdoms. Tremendous tempests with fierce gales and waves the size of this palace. We were not completely dry until we returned to the Island Kingdoms, especially after our encounter with a monstrous whirlpool," said Rhinauld.

"Waves the size of the palace?" Aaliyah asked skeptically. She was shushed by one of her siblings.

"Once the storm subsided, we were attacked by a number of sea monsters," said Rhinauld.

"What kind?" asked a child.

"Sea serpents, a leviathan, sharks, a kraken," began Rhinauld.

"What is a leviathan?" asked Lae.

"A large whale with an incredibly tough skin," replied Andraste.

"A ginormous whale that has virtually impenetrable skin," continued Rhinauld.

"How did you defeat it?" asked Aaliyah.

"We had to outsail the leviathan. We did not have the weapons to defeat it," admitted Rhinauld.

"Tell me, brother, did they come all at once or separately?" asked Andraste.

"It seemed as though we would defeat one and then we would be attacked by another. This went on for four days," said Rhinauld.

Aayilah looked at Rhinauld skeptically.

"I have seen such creatures, and my brother does not lie," Andraste told Aaliyah.

"How did you defeat them?" asked Lae.

"The men of the Island Kingdoms are fierce fishermen. We fought with nets and harpoons. Henry jumped onto the sea serpent's back and sliced off its head with one mighty blow," said Rhinauld. He pretended to fight a giant sea creature. The children laughed.

"What happened next?" Andraste asked as eager as the children.

"We heard the most beautiful music. The melody drifted across the azure seas, and drifted towards our deck, where we stood almost spellbound, helpless against its beauty. The sound that serenaded our ears was the sound of a chorus of angels singing. Sumptuous, exquisite women emerged from the waters and invited us to go with them," said Rhinauld.

"Sirens?" asked Andraste.

"Do not ruin the story," replied Rhinauld. He glared at Andraste.

"Some of my men attempted to go with them, but Henry and I stopped them. We made the men put rags into their ears, so they could not be lured by the singing," said Rhinauld.

"How were you able to resist?" asked Aayliah.

"My Empress is far more beautiful than any of the sirens, and she sings even more beautifully," replied Rhinauld.

The oldest girls giggled, while the boys made disgusted sounds.

"So my brother does lie," Andraste amended. Aaliyah giggled, but Rhinauld ignored them both.

"The sirens turned into evil-looking creatures and their songs into screeches," told Rhinauld.

"Imagine that? You rejected the women and they turned into horrible beasts," said Andraste, "Are you sure they did not reject you brother?"

"The calm seas once more turned tempestuous, but with my skilled crew, we were able to sail on. We reached a deserted island and found the Spirit of the Ruin," said Rhinauld.

The children were not impressed.

"So for most of your journey you just out-sailed the danger?" asked one of the children.

"That is an impressive skill," protested Rhinauld.

"What form did the Spirit assume?" asked Andraste.

"Let us just call it the Spirit of the Ruin," replied Rhinauld.

"I want to know. What was it?" inquired Andraste.

"It took the form of a seagull," admitted Rhinauld.

The children laughed, but not as hard as Andraste. Rhinauld looked like the wind had been let out of his sails.

"A seagull?" repeated Aaliyah.

"What did this fierce Spirit propose?" Andraste asked as she wiped the tears from her eyes.

"As we had made it to the island, past all of its monstrous allies, it granted us the option of one treasure or one wish," answered Rhinauld.

"All of you?" asked Lae.

"Just one," replied Rhinauld.

"What did you ask for?" inquired Aaliyah.

"A piece of the relic that I gave to the Empress," said Rhinauld.

"Many thanks," replied Andraste.

"Any wish in the world and you asked for a piece of junk?" asked another child.

"It is what my Empress requested," replied Rhinauld. He looked even more deflated.

"So Rhiannon could marry Brion?" asked one of the older girls.

"That is so romantic!" said her companion.

"That is enough of that!" announced one of the boys, "Let us play blind man's bluff."

"I want to be it!" declared Lae.

One of the girls took off her sash. Andraste took it and tied it around Lae's eyes. Rhinauld spun him three times and then backed away. Lae was too little to get the other children. Andraste stepped forward. She playfully teased Lae for a few minutes, and then let him tag her.

Rhinauld tied the blindfold around her eyes. She picked up the hem of her gown in one hand and extended the other hand forward. She listened. The children were giggling, but had a head start from Lae's first round.

"Not too far!" Rhinauld called to the children. Andraste turned towards the sound of his voice.

"The name of the game is blind man's bluff. Is it not played in the South?" Rhinauld was asking.

Andraste reached out. She was sure Rhinauld was right in front of her. She tripped over a rock. She felt strong arms reach out and catch her from her fall. The arms were strong and the bare chest muscular.

"Rhinauld?" asked Andraste.

"No, I am here, Empress," replied Rhinauld.

Andraste blushed. She reached a hand to her rescuer's face.

"Henry?" inquired Andraste.

"Wrong again," confirmed Rhinauld.

Andraste removed the scarf. She looked at Aldrich in surprise. Aldrich released her.

"If this was played as a parlor game, since she was wrong, she would have had to kiss you," advised Henry, who was standing beside Rhinauld. Aldrich did not seem amused.

"Have you been watching long?" asked Andraste. Her blush deepened. She passed the scarf to an approaching child and the children resumed their game.

"We witnessed the tale of the third Ruin," answered Aldrich.

"Have you lost your shirt?" asked Andraste.

"I was training the recruits. I am on my way to the pools," replied Aldrich.

"I should have helped with the recruits. I am sorry," said Andraste.

"Your time was better spent here," said Aldrich. He smiled as he looked at the children behind her.

"Pools?" inquired Henry.

"The city offers several pools for the public. It can be so hot here, that at times, swimming is the only way for relief," replied Aldrich.

"I would like to see these pools," indicated Rhinauld.

"I will return to my study. I still have not yet read the reports you sent me," said Andraste.

"Nothing momentous. I will tell you about them as we walk," replied Aldrich. He offered her his arm. Andraste glanced to Rhinauld, who nodded. She took Aldrich's arm.

"Is your nose bleeding?" asked Andraste.

"Was. Henry struck me in a moment of distraction during our duel in the training yard," said Aldrich. She saw Henry shoot Rhinauld an evil grin.

"While I was dueling the prince, Felix called out, 'Andraste,' and the prince dropped his guard as he turned to look," said Henry.

Aldrich blushed crimson underneath Andraste's scrutiny, but he saw it was Henry that she was judging.

"Striking a man in a moment of weakness? Hardly befitting a knight of the Island Kingdoms," reproved Rhinauld, but he laughed anyway. Aldrich glared at both of the warriors.

"Who won?" asked Andraste.

"Aldrich," admitted Henry.

"Defeated both of you, has he? It appears that my dear knights should have trained harder on their pleasure cruise," mentioned Andraste.

"A Ruin conquest a pleasure cruise?" snorted Rhinauld, "This was the last time I enter Ruins on your behalf."

"It was for Rhiannon," reminded Henry.

"Henry would not partake such a quest on my behalf," alleged Andraste.

"No, I would not," agreed Henry.

"But you would challenge her suitors?" inquired Rhinauld.

"No. It was curiosity. I wanted to fight the swordsmen who bested you," replied Henry. Rhinauld's face darkened at his comrade's words. Andraste laughed softly and turned towards Aldrich.

"Let me see," commanded Andraste. She raised a hand to Aldrich's face. As she did so, gold light began to radiate from her palm to his face.

"I still do not understand how this is possible," stated Aldrich.

"Why question a gift from the gods?" asked Henry.

"Perhaps it is because we conquered the Ruin together. I assumed that is why you can lift my sword," said Andraste.

"I do not follow," admitted Aldrich.

Andraste took off her sword and threw it at Rhinauld. He caught it but was unable to hold it for long. It fell from his grasp to the floor. Henry tried to pick up the sword, but could not.

"A Ruin item can only be used by those who conquered the Ruin," said Andraste.

"But you won the sword," replied Aldrich.

"No. We won it together," contradicted Andraste. She raised her azure eyes to Aldrich as he studied her. She lowered her hand as the light between them diminished.

"But then why could you not heal yourself or the Victorious from the poisoned arrows?" asked Rhinauld.

"I have not studied magic. Maybe I can only heal the prince since his powers will not allow him to heal himself?" returned Andraste.

"We should ask Brion, but I imagine he is locked away with his head in a book in the Sorcerer's tower," said Henry.

"He spends most of his time there," replied Andraste.

"Speaking of spending time, are you ready to return to our ship? I have your cabin prepared," said Rhinauld.

"Surely a lady would be more comfortable within the palace," said Aldrich. His grip tightened on Andraste's arm.

"Nonsense. Andra has spent time aboard my ship since she was a girl. It is a second home to her. We are from the Island Kingdoms. We live to be on the sea," said Rhinauld.

Aldrich and Rhinauld glared at each other.

"I will stay at the palace. I wish to be near my Victorious, and their families are already settled. I would not uproot them again," said Andraste, "Ah, Laelius, perfect timing."

Laelius approached them; although, he was ignored by the two glowering lords.

"There is a counsel in the War Chambers. Commander, Prince Aldrich, lords, you are all summoned by the Queen," advised Laelius.

"Thank you, Laelius," said Andraste.

Laelius bowed to her and joined Rhinauld and Henry. She glanced up at Aldrich, who looked annoyed.

"I will show you the pools another time," said Aldrich.

They made their way to the War Chambers. Upon approach, she heard a heated conversation. Andraste released Aldrich's arm and entered the room. Everywhere that Andraste looked there was arguing. It sounded like the persistent hum of a bee hive. Andraste joined the King's side and the arguments subsided.

"Andraste," welcomed the King. He took a moment to study the council before turning his sea-green eyes to Andraste. He ordered, "Explain to the Southern lords, why we cannot take the Ice Palace."

"There is no need to take the Ice Palace," countered Andraste.

"I already said that," stated the Queen. She eyed the men furiously.

"Thank you, Queen Marian. Andraste, please explain the Ice Palace. Our Southern comrades are not permitted to enter that far North," said the King tiredly.

"I began my training at the Ice Palace. I was not strong enough to make the ranks. We cannot match the sorcery or the power that dwells there," affirmed Andraste.

There were murmurs of surprise throughout the room.

"That is all you are going to say?" asked the King.

"Why do you not explain yourself?" retorted Andraste.

"Men are not allowed there- other than the Emperor," explained Brion, "You and the Queen are the only ones present who have seen the Ice Palace."

"We are not going to attack a palace guarded only by women?" asked Lord Arnold.

"Not all are as weak as the women you keep in chains," said the Queen icily. The room fell silent.

"And yet the Ice Palace is the fastest way to the Emperor and to victory," alleged Kasimir.

"Yes, but I would remind you that the grounds of the Ice Palace are sacred and not ruled by the Emperor. The Ice Palace was built as a sanctuary and is a vault for the relics from Ruins. The palace is a tower of learning similar to the tower at the City of Sorcery. The Emperor resides in the Citadel. He can only enter the Ice Palace by day and does so rarely. It is not the Ice Palace we want to attack, but the Citadel," advised Andraste.

Brion shivered and the Southern lords looked alarmed by his reaction.

"Is it that bad?" asked Eadbehrt.

"The Emperor's experiments are terrifying. If I had the option, I would never return. Additionally, in our way will be the Imperial Army, some 50,000 strong, drawing from the best soldiers from across the Empire," said Andraste.

"Experiments?" questioned the Queen. Her eyes turned to the King of the Island Kingdoms. However, he looked to Brion for a response.

"There is an army of the undead. We call them the Arisen," answered Brion.

"The Emperor tried to save our defeated soldiers and it backfired terribly," elucidated Andraste reluctantly. She did not like the look on Aldrich's face.

"The Northern lords permitted this?" asked Lord Arnold.

"Death is the punishment for dissent," responded Brion.

"Is death the punishment for everything in the North?" inquired Aldrich.

Andraste ignored the question. She went to stand between Rhinauld and Henry. She studied the maps on the table.

"Can the Arisen be defeated?" asked the Queen.

"Only with sorcery. In this matter, the Ice Palace may come to our aid. The warriors have been hunting down any of the Arisen that they find," responded Andraste.

"The Emperor allows this?" asked Kasimir.

"He cannot control the Arisen," eluded Brion.

"Our best plan is to draw out the main forces away from the Citadel. We will only have to deal with the Emperor's monsters and the Arisen. I advise that you lead our combined armies against the Emperor's forces, and that I take the Victorious to fight our way into the Citadel," recommended Andraste.

"You want to lead a Northern force to defeat your own father?" snarled Lord Arnold, "How do we know it is not a ruse? You could sell us out for your own redemption. What is your proof that you will not turn on us?"

"You question my lady's honor?" asked Rhinauld darkly. His hand rested on his sword.

"A traitor and an exile?" retorted Lord Arnold.

Aldrich stepped between the two men. Andraste thought he was going to pacify the situation. However, Aldrich punched the smaller lord squarely in the face. Lord Arnold let out a comical sound of disbelief as he flew backwards and hit the ground hard. The lord put a hand to his bleeding lip.

"The Emperor already once offered amnesty. My Commander refused said offer. The proof of this statement is in her and three of our warriors' scars from the encounter," stated Laelius.

"She is a sorceress just like her mother. She has you wrapped around her finger-" started Lord Arnold. He stopped as fifteen Northern blades and two Eastern blades surrounded his throat. However, Aldrich's glowering stare was more menacing.

"Andraste Paramerion has done more to secure our nation's freedom than anyone else in this room. She has sacrificed her birthright and fortune to aid us in our cause. She has shown tremendous courage. I am honored to stand with her," avouched the Queen.

Lord Arnold rose to his feet shakily and snarled at Aldrich, "Just bed her and be done with it. You are letting the North interfere with our future!"

Aldrich's hand went to his blade. There was murder in his eyes.

"She already has one child out of wedlock! Surely you have heard the rumors! How can you pursue such a woman as our future Queen?" snarled Lord Arnold.

Rhiannon stood from her place by Marcella's side.

"No!" commanded Andraste.

"The child in question is mine. Brion is the father. As we are to be married, our son will be accepted into our household with proper course and honor as is the tradition in the Island Kingdoms and the North," said Rhiannon. She blushed crimson.

Brion took Rhiannon's hand in his and kissed it.

The Queen rose.

"Lord Arnold, you are no longer a member of this Council. Insulting our guest and allies? I have never seen such a display. The Northern lords have every right to behead you now for the insults you have reaped on their princess. Now leave," ordered the Queen. She shook with rage.

"But you have heard the rumors yourself? The prince entering in and out of her chamber in the middle of the night-" started Lord Arnold.

"The princess has been unwell. Marcella and Rhiannon witnessed the prince's healing power themselves. Have there been any acts that have ruined the princess's honor?" retorted the Queen.

"No, your Majesty," answered Rhinauld and Brion together.

"The other Northern Commanders would have slain you for spurting such nonsense," stated Laelius. There was no forgiveness in his eyes.

"Even more importantly," said Andraste, not looking up from the map, "Your petty qualms are interfering with the success of this mission and distracting the focus of this Council. If you are not here to aid us, then there is no place for you."

"I am a citizen of this city. The future you could damage is mine own!" exclaimed Lord Arnold in outrage, "Why do you cry for war? We are safe within the city's walls. We can withstand a siege. We can appease the Emperor."

"Do you hear that, Lord Arnold? The sound of the Northern wind? It brings the sound of Imperial troops marching upon this city. That Northern gale resounds with the clash of arms as your fair Capitol is rendered into ash. It echoes terribly in the sound of nothing. You will bring the creation of another Ruin by your inaction," stated Andraste.

"I will not witness the implements of war. We would be better off not provoking the wrath of the Emperor. You are the harbinger of our mutual destruction," retorted Lord Arnold.

"You will not speak so to your future Queen. Forgive me, I meant Empress," said Aldrich. He blushed crimson at his error and would not look at Andraste. The room grew silent as Lord Arnold calculated his next words.

"Aldrich Caelius, crowned Prince of the Southern lands, based on the laws of the South, I challenge your right to the throne on grounds of honor," proclaimed Lord Arnold.

"Lord Arnold, you may have bought your title and lands, but as you are a foreign born citizen, you hold no such right. You cannot issue the challenge," intervened the Queen, "Does anyone in this room doubt the righteousness of my words?"

Not one of the Southern lords objected.

"Does anyone else believe I lack the honor for my position?" asked Aldrich. His sapphire eyes were pained as he looked to the faces of each of the Southern lords, but again none made a motion. Lord Arnold was near magenta with rage.

"There will come a time when you wished that you had heeded my counsel. As of now, I return to the Lionden Empire," foretold Lord Arnold.

Lord Arnold looked from the Queen to the prince. They offered no words of reconciliation. They only stared at him with loathing. Lord Arnold turned smartly on his heel and left without another word.

"The King of the Island Kingdoms and Captain Egnatius will lead attacks on the Empire on all fronts. I will ride with your Victorious to the Citadel. It is our combined power that will defeat the Emperor. None one of us can do it alone," said Aldrich. He addressed the whole chamber, but Andraste knew he spoke only to her.

"As you wish," Andraste responded at last.

She did not look at Aldrich. She would have to be very careful how she acted with such rumors floating around the palace. She kept her attention firmly on the map before her.

"But a princess-" frowned the Queen.

"I am Paramerion, leader of the Victorious, and sworn warrior and protector of the Empire. I will waste no more time with this farce. I am a warrior of the North. I was a Commander of the Imperial Army. Do not speak to me of archaic customs and prude traditions. In the North, any who pick up a spear can fight regardless of their gender or station. I will fight and I will defeat any who stand in my way! To those who can swallow their pride and follow a female warrior, my Victorious leave in three days' time. Ride with me if you have the courage, but those cowards, who stay behind safe behind this city's walls have no right to judge me!" cried Andraste. Her sea-green eyes flashed as she slammed down her fists on the table. She looked dangerous.

"Fine words, Commander," approved Laelius.

"Is there anything else?" asked Andraste.

The King of the Island Kingdoms shook his head. Andraste left the room. She heard footsteps in the hall.

"Princess-" started Aldrich. She swung around in anger.

"Do not call me that," she said vehemently.

Andraste heard whispering down the hall.

"I thank you for your aid, but I cannot continue like this. I will dishonor us both," said Andraste. She did not look at him.

"Paramerion-" started Aldrich. However, seeing the eyes upon them, he stopped. He bowed to her and retreated to the War Chambers.

She saw Rhiannon and Marcella whispering together across the hall. Andraste ignored them and returned to her chambers. She changed from her dress to her uniform. She paced around the library.

"So scary," disapproved Rhiannon at her door.

"This is who I am," stated Andraste.

"You should not have been so cruel to him," chastised Rhiannon.

"We are from the North. It is our way," said Andraste.

"He defended your honor," said Rhiannon, "Do not fear him."

"I am not afraid," objected Andraste.

"You should make an effort to meet the Southern ladies. They are quite friendly. Come to the sewing room with me," Rhiannon tried a different path. Andraste glared at her sister.

"I will ride," said Andraste. Rhiannon sighed.

"Do you need yet another scar? Rhinauld and Henry will accompany you. It is not safe for any of us to ride alone," compromised Rhiannon. Andraste relented. She waited for the knights to join her.

"I do not remember you being so petrifying," commented Henry.

"I do not recall you being so nice," retorted Andraste.

"I like you better now that I know you are not trying to cap your hat at my lord," said Henry. Rhinauld looked abashed and cleared his throat.

"Henry, that is enough," ordered Rhinauld. The two men shared a look of understanding that made Andraste increasingly uncomfortable.

"Shall we go?" asked Andraste. She did not wait for a response. She left her rooms hastily.

"Will you not join us?" Egnatius called out to them as they passed Aldrich's chambers.

Andraste paused in the doorway and surveyed the seven Southern ladies that she had encountered the day before. They were joined by ten Southern lords.

"In the hottest hours of the day, we often retire indoors," explained Egnatius.

Rhinauld pushed Andraste gently in her back, so that she would enter the room. She glared at him.

"We would be delighted," said Rhinauld. He bowed gallantly to the Southern ladies, "I am Rhinauld, Lord of the Salt Islands, and this is Sir Henry also of the Salt Islands. You will already know my sister."

"Is it true you have conquered three Ruins?" asked Gerlinde.

"Two with my sister, and one with Henry," replied Rhinauld.

"Rhiannon?" asked Gerlinde in amazement.

"No, Andra," responded Rhinauld. He took Andraste's hand and kissed it. At the same time he pulled her further into the room.

"Henry? Must I do the same to you? Come in at once. They are not going to attack us," said Rhinauld.

Andraste and Henry exchanged glances. Henry reluctantly entered the room and took the free space by Andraste's side.

"What are the Ruins like?" asked Eadbehrt. Rhinauld turned his back on the Southern lord and looked to Andraste.

"Challenging," replied Andraste.

"Andra, seriously," sighed Rhinauld, "They are all different. There can be monsters, mazes, duels, riddles, traps. Each one I have seen has been completely different. The Ruins test you in cruel ways."

"You entered the Southern Ruin?" asked Kasimir. All eyes turned to Andraste.

"Did Felix not tell you?" questioned Andraste as she raised her eyes to Rhinauld. He shook his head, but he slowly smiled. They held their gaze for a moment.

"Four?" asked Henry, "You have taken the lead, Empress."

"Why do you call her 'Empress'?" asked Kasimir.

"The Northern traditions allow the eldest daughter to assume the rolls, duties and privileges of the lady of the house if the widower does not remarry," answered Henry.

"I thought the Emperor had four wives," interjected Gerlinde.

"Currently the Emperor possesses four consorts. However, he only married twice. His first wife betrayed him, and was executed for her treason, which nullified any claims of her three children. The second wife,

Victoria, is my lady's mother, and so, as the only heir of the union, Andraste Valerianus is regarded by the majority of the North as the Empress and only true heir of the Emperor," replied Henry.

The Southerners did not approve this arrangement, but Rhinauld ignored them all. He turned his attention to Andraste.

"What did you obtain from the Ruin?" inquired Rhinauld.

"I asked for nothing. I went to speak to the Spirit," replied Andraste.

"Whatever for?" asked Rhinauld in surprise.

Gerlinde was doing her best to get Rhinauld's attention focused on her once more. She glared at Andraste. Henry whispered something into Andraste's ear and she laughed. Gerlinde bristled. Andraste surveyed Gerlinde with a calculating gaze.

"What is the most frightening thing you have ever witnessed?" asked Gerlinde to Rhinauld.

"The kraken," responded Henry immediately.

"If you had been a fan of seafood, it would not have been that bad," replied Rhinauld. The ladies laughed. Andraste rolled her eyes at Henry.

The ladies curtsied and the lords bowed as Aldrich walked into the room. He surveyed Andraste dressed for riding and the knights at her side.

"And you, Lord Rhinauld?" asked Gerlinde.

"The scariest thing I have ever seen?" repeated Rhinauld. Gerlinde nodded.

"Without a doubt, Andraste," replied Rhinauld.

Gerlinde unsuccessively stifled a laugh behind her fan. The Southerners looked to the Andraste in alarm as they awaited her response. However, Andraste laughed.

"I have traveled so little, whereas you have traveled greatly throughout the Empire. What has been your most terrifying encounter, princess?" asked Sonje shyly.

The smile from Andraste's face faded.

"My Empress has seen too many terrible things to name just one," intervened Henry. Although, he spoke softly, the words carried throughout the room.

"Yes, but our travels have shown many beautiful things as well," said

Rhinauld quickly.

"So what is the most beautiful thing you have ever seen?" asked Aldrich. He raised his sapphire eyes to Andraste.

"The sun setting over the beaches here is remarkable. I have never seen its equal," responded Andraste. Aldrich smiled at her in return.

"And you, Sir Henry?" asked Gerlinde.

"My Empress dancing," admitted Henry. Andraste hit him in the stomach with the back of her hand. The knight was unbothered.

"It is true. I have to agree. It is truly a shame. If we were in the North, you would have all witnessed one of the traditional fan dances that my Empress is so talented at performing," said Rhinauld. He was too far out of Andraste's reach to be silenced by a blow.

"Yes, you danced the Island Kingdom dances so perfectly," praised Sonje.

"You should see her dance the Southern waltz," suggested Rhinauld.

"I thought you did not know our dances," stated Aldrich. His smile had faded.

"Of course she does! After all she is a princess of the Empire. We learned all of the dances as children," replied Rhinauld. He glanced to Andraste and saw the firm set of her jaw.

"You have only danced one night since you have been here?" asked Henry.

"So the rumors are true. You have not been well," stated Rhinauld. Both of her knights turned to her in concern. Andraste felt all of the eyes upon her in the room.

"When did you two turn into my nursing maids? I expected men from the Island Kingdoms to have more metal to them," replied Andraste. The Southern lords laughed.

"Andra," sighed Rhinauld.

"My knights and I are going riding. I will not stray as far as I did before," said Andraste. She left the room before Aldrich could respond.

"We were going to have a Northern tea. Would you pour for us?" asked Egnatius.

"Do you know how?" asked Gerlinde skeptically. She already had her hand on the pot. Rhinauld and Henry both glowered at the Southern lady.

"The princess and I have shared tea on our travels," said Aldrich. His back was to Andraste, so she could not see his face. She continued out of the room.

"Did the prince just lie for you?" asked Henry when they were out of earshot.

"Not quite what you are imagining," replied Andraste.

"I knew I liked him," replied Rhinauld, "But now you will have to make him tea."

Andraste decided to ignore her knights as she proceeded towards the stables. She mounted her horse before Rhinauld could assist her. She did not wait for her knights. She spurred her horse forward. She jumped over the practice barrels and raced out of the courtyard. They rode down the hill towards the port, and then onto the beaches. Andraste felt freer then she had in some time.

They found a deserted cove and dismounted. Rhinauld set about fashioning fishing poles, while Henry dug for worms. The two knights seemed to be utterly content together. Without speaking they seemed to move in sink. Andraste sat lazily in the sand. They spent the morning fishing. Henry was the only one to catch anything. They cooked Henry's catch over the fire. The knights went swimming, while Andraste laughed at them from the beach. It was hard to believe that they were planning a war. After lunch, they reluctantly rode back to the city. The sun was setting as their horses were led away to their stables.

"Shall we join the feast?" asked Rhinauld.

Andraste sighed. She followed the knights to the dining hall.

The dining hall was filled with loud voices and laughing. Rhinauld waited for Andraste to pass him. She chose to sit with the Victorious and their families, and her knights followed. There was an exchange of greetings and hugs amongst the two knights and her people. Rhinauld and Henry began to describe some of their adventures.

Andraste scanned the great hall. Aldrich was not seated with the Queen, the King, or his sisters. She saw Aldrich enter some time later. He looked straight to the dais and not seeing her, he joined the table with his men. Aldrich looked exhausted, but he smiled and spoke warmly to his fellows.

"Empress?" Rhinauld was asking. She turned her head to look at him.
"What?" asked Andraste.

"They have asked for a Northern dance. The women are rising. Do you
wish to join them? I or Henry would dance with you," offered Rhinauld.

Andraste saw that many of the Northern women were pants as she did.
She saw that this scandalized the Southern ladies.

"I do not wish to dance," refused Andraste.

Rhinauld shrugged and then asked Laelius's oldest daughter to dance
with him.

"What is with these Southerners and dancing?" Andraste asked Henry.

"It is a fine custom. They are a little repressed, our Southern brethren. They only allow ladies and gentleman to touch by dancing and walking arm and arm. Does that not strike you as strange?" asked Henry. He
pierced her with his brown eyes, but she realized he was looking down the
table to Aldrich.

"Would my Empress prefer a song instead?" asked Henry. He did her
great honor. He was renowned as one of the greatest singers of the Island
Kingdoms. He did not often choose to perform. He would not sing even
when Rhinauld demanded it.

"I would be honored, Sir Henry," said Andraste.

"After their dance then," said Henry.

Henry turned his eyes to Rhinauld, who was quick on his feet. The
Northern dances did not suit the tall Lord of the Salt Islands, but Rhinauld
laughed heartedly and kept up as best he could. Henry and Andraste both
laughed at him. Rhinauld once more tried to get her to dance, but she
refused. Rhinauld lowered her hood so that he could see her face, and
rumpled her hair like he did when she was a child.

"Rhinauld!" Andraste muttered and swiped his hand away.

"You are angering our host again," commented Henry dryly as he
glanced down the table.

Aldrich did look seriously displeased. Rhinauld made a face at them
both and then harassed Rhiannon into dancing with him. They made an
elegant pair as they danced to a tune from the Salt Islands. Rhinauld and
Rhiannon stopped to address Aldrich on their way back to their table.

"I really hate him sometimes," said Andraste, glaring at her foster brother.

"He does so enjoy meddling," stated Henry tiredly.

The conversation between Rhinauld and Aldrich seemed civil enough; although, despite his best efforts, Aldrich still eyed Rhinauld with scarcely contained loathing.

"You know, that prince is as scary as you are. After a night of drinking, telling stories and brawling, any other men would be friends," commented Henry.

Andraste jabbed Henry mercilessly in his ribs with a serving spoon. Henry showed no signs of it bothering him or even noticing.

"What did you say to him?" Andraste inquired as Rhinauld helped Rhiannon to a seat beside Andraste.

"That it would please my Empress to hear a song from her homeland," whispered Rhinauld in her ear as he sat beside her.

Rhiannon giggled behind her fan. Andraste blushed. She turned her eyes to Aldrich. He was watching them carefully. Aldrich rose and signaled for quiet.

"Sir Henry of the Salt Islands will entertain us with a song from his homeland," Aldrich introduced.

Aldrich positioned himself so that he could face Henry, which put Andraste in his direct line of sight. However, she turned her back on him and focused her attention completely on Henry. Henry had stood and walked to the center of the aisle. Henry began to sing. Andraste had not heard the ballad for some time.

"Lost to me are those I loved, though I raised my sword,
You know me not, and trust me not, but I pray a word.
That that comes you cannot stop, fiercely though you try,
I and mine would fight with you, though we all may die.
My country gone that I will never know once more,
I would never see you lose as I did before.
True never together have we fought side by side,
Our ways and traditions wore too great a divide.
None of that matters now, as I stand at your door,

The enemy makes haste and war will destroy more.
The great Eastern ships we sail bring men strong and true,
Never together have we fought, but today we fight with you.
If we fall for your cause all we ask in return,
For our bones be laid to rest where our loved ones burnt.
May our bones rest with their ashes on a land soon forgot,
But if we die, we die at your side, and friendless you were not."

Henry's song ended to thunderous applause.

"Political brute," said Rhinauld with pride as Henry bowed.

"What do you mean?" asked Rhiannon.

"He makes a good point. Particularly after that nasty council meeting this morning," replied Rhinauld. Henry rejoined them and Rhinauld clapped him on the back perhaps too enthusiastically.

"Where did you learn that song?" Aldrich asked from his table.

"My Empress taught it to me. It is a song from the Island Kingdoms regarding the time before the First Republic," replied Henry.

Henry bowed to Andraste before he took his seat. Aldrich and his lords returned to their table's discussion.

"Is that a tear?" Rhinauld asked in alarm as he looked at Andraste.

"My mother used to sing that song," Andraste said. She hastily brushed a tear from her face as if she was moving a strand of hair.

"Andra," consoled Rhinauld. All of his merriment had faded. He reached for her, but she rose from the table. Her face was once more composed.

"Thank you, Henry. It was beautifully delivered," Andraste said. Henry did not respond.

"There you are, princess. I could not find you due to your current attire. You were missed at the head table," commented Marcella as she walked by their table.

Marcella was greeted by all. Rhiannon shot Marcella a look of warning.

"Are you well?" asked Marcella. She looked at Andraste with sisterly concern.

"Could I trouble you for a sleeping draft?" asked Andraste.

Andraste was exhausted, but she feared her dreams. She feared causing another disturbance and waking again in the prince's arms.

"Of course, I will have one sent to your chambers," said Marcella. She continued on her way.

"Sleeping draft?" asked Rhinauld.

Brion had already informed Rhiannon of Andraste's nightmares, who in turn had told her brother. Rhiannon and Rhinauld exchanged glances.

"I will retire for the evening," said Andraste.

Rhiannon rose to join her and led the way down the hall. Rhiannon stopped in front of Aldrich's table. Andraste almost walked into Rhiannon due to the abrupt stop.

"Good night, we are retiring for the evening. We are so enjoying your hospitality," said Rhiannon. She curtsied prettily.

Aldrich rose and bowed to them both. Andraste inclined her head in acknowledgement. She continued on her way.

"How was your ride?" asked Aldrich politely. Andraste turned to address the prince.

"The beaches are lovely. We found the fishing quite satisfactory," replied Andraste.

"I hear that your largest festival approaches," prodded Rhiannon.

"Yes, it is the Festival of the Gods. It is a costumed ball full of much revelry," said Aldrich.

"Costumes?" purred Rhiannon, "What do we dress as?"

"Aldrich will be the God of War," interjected Kasimir.

"And you will be the God of Wine," commented Eadbehrt and the lords laughed.

"I did not bring anything suitable," pouted Rhiannon.

"You do not dress like gods in the Island Kingdoms?" asked Andraste. Rhiannon nudged her with her fan.

"I will have my sister and Decima help coordinate your outfits," said Aldrich. He looked to Andraste for approval.

"I thank you, but we plan to leave early on the following morning-" started Andraste, but was stopped as Rhiannon stepped on her foot.

"My sister can delay her journey a few days. We thank you. We will be delighted to attend. My sister and I appreciate your favor," interrupted Rhiannon.

Rhiannon curtsied once more to Aldrich, who again bowed. Rhiannon wrapped her arm in Andraste's and pulled her down the hallway before Andraste could object.

"And people say I am scary, you devious little gutter-" Andraste whispered to Rhiannon's ear.

"Language, niece," said the King of the Island Kingdoms. They were passing by the dais.

"Sorry, your Majesty," the girls chimed together and Rhiannon curtsied perfunctorily. He dismissed them with a wave of his hand.

Andraste was so furious that by the time she reached her chambers, she did not even say goodnight to Rhiannon. Rhiannon was not perplexed. She followed Andraste into her chambers.

"Look, a present!" exclaimed Rhiannon.

Andraste saw a box waiting on the table. She opened it gingerly and found a traditional Northern tea set waiting for her. She shook her head as she opened the card.

"Rhinauld," said Andraste.

"But why a tea set?" asked Rhiannon.

"He thinks I owe the prince tea," responded Andraste. She glanced at her smiling sister, "But he already told you."

"I picked it out this afternoon," responded Rhiannon.

"It is beautiful, and I will admit, this is one Northern tradition that I miss," conceded Andraste.

"There is tea from the Salt Islands in the box, I thought it might help you sleep," encouraged Rhiannon.

"Many thanks," said Andraste.

Andraste picked up the box and opened it, the fragrance of lavender, mint and chamomile filled the room. It smelled like the gardens of Rhinauld's castle. It reminded her of home.

"Are you still with me?" asked Rhiannon, "Still my same day-dreaming, sister?"

"I was thinking of the Salt Islands," replied Andraste.

"I will leave you to your thoughts. You looked so happy," announced Rhiannon.

"No, stay for tea," said Andraste, "It would be so sad to drink alone."

Rhiannon removed her shoes and sat on Andraste's sofa. She curled her feet up underneath her. Andraste rinsed the pot out, filled it again with clear water, and then set the pot on a hook over the fireplace.

"You are actually making tea?" laughed Rhinauld from the doorway.

"I love tea. I always have," stated Andraste. She did not turn to face him.

"So you like our gift?" asked Rhinauld.

"Yes, thank you, but it was not necessary," replied Andraste.

"Should not a brother dote on his sisters?" Rhinauld asked. He kissed Rhiannon on the forehead and then Andraste.

"Go away, Rhinauld!" said Andraste. She shoved him playfully. She turned and saw Aldrich and Henry in the doorway.

"Henry, please take Rhinauld away," requested Andraste. She turned her back on the men as she poured hot water into the tea pot.

"Yes, Empress. Where would you have us go?" questioned Henry.

"You may decide," replied Andraste.

"We were going to have a drink with the prince. Do you not want to join us?" Rhinauld asked them both.

"We are going to enjoy our tea," replied Rhiannon. She rose, "Or perhaps the prince would like to join us for tea instead?"

"I would be honored," said Aldrich. He bowed low to both ladies in one sweeping gesture.

"We will find a real drink elsewhere," said Henry.

Andraste heard Aldrich enter the room. She turned and bowed to him. Aldrich bowed to her in the Northern style. Rhinauld and Henry exchanged looks and left. The both made over-exaggerated bows to the ladies before they departed. Rhiannon giggled. Andraste turned her back towards them, so she could examine the status of the kettle.

"Please make yourself comfortable," invited Andraste.

Aldrich sat in the chair nearest the fire. Aldrich watched Andraste as she cleaned each of the cups, tea whisk and tea scoop with graceful movements. As the kettle began to whistle, she discarded the hot water in the tea pot and set tea in the strainer. She retrieved the kettle and poured hot water into the tea pot slowly. She did not spill a drop. She set the kettle on the hearth. She returned the lid to the tea pot.

"Do you drink much tea in the South?" asked Andraste.

"No, we do not, but my mother does. I assume it is a habit that she picked up from her time in the North," responded Aldrich.

"This tea is actually from the Salt Islands. Northern tea is much bitter," said Andraste.

"As are most things from the North," amended Rhiannon. Andraste laughed.

"That is true, better things come from the Salt Islands, I suppose it is due to the warmth there," said Andraste. She poured weak tea into the cups to warm them and explained the movement to Aldrich, "This way the cups will already be warm."

"When this business is over, you will have to come to me and Brion in the Salt Islands. You are also welcome, Prince Aldrich," said Rhiannon.

"I would like to see them," responded Aldrich.

"What if Brion wishes to stay in the North?" asked Andraste.

"He seems to think that will not be an option with whatever you have planned," replied Rhiannon. She looked at Andraste questioningly.

"He already guessed? No, I will not remain in the North," responded Andraste.

Andraste discarded the tea in the cups and poured the first cup from the steeped tea in the teapot. She offered the cup in both hands to Aldrich. He bowed to her before accepting. His fingers grazed her hand as he took the cup. He took a slow sip from the cup, before meticulously examining the cup in his hand.

"It is delicious. This cup is lovely," said Aldrich. He offered the cup to Rhiannon.

"You know the ways of the North?" approved Andraste. She smiled at him in delight.

"My court made me practice earlier," responded Aldrich. He looked uncomfortable.

"Gerlinde seemed quite proficient," said Andraste.

"It was Kasimir and Eadbehrt that instructed me," admitted Aldrich.

Andraste laughed as she imagined the Southern lords teaching Aldrich the Northern tea ceremony. She offered Rhiannon a cup of tea. Rhiannon bowed to Andraste and took the tea. She took a sip and then returned it to Andraste.

"If you wish to learn Northern ways, you could ask me," said Andraste as she poured another cup of tea and offered it to Aldrich. His fingers gently touched her wrist as the cup was passed. Andraste turned quickly to refill Rhiannon's cup. She poured herself a cup and took a sip.

"Would you be the best teacher?" inquired Rhiannon.

"I may not be a courtier, but I am lady enough to serve tea to Aldrich Caelius better then Southern lords," commented Andraste.

"I find nothing lacking in your service," said Aldrich.

"Just do not eat anything my sister cooks. You may die," warned Rhiannon. Aldrich stifled a smile, but turned his sapphire eyes to Andraste. She ignored Rhiannon.

"So who actually are the ladies I have met twice in your chambers?" asked Andraste.

"My harem?" inquired Aldrich. His eyes sparkled over his cup of tea.

Rhiannon spat out the tea she was drinking.

"Your sister accused me of keeping a harem in my chambers. The ladies told me what Gerlinde had implied, so I can recognize the misunderstanding. I apologize on her behalf. As Egnatius later told you, I was speaking with my commanders on the veranda, but the doors were shut so we missed each other," explained Aldrich.

"Do your commanders often bring their wives to war councils?" asked Andraste.

"As I said before, in the South we see marriage as a partnership. It is common for married couples to go everywhere together," responded Aldrich.

"But the ladies did not partake in the discussion?" inquired Andraste.

"They can if they wish. At that moment, they were discussing other things," responded Aldrich. He blushed.

"What could be more important than the rebellion?" asked Andraste.

"The prince needs more tea, Andra," interjected Rhiannon. She cast Andraste a look of warning. Andraste poured the prince another cup of tea.

"Why did you not want Rhinauld and Henry to stay? I had thought after so long apart, you would want to see them?" asked Aldrich.

"I can only take my brothers in small doses," replied Andraste.

"We are immensely fond of Rhinauld, but he is a character," agreed Rhiannon, "Although, you must have made a strong impression on him, he never leaves Andraste alone with another man."

"Or he does not see me as a threat," responded Aldrich. He glanced to Andraste.

"We are from the North. Everyone is a threat," replied Andraste.

She reached again for his cup and went to the pour the tea pot, but it was empty.

"I will take my leave," said Aldrich and he rose.

"We can make more," offered Rhiannon.

"No, I will not trouble you," said Aldrich.

He bowed to them both and left the room. He closed the door softly behind him. They heard him enter his chambers.

"Months on the road with that gentleman? I am surprised on two accounts," repudiated Rhiannon.

"Which are?" Andraste inquired as she started to add more water to the kettle.

"I would have thought one of two things would have happened and yet miracles of miracles, both have not. The first being that you did not kill each other, and the second that you are not already sharing chambers," alleged Rhiannon.

"Rhiannon!" exclaimed Andraste. She dropped the kettle and jumped back as water sprouted across the hearth.

"So you do like him?" asked Rhiannon innocently.

"It does not matter. He refused me," said Andraste.

"Tell me what happened," ordered Rhiannon. Andraste relayed the circumstances to Rhiannon.

"But he proposed, or tried to, before you slapped him," stated Rhiannon.

"I think he only proposed out of honor, in order to rectify my error. Regardless, I cannot marry him now. Surely you must see the reasons," rationed Andraste.

"And some day?" asked Rhiannon.

"He is not interested. I refused him. What man would ask again after such a refusal? I did not know the Court was watching. They all saw me slap him, his sister and mother too," sighed Andraste.

"Andra, do you not see how he looks at you? He is always watching you. Are you so indifferent as to not notice the way he scowls at Rhinauld and Henry when they are near you?" asked Rhiannon.

"It is because he loathes us. He detests the North. He despises everything that I am. Do you not see the difference in how he looks at Decima or the Southern ladies? Or how relaxed he is with Decima? He never fights or scolds her," replied Andraste.

"By the gods! I never thought I would witness the day. You are jealous!" laughed Rhiannon.

"Some sister you are!" cried Andraste.

Rhiannon giggled and Andraste could not help but laugh with her. They cleaned the tea set, dried it, and then set each dish back in the box.

"I did spend one night with him," said Andraste. She glanced to Rhiannon to see her sister's reaction.

"And why not more?" asked Rhiannon.

"He distracts me. I thought if I spent one night with him that it would pass, but it has made it worse. My thoughts, now . . . " sighed Andraste.

"Is that why you are so mean to him?" questioned Rhiannon.

"I am not mean. I treat him as I do the other warriors. Besides, after that council meeting, I cannot go to him again. I did not think they would seriously try to depose him for so small a thing," replied Andraste.

"You need to take care, Andra. The Southerners abide by their code of honor. It is not just words. It is their way of life. However, what is the prince to think? You allow him to make love to you and then you ignore him? Berate him? Show him no care what so ever? Then invite him for tea?" asked Rhiannon.

"I cannot imagine his thoughts. I do not know what I think," replied Andraste.

"My poor, scatter-brained sister," sighed Rhiannon, "And poor Southern prince to fall for such a silly duck."

"He has not fallen for me. It will pass," said Andraste, "We will complete our mission, and go our separate ways."

"Are you so sure?" asked Rhiannon.

"How else can it end? Even if we are successful in our mission, we are divided in our views for the Empire. He will destroy it if he has his way. I will preserve it if I have mine. It is most likely we will wage a war against each other. It is a doomed affair," replied Andraste.

"You do not know how many times a stone will skip until you throw it," said Rhiannon.

"You think I am getting ahead of myself?" asked Andraste.

"You never let others close to you. You are waging hypothetical wars in your mind to keep this excellent man at a distance. He is reasonable. He is intelligent. And I am sure that he loves you. You do not think you can find a compromise?" asked Rhiannon. She surveyed her sister with her emerald eyes.

"He has the power to harm me like no other," said Andraste softly.

"You are fearless. Will you let your fear blind you? You take chances all of the time. I see no reason to not take a chance on the prince," stated Rhiannon.

"He is a Caelius. His parents ordered the death of my mother. He is a leader of the Resistance, trying to decimate the Empire. He hates the North," started Andraste.

"There is a negative history there, but we are talking about your future, not the past," said Rhiannon.

"What if he is after the Empire? What if he is just using me?" asked Andraste.

"Look into those gorgeous, sapphire eyes and tell me if you truly need to ask such a question. The prince is earnest. If he had such an agenda, he would tell it to your face," said Rhiannon.

"How did you become his biggest fan?" asked Andraste.

"When I saw him look at you," replied Rhiannon, "If ever there was man, who was your equal, it would be Aldrich Caelius."

"The gods are cruel," said Andraste. Rhiannon laughed softly at her sister. She put the last tea cup in its proper place.

"Can I stay with you? I do not know if I can find my way back to my chambers in this massive palace," requested Rhiannon.

"Of course, there is room for a family of five in my bed," responded Andraste.

Rhiannon proceeded into the bedchamber and laughed.

"You are right. You could have three men in this bed," replied Rhiannon.

"How do you know of such things?" asked Andraste, "You are supposed to be the sweet, innocent sister."

"How have you not tried such things with your freedom and wild nature?" retorted Rhiannon. They laughed together.

Andraste threw a nightgown at her sister, and then changed herself. Andraste climbed into her bed and did not dream that night.

Chapter Nine

Andraste and Rhiannon were taking breakfast on her balcony, when they were interrupted by a knock. Andraste let in Rhinauld and Henry. As she shut the door, she saw the door was open to Aldrich's chamber. She caught a glimpse of the sleeping prince on the sofa.

"He probably wanted to be near enough to hear if you called out," commented Henry. Andraste shut the door firmly. She chose to ignore Henry.

"He is an excellent sort of man, even if he glowers at me a bit too much, but I guess that is my punishment for having such a sister," relented Rhinauld.

"Do you think he heard our conversation last night?" asked Rhiannon in wide-eyed horror to Andraste.

"No, we did not, but we did hear an unseemly amount of giggling. It amused the Southern lords immensely," replied Rhinauld.

"You were with the prince?" interrogated Andraste. She tried to not sound too concerned.

"As we were leaving, we saw some of the Southern lords had already opened the prince's wine. Kasimir and Eadbehrt are fine fellows," responded Henry.

"They know Rhiannon was in the room with us?" asked Andraste.

"Yes, sweet sister," replied Rhinauld.

"What did you discuss?" inquired Rhiannon.

"The relics," responded Henry.

"Why do you think the Emperor wanted those relics?" asked Rhiannon.

"For nothing good," commented Rhinauld. He fixed Andraste with emerald eyes, "What are you planning?"

"My best guess is that if the Emperor requested pieces, that he has accumulated other pieces that will be stored in the Ice Palace," answered Andraste.

"You yourself said you could not go there, and we saw what happened when you touched the pieces we already have," warned Rhinauld.

"No. I said men could not go there," corrected Andraste.

"You wish to stop at the Ice Palace on the way to the Citadel," stated Henry.

"I agree with your prince. I do not think you two should be separated. I think that there are forces beyond our comprehension at work here. Whatever exists between you and the prince is more than simple infatuation. Our King spoke of a prophecy," identified Rhinauld.

"I do not believe in prophecy. We make our own fate. We cannot let the relic fall into the hands of the Emperor. I know this to be true," said Andraste. Her eyes shone fiercely as she looked at the two knights.

"You have heard the prophecy?" asked Rhinauld.

"It is vague. It is nothing that we were not going to do already. The prince and I will continue to the North, and the Resistance forces will attack the Empire as planned," replied Andraste.

"We are not joining the battle, are we?" asked Henry.

"I want you two to capture as many more Ruins as you can. I feel that we need that shield. The same feeling directs me to go to the Ice Palace," answered Andraste.

"Yes, Empress," said Rhinauld and Henry together.

"I want you to take Gnaeus with you," ordered Andraste.

Rhinauld nodded but did not question her.

There was a knock on her door and Laelius entered. Andraste informed him of the new plan and then asked, "Are our preparations made for our departure?"

"Yes, Commander," confirmed Laelius.

"Instruct our men to enjoy themselves but not too much at tonight's revelries. We will leave at first light," ordered Andraste. Laelius bowed and left the room.

"I will also take my leave. The Southern ladies invited me to join them," said Rhiannon. Henry took Rhiannon's arm to escort her to the sewing room.

Andraste spent the rest of the afternoon pouring over the maps and discussing strategy with Rhinauld. When Henry returned, he took a nap on the sofa. Brion and the Victorious came in and out between their other duties.

"Marcella and some of the other sorcerers are going to demonstrate their water magic. Do you want to see?" asked Brion.

Andraste was on her feet almost immediately. She was curious to see the Southern specialty for herself. Rhinauld and Henry decided to join as well. Brion led them to the public pools. The pools consisted of four levels, each leading down a level into the next pool, making a waterfall on each level.

"They have closed the pools for this demonstration, but usually they are open to the public," commented Brion. He raised a hand in greeting as he saw Marcella and three sorcerers approaching them.

"This is Ahmose, Nephthys and Madu, sorcerers of the first circle," introduced Marcella.

"It is an honor," said Brion. He bowed to the sorcerers.

Ahmose summoned a large tidal wave from the first pool and let it crash down to the second level, which got only larger as it crashed on the third, and was breathtaking as it approached them as a tidal wave on the fourth level. Ahmose paused the wave in front of them, so that they could see its might. Madu interfered and with a snap of his fingers the wave dissipated and the water redistributed between the four levels. Not to be out down, Nephthys summoned a large warrior made out of water. She created him a bow and arrows. Her warrior shot arrows at them, but Ahmose summoned a water shield to block the attack.

"Lightning magic is the specialty in the North, yes?" asked Nephthys.

"That is true," confirmed Andraste.

"Will you show us?" inquired Nephthys.

"I would, but I do not have that power," said Andraste.

Nephthys looked at Andraste in disbelief.

"It is true. My sister did not inherit that power," stated Brion, "I myself have not yet learned lightning magic."

"It is safer to start with water or wind," approved Marcella. Her attention was drawn by loud voices from the entrance.

Andraste turned to look as well. It looked like a group of Southern guardsmen and some of her Victorious were entering the pool entrance. Laelius had brought some of his children.

"That is enough for today. We should reopen the pools to the public," Marcella said to her fellow sorcerers. Brion left with them.

"We thank you for your demonstration," said Andraste.

The sorcerers returned to the palace. Laelius's children approached her. Laelius watched them cautiously, but continued his conversation with the Southern guardsmen. Rhinauld and Henry went to join him.

"Do you mean to swim as well?" Lae asked Andraste.

"It is acceptable. There are water clothes for ladies," said Marcella.

"No, thank you. I will return to the palace. There are some reports I would like to go over before dinner," said Andraste. Lae's face fell.

"But I will stay a while with you. Shall we explore the shallowest pool together?" Andraste asked, offering her hand to Lae. He took it in his tiny hand, and his sister, Plumeria, grabbed Andraste's other hand.

"That would be the top level. It is the safest for children," Marcella said. She waved goodbye as they passed.

Andraste signaled to Laelius that she was taking the children to the top level. He nodded. The children climbed the steps to the top pool. Once they reached the top, she rolled up her pant legs to her knees, so that she could wade in with the children.

"Not too deep," cautioned Andraste.

"What sort of game is that?" Plumeria asked her.

Andraste looked to where Plumeria was pointing. Northern and Southern men had entered the deepest pool and were playing some sort of game that involved a ball and hoops.

"I do not know that game," answered Andraste.

She saw that Aldrich had arrived at the pool. He took off his sandals and placed them against the wall. He took off his cape and tunic and left them on the floor. He was greeted by his men. He spotted Rhinauld and Henry and then scanned the pool before him. Rhinauld pointed in her direction. Andraste looked down to Plumeria hastily. Lae was trying to go into the deeper part of the pool, but his older brother was pushing him back. Andraste went to the rescue and scooped Lae up in her arms.

"But I want to go to!" cried Lae.

As he struggled against her, Andraste lost her balance and they both went down into the cold water. Lae and the children laughed. Andraste composed herself.

"Let us play a game in the shallow end," soothed Andraste. Lae was pacified. They began to play sharks and minnows in the shallow water.

"Daddy! Daddy! Come play with us!" Plumeria yelled to her father.

Laelius laughed and joined in their game. Andraste played for a little longer and then made her exit. She picked up her boots and socks in one hand and descended the stairs barefoot to the bottom level.

"Sneaking off are you? Come join the game. You are already soaked. It is similar to water basketball we play in the Salt Islands," said Henry from the edge of the pool.

"You can look at your maps later. Come here," said Rhinauld.

He was already out of the pool, water dripping off his bare chest and from his black curls. His smile faded as he saw Andraste's tension. Instead he picked his emerald cloak from against the wall and wrapped it around her shoulders. Andraste grew conscious of her soaked clothing clinging to her skin and her hair becoming undone from her braids.

"What is it, Andra?" asked Rhinauld. He tussled her hair and she glared at him. He raised her hood so that he could not see her icy stare.

"That is better. This is more you. Now tell me what is wrong," said Rhinauld.

"It is nothing. I just feel like I have forgotten something important. My head has been hurting for days. I just cannot remember," replied Andraste.

"My ship is moored not far from here. It is closer than the palace. You could rest there a while," said Rhinauld.

"I am headed back to the palace. I will escort you. You will need to get ready for the festival," said Aldrich.

Aldrich had already reached for his own shirt and put it over his head. Andraste turned to look away, but still caught a glimpse of his muscles. She was reminded of their last evening together. She started repeating the names of Northern kings in her mind to remain focused.

"You just arrived. I will not trouble you," said Andraste.

"Go with the prince. His healing powers will help your headache. I will see you at dinner," said Rhinauld. He tussled her hair again just to irritate her.

Aldrich picked up his own sandals in his hand and walked barefoot as she did. He went a few steps ahead and then turned to wait for her. Andraste followed after him. He did not speak to her.

"How were the Chambers of Justice?" asked Andraste.

"About the usual, farmers squabbling over livestock, lords fighting over a boundary line, merchants quibbling over rights," answered Aldrich.

"Do all disputes come before you?" inquired Andraste.

"Only the cases that cannot be resolved in the lower courts. What is the system in the North?" asked Aldrich.

"I am not familiar with our legal system. I did not spend much time at court," said Andraste, though all she could think of was the courtyard of the Citadel, when she had interfered with the Emperor's justice. Aldrich seemed to sense her retreat and did not ask her further questions. They continued to the palace in silence. Aldrich hesitated as they reached the steps of the palace.

"I am sorry to take you from your game," apologized Andraste.

"It is nothing. I enjoyed our walk," returned Aldrich. He took a tentative step closer.

"We have not been alone since that night. You have not sought my company. In fact, I think you are avoiding me. It was Rhiannon who invited me for tea. Are you angry with me? Have I offended you?" asked Aldrich.

Andraste was saved from a response as she saw the Queen and some of her ladies, including Rhiannon and Shannon, stop in the entrance corridor to watch them. Aldrich sighed and took a step back.

"I know the rest of the way from here, thank you," said Andraste loudly.

Aldrich bowed to her as she passed. She made her way quickly to Rhiannon and Shannon. Gerlinde glared at Andraste as they brushed shoulders on the stairs. Gerlinde misstepped, the heel of her delicate shoe napped in two, and the lady slid down two stairs. She landed in a heap. Andraste glanced over her shoulder and saw that Aldrich was already at the fallen lady's side. Gerlinde was near fuchsia with embarrassment.

Andraste had reached Rhiannon and Shannon's sides. Rhiannon's eyes narrowed as she watched Gerlinde.

"Definitely on purpose," whispered Shannon. Rhiannon nodded her consent.

"Go back," said Rhiannon.

"Whatever for? If she is injured, Aldrich he will heal her. If she is not, he will proceed with his business. Regardless of either option, I would be superfluous," replied Andraste.

"He has a free afternoon, and she is about to steal it from you," stated Rhiannon. She nudged Andraste in her side.

Andraste turned back to look at Gerlinde. Aldrich was examining the lady's ankle from a distance. Andraste laughed heartedly. Aldrich stopped his efforts and turned to survey her. Gerlinde lowered her foot and lifted long, elegant fingers to Aldrich for assistance. She regained his attention and he helped her to her feet.

"I am unharmed after all. Would you care for a walk in the gardens, my lord?" asked Gerlinde.

"Your footwear will not permit such a feat," said Aldrich. Gerlinde daintily stepped out of her shoes.

"Now, I will go about as you are," said Gerlinde.

"Devious fox, although well played," admitted Shannon. She glared at Gerlinde for Andraste.

"You really do not care?" asked Rhiannon.

"We have no understanding. I have no right to care," said Andraste, "Besides I was coming for you two. Do either of you fancy a sail?"

"Have you a ship, my lady?" asked Shannon.

"I was hoping to borrow yours," replied Andraste.

"Mine is docked for repairs," replied Shannon.

"Then we will commandeer Rhinauld's. I know his crew very well," said Rhiannon, "But you should tell the prince that you are leaving the Capitol."

"We will not go far. I will not intrude on his social time," said Andraste. Shannon and Rhiannon exchanged looks.

"I believe the Queen desires a word," said Rhiannon.

"Of course she does, I am soaked from head to foot, barefoot, and in total disarray," replied Andraste. Shannon laughed behind her. They approached the Queen and Andraste bowed in the Northern style.

"Good morrow, your Majesty," said Andraste.

"Have you been for a swim?" asked the Queen.

"Laelius's children," responded Andraste.

"You both let them get away with murder," stated Rhiannon. She eyed her sister's soaking clothes in disapproval.

"I did say there were water clothes for ladies," commented Marcella, "Whose cloak is that?"

"Rhinauld's," answered Andraste.

"And barefoot? Andraste, they are going to think we are wolves, not ladies," sighed Rhiannon.

"I go about barefoot most of the time. Leave her alone," commented Decima.

"The gardens are suitable for bare feet. Perhaps my son could show you the grounds?" asked the Queen.

"I have seen the gardens already. They are quite beautiful. I would not intrude on his time. I have been so much trouble. I do not wish to bother him," replied Andraste. She ignored Rhiannon's elbow nudging her in the ribs.

"We have a bit of mischief planned this afternoon already," said Shannon.

"Indeed?" asked the Queen.

"I plan to commandeer a ship, your Majesty," answered Andraste.

Behind her the Southern ladies were torn between laughter and looks of mortification.

"Aldrich would take you on his ship, if you asked," said the Queen.

"But, that would rob us of the look on Rhinauld's face, when he finds his ship has been taken by three women from the Island Kingdoms. It also looks as though the prince has been commandeered himself," replied Shannon.

Andraste glanced over her shoulder and saw that Gerlinde had succeeded in wooing the prince towards the gardens; although, Aldrich was watching Andraste and the Queen closely.

"She won this round," conceded Rhiannon.

"Enjoy your afternoon, your Majesty," said Andraste. She bowed in the Northern style while Shannon and Rhiannon both curtsied. They hurried quickly down the stairs before the Queen could respond.

"Do you not want to change?" asked Rhiannon.

"If we tarry too long, we will lose the wind," answered Shannon.

"I am more worried about the tide," replied Andraste.

"You are both incorrigible," stated Rhiannon.

"You are slowing us down, Rhiannon," said Andraste.

She and Shannon smiled conspiratorially and began to run towards the port. Rhiannon removed her heels and then ran after them. They all arrived winded at Rhinauld's ship.

"What is the occasion?" asked Henry. He leaned over the ship's edge to help them aboard. He steadied Shannon and pulled her across.

"We have come to commandeer your ship," stated Shannon.

"You know better than to tell a rival crew of your intentions," snorted Henry.

"Is your lord on board?" asked Andraste.

"Aye," said Henry. Andraste leapt across her own, leaving Henry to guide Rhiannon across.

"Is that my Andra's voice?" asked Rhinauld. He came from below deck, Kasimir and Eadbehrt in tow.

"I have come to steal your ship," replied Andraste.

"You need only ask. Where you do you want to go?" asked Rhinauld.

"Anywhere, as far as we can, but in time to return for dinner," replied Andraste.

"Are you not concerned for your prince's safety?" asked Kasimir.

"The prince chose to spend the afternoon with Lady Gerlinde. Let us see how she fares as a protector," replied Andraste.

"Is that wise?" asked Rhinauld. Andraste paused to listen.

"Are my Victorious already on board?" asked Andraste.

"All save five that are guarding the Caelius family," replied Henry.

"What are you up to?" inquired Andraste. Rhinauld only flashed a pearly grin. He looked past her to the Southern lords.

"My lords, you wished to see the *Sea-Demon* out on the ocean? Do you wish to join us or are you going ashore?" asked Rhinauld.

"We will remain," answered Kasimir.

"Do you still have some of my things in your cabin?" asked Andraste.

"Go on ahead," replied Rhinauld. He caught her hand and kissed it as she passed. Andraste laughed at him.

"When my sister is aboard she stays in Rhinauld's cabin, and Rhinauld stays with Henry," said Rhiannon quickly. The Southern lords looked unconvinced.

Andraste found her way to Rhinauld's cabin and found it in its usual state of disarray. She opened her drawer and found that she had a stash of clothes still stored away. She removed her wet clothes and dressed in thick leggings, a linen undershirt, wool socks, and a thick leather tunic from the Island Kingdoms. She found a pair of her boots stored in Rhinauld's cabinet. She used his comb to untangle her tresses, than she pulled all of her hair back in a braid. She remerged feeling substantially better.

"At last, there is my goddess from the Island Kingdoms," said Rhinauld.

"Still only a sea monster awaits me," replied Andraste.

"Do you not mean goddesses?" asked Shannon. Rhinauld laughed at her.

"Your rigging is loose," stated Andraste as she surveyed the ship.

"My rigging is exactly as it should be, my lady," replied Rhinauld with a rakish grin. He turned to see her study the rigging.

"She is right, look at the mast," said Henry. Rhinauld and the Southern lords turned to study the mast. Andraste was already climbing the robes and making her way to the faulty area.

"Whatever makes you happy, Empress," called Rhinauld. Andraste laughed from her position. She redid the rigging and then paused to view the horizon.

"Is that smoke?" asked Andraste.

"What do we approach?" asked Rhinauld.

"It is only small fishing villages in this direction," replied Eadbehrt.

"What do you see?" Rhinauld called to the crow's nest.

"It is a village in flames," replied the sailor.

"Change direction, head twenty degrees starboard. Full speed ahead," commanded Rhinauld, "Andra, at my side, at once."

Andraste jumped forwards, and slid down a rope, landing gracefully on her feet.

"Not even a broken shoe," commented Shannon. Rhiannon laughed at her side.

"You obey the Lord of the Salt Islands?" asked Kasimir. Andraste turned sea-green eyes towards the Southern lord.

"He is the Captain of this ship," replied Andraste.

She pursued Rhinauld to the bow. Henry threw Rhinauld a spyglass, which Rhinauld caught and turned towards the flaming village.

"What do you see?" asked Andraste.

"Nothing living," replied Rhinauld. He handed Andraste the spyglass. She took it and looked towards the village. She did not see a single living creature moving about. No one tried to extinguish the wild flames.

"I see no attackers either," said Andraste.

"At this rate and the size of those flames, they could be long gone," stated Rhinauld. Kasimir and Eadbehrt joined them at the bow. Andraste handed the spyglass to Kasimir.

"Whose lands are these?" asked Andraste.

"Aldrich's," replied Kasimir.

"There is no reason to attack this village. It is a simple, peaceful," said Eadbehrt, "They have no quarrel with anyone. They have nothing to steal."

"We will have to go ashore in row boats. The waters are too shallow," warned Kasimir. Rhinauld nodded his consent.

"The waters will look deeper than they are," added Eadbehrt.

"Just let us know when we should anchor," said Henry.

"You will stay on ship," said Rhinauld. He addressed Andraste but his eyes were still locked on the village.

"You are short warriors. You will need Shannon and me," said Andraste.

"I can wield my bow," added Rhiannon.

"No," declared Rhinauld and Andraste in unison.

"Dear one, there are things you do not need to see," amended Rhinauld.

"Rhinauld is right," agreed Shannon.

Rhiannon looked to Henry, but he shook his head in response. Andraste whistled and they heard the laughing below deck subside; shortly afterwards her Victorious emerged on deck.

"So we are at sea?" asked Maximianus.

"Nice of you to join us," commented Otho.

"She is never far from my lord," replied Felix.

"You have been drinking?" asked Andraste.

"Yes, Commander," replied Maximianus.

"You will stay aboard and guard Rhiannon," ordered Andraste.

"Aboard? From what?" asked Otho. Andraste inclined her head towards the village. Otho turned on Maximianus, "You said we would just come aboard and play cards."

"I can never predict the Commander's whims," responded Maximianus.

"Shame of the North," sighed Andraste.

"I can still fight," alleged Maximianus.

"Even drunk, they are better than most," commented Rhinauld.

"Recite the last ten Kings of the North," ordered Andraste.

"I could not do that sober," replied Maximianus.

"Fair enough," commented Shannon.

"Go, drink water," ordered Andraste, "And eat something."

"Are you their mother?" inquired Henry.

"Shut up," replied Andraste, "This is worse than Cato falling off his horse."

"Will no one forget? By the gods! I was shot and poisoned!" cried Cato.

"As were the Commander, Laurentius, and Glaucio, but they all remained on horseback," commented Avitus.

"Ladies present," cautioned Rhinauld as Cato let out an unforgiveable stream of curses. Rhiannon pretended not to hear, but Andraste and Shannon laughed whole-heartedly. Andraste made her way to one of the row boats.

"Stay aboard," ordered Rhinauld.

"It is undisputed that you are Captain of this vessel at sea. However, on land, I follow not your commands," said Andraste.

"I will confine you to the brig," threatened Rhinauld.

"I have broken out before, and I can swim to shore from this distance," replied Andraste.

"The Empress will go," stated Henry.

"She is your responsibility on shore," said Rhinauld.

"Ours," replied Henry. He shared looks with Rhinauld.

"Mine," said Felix.

"Granted," replied Rhinauld.

"Fie!" cried Andraste in exasperation.

"Use your words, Andra," chided Rhinauld, who only glared at her foster brother in response. Shannon, Henry, Felix, Maximianus, Kasimir and Eadbehrt joined her in the first boat. They were lowered down into the Southern waters.

"What is that stench?" asked Eadbehrt.

"Burning corpses," replied Andraste. They fell silent as Henry and Kasimir rowed towards the shore.

They found not a single survivor. Andraste was the first to find a shovel from one of the huts. She began to dig graves behind the village. The others were quick to join her in her gruesome task. Andraste hesitated as they buried the elderly fisherman she had not seen but days before. She closed his eyes and said a prayer to the gods. They dug near ninety graves.

"Mostly women and children; the fishermen must still be at sea," commented Kasimir.

"We must tell our lord," said Eadbehrt.

"We will head back at once," replied Andraste. She brushed a hand through her soot- and sweat-covered hair.

"The wind is favorable," remarked Rhinauld. He lifted his hand to help her into the waiting boat. Rhiannon did not ask any questions as she saw their apparel soaked in blood, soot and grime. They did not speak on the journey back. Andraste stood by Rhinauld's side at the helm.

They continued in silence once they reached the port and as they walked up the hill towards the golden palace. The merriment faded in the banquet hall at they entered. They made their way outside to the veranda where they say Aldrich laughing with the Southern nobility. His back was towards them, so he did not see them approach. Gerlinde was on his arm and whispering into his ear. Her smile was radiant and he laughed at her words.

"My lord, we must speak with you," said Eadbehrt.

Aldrich turned to face his friend, but his smile fell as he saw Andraste.

"Another time," said Aldrich.

"It is of great importance, my lord," said Eadbehrt. Aldrich dropped Gerlinde's arm and folded his arms across his chest.

"Speak," ordered Aldrich.

"Is that blood I smell?" asked Gerlinde. Her rosy cheeks paled, and her emerald eyes widened as she looked to Kasimir.

"It is not ours," reassured Kasimir.

Out of the corner of her eye, Andraste saw the glint of silver. She turned away from Aldrich and surveyed the crowd looking for someone out of place. She saw a flash of dark clothing moving across the veranda. The figure was too small for one of her Victorious.

"Victorious to me!" ordered Andraste. Her men began to push their way through the crowd. Andraste put herself between Aldrich and his assailant. She stepped back into him protectively, but a needle still grazed her leather tunic. Andraste threw off her cloak and the leather tunic immediately.

"Do not touch it!" said Andraste. Her eyes followed see a petite figure running down the veranda towards the stairs to the beach.

Aldrich took a step forward. Andraste slammed her Ruin sword on the stone floor and a ruby circle of light encircled Aldrich. He could not proceed, but no one could touch him either.

"Paramerion!" swore Aldrich.

Andraste jumped onto the stone ledge and raced after the assassin. Her men were still too far because of the crowd. Andraste reached the end of the stone ledge and looked at the steep stairs. She had too much speed to stop. She jumped into the air and landed on the stair railing, sliding to the bottom. The assassin had reached the bottom of the stairs.

Andraste jumped from the railing and nailed the assassin to the ground. The assassin's cowl had been removed. She was the image of Varinia, so alike in features and coloring, except that this woman had cut her hair short, and she had purple swirls tattooed onto the left side of her temple.

"Mavourneen," said Andraste.

"Sister, I have been cursed. Kill me while you have the chance. I cannot control my actions," pled the assassin.

Mavourneen trembled as she tried to hold back her hands. She swept at Andraste with her hand, four needles between each of her knuckles. The tips of each laced with a lethal poison. The Victorious approached and encircled them.

"What do you do, Mavourneen?" cried Laurentius.

"I can help you," avowed Andraste.

She raised her Ruin sword and summoned Aldrich's spirit phoenix. It hit Mavourneen full on and she went to her knees. The purple markings faded from her temple. She dropped the needles in the sand.

"The Emperor will still find me. I cannot escape. We are both condemned to death," alleged Mavourneen.

"If you remain, we will protect you," promised Andraste.

"No, sister. I will go to the Far East," answered Mavourneen, "Take care. More will come."

With lightning like speed, Mavourneen once more had needles in her hands, and she threw them towards all of the Victorious. They were deflected, but when they looked up, the assassin was gone.

"Laurentius, I release you. Go with her," said Andraste.

"No, Commander. She did not want me to follow," said Laurentius. Andraste studied her warrior and realized that he had been struck by one of the needles. Two more lay at his feet.

"Paralytic," said Laurentius. He could not move from his place, nor could he utter another syllable.

"You should release Aldrich," commented Laelius. They could hear his yelling from the veranda.

Andraste sheathed her Ruin sword. They heard running footsteps from the veranda. Aldrich was the first to reach them followed by his Southern lords and Marcella.

"Look how cautious they are being. They are taking the stairs," remarked Otho.

"This why you have a reputation as a show boat," said Maximianus. He cast a grin towards Andraste but her attention was focused on Laurentius.

Aldrich hesitated as he found Andraste kneeling at Laurentius's side. He summoned his spirit phoenix and it healed the wounded warrior. Andraste pulled Laurentius to his feet.

"If you want to go with her, go," commanded Andraste.

"No. There was madness in her eyes," replied Laurentius.

"All the more reason for you to go," stated Laelius.

"You let the assassin escape? All of you?" asked Kasimir incredulously.

"She was innocent. She was bespelled," said Laurentius.

"Who was it?" asked Egnatius.

"Mavourneen Valerianus," admitted Laelius. The Southern lords tensed. They looked to Aldrich for his orders. Andraste turned to face Aldrich.

"You judge my sister too harshly. She is but seventeen. She cannot defeat the Emperor's control. If it was her intention, you would be dead. She needed my help," said Andraste.

"Forgive me, for not forgiving assassins sent to murder my lord," remarked Kasimir.

"That is enough," said Aldrich.

"She was aiming for the Commander," stated Laelius. Andraste ignored them all, and addressed Laurentius once more.

"Go after her," ordered Andraste.

"No, Commander. She has chosen to flee. I have chosen to fight. She will never be free until the Emperor is defeated. As I love her, this I must do, even though I want to pursue her," replied Laurentius.

"Then I accept you back into my service," said Andraste. She offered her hand to Laurentius and he grasped it. They held each other's eyes for a moment.

"Engaged to a Valerianus assassin?" asked Egnatius.

"We all make mistakes," answered Otho. The Victorious laughed and even Laurentius smiled slightly.

Rhinauld removed his own tunic and placed it around Andraste's bare shoulders.

"V? Is it for Victorious?" asked Kasimir as he surveyed Andraste's tattoo on her back shoulder.

"We all bare the mark," replied Laelius.

"Do not go drinking with the Commander in the Far East," cautioned Felix. Laelius shot him a look of warning.

Andraste pulled Rhinauld's tunic over her head. She turned towards the port.

"Paramerion?" asked Aldrich.

"I will stay with my kin tonight," replied Andraste. Rhinauld and Henry fell into step behind her, as did Shannon and Felix.

"I cannot protect against such assassins. My magic was not adequate," stated Marcella.

"They will come for Andra, not for Aldrich. Do not worry. He will be safer if she is not near," responded Rhinauld.

"That is what worries me. He can heal her if such an attack occurs, but not if she is far away," said Marcella.

"We thank you for your concern, but we can protect our own," replied Rhinauld.

"My Victorious will protect me as they have always done. Do not trouble yourself," said Andraste. Aldrich proceeded to follow her.

"Return to your lady. She will care for you better than I can, and be less of a threat," said Andraste. Aldrich approached her, but said nothing. The look in his eyes did not need words.

"Well come if you must, but I stay aboard the *Sea-Demon* tonight," stated Andraste.

"The more the merrier," said Rhinauld.

"What did you want to tell me earlier?" asked Aldrich.

"Lord Eadbehrt should report," replied Andraste. She looked towards the sea and moved closer to Rhinauld.

"The nearest fishing village to the South was attacked. We found not a single living soul," said Eadbehrt.

"Who is responsible?" asked Aldrich.

"We think it an attack from the North," stated Kasimir.

"Most likely Varinia. It was her style," mentioned Andraste softly.

"But there was no reason for such butchery," said Aldrich. His eyes flashed.

"You should signal for your people from the surrounding villages to come within the security of the city's walls," advised Andraste.

"You do not need to remind me my duty," remarked Aldrich.

Andraste bowed her head slightly to Aldrich and headed towards the port. Rhinauld and Henry fell into step behind her.

"He spoke out of anger, not at you but at the events," said Henry.

"I know," replied Andraste, "But I am also of the North. He finds difficulty separating me from the actions of the North."

"Give him time," suggested Henry, "He is a reasonable man."

"I just want to hear our music underneath the stars," said Andraste.

"Wish granted," replied Rhinauld. He wrapped his arm around her shoulders as they walked to the port. As they approached the ship, they heard a melancholy fiddle tune.

"That is truly depressing, so it must be your taste, Andra," commented Rhinauld.

"It does speak to my heart," admitted Andraste.

They had reached the plank to cross over to Rhinauld's ship. Rhinauld effortlessly took Andraste in his arms and carried her across. He set Andraste down on her feet but he kept a hand about her waist. They turned to watch Shannon and Felix approach.

"Felix?" asked Shannon. Felix sighed and replicated the gesture. However, he took his time crossing the plank.

A lighter and merrier tune began to be played by the fiddler. He was joined by other musicians. Andraste made her way into Rhinauld's cabin and bathed. She dressed in leggings from her drawer and one of Rhinauld's tunics. She remerged and sat by the ship's wheel. She could survey the merriment below.

Rhinauld placed a thick blanket about Andraste's shoulders and then went to check on Rhiannon. Two more songs were played before Aldrich crossed the plank. Andraste ignored him, although Rhinauld greeted him warmly. Aldrich made his way to her and sat by her side. Felix brought Aldrich a silver mug before returning to Shannon.

"Do not drink that," advised Andraste.

"Why?" asked Aldrich. He smelled the contents.

"They dump whatever cheap liquor they can find into it. You will regret it in the morning," said Andraste.

"It is not that bad," commented Aldrich. Andraste returned her attention to the musicians.

"I apologize for my words earlier," said Aldrich.

"It was not my place," returned Andraste.

"It was sound counsel," stated Aldrich.

"I know," responded Andraste.

"Eadbehrt and Kasimir told me how you tended our dead. I thank you," said Aldrich.

"It is what should have been done," replied Andraste.

"Andraste," addressed Aldrich.

Andraste turned her sea-green eyes from the musicians to study Aldrich.

"I thank you," said Aldrich.

"How was your garden stroll?" asked Andraste. Aldrich sighed and moved away from her.

"Do not be angry at Gerlinde. Her father pushes her to behave so. He believes that it is time their family line was joined with the Southern Crown. Without her family, Gerlinde is a sweet girl," stated Aldrich. Andraste's lips were pursed in irritation but she did not respond.

"Jealous, my lady?" asked Aldrich. He smiled at her and Andraste's heart skipped a beat. As he stretched his arm behind him for support, he brushed her hip with his thumb.

"I do not know the meaning of jealous. It is not a Northern emotion," said Andraste. She sat up even straighter and raised her head proudly.

"Then let me explain it to you. Every time I see Rhinauld's hands on you, I start contemplating a hundred ways to lead him to an early demise," remarked Aldrich.

"You may not speak so of my kin," stated Andraste.

"Kin? If only that were true," said Aldrich. He moved a strand of hair from her eyes, "Will you return to the palace with me?"

"No. I will listen to the music for a while," said Andraste.

"We could check my room for snakes," suggested Aldrich. Andraste smiled slightly but she shook her head.

"We could check your room for snakes," amended Aldrich.

"We could check my cabin for snakes," rejoined Andraste.

"Your cabin?" frowned Aldrich.

"Rhinauld is loaning me his cabin. Before you turn green with envy, you should know he is bunking with Henry," replied Andraste.

Aldrich surveyed her and accepted a refill from Henry as he passed with a pitcher. They sat and listened to the musicians and watched the Southern stars. Although it was not before long that they were the only ones left on deck, and even the musicians went to find their bunks.

"This may be stronger than I thought," admitted Aldrich as he surveyed his empty mug. Andraste rose to her feet and offered a hand to Aldrich.

"You should bunk with me tonight. I do not think you will find your way back to the palace," said Andraste. She wrapped his arm about her shoulders.

"My palace? Is it far?" asked Aldrich.

Andraste led to her cabin and settled him in the bed. She removed his boots and pushed him down on the bed. She removed her own leggings and boots and climbed in next to him. She watched him for a while. He was already sound asleep.

Aldrich was awoken by the unmistakable feeling of cold steel against his throat. Aldrich quickly opened his eyes and found Rhinauld, Henry and Felix towering over him, each directing an Eastern blade at his jugular. Aldrich realized that his hand was resting on Andraste's bare leg. Aldrich quickly brought the covers around Andraste to conceal her.

"Outside, Caelius," ordered Rhinauld.

Aldrich tried to move, but found he was secured by one of Andraste's arms.

"My head feels as though it has been struck by a hammer," said Aldrich.

"It very well could be," growled Rhinauld.

Aldrich felt Andraste stir beside him. She opened her sea-green eyes and smiled at him. He gestured his head to the men behind her.

"Are we under attack?" asked Andraste. She sat up quickly.

"Personally, not as a people," replied Aldrich dryly.

"Then get out," said Andraste as she turned her head to survey Rhinauld, Henry, and Felix. She laid a hand on Aldrich's chest as he tried to rise. Henry and Felix sheathed their swords.

"Not you, them," said Andraste.

"Andra, this is serious," said Rhinauld. He did not sheath his sword. He turned his emerald eyes to Aldrich, "I demand you marry her."

"I would marry her this instant if she would have me," swore Aldrich.

"Perhaps a poor choice of words," commented Henry. Felix did not smile.

"We would lose many allies from the North and the West if I married the prince. The South would have a claim for rule of the Empire," said Andraste softly.

"I will send Rhiannon to talk you," stated Rhinauld.

"I would prefer to duel," said Andraste, "Did you not notice? He is fully-clothed. Nothing happened. It is no different from me sleeping by his side as we did for months on the road."

"During that time, he thought you were a man," remarked Rhinauld.

"But I knew I was not," replied Andraste. She blushed and looked away.

"See how maidenly she blushes. Leave her be, Rhinauld," said Henry.

"She only blushes when she is guilty," responded Rhinauld. He eyed Andraste and then Aldrich. He reluctantly sheathed his sword.

"If I find you in her bed again, without an understanding between you, I will kill you," vowed Rhinauld.

"I think it will be more like you find her sneaking into his bed," said Felix.

"Felix!" cried Andraste. Henry and Felix both laughed, but Rhinauld's eyes were still murderous.

"The Southern lords approach," informed Shannon from the doorway.

"They probably think I have been abducted," suggested Aldrich.

"Not too smart your brethren," said Rhinauld.

"Easy," said Andraste, "Now if you gentleman will leave so I can get dressed, or I could greet them in your tunic Rhinauld."

"You are going to develop quiet a reputation, my lady. Waking with one lord and dressed in another lord's tunic? You must take care," cautioned Shannon.

"Explain these things to her," said Rhinauld.

"Yes, my lord," replied Shannon.

"Perhaps we should find a woman without such loose morals to be her instructor," suggested Henry.

"Is there such a woman in the Island Kingdoms?" asked Felix. Shannon slapped Felix soundly. The men all winced.

"So I am not the only one so abused," commented Rhinauld.

"Or I," added Aldrich. For a moment they exchanged grins, but Rhinauld's quickly faded as he saw Andraste. Aldrich quickly climbed out of bed. He was very careful to not touch her, nor did he look at her. He followed the Eastern lords out of the cabin.

"Really? All that trouble and you did not sleep with him?" asked Shannon.

Rhiannon paused in the doorway at that moment. Andraste began to laugh and could not stop. Rhiannon and Shannon joined in.

"They are laughing," sighed Rhinauld.

Rhiannon shut the door behind her. She carried a silvery silk gown from the Island Kingdoms. She gestured for Andraste to start getting ready.

"If he were any other man, I would not object and say it is your business. However, you are putting Aldrich at risk. Your lack of discretion reflects poor judgment. A lord has already challenged his right to the throne due to rumors of dishonor," said Rhiannon, "We need the alliance with the South. The King will be angry if we lose our ally because of your romantic involvement."

"Romantic involvement? Is that what we are going to refer to it as?" asked Shannon. Rhiannon silenced her with a look. She began to comb Andraste's hair with a vengeance.

"Ouch!" cried Andraste. Rhiannon ignored her, but she did attack Andraste's hair with less gusto.

"Your penance will be that you must behave as a lady for the rest of the time in the Island Kingdoms. We will expect your best behavior. You will spend the mornings in the sewing chambers with the Southern ladies. You will not move without Felix at your side, and for no reason will you stray into Aldrich's bedchamber unaccompanied," dictated Rhiannon.

"Sewing chambers?" asked Andraste.

"There will be no discussion, or I will tell your uncle," threatened Rhiannon.

"And then he will have to call Aldrich out," advised Shannon.

"I understand," replied Andraste. She rose and looked fully as a princess of the Island Kingdoms should.

"Aldrich will have to look at you now. He was so embarrassed. It was adorable," said Shannon.

"Leave him alone," growled Andraste. She reached for her boots, but Rhiannon held her a pair of slippers instead.

"Really? No one will know," said Andraste.

"No negotiating," dictated Rhiannon, "This way there will be no dueling, no sliding down banisters, or climbing the rigging."

"That sounds like a challenge," said Shannon.

"Do not encourage her," replied Rhiannon.

"I know. We are all to be on our best behavior by order of the Eldgrimson," sighed Shannon.

Rhiannon opened the door for Andraste and she headed out into the sunlight. As she came onto the deck, all of the sailors and soldiers stopped what they there doing to bow to her. Andraste acknowledged them. She heard the discussion on shore pause as the lords turned to survey the response from the men. Aldrich did not finish his sentence as he watched Andraste approach the plank.

Henry came for Rhiannon, carried her across the plank, and set her lightly on her feet. Aldrich risked potential skewering by Rhinauld, but he made it to Andraste's side first.

"If I may?" asked Aldrich. He picked her up in his arms and carried her across the plank. He turned his eyes on Rhinauld, "Lord of the Salt Islands, may I suggest a gangway?"

"Hardly defensible," said Henry.

"And then we cannot assist the ladies," added Felix as he joined Shannon's side.

"You are a rake, Lord Felix," said Shannon. Felix still swooped her up in his arms and grinned broadly as he carried her across.

Aldrich set Andraste gently on her feet and offered her his arm. He led her to one of the carriage-laden elephants. Andraste saw that his horse was saddled.

"I will be aiding in the settlement of the refugees," said Aldrich. Andraste glanced to Rhiannon who shook her head.

"I will be slowly dying in the sewing chamber," replied Andraste. Rhiannon glared at Andraste.

"I will be enjoying my time with the Southern ladies," amended Andraste.

"I would rather battle the Imperial officers then deal with that lot," said Aldrich. Rhiannon turned her glare on Aldrich.

Andraste turned her attention to the elephant as it reared. His handler was unable to control it. The elephant began to run towards the city. One of the Southern lords picked up a spear.

"No!" ordered Andraste. She turned her sea-green eyes on the elephant. It locked eyes with her and quieted. It approached and bowed to Andraste. She let the elephant wrap its trunk around her hand.

"How?" asked Aldrich.

"My lady has a gift with animals," said Felix at Andraste's side. He led her away from Aldrich and helped her into the carriage. She was joined by Rhiannon and Shannon.

"I will see you at the festival," said Aldrich.

"I will be seen," replied Andraste. Aldrich bowed to them and returned to his comrades.

"Is it me or is it warm in here?" asked Shannon. She began to fan herself.

"I know, I love Brion, but I wish he would look at me with such passion," said Rhiannon.

Andraste turned so that she could watch the Southern lords. She saw that Aldrich still had his eyes locked on her. She blushed and Shannon began to fan her. Andraste knocked the fan aside, and they laughed.

"Is Rhinauld accompanying the prince?" asked Andraste.

"So it would appear," replied Shannon.

The elephant rose to its feet and they began their journey upwards towards the palace. Once on the grounds, they were directed towards the music room. Andraste and her ladies curtsied to the Queen as they entered. Rhiannon started to lead the way to the Queen, but Andraste retired to an alcove. Shannon sat by her side. As Sonje was in the middle of playing a harp, Rhiannon could not speak. Andraste sat behind the curtain so that the Southern ladies could not see her. Shannon picked up a book from a shelf and began to read.

"Gardening," mouthed Shannon. She exchanged looks with Andraste. Rhiannon slapped Shannon's knee and Shannon composed herself. Andraste closed her eyes and was soothed by the sound of Sonje's harp. She nodded off and laid her head against the back cushion. She was awoken with a start an hour later by the sound of shrill singing.

"Shhh," chided Felix. He motioned for her to be silent.

Andraste saw that Henry had also joined them. Henry was gritting his teeth and Rhiannon was glaring at them all. Andraste peered around the curtain and saw it was Gerlinde that was berating their ears. Andraste quickly resumed her position and looked away from Felix so that she would not laugh. Gerlinde's song concluded.

"Perhaps one of the lovelies from the Island Kingdoms would wish to entertain us?" asked the Queen.

"Henry?" suggested Andraste loudly. Shannon elbowed her in the ribs.

"With pleasure, your Majesty," said Rhiannon. She rose and took her place in the center of the room. She began to sing a ballad from the Island Kingdoms. Henry and Felix both straightened and turned their attention to Rhiannon. Shannon closed her book. Andraste decided to go back to sleep.

"I thought that was our Rhiannon," said the King from the doorway, as Rhiannon's song concluded to polite applause. All of the assembled rose and curtsied or bowed to the King.

"But where is my niece?" asked the King.

"I am in attendance as requested," replied Andraste. She rose and surveyed the King.

"I would hear you sing," said the King.

"As you wish, Uncle," replied Andraste.

"5 gold pieces if you sing, '120 ways to kill a man,'" whispered Felix.

"Perhaps, your Majesty would like to request a song?" asked Rhiannon quickly.

"Did she hear that from so far away?" asked Shannon.

"'When my love returns', a good, old-fashioned tune from the Island Kingdoms," said the King. Andraste rolled her eyes at Henry and Felix, but she rose. However, she did not go to the center of the room. She stood behind the curtain and sang clearly:

"When my love returns we will walk along the glade,
Hand in hand, or arm in arm, or just side by side,
All the afternoon I will whisper sweet words in his ear,
And with sweet caresses I will massage away his pain,
I will kiss away all thoughts of battle and fear,
And if only for an afternoon I will be his queen,
A crown of wild flowers I will weave for my love,
To lengthen our time alone in the secluded glade,
For when my love departs, there will be no more walks in the glen,
Never more will I smile, will I laugh, until my love returns.
Until my love returns, forever lonely will I be,
For it takes two hands to hold and two arms to embrace,
For it takes two hearts to love and two lips to kiss,
When my love returns the two will become one,
For when we are divided, I just cannot be."

"That was actually quite good, Empress," said Henry as the room filled with applause.

"I never much liked that song," admitted Andraste.

"It is patronizing" affirmed Shannon.

"Come Shannon, you are just as melancholy when Felix is gone," stated Rhiannon.

"You must be daydreaming," contradicted Shannon.

"It is a beautiful song. What man does not want a woman who will miss him when he is gone and care for him when he is home?" asked Felix.

"Perhaps I would feel differently if I had a man who wrote me letters," replied Shannon.

"Oh!" cried Felix in exasperation.

Andraste turned as she heard Aldrich's laughter from the doorway. He had been following their discussion. His sapphire eyes sparkled at her from across the room. Andraste looked away quickly and stepped behind the protection of the curtain.

"Come in, Aldrich," bade the Queen.

"I was drawn in by the singing, but I must attend my duties. Good day, ladies," replied Aldrich. He bowed to the room before proceeding down the hall.

"Andra," summoned the King.

"Yes, Uncle," said Andraste. She rose and followed after the King as he swept out of the hall. She hastened to keep up with him. He glanced down at her.

"Good, I was worried you would have been injured after your tumble yesterday. Although in retrospect, maybe I should not have stopped you from banister diving when you were younger. Apparently it was useful after all," said the King.

"We are Eldgrimsons. I am not so easily broken," replied Andraste.

"That and the prince's healing powers. You are more reckless than usual. Take care. There are some injuries even he may not be able to save you from," said the King.

"Yes, Uncle," replied Andraste.

"I also heard about your tumble this morning," said the King as they moved away from the room, "Your actions can have repercussions on the Empire. You must think before you act."

"Yes, Uncle," said Andraste. She blushed as she surveyed the stone floor.

"That being said, at the festival it would be awkward if Aldrich did not escort you. The Queen has arranged and expects it. It would raise too many questions if he did not escort you. That being said, you must be on your best behavior. All eyes will be upon you. Your represent the North and the Island Kingdoms. Your actions must be beyond reproach," said the King, "We are warriors, you and I, so the court life is irritating, but we are guests here. The Caelius family is our ally and can do them no harm.

After the festival you will spend as little time with the prince as possible. Rhinauld, Henry, Felix or Brion will be with you at all times, as will Rhiannon and Shannon. Two of the Victorious will guard you as well. It is not safe here for a Valerianus. You are not behaving like yourself. You are overlooking threats and being careless. We must execute constant vigilance. You are the last of our house as such we cannot risk you."

They had reached her chambers.

"You will stay in your rooms until Rhiannon comes for you. Rhinauld and Henry will keep you company," ordered the King.

"As you command, your Majesty," said Andraste.

"No fight? No protests?" asked the King.

"I would prefer to be confined to my chambers then the music hall or sewing room," answered Andraste.

The King kissed her fondly on her forehead and chuckled as he departed. Andraste entered her study and began to scan the reports on her desk. She heard a knock on her door and found her foster brothers studying her.

"I am confined to quarters," said Andraste.

"Commander will accept orders from the King of the Island Kingdoms?" asked Felix.

"I no longer have my rank, wealth, or privileges. I must obey my uncle," replied Andraste, "And in this circumstance, he is right."

"The fierce Andraste Valerianus tamed. I never thought I would see the day," said Henry.

"Are you going to stand there or are you going to enter?" questioned Andraste.

Felix was the first to enter. He produced a deck of cards from his pocket and shuffled them masterly in his hands.

"Pray be seated," said Andraste. Rhinauld and Henry came in as well. Felix all dealt them a hand of cards.

"Should we play some fancy Southern game?" asked Felix.

"I am tired of these Southern ways," replied Rhinauld.

"Poker it is," said Felix.

"What are you doing?" asked Maximianus from the doorway.

"We are playing house," replied Andraste, "Why are you here?"

"Laelius ordered us on sentry duty because he was ordered by the King," said Otho.

"This is ridiculous. Six warriors confined to guard an Imperial Commander on a beautiful day. Come in and join our game," said Andraste.

"You are exiled, condemned to death, and the Emperor has sent assassins and his personal guard after you," commented Rhinauld. He did not raise his eyes from his cards.

"You are not taking the situation seriously," added Henry.

"I am raising the stakes," said Andraste. She added in all of her coins.

"Fold," said Rhinauld and Henry together.

"I think you are bluffing," said Felix.

"Fold," said Maximianus.

"I match your wager," said Otho. Felix and Otho put in their coins.

Andraste revealed her hand and Rhinauld laughed, while Felix swore. Andraste retrieved all of the coins.

"So this is where you escaped to?" asked Shannon as she swept into the room.

"Escaped? I am imprisoned," replied Andraste.

"Deal me in," demanded Shannon. She sat on the floor by Felix's feet. He rose to give her his seat, but she shook her head. She leaned against his legs.

"I can see your cards from here," said Felix.

"Then do not look," replied Shannon. Felix dealt her a new hand and she concealed them.

"It does not matter. You cheat," retorted Maximianus.

"We should go to the sewing chambers," said Rhiannon.

"Andra has been ordered to remain here," said Rhinauld.

"Go on ahead," said Andraste, "I know you do not care for cards."

"As you wish," said Rhiannon, "I will return with Decima and Marcella, so we can get ready for the festival together."

Chapter Ten

Decima produced a costume from a box and held it up to Andraste for inspection.

"Where is the rest of it?" asked Andraste. The breast plate was missing the rest of the armor that should protect her stomach.

"This was the fashion. In the portraits nearest the Chamber of Justice this is what the Goddess of Victory is depicted as wearing," explained Marcella. She also held up a long glittering gold skirt made of a very fine gold cloth. When the light hit it, it resembled fine chain mail.

"What are you wearing?" asked Andraste.

"I am going as the Goddess of the Hearth," replied Marcella, "But I am the mother of three children. I went as the Goddess of Victory in my first season. The design of Decima's costume is similar to your own."

"Goddess of Agriculture," explained Decima.

"And you?" asked Andraste.

"Goddess of the Sea," blushed Rhiannon. She held up a turquoise gown that did not possess sleeves. It looked like it had a very clinging fabric.

"Such apparel for such strict codes of conduct," remarked Andraste.

"It is one day a year," laughed Marcella.

"We are guests. We must follow the traditions of these lands," said Rhiannon.

"I was once a Commander of thousands," sighed Andraste. She picked up the breast plate and held it out far in front of her.

"And I imagine you will be again. Cheer up. It is a festival! I have heard no other festival can rival it in all the Empire," said Rhiannon. Her eyes sparkled with excitement.

"Rhinauld will call me a lady of the night," stated Andraste.

"He will not!" stated Rhiannon.

"I bet you a gold coin that he will," said Andraste.

"I will take that bet and I will slap him if he does," offered Decima. Andraste and Rhiannon laughed, while Marcella looked equally mortified and concerned.

"What do the men wear?" asked Andraste.

"Do not fret. They will be as scantily clad as we are," stated Decima. Andraste looked alarmed, while Rhiannon giggled.

The ladies dressed and helped each other with their hair. Andraste felt exposed by her bare midriff, but Decima did not seem to mind in the least. Andraste reminded herself that she was raised as a princess of the Empire. She drew herself up to her full height.

"The rules are slightly changed for this festival," commented Marcella as they approached the dining hall, "You are both assigned an escort for the entire evening. Rhiannon will be escorted by her betrothed, and because of your rank, you will be escorted by Aldrich. He is not pleased either. Nor are many of the Southern ladies. I would stay clear of Gerlinde if I were you."

They passed through the courtyard. Andraste swept past the Victorious. They did not recognize her at first. Felix for once was lost for words, but Otho opened his mouth to speak.

"Not a word," commanded Andraste.

"Yes, Commander," said Maximianus. He kept his eyes locked on the horizon. Not one of her men would look at her.

Rhinauld left his knights to approach Andraste. He surveyed both of his sisters. He was not pleased. Brion and Henry followed behind him.

"Do you not think this is too ... revealing?" inquired Rhinauld. Decima laughed in his face.

"Lord Brion, do you object?" questioned Rhiannon as her betrothed took her hand.

"You look beautiful. Are you content?" asked Brion as he kissed her hand. Rhiannon blushed.

"As you are spoken for, I will leave it to your future husband. But

Andraste-" started Rhinauld.

"My lady, you could tempt even me in that costume," agreed Henry.

Rhinauld quickly reached to wrap his cape around Andraste's shoulders. Decima laughed and shielded Andraste from Rhinauld's advance.

"Would you so offend your Southern hosts by so disparaging our traditions?" asked Marcella.

"If you dress my sisters like common strumpets, yes," replied Rhinauld.

"Strumpet is better than lady of the night," pacified Marcella. She tried to block Andraste's path.

"Really?" questioned Rhiannon.

"What?" asked Rhinauld.

Andraste stepped out of Decima's protection and towards Rhinauld. She forcefully slapped Rhinauld across his face. He stood for a moment stunned. The Victorious and the knights of the Island Kingdoms laughed. Rhinauld turned to look at her again and laughed. He rubbed his jaw as Andraste glared at him. She walked past him. Decima handed a gold coin to Andraste she placed it in her chest plate.

"Andra!" Rhinauld called after her as she proceeded into the banquet hall.

The lords from the Island Kingdoms bowed to her as she passed. They gave her room. Decima and Marcella followed after her. Andraste paused on the top of the steps as Gregor came for Marcella and seized her boldly by the waist. Marcella laughed like a girl. Decima accepted the arm of a Southern lord that Andraste did not know.

Andraste waited. She surveyed the crowded hall. It was more filled then she had ever seen it. There was barely room to stand. She stood waiting on top of the stairs. She looked to a group of Southern lords, who were not discreet in their admiration. She was rewarded by the sight of a pair of fine sapphire eyes studying her intently. Aldrich began to slowly make his way through the crowd to her side.

Her eyes rested on Aldrich's broad shoulders. He was bare-chested once more. Andraste tried not to stare at his muscular torso. The candlelight was reflected in his gold and lapis collar. He wore two large gold cuffs on his arms. His auburn hair was loose on his back. He wore a shendyt made from linen that went down to his stalwart calves.

He stood three stairs below her. His eyes rested on her exposed midriff. He offered her his arm. She descended the stairs and took his arm lightly in her own arm. Drumming started in the ballroom. The crowd parted so that they could pass. It was so tight in the ballroom that she was pressed up against his exposed chest. Her hips met his own as she was pushed by the movement of the crowd.

"My apologies," Andraste said hastily.

Aldrich's hand moved slightly lower on her back, so he could guide her better from the other dancers and lead her through the unfamiliar movements. The first song ended. Andraste was breathless and invigorated. Her eyes sparkled.

"Do you want to retire to the banquet rooms?" asked Aldrich.

He had taken two steps away from her. It was as far as he could get from her in the current situation.

"Still so formal? I thought the decorum was different at festival?" asked Andraste. Aldrich shifted uncomfortably before her. His eyes glanced to Rhinauld in the distance.

"Another dance, if you do not mind?" asked Andraste.

She stared at his sandals.

Aldrich reached for her and twirled her into the next formation. She laughed and he seemed to relax. He guided her through the movements. The beating of the drums seemed to be getting faster and faster, which led them closer and closer. Andraste glanced up at Aldrich and found that he was surveying the ceiling tiles. She realized that he was still keeping distance between them unlike the other couples.

She paused and he sensed her hesitation. She stepped an inch closer. His hand on her waist kept her firmly in place, not allowing her any closer. He smiled down at her for the first time that evening. No matter how she moved, he countered her and kept the space between them. Andraste laughed and Aldrich's sapphire eyes effervesced. The music came to an end.

Marcella and Decima came and grabbed Andraste's hands as a new dance started.

It was a woman's dance. It was one of the old tunes that somehow seemed to have survived in each realm of the Empire. The women all grabbed hands in a circle dance. Outside the circle, the men started clapping. The women wove in and out, dancing faster and faster until they could hold hands no longer. Rhiannon lost her footing but was steadied by Marcella and Andraste, all three nearly tumbling to the floor. They laughed and laughed. As she turned to find her partner, she saw Aldrich eyes locked on her. He stood with his hands crossed his chest. His face set in stone. Gregor was whispering something in his ear to the laughter of the Southern lords. Aldrich was not amused.

The ladies moved to rejoin their partners as the music changed.

Andraste stopped within arms' reach of Aldrich and twirled. Aldrich reached for her, but she dodged him elegantly. He approached and she twirled beautifully again out of his reach. She laughed and his face softened. However, try as he may, she would not permit him to touch her. He was graceful as he attempted to catch her. For a man of his height and build, he was surprisingly quick.

She caught the movement of the other dancers and raised her arms above her head, rotating her wrists. Aldrich's eyes lowered as her breast plate inched up her side. He flushed. She again twirled out of his reach. As she lowered her arm, he caught her by the wrist and pulled her to him hard. There was a cheer from his comrades and laughter from the ladies.

Aldrich picked her up from below her waist and lifted her in his arms. Andraste laughed. She slid down his body as he put her down. His eyes were determined. It was the same look as in the training field. He held her to him tightly so she could not slip away again. She laughed and raised her arms around his neck. His hands on her exposed back made her skin tingle. She felt lightheaded. Her face was flushed.

"I think we both need some air," said Aldrich.

"One more dance," countered Andraste.

Aldrich hade made up his mind. He wrapped her arm in his and swept from the ball room, once again keeping her distant. He led her on to the veranda. He leaned against the railing overlooking the sea. He kept his eyes on the horizon. He was all too aware of the presence of Rhinauld and the Victorious watching them from a distance. Andraste seemed oblivious.

"Why did you slap Rhinauld?" asked Aldrich.

"Which time?" inquired Andraste with a smile. She stepped closer to him.

"Do you strike him often?" questioned Aldrich.

"Yes," replied Andraste. Aldrich surveyed her.

"No," admitted Andraste.

"Is it common in the North for ladies to strike gentlemen?" asked Aldrich.

"Rhinauld is not a gentleman. He is a pirate. And we are from the Island Kingdoms. In the Island Kingdoms we are permitted to live," responded Andraste.

"You are different around him," remarked Aldrich.

"What do you mean?" asked Andraste.

"You drink. You dance. You laugh more. You are more approachable," answered Aldrich.

"He is my favorite brother and my truest friend," said Andraste.

"That seems unfair when Brion has been by your side for all this time," alleged Aldrich.

"Brion keeps secrets," replied Andraste.

"As do you," countered Aldrich.

Andraste stepped away from Aldrich. She traced her fingers on the railing as she walked along the passageway.

"Why did you strike him in the courtyard?" asked Aldrich. Andraste turned to face Aldrich.

"Why do you think?" asked Andraste.

"Another marriage proposal?" inquired Aldrich. Andraste blushed crimson.

"He did not like my costume," Andraste replied hastily.

"Really?" asked Aldrich. He turned his full attention on her as he surveyed her from head to toe. His gaze lingered on her breast plate. She took a few steps back. She lowered her eyes to his torso.

"What is that scar from?" asked Andraste.

"Arrow wound from Thoran," replied Aldrich. He surveyed her midriff,

"And that one?"

"Flail at Alexius. It bent my armor like paper," said Andraste. She raised her eyes to the scar on his chest.

"Battle axe in the Forest Wars," answered Aldrich.

"I saw some of the strangest things I have ever seen in the Forest Wars," admitted Andraste.

"For example?" asked Aldrich.

"That is when the Emperor's first experiments started. He tried to make his own mythical creatures. He tried to make Griffins, Hydras, and the like by combining animals. It was terrible. The results are just monstrous," stated Andraste.

"Why did not anyone stop him?" questioned Aldrich.

"His power is unmatchable," replied Andraste.

She turned away from him and looked out across the sea.

"Those scars on your back?" asked Aldrich.

Andraste did not respond, but she quickly turned so her back was towards the sea.

"Were you whipped? By who?" questioned Aldrich. His sapphire eyes flashed.

"I have never been obedient. My father views acts of mercy as weakness. He wanted me to be stronger," replied Andraste. She stepped away from him. She changed the subject.

"Do you think it odd that we were both at the Forest Wars and Thoran and we never met?" asked Andraste.

"Southern troops were not allowed to fight beside Northern," stated Aldrich, "But I did see you with the Victorious. You were fearless."

"Fortune favors the brave," replied Andraste. She looked at her sandals. The silence between them lengthened.

"You were cloaked even then," said Aldrich.

"Once my mother died, the Emperor ordered I never show my face in his presence. It has become a habit," responded Andraste, "But we are in the South and you prefer me uncloaked."

"Paramerion," warned Aldrich.

"I know such things are not spoken of," said Andraste. She smiled up at him and joined his side. Her fingers brushed his elbow. He slipped on the railing.

"We may need to postpone our journey," Aldrich said as he tried to regain his composure.

"Why?" asked Andraste angrily.

"There are delegations from the West and the North arriving tomorrow," answered Aldrich.

"The King and the Queen can deal with them," protested Andraste.

"They come for you, my lady," stated Aldrich.

"Me?" asked Andraste. Aldrich looked increasingly uncomfortable.

"You mean for an alliance through marriage, so one of their lords can pursue the title of Emperor," alleged Andraste finally.

Aldrich did not respond.

"Anyone I marry will be labeled a traitor. His lands and people will be forfeit to the Empire," said Andraste, "Men are such fools."

To her surprise Aldrich laughed. He seemed more like her travel companion from the road then the crowned prince of the Southern lands.

"What do you want to do?" questioned Aldrich.

"I will take care of the delegations," declared Andraste.

The look in her eyes was terrifying. She took her leave, while Aldrich returned alone to the ballroom, wishing he had agreed to another dance when he had the opportunity. He watched her move farther away across the ballroom. However, he saw her hesitate as the great doors were thrown open.

The drums stopped in mid beat and silence swept across the dance hall. Fifteen Imperial officers came striding into the feast hall. The crowd parted so that Aldrich could reach Andraste. However, her Victorious reached her first. She stood at the front of a triangle. Laelius and Felix stood directly behind her. The Victorious kept Aldrich safely shielded from the Imperial officers. Kasimir, Eadbehrt, and Egnatius formed the rearguard of the triangle.

"Commander Vespasian," greeted Andraste.

The Victorious all had their hands on their weapons. The fifteen Imperial officers met them in a mirror image of the triangle. The officer at their center removed his helmet and showed golden locks and icy, blue eyes. The officer approached Andraste and knelt at her feet. His face nearly grazed her midriff as he looked up at her.

"It does my heart good to see you so well," said the officer.

"Vesp!" cried Rhiannon as she recognized the officer. She flew across the room to Andraste's side. Andraste put her arm out and kept Rhiannon behind her.

"He is still our foster brother," cried Rhiannon.

"How many foster brothers do you have?" questioned Kasimir. Andraste ignored the question.

"He is still a Commander of thousands of Imperial troops," replied Andraste. Vespasian lowered his eyes to the floor.

"Empress, I bring you news," said Vespasian.

"Proceed," replied Andraste.

"Commander Titus has defected, as did near half of his forces. He leads the Northern Resistance. As I commanded your Eastern forces, I must report that we have all defected," said Vespasian. Andraste heard disbelief circulate through the ball room.

"Furthermore, I bring ten thousand men with me. The remainder I left behind to protect the Island Kingdoms, including the Island of Fortune. There are many refugees in need of assistance. We are camped not two miles from here. Forgive my coming without invitation, but I came only to make my report and to let the Southern Crown know that we were not hostile," reported Vespasian.

Andraste lowered her arm and Rhiannon threw herself into Vespasian's arms. Rhinauld, Henry, and Felix joined them as well. Rhinauld tussled Vespasian's hair and Vespasian swatted his hand away. Henry grasped Vespasian's hand in his and clamped his arm with his free hand. Felix embraced Vespasian warmly. The Victorious stepped forward to grasp hands with the Imperial officers. However, Vespasian's eyes remained on Andraste.

"You have gone native," commented Vespasian, "It is a good look for you."

"Rhinauld does not think so," said Andraste.

"Well, if even one of our brothers is tempted by such a costume," muttered Rhinauld. He stepped between Andraste and Vespasian, but she retook her position.

"You and the other three hail from the Island Kingdoms. Andra and I hail from the North, so your puritanical rules do not apply to us. I will admire beauty when I see it," stated Vespasian.

Andraste blushed deeply and lowered her eyes. Aldrich reached her side and also blocked her with his shoulder. Andraste did not move in front of him. However, she turned her attention to Vespasian's officers. Vespasian and Aldrich wordlessly judged each other.

"Your command has altered. Where are Riona? Cathair? Fearghal? Rorie?" questioned Andraste.

"They fell. We lost many in the march. The Arisen are out of control," said Vespasian.

"It honors us that you would remember them," said Vespasian's second in command.

"Vitus, I have fought with you all for years. Of course I remember," said Andraste. She scanned the faces of the men before her again and for faces that were no longer there.

"And where is your squire? Where is young Rico? I long to see him," asked Andraste. She tried to conceal her alarm.

A hush fell over Vespasian's warriors, the merriment that had been restored faded. Vespasian stepped forward with deep regret in his eyes and a somber expression. Rhinauld allowed Vespasian to reach for Andraste's arm and grasp her hand. Vitus stepped forward and knelt at her feet, removing a sword that was slung across his back. He kept his head bowed as he raised the sword to her.

"Speak, Vitus," commanded Andraste. She tried to keep her voice from trembling as her heart pounded in her chest.

"Rico Valerianus was slain in our retreat from the North. He was taken by the Arisen," said Vitus. He offered the sword to Andraste.

"I did not want my sword returned to me in this way," said Andraste softly. Her grasp around Vespasian's wrist tightened.

"Did you recover the body?" asked Andraste.

"We burned them as is our way," replied Vespasian. Andraste took the sword from him.

"The rights?" questioned Brion. He appeared at her side and took the sword from Vitus.

"As we are at war, we will honor all of our dead at its completion as is suiting to our traditions," replied Vespasian.

"Thank you for returning our brother's sword. I know you did your best," said Brion.

"He was so young, not yet fifteen," said Andraste. She took a deep breath to steady herself.

"Andra," said Rhinauld. Andraste waived him away. She turned around so that she would not face the Imperial officers and her eyes landed on Aldrich. She looked away from his as well.

"You should meet our host," said Rhiannon. She wrapped Vespasian's arm in her own. Vespasian released Andraste's arm, but he kept his eyes on her. She nodded and Vespasian allowed Rhiannon to lead him forward.

"Prince Aldrich, may I introduce Commander Vespasian of the Eastern Imperial Forces. He was fostered with us in the East," introduced Rhiannon.

Vespasian bowed awkwardly to Aldrich as Rhiannon still had a firm grasp on his arm.

"You and your men are welcome," said Aldrich, "It sounds as though your way was arduous. Are you in need of medical attention?"

"We are tending our own, but I thank you. I did not expect a welcome, but we are humbled by your generosity," said Vespasian, "I see we are intruding on a feast. We will take our leave, and return once properly invited."

"Nonsense, you are brothers to our cause. You need no invitation," said Aldrich.

He offered his hand to Vespasian, who took it. Vespasian glanced sideways to Andraste. She nodded her head.

"We look forward to fighting with you," said Vespasian.

"Vesp," chided Rhiannon. Vespasian offered her a smile and she laughed prettily. She let go of him so that Brion could grasp his hand and embrace him in the Northern style.

"So, at least all of you are together again. The Hope of the East is together once more," said King Aelius. He clamped a hand on Vespasian's shoulder.

"It has been near five years since we were all under one roof," said Rhinauld.

"Queen Marian, I apologize for whatever ensues. My charges are all rascals, except for Rhiannon," said King Aelius.

"Always the favorite," remarked Rhinauld.

"Where is Andra?" asked Rhiannon.

"She has fled," replied Henry. Rhinauld moved to follow.

"Leave her be," said Rhiannon.

"But-" started Henry.

"She does not want us," replied Rhiannon. She glanced to Aldrich. She took Brion's offered arm and allowed him to convey her back to the dance hall. She said over her shoulder, "Come, Vesp. The ladies of the Island Kingdoms will want to see you."

Vespasian bowed once to Aldrich before following after Rhiannon. Rhinauld and Henry began a conversation and leisurely made their way to the lords and ladies of the Island Kingdoms. Aldrich surveyed the dance hall before making his exit. He went directly to Andraste's chambers. He knocked on the door, but received no answer.

Andraste paused in front of Aldrich's chambers. She saw him sleeping soundly on his sofa. He still wore his attire from the festival. She went in silently and knelt by his side. She started to reach for him but stopped herself. Instead she took off her cloak and wrapped it around him. Aldrich stirred but went back to sleep. Andraste rose soundlessly and returned to her own chambers, gently shutting the doors behind her. She removed her costume and climbed into the bed. She was asleep as soon as her head hit the pillow.

"Let her sleep. Rhinauld and Henry can deal with the suitors," whispered Rhiannon.

"She said she wanted to deal with them herself," replied Aldrich.

"She rode all night. She did not return until dawn. Let her sleep. She may not show it, but she is grieving for Rico," said Rhiannon.

"Where did she go?" asked Aldrich.

"Felix says that she rode to Tobias's and Matthias's graves. She left Rico's sword there," said Rhiannon.

"Alone?" asked Aldrich.

"The Victorious followed. She is rarely alone," replied Rhiannon.

Andraste heard Aldrich pacing in front of the door to her bedchamber.

"She is not decent. You cannot enter," ordered Rhiannon. Aldrich hesitated outside of her door, debating between his desire and decorum.

"Please have her come to me before we receive the delegations. I will be in my chambers," requested Aldrich.

"Yes, Prince Aldrich," replied Rhiannon.

"Please call me Aldrich," replied the prince.

"Yes, my lord," responded Rhiannon. Aldrich's footsteps faded down the hall. Andraste rose and wrapped her robe around her.

"I thought you were awake," said Rhiannon as she came into the room.

"How much time before we receive the delegations?" asked Andraste.

"Not much. I have brought you your armor from the Island Kingdoms," said Rhiannon.

"Will you dress as well?" asked Andraste.

"Are we to be dueling suitors once more?" asked Rhiannon.

"That is my intention," replied Andraste.

"I thought as much. I have sent for Shannon," said Rhiannon.

Andraste bathed quickly and then dressed in her armor from the Island Kingdoms. She found Rhiannon and Shannon already dressed in their own armor and waiting for her. They both carried the long bows so revered by the Island Kingdoms.

"Let us go," said Andraste.

"Aldrich awaits-" started Rhiannon.

"This is Island business," replied Andraste. She swept down the hall. Rhiannon and Shannon followed.

They arrived late to the reception of the delegations. The introductions had already been made. The King of the Island Kingdoms looked grumpier than usual. It was as she had feared: many of the delegations had produced an heir who wanted to pursue her hand.

"We will resolve this soon enough in the style of the North," said Andraste, "We will duel. The one who can beat me, I will accept as a husband."

"A duel?" asked one of the Western lords. He laughed in Andraste's face. He was a large man. His face was heavily scarred and he was missing an eye.

"A suggestion, princess," proposed Aldrich. He did not seem surprised by her proposition. Andraste turned to him.

"Let the suitors duel amongst themselves and you fight the victor," suggested Aldrich.

"We will enter as well," said Shannon. Andraste saw Felix watching Shannon closely from across the field.

"Do I have to marry you if win?" asked Andraste. Shannon laughed heartedly.

"No, my lady, but no woman should have to put up with these consent attacks. We are not prizes to be won. We are creatures capable of thought and choice. I will not sit aside and watch you so abused," replied Shannon. Andraste grasped hands with Shannon.

"You will not enter?" asked the large Western lord to Aldrich's back. Aldrich was already half way out of the hall.

"In the South a lady chooses her husband, a gentleman does not duel for her," said Aldrich, and then over his shoulder, "Besides, you will all lose."

Rhinauld laughed heartily. He had not entered either. Aldrich left the hall. It was decided to have the duels in the training arena.

Rhiannon took on the first opponent. The Northern lord was unfazed by her gender. He surveyed her as he would any other opponent. He struck at Rhiannon first. She dodged him and removed the bow from her shoulder. She struck her opponent in the jaw in the same gesture. He fell unconscious to the ground. Simultaneously, Shannon had already defeated her own opponent.

Andraste watched each of the duels carefully. Not one of the contestants possessed more than ordinary training and ability. The Western lord who won the contest did it mostly based on his own strength. The discontented, defeated seven lords muttered around the sidelines as Andraste approached the brute. She partially unsheathed her sword and the blade flashed red in the sunlight. She let it sink back down into the sheath.

"That is a Ruin sword!" recognized the Western lord.

"I am a Ruin conqueror," stated Andraste.

The Western lord hesitated. However, a look of determination crossed his face.

"I am Orthos of the Western plains, Chief of the Free Peoples," was all that he said.

The Western lord saluted her. She returned the salute.

He raised his axe and charged. It was a fatal mistake. Andraste easily dodged his attack and hit him squarely in the stomach with her hilt. The Western lord went barreling to the ground unable to breathe.

"She did not even unsheathe her sword!" said one of the lords.

"Do you concede?" asked Andraste.

The Western lord's face was flushed and he gasped for air. He nodded.

"Now that is settled. If any of you are serious about joining the resistance, I suggest you follow me to the War Chambers. You should know that my hand is not a prize or dealing chip. I am the leader of the Victorious and have little time for such nonsense," acknowledged Andraste.

"A moment, Commander," said Kasimir. He approached the field and bowed to Andraste and her ladies.

"I would challenge the lady knight from the Island Kingdoms," said Kasimir.

"You will do no such thing," growled Felix. He was between Kasimir and Shannon in an instant.

"I fight my own battles," said Shannon.

"Not today," replied Felix. His normal jovial disposition was replaced by a sinister nature. He unsheathed his sword and approached the Southern lord.

"Uh-oh," said Rhiannon.

"I forbid the drawing of blood," called Andraste.

"I will beat him just the same," replied Felix.

The duel between Felix and Kasimir only took moments. Felix moved with such purpose and speed that the Southern lord had no chance. Felix kept his blade under Kasimir's chin and stared at him with undisguised loathing.

"That is enough," said Andraste. Felix withdrew his sword and saluted Andraste before sheathing it. He approached Shannon.

"You had no right to interfere," said Shannon.

"I would not see you defeated," replied Felix.

"He would not have defeated me," stated Shannon, "And you did not interfere when I dueled the Western lords."

"They were no competition," replied Felix.

"He speaks the truth," said Andraste.

"Do not interfere," chided Rhiannon. She smiled as Valens brought Felix overly-packed saddlebags. Felix took it from his comrade.

"What do you have there?" asked Shannon.

"The letters that I should have written you. One for every day of our separation," replied Felix.

"Oh!" cried Rhiannon.

"I would make sure they are not the same letter written over and over," stated Otho.

"I will. I do not expect Felix to know so many words," replied Shannon. However, she was obviously pleased by his gesture.

"I would read each one to you, if you wish," replied Felix. He took Shannon's hand in his and she allowed him to kiss it.

"The Southern gardens are so lovely," suggested Rhiannon.

"This gesture has you written all over it," replied Shannon.

"It was not I!" cried Rhiannon.

"Nor I, although I may have financed the ink and paper," admitted Andraste.

Felix threw the saddlebags over his shoulder and offered Shannon his arm. She took it and they retreated to the Southern gardens.

"I never took you for a romantic," said Kasimir as he turned his scrutiny to Andraste.

"You have no idea," replied Rhiannon.

Andraste nudged her sister painfully in the ribs before heading to the War Chambers. Rhinauld and Henry flanked her either side.

"That was cruel, little Empress," commented Rhinauld, "You did not even give the Western lord a chance."

"I have no time for hand-holding," replied Andraste.

"Truly petrifying," alleged Henry. He granted her a rare smile.

They entered the War Chambers. Aldrich was reading a book. His feet were resting on the table. The Victorious and the Southern lords were discussing the different duels. The King and the Queen were discussing a map.

"All settled?" inquired Aldrich, not looking up from his book.

"Settled," confirmed Rhinauld, "What do you think, Henry? 187 failed proposals?"

"188," corrected Henry. He glanced to Aldrich, but the prince did not respond.

Andraste moved to the window behind Aldrich. It had a fine view of the courtyard. She sat in the window seat and began cleaning her sword menacingly.

"Empress," said a familiar voice at her side.

Vespasian had the bearing and the physique to wear his full Imperial armor to the fullest potential. He bowed to her with the utmost respect and remained bowed.

"Vespasian," greeted Andraste.

"Commander," returned Vespasian, "I fear I missed your duels."

"I will duel you later if you wish," said Andraste.

"That is not our way. If you want me, you will make your pledge," said Vespasian. He flashed her a smile and Andraste retreated to the window. Aldrich shut his book and examined her reaction. Rhinauld and Henry exchanged glances.

"How fare your sisters?" inquired Andraste.

"They are well. Your brother, Titus, had them sent to, and they are now settled at your castle on the Island of Fortune. The King of the Island Kingdoms refused to surrender your lands to the North. At present, the Emperor is too engaged elsewhere to reclaim it," replied Vespasian.

"I saw Tacita at the Refuge and have been worried since. It lightens my heart to know that they are safe, and to see a friendly face. I miss my time with them. I have not seen them since my years at the Ice Palace. Nor have I seen you since Gardenia," said Andraste.

"My promotion has taken me to places far from those I love," replied Vespasian.

"Yes, but I hear you have done well," said Andraste.

"I do my duty, Empress," answered Vespasian.

"It seems like only yesterday that we were all in the Salt Islands," sighed Andraste.

"It has been near ten years, Empress," mentioned Vespasian.

"To me, you are still that same little boy who followed behind Rhinauld and me," laughed Andraste.

"And you all trailed after me," commented Henry from the window. Rhinauld laughed at his side.

"What news from the North? Do you know the Northern delegation? Is there anyone else I know, or should be weary of?" asked Andraste.

"I have just come myself. It took me longer to arrive as I have brought all of my squadrons. We had a time traversing the Northern Mountains. The Emperor's experiments have multiplied exponentially and the way was a demon filled nightmare. I lost near one hundred men," answered Vespasian.

"I am sorry," responded Andraste. She studied her friend and realized how much older he seemed since she had last seen him. When she had last known him he was a boy, but he had grown into a fierce warrior.

"And your wounds?" asked Henry.

"It is nothing," replied Vespasian.

Andraste surveyed the warrior before her. His posture was impeccable. He did not shift his weight from foot to foot. He stood at absolute attention.

"It is nothing," restated Vespasian, although his eyes looked pained.

"Were many wounded?" asked Andraste.

"We were in sorry shape when we reached the Capitol. We fought a Northern force near the coast, but we forced them to retreat," answered Vespasian.

"I would see your warriors. I would like to thank them for their service," said Andraste.

"We would be honored. Some of the Northern ladies will entertain the wounded after dinner. Others are there now tending to the wounded," alleged Vespasian.

"I am obliged to my host to attend the dinner hour, but afterwards I will go with you," responded Andraste.

"What sort of man is Aldrich Caelius?" asked Vespasian.

"He is a man without fault," replied Andraste.

Vespasian raised an eyebrow. However, their conversation was cut short as the Western and Northern delegations filed in. Vespasian bowed to Andraste once more. Andraste retook her seat in the window and Vespasian took his place among the Northern delegation.

"We have accepted you into this council because you were vouched for by the King of the Island Kingdoms and the Queen of the Southern lands. I will not waste time debating merits or claims to territory. The only purpose of this union is to defeat the Emperor and restore order to our currently established lands," addressed Aldrich.

"Such trust is so noble, Prince Aldrich," said a voice from the back of the room.

Andraste looked up from the window and rose. Brion, Rhinauld and Henry had the same reaction. She noticed their swords were already drawn.

"You heard, *Empress*, I am welcomed here by your hosts, and I am leader of the Northern delegation. Would you slay me here in front of your new sworn brethren?" asked the man. His voice was soft, like a whisper, but deadly like the hiss of a cobra. He was small, slender, with a hawkish face and cold dark brown eyes. When Andraste looked into Toxin's eyes, she saw only hard, calculating reality. His eyes viewed her and seemed to be estimating how many days she had yet to live and how much of a threat she might prove to be. It was for this reason his eyes reminded her of the vultures that she had encountered on her travels.

"Without a doubt," alleged Andraste.

"Who is the Demon of the North to judge me?" asked the man.

"I have only killed when absolutely necessary, never for pleasure. I am not a butcher of villagers and townspeople, of women and children," hissed Andraste.

"And if our positions had been reversed? Would you have been able to defy the Emperor?" asked the man.

"I am here, am I not?" rejoined Andraste.

"This man is the Earl of the Icelands but you will know him as Toxin. He is a militant sorcerer," declared Brion.

"For those of you who need it spelled out, he is not to be trusted," expanded Rhinauld.

"I know the reasons for the Earl joining, and he has sworn a life oath. If he breaks his oath, he will die," said the Queen.

The Southern lords looked uncomfortable.

"Who do you think made the poison that coated the arrows of the Emperor's personal guards?" asked Andraste. She stared at Aldrich. He returned her gaze.

"As I said everyone here is vouched for by the King of the Island Kingdoms and my Queen," stated Aldrich calmly.

Andraste sheathed her blade and the others followed suit. She retreated to her window seat. She did not speak for the rest of the meeting. Aldrich went over the plans that had been made for the military advances. Andraste did not take her eyes off the Earl of the Icelands. During the first break, Laelius approached her. Rhinauld, Henry and Brion inched closer to hear.

"We leave as soon as possible," whispered Andraste.

"Two days?" asked Laelius. Andraste pursed her lips but nodded her agreement.

"Is that wise, my Empress?" asked Rhinauld.

"We cannot stay here. We will not be safe while Toxin is in the palace," said Andraste.

"But to leave without-" started Rhinauld.

"Toxin's special gifts also include assassination. He has powers that we cannot dream of. I do not want him to discover my mission or yours. More importantly, we need to get Rhiannon home to the Salt Islands. You know this," cautioned Andraste.

"As you wish, my Empress," relented Rhinauld, but he frowned. He nodded to Henry, who went to inform Rhiannon.

"As there is nothing new to discuss, the Island delegation will retire," Rhinauld said to Aldrich. Aldrich frowned but inclined his head in acknowledgment. Andraste smiled to Vespasian in passing. Andraste continued down the hall. Rhinauld walked by her side.

"Are you going to change for the feast?" asked Rhinauld.

"I am tired of these Southern traditions. I feel like I am two people: soldier by day and courtier at night. I have had unusually strong headaches. I know I have forgotten something," replied Andraste.

"You have always worn two faces. It is nothing new. However, Rhiannon had clothes made for you in the Salt Islands. She thought you may need some things. Perhaps her gifts will help you feel more like yourself again," said Rhinauld.

"I will be sure to wear one of her gifts," conceded Andraste. They walked in silence back to her chamber.

"I will collect you before dinner," said Rhinauld.

Andraste grunted in response. Rhinauld bowed gallantly to her and returned to his own chambers. Andraste read the new reports that had been forwarded to her and then took a long bath.

Andraste prepared herself for dinner. She found that boxes had been delivered to her chambers. The enclosed gowns were beautiful. Andraste examined the embroidery; she was sure Rhiannon had done it herself. The stitches were tiny, perfect. Andraste dressed in a sea-green gown. Tiny hummingbirds had been embroidered around the neckline and the trim of her dress. She secured her hair in a bun.

She heard a knock on her door and Rhinauld entered.

"Truly lovely," Rhinauld said. He offered her his arm. Once she had taken it, he paused.

"I brought you a gift from my travels. I know you never wear jewelry, but it made me think of you," he said.

Rhinauld pulled out a necklace from his pocket. It was a simple silver chain with a round tourmaline gemstone also set in silver.

"It is lovely," praised Andraste.

Rhinauld fastened it around her neck. She felt the cold gemstone with her hand.

"Thank you, Rhinauld," said Andraste.

Rhinauld took her arm back in his. They started down the hall. They passed Rhiannon's door and they were joined by Rhiannon, Brion, and Henry as well as other ladies and lords from the Island Kingdoms.

"So this is where the celebration commenced," commented Andraste.

"Rhiannon has seemed to have developed a taste for the South's sparkling wines," said Rhinauld. Andraste laughed.

Aldrich was a head of them down the hall with a group of Southern lords. He turned at the sound of her laughter. Rhinauld bowed to the prince in greeting. The prince returned the gesture and continued down the hallway with the Southern lords.

"Due to the new arrivals, I hear that you are sitting with us tonight," Rhiannon said gaily to Andraste.

"I am glad to hear it," said Andraste, "But before we sit, I must speak to the Northern delegation."

"You expect a welcome?" asked Rhinauld.

"They too are traitors and exiles. I want to see who else has left the North," said Andraste.

"You mean you are looking for spies," replied Henry.

"Toxin is our only threat. I surveyed the new arrivals after we parted earlier this afternoon," said Rhinauld.

"Pretenses must be maintained. I will welcome these new allies," said Andraste.

"You should know Tobias' wife and son have come. Their lands were usurped by the Emperor for their lord's defeat," said Rhinauld. He watched Andraste's face carefully, but her face showed no signs of emotion.

"Where are they?" asked Andraste.

"Nearest Aldrich's men," answered Rhinauld.

Andraste scanned the dining hall. The Southern lords and ladies halted their conversations to watch the Northerners' reception of Andraste. As she passed by the Northern delegation, the Northern lords and ladies rose and bowed to her. She acknowledged them with a bow of her head, but she continued down the row, followed by Rhinauld and Henry, while the rest of the Island delegation proceeded to their table. She stopped before the Lady of the Mystic Caverns, who bowed before Andraste. She did not raise her head.

"I am sorry for your loss and troubles, Lady Vita. Lord Tobias was the best and most noble man of my acquaintance. I doubt I will ever again meet his equal. I will never forgive myself for my part in his death. At present I have no means to pay the blood debt, or restore what has been taken from you, but some day, I will make this right," swore Andraste.

"Empress, I have heard the details of my husband's death. I know you are not at fault. It was Varinia's order and her deviousness. I know he died for the lives of his men, and he died with a clean conscience. My husband never stopped in believing in you.

I thank you for properly burying my husband. We stopped by the grave on our journey. I must also thank you for sending his sword to our son.

All I ask is that you take my son into your service. I wish him to be raised by the warriors that knew his father best. I hope that through such a situation, he will be the man his father was, and one day join the Victorious," said Lady Vita. She still did not rise from her bowed position.

"How old is the boy?" asked Andraste.

"He has seen seven winters, but he is big and strong for his age," replied Lady Vita.

"I cannot deny such a request. I know it would also be the wish of his father; however, my way is too dangerous for so young a child. When he reaches his fourteenth winter, I will accept him as my squire. If we see a peaceful time before then, I will welcome him into my service as a page if that is agreeable to you," said Andraste.

"Thank you, Empress," replied Lady Vita. She slowly rose, but would not meet Andraste's gaze.

"Where is the boy?" asked Andraste.

"Andrew," called Lady Vita.

A boy with brown hair and dark eyes appeared instantly at his mother's die. He wore his father's sword across his broad shoulders. It was a mighty weapon for such a young child.

"This is the Empress Andraste Valerianus," introduced Lady Vita. The boy bowed in the Northern fashion.

"You are the image of your father," said Andraste. The boy's eyes darted to her face but then back to the floor. He remained bowed.

"He is the same age as our nephew," commented Rhinauld. Andraste looked to her foster brother.

"Lady Vita, perhaps you and your son would like to join our sister, Rhiannon, on her voyage to the Salt Islands. She will need a companion, and our nephew could use someone to train with. It will not be safe to remain in the mainland once the war commences," said Rhinauld.

"We would be honored, Lord Rhinauld. I am grateful. I fear for my son's life and my own protection," said Lady Vita. She bowed once more to Andraste and Rhinauld. Andraste could not take her eyes off Andrew.

"Have you had trouble?" asked Rhinauld.

"I had thought some of my husband's contemporaries would have protected us on our journey, but everything has a price," replied Lady Vita. She lowered her eyes in shame.

"Seeking the protection of your husband's murderer? I had not thought you could fall any lower, Vita. However, I have been wrong before," said the nearest Northern lord.

Andrew was so quick that the Northern lord could not block his attack. He had already taken the sheathed sword and slammed it down on the lord's shoulder with all of his might. The lord rose in outrage almost knocking over the bench in the process. His tablemates were scattered in the process. The lord dove at Andrew, but Andraste shielded Andrew behind her body. She raised her fists in a protective stance. Rhinauld and Henry stepped protectively in front of Andraste. Lady Vita wrapped her arms around her son.

"Stand down, Lord Blasius," ordered Andraste.

"I will let this pass just once since you are a fatherless mongrel," snarled Blasius. He glared at Andrew. Rhinauld and Henry did not move an inch.

"Is that any way to speak to a child? Or to speak to widow?" asked Aldrich quietly as he came up behind them. He stopped by Andraste's side. Rhinauld and Henry stepped aside so that Aldrich could address the Northern lord.

"My apologies, Prince Aldrich," said Blasius. He bowed to Aldrich.

"Are you hurt?" asked Aldrich to Andraste.

"No," answered Andraste. Aldrich looked once more to the bowing Northern lord and then to Lady Vita and her son.

"I suggest we all be seated for dinner," said Aldrich. He offered his arm to Lady Vita.

"Lady Vita wishes to be reacquainted with the Victorious. Andrew will know Laelius's children as well," said Andraste.

"Forgive my lack of consideration if I had known, I would have had you seated there first. Please let me show you the way," said Aldrich. He still offered his arm to Lady Vita.

"It is a Southern custom. It is no breach of honor to accept his arm," said Andraste.

Gingerly Lady Vita took Aldrich's arm. Aldrich smiled kindly at Lady Vita and guided her across the hall to the Victorious's table. The Victorious rose and bowed to Lady Vita.

"I expect that no such further displays will occur while we are guests in the Southern lands," said Andraste to Blasius.

"Yes, Empress," replied Blasius. He did not look at her.

"Come, Andra, we must proceed to our table," said Rhinauld.

Andraste turned her eyes back to the passage. Rhinauld retook her arm in his and they proceeded to their table. They passed Aldrich as he returned from the Victorious's table. He glowered at Rhinauld's firm grasp on Andraste's arm.

"My lord?" asked Andraste. Aldrich paused at her side and looked down at her.

"Thank you," said Andraste softly. Aldrich inclined his head to her and continued on his way.

Andraste sat between Henry and Rhinauld. They ate heartily, laughed merrily and drank deeply. Andraste surveyed the feast. Lady Vita was sitting beside Paulina and they were deep in conversation. Andrew was silently listening to the children's conversation, but he did not join in.

"Where is Vespasian?" asked Andraste.

"Aldrich invited him to sit beside him. After you showed Vespasian such favor, Aldrich must be intrigued," replied Henry.

"I did not," said Andraste.

"Did you address any of the remaining Northern lords?" asked Henry.

"We have known Vespasian since we were children," replied Andraste.

Andraste glanced to the Southern table and saw Aldrich and Vespasian deep in conversation. Andraste turned her attention back to the Northern delegation. There was one table that was only inhabited by two individuals. The first being Toxin, the second a young girl with a mournful face and long raven hair.

"Who is that lady by Toxin?" inquired Andraste.

"That is his daughter, Hyacinth. She has not yet seen seventeen winters," answered Henry.

"I did not know he had any children," said Andraste.

"He swore allegiance to the Caelius family and took the blood oath in order for his daughter to be fostered by Marcella and Gregor. Marcella is going to train her to be a sorceress," explained Henry.

"If Toxin had not freed her from the North, she would have had to be a militant sorcerer. Here at least she has a chance. She can learn the healing arts, which I hear is her wish," said Rhinauld over his glass of wine.

"That does not change his previous sins," commented Henry.

"She is the same age as Aurelia," said Andraste, "Or would have been."

Rhinauld's arm rested around her waist.

"They were sweet girls. They did not deserve that fate," stated Henry.

"I am sorry for their loss, Empress. We should have gone with you," said Rhinauld.

"And we could have all been cursed together? Or worse, he would have killed you both immediately," said Andraste. Rhinauld's grasp tightened around her waist. Andraste looked up to see who approached.

One of the defeated Western suitors approached their table. Henry and Rhinauld stared the man down. The Western suitor continued on his path. Rhiannon giggled.

"Surely Andra can decide for herself," suggested Shannon.

"They know the rule. My Victorious and the knights of the Salt Islands may approach me," said Andraste.

"You actually have a rule?" inquired Rhiannon, "And what about the Southern prince?"

"As he defeated me in a duel, we will permit him to approach Andra," replied Rhinauld.

"You three are ridiculous," stated Rhiannon.

"Do not be jealous, sister. The rule applies to you as well. However, as you have no sword skills, we will eliminate the Victorious as potential dance partners. The knights of the Salt Islands and Brion are the only ones we will allow approach you," said Andraste.

"I will dance with whomever I so choose," responded Rhiannon.

"So long as it is me, I will not object," said Brion. Brion kissed her hand, and Rhiannon blushed.

Andraste looked back to the table where Toxin and his daughter were sitting. She saw that Aldrich and Marcella had gone to speak to them. Aldrich saw her gaze and he faltered for a moment in his response to Toxin. Rhinauld removed his arm from her waist. When Andraste looked back at their table, she saw that Aldrich had returned to his place with the Southern lords. His back was towards her.

The music had started and couples were taking their places.

"Do you remember Aurelia at her first season? How she agonized if someone would ask her to dance? She was always practicing, even when she should have been at her lessons," said Andraste. She smiled at the memory.

She looked to Hyacinth sitting alone at the table with her father. Hyacinth had glanced up to watch the beginning of the dance but quickly averted her gaze.

Rhinauld took one last sip of wine and rose from the table. He bowed to Andraste and approached Toxin's table. He spoke a few words to Toxin, who inclined his head in response. Rhinauld bowed and offered his arm to Hyacinth. The girl blushed and stood up with Rhinauld.

"Sometimes he does something redeeming," commented Henry.

"But look, the other couples are leaving the floor!" exclaimed Rhiannon.

Andraste stood. Henry immediately rose and offered her his arm. He held her hand loosely in the Northern style.

The music had stopped. Hyacinth's cheeks were burning as she and Rhinauld stood alone on the dance floor. Rhinauld was trying to amuse her with a story. Andraste and Henry joined them. She saw that Brion and Rhiannon, as well as the lords and ladies of the Island Kingdom delegation had joined them. She saw a few of the Southern lords and ladies join as well.

Andraste looked to the music, as she heard a fiddle begin to play. She saw that Felix had bullied a musician into relinquishing his instrument. Felix began playing a song the Salt Islands. It was one of the country dances. The ladies stood on one side and the gentleman on the other. The gentleman bowed and the ladies curtsied. Each set of four couples joined hands. Andraste offered her hand to Hyacinth.

"Empress!" Hyacinth said in alarm as she realized Andraste was by her side.

"You will miss the movement," Andraste said kindly.

She guided Hyacinth in the right direction. Hyacinth smiled throughout the remainder of the dance and giggled at whatever Rhinauld was saying to her.

At the end of the dance, Felix began to play a faster tune from the Island Kingdoms. Some of the other musicians joined in with him. Henry twirled Andraste to Rhinauld's arms, and then bowed to Hyacinth extending his hand in invitation.

"No!" Andraste said as Rhinauld led her to the dance, but his grasp on her was firm. He laughed at her. Andraste relented and laughed as well. By the time the dance had concluded, her cheeks were rosy, her eyes bright, and her stomach ached from laughing so hard.

For the next song, all of the musicians began to play a slow Southern waltz. Felix had relinquished the fiddle back to its rightful owner.

"One more dance. I know it is all an act to keep off suitors. But it is me, Andra, and I know you. You have been dying to dance the Southern dances. We have not danced this since Gardenia," said Rhinauld.

He had already taken her left hand in his, and placed his other hand on her waist. He drew her to him.

"I cannot dance two dances with you. It would be scandalous!" Andraste mocked. She allowed Rhinauld to turn her. She struggled to escape.

"By the look the prince shot us, I assume I should not wrap my arm around you anymore. In that case, I should probably sit across from you at dinner as well. That being said, I am your foster-brother. Aldrich has danced multiple dances with Decima. If you ever stayed past three songs, you would have realized it," teased Rhinauld.

Andraste placed her right hand on his shoulder. Rhinauld grinned with triumph. He turned her beautifully and took her once again into his arms. They did not speak for the rest of the dance. At the end Andraste curtsied low to Rhinauld.

"Thank you, my lord," Andraste said.

Rhinauld bowed deeply to her and kissed her hand. As she rose, she saw that she was an item of fascination for the Southern nobility. She sighed and shook her head at Rhinauld.

"Always watched, but how can you blame them? You can be quite charming when you want to be. Or perhaps the South agrees with you better than the North?" asked Rhinauld.

"I have always enjoyed the Island Kingdoms best- the merriment, the freedom, the sense of adventure, the love of life. I miss the Salt Islands. We spent our happiest times there," responded Andraste.

Rhinauld had taken her arm in his. Andraste beamed up at him. He smiled down on her. Her smile faded as she recalled her imminent journey, and that they would be parted once more. She forced a smile for Rhinauld.

"Let us find Vespasian. He is taking me to see the Northern Resistance troops," said Andraste.

They approached a party of Southern lords and ladies, Aldrich and Vespasian stood in the middle. Vespasian was composed, but Andraste could tell that he was irritated by the set of his jaw.

"The North allows common soldiers to attend noble banquets?" asked Gerlinde.

"There is nothing common about Vespasian. In the North, intelligence, honor, and bravery can promote a man beyond the chance of his birth," said Andraste as she approached. Vespasian bowed low to Andraste.

"As demonstrated by Captain Egnatius as well," commented Aldrich.

"He is not a lord?" asked Andraste.

"No, he was born to peasants. He is hardly to be confused with a Southern lord. It would not do to dance with such a fellow," stated Gerlinde. She eyed the other ladies meaningfully.

"Neither he nor Commander Vespasian asked you, Gerlinde," said Aldrich.

"I would dance with you," said Andraste. Aldrich turned quickly at her words, but realized that she was addressing Vespasian.

"You honor me, Empress. Thank you, but no. Do you still wish to proceed to the Northern camp? I stand at the ready," said Vespasian.

"Your wounds from the defense of this city must be bothering you. Let us get you some well-earned rest, and I will dance for you. It was your sister, Aelia, who taught me the fan dances. You can tell her how her student fares in your next letter," said Andraste.

Vespasian bowed once more to Andraste, and stood without making a response. He looked to Aldrich.

"I will accompany you. Some of my men wish to meet the Northern officers. Kasimir, Eadbehrt, and Egnatius will come as well, as they will be working closely with the Northern Resistance," said Aldrich.

"As you wish," replied Andraste.

"I will take my leave. There is some business that Henry and I must attend to," said Rhinauld. He bowed to Andraste before retreating to the table of the Island Kingdoms.

"Lead on," commanded Aldrich.

Andraste bristled under his tone. Vespasian looked to Andraste for direction.

"If you would be so kind," said Andraste.

"Yes, Empress," replied Vespasian.

Vespasian headed towards the exit. As they passed by the Northern table, several Northern officers and ladies joined them as well. Andraste was relieved that the officers were all men that she knew. Many had fought underneath her command before. The remaining Northern lords and ladies rose and bowed to Andraste as she passed. The officers fell in step behind her.

"Heiyoh!" called a Northern officer as he approached. The other officers laughed.

"But you are not one of my men. Frederick? You served under Titus," said Andraste.

"I serve the Empire," replied the officer. He bowed to Andraste.

"Well met. I heard you were dead," said Andraste.

"Perhaps we both are? I heard the same about you," replied Frederick.

"Worse. I heard you were cursed," said a second officer. Andraste grasped hands with him.

"Better than an oath breaker, Martin. After Gardenia, you swore you would never return to the South, and yet you found your way?" questioned Andraste.

"I go where my unit goes, oaths or no," replied Martin.

"Well said," stated Vespasian.

"The Victorious do not lie. Laelius said you had gone native," commented Frederick.

"I must agree. It is a wonder. In all of our years of service, I have never seen you out of uniform," said Martin.

"Order!" snapped Vespasian. He turned to reprimand the officer and was halted in his tracks by the bemused expressions of the Southern lords.

"I could say the same thing about you, Martin," rejoined Andraste. The Northern officers laughed.

"Although I have heard varying accounts . . . what exactly did you and Paulina wear at the Gardenia prison break?" asked Frederick.

"No comment," replied Andraste.

"Irena, gods bless her soul, was with you as well. The Victorious have lost some of their edge without Paulina and Irena. To think you three rescued the other twelve out of the Gardenia prison. We cannot let Laelius live that one down," said Vespasian. He smiled at the memory.

"We 'three' did not get captured in the first place," commented Andraste.

"So how did you break into the most formidable prison in the South?"

asked Aldrich.

"That would be classified under Victorious intelligence," replied Andraste.

"It is a good story and I know how the Victorious love to tell tales of their deeds. You really are not going to say?" asked Martin.

"It was less then ladylike behavior. It would burst the standards of Southern propriety and our Southern lords may never fully recover," stated Andraste.

"Ladylike behavior?" snorted Martin. Andraste silenced him with a look.

"Ask Felix. He will tell you," advised Vespasian.

"Heiyoh!" greeted an officer as they reached the stables. Andraste returned the salute.

"I do not even know him," commented Andraste.

"Heiyoh has spread throughout the Imperial army," said Vespasian.

Andraste looked exasperated, and the officers laughed. Andraste saw that carriages had been readied to convey the Northern ladies. Vespasian and the Northern officers mounted their horses.

"Boreas, I am glad to see you are well," said Andraste as she approached Vespasian's black stallion.

"You speak more kindly to Boreas than any man," commented Vespasian.

"Well just look at him," said Andraste. She stroked Boreas's neck. Boreas watched her with large golden eyes. He nudged his head into her shoulder and Andraste laughed.

"Is it far?" inquired Andraste.

"No, Empress," replied Vespasian.

"Then I will ride with you," said Andraste.

Vespasian reached for her and swung her up behind him. Aldrich headed towards his own horse, and was followed by the Southern lords. Andraste shivered as a cool breeze blew from the North. Vespasian undid his Imperial cape. Andraste took it from him and wrapped it around her shoulders.

"Did you see your prince's expression?" asked Vespasian.

Andraste glanced over her shoulder. Aldrich's back was turned to her as his horse was brought around. She could not hear what he was saying to the Southern lords but he did seem vexed.

"The Southern lords are ready," said Martin.

"Can they ride?" asked Frederick.

"Aldrich is a better rider then I," admitted Andraste.

"And he is a man without fault," said Vespasian. Andraste blushed. She hid her head behind Vespasian's shoulder.

"You have been lied to. Who so described him?" asked Kasimir.

"My Empress, and she does not lie," responded Vespasian. Andraste saw a ghost of a smile flicker on Aldrich's lips.

"That was before I knew you accepted Toxin as an ally. You are a fool, Aldrich Caelius," said Andraste.

"That I already knew," remarked Aldrich dryly.

"Shall we go?" asked Vespasian.

"Lead on," replied Aldrich.

Vespasian's horse nearly flew into the night. Andraste held on tightly to Vespasian, who only laughed. Vespasian urged his horse faster and faster. They approached a gate, but Vespasian did not slow. His horse leapt over the gate and landed on the ground. Andraste heard the sound of Kasimir swearing in the night. The Northern officers, all save one, also leapt over the gate. The remaining officer opened the gate for the carriages.

"You have left behind the Southern lords," said Andraste.

"It is their country. They will know the way," replied Vespasian, "Besides your prince has taken the lead? Did you not notice?"

"Stop calling him my prince. He could not outride the greatest horseman in the North," stated Andraste.

"Look there," said Vespasian. He flicked his head to the right. Andraste could see that Aldrich was already waiting for them at the army camp. He ignored Andraste completely. He spoke to some of the Northern soldiers. Andraste turned her attention back to Vespasian. He was moving slowly and obviously in pain.

"Are you alright?" asked Andraste.

"My stitches may have come undone," admitted Vespasian.

"Why would you ride so hard with such a wound? It is careless," scolded Andraste.

"It was a matter of principle, Empress, a matter of Northern pride," replied Vespasian.

Andraste sighed in response. She dismounted gracefully, and then extended an arm to Vespasian. He laughed at the gesture and dismounted on his own. However, he faltered a step. Andraste could see blood start to seep through his tunic. Andraste wrapped his arm around her shoulders.

"Straight ahead," directed Vespasian. Andraste saw a massive red meeting tent before them. The Southern lords had finally met up with the party.

"The ladies must be frightened from such a ride," said Egnatius. He bowed eloquently to the Northern ladies.

"We are Northern women. We fear nothing," replied a Northern lady. She rejoined the other Northern ladies and they headed toward the meeting tent.

"Fear is afraid of Andraste Valerianus," stated Martin.

Andraste laughed along with the Northern officers. Due to the commotion, a healer poked his head out of the tent.

"Tore out his stitches, did he not?" asked a healer.

"I suppose so," said Andraste.

"I see he has brought me an additional patient. How are you holding up?" asked the healer.

"I am as you see me," responded Andraste.

"Well that is better than we hoped," replied the healer. He moved to help Andraste.

"I have him, if you would just open the tent flap?" asked Andraste. The healer opened the tent for her.

Andraste paused in her tracks as she saw the number of wounded.

"Courage, Empress," said Vespasian.

"It is more my resolve. Is it worth such a cost?" whispered Andraste.

"Yes," replied Vespasian.

The healer pointed to a clean bedroll and Andraste deposited Vespasian to the spot.

"I can tend to him," said Andraste.

"Yes, Empress," said the healer. He left with her with the supplies that she would need. She removed Vespasian's shirt. She could see fresh blood stains on his bandages.

"So many stiches," said Andraste, "Animal attack?"

"One of the experiments, a failed jiufeng, poor thing only had five heads," said Vespasian.

"You would not have survived if it had possessed the other four," replied Andraste.

She removed the Imperial cape, and took her place at Vespasian's side. She paused as she heard one of the Northern ladies begin to sing. Vitus watched her movements carefully. She gestured towards Aldrich and the Southern lords. Vitus bowed and then went to introduce the Southern lords to the other Northern officers.

Andraste worked quickly and expertly on restitching Vespasian's wounds. He did not cry out in pain, although he took labored breaths. Andraste finished and reapplied his bandages.

"We should rejoin the Southerners," said Vespasian.

"Vitus has them in hand. You will sit. I told you I would entertain you," said Andraste. One of the Northern ladies brought her a bowl of clean water and soap to wash her hands.

Andraste retook her seat at Vespasian's side. She saw that someone had left them a tray with a carafe of rice wine and two small pottery glasses. Vespasian reached to serve the wine, and Andraste slapped his hand away. He rolled his eyes at her. She poured him a glass and offered it to him.

"What is the origin of this rice wine?" asked Andraste in surprise as she tasted.

"It is quite good," replied Vespasian with a grin, "We helped ourselves to the Emperor's rice stores and rice wine as we left the North."

Andraste laughed heartily as she took another sip. She saw some heads turns at the sound. Andraste poured him another glass and one for herself. She returned her attention back to the dancers. Andraste saw Vitus leading the Southern lords around. Aldrich would stop and talk to some of the wounded soldiers. On the direst cases, he would use his spirit phoenix to heal the wounded.

"A remarkable power," commented Vespasian as he followed

Andraste's glaze.

"He is a formidable ally," replied Andraste.

Aldrich and the Southern lords had finished making the rounds. Vitus seated them with the Northern officers. The Northern ladies brought rice wine and poured for the Southern lords and Northern officers. Andraste saw Maximianus and Nero glowering at the back of the tent. She gestured for them to come to her.

"Why so sinister?" asked Andraste.

She followed Maximianus's gaze to the Northern lady, Iunia. She was pouring rice wine for Eadbehrt, who was trying valiantly to get her to speak. The lady said nothing and lowered her eyes to the ground.

"I expect you to welcome the Southern lords. The men will look to your example, and follow your lead," said Andraste.

"Yes, Commander," said Maximianus and Nero in unison.

"Iunia," called Andraste. Maximianus stood to his full attention as the lady approached. However, he kept his eyes on Andraste.

"I have requested Maximianus demonstrate a Northern dance, but he is lacking a partner," said Andraste.

"Yes, Empress," said Iunia. She smiled brightly and raised her dark eyes to Maximianus and then quickly to the ground.

Maximianus turned towards the center of the tent and Iunia followed a few steps behind. When they reached the center, he turned to speak gently to the lady and she raised her eyes to him. She smiled sweetly and said a few words. Maximianus bowed low to Iunia in response.

"Perhaps the sweetest lady of the North," commented Nero.

"And who are you seeking?" asked Vespasian, "The Empress could summon you a partner as well."

"If she wishes to see me, she will come to me. It is her choice," replied Nero. He bowed low to Andraste and then joined the Southern lords. A Northern lady Andraste did not know served him a glass of rice wine. Nero said nothing, but he looked pleased.

"For a war, there is a peculiar amount of matchmaking," stated Vespasian.

Andraste laughed softly and turned her eyes to the dancing couple. She poured Vespasian another glass of rice wine.

As the music finished, Andraste rose. A Northern lady approached her and brought her two large red fans. She bowed low before presenting them to Andraste. Andraste took the fans and inclined her head towards the lady. The lady backed away and took a seat on the ground beside an injured warrior. All eyes turned towards Andraste. Andraste took a few steps forward and then turned to face Vespasian.

"Why is it so quiet?" Kasimir asked across the room. A Northern lady began to play a shamisen. It was a slow, mournful tune.

"The Empress will dance," replied Vitus. He turned his intention back to Andraste.

Andraste stood perfectly still with the two open fans. The first she spread in front of her to block her face. The second she held in her left hand behind her back. As the music started, she slowly turned in three circles, her skirts sweeping out around her, and holding her fans stationary. She paused, made the slightest of curtsies, and swept the front fan towards the audience, sweeping her hand downward and then upward, and then raising the fan to the ceiling. She repeated the motion before raising both fans towards the ceiling and turning in three circles. She raised the first fan before her face and the second fan behind her back. She closed the first fan and almost touched her face with it and then swept downwards lightly touching her knee before opening it and sweeping both hands towards the ceiling as she spun in a circle. She momentarily froze in a curtsey, lifting her front fan to her side and the second fan to the ceiling. Then raising her first fan to the ceiling she rotated in three circles once more. She closed both fans and alternated her arms moving up and down, stepping backwards as she did so. She turned in a circle and opened her fans, putting them behind her back and then opened them to the front. When she brought them to the center she curtsied before settling to the floor. She spread out both hands in front of her, one raised to the ceiling, and the other just below her chin. She swept the fan towards the ceiling downwards and held it behind her, while the fan in front of her was swept towards the side and towards the ceiling. She swept the fan in front of her face while rising to one knee and then standing. She closed both fans and swayed from side to side as she raised them to the ceiling. She opened one fan and turned in three circles, before closing it as she opened the second fan and turned three circles in the opposite direction. She resumed her opening stance as the music ended.

Andraste wordlessly resumed her place by Vespasian as another Northern lady started a dance in the center of the tent. She lifted her glass to her lips.

"You are rusty," said Vespasian. The nearest Victorious laughed. She threw the contents of her glass in Vespasian's face.

"It is cruel to torment an injured man," advised Vespasian.

"I am sterilizing your wounds," replied Andraste.

"I have seen you dance while a thousand people waited on bated breath," reminded Vespasian.

"I am tired," responded Andraste.

"Shall I return you to the castle?" asked Vespasian.

"You will rest. I will listen to the war council," said Andraste.

Vespasian lifted his empty glass to her and Andraste poured him more wine.

"It as if there is no direction in the North. The Empress was exiled. Tobias and Matthias were slain. The only Northern pillar remaining is Titus, and he has defected to the Resistance," said Vitus.

"Who leads the Imperial Army?" asked Aldrich.

"The Emperor's personal guards have usurped control. However, they are more feared than trusted. They have no regard to human life or sacrifice. They send troops out without the means to fulfill their missions, but if the troops hesitate in the slightest, they are executed," answered Vitus.

"From our reports, it seems as though the Emperor is keeping the majority of his forces in the North," said Aldrich.

"Agreed. It is as though he is waiting for us to come to him," replied Vitus.

"He knows I will come for him," said Andraste to Vespasian.

"Is that your intention?" questioned Vespasian. Andraste raised her eyes, filled with sorrow, and poured Vespasian another glass of rice wine.

"Where is Titus?" asked Aldrich.

"He is currently stationed in the east but he plans on moving his forces north," responded Vitus.

"Are we sure he is to be trusted?" asked Kasimir.

"His mother and brother were executed by the Emperor's will and his second brother cursed by the Emperor. Titus is both hard and cruel, but he abides by honor. He will give her hell, but when the time comes, he will follow the Empress as he always has," stated Vitus.

"Debatable," commented Andraste.

"He challenges you and fights you, but when you make a decision, he is the first to lend you aid," replied Vespasian.

"Vitus speaks a great deal in your place," stated Andraste.

"I will interject if he is wrong," responded Vespasian.

"You have such faith in your second?" asked Andraste.

"We have been through a great deal together," responded Vespasian, "As have you with Laelius and Mikhael."

"I have not heard from Mikhael. I do not know the fate of my squadrons," said Andraste.

"Shortly after the rumors of your death at the hands of the Emperor, Mikhael and the equivalent of three of your squadrons defected to the Resistance. The remaining two defected on the return to the North after the deaths of Tobias and Matthias. There was a bloody skirmish with Varinia's forces. However, your men were aided by Matthias's men, and they all headed towards the East to join Titus," described Vespasian.

"Where will you go?" asked Andraste.

"The men of the Island Kingdoms are holding the sea to prevent supplies from reaching the Northern lands from the other Empires. They are also thwarting the movement of Northern ships. As Titus is moving from the Northeast, I will move from the Southwest, and we will invade the North from either side to thin out the Imperial lines," replied Vespasian.

Andraste realized that the conversation of the officers had faded as they listened to her own discussion.

"You will ride with us?" asked Vespasian.

"There is something I must do," responded Andraste.

"I see," replied Vespasian. He glanced to Aldrich, "And the Southern prince will accompany you?"

"I will only take Brion, my Victorious, and Aldrich Caelius for our mission," said Andraste.

"Be careful when you are North, the Arisen and experiments are at their highest numbers yet. They are uncontrollable and powerful," warned Vespasian.

"Rest a few days so that your men can heal their wounds. I will not leave for at least two days," said Andraste.

"So soon?" asked Vespasian.

"We must move before the Emperor has time to regroup," said Andraste. She turned her eyes towards Aldrich, who was already watching her intently.

"I thank you for your hospitality," said Aldrich.

Aldrich rose and bowed to the Northern officers and ladies. The Southern lords began to rouse themselves but Aldrich shook his head. He turned and departed the tent.

"Thank you for coming. It restored our spirits," said Vespasian.

"Am I dismissed?" asked Andraste.

She smiled at her friend. She rose and proceeded into the night. The night air was cold for the Southern climate. She saw Aldrich studying the stars as his horse was brought for him. She joined his side and looked to the stars.

"It is said our fate is written in the stars," said Aldrich.

"The stars may guide us, but we move our own feet," replied Andraste.

A soldier brought forth Aldrich's horse and Vespasian's black stallion. Aldrich looked over his shoulder for the Northern Commander.

"I cannot take Boreas," said Andraste. She stroked the stallion's neck.

"My Commander insisted. He trusted no other to take you safely," said the soldier.

"Tell Vespasian that I will return him tomorrow," said Andraste. The soldier saluted her and went into the red tent.

"So you can ride with a lord, but you cannot take his horse?" asked Aldrich.

"Boreas is the finest stallion of the North. His worth is perhaps more than Vespasian's command," said Andraste. She mounted the great stallion.

"You put such value in animals?" asked Aldrich. Boreas is snorted and flipped his mane.

"Boreas is a war horse. He is well-trained and shows no fear. He is extremely intelligent," answered Andraste. She bent forward to stroke Boreas's neck.

"Well, at least you have found a male who will please you," replied Aldrich.

Andraste laughed softly before turning Boreas towards the Southern palace. Aldrich mounted quickly and urged his horse beside her. Out of the corner of her eye, she saw Felix following them at a distance.

"Are all Northern ladies schooled in the healing arts? I did not see one lady here who was not aiding the wounded," said Aldrich.

"It is our survival. We all learn. The North-" started Andraste.

"Is a dangerous place," finished Aldrich. Andraste smiled in spite of herself.

"I do admire Northern strength. I heard tales of what your countrymen encountered on their journey. It sounds like hell would have been more inviting. And, yet, they still laugh. They still make merry and carry on. It is impressive fortitude," said Aldrich.

"We do what we must," replied Andraste.

Aldrich looked at her questioningly but he said nothing.

"Do you have any other questions regarding the North?" asked Andraste.

"Is it common for noble ladies to dance among commoners?" inquired Aldrich.

"The concept of rank evolved with the Empire. It came from the South. Before the Empire, there were leaders of tribes or a head warrior. We do not see the difference in ranks as the Southerners do. A member of the tribe is rewarded by his deeds, not his birth," answered Andraste.

"So a lady could become a Muse even of a common-born man?" asked Aldrich.

"I have no such intention, if that is what you are truly asking. Vespasian is a fine officer, and a fearless warrior. However, he has rendered me no such service to offer such a prize," responded Andraste.

"He has brought you 10,000 warriors and saved the South from the

Emperor's attack," said Aldrich.

"He did not do it for me. They are fighting for their freedom as well," said Andraste. She glanced back to the prince, "Have you reconsidered my offer?"

"Many times, but my answer is the same," replied Aldrich. He quickened his stallion's pace, which made conversation become more difficult.

The palace was near silent as they rode into the courtyard. There were very few lights in the windows. Aldrich dismounted and turned to survey Andraste.

"The city sleeps," commented Andraste.

"It will awaken soon. It is near dawn," replied Aldrich.

Andraste dismounted and a stable boy, rubbing sleep from his eyes, came to take their horses. She proceeded down the corridor and Aldrich followed. They did not speak again until they reached the doors to their chambers.

"I will come for you near the evening meal to escort you back to the castle," said Aldrich.

"As you wish," replied Andraste. They bowed to each other in the corridor, before each retreated to their chambers.

Chapter Eleven

"Lords," said Andraste as she entered Aldrich's chambers. Rhinauld and Henry followed behind her. The tension in the room was palpable.

"Commander," said Egnatius. He bowed to her as she passed. Andraste stopped before him. She surveyed the filled room but did not see Aldrich.

"He is not well," stated Egnatius.

"What do you mean?" asked Andraste. She surveyed the group of healers and sorcerers assembled. Marcella was very pale, and in deep discussion with Brion.

"We think he has been poisoned," said Egnatius. Andraste's hand went to her hilt and she searched the room for Toxin.

"It is not a Northern poison," rejoined Toxin quickly.

"If Toxin was guilty, he would be dead. The blood oath binds him," stated Marcella.

"Nor is it a poison I have encountered on my travels," interjected Brion.

"Why did you not send for me?" asked Andraste angrily.

"What could you do?" retorted Marcella.

"She shares Aldrich's healing power. We are not sure why, but it only seems to work on him," said Rhinauld. Marcella sent Brion an accusatory glance.

"I did not know," said Brion.

Andraste was already sweeping past the Southern lords to Aldrich's bedchamber. Eadbehrt stood in her way.

"Perhaps not the best time, Commander," said Eadbehrt. His eyes darted to Marcella.

"The prince is not himself," stated Kasimir. He too joined Eadbehrt, and barred Andraste from the room.

"Step aside. She may be able to heal him," ordered Marcella.

"The prince would not want her to see him in such a state," advised Kasimir.

"This is no time for Southern propriety," stated Andraste angrily.

Marcella laid a hand on Andraste's shoulder and gently pushed her forward. The Southern lords stepped aside and bowed to Andraste as she passed.

"We are trying to keep him awake. Sleep could be fatal," said Marcella, "However, he is proving a troublesome patient. My mother is with him now."

They entered the chamber and Andraste saw the Queen and Aldrich both sitting cross legged on the bed playing cards.

"You are cheating," alleged Aldrich.

"You are not following the rules," protested the Queen.

"A card game? Deal me in," said Andraste. The Queen smiled at her approvingly.

"Pulchritudinous," said Aldrich as his eyes landed on Andraste. He smiled at her.

"What?" asked Andraste.

"Beauteous, bewitching, ravishing, elegant, alluring," replied Aldrich. His eyes followed her every movement. Andraste looked to the Queen.

"In other words, Andraste," said Aldrich.

"Ill or not, I will beat you if you continue in such a state," stated Andraste. The Queen passed her a hand of cards.

"Please be seated," invited the Queen.

"I may have to do a running leap to climb into this bed," said Andraste as she eyed Aldrich's four poster bed.

"Please do," encouraged Aldrich.

"This is serious," disapproved Marcella.

"It is not an opponent. It is a piece of furniture," said Aldrich.

He rose from the bed and picked Andraste effortlessly in his arms.

Golden light seemed to envelop wherever they touched. The light was so fierce that it was near blinding. Aldrich paused and watched the light memorized.

"I have never seen the like," said Marcella, "How do you do it?"

"Nothing," replied Andraste.

"Can you make a phoenix?" asked Marcella.

"No," said Andraste, "Aldrich, put me down."

Aldrich regained his focus and placed her gently on the bed. The cards dispersed in every direction.

"Alas, the cards have flown," said the Queen.

Aldrich was fascinated by the cards and started picking them up one by one. He would pick up a card put it in the pile on the center of the bed and then find the next card.

"What was the game?" asked Andraste.

"A child's game, I could not get him to focus," said the Queen.

"How long will it take to heal him?" asked Marcella impatiently.

"I will need to be close to him. When the light stops between us, he should be healed," said Andraste.

"We will leave you. Perhaps if he is not distracted and he stays still, he will heal faster," said Marcella.

"Suggestions?" asked Andraste.

"Read to him," said Marcella.

"Would you like the princess to read to you?" asked the Queen.

Aldrich surveyed Andraste in his bed and forgot about the cards. Andraste repositioned to a cross-legged position on the bed with her back against the headboard. She laid her Ruin sword across her knees.

"Why would we read?" questioned Aldrich as he ogled Andraste. Andraste blushed and looked away from the prince.

"Return to bed," commanded Marcella.

Aldrich did not require a second invitation. He propped himself on his side so that he could watch Andraste. He just barely touched her knee and the light grew between them once more.

"Do not stare at me," ordered Andraste.

"No," returned Aldrich with a smile. His sapphire eyes laughed at her.

"No?" repeated Andraste.

"How could I not admire such beauty?" asked Aldrich.

"Seriously?" questioned Andraste.

She judged Aldrich with her sea-green eyes. He was undeterred by her hostility. She looked up as she heard the door close. Marcella and the Queen had stealthily left the room. Aldrich gently laid his head on Andraste's lap and said:

"My lady fair, do not cast me aside,
For I will love you as no other can,
Do not exile me by your unfair ban,
For I love you as no other has tried,
My love increases even when denied,
At first sight my love of you began,
For only you every moment I plan.
Never alter or change, my lady fair,
I will always love you as you are now,
Every feeling, every thought is bare,
For your love I will return, I avow,
Your love is the only shield I will wear,
If my constant love your heart will allow."

Andraste did not know how to respond. She studied the tapestry on the wall before her. The silence lengthened between them, and Aldrich's eyes slowly closed. Andraste shook him gently.

"It is too early to sleep. Tell me another poem," said Andraste.

"It is a sonnet," corrected Aldrich.

"I will hear another," ordered Andraste.

Aldrich opened his sapphire eyes to gaze upon her. He stared at her as if he was committing every curve of her face to memory. He stretched beside her, but then did as she bade:

"No entity can meet her allure with ease,
Nor compare to the beauty of her eyes,
Not the azure waters of the Southern seas,

Nor the diamonds of the midnight skies,
Nor the beryl gleam of a gemstone prize.
Her beauty grows exponentially by the hour;
Other charms fade away but hers never die.
With such beauty she needs no other power.
The alabaster petals of a wild flower
Cannot equal the fairness of her complexion.
But not to tempt the light-hearted vower,
The insincere will not pass by her detection,
More suitors than stars in the skies has she,
But yet is she to declare, 'This one pleases me.'"

"I do not know these poems. Recite another," said Andraste.

"I cannot compose on demand," said Aldrich, "Recite a Northern poem for me."

"I know very little poetry," said Andraste.

"Not part of Northern education?" teased Aldrich. Andraste glared at him in response.

"Does not your father write poetry?" asked Aldrich.

"When I was a child, he wrote poems for my mother, but that was a long time ago," said Andraste sadly. Her thoughts turned to the past.

"Andraste," said Aldrich. Andraste turned her attention back to the prince and said:

"I am beside you
Two cannot cry the same tears
Think not of sorrow."

Aldrich kissed her hand and resettled his head in her lap. Andraste blushed but she did not push him away. The light between them was beginning to dissipate. Aldrich closed his eyes and drifted off to sleep. Andraste placed both of her hands on Aldrich's back, so that the light would maximize. Aldrich slept for no more than an hour, but when he awoke, he seemed to be himself. It took a moment for his eyes to focus.

"Am I dreaming?" asked Aldrich.

"Yes," replied Andraste with a smile. He nestled his head in her lap.

"You smell of lavender and the seaside," said Aldrich.

"I went to the shore today," replied Andraste. She adjusted to make him more comfortable. He felt her against him, and he hastily moved to remove himself.

"I am not dreaming. You are in my bed," stated Aldrich.

"You have been poisoned. You find me thus in order to heal you," said Andraste.

"How long have you been here?" asked Aldrich.

"I am not certain. I returned from the Northern camp this evening and found you thus," said Andraste.

"I did not meet you as promised. I apologize," said Aldrich. He shifted on the bed uncomfortably.

"Stay where you are. I need to be close to you," said Andraste. Aldrich looked at her sharply. She raised a hand so that he could see the light glowing between them.

"Thanks to the Ruin," said Aldrich. Andraste's attention fell to the reports on his bedside table.

"Shall I read to you?" asked Andraste.

"Not those. Those are agricultural reports. I read them when I cannot sleep," admitted Aldrich. She picked up a book on the bedside table instead.

"On Northern customs?" inquired Andraste. Aldrich took it out of her hands.

"What do you want to know? I am more of an authority than this book. When was it written?" asked Andraste. She took it back from him.

"Probably before our parents' time," said Aldrich. Andraste laughed and opened the book to the table of contents.

"There is not a section on courtship or Muses," commented Andraste.

Aldrich wrestled the book from her and threw it across the room. Andraste laughed at him.

"That was not my desire–" started Aldrich. He froze as he realized he had Andraste pinned to the bed underneath him. He hastily retreated to his side of the bed. Andraste raised herself on one elbow.

"I like you best when you are unwell," said Andraste.

"You would prefer I was poisoned on a regular basis?" asked Aldrich.

"If you will allow me to tend you, I do have a debt to repay," said Andraste.

"You are here because of your debt?" inquired Aldrich. He surveyed her with his sapphire eyes.

"You may think me heartless and cruel, but I do care what happens to you," said Andraste softly. She would not look at him. She changed the subject before he could respond, "But who poisoned you? Have you eaten anything suspicious?"

"Well, yes. A foreign man came to me and offered me heliotrope mushrooms," replied Aldrich. His eyes laughed at her.

"You are being sarcastic?" inquired Andraste.

"Of course, I am. I ate nothing unusual, and accepted nothing from anyone sinister," replied Aldrich.

"No one else is ill, so it could not have occurred at the feast. At the Northern tent? Did you partake of the rice wine?" asked Andraste.

"Rice wine?" inquired Aldrich.

"Vespasian stole the Emperor's rice wine stores," admitted Andraste.

"Alas, I missed that, and I thought at least we were friends. A friend would have shared such bounty," said Aldrich, "No. I did not eat or drink at the Northern tent. You seem relieved. Were you worried your men had poisoned me?"

"It would have been awkward," responded Andraste.

"Awkward?" cried Aldrich, "You define my hypothetical death as 'awkward'?"

"You are twisting my sentiment. What am I supposed to say? It most likely would have created civil war, the Northern forces would return to the North, and the Emperor would prevail," said Andraste. She and Aldrich surveyed each other.

"You think a militant sorcerer then? Is Toxin still living?" asked Aldrich.

"Yes," answered Andraste, "But what if he had someone else administer the poison?"

"Ancient magic cannot be deceived so simply," replied Aldrich.

"But who else could have gotten to you?" asked Andraste. Aldrich did not reply.

"Gerlinde?" asked Andraste.

"No!" cried Aldrich. He flushed angrily.

"Why are you so angry? It is just a question," said Andraste.

"Why are you so infuriating?" asked Aldrich.

"Infuriating? I, who have sat devotedly by your bedside all evening, saving your life, am infuriating?" rejoined Andraste. Her sea-green eyes flashed.

"I apologize. I am not myself today," replied Aldrich, "I am sorry I could not go the Northern camp. Fewer things give me as much pleasure as seeing you dance."

Andraste turned her full attention to the prince. She put a hand to his brow.

"You are feverish again," said Andraste.

"Then come closer, heal me," said Aldrich. He pulled her to him. The Ruin sword fell to the floor.

"I will only warn you once, my prince. I am armed," said Andraste. She pushed him away as she blushed.

"You are always armed," said Aldrich. He removed a dagger from her sleeve and tossed it to the floor.

"My lord, you are not yourself," said Andraste. Her heart began to race. He moved a strand of hair from her face and asked, "Do you not want-"

There was a knock on the door. Aldrich hastily dropped his hand and returned to his side of the bed. Marcella entered followed behind by Brion, who carried a tray of food. Brion looked to Andraste and then shot a look of warning to Aldrich. He deposited the tray on the bed and left the room. Marcella moved to follow him.

"Please stay," requested Andraste.

"Go," ordered Aldrich.

"His fever has returned. I think we may need a professional healer," said Andraste.

"Andraste will heal me. Go!" ordered Aldrich. Andraste blushed as he said her name.

"I see," said Marcella.

"Perhaps a sleeping draft for the prince?" asked Andraste.

"That would be dangerous as we do not know the nature of the poison," responded Marcella.

"See, your presence is needed here! I could kill him with kindness," alleged Andraste. Marcella drew up a chair beside Aldrich, who sighed in defeat.

"Do you think it a militant sorcerer underneath the Emperor's control?" asked Andraste.

"No, we have found traces of a blue flower in the sample, but I know of no poison of that nature," replied Marcella.

"Could it be a Reaper's Boutonniere? It is an indigo flower that grows only in the West. It is extremely rare and hard to come by, but it is nearly untraceable," said Andraste.

Marcella set down the soup that she had been eating.

"Two score healers and sorcerers have been outside for near eight hours, and not one suggested that," said Marcella.

"Not even Brion? We have run into it before. Someone tried to poison me in the West with such a flower," replied Andraste.

She frowned as she surveyed her own food. She was no longer hungry. Brion returned to the room with a pitcher of water. He had heard their exchange, but did not respond until he had closed the door.

"I did not poison the prince," said Brion, "It seemed too great a coincidence for you both to have attempted assassinations from the same extremely rare flower."

"How rare is this flower?" inquired Marcella.

"One in a million," responded Brion, "It blooms only once every twenty years in the farthest corner of the Western plains. It would take nearly two years to get there. However, if it has not had the right conditions, it will wait another twenty years before blooming. When the flowers are in bloom, they create a fragrance that if inhaled, can kill a man. Furthermore, the process to make such a poison is both tedious and arduous. It would take a master sorcerer to produce said poison, or someone would have to sell their kingdom to afford it. Once made, it would need to be used within one day."

"Which rules out all of our suspects," sighed Marcella.

"At this point, I do not care who did it. Just find an anecdote and heal him," said Andraste.

"Your magic did not heal him completely?" questioned Brion.

"He is feverish," responded Andraste.

"So were you even after he healed you from the poisoned arrow," reminded Brion.

"I do not recall," said Andraste.

"You attacked three of your men and Brion," said Aldrich.

"I did no such thing," bristled Andraste. Aldrich and Brion exchanged glances. Andraste looked at them thoughtfully.

"You bade me return your Ruin sword for a kiss," said Aldrich. He laughed at her. Marcella and Brion looked at Andraste in shock.

"That is an utter and complete fabrication," alleged Andraste.

"Now that he has eaten, his color seems to have improved," said Marcella as she studied her brother.

"Andra, I am sure it would return to normal if you sat farther away," commented Brion dryly.

"The light still glows between us. He is not fully recovered. I will stay with him until the light dissipates," said Andraste.

"I fear we have no other alternative," admitted Brion. He took the tray from Marcella and they left the room together.

Andraste resumed her cross-legged position against the headboard. Her knee was barely touching Aldrich. She closed her eyes.

"That position cannot be comfortable," stated Aldrich.

"Keep your distance," ordered Andraste. She opened one eye to study him. He was just within touching distance. The light continued to flow between them.

"As you wish," said Aldrich.

She could feel him watching her as she tried to fall sleep. When he thought that she had fallen asleep, he inched closer to her so that they were just barely touching, but he came no further.

Andraste woke as the morning light streamed in through the blinds of the windows. Her neck and back ached terribly from sleeping against the headboard in her upright position. She surveyed her patient. She lifted a hand to his chest, but did not touch him. No light emerged from her fingertips.

"What are you doing?" inquired Aldrich. Andraste removed her hand hastily.

"I was seeing if you were healed," replied Andraste.

"Did you determine who poisoned me?" asked Aldrich.

"No," said Andraste. She lifted a hand once more to his chest. No light omitted from her finger trips.

"You seem disappointed," said Aldrich.

"Not at all. I am relieved that you are healed. I will return to my chambers. You have long desired my absence," said Andraste. She removed herself from the bed.

"Paramerion," said Aldrich. He reached for her hand, "I owe you my life."

"As I owe you mine," said Andraste, "Once you are fully recovered, we need to travel to the North. We cannot wait for the Emperor to kills us in our beds."

"If it suits you, we will leave at first light tomorrow," said Aldrich.

"Agreed," responded Andraste. She turned to look at him at the doorway.

"I am well," said Aldrich.

Andraste stepped out of the room quickly. Egnatius rose as she exited the chamber and she paused in the doorway.

"Are you ready for visitors: Captain Egnatius, Lords Kasimir and Eadbehrt?" asked Andraste. Aldrich rose and stretched.

"He is coming," said Andraste.

"Thank you, Commander," said Egnatius. He bowed low to Andraste. Kasimir and Eadbehrt followed suit.

Andraste brushed past them and returned to her chambers. She shut the door behind her, and headed to her own bedroom. She took a long bath and then slept for a few hours. She woke feeling groggy and disoriented.

She dressed in a buttercup-colored gown and secured her hair in the Southern fashion.

"I did not know you were waiting. I apologize, Vesp," said Andraste as she entered her study. Vespasian was studying her map.

"I am on guard duty so that your brothers could get some sleep," replied Vespasian. He bowed to her, "By these movements, you are planning for a Northern attack."

"I think our intelligence is wrong. Ricimer Valerianus is not known for restraint. The attack will come quickly and without warning. I believe he will attack from all sides," said Andraste.

"You would have me quarter my troops in the Capitol? That will create tension," advised Vespasian.

"I will not have you and your men stuck between two forces. The losses would be catastrophic. We must find ways to work together," replied Andraste. Vespasian bent to examine the map more closely. Andraste joined his side.

"I understand the Island Kingdoms on the ocean, guarding the East. You have my forces and the Southern guarding the North and South. Why are you and your Victorious are guarding the West?" asked Vespasian.

"It is the only direction unguarded by sand," replied Andraste.

"You think the Arisen will come?" asked Vespasian. He reached across her to move one of the pieces on the board.

"I know they will," responded Andraste, "Your forces have no magic users. You will be safest in the city."

She moved his piece back.

"You two look cozy," said Aldrich from the doorway. His sapphire eyes narrowed as he surveyed Vespasian's arm.

"The Commander suspects a Northern invasion," said Vespasian. Andraste stepped away from Vespasian.

"I heard your discussion," said Aldrich. He examined the map, "You have me with the Southern forces?"

"You must lead your people. Additionally, you are most valuable for your healing powers. If you are with the sorcerers on the battlements, you will be away from the front lines, and thus more able to heal the wounded," stated Andraste.

"It is sound reasoning," said Vespasian. He was distracted as one of his soldiers knocked on the door.

"Excuse me," said Vespasian. He stood just outside the door, but he turned so that he could watch Aldrich.

"You are angry with me," said Andraste.

"How long have you been planning for an attack?" asked Aldrich.

"It is a possibility," replied Andraste, "I often plan for many possible situations. If we had proof of such a force, I would give you my recommendations."

"But you will discuss it with Vespasian?" inquired Aldrich.

"We have fought together on campaigns before. He knows my mind and often sees holes in my strategies. I appreciate his counsel," replied Andraste.

"And Rhinauld does he know your plans?" questioned Aldrich.

"He has seen the map and read the same reports, as befits his duty as Commander of the Island Kingdoms Armada," responded Andraste. She shifted uncomfortably as Vespasian disappeared from view.

"You should not be here, my lord," said Andraste.

"And yet, you will permit Vespasian, Felix and Rhinauld alone in this room with you," said Aldrich.

"It is the traditions of your lands. All three are my foster brothers. Decima has been alone in your room with you," rejoined Andraste.

"Yes, but her reputation is beyond on reproach. There is no question of her honor. There is no other name associated with her own, unlike you, who have three names associated with. The court believes that you have multiple lovers. And why should they not, when you behave like a common woman? Decima does not toy with the genuine feelings of lords. She does not flaunt her independence so wantonly," said Aldrich.

"Question my honor? Common? Wantonly? Do you believe me to be a harlot?" asked Andraste.

"That is not what I said. I know you to have spent one night with me. What about with the others? Your conduct is shameless, but-" started Aldrich. He stopped himself as Vespasian reappeared in the room.

"If you have such misgivings about my honor, then you should not remain in the same room with me. Although it is you who entered my chambers and remained unchaperoned. Get out and do not enter again," said Andraste. Aldrich did not move.

"The Commander asked you to leave," said Vespasian, "It is only because you are our host that I have not called you out on those insults. Our ways forbid me from dueling our host."

"Andraste-" started Aldrich.

"Do not address me so informally," said Andraste.

"I-" began Aldrich. He stepped forward to approach her.

"Get out," commanded Andraste, "I cannot leave. I am confined to chambers by order of my King."

"As you wish," said Aldrich. He bowed stiffly to Andraste and left the room. He brushed against Vespasian's shoulder as he passed. Andraste struck the figures on the board and they flew across the room. She took a deep breath and regained her composure.

"What news?" asked Andraste.

"Your foresight is uncanny, Commander. We are being approached from all directions. They will be here by dawn," said Vespasian.

"Summon the Victorious and your officers. We will meet at the Imperial camp," said Andraste.

"Yes, Commander," said Vespasian.

He turned smartly on his heel and closed the doors behind him. Andraste returned to her study and dressed in her travel clothes. She strapped the Ruin sword about her hip and concealed her daggers. She was half way to the stables before she encountered the King of the Island Kingdoms.

"You have heard," stated the King.

"Yes. I am on my way to meet with the Northern officers," replied Andraste.

"Aldrich has convened the War Council," said the King.

"He knows my recommendations," said Andraste, "We will start moving Vespasian's troops to the city, and then my Victorious and I will position ourselves in the West."

"That is what I would do," replied the King, "But we are in his lands."

"If he instructs otherwise, I will be at the Northern camp," said Andraste.

"Where are your guards?" asked the King.

"First, I have born that nonsense for as long as I can. Second, there is no need. Aldrich called me a wantonly common woman without honor or shame. He will not be near me again," replied Andraste.

"Are those his exact words? Are you positive he was not trying to tell you something different?" asked the King.

"We are going to battle. It does not matter," said Andraste. She mounted her horse. She paused as she saw Rhiannon running down the hall towards them.

"I wish to fight," said Rhiannon.

"No," said the King.

"I am older than many of your soldiers. I have more training then many of your officers. I have the right to fight for our lands and for my family," said Rhiannon, "Let me serve, my King."

The King looked to Andraste, she nodded.

"Return to Rhinauld's ship and retrieve your armor. Then you will board and remain on my flagship. From that moment, you will not leave my side. You will do as I do," said the King. Rhiannon bowed to the King.

"I doubt I will see either of you again before this is over," said Andraste.

"Victory loves fools," said the King.

"Fortune favors the brave," replied Andraste.

She bent to grasp hands with the King and then she turned her horse towards the Northern road. She set off at a fierce gallop. The palace gates were already being closed. Andraste urged her horse faster and jumped through the opening. As she approached Vespasian's camp, she saw that they were already being mobilized. The first squadrons were already being moved towards the city. Vespasian rode out to meet her.

"Aldrich already gave the order," explained Vespasian as he rode to her side, "He heard the news before we did."

"That is why he was so angry. He thought I was concealing information," said Andraste.

"One of the reasons," commented Vespasian.

"My Victorious?" asked Andraste.

"I bade them meet you on the Western road. I will coordinate with Egnatius once my troops are within the city," said Vespasian. He saluted her and she returned the salute. Andraste turned her horse west and rode towards the plains.

"Heiyoh!" called Andraste as she approached the Victorious.

"Arisen?" asked Laelius. Andraste slowed her horse as she reached his side.

"Vespasian says you think there will be Arisen," said Laelius. Andraste nodded her head once. She heard swearing amongst her men.

"We have fought them before and survived. We will do so again," said Andraste.

"Yes, Commander," replied Laelius.

"We will camp on the Western road?" asked Felix.

"Yes. We will stay within sight of the city. We will hold our ground," replied Andraste.

"Head out," ordered Laelius.

The Victorious followed the Western road and stopped short of reaching the plains. Andraste turned towards the South. They could see the palace in the distance.

"The Southerners will be able to see us," stated Laelius.

"We cannot conceal our secret forever. Sorcery is authorized. I will not have you all risk your lives needlessly," said Andraste, "We will attack in teams and rotate the use of magic users."

"Will the Southern sorcerers be able to aid us from such a distance?" asked Gnaeus.

"Their power is mostly for healing. They will not be of use against the Arisen," replied Andraste.

"Yes, but they could heal us," stated Otho.

"We will approach the palace," conceded Andraste. They rode halfway towards the palace and then stopped their horses.

"Do you think we will wait long?" asked Felix.

"No. I think they will attack before the main forces under the cover of darkness," said Andraste. The sun was already setting.

"Rest the horses for now, let them graze. Thracius, Priscus, on sentry duty," ordered Laelius. The warriors did as they were told.

"You did not bring Aldrich," said Laelius.

"His duty is to his people," replied Andraste.

"Vespasian says you quarreled," said Laelius.

"Remind me to remove Vespasian's tongue when we return," said Andraste. Felix laughed softly, but Andraste silenced with him a glare.

"What now?" asked Gnaeus.

"We wait," replied Laelius.

"Valens, Felix, you will ride at my flanks. Gnaeus you will ride behind me. Give each other room, so that Thracius, Priscus, and Nero do not strike you," said Andraste.

"Yes, Commander," answered Valens, Felix and Gnaeus.

"Maximianus and Hadrian, you will take over as needed from the magic users. Otho, Cato, Glaucio, you will use flaming arrows on the corpses. The remainder of you will deal with any who get past us. I will not allow a single Arisen to reach the city," commanded Andraste.

"Yes, Commander," answered her warriors. Andraste turned her eyes to the horizon. She saw flashes of grey start to move from across the plain.

"They move despite the sunlight. These are not normal Arisen. Be cautious," warned Laelius.

"Riders approach from the South. It looks like Kasimir, Eadbhert and Aldrich. They bring their squadrons," reported Glaucio.

Andraste did not move her eyes from the approaching horde.

"Who do we protect?" asked Andraste.

"The helpless," replied the warriors.

"Who we fight for?" asked Andraste.

"Each other," replied the warriors.

Andraste unsheathed her Ruin sword and her paramerion, taking swords in both hands, she urged her horse forward. Valens, Felix and Gnaeus gave her space, but each took one of her sides. She heard the sound of crackling before she saw the waves of white lightning that passed by their shoulders towards the Arisen.

"Heiyoh!" cheered Gnaeus.

"Focus!" ordered Andraste.

She drove her blade at an Arisen warrior, slicing his head clean from his body. She rode forward. Two Arisen came hurtling at her from two different sides. She decapitated the first and Valens the second. She saw only saw a flash of orange light as his axes moved through the air. She continued riding towards the Arisen. The Arisen did not move tactically. They seemed to be driven towards the living. They began to charge towards Andraste and her three comrades.

"By the gods," swore Gnaeus.

"Courage, son of Laelius," called Valens.

Andraste again urged her horse forward, swinging her blades in every direction. She did not know how many she struck down, but she continued forwards. She glanced behind her and saw flaming arrows hurtling towards the corpses of the Arisen. Avitus, Laurentius and Laelius had joined the melee on her right. The Southern guardsmen were taking up flaming arrows from Cato, Glaucio and Otho. Accordingly, the three Victorious urged their horses towards the Arisen.

There was a pause in the onslaught, and Andraste pulled her horse to a sudden stop.

"What is that?" asked Felix.

"Leave it to me," ordered Andraste, "Spread out. Do not let the Arisen through."

"Yes, Commander," answered the warriors.

Andraste approached the creature in question. It had the head of a crocodile, the body of a bull, a tail of a scorpion, and large powerful wings. It was gigantic. It gnashed its large teeth at Andraste and the tail raised its stinger. Andraste faked to the right, and the creature's stinger came down at her, but she leaned left and slashed at the creature's stomach. Her paramerion was broken in twain. Andraste swore and she could hear Felix laughing.

The creature bore into her horse's flank with its shoulder and it snapped its head around. Andraste was thrown from her horse. She somersaulted across the ground and rose to her feet dizzily. A blue wave of radiating energy passed over her and evaporated the two lunging Arisen. She raised her sword to Maximianus and then turned her attention back on the creature. It was charging her at a rapid pace. Andraste raised her sword and yelled at the top of her lungs. She charged the creature. It hesitated for but a moment. Andraste jumped through the air and sliced through its great head with her Ruin sword. She rolled to the ground as the stinger nearly pierced her side.

"Crazier then all reason," swore Felix. He was no longer laughing.

Andraste whistled for her horse, who limped towards her side. Andraste ran her fingers across its injured flank.

"Go," said Andraste. The horse nuzzled her and headed towards the Southern lines. Felix offered her his hand to pull her up behind him, but she shook her head.

"You will fight better with one rider," said Andraste.

"Take my horse," said Felix.

"No," said Andraste.

"Left," called Laelius. Andraste raised her blade and struck the Arisen hurtling at her side.

"Gnaeus!" said Andraste.

Felix turned to his right and hurtled his horse towards the young warrior, who was fighting three Arisen at once. Andraste swept her eyes across the battlefield. She rested her sword against her back for a moment. The Southern guardsmen were holding their own against the Arisen. They were being aided by the Victorious's magic and Aldrich's healing power. She met Aldrich's eyes. He was following her every movement like a hawk, but he heeded her advice. He did not approach. She felt his spirit phoenix swoop over her shoulder and she turned to see its progress. It healed Gnaeus instantly.

Andraste saw another creature coming across the plain. It was a five-headed bird with the body of a lion, but the talons of an eagle.

"Ours," said Felix. He and Valens rode towards the monster.

Andraste removed her cloak and threw it to the ground. She caught her breath and then charged towards the next line of Arisen.

Red lightning forged a path for her, so that the Arisen would approach her individually. Andraste moved across the field, swinging her blade continuously. She paused as blue flames were produced from the Southern tower. Andraste hesitated for a moment in apprehension but saw the flames only consumed the corpses of the Arisen. The archers were then able to join the battle.

Andraste proceeded forwards as she saw flashes of gray beginning to shoot across the plains. They were halted by a combined wave of white and red lightning, and a tidal wave of radiating blue energy. Andraste paused as she surveyed the field. Nothing ahead of her moved. She looked behind her once more and saw that there were no Arisen between her and the Southern line. She heard cheering from the guardsmen. Her Victorious began to move across the field towards her.

"Hold your position," ordered Andraste. The Victorious froze and the guardsmen fell silent. Andraste used her war fan to direct the Victorious. They took positions across the field.

The wind picked up from the North. Andraste turned her head to the sky and saw clouds as black as night beginning to consolidate on the horizon. The horizon crackled with an emerald light in the distance.

"Sorcerer's fire," called Laelius, "What do you want to do? We cannot fight against it. We cannot put it out."

"It is headed towards the city. They will be destroyed without a chance," said Kasimir.

"Commander?" asked Laelius.

"More Arisen approach, more than before," called Felix.

Andraste placed both of her hands on the hilt of her Ruin sword and placed the tip of the blade on the ground. She held her position. The wind picked up around her and tossed her hazel hair. As the emerald flames shot from the clouds towards the city, a cyclone of ruby light radiated from around Andraste and directed the emerald flames to consume the approaching Arisen and monsters.

Andraste watched until the last of the corpses were consumed. She cleaned her Ruin sword on the grass and sheathed it. She turned back towards the palace. There was silence across the field. Slowly her Victorious approached her. Laelius offered her his arm and he pulled her up behind him on his horse. Andraste surveyed her warriors and saw that they had lost none, although the Southern guardsmen were not so lucky.

"Let us return to the palace. I am hungry," said Andraste. Felix began to laugh, and the Victorious all began to laugh.

"Yes, Commander," replied Laelius. He urged his horse forward at a slow trot.

"Ride on," ordered Andraste. Laelius did not stop to speak to Aldrich or the Southern forces. However, he did return their salute.

"Ride to the port, I want to see how our brethren fared," said Andraste. Laelius did so and they rode towards the port. The remnants of a fearsome battle and wreckage floated across the harbor. Andraste scanned the Island Kingdoms ships.

"The *Sea-Demon* is not there," said Felix.

Andraste scanned the harbor again and her eyes registered on the King's flagship. She saw the familiar sight of her uncle and Rhiannon at the helm. They appeared uninjured. As they approached the city's gates, the riders crossed over a field of corpses. Most of the bodies were dressed in the amethyst uniform of the Emperor's personal guard, but there were Imperial troops as well.

They met the King's flagship as it docked.

"I see you were foolish," said the King.

"I see you were brave," answered Andraste, "Where is the *Sea-Demon*?"

"Destroyed. They used sorcerer's fire on its planks. It went up in smoke. However, Rhinauld sailed it into their formation until the last moment. We were lucky. A wind picked up and blew the *Sea-Demon* into the Imperial ships. They were nearly all destroyed. Most of his crew swam ashore, but we have not yet found him," said the King. Andraste dismounted and took Rhiannon into her arms.

"We will find him," promised Felix. He put a hand on Rhiannon's shoulder.

"Have you seen Brion? Is he not with you?" asked Rhiannon.

"No, he did not fight with us," answered Andraste. Her heart quickened.

"He remained with the Southern sorcerers. I bet he told them to use the ceremonial flames to vanquish the Arisen corpses. It was quite a battle, Andra. We could see you fighting in the distance. You have done the Island Kingdoms proud," said the King.

"Henry? Shannon? How did their crews fare?" asked Andraste.

"Fools all. They are well. They are searching the sea for Rhinauld," said the King.

"It looks like the *Gambit* is returning to port, and the *Kraken*," announced Valens.

Andraste jumped aboard the flagship and across the desk to the portside. She jumped onto the railing, so that she could look across the harbor. From the merrymaking on both ships, she concluded that they were celebrating. The *Gambit* passed the flagship.

"Really, Rhinauld? Is now the best time for a swim?" called Andraste.

"You should take one. You look like one of the Arisen yourself. You probably smell like one too. Stay down wind, Empress," rejoined Rhinauld.

"Glory seeker!" yelled Andraste.

"Showboat!" rejoined Rhinauld.

Andraste turned to find Aldrich conversing with the King. He did not smile as he watched Andraste's exchange with Rhinauld. Andraste was knocked to the ground as two hurtling sailors swung across on ropes. Andraste laughed herself near silly.

"Decorum," reprimanded the King, but his disapproval turned into hearty laughter. His crew and the Victorious began to laugh as well.

"You turned at the wrong moment," swore Rhinauld. He pulled her to her feet. Andraste embraced him and then Henry.

"Where is Shannon?" asked Felix.

"She is taking her time as usual," replied Rhinauld.

"Her ship was damaged in the battle. She has lost a mast and can only turn left at the moment," said Henry.

"And still she went to look for you, ungrateful wretch, only the gods know why," said Andraste. Rhiannon hurled herself at Rhinauld and then Henry.

"No tears," ordered Rhinauld.

"I am not crying!" protested Rhiannon, "That was the bravest, stupidest thing I have ever seen."

"I think attacking a winged crocbullorprion on foot, alone, after losing a blade, might surpass me," said Rhinauld.

"What was that thing?" asked Henry.

"One of the Emperor's experiments," replied Andraste.

"Did it really break your blade?" asked Henry.

"The Imperial steel, but not the Ruin blade," answered Andraste.

"Any news from Vespasian?" asked Rhinauld. Andraste's smile faded and she shook her head.

"We should return to the palace, and see if we can be of any use to the city," said the King.

Aldrich was already proceeding in that direction. He was met by Vespasian and his officers on horseback. Andraste quickened her pace to reach them.

"Our losses would have been significant without the aid of the Southern sorcerers. As you see, we let none of the Imperial army through. There was little damage to the city," reported Vespasian to Aldrich, but his eyes were on Andraste.

"I am well. Our family suffered no losses," said Andraste.

Vespasian looked past her to the approaching Island Kingdom's party. Vespasian seemed relieved. He directed his full attention back to Aldrich.

"There will be supper in the main hall if you and your officers would care to attend," said Aldrich. He rode his horse forward. He glanced over his shoulder towards Andraste.

"You bade me remind you that you desire to cut off Vespasian's tongue when we returned to the city," said Laelius. A ghost of a smile appeared on Aldrich's lips before he returned his eyes forward.

"You must be exhausted. Let me convey you to the palace," said Vespasian. He chose to ignore Laelius's remarks.

"I would like to walk," said Andraste.

"That rolled ankle would beg otherwise," commented Laelius. Vespasian dismounted and offered her Boreas's reins.

"Damn crocbullorpion," said Andraste. She swung herself onto Boreas.

"Just send him home. He will find his way," said Vespasian.

"Many thanks," said Andraste.

"I expect to see you at dinner," called the King.

Andraste only raised her hand in response. The Victorious followed Andraste towards the palace but she gave them leave to stop at their cottages to see their families. She continued onwards alone. The road cleared for her when she passed, and everyone bowed or curtsied to her.

Upon reaching the palace, she stroked Boreas's neck before releasing him. He turned back and galloped towards the port. Andraste made her way to her chambers. The sounds of a fierce raucous gathering emerged from Aldrich's chambers.

"Commander, will you not join us?" asked Kasimir. The voices inside the room quieted.

"I thank you, but no," replied Andraste.

"But you are alone, surely you would want to rejoice with us?" inquired Kasimir.

"Thank you, but no," answered Andraste.

"Are you limping?" inquired Egnatius.

"It is nothing," replied Andraste.

"It was a fierce battle. I have never seen a warrior that was your equal," said Eadbehrt.

"There were many fine warriors on the field," replied Andraste.

"The cyclone- how did you summon it?" asked Marcella.

"The power of the Ruin sword," replied Andraste, "Please forgive me. I am tired."

"Of course, forgive us," said Egnatius. The lords bowed to her.

Andraste proceeded into her chambers and locked the doors behind her. She showered first and scrubbed herself thoroughly before drawing herself a hot bath. She soaked in the waters until they became cool. She secured a thick robe about herself before climbing into her bed. She collapsed and fell into an exhausted slumber.

"Andra," said Rhiannon.

"How did you get in?" muttered Andraste.

"Rhinauld climbed over the adjoining terrace and then let me in through the front door," replied Rhiannon, "It is time for dinner. You are missed in the banquet hall."

Rhiannon pulled back Andraste's covers and took in her breath as she saw Andraste's ankle.

"It is an eggplant," said Rhiannon.

"It is not that bad," replied Andraste.

"Does Aldrich know?" asked Rhiannon.

"It is none of his concern," answered Andraste. She hid her ankle underneath the covers.

"Have you quarreled?" inquired Rhiannon.

"Vespasian probably already told you," said Andraste.

"That is true. He gossips more than the Southern Court," replied Rhiannon, "Aldrich feels badly about his words earlier. He spoke out of anger."

"You spoke to Aldrich?" asked Andraste furiously.

"He has not yet come to the hall either. He is waiting for you," responded Rhiannon.

"I do not wish to see him," replied Andraste.

"That will make your journey north difficult," stated Rhiannon. She handed Andraste a fine golden gown.

"No. I am not playing this game anymore. I will never fit in with their ways. I will never fit their image. I will go as myself, and if they do not like it, then they can go and-" started Andraste.

"Language, dear one," called Rhinauld from the adjoining chamber.

"As you wish," replied Rhiannon, "Just come to dinner."

Andraste dressed slowly in breeches and a tunic. She painfully pulled her boot over her swollen ankle. She only pulled her hair back in a ponytail. She rose and went into the adjoining room.

"Good now both heroes of the day are in the same room," said Rhiannon.

"Doting sister," sighed Rhinauld.

"Let us get this over with," responded Andraste.

"You were more thrilled about the battle," commented Felix.

"I just want to sleep," replied Andraste.

"You should eat after using magic," advised Brion.

"Where have you been?" asked Andraste.

"I remained with the Southern sorcerers. I thought my knowledge might be useful to them," replied Brion.

"He also used some powerful magic," praised Marcella. Andraste turned to the corner. She had not seen Marcella seated.

"My brother apologizes. He had to proceed to commence the feast without you. He would have told you himself, but he has been barred from your rooms?" asked Marcella.

"That is correct," answered Andraste, "Shall we proceed?"

Andraste ignored the pain from her ankle and hastened to the dining hall without waiting for a response. She made her way to the main hall and found it bustling with activity. As she entered the hall, the assembled lords and ladies rose. Aldrich rose at the dais, but she made her way to the Victorious table. She squeezed between Gnaeus and Laelius. Laelius clamped a hand on her shoulder and then returned to listening to Valens' story.

Andraste saw her kin proceed towards the tables for the Island Kingdoms. Rhinauld shook his head at her as he passed and Rhiannon scowled. Felix joined the Victorious table and was shortly joined by Shannon. Andraste scanned the hall. Vespasian was seated with the Northern officers. They were subdued, but they seemed to be speaking conspiratorially. They fell silent as they saw Andraste's gaze.

"Aldrich spoke well. Not too long, sincere, and glowing in his praise for the North," said Laelius.

"We did save his city," commented Nero.

"It was a joint effort," replied Laelius. He stifled a smile as Vespasian approached.

Vespasian laid a single flower on Andraste's plate and proceeded on his way. He was followed by each of the Northern officers. One by one each of Andraste's Victorious laid a flower on her plate, as did the lords and knights from the Island Kingdoms, including the King. The last flowers given to her were from Kasimir, Eadbehrt and Egnatius. As the Southern lords returned to her table, her eyes narrowed as she viewed her Victorious.

"Are you mocking me?" asked Andraste.

"We are honoring a valiant and sweet lady for her deeds of legend," replied Felix.

"Even without sorcery, your battles today were remarkable," said Laelius.

"Absolutely fearless," said Maximianus. He raised his glass to her.

"It is expected that you say a few words," said Laelius.

Andraste was unable to speak. She looked to Laelius for guidance. Laelius rose and put a hand to her shoulder.

"My Commander is a loss for words as she is so moved by your gesture," said Laelius. He sat back down. The conversations in the hall resumed.

"Aldrich did not bring me a flower," stated Andraste.

"He was not included in our plans," replied Felix, "Besides it was Vespasian's idea."

"I did not know Northern lords could be so romantic. It seems like something a Southern lord would do," commented Shannon.

"I imagine you could find yourself a Southern lord with pretty gestures, but then you would have to live with him," said Felix.

"That is a good point," replied Shannon. Felix silenced her with a kiss.

"Get a room already," commented Maximianus.

Shannon blushed prettily and looked to Andraste to share in her laughter. However, Andraste was paying them no heed. Andraste picked up the yellow rose that Vespasian had brought her. As she examined it, she noticed that the outer edges of the petals were lined in scarlet. She dropped it on the table as Aldrich approached.

"I am all too aware that you do not wish to see me, and I will respect your wishes. However, Rhiannon said you were injured. I apologize for not recognizing earlier. Your strength is blinding at times," said Aldrich.

Andraste did not respond. She started playing with the rose again.

"It is her right ankle," said Felix.

"May I?" asked Aldrich.

Andraste swung around the bench so that she was facing Aldrich. He knelt at her feet and put a hand to her ankle. He summoned his healing powers and the golden light grew between them, when it faded Aldrich rose and bowed to her. He hesitated for a moment for a response. He raised his sapphire eyes to her, but still Andraste said nothing. He produced from his tunic a dried, white flower. He set it on the table before Andraste and wordlessly returned to his own table.

"What is it?" inquired Shannon.

"A Northern stargazer. I gave him such a flower when we first met," answered Andraste.

"You think he has kept it near his heart all this time?" asked Shannon.

"That would be peculiar. He thought I was a man when we met," replied Andraste. However, she picked up the flower and examined it with her fingers.

"I think he knew all along," commented Laelius.

"But he was so angry on the ship," contradicted Felix.

"It is irrelevant," stated Andraste. She set the flower on the table.

"You cannot be angry forever," advised Shannon.

"You are one to speak," remarked Felix.

"It reminds me of that Northern song," said Maximianus.

"Do not sing," pleaded Otho.

"When we met, I was picking flowers . . ." began Maximianus loudly and off key. Andraste and the other Victorious laughed heartedly.

"And I picked a flower for your love," sang Maximianus.

"Please stop," begged Paulina, "My lady!"

Maximianus hesitated in his serenade. Andraste picked up the rose and played with it. She sighed, but she smiled and sang:

"When we met, I was picking flowers,
And I picked a flower for your love.
When you came a courting, you brought flowers.
When I met your mother, I took her flowers.
You asked for my hand in a field of flowers.
When we wed, I wore flowers in my hair.
When we had our first home, you planted flowers.
When at home, I picked flowers for our table.
When our child was born, we took flowers to the temple.
When we renewed our vows, I wore flowers.
When you grew ill, I kept flowers by your bed.

And when you died, I brought flowers to your grave.
Our love can be measured in fallen petals.
And when I pick flowers, I remember your love."

Andraste was applauded by her comrades.

"Such a sweet and gently lady," commented Felix.

"So pure and innocent," said Otho.

"I will take you both outside and beat you soundly," said Andraste.
However, she smiled at her Victorious.

Andraste moved as a servant picked up the remaining flowers.

"I will put them in your chambers, princess," said the servant.

"Not this one," said Andraste. She took back Vespasian's rose. The servant curtsied and proceeded on her way. Felix took the rose and cut off the stem with his dagger. Shannon picked up the blossom and fixed it in Andraste's hair.

Andraste ate and drank heartedly. They stayed up late into the night laughing and singing songs. They were the last ones to leave the banquet hall. Andraste saw the dried Northern stargazer had not been moved from the table. She picked it up and put it in her pocket hastily.

Andraste made her way silently towards her chambers. As she locked the doors behind her, she saw that Aldrich was sound asleep on his sofa, facing the door. She quietly closed the doors behind her and headed to her own bed.

"Good morrow, Commander," said Kasimir as Andraste entered the training field. She nodded her head in greeting.

"Our lord is not here. He is tending the wounded with the Southern sorcerers," said Kasimir.

"I do not seek him," replied Andraste.

Kasimir colored slightly and bowed to her. She surveyed the training yard and her eyes landed on the Victorious. They were seated on benches and laughing amongst themselves. Their smiles fell as she approached. She noted that none of the Southern guardsmen or recruits were training.

"Our youngest member fought well yesterday," said Felix.

"If not for Aldrich Caelius, Gnaeus would be dead. I expect you to train harder," responded Andraste.

"Easy," sighed Felix. He put a hand to Gnaeus's shoulder.

"The Commander is right. You were lucky, Gnaeus. You only survived because the Commander and Felix were watching over you. You are still young and have much to learn," reprimanded Laelius.

Gnaeus bowed to Andraste and Laelius.

"Am I relieved of my duties?" asked Gnaeus.

"No. We are saying train harder. The Victorious train every day. Even the day after battle," said Laelius.

"Yes, sir," said Gnaeus. He rose and picked up his spear.

"Heiyoh," called Andraste. Cato tossed her a spear. She turned to face Gnaeus.

"It is because she cares," said Felix.

"Tell that to my future bruises," grumbled Gnaeus.

"We are only as strong as our weakest member," said Andraste. Gnaeus blushed unhappily and looked to the other Victorious.

"Anyone else wish the prince had not healed her ankle for a day or two?" asked Otho. There was a chorus of agreement, but Andraste silenced them with a glare. She removed her leather vest and flipped her spear into her hand. The Victorious rose as well.

"Come," said Andraste.

Gnaeus advanced repeatedly, but he never got close enough to strike Andraste. He increased his speed, but still had no success. Felix intervened and knocked Andraste's spear. He gestured for her to step aside. Andraste considered for a moment and relented. Felix took up training with Gnaeus.

"You could use some work on wielding two swords," commented Laelius.

Andraste turned and stared at Laelius. The other Victorious laughed. Valens approached with his two twin axes. Laelius tossed Andraste two swords. She caught them and turned on Valens, but he was already at her side. She laughed as she jumped back. They went a few rounds, neither being able to hit the other. Andraste disarmed Valens's right hand first and then his left-hand in a fluid gesture. He bowed to Andraste and went to retrieve his axes.

Andraste turned to see how Gnaeus was progressing and found instead that she was being watched by Aldrich and his commanders. Aldrich began to approach purposefully across the field. Andraste paused as she felt a blade raised to her shoulder blade.

"Dead," declared Otho.

"Not yet," replied Andraste. She kneed Otho soundly in the ribs and he went down winded.

"That is enough for today," called Andraste, "Go spend time with your families."

She moved across the field to Felix and he threw her leather vest. She secured it as she walked. She saw Laelius and Gnaeus bar Aldrich's path.

"I would speak to your Commander," said Aldrich.

"You may to speak to me," stated Laelius.

"You have never stopped my approach before," commented Aldrich.

"She will not see you," informed Laelius.

"It is a matter of our mission," stated Aldrich.

"Then you will have no qualms discussing it with me," said Laelius. Aldrich watched Andraste cross the field to talk to Felix. She kept her back purposefully towards him.

"When do we plan to depart?" asked Aldrich.

"The Commander feels that the Capitol's defenses should be restored, and then we shall leave directly," replied Laelius.

"Three days?" questioned Aldrich.

"That seems probable," answered Laelius.

They fell silent as Vespasian and some of his Northern officers rode into the courtyard. Vespasian dismounted and approached Andraste. He carried a second sword over his shoulder.

"I hear one of your swords was broken in battle," said Vespasian, "I have brought a spare from our arsenal."

He tossed the sword and Andraste caught it. Her eyes sparkled as she unsheathed the blade.

"Imperial steel. It is a fine weapon," praised Andraste. She saluted Vespasian with it and he returned her salute.

"Where is our Lord of the Salt Islands?" asked Vespasian.

"Mourning the loss of the *Sea-Demon*," replied Andraste.

"You would think it were a woman the way he carried on," commented Vitus.

"It was his first love," said Felix.

"How fare your wounded?" asked Andraste.

"We are well as can be expected. We will need a few days to regroup," answered Vespasian, "I have business to discuss with the Southern commanders."

"Carry on," said Andraste. She stepped aside.

"You may want to hear," said Vitus.

"I trust your judgment," replied Andraste. Vespasian gestured for his officers to proceed.

"Are you alright?" asked Vespasian.

"I am fine," responded Andraste.

"Host or not, I will call him out if that is your wish," said Vespasian.

"I have already forgotten his insults," replied Andraste. Vespasian exchanged looks with Felix.

"Good," said the King of the Island Kingdoms as he approached, "Because we have much to discuss, and it will be easier if you two are speaking. Come, we keep them waiting."

The King proceeded across the training yard to the Southern commanders. Rhinauld and Henry followed behind the King. Henry bowed to Andraste before continuing. Rhinauld kissed her hand and tried to pull her across the field.

"I would not try," commented Vespasian.

Rhinauld released her but paused to make sure she would follow. Vespasian joined Rhinauld and they proceeded to the Southern lords together. Andraste waited for Laelius and Felix to join her before she also made her way to the Southern commanders. She stood fifteen paces away from the Southern commanders and kept her eyes on the King of the Island Kingdoms. Seeing that she was convinced on ignoring him, Aldrich also turned his eyes to the King.

"We all need a few days to tend to our wounds, replenish our defenses, and mend our equipment. I would also use this time to get to know our allies. My people have been ordered to pay the utmost respect to Southern traditions and customs. We appreciate your hospitality," said the King. He glanced to Andraste.

"We are honored to have you fight with us," replied Aldrich, "We appreciate your respect, but we would not have you change your ways on our account. As we have fought and bled together, are we not brothers? Do families not respect each other's differences?"

"Fine words, do you not think, Lady Eldgrimson?" asked the King.

Rhinauld nudged Andraste in her ribs.

"Me?" asked Andraste, "Yes, Uncle."

"In the spirit of our allegiance, why do you not spend the day with the prince? We must be seen as working together. It would make the Eastern and Northern troops more amiable, if they could follow your example," said the King.

"Is this a command?" asked Andraste.

"Yes, dear one," replied the King. His eyes narrowed as he studied Andraste.

"Our Commander does not submit to Eastern commands," said Vespasian. He held the King's eyes.

"The insolent pup has grown fangs," remarked the King.

"Let us leave our family quarrels for behind closed doors," intervened Rhinauld.

"This morning Rhinauld and I were aiding the wounded with the prince and viewing the city's defenses. There is much to be done. Why do you not join us this afternoon? We could use your wisdom," pacified Henry.

"As you wish," said Andraste, "But Vesp, you had business to discuss with the Southern commanders?"

"Vitus will remain in my stead," responded Vespasian.

"It will be so," acknowledged Vitus.

"We will all go," said Aldrich.

"Laelius, you and the Victorious are free to go. Spend the day with your families or aid in the rebuilding, I leave it to your will," said Andraste. She looked up at the three men surrounding her, "Well then, brothers, let us continue our family quarrel at the port."

"No dueling, no duels, no bets, no shenanigans," ordered the King.

"We command thousands," replied Vespasian.

"I have every confidence in you, Vespasian. You always were the most capable and responsible of the six. I was speaking to Rhinauld, Felix, my niece, and to Henry's better judgment," replied the King, "If I hear of any mischief, I will send Rhiannon to deal with you."

"What is wrong with you?" asked Vespasian. He turned his icy blue eyes on Andraste, "No protest? No fighting? No fire? Are you unwell?"

"Leave her be," growled Henry. Even Rhinauld was taken back by Henry's defense.

"We go," said Andraste. She turned towards the port and proceeded across the field. She found herself boxed in by her four foster brothers. Aldrich and the Southern lords were unable to approach from any angle.

"We will not harm her. Besides she is a fierce warrior. She could slay any of us with a flick of her wrist," commented Kasimir as he approached.

"I will remind you, sir, that you are addressing a princess of the Islands Kingdoms, and a lady above reproach," said Henry.

"He did not mean insult," said Andraste. She half-smiled at Kasimir over her shoulder. She turned her eyes to Henry, "I am not Rhiannon. You need not guard so closely."

"We guard what is precious," said Rhinauld. He glared at Aldrich.

"As do we," said Kasimir, "But how will Caelius ever make his apology if he cannot get near or speak to her?"

"Kasimir, I will make it right on my own," said Aldrich. Rhinauld glanced down to Andraste.

"What was the method of attack?" asked Andraste.

"Words most foul," replied Vespasian. Her porcelain skin was near crimson when she turned to face Vespasian. He put a hand to his hilt defensively.

"Northern standard procedure. It was what I would have done," interceded Vitus.

"I saw no signs of towers. Battering rams and ladders?" questioned Andraste.

"They would have had to bring them from the North. The trees here are sparse," responded Vespasian.

"They came so quickly. Do you think sorcery?" questioned Andraste.

"Yes, without a doubt. The Emperor grows stronger. I did not think moving so many troops would be possible," replied Vespasian.

"Varinia?" asked Andraste.

"Not present," replied Vespasian.

"Did you discuss defending against Northern attacks with the Southern commanders?" asked Andraste.

"Yes, Commander," answered Vespasian.

"Did they listen to your advice?" questioned Andraste.

"Yes, Commander," acknowledged Vespasian.

"Were there any problems from the troops? Mutiny? Refusal to fighting with the Southerners?" inquired Andraste.

"No, but we could see your battle from the battlements. It waived away any doubt. However, we did wonder why the Victorious were in the front and the Southerners arrived late and in the rear," said Vespasian. He glanced at the Southern commanders, who eyed him with equal contempt.

"I told Caelius not to come, but he did anyway. I told him to remain behind because his healing power is so valuable," replied Andraste.

"It was a solid effort. You both fought with great honor and courage," stated Vespasian.

"Unquestionable honor," stated Henry. He glared at Aldrich, who kept his eyes firmly on the road ahead of them.

"So hostile, Henry. Usually you only reserve such hostility for Andra. Tell me, Caelius, what exactly did you say to my sister?" asked Rhinauld. Rhinauld's words were spoken lightly but his eyes gleamed with rage.

"I love our sister as much as any of you. Should those words be repeated, I will slay you," forewarned Vespasian. He also turned to glare at Aldrich.

"Enough," ordered Andraste, "Focus on the task at hand. We have people to aid and to protect. Caelius, you are forgiven. We will not speak of this again."

Her foster brothers exchanged glances.

"I would formally apologize-" started Aldrich. He tried to catch her attention.

"I said enough," said Andraste. Her eyes flashed as she turned to address Aldrich. He hesitated as he watched her. Before he could speak, she had resumed her pace again.

"What are you going to do about the fallen wall?" asked Andraste.

"The Southern sorcerers have already repaired it," answered Egnatius.

"Will it hold?" inquired Andraste.

"Yes, Commander," replied Egnatius.

"And the houses that were damaged or destroyed?" inquired Rhinauld.

"In the process of being repaired by the Southern sorcerers. Our strength lies in our powers to heal and rebuild," answered Egnatius.

"They do not rely on potions and herbs as we do. The sorcerers moved through our troops and healed them with magic," explained Vespasian.

"You cannot trust magic," frowned Andraste.

Vespasian pulled back his sleeve and showed her his arm. She saw a new, thin red scar around his forearm.

"I lost my arm in battle yesterday. I could have died from bleeding out," stated Vespasian. Andraste examined his arm thoroughly. He laughed at her disbelief. She removed her hands quickly.

"And still you had time to pick flowers," said Andraste.

"Just one," replied Vespasian. Andraste smiled slightly.

"Two. Rhiannon says you are seeing a Northern lady?" asked Andraste slyly. Vespasian missed a step and Rhinauld and Felix laughed soundly.

"Who is it?" inquired Andraste. Vespasian blushed deeply.

"It may be a matter of security. Who is it?" asked Andraste. Vespasian quickened his pace.

"You never keep secrets from me," frowned Andraste.

"Better tell her or she will angry when she finds out," said Henry.

"When I reach an understanding, I will inform you. Otherwise, I will not speak so lightly of a lady," said Vespasian.

"Prude," said Felix.

"He is right. I should not have pried," said Andraste.

"Your intentions are not towards Lady Eldgrimson?" inquired Kasimir.

"She will not have me," stated Vespasian.

"And she is a higher ranked officer," said Rhinauld.

"Was," replied Andraste, "The Imperial Army does discourage fraternization."

"You were engaged to-" started Rhinauld. Andraste's blade was at this throat before he could finish his sentence.

"You know that was a farce, and never a question of honor. Question me if you must, but you will not speak ill against Tobias in my presence ever," said Andraste.

"You will draw blood, Empress," cautioned Henry. Andraste sheathed her dagger and proceeded ahead alone.

"She is unstable," commented Rhinauld.

"The prince wounded her deeply," rejoined Vespasian, "Before this instance, I never saw her try to please a lord."

"How do I make it right?" asked Aldrich.

"Whatever you hoped for, recognize it as lost. She will not let you close again. Forgiving is not one of the adjectives used to describe her. She is also a Valerianus and proud. She will never forget your insults," said Rhinauld.

"She is returning to the palace? Do we follow?" asked Henry.

"Felix," said Rhinauld. Felix nodded to his lord and followed Andraste at a distance.

"She will also be angry that you witnessed her outburst," advised Rhinauld, "We should give her space so that she can cool down. We should complete our review of the city's defenses. Caelius, you should try reporting to her later. If it is official business, she may see you."

"She would not see you?" inquired Rhinauld. Aldrich shook his head and entered his own chambers. He left the door open so that Rhinauld could follow.

"Sit beside her at dinner," suggested Rhinauld.

"That is not our way," said Aldrich.

"But it is the way of her people. You must try to reach her halfway. You will earn her attention and respect," said Rhinauld, "But brace yourself for hostility and possible loss of limb."

They paused as they heard Andraste's door open and her footsteps proceed down the hall.

"Felix," called Rhinauld. Felix stuck his head in through the doorway.

"Permit Aldrich to approach Andraste at dinner," said Rhinauld.

"Yes, my lord," replied Felix, but he raised his dark eyes to Aldrich, "But if you hurt her again, I will kill you."

"Fair enough," said Aldrich. He rose and they made their way to the great hall.

Andraste had once again seated herself at the Victorious table. She remained in her training clothes. Aldrich saw disapproving looks from the Queen and Marcella, as well as many of the Southern lords and ladies. Gerlinde's triumphant smile was glowing as she whispered criticisms to the other Southern ladies. Decima's eyes went from Aldrich to Andraste and she smiled sadly. Rhinauld clamped his hand on Aldrich's shoulder and then joined the table for the Island Kingdoms. He gestured for Felix to follow him.

Aldrich sat beside her.

"Felix, you are not much of a protector. I have been near ten minutes without you," said Andraste. She turned and started as she realized Aldrich sat beside her. She scanned the hall and saw Felix sitting with Rhinauld.

"Seditious wretches," muttered Andraste. They laughed as they read her lips. She took a drink from her stein and surveyed Aldrich under lowered eyes, "What do you want?"

"To be allowed to remain at your side," answered Aldrich.

"Do as you wish," replied Andraste. She turned her attention back to Paulina. Her braids brushed Aldrich's arm as she turned. He reached for a pitcher to refill her stein. His arm brushed against her own, but she ignored him.

"They add sugar instead of honey and use white flour instead of buckwheat, which makes their pancakes much sweeter and full of air. They are quite delicious," concluded Paulina, "And then they add insects and roll them in dirt."

"That must be good," replied Andraste.

"You are not listening," stated Paulina to Andraste. Paulina glanced to Aldrich at Andraste's side.

"You will find our bread is much different as well," said Aldrich.

"In what way?" asked Paulina.

"Northern bread is dark and dry, while ours is light and airy," replied Aldrich.

"I prefer the Southern breads," stated Laelius.

"My lady, I remember one time when you were home on leave, not yet fifteen, you near burnt down my kitchen trying to bake bread," said Paulina. Andraste nearly choked on her ale.

"Do not worry, Commander, you have other talents," said Laelius.

"It was awful," said Maximianus, "Laelius ordered us to eat it."

"I did so willingly. It was not that bad," said Paulina. She smiled kindly at Andraste. She looked to Aldrich, "I understand baking is a male profession in the South. Have you ever tried baking?"

"I cannot say that I have," replied Aldrich.

"What a question to ask the Prince of the Southern lands! Polly, you have seen his swordsmanship, such dedication to his craft would leave little time for baking," reprimanded Laelius.

"And ruling a country," commented Maximianus.

"We have to talk about something," replied Paulina, "I imagine we could sit through this long, delicious Southern dinner in silence. Northern state dinners can last four hours as they are served one course at a time, up to twenty courses. The only ones allowed to speak are at the head table."

"That sounds miserable," said Aldrich.

"It is," affirmed Laelius.

"The music is starting early this evening," commented Paulina.

"A Northern song," approved Laelius as he rose and offered his hand to Paulina.

"The gods help us," said Maximianus.

"Should we warn the other dancers?" asked Otho. Laelius scowled at both of the warriors.

"Do not worry, Laelius, you have other talents," commented Andraste.

Paulina laughed heartedly and allowed her husband to lead her to the dance floor. Andraste laughed as well until she realized all of her Victorious had also left for the dance floor.

"Do you wish to dance?" asked Aldrich.

"Not with you," replied Andraste.

"I would dance with you, my lord. Even if it is one of these barbaric

Northern dances," said Gerlinde as she passed by.

"I find them quite civilized," replied Aldrich. He took a sip from his stein.

"Oh?" asked Gerlinde. She continued on her away as she saw no invitation forthcoming.

Andraste swung her feet around on the bench so that she could watch the dancers. She smiled as she saw Laelius hopping about. Aldrich swung one leg over the bench so that he could face her.

"Paramerion," said Aldrich. Andraste did not remove her eyes from the dancers.

"I regret-" started Aldrich.

Andraste rose abruptly. Aldrich reached for her hand, but she gracefully dodged him and swept out of the hall. She went first to the stables to check on her horse.

"She was healed by my lord, princess. You will not even be able to tell she was ever injured," said the stable boy. He bowed at least three times before he carried on his other duties.

Andraste put her hand to the previously injured flank. Her horse did not even blink. She continued to eat her oats and swish her tail at flies.

Andraste headed back to her room. She passed Aldrich's doors quickly as she saw that they were open. She entered her own chambers and placed her Ruin sword on the desk. She did not turn on any lights as she feared Aldrich would realize she had returned. She went into her bedchamber. It felt stuffy to her, so she opened the doors to the veranda. She put on a night gown before climbing into bed. The fresh air aided with the stuffiness. However, it was an unusually cool night in the South. Andraste reached for her blankets, but found that she could not move.

The air was becoming heavier, almost thick. Andraste could no longer see before her, the air had become thick, velvety, amethyst clouds of smoke. Still Andraste could not move. She could not call out. She was pinned, suffocating where she was. It was as if she was held in place by invisible threads. Whenever she tried to move, they cut into her throat in an indiscernible snare. She could see the top of her Ruin blade growing ruby in the darkness. She knew it was sitting on her desk, waiting for her, but she could not move her limbs. She gasped for air but to no avail.

Andraste heard footsteps running across the study. Double, golden phoenixes burst threw her door and flew into the room. She saw the Ruin blade begin to slash at the webbing that ensnared her. As the phoenixes continued to circle and dive, the smoke began to evaporate. Not before long, she and Aldrich were the only ones in the room. She sat up gasping for breath. She put her hands to her throat and found blood on her hands from the invisible wires.

"We need to get out of here," said Aldrich.

He lifted her in his arms, carrying her out of the room and towards his own chambers. A golden light was already growing between them. Andraste winced as she saw her own blood on Aldrich's white tunic. Aldrich kicked his door fully open with his foot.

"Search the castle," ordered Aldrich.

"Is she-" started Eadbehrt.

"Go now! Assassin in the castle," said Aldrich.

Kasimir, Eadbehrt and Egnatius left the room at once. Aldrich carried Andraste to his bed and gently laid her down. He sat by her side and raised his hand to Andraste's throat. She whimpered in pain. He removed his hand quickly.

"Andraste," said Aldrich softly.

She moved her hair and looked away so that he could try again. He barely touched her skin, but she still felt like she was being choked. Angry tears filled her eyes. She blinked quickly so they would not fall. He did not move until the light had faded between them.

"Come here," said Aldrich.

Andraste nearly dove into his arms. He held her to him and comforted her. She raised her lips to his but he withdrew.

"You were badly wounded and frightened. I will not take advantage of this moment," said Aldrich. He raised her hand to his lips. He slowly raised a hand to her face to turn her eyes to him. When he saw there was absolutely no light growing between them, he removed his hand.

"My lord," called Egnatius from the study.

"Stay here. You are safe. I will only be a moment," said Aldrich. He went into his study and spoke quietly with Egnatius, but Andraste could still hear.

"We found no trace, my lord. No one saw anything. It must have been sorcery," said Egnatius.

"I have never seen its like," replied Aldrich, "I do not know how we will fight such evil."

"She was afraid. That is what I found most unnerving," said Kasimir.

"How fares the princess?" asked Eadbehrt.

"I have healed her wounds, but she is not herself. She will have my chambers tonight, and I will stay in the study," said Aldrich.

"Shall we send for her brothers?" asked Kasimir.

"No," said Andraste, "They can do nothing."

"We will be across the hall in case it returns," informed Egnatius.

"Thank you, my friends," replied Aldrich. Andraste heard the other lords depart to the chambers across the hall.

"They are excellent men," said Andraste.

Aldrich leaned into the doorway to the bedchamber and raised his sapphire eyes to her face.

"If you go through that door, you will find my bath chamber. It is filled by the hot springs. The waters will help you relax," said Aldrich.

"Would you," started Andraste. Her voice shook slightly, "Would you check?"

She did not look at him. Aldrich wordlessly crossed the room and conducted a thorough search of the bath chamber. He also disappeared into his study for a moment and reappeared with her Ruin sword. He left it near the edge of the pool.

"What attacked me?" asked Andraste.

"I do not know," replied Aldrich, "But I will be just outside if you need me. You are not alone. Furthermore, now you have your Ruin sword. You will not be defenseless again."

Andraste cringed at the word and lowered her eyes.

"You are still the bravest, fiercest warrior I have ever seen," said Aldrich.

He turned and went into his study. She heard him sit at his desk and pour a glass of wine. She rose slowly. She felt like she could barely control her movements. She had so little energy. Her joints ached. She raised a hand to her throat. She knew there was no blood, but she still smelled it. She could still feel the cuts on her flesh. She shook her head. She knew it was only mental.

She went into Aldrich's bath chamber, and was astounded by the tile-inlaid bath chamber that awaited her. She had expected a porcelain bath tab, but instead it was a small pool laid out in front of her. She discarded her nightgown in a heap by the door and gingerly put her foot into the pool. She turned as she heard the sound of a glass breaking on the floor. She realized that the doors to the bedchamber and bath were still wide open.

"It is nothing. I dropped my wine," called Aldrich from below his desk.

Andraste realized his words were more for his men across the hall then for her. She laughed softly and the sounds of cleaning stopped.

"You could join me," said Andraste. She stepped into the bath and waded into the waters. She turned to face the doorway.

"You cannot say such things!" rejoined Aldrich. By his tone, she could sense his blush from the next room. She could hear him cleaning up the glass shards.

"You just said that to irritate me," alleged Aldrich.

"Yes, my lord," replied Andraste.

She could see that he had repositioned his chair so he was no longer looking towards the bath chamber. She saw the front toes of his boots on the desk. She went deeper into the waters and found that they came above her head. She swam in the deeper part of the pool. She resurfaced and turned towards the door.

"Since I have already caught you peeping, you should bring me a glass of wine as penance," said Andraste.

"No," replied Aldrich.

"It could help me sleep," alleged Andraste.

"I will leave a glass by your bed," responded Aldrich.

"Your bed, my lord," corrected Andraste. She saw him rise and pour a second glass of wine. He was smiling.

"At least your spirits have improved," said Aldrich. He headed towards the bedroom. He froze as two sea-green eyes watched his movements. She folded her arms on the edge of the pool.

"You should say at least you are talking to me," rejoined Andraste.

"I am getting used to your ways, my lady. I have either all of your attention or none of your attention. All of your favor, or none," replied Aldrich.

Andraste found his words unpleasing. She turned her back on him and ignored him.

"A perfect example," said Aldrich. He set the glass of wine down by her shoulder.

"Aldrich!" swore Andraste.

She wrapped her arms around herself and ducked so that only her head was above water. He laughed softly and returned to his study. His boots reappeared on the edge of his desk. Andraste stuck her head under water once more and then rose out of the pool. She saw that he had also set a towel and robe by the wine. She dried herself off and wrapped herself in the robe. It smelled like Aldrich. She picked up the wine and went to the doorway of the study. Aldrich was intently reading a report.

"Good night," said Andraste. Aldrich quickly removed his feet from the desk and nearly dropped his wine glass.

"How would you explain the second glass breaking to your men?" asked Andraste.

"I would say you did both," replied Aldrich. He repositioned his candelabra so that he could read better. Andraste took a sip of her wine.

"I will sleep on your couch," said Andraste.

"Nonsense," replied Aldrich. He returned to reading his report.

"I would fit better," protested Andraste.

"That would hardly demonstrate Southern chivalry. Go to bed," retorted Aldrich. She hesitated in the doorway but he did not raise his eyes.

Andraste returned to the bedchamber but kept the door open. She blew out the candles and then returned to the bed. She repositioned herself so she could watch Aldrich reading. He was only outlined by the flickering of the candle flames. She sipped on her wine. Once all of the wine was consumed, she became more aware of the darkness surrounding her. She lit the candle on the bedside table.

"Still awake?" asked Aldrich softly. He came to stand in the doorway.

"Earlier, the darkness felt like Ricimer Valerianus, and yet something much more sinister was there in that room. It felt like my father was cursing me again," said Andraste.

"He will never lay a hand on you again," swore Aldrich, "I will never permit it."

He approached and put a chair by the side of her bed.

"I will stay with you until you fall asleep," said Aldrich. The silence lengthened between them. She rested her fingers against his knee, and he took her hand in his. Aldrich began to sing softly:

"Have no fear dear one.
While you lie sleeping,
I am here safekeeping.
When the night is done,
Golden rays are creeping.
Together we greet the sun,
And fear there is none."

"If I had known you could sing like that, I would not have refused your proposal," said Andraste sleepily.

"It is just a lullaby," said Aldrich. However, his hand tightened in her own. He sang it to her again, and when his song completed, she had fallen asleep. Aldrich blew out the candle on her table but he did not leave her side until the first rays of golden light came in through the blinds. He gently removed her hand from his own and collapsed on the sofa in the study for a few hours of sleep.

Chapter Twelve

"Aldrich," said Marcella. Aldrich's sapphire eyes opened quickly. It was the unmistakable tone of an older sister that was not going to be appeased.

"Shh!" said Aldrich. He looked to his bedchamber.

"She left hours ago in a particularly luxurious bath robe. She ordered us not to wake you in that way of hers," said Kasimir.

"As if the choices are only to obey or die," commented Eadbehrt.

"Where is she?" asked Aldrich.

"She is in her chambers with Brion. They are doing some sort of Northern magic; a tracing spell of some sort. Brion said it would be too dangerous to have so many present," answered Marcella.

Aldrich was already on his feet.

"If they want to play with fire, let them," said Kasimir, "But you are no magic user, Caelius."

"We always get burned when we do not heed her warnings," remarked Eadbehrt.

Aldrich paced back and forth across his study. He opened the doors to his chambers and was surprised to find Rhinauld, Henry, Felix and Rhiannon listening at Andraste's door.

"Undertaking dark magic was a ruse. They are fighting," admitted Rhinauld.

"What about?" asked Kasimir.

"Rude!" swore Marcella and Rhiannon at the same time.

"She wants to leave immediately. He says no," informed Henry.

"But the real issue is she wants to leave Aldrich behind. She fears the North will be too dangerous for you after what she encountered last night," stated Rhinauld. He turned his ear back to the door.

"Brion says you have to come for the allegiance and in order to fulfill the prophecy," informed Felix.

"If it was me, I would have left you," commented Rhinauld.

"That is because you have never said 'no' to the Empress once in your entire life," replied Henry.

"You trying being mother and father to two tiny, adorable girls, and see how you do," rejoined Rhinauld.

"I was there as well. You have been too easy on them. That is why they are obstinate, head-strong, and spoiled. Additionally, they have unrealistic expectations for both of their men; in fact, all men," stated Henry.

"Neither is good enough for them," remarked Rhinauld.

"Are you finished?" growled Rhiannon. Her emerald eyes flashed dangerously. However, it was Aldrich that Rhinauld and Felix stepped back from.

"Before you add more fuel to the fire, realize that it is because she cares for you. She will listen to Brion. If we interfere, she will only become less reasonable," advised Henry.

"Should we summon the Eldgrimson?" asked Rhinauld.

"No, let Brion speak to her," replied Rhiannon.

They all jumped as both doors to Andraste's room flew open. Andraste let Brion out of her chambers.

"Might I speak with you, Caelius?" inquired Andraste. As she saw Aldrich hesitate, she said, "Rhinauld, come chaperone."

Rhinauld proceeded into Andraste's chambers and onto the veranda, where he stood surveying the sea. Aldrich glanced to the Southern lords and then entered Andraste's chambers. Brion closed the doors of the room behind Aldrich.

"How long were you eavesdropping at the door? I just want to know how long I need to repeat myself," said Andraste. Aldrich seized her by the waist and pulled her to him.

"I am going with you," said Aldrich. He kissed her before she could object. Andraste pulled free from his grasp.

"I am unconvinced by your argument," replied Andraste. Aldrich seized her again.

"Can your eavesdroppers see through that keyhole?" asked Andraste, "I am beginning to worry for your honor."

"I care not for honor. By my love for you, I will follow," swore Aldrich.

"Love is fleeting. Honor is constant," replied Andraste. She freed herself from his embrace again and glanced towards the veranda.

"I do not care what methods you try to keep me away from you. It does not matter. Regardless, I will be at your side, and I will go North with you," declared Aldrich.

"Aldrich," warned Andraste.

"You need me as much as I need you. We must go together or we will both fail," said Aldrich.

"As of yesterday, for the first time, you witnessed the true power of the Emperor. We may not succeed," claimed Andraste.

"I defeated it and protected you yesterday. I will do so again," replied Aldrich. He raised her face to his and his sapphire eyes filled with recognition, "You are afraid."

"Only fools know no fear," said Andraste softly.

"Our way is together," insisted Aldrich.

"At what point does your code of honor insist that I interfere?" asked Rhinauld as he walked into the chamber. Aldrich released Andraste from his hold reluctantly. He met Rhinauld's eyes and Rhinauld said, "By ours, you should have a clear understanding by the words I just heard."

"Enough," ordered Andraste. Rhinauld folded his arms across his chest and leaned into the doorway. He did not take his eyes from Aldrich, who shifted uncomfortably, and took a few steps away from Andraste.

There was a knock on the door. Before Andraste could respond, Kasimir stormed into the room. Kasimir put a hand to his hilt. His entire body was tense with rage. His dark-brown eyes were unforgiving.

"What is it?" asked Aldrich.

"I challenge your right to the throne on grounds of honor," said Kasimir coldly. Aldrich stood stunned as he surveyed his friend.

"On what grounds?" asked Rhinauld.

"Lady Gerlinde's father just announced your engagement to his daughter," responded Kasimir.

Rhinauld and Aldrich both looked to Andraste for her response. Her face remained neutral, but she kept her attention on Kasimir.

"I have made no such proposal," said Aldrich.

"So the exchange for her family's army and wealth signifies nothing to you?" inquired Kasimir. He flushed with rage.

"You know me better than that," replied Aldrich.

"I thought I did, but instead you are a false, backstabbing lecher without honor. What are you playing at? You pursue two ladies at once and whisper false promises to both? I will not allow it, not in these lands, not against our ways," said Kasimir.

"I find I must repeat myself. I have made no such proposal. My intentions have always been towards a different lady, and Lady Gerlinde knows this. We have spoken about it at length, as have you and I," replied Aldrich.

There was a second knock on the door and the Queen and the King of the Island Kingdoms entered. The Queen surveyed her son with her sapphire eyes, while the King looked to Andraste.

"Lady Gerlinde has been to see me. She is most distraught and confused," said the Queen.

"I promise you, I am equally confounded," said Aldrich.

"I did not think you would enter such an arrangement without speaking to me first," replied the Queen. She surveyed her son with her piercing gaze.

"A challenge has been issued," said Rhinauld softly.

The Queen looked from Aldrich to Kasimir. Her gaze hesitated on Andraste for a moment.

"Let us resolve this amicably first. You will both look foolish indeed, if you come to blows over a fabrication. Let us not tar the friendship that has so long sustained you both. It grieves me to see such distrust between you," replied the Queen. She turned to leave and the lords bowed to her. She paused in the doorway.

"Princess, please attend us," said the Queen.

"It is a family matter. I will not intrude. The prince must do what is best for his kingdom," said Andraste.

"Do you also not have a claim in this matter?" asked Rhinauld.

"I can offer the prince nothing," answered Andraste. She turned her attention the King, "Uncle, I imagine you came to speak to me on a different matter."

"So you sense it, too?" asked the King. The Queen lingered in the doorway.

"Sense what?" inquired Aldrich.

"We will take care of this. You have bigger problems to contend with," replied the King.

The wind blew the veranda doors open. Andraste swore a voice was calling to her.

"We must send someone to the East," said Andraste.

"I will leave at once," stated Rhinauld.

"No, you have your orders," replied Andraste.

"The East? The evil I sense is from the North," stated the King. He frowned as he studied Andraste.

"No, it is the East. Something important, something I have forgotten," said Andraste. She involuntarily put a hand to her forehead. Rhinauld and Aldrich both stepped towards her. They glared at each other, but Rhinauld allowed Aldrich to raise a hand to Andraste. However, no light resonated from his fingertips.

"It is nothing," said Andraste.

The King approached Andraste and put a hand underneath her chin so that he could examine her eyes. He said a few words and a red light grew between them.

"What sort of magic is that?" asked the Queen. She frowned as she watched the gesture.

"A form of healing magic," replied the King. However, he did not meet the Queen's eyes. He looked to Andraste, "Is that better?"

"But why would Aldrich's magic not heal her?" questioned the Queen.

"There is probably an answer to that question in one of your precious books. Were you not on your way to resolve a dispute?" inquired the King.

"If you both sense an attack, then we must prepare ourselves," replied Aldrich.

"You cannot lead your people while they are divided. Resolve this issue and then we will talk," said Andraste. Aldrich frowned, but he bowed to her and then proceeded out of the room. Kasimir followed at his heels.

"If your headaches continue, please see Marcella," said the Queen before she left the room.

"Rest a while. I will speak with the Southern sorcerers. Perhaps they have more knowledge of what approaches from the North. Rhinauld, stay with her," ordered the King. Rhinauld bowed to the King as he passed.

Andraste settled herself on the sofa.

"You are not going to object?" asked Rhinauld. He raised an eyebrow.

"I feel strange, Rhinauld," replied Andraste.

"Do you think it an effect from the assassin?" inquired Rhinauld.

"I know not," responded Andraste. She picked up a book, and pretended to read it. Rhinauld headed towards the veranda.

Andraste.

Andraste dropped her book in surprise.

Good. Now you can hear me.

She scanned the room, but saw no one. Rhinauld approached and knelt at her feet to pick up the book. He hesitated as he offered it to her.

"What?" asked Andraste.

"For a moment, your eyes turned ruby red," replied Rhinauld. He studied her with concern.

"I need to get out of these rooms. I will stay at the Northern camp," said Andraste. She rose hurriedly and felt dizzy as she stood. Rhinauld came to her aid but she waved him away. She left the room quickly and Rhinauld hastened to catch up with her as she made her way to the stables.

"Of course she is out of sorts. Your King has confined her to chambers for near a week. Any of us would go mad!" exclaimed Laelius.

"She remains within of her own choice," responded Rhinauld softly.

"Do you think she is so angry with the prince?" asked Felix.

"She is not herself. I have never seen her like this," replied Rhinauld,

"She asked me if the troops were ready to take the beaches of Gardenia."

"Do you think she meant-" started Felix.

"She meant Gardenia," finished Rhinauld.

"So it is on purpose that you keep her from the Southern court," said Laelius.

"I thought it would let up after a few days, but she shows no sign of improvement," replied Rhinauld.

"Do you think it a concussion?" asked Laelius.

"She has received no such injury. We have not allowed her near the training field for at least a week," replied Rhinauld.

"She does not sleep. She walks the beaches at night. Sometime she talks to herself," added Felix.

"Really?" asked Rhinauld. Felix nodded without looking at his lord.

"Have you let Aldrich see her? He should be able to heal any illness with the power bestowed upon him by the Ruins," said Laelius.

"He saw her when it started near a week ago, but to no avail. Only the King of the Island Kingdoms seems to be able to sooth her," reported Rhinauld. He paused as he revisited his words and he frowned. He met Laelius's eyes.

"You think she is bewitched?" asked Laelius.

"That is a serious accusation," remarked Felix.

"How would we know for certain?" questioned Rhinauld.

"Take her to the Queen," ordered Laelius.

"But then they will know. All will know her illness," protested Rhinauld.

"We need help. She cannot lead in such a state," said Laelius.

"Lead? I just want her to be normal again," sighed Rhinauld.

"We should summon Vespasian and Henry," stated Felix.

"Go now," replied Rhinauld. Felix left immediately. Rhiannon left from Andraste's inner chambers and studied her brother.

"Get her ready to go to the palace," said Rhinauld.

"She is ready, but is that wise?" asked Rhiannon.

"We have no other choice," replied Rhinauld. They fell silent as Andraste emerged from her rooms. She was dressed in an indigo silk Southern-style gown and her hair was pulled back in the Southern style.

She had a faraway look about her. She turned in surprise as she registered Laelius and Rhinauld.

"Do you hear music?" asked Andraste.

"Yes. It is coming from the gardens," answered Rhiannon.

"Come. Let us go listen," said Rhinauld. He offered her his arm and Andraste went to him. He wrapped her arm in his protectively. Rhiannon approached with a silver cloak and wrapped it around Andraste's shoulders.

"It is cold. Is it not?" asked Andraste.

"Yes, my lady," answered Rhinauld. Andraste drew the hood over her head and it concealed her face. They headed into the central meeting area of the Northern camp.

"Why do we linger?" inquired Andraste.

"We are waiting on Henry and Vesp. We will all go together like old times. Will that not make you happy?" questioned Rhinauld.

"Old times? We have been together all this time," replied Andraste.

"No. It has been some time since we were all together," corrected Rhiannon. She looked to Rhinauld for confirmation but he shook his head.

"Where are we going?" asked Andraste.

"The palace to hear the music," answered Rhinauld.

"But that is several days ride from here. We cannot make it in time," stated Andraste.

"No, my lady. We are not half an hour from the Southern palace," said Rhinauld.

"We made good time," replied Andraste. Rhiannon looked to Rhinauld in confusion but he shook his head once more. He frowned as Vespasian, Henry and Felix approached. Vespasian kept his eyes locked on Andraste. He approached her with purpose.

"I hear you have been wounded, Commander. It is nothing shameful. We have all been concussed at point or another. I imagine it is my time to take care of you, as you tended me so attentively the last time I was wounded," alleged Vespasian. He bowed to her in the Northern style.

"You are so changed, Vesp," stated Andraste, "You are such a handsome man. Not the gangly boy that followed me around last summer."

"I will take a compliment when it's given. Even if it is a decade too late," responded Vespasian. Andraste approached him and offered her arm to him.

"He does love her best. He did not even bat an eye," commented Henry to Felix.

"If a woman that lovely told me it was the time of the full moon, while the sun was at its apex, I would agree," returned Felix. Rhinauld silenced them both with a glare and turned his intention back to Andraste. Vespasian had helped her mount Boreas and already swung up behind her.

"What did you say to him?" asked Rhinauld.

"I said she had a concussion. It seemed the most believable excuse," answered Felix.

"For a week?" inquired Rhiannon.

"If you wanted to lie to our brother, you should have gone yourself," rejoined Felix.

"You told him to take her directly to the Queen?" asked Rhinauld.

"Well, no. I thought she would be under your care. I gave no such instruction," said Felix. Rhinauld and Rhiannon quickly exchanged looks.

"Henry," began Rhinauld.

"I will take Rhiannon. Go," responded Henry.

Rhinauld quickly urged his horse into the night towards the Southern palace. He entered the stables and left his horse with a stable boy. He could hear the sound of Northern music coming from the palace gardens. He headed towards the sound along a path lit with hundreds of torches. He entered the main garden and saw a Northern dance being performed in the center of the garden. His eyes narrowed on Vespasian and Andraste almost immediately. The other dancers were already giving the couple a large berth in order to better watch the couple. Andraste was absolutely enchanting. She was beautiful in the torchlight, not missing a beat, laughing and guiding Vespasian through the movements. Rhinauld stopped to watch her. It was if she was a young girl again without the decade of memories of war and suffering. Rhinauld paused as he came across Aldrich, who stood with Egnatius and Eadbehrt. They also watched the Northern princess dance.

"You look exhausted," commented Eadbehrt. Rhinauld ignored him and turned his attention to Aldrich.

"We came to the see the Queen, but I do not see her. Do you know where I could find her?" questioned Rhinauld.

"She has already retired as have most of the Southern ladies," replied Eadbehrt.

"It is said your princess was wounded. Is she well? She looks well enough," said Egnatius.

"That is why we wish to see the Queen. My lady has been in a delicate mental state due to a concussion. We wish to see if the Queen's healing powers will have any effect," said Rhinauld. He kept his eyes focused on Andraste.

"A delicate mental state?" questioned Eadbehrt.

"Why do you not see, my lord?" asked Egnatius.

"His magic had no effect," replied Rhinauld.

"And the King of the Island Kingdoms?" asked Aldrich.

"I would prefer not to answer that question," replied Rhinauld, "We will come again tomorrow if the Queen will see us."

"She will, but I will see your princess before she leaves. She has refused to see me all week," said Aldrich.

"I will try. I cannot control her as of late," muttered Rhinauld.

"You may be better off asking Vespasian for an audience," said Henry. He came to Rhinauld's side with Rhiannon on his arm and they surveyed the dancers. Vespasian whispered into Andraste's ear and she laughed heartily. Her cheeks crimsoned with the effort and her sea-green eyes sparkled. However, her eyes seemed not to register Aldrich or the Southern lords. She paused as she saw Rhinauld watching her. She smiled at him invitingly.

"My lady calls," said Rhinauld. He half-bowed to the Southern lords before pursuing Andraste. Henry followed at his side.

"It seems as though you have found your shadow, my lord. Although, he follows awfully close even for a shade," said Andraste.

"And, yet, I come of my own free will," replied Henry.

"Silence, Shade. Shadows are silent," chided Andraste.

"Only a madwoman would catechize a shadow," rejoined Henry.

"A shadow would know only a madwoman would listen," replied Andraste.

"But I am not a shadow, so you cannot be mad," replied Henry.

"Do you not know, sir? Madness runs in my family," answered Andraste.

"We do not mention that word," said Rhinauld wearily, "And pull it together for a few minutes, the prince wishes to address you."

"Which prince?" asked Andraste.

"The Prince of the Southern lands," answered Rhinauld.

"Good. I have been longing to meet him," replied Andraste.

"Meet him? You have been at his side for months," said Vespasian. He frowned as he studied Andraste.

"I am sure I would have noticed such an acquaintance," returned Andraste.

"Do me a favor and pretend to know him. You have known him, but you were recently injured and you may not remember him as you should," cautioned Rhinauld. He fell silent as Aldrich and his Southern lords approached.

"Good evening," said Aldrich. His eyes were only focused on Andraste. She paused and studied him in return, but did not speak. She seemed surprised as her sea-green eyes met his sapphire eyes.

"We have met before," said Andraste.

"Indeed. You have traveled for months on the road together," said Rhinauld with a forced laugh.

"No. I met you in Thoran. I met you in the dances during the celebration after the expulsion of the Lionden troops from the Empire. We danced together," said Andraste.

Aldrich paused to consider her words and slowly smiled in remembrance.

"That was you? Yes. We met long ago, but I did not think of it until this moment," said Aldrich.

"We should return to our camp, my lady," interjected Henry.

"But we came for someone. We leave no one behind," protested Andraste.

"We will see the Queen tomorrow," pacified Rhinauld.

"The Queen? It was not the Queen I came for," responded Andraste. She frowned and looked confused. Vespasian offered his arm to her and she smiled. As she took his arm, he drew her to him protectively.

"I will take you to the Queen now if that is your wish," said Aldrich.

He offered his arm to Andraste, but she held onto Vespasian's arms. She turned to survey Aldrich again. She frowned and she tensed on Vespasian's arm.

"No, you are not the soldier from the Thoran. You are the lord, who called me-" started Andraste.

"Andra, Vespasian will return you to the Northern camp. You are tired from the events of the day," interrupted Rhinauld.

"Am I?" asked Andraste.

"Yes," answered Vespasian, "Come, I will see you to your tent."

"As will Henry," said Rhinauld. Henry quickly took Andraste's free arm.

"You?" inquired Andraste.

"We are friends now. Remember?" questioned Henry.

"No. I must be dreaming," replied Andraste. She looked to Rhinauld in confusion.

"Please have the Queen attend us in the morning if she is able," said Rhinauld. He bowed to the Southern lords, while Henry pulled Andraste towards the stable. Vespasian was distracting her with his conversation and she laughed prettily. The sound carried across the night air towards the Southern lords.

"A concussion?" asked Aldrich as he watched her in the distance. Henry put himself between Andraste and Vespasian.

"That would explain the confusion," said Egnatius.

"But the lady seemed altered. She is not herself," stated Eadbehrt.

"What are you not telling us?" inquired Aldrich.

"Her condition worsens. Please have the Queen see us in the morning," replied Rhinauld. He bowed to the Southern lords.

"Laelius?" asked Aldrich. Laelius only bowed in response. He followed the Lord of the Salt Islands towards the stables. Once they had reached the stables, Rhinauld turned to face Laelius.

"Did you notice?" asked Laelius.

"Her eyes were sea-green again when she was near the prince but ruby when she left his presence," answered Rhinauld.

"So she is bewitched," stated Laelius.

"Bewitched?" asked a voice from the shadows. Laelius was not used to being caught by surprise; yet, he jumped at the sound and drew his blade.

"Your Majesty," said Rhinauld. He bowed deeply to the Queen.

"Your Majesty, where are the Victorious I assigned to protect you? You will not be safe left on your own," said Laelius in concern. The Queen silenced him with a penetrating gaze.

"Bewitched?" repeated the Queen.

"We believe Andraste has been bewitched. Aldrich's magic has not healed her. We came to see if the Southern sorcerers may have a cure," replied Rhinauld.

"Take me to the Northern camp," ordered the Queen, "Immediately. We have no time to waste. Why did Aelius not come himself?"

Laelius and Rhinauld exchanged looks again.

"You suspect the King?" asked the Queen in shock. She quickly composed herself, "Why?"

"Let me be absolutely clear. We only have suspicions, not proof. However, she has not improved underneath his care. She seems even more confused after he visits. I have never seen him use healing magic before, or even magic so openly. Something is not right," said Rhinauld.

"Nor I, now that you mention it. The Eldgrimsons have always been secretive about their magic," agreed the Queen.

"I will call for a carriage," said Laelius.

"It will take too long. I can ride as well as you although I do admit it has been some time," insisted the Queen.

"We apologize for the inconvenience," blushed Rhinauld. He bowed eloquently again to the Queen.

"I am glad we ran into one another. I have been worrying about the princess," said the Queen, "It seemed strange that she was so calm regarding Aldrich's engagement to Gerlinde yet ignored him for a week once the matter was resolved."

"It is true Andraste remains in her tent of her own volition. However, the King has not allowed her visitors other than Laelius and my siblings," replied Rhinauld. He helped the Queen mount and then mounted his own horse.

"I really do apologize. If I had known you were about, I would not have returned Andraste to the Northern camp," said Rhinauld.

"It will be more discreet this way. Aelius may not even notice," responded the Queen.

She turned her horse towards the road. Rhinauld urged his horse to her side and Laelius followed behind. The riders were observed by a thousand sparkling stars and a full glowing moon. There was a gentle hum from the main tent but the rest of the camp was quiet. They left their horses and made their way to Andraste's tent. Felix was at his post where he eyed the hooded figure of the Queen warily.

"My lord, the King was strict in his orders," started Felix.

"Remember, we serve the Empress, not the King," replied Rhinauld. The Queen paused as she passed Felix and put a hand to his arm. Felix stepped back in surprise and bowed deeply to the Queen.

"My apologies," said Felix.

"How is she?" asked Rhinauld.

"She is subdued," answered Felix, "which usually means trouble."

Rhinauld led the way into the tent and Felix followed, while Laelius took his place at the tent door. The Queen made her way into the tent and was surprised by the amount of comfort and luxury.

"She is not alone. I sense three souls," said the Queen.

"But there is no one here," stated Felix.

"Not in the flesh, but there are three souls here," replied the Queen.

"Andra, are you awake?" called Rhinauld, "I have brought you a visitor."

Andraste emerged from the curtained area at the back of the tent and approached cautiously. She surveyed the three figures before her.

"This is the-" started Rhinauld.

"Really, Rhinauld, I know my own godmother when I see her," replied Andraste.

"Godmother?" questioned Felix.

"She is correct, although I thought she had forgotten," responded the Queen sadly. She lifted a crystal from her pocket and turned her full attention to Andraste, "Come here child."

Andraste stood before the Queen and allowed the Queen to lift the crystal towards her. The crystal turned crimson and began to radiate heat.

The Queen dropped it on the floor. Andraste knelt to pick it up.

"Wait! It may be hot!" exclaimed the Queen. However, as Andraste picked up the crystal it cooled to her touch. She lifted it in her open palm to the Queen. The crystal had transformed into a ruby. The Queen accepted it and examined it closely while Andraste returned to her blankets.

"What does it signify?" asked Laelius.

"I do not know. Never before have I heard of a crystal turning into a ruby. I will have to consult the elders," frowned the Queen, adding, "But you are correct, she is bewitched. Continue to keep her sequestered in her chambers. I will return in the morning with council."

"Laelius and Felix will escort you back to the castle," said Rhinauld.

"And, Rhinauld," said the Queen before she left the tent, "Do not let the King within ten feet of her."

"I will do as you say," replied Rhinauld.

Over a week had passed since she encountered the assassin, and Andraste had not slept for a minute. Her thoughts were plagued by the emerald dragon and a giant white tiger with gleaming beryl eyes. Sometimes the dragon and tiger spoke and seemed familiar. Other times they spoke and she did not understand their words; however, she could sense their anger and sense of betrayal. They never spoke ill towards her. They treated her like a child privy to their conversations. Sometimes she heard their voices even during the daylight. She could not always tell who was speaking.

She is beginning to remember.

Will she come for us?

We shall see.

"The prince seeks an audience. He is concerned after your encounter in the gardens last night," said Rhiannon.

"He is overly familiar," replied Andraste. She frowned as she considered the request.

See the prince. Trust him. He will help us.

"It has been over a week since you have accepted his visit. He tries three times a day. Will you not see the prince? Rhinauld says Aldrich nearly slayed Gerlinde's father in the Queen's audience rooms. Aldrich gave a speech on freedom and love that will shake these halls for centuries. Rhinauld nearly swooned," said Rhiannon.

"I do not see how such a speech would have anything to do with me. I have no business with the prince," replied Andraste.

Remember. He does have business with you. You share a common goal.

Andraste paused as flashes of the battle with the Arisen on the Southern plains came back to her. She rubbed her temples, and said, "We are in a holding pattern until we depart for our mission. It may not seem like it, but my men, the Victorious, are still recovering from the battle with the Arisen. Resorting to the use of their magical powers has exhausted the troops and they must have time to recover."

Yes. It is magic that has weakened you. However, it is magic which will set you free. Be as you should be.

Remember the truth.

"As did you," said Rhiannon.

"As did I," said Andraste, "I am weakened from my encounter with the assassin. It is not a physical complaint which ails me. The Prince managed to heal my physical complaints already, but there is something far deeper which continues to plague me."

No, the assassin is not what weakened you. Do you not remember?

Concentrate! Listen to us.

You will recover in time. Think. What must you do to recover?

"Why did you not say anything?" asked Rhiannon.

"The Eldgrimson knows my reasons. He is delaying the plans accordingly," replied Andraste.

Do not trust the Eldgrimson.

The Eldgrimson loves you.

I curse the Eldgrimson.

"The prince could heal you," said Rhiannon.

"It is not physical. He healed me that night. It is something deeper that wounds me," said Andraste.

I am wounded by your forgetting. How can you not remember my love?

"What have I forgotten?" asked Andraste.

"You moved all of your belongings from the palace. You have asked me exactly what it is you have forgotten for two days now. Are you sure you are well?" asked Rhiannon. Andraste tried to focus as she realized Rhiannon was still speaking.

It is my doing. The remembrance is my doing. I should have never asked the Eldgrimson.

"You would be better off staying at the palace with the Southern sorcerers and the prince. Not that I mind sharing my tent. The Northern camp has been more than kind to house us since the loss of the *Sea-Demon*. Let us go seek the aid of the healers," entreated Rhiannon.

"It is so loud at the palace. I can think better here. I plan to go to the Southern Ruins and speak with the Spirit once more," responded Andraste.

Yes. Go to the Spirit. Go now.

That is the answer. The Spirit will release you. Ask him.

"Rhinauld was specific. He said you were not to leave the tent this morning. Let me get him. He and Henry will go with you. I will summon them," said Rhiannon.

"No. There is no need for summoning. A warrior was not necessary last time and I do not need an escort now," replied Andraste.

You will need to summon me.

"Then I will go with you," said Rhiannon.

"No, dear one. Your place is here. I will not be alone," answered Andraste.

Dear one, we are with you.

"Who are you taking with you? What if you are caught by Northern forces like last time?" asked Rhiannon.

"There is a series of caves that lead to the Ruins. I will take that path," replied Andraste.

Anima, follow the path. Read the threads of life. The web of time is tangled.

"If you do not permit me to come then I will go straight to the prince," fulminated Rhiannon.

"You would threaten me?" questioned Andraste. She half-smiled at her foster-sister, but it was not kind, "I could render you unconscious with a singular blow from which you will not awaken for two days and when you do, your headache will make you wish you were dead."

Dear one, I would never threaten you.

"Never before would you threaten one of your kin. Something is wrong. Let me summon the Eldgrimson," pleaded Rhiannon.

Do not see the Eldgrimson. He will harm you further.

"No, he cannot help me. None of them can help me," replied Andraste. She picked up her Ruin sword and headed towards the tent flap.

"I have forgotten something. I know it. I forgot it at the Southern Ruin the last time I spoke with the Spirit. That must be it," said Andraste.

"You are not making sense and I know you are not listening to me. Your responses are getting more and more delayed. Please, Andra," begged Rhiannon, but before she could finish her sentence, Andraste was already gone. Rhiannon ran outside of the tent.

"What is it?" called Felix.

"You did not see her? She left. She is not well. I do not think she heard a word I said. She is headed towards the Southern Ruins," responded Rhiannon.

"I will get Rhinauld and Henry," said Felix.

"I will tell the Eldgrimson," replied Rhiannon.

I have not been in these halls for some time. How sad these Ruins are. Once it was a great castle.

Andraste shook her head and made herself focus on the trail leading up to the caves.

Do not block me. I can teach you to be great. You can succeed where I failed.

Andraste wandered through the caves. A small bright light appeared before her twinkling like a star and leading her through the labyrinth to a set of stone stairs. She began her ascent, feeling a breeze ahead in the corridor. As she turned a corner the guiding light faded as she reached a doorway; entering it she emerged into the derelict throne room of the Southern Ruin.

It is nearly time.

I can taste freedom.

"Your mind is not as it should be. Your latest battle has left you weakened. You cannot tell dreams from reality now, can you?" asked the white stag.

As the white stag appeared before her, the voices in her mind were blocked out. Andraste took a deep breath and felt clear for the first time in days. The stag waited for her to compose herself.

"It is more my memories of the past. I cannot tell what was a dream and what was not," answered Andraste, "My dreams . . ."

"Your dreams are also real. You are traversing the vortex, a place where time circumnavigates," explained the stag.

"I do not understand," replied Andraste.

"You do not, but you will," foretold the stag.

"How did I become this way?" asked Andraste.

"There are things you must remember. There are gaps in your memories. You have been betrayed, Empress. One who you viewed as a protector has harmed you," answered the stag.

"Who?" inquired Andraste.

"Do you not know?" asked the stag.

"The Eldgrimson. The voices in my head said the Eldgrimson. One voice trusts him and the other does not," replied Andraste.

Andraste heard footsteps on the stairs.

"You must go, Anima. You can traverse here freely as can any you bring. But those who enter of their own accord must face the challenges as those are the rules given to me. They may not survive," stated the stag.

"What should I do next?" asked Andraste.

"That is for you to decide," replied the stag.

"I feel so lost and hopeless," said Andraste.

"You have a path to follow. You must choose to do so. The god of all gods gave mankind freewill," said the stag. He began to fade away.

"Wait!" plead Andraste, but the stag had already disappeared. She was left alone in the Ruins.

"Andra!" called Rhiannon. She came running across the Ruins and knelt at Andraste's side, setting her long bow on the ground next to Andraste. She put her hands on Andraste's shoulders in order to examine her.

"You are deathly cold," cried Rhiannon. She removed her cloak and wrapped it around Andraste's shoulders.

"Why did you come? Alone?" asked Andraste angrily. She rose to her feet and unsheathed her Ruin sword.

"I am not alone," said Rhiannon. She did not move from her position. Andraste looked to the ruined doorway and saw Aldrich standing in the doorway.

"We must leave at once," said Andraste, "You will both be in danger."

She pulled Rhiannon to her feet and led her from the Ruins. Already the caves were beginning to transform. Andraste started running and nearly dragged Rhiannon from the perimeter. She used her Ruin sword to cut through the plant maze. As they emerged onto the beach, the Ruins began to quiet.

"I told you I would be fine. Why did you come?" asked Andraste.

"Do not scold her," replied Aldrich.

Andraste turned her eyes to Aldrich. Observing that her eyes had turned to their ruby shade, he cautiously put a hand to his sword. A gentle breeze blew from the Ruins and carried white petals towards Andraste. Andraste turned to watch them. When she looked back to the others, her eyes had resumed their normal sea green shade though they still held the look of a wounded animal.

"Andraste," commanded the King of the Island Kingdoms.

Andraste turned at the sound of his voice. The King and his knights were riding towards them from the beach. They were dressed in their full battle armor.

"We have been betrayed," said Andraste.

"Who?" asked Aldrich.

"Send for my brother," commanded Andraste. Her eyes were locked on her uncle. Her hands went to her hilt as her uncle raised a hand to her. He made an encircled star in the air.

"Which one? Brion?" asked Rhiannon.

"Eldgrimson," replied Andraste. The King was unfazed by her response.

"That does not make sense," stated Rhinauld at the King's side.

"You are unwell. Calm yourself," ordered the King. He put his hand in the center of the star.

Do not forget.

"I will come for you," swore Andraste.

Rhinauld stepped between the King and Andraste, blocking her from the King's spell.

"You fool!" swore the King.

Andraste was on higher ground and leaping over Rhinauld's shoulder, she raised her Ruin sword towards the King. However, her blade was countered by Aldrich's.

"Let us talk," mediated Aldrich, "We are all friends here."

"I remember, Uncle. I know what you have done," hissed Andraste. She turned on the King.

"Sleep," commanded the King. His spell hit her directly and she fell unconscious to the ground. Aldrich caught her in his arms, dropping his sword in the process. His only concern was Andraste, who now bewitched, was fully asleep in his embrace. He looked up the King in rage. Rhiannon tried to restore calm while the Island Kingdom knights divided into two sides.

It took six knights to keep Rhinauld from the King. The knights first tried to restrain Rhinauld by the points of their swords, and when that failed, they wrestled him to the ground.

Chapter Thirteen

"Andra," called Rhinauld.

Andraste opened her eyes and looked at him. She felt groggy and uncertain. It took a moment for her eyes to adjust. Her headache had returned but was not as debilitating as before. She was in her chambers at the palace. She had no idea how she had arrived there.

"Ask no questions. Pretend like nothing is wrong. We will speak later after the meeting," said Rhinauld. He spoke with utmost sincerity. He raised his voice and looked pointedly towards the adjoining chamber, "You are needed at the War Council."

"What more could there be to discuss?" Andraste asked irritably. Her head felt as though it would split in two. However, upon reflection she realized she was no longer hearing two voices.

"You must go," urged Rhinauld.

"I know my part. How many times must I learn the others?" inquired Andraste.

"I will leave you to get ready," said Rhinauld. He patted her on the head and she knocked his hand away. He left her chambers, but he poked his head back in her room, "Do not go back to sleep."

Andraste sat up slowly in the bed and she heard Rhinauld's voice, "No, Caelius, she is not ready."

"She still will not see me?" asked Aldrich.

"She has just awakened," replied Rhinauld.

"And none of you will comment on the events of yesterday?" inquired Aldrich. Rhinauld did not respond.

"How long do you expect me to just follow blindly? How many secrets will you withhold? She attacked her own uncle. Is the madness hereditary? Is she has mad as the Emperor?" asked Aldrich.

"For a good time I have suspected she was bewitched, but yesterday solidified my doubts. She had become more lucid since her time with you but within the last few days, she has fallen once again into a downward spiral. There are words that I will say to you, but not here, and not now. Andraste is my priority. I will do anything to keep her safe," answered Rhinauld. There was silence as Aldrich considered Rhinauld's words.

"But if she was bewitched, would not my healing power heal her?" inquired Aldrich.

"Not if she was bewitched by another Ruin conqueror," responded Rhinauld.

"We will speak soon," said Aldrich. He left the room with apprehension.

Andraste dressed in dark breeches and a tunic. She hastily braided her hair, before fastening her tourmaline necklace. She proceeded into the adjoining chamber. Rhinauld acted as though the conversation had not occurred.

"Vespasian will not attend due to his duties. Vitus will be there in his stead," informed Rhinauld.

"Okay," said Andraste.

"You need to know. It is said that you lead the assembled Northern forces," replied Rhinauld.

"Me? They are Vespasian's men," rejoined Andraste.

"Vesp and Vitus both said to defer to your judgment," said Rhinauld.

"How long until we sup?" asked Andraste.

"Perhaps an hour or two. I imagine we will attend after the War Council finishes," answered Rhinauld. They fell silent as a soft knock sounded on the door. Rhinauld opened it and the Queen entered. She surveyed Andraste with concern.

"Your Majesty," greeted Andraste. The Queen already had her crystal in hand. She raised it to Andraste but it remained neutral.

"I saw Aelius on his way to the War Council so I thought it would be a good time to try our solution. It appears as you are already recovered. The

Spirit healed you?" asked the Queen.

"He said it would take time for me to remember everything," answered Andraste.

"You remember the Queen visiting you two nights ago?" inquired Rhinauld.

"I do. I thank you for your pains," replied Andraste.

"As I can be of no use, I will depart. You are both expected at the War Council. Make haste or Aelius will know something is amiss," said the Queen. She departed quickly and turned down the opposite hallway. Andraste and Rhinauld exchanged glances before proceeding to the War Chambers.

"Do you-" started Andraste.

"We cannot speak. We do not know who is listening," interrupted Rhinauld. He surveyed her with his emerald gaze and she fell silent.

"How do you feel?" asked Rhinauld.

"I do not know how long I will be able to maintain this farce," replied Andraste.

"When we have enough support, we will call a gathering. Until then, you must maintain that you are still under his spell. If he knows otherwise, I do not know what he will do," responded Rhinauld.

"But it is different now, Rhinauld. Not only is his spell broken, but I remember. I remember everything," said Andraste.

"What do you mean?" asked Rhinauld.

They had reached the War Chambers and the discussions within paused as the warriors surveyed Andraste. Food and drink had been laid out in the back of the room. She started towards it but saw that Aldrich had risen and was waiting for her. Rhinauld conveyed her to the empty chair next to him. She glared at Rhinauld. He helped her to her seat. Helping Andraste into her seat, he then kissed her hand before hastening to the back of the room. Aldrich was watching her closely.

"Why are we meeting?" asked Andraste.

"It is the will of the Council," responded Aldrich.

He retook his seat. He saw Andraste's eyes following Rhinauld's every movement. Rhinauld turned to face her. He pointed at the appetizers and she shook her head. He pointed at the basket of Northern apples and she nodded.

"You have not eaten today?" asked Aldrich.

Andraste shook her head. Aldrich reached in front of her as an apple hurtled across the room. Wordlessly, he took a knife from his belt and began to cut the apple into pieces, then offered her the first piece. Andraste was too hungry to not accept the offering.

"You are not angry with me?" inquired Aldrich.

"Why would I be angry with you?" rejoined Andraste. She looked at Aldrich's eyes questioningly and Aldrich frowned. Rhinauld had returned to her side and offered her a glass of water. She eyed the stein in his other hand.

"Not until you have eaten. We do not want another incident like Gardenia," said Rhinauld.

"I was on my best behavior in Gardenia. You mean the Northern Mountains," rejoined Andraste. Rhinauld bowed to her and retreated before she could say more.

Aldrich offered her another piece of apple.

"Do lords often throw food at ladies in the North?" asked Aldrich.

"Never, but in the Island Kingdoms, it has been known to happen," replied Andraste.

Aldrich handed her another piece of apple. The Northern and Western delegations were filing into the chamber.

"Are the Southern lords always so punctual?" asked Andraste.

"Always," replied Aldrich. The corners of his mouth twitched. Andraste and Aldrich both rose as the King of the Island Kingdoms swept down the hallway towards them.

"The Queen will not be joining us?" asked the King.

"She is preparing for dinner," replied Aldrich.

The King gestured to one of his men who brought him a stein of beer. The King handed it to Andraste who grinned triumphantly at Rhinauld. Rhinauld stared darkly at the King. Aldrich surveyed the King with distrust.

"Are you sure-" started Aldrich.

"Have you asked Rhinauld about his day? What he has been up to while you slept?" asked the King. His man brought him a second stein of beer.

"What did he do?" inquired Andraste.

"There was another skirmish outside of the city. Egnatius, Vitus, Rhinauld and their combined forces drove back the Imperial troops," said Aldrich. Andraste frowned.

"But all of our reports detected no movement from the North," said Andraste.

"Our communication network is evidently lacking," replied the King.

"Will you leave at such a time, when your lands could be under attack?" asked Andraste.

Aldrich took his time to respond. He slowly cut Andraste another piece of apple and then offered it to her.

"The Queen has held the city in times of war before. I have faith in my men. I would prefer to remain with them, but our greatest chance of success is to pursue the Emperor in the North. Otherwise, we could be in for a long siege," replied Aldrich.

"Well-reasoned," approved the King.

"May I be excused? I want to make sure our preparations are made for our journey," said Andraste.

"As I have said before, we must be seen as working together and not apart," replied Aldrich. He offered her another piece of apple.

"There are many more apples here," said the King, addressing Aldrich, "They are her favorite."

"Would you care for another?" asked Aldrich. Andraste shook her head.

"We are all assembled," said the King as he scanned the room. Aldrich stood and surveyed the room.

"This meeting is to confirm our plans. Paramerion, the Victorious and I will be leaving on the morrow. The King of the Island Kingdoms will be pushing his ships north. Vespasian will be pushing from the West with our Western and Northern allies assembled here, and we hear that Titus will be pushing further from the East. The Queen will be remaining in the

Southern capitol to hold the city," said Aldrich, "I would ask each of the Commanders to state their readiness."

Aldrich took his seat and Orthos, Chief of the Western Plains rose. Andraste glanced to Aldrich; she could not tell what he was thinking. He offered her another piece of apple but kept his eyes on the Western chieftain. Orthos had been so succinct that by the time Andraste returned her attention to the Chief, he had reseated.

The great doors of the Chambers were opened. Andraste frowned as she saw Vespasian enter the hall, moving resolutely. He had an agitated look to his eyes and his face was set in a firm frown. Aldrich handed Andraste another piece of apple but she did not take it. She did not like the look on Vespasian's face who knelt without ceremony at her feet.

"There is news from the North, Empress," informed Vespasian. He did not raise his head.

"Proceed," said Andraste.

"Civil war has erupted in the North. The Lady Claudia tried to return to her homeland for safety but the Emperor viewed it as an act of treason," said Vespasian. He did not look at Andraste.

"Lady Claudia's children-- my siblings?" questioned Andraste.

"All three executed along with the Lady," replied Vespasian.

"What was the manner?" inquired Andraste.

"Poison. It was not two weeks ago," responded Vespasian.

Andraste's eyes flew to Toxin who was closely watching her exchange with Vespasian. Andraste's eyes burned with tears as she turned accusingly to Aldrich.

"There is no proof. Our deal with the Earl was made but a week ago," said Aldrich.

"Gratiana was fourteen, Crispus was twelve, and Paulus was nine!" ranted Andraste.

"It is not Aldrich's fault," stated the King. Andraste looked away. She blinked back tears.

"I am sorry for your loss," said Aldrich. Andraste composed herself.

"Five poisonings in two weeks?" questioned Andraste aloud.

"It is the preferred method of the Northern militant sorcerers," responded Aldrich.

"Forgive me, Empress, but there is more you must know. Your sister, Herminia, is also dead. She intervened on behalf of the children and was so executed by the Emperor's orders," said Vespasian.

"By whose hand?" asked Andraste.

"Your brother, Sulla. He was given the choice to die or to execute the Lady. For his service, he has been appointed Supreme Commander of the Imperial Army. He and Varinia ride towards the South," responded Vespasian.

Andraste rose angrily and stood unsure of the appropriate action. Her hand tightened on the hilt of her Ruin sword. Brion rose from his seat in the back of the room. Andraste locked eyes on Brion and began to regain her composure. As she headed down the aisle, Brion took his place by her side and they left the Chambers.

"We already leave at first light," cautioned Brion.

"I know," responded Andraste, "I am just so angry. I feel as though I just rip someone's eyes out with my bare hands!"

"Such rage is dangerous," replied Rhinauld as he caught up with them, "A duel would clear your head."

"Lead on," ordered Andraste.

Rhinauld quickened their pace to the training yard. The recruits were no longer running drills. The three of them were alone in the training yard. The sun was beginning to set behind the stone wall as the wind blew dust and bits of grass across the training yard.

Andraste unsheathed her sword and faced Rhinauld. Unequivocal rage was building inside of her as she thought of all the people she had lost in the last years. Andraste took a step forward and Rhinauld hastily drew his sword. His normal merry disposition had faded as he eyed Andraste with apprehension. His gaze was calculating. Andraste did not take her eyes from him as she advanced.

Andraste did not hold back. Rhinauld was driven back several paces yet he held his ground. Andraste quickened her attack but this time, Rhinauld was forced to give ground as Andraste backed him into a corner of the courtyard.

"Andraste," cautioned Brion.

Andraste did not hear him. She raised her sword against her foster brother.

Rhinauld changed his tactics. His years at sea had produced unparalleled footwork and balance. Darting this way and that, Rhinauld countered and advanced as though in a dead dance to the end. Andraste gracefully deflected his attacks. Once more she cornered him against the wall of the training yard.

"I yield," said Rhinauld.

Andraste froze in her position. Rhinauld threw his sword to the ground. The action turned Andraste's gaze to the ground. She saw trails of violet magically trailing from her cloak. Crystalline violet particles reached her hand which was still clutching the hilt of her Ruin sword. The sword heated suddenly, radiating with red energy and scorching Andraste who instinctively dropped the molten sword to the ground.

"What is it?" asked Rhinauld.

"Dark energy," replied Andraste.

"You can see it?" asked Brion.

Andraste turned to see that he and the King were watching from the opposite side of the field.

"Rhinauld cannot?" inquired Andraste. She looked to Rhinauld.

"Complex magic," explained Brion, "You are seeing auras. What do you see when you look at me?"

"I see blue light, but a red chain ensnares your heart," said Andraste.

"You can see the seal?" asked Brion.

"Is that what it is?" asked Andraste.

"I do not understand. How can you wield this magic if you are not a magic user?" asked Brion. He looked to the King of the Island Kingdoms.

"But I am, I was," answered Andraste in confusion.

"Do you remember? It was in this very place," said the King.

"Mother sealed my magic. If I had the need, my brother would protect me. I was told to never use magic," replied Andraste.

"But why?" asked Brion.

"Andraste and I were here when the Empress fell. The Empress's last action was to seal Andraste's powers away. She feared that Andraste would follow her path. She asked me to remove Andraste's earliest memories," said the King.

"But then why does she not remember later events such as attacking her own men?" asked Brion.

"I removed later memories because they created confusion. They made her try to think of the past. Additionally, on the night she attacked her men I spoke with her afterwards before approaching the Southern court. There are things she must know in case I am killed in battle. Understanding my reasons, the Spirit restored all of Andraste's memories except for this one particular conversation. Her full memory will be restored if I am killed. If not, then we can discuss after the defeat of the Emperor," said the King.

"Andra is strong. What could be so terrible that she could not handle it?" inquired Rhinauld.

"What could be more important?" questioned Brion.

"It is not time," replied the King.

"Why did the Ruin sword attack me?" asked Andraste.

"The dark, ancient magic of the curse will always remain with you. It will grow more powerful with your anger and fear. You must do your best to remain calm. The Ruin sword protected you. It is helping to seal away the curse," answered the King.

Andraste surveyed her clothes. The mist of amethyst energy had disappeared.

She gingerly reached for the Ruin sword which lay on the ground as though nothing had happened and having resumed normal appearances. Andraste eyed it cautiously before picking it up with a mixture of increased respect and bewilderment. She returned the sword to its sheath.

"Do not use magic! I cannot contain your power anymore. The curse has unsealed my spell. It is your choice, but again, I beseech you: do not use magic! Heed your mother's warning," pleaded the King.

"I remember. I am an Anima. I restore the balance. I read the web of time. I correct the threads of life. Brion is not as he should be. I must make it right," said Andraste.

The King stepped forward to stop her. He raised his sea-green eyes in pleading as Andraste resolutely raised her outstretched palm towards the King who was thrown forcefully into the training yard wall. Rhinauld went to the King's aid and in doing so, drew his sword and thrust himself between Andraste and the King.

He drew his sword and put himself between Andraste and the King.

"Andra," warned Rhinauld.

The skies had darkened overhead. The wind blew from the East and blew Andraste's tresses about her. She brushed her long, hazel hair out of her eyes. Brion stood ten paces from her. She raised her hand to Brion, who looked at Andraste with absolute trust. He did not flinch.

Andraste made a circle in the air with her index finger, as she did so, red light followed and made a pattern in the air. When she reached the top of the circle, she then created a five pointed star. Placing her hand in the center of the star, she raised her eyes to Brion.

"Be as you should be," commanded Andraste.

The entire circle and star radiated with red energy before flashing into a beam of ruby light, which squarely hit Brion's chest. The chains that ensnared his heart fell to the ground evaporating on contact with the earth. Brion dropped to one knee before her.

"Are you hurt?" asked Rhinauld in concern.

Brion laughed. It was not a laugh filled with mirth. It was a laugh that made both Rhinauld and the King uneasy.

"I have never felt better," replied Brion as he rose to his feet.

"Easy," said the King, "It will take time to get used to such great power."

Brion nodded to the King. His eyes turned to Andraste. She was surveying the King.

"You will not meddle with my memories again. Uncle or not, ally or not, if you do so again, I will kill you," said Andraste. Her sea-green eyes turned on the King. It was as if she did not see him.

"Andra!" exclaimed Rhinauld.

"Do not interfere," said Andraste. She surveyed Rhinauld. He sheathed his sword and bowed to her.

"You sound like the Emperor," said Brion. His smiled had faded.

"You are calculating me as if I am your enemy," responded Andraste.

"Your powers were sealed for a reason," said Brion.

"As were yours," replied Andraste. The look between the siblings was hostile. The King interceded, "You had to develop the physical, emotional, and intellectual state to be able to wield such a power. Your mother failed. On top of that, you have your father's powers as well."

Rhinauld pulled the King to his feet. The King approached Andraste wearily.

"You betrayed me, weakened me, and lied to me. In essence the trust we once shared was only an invention," said Andraste.

"My actions were performed reluctantly and only in order to protect you. I love no one in this world as much as my family," replied the King. He besought Andraste earnestly.

"You have also used dark magic in a manner unbefitting the King of the Island Kingdoms. You have wounded your own kin. You could be deposed," said Rhinauld.

"All you say is true. My honor is tarnished by this act, but I would do it again if it would have protected my daughters or Andra," stated the King.

"Why did the Empress say your brother will use magic to protect you? My power was sealed and we have no brother, whose power could rival the Emperor's," inquired Brion.

"Victoria had a son by her first union," replied the King reluctantly.

"What?" asked Brion. He frowned at Andraste and the King.

"Yes, Sveinbiorn Eldgrimson," said Andraste softly. She turned her eyes on the King.

"Where are you headed?" asked Brion.

"The transport circle in the Sorcerer's tower," said Andraste. Brion hastened after her as did the King and Rhinauld.

"Andraste and I are the only ones who knew," said the King.

"You made me forget my own brother," stated Andraste. There was no forgiveness in her eyes.

"He is half-demon. Victoria had no reason to try to pull him through the barrier. If it was meant to be done it would not have been so hard. She would not have been wounded," replied the King.

"He is half-human," retaliated Andraste.

"Barrier?" asked Rhinauld.

"Victoria studied across the seas. She encountered a race of demons, which, centuries ago, had been sealed behind a vapor barrier by our ancient ancestors. Victoria could come and go as she pleased. However, to learn ancient magic, the Demon lord bade her bare him a child. A child, who, cannot cross the barrier due to his demon blood," answered the King reluctantly.

"You would free a demon?" asked Rhinauld. He saw the look on Andraste's face and amended, "Half-demon?"

"He will never be one with the other demons. They disparage him because of his human blood. He belongs with me. He is my mother's child. He is human. My mother died in pursuit of his freedom," said Andraste.

"Do we not have enough to deal with at the present?" asked Brion.

"Sveinbiorn will be our greatest ally. His power will rival the Emperor's," stated Andraste.

"If you can control him," replied the King.

"Should we not ask Aldrich Caelius before you summon a demon to his lands?" questioned Rhinauld.

"I am through taking orders from men. Look at the mess you all have created. Better I follow my own heart. I am summoning my brother," said Andraste, "Besides can you not feel the negative energy radiating throughout the castle? Malicious intent is in the air! Those darkened skies were not my doing. The Emperor's next attack will be by sorcery. He will curse the entire city. Even my full power will not stop it."

"We will find another way," said the King.

"At what cost? How many more must die?" asked Andraste.

"That is the cost of war," replied the King.

"Can you not feel the power that comes?" questioned Brion, "She is the right. The Southern tower will not be able to stop it."

Andraste pushed the great doors open into the transport room. She proceeded and stood before a large silver circle that was engraved into the floor in the pattern of a star. The room had evidently not been used for some time. Rhinauld eyed the silver markings on the floor.

"What is that?" asked Rhinauld.

"It is ancient magic. The transport circles are placed throughout the First Republic. In days of old, transport circles were used to ferry people and goods from one end of the Republic to the other within minutes," explained Brion, "There are a few still in use in the North."

"So that is how the Empire moved the troops so quickly," said Rhinauld.

"Typically, the South has banned their use as they know so little about them which is a waste. The Southern transport circle is the largest and the most powerful due to its location. It is located above substantial lay lines that run throughout the lands," replied Brion.

"Save your lecture, professor," said Andraste.

"I still say, do not summon the demon, but if you feel you *must*, do it now," said the King.

"How does one summon a demon?" asked Rhinauld.

Andraste drew a circle in the air before her. She took the dagger from her sleeve and cut the palm of her hand. She dropped blood into the circle she had drawn in the air.

"Sveinbiorn Eldgrimson, Sveinbiorn Eldgrimson, Sveinbiorn Eldgrimson," called Andraste.

The circle shimmered and turned into a mirror but instead of reflecting Andraste's image, an enormous snow tiger, apparently sleeping within a dark cave, appeared. Raising its head, the tiger slowly gazed into the mystical mirror. Its two front fangs protruded over his bottom lip. The look in its eyes, which were the same color as Andraste's, was true sorrow. The intensity of the pain was almost human.

The great snow tiger arose and padded silently towards the mirror; sitting upon its hind legs, it surveyed Andraste. Brion and Rhinauld both stepped back from the mirror. The King took a step forward and eyed the tiger with distrust. Likewise, the tiger returned the King's gaze but then turned his full attention to Andraste.

"Little one," greeted the tiger. Brion jumped as he heard the tiger speak. Andraste recognized the voice as one that she had been hearing in her thoughts.

"Sveinbiorn, I am sorry. So very, very sorry," whispered Andraste.

"So you have not forgotten me?" asked the tiger.

"Forgive me. I promise I will explain everything later but for now, our need is dire. You once made a contract with our mother for your freedom. Will you make the same deal with me?" questioned Andraste.

"I will serve you and your children for all of my days if you free me and grant my two conditions," said Sveinbiorn.

"For such service, I will free you. I will find you a consenting companion. I will release you once our war is fought but first we must pursue the Lionden Emperor," said Andraste.

"That could mean a second war," cautioned Brion.

"Lionden will come for us anyway, and we will have to combat the Arisen one way or another," replied Andraste.

"I accept your contract," said Sveinbiorn, "But-- have care, little one! Our mother could not free me. I would not see you come to harm."

"Swear by the blood that binds us," ordered Andraste.

The tiger pierced his paw with his fang and touched the mirror.

"I swear to uphold our contract," vowed Sveinbiorn.

"As do I," said Andraste, "Please arrive in your human form."

She stepped into the center of the transport circle. She raised a hand to make a second magic circle.

"You are going to try to release him without a second transport circle?" asked the King.

"There is no time," replied Andraste. She used her own blood to draw a doorway. A portal appeared before her. She could see the tiger pacing back forth. The patterns of the transport circle engraved in the floor began to emanate blinding silver light towards the ceiling. Andraste and the King kept their eyes fixed on the doorway, but Rhinauld and Brion diverted their eyes. The doorway had turned into a silver beacon of light.

"Now," ordered Andraste.

The tiger transformed into his human form. He opened the door on his side and stepped through the portal. He quickly turned to shut the door behind him. Through the mirror, Andraste saw shapes beginning to materialize in the dark shadows of the cave. Sveinbiorn used his own magic to rid the room of the portal, while Andraste dismissed the mirror. The light from the transport circle faded and they were left once more in near darkness.

"Your cloak," demanded Andraste.

Brion threw his charcoal cloak to Andraste. She handed it to Sveinbiorn as he stood bare before them. His long, silvery hair was loose upon his fair-skinned broad shoulders that were covered in faint scars. He knelt at Andraste's feet. She rested her hand on the top of his head.

"That is a demon?" asked Rhinauld incredulously.

"Your people once referred to mine as gods," replied Sveinbiorn. He rose, towering over Andraste, and turned his narrow beryl eyes to survey the speaker. Rhinauld looked to the King for explanation.

"Later I will tell you why the barrier was built," said the King.

"Uncle," greeted Sveinbiorn. There was no welcome in his tone or kindness.

"Nephew," replied the King just as surly.

"You are tainted with dark magic," said Sveinbiorn as he surveyed his half-sister. His sea-green eyes flashed as he turned to their uncle, "Was this your doing?"

"No," answered the King.

"I sense your magic," stated Sveinbiorn.

"I tampered with her memories as was the wish of your mother, but I have done nothing to harm her," replied the King.

"Tampering with her memories is harming her," stated Rhinauld. The look in his eyes was unforgiving.

"This must wait. I am sorry to ask so soon. The Emperor sends-" started Andraste.

"I feel it. It will undo the web of time. He has no right to meddle with such ancient magic. He will destroy these lands," said Sveinbiorn. He made no sound as he turned to the doorway.

"We must face the attack outdoors. Are there battlements?" asked Sveinbiorn.

"We should go to the roof. We are in a sorcerer's tower," replied Andraste.

Sveinbiorn bolted for the stairs, with long, purposeful strides. Andraste proceeded at his side, although it took her more steps to keep up with him.

She heard the footsteps of the other three following behind. They emerged onto the roof into fierce winds. The gale almost knocked Andraste off her feet. Sveinbiorn stepped in front of her and she placed a hand on his back for balance.

A massive thunderstorm was approaching from the North. Although the dark clouds ruled the skies, the sky itself had turned into a deep shade of violet. Five violent rotating columns of air extended from the thunderstorms to the ground. The winds were so fierce that they were lifting trees and structures from the ground.

Southern sorcerers lined around the edge of the tower, firing spells at the colossal storm but nothing weakened it. Despite the lack of any signs of improvement, the sorcerers stood strong and resolute in their attempts to come up with spells that would defeat the storm of sorcery. Marcella's concentration was broken as she turned to look at Andraste and surveyed the newcomer. Sveinbiorn turned to speak to Andraste but the words were lost on the wind. He pointed towards the distance.

Sveinbiorn used one arm to draw Andraste to him and the other to draw an encircled star before him. He chanted an incantation, but Andraste could not distinguish the words. With a motion of her hand, Andraste made the same encircled star, moving in sync with Sveinbiorn. When he placed his hand on the center of his star, she did the same.

"Follow," commanded Andraste.

Ruby light radiated from their stars although Andraste's spell wrapped around and fortified Sveinbiorn's spell. The ghost of a smile flickered across Sveinbiorn's face but it quickly faded. Andraste's spell strengthened and propelled Sveinbiorn's spell, but she could not sustain her spell for long. Her ruby light was quickly fading.

A cheer went up from the Southern sorcerers as the winds began to lessen. The massive wind columns disappeared and the sky to lose its violet tinge. Andraste began to feel weak. Sveinbiorn was studying her intently. When he spoke to her, she did not understand. He drew a flower in the air which materialized before him. Sveinbiorn plucked the snow-white orchid with magenta lined petals from the air and delicately put it behind her ear. The orchid began to radiate a soft rosy light. Andraste felt her head begin to clear.

"Impressive for a human," said Sveinbiorn. As he saw her weakening, he swept her up in his arms as if she weighed nothing.

"Take me to her chambers," ordered Sveinbiorn. Rhinauld did not move.

"She needs rest," stated Sveinbiorn.

Rhinauld looked to the King of the Island Kingdoms and Brion who both stepped aside. Rhinauld led the long way back down the spiral staircase. They did not speak. Half way down the stairwell, they encountered Aldrich. His eyes widened in concern. He stepped to take Andraste from Sveinbiorn, but the half-demon only eyed him coldly and with suspicion.

"Is she-" started Aldrich.

"She is sleeping," responded Sveinbiorn.

"And you are-" began Aldrich.

"You may call me, Eldgrimson," replied Sveinbiorn. He took a step forward, and Aldrich stepped aside so that he could pass. Aldrich looked to the King of the Island Kingdoms.

"No one was injured. Your sister and the other sorcerers are well," said the King. He continued to follow after Sveinbiorn, leaving a disgruntled prince on the stairs.

Upon reaching Andraste's chambers, Sveinbiorn laid her gently on the sofa. Seeing a tea tray had been laid out, he brought it to her side.

"Awaken," said Sveinbiorn gently.

Andraste's eyes opened. He lifted a glass of water to her lips. He fed her a confection. He took a bite of a second and made a face. Andraste laughed softly.

"It is like eating air and sickly sweet. What is this trash?" asked Sveinbiorn.

"It is a cookie," replied Andraste. She looked past Sveinbiorn to Rhinauld.

"Will you bring him some clothes?" asked Andraste. Rhinauld bowed to her and turned to leave.

"Rhinauld," called Andraste. He turned to face her, "Do not tell anyone, not even Rhiannon of my brother's origins or true nature. In fact, tell no one that he is my brother. It will raise too many questions."

"Yes, Empress," said Rhinauld. He bowed once more and left the room. Brion shut the door.

"I will never hurt her," said Sveinbiorn. He did not glance up from Andraste. The King and Brion still watched him carefully.

"I am glad to see that she has such protectors. However, I swore by blood to enter her service, and she is my only family. I will never hurt her," repeated Sveinbiorn.

"You are still a demon," stated the King.

"And you my captor," replied Sveinbiorn, "I have not forgotten, Aelius. For her sake and by my oath, I am permitting you to live."

"All I ask is that you tell her nothing. There is much that she does not know. Listen to her story and her directions, but do not speak. If you want to protect her, you will do this," said the King.

Sveinbiorn turned his sea-green eyes on the King and studied him.

"Two decades I spent in hell because you tampered with her memories," said Sveinbiorn, "Your debt grows."

"And true to your kind, you will not forget it. In time you may understand my actions. Everything I have done has been for her," replied the King.

Sveinbiorn did not respond. He only stared at the King with his calculating sea-green eyes.

"Come, Brion," ordered the King. Then, holding a steady gaze upon Sveinbiorn, the King continued, "Let her rest and return to the dining hall at sunset."

"I will consider it," replied Sveinbiorn.

"I am fine," said Andraste. She sat up slowly. She put a hand to the orchid in her hair, "Is it magic?"

"It has healing properties," concluded Sveinbiorn.

Sveinbiorn rose from her side and surveyed her surroundings. He examined the books on the shelves but turned as Rhinauld reappeared and set an arm full of clothes on the table. The King motioned for Brion and Rhinauld to follow him. They left the room and Rhinauld paused to study Sveinbiorn once last time.

"Woof," said Sveinbiorn. Rhinauld shut the door quickly.

"I will give you a minute to dress," said Andraste. Sveinbiorn did not respond.

Andraste went into her bedchamber. She caught a glimpse of herself in the mirror. Her hair was knotted and tangled from the wind on the tower. Her clothes were wrinkled and stained from the day's events. Andraste quickly changed into Northern charcoal colored robes and set herself to rights. She smoothed the coarse linen of her robes, picked up her hair brush and then proceeded to walk into the antechamber.

"Are the boots too small?" asked Andraste.

"I do not wear footwear," replied Sveinbiorn. She passed him the brush but he only looked at it in confusion. Andraste sat beside him on the sofa and began to comb his hair.

"What are you doing?" asked Sveinbiorn.

"I am combing your hair," replied Andraste.

"Whatever for?" asked Sveinbiorn.

"It is what we do," responded Andraste.

Sveinbiorn permitted her to comb his hair. She fastened his hair into a ponytail in the Southern fashion. With his hair pulled back, his sea-green eyes were even more striking against his fair skin.

"What now?" asked Sveinbiorn. He was uncomfortable by her scrutiny.

"I see mother in your face," said Andraste softly. Sveinbiorn's face softened, but he said nothing.

"Let us go," said Andraste. She rose and Sveinbiorn followed her. She strapped the Ruin sword around her waist.

"That is a weapon of great power. It is a demon slayer," stated Sveinbiorn. He looked at it curiously but did not reach for it.

"How can you tell?" asked Andraste.

"I can smell demon blood," replied Sveinbiorn.

"When we are among others, let us not speak of such things," cautioned Andraste.

"You are ashamed of me?" questioned Sveinbiorn.

"I do not want you to face prejudice," replied Andraste.

"I will exercise caution," said Sveinbiorn.

"We will see if the Queen will see us," said Andraste.

She made her way to the Queen's chambers and Sveinbiorn followed at her side. As they passed the music chambers Andraste heard the room buzzing with discussion.

"Surely only the gods have such magic!"

"Who is he?"

"Who is she? Why did she hide such power?"

"The Island Kingdoms are in an uproar. There is talk of deposing the King."

"Depose a king? Has that been done before?"

"They say he bewitched the princess to the point of madness."

"Who would take his place?"

Silence fell on the room as Andraste and Sveinbiorn passed. Sveinbiorn surveyed the room with interest, but Andraste kept her eyes on the Queen's chambers. She saw two of her Victorious stationed outside of the Queen's chambers as well as two Southern guardsmen.

"Where is Laelius?" asked Andraste.

"He went to find you," replied Maximianus.

"Is the Queen-" started Andraste.

"Please enter," replied the Queen from within her chambers.

Andraste entered the rooms and pulled Sveinbiorn inside by his tunic. He was distracted trying to study everything he encountered. She found the Queen seated on her veranda with a book. Andraste bade Maximianus close the doors. She approached the Queen.

"Forgive the intrusion. Pray may we have an audience with you?" inquired Andraste.

"Of course, I have been hoping you would visit. I would have thought you would have called sooner," replied the Queen.

"My apologies, your Majesty. In the North, we do not approach the Emperor without being summoned. I thought that it would be the same in the South," returned Andraste.

"I would be happy to instruct you in the ways of the Southern court," said the Queen. Andraste blushed unhappily and looked to Sveinbiorn.

"May I present, Sveinbiorn Eldgrimson, a sorcerer from the East," said Andraste. Sveinbiorn bowed and kissed the Queen's hand.

"Those eyes! There is no question. He is an Eldgrimson," replied the Queen, "You are welcome, Lord Eldgrimson. Please be seated."

Andraste sat at the Queen's table but Sveinbiorn turned to survey the sea. He turned his back on their conversation.

"Many rumors have reached my ear," said the Queen. She poured Andraste a cup of tea.

"That is why I have come to speak with you," replied Andraste.

"You seem different, more composed," said the Queen as she studied Andraste.

"I am myself again," responded Andraste.

"And who were you before?" asked the Queen with a small smile.

"Aelius tampered with her memories to suit his purposes," replied Sveinbiorn. The Queen's smile faded and she flushed with anger.

"That would explain your splintered personalities but to use dark magic on your own kin. For what purpose?" asked the Queen.

"He says now is not the time to tell me. He says we must defeat the Emperor and then he will defend his actions," replied Andraste.

"This is inexcusable," said the Queen, "So the Island Kingdoms are rightfully talking of deposing the King."

"I will forbid it. Not during a time of war. We cannot risk divisions that could lead to civil war. I am furious with my uncle and I will never trust him again, but he is the King of the Island Kingdoms. He will protect our people," said Andraste.

The Queen considered Andraste's words and took a sip from her tea cup. She raised her sapphire eyes to Andraste and asked, "Why do you speak of this with me and not my son?"

"My memories are returning but there are some matters that I am unclear of," said Andraste. She blushed and stirred her tea.

"Then speak to me not as Queen, but as woman to woman. I would do anything for the daughter of Victoria Eldgrimson. Please let me know how I may be of assistance," said the Queen.

"Am I engaged to Aldrich Caelius?" asked Andraste. The Queen set down her cup.

"No, my dear, and I believe if you were I would be the first one he would tell," said the Queen. She patted Andraste's hand.

"May I ask a favor, your Majesty?" asked Andraste. She blushed even deeper.

"What is it, my child?" inquired the Queen. She did not remove her hand.

"Would you check me for spells one more time, please?" requested Andraste. She did not meet the Queen's eyes.

"What sort of spells?" asked the Queen.

"My uncle has pushed me towards your son since we entered the Ruins of the Darklands. I want to know if-" Andraste stopped.

"You want to know if your feelings are real?" questioned the Queen kindly. She removed a crystal from her pocket and ran it over Andraste. The crystal remained in its natural form. Sveinbiorn watched the gesture with interest.

"No spells," said the Queen, "But could you not ask Lord Eldgrimson?"

"I wanted a second opinion," replied Andraste.

There was a knock on the Queen's doors and then Aldrich entered. He halted in surprise as he found Andraste seated before the Queen and Sveinbiorn surveying the sea. He shifted uncomfortably as both women turned expectantly towards him.

"Am I intruding?" asked Aldrich.

"No, of course not," replied the Queen, "We are discussing the state of the Island Kingdoms."

"The King and Rhinauld follow behind," said Aldrich. He approached and stood at the opposite side of the veranda surveying the sea.

"Is this your son?" asked Sveinbiorn.

"Yes, this is my son, Aldrich Caelius," answered the Queen.

"We have already met in an unofficial capacity," said Aldrich dryly. The two men stood studying each other. Sveinbiorn looked to Andraste.

"No questions. We will talk later," instructed Andraste.

"I had no notice of your arrival. How exactly did you arrive in our city?" asked Aldrich. Sveinbiorn looked to Andraste.

"I summoned him," said Andraste.

"That is not an answer," replied Aldrich irritably. He turned his eyes back to Sveinbiorn, "I am told you are from the Island Kingdoms."

"I am from the Far East," answered Sveinbiorn.

Aldrich's sapphire eyes flashed and he opened his mouth to ask another question.

"That is enough, Aldrich. Basic grace and courtesy, please. This is not an interrogation," said the Queen. She took a sip from her tea. Andraste looked to the Queen in surprise.

"I will speak with the King and Rhinauld in my receiving room. I imagine the princess has things she wishes to discuss with you," said the Queen. She rose and proceeded towards her chambers.

"I should be-" started Aldrich.

"You will remain with the princess," ordered the Queen. Aldrich bowed to his mother as she swept past him.

"Sveinbiorn attend the meeting and let me know what is decided," said Andraste.

Sveinbiorn looked from Andraste and then to Aldrich before following after the Queen. The Queen took his arm in her own. He hesitated and looked to Andraste once more. She nodded. Sveinbiorn proceeded stiffly with the Queen on his arm to the receiving room.

Andraste raised a slender wrist and reached for the tea pot. She poured Aldrich a cup of tea and set it on the table. Aldrich took it but did not sit down. He took a gratuitous sip and then set it back down on the table. Andraste raised her sea-green eyes to Aldrich and watched his movements. Aware of her observations, Aldrich took another sip of his tea but still said nothing.

"What do you know?" asked Andraste at last.

"Rhinauld came to see me earlier," replied Aldrich.

"I am still confused regarding some details of the last few weeks," said Andraste. She blushed as she stirred her tea. Aldrich seated himself at the table and drew his chair near her.

"Ask me whatever you wish," said Aldrich.

"When I was attacked by the assassin, did you sing me to sleep?" asked Andraste.

"Yes," replied Aldrich.

"And you stayed all night?" asked Andraste.

"Yes," said Aldrich.

"Do we share chambers?" questioned Andraste.

"No, you have your own rooms," responded Aldrich.

"Have you ever made love to me?" inquired Andraste.

"Yes," replied Aldrich. Andraste's blush was deeper than the Southern roses blooming behind her shoulders.

"Many times?" asked Andraste, staring at the contents of her tea cup.

"We have spent night one night together," replied Aldrich.

"And yet, I gave you my pledge but you did not accept it?" inquired Andraste.

"I do not understand your meaning," replied Aldrich.

"You are engaged to Gerlinde?" questioned Andraste.

"No, I am not. I have tried to tell you for days," said Aldrich. He rose angrily and went to survey the sea.

"What do you mean by pledge?" asked Aldrich. However, as he turned, he saw Andraste had risen to greet Rhinauld as he walked into the room.

"An Island gathering has been called. We must go, Andra," said Rhinauld. He offered her his arm and she went to him. She glanced back towards Aldrich.

"Outsiders are rarely permitted at the gathering of the clans. However, the Queen wishes for you to attend as well. Please come as our guest," said Rhinauld.

"As you wish," responded Aldrich. He followed behind them and watched Rhinauld closely. Sveinbiorn stepped out of the shadows and joined Andraste's side. Rhinauld's hand went to his hilt. Sveinbiorn did not pay him any attention. Aldrich surveyed the interaction wearily.

"Where will the gathering be held?" asked Aldrich.

"On the King's flagship," replied Rhinauld. He glanced down to Andraste.

"Where are the others?" inquired Andraste.

"They went ahead of us," answered Rhinauld.

They made their way quickly and silently to the palace steps. Andraste saw a carriage laden elephant awaited. Aldrich and Rhinauld both offered Andraste their arms. Aldrich withdrew and Rhinauld helped her to her seat. He sat beside her, but his eyes were on Sveinbiorn. Aldrich sat across from them. He kept his eyes fixed on the sea. Andraste smiled as she saw Sveinbiorn jump onto the elephant and then on top of the carriage.

"He is as much a showboat as you are," alleged Rhinauld. A ghost of a smile flickered on his face.

"Worse," replied Andraste.

The elephant rose and they were conveyed to the port. It was a hot and uncomfortable trip, although brief. Sveinbiorn jumped from the carriage as they came to a stop. He offered his hand to Andraste. She had no more then took it, when he swept her into his arms and jumped to the ground below. Andraste laughed as he set her on her feet. She wrapped her arm in his and led the way to the flagship. The passengers boarded a small row boat which ferried them across the narrow channel leading to the flagship.

"What is a gathering?" asked Sveinbiorn. Aldrich seemed puzzled by the question.

"Sveinbiorn has not been spent much time at Court," explained Andraste quickly.

"When the decisions that affect us all are debated, nobility meets to decide on our fate," answered Rhinauld.

"A King with a democracy?" asked Sveinbiorn. He cocked his head to the side, "That cannot be efficient."

"We have not faced a tyrant in two thousand years with our system," responded Rhinauld proudly.

"Little one, perhaps your bloodline is not meant to lead," said Sveinbiorn. Rhinauld began to protest but was silenced by Andraste's soft laughter.

Arriving at their destination, the transport boat was secured and hoisted to the top of the flagship. Rhinauld leapt out first and then turned to lift Andraste safely to the deck. Aldrich made his way across and went to stand with Felix, Valens and Hadrian. They acknowledged him but returned their attention promptly to the King. The mood on the ship was somber. Aldrich was unnerved by the lack of merriment that usually accompanied the Islanders.

"The last have arrived," announced the King.

Andraste surveyed the lords and ladies on board. They all bowed or curtsied to her as Andraste made her way across the ship towards the helm. Her eyes were locked on the King. She took her place dutifully at his right. Already an angry murmur was beginning to grow. Rhinauld broke protocol and went to stand between the King and Andraste. He stood at attention with his hand on his hilt.

Sveinbiorn emerged from the shadows and went to stand on Andraste's free side. The ship fell silent as the lords and ladies were scrutinized under Sveinbiorn's emerald gaze. He turned his full attention to Andraste.

"I would speak, Uncle," said Andraste. The King nodded his head.

"I will be brief. This is a family matter and not your concern. We are at war. Only hours ago, we were attacked by a fierce, limitless power. It is not the time to depose a King," said Andraste.

"That was very brief," commented Shannon. Her voice carried across the deck and there was some laughter. However, the tension still remained.

"I object," said Cuán.

"On what grounds?" asked the King.

"Upon a lady being wronged; upon the honor that binds us; and upon the Code that we all follow," roared Cuán.

"As the lady wronged, I do not pursue a claim. I am fully capable to speak in own my defense," retaliated Andraste. Rhinauld gritted his teeth at her side, but did not intervene.

"Two charges have been brought that we must address," said the King, "First, let us speak regarding the honor that binds us."

"You willingly and with full knowledge bewitched a child, who was under your protection and guardianship. You continuously and purposeful-ly meddled with her welfare to the point of madness," indicted Rhinauld.

Silence had fallen on the deck even though Rhinauld spoke softly his words carried across the ship. Andraste felt him tense at her side. She put a hand on his arm to restrain him.

"What say you in your defense?" asked Rhinauld.

"I have nothing to confess. No defense to propose. It is as you say," re-plied the King. Angry muttering had turned to outward yelling and insults. The King remained unmoved.

"And upon the Code that binds us, we ask again: what is your defense?"

inquired Rhinauld.

"There is nothing stated in the Code that outlaws the use of dark magic or disciplining children," answered Andraste.

"Disciplining children?" roared Rhinauld, "Andra, this is more than discipline and you know it. Stop protecting him!"

"The only charge is that of honor," stated Andraste calmly.

"I agree with Lady Eldgrimson. She is correct. The Code does not outlaw the use of dark magic," said Henry.

"But think of our history! Look at what happened the last time dark magic was used in the Eastern lands," claimed Rhiannon.

"It is not prohibited in the Code," repeated Andraste.

"The lack of honor is still a solid ground to dispose a King," asserted Cuán.

"And then what? Who here has more service then my uncle in defending the Island Kingdoms? Who else has served without question for near forty years? Who else has protected us and kept us from the wrath of the Emperor? In all state matters, my uncle is beyond reproach. Already his name is associated with legend. There is not a better man or woman who stands amongst us!" cried Andraste.

"The Lord of the Salt Islands," alleged Cuán, "I would follow him into battle. I have before and I will do it again."

"I would follow Andraste Eldgrimson," swore Shannon. She eyed the King with loathing.

"Now is not the time to be divided. We must stand together and strong!" proclaimed Andraste.

"I would follow Rhinauld and Andraste. It would be a pairing that could never be beaten," said Murchadh.

"As would I," said Gormlaith. There was an almost unanimous chorus of throughout the assembled.

"It is a union that would bring the Island Kingdoms to glory," claimed Lorcán.

"I will never marry for an allegiance," swore Andraste, "Our people have thrived for the last two millennia pursuing freedom. We have never married for allegiance. We follow our hearts. We have become strong through following our own path. We have become strong because we have not limited our options to aristocracy or equitable distribution. We are a nation of equals. No, I will not marry for allegiance. I need not a man to be strong, or to pursue my claims.

We are Island people. We go where the wind takes us, we sail the seas without fear, and we abide by no other man's law. This is the way of the First People. Ours is a way built on choice. We are independent and fierce so that may we can forge our own way. We are a nation built on adventurers and dreamers. Would you change our ways now when we are most in need of our strength and our traditions? What do we fight for if not for our way of life, our equality, our freedom?"

The lords and ladies surveyed Andraste and waited for her to speak again.

"My brethren, I would also remind you that it is also treason to speak of other choices before a king is deposed. Lady Eldgrimson's earlier questions were rhetorical," mentioned Henry.

"The King of the Island Kingdoms acted wrongly in my case, but as I said, it is a family a matter. He did not speak in his defense, but I feel as though this is also due to a family matter. As I see it, the gathering has no place in this family quarrel," concluded Andraste.

"The vote to depose a King must be unanimous," stated Henry.

"Raise your hand if you would depose the King," ordered Rhinauld.

Andraste surveyed the lords and ladies before her. Not one person raised their hand under her cool gaze.

"Then this matter is decided. As in all matters that come before us, once resolved we do not speak of it again. We move always forwards!" said the King.

"Together and onwards," replied Andraste. She looked pointedly at her foster brothers.

"Together and onwards," said the assembled.

"Andraste--," said the King quietly.

Andraste did not stop. She continued on her way to the row boats. Aldrich helped her into the row boat and sat at her side. Andraste raised her hood against the Eastern wind. She adjusted and part of her cloak cascaded onto his lap. Aldrich watched her under lowered eyes, but said nothing. Under the folds of her cloak her fingers rested beside his. Aldrich did not move. Once the boat was full, they were rowed to shore.

"I will walk from here," said Andraste. Aldrich moved to say something.

"Sveinbiorn," called Andraste.

Her brother appeared at her side instantly. Aldrich had not even seen him in the boat. Andraste wrapped her arm in Sveinbiorn's and they began the ascent to the palace. Aldrich did not follow them.

Chapter Fourteen

The Northern lords and ladies rose as Andraste entered the hall. Sveinbiorn hesitated before entering the dining hall. Andraste turned to look at him.

"So many people," said Sveinbiorn. He eyed the tables curiously.

"They will not bite," stated Andraste.

"Their teeth would not harm me," replied Sveinbiorn.

Andraste pulled on his sleeve and he proceeded down the hall. Andraste surveyed the Northern delegation. She noted that Toxin and Hyacinth were nowhere to be seen. She led Sveinbiorn towards the Northern tables.

"Empress, I am sorry for your loss. They were such dear children," consoled Iunia. Andraste took her offered hand and held it.

"We are reminded by this news of why we have left our homeland. We are more confident and resolute in our purpose than ever. It is our oath to protect those who are weaker then ourselves. Never forget this as you leave for your stations. We fight to protect our people. We must stand strong and we must stand together," said Andraste.

"You do not mean to persecute Toxin?" asked Blasius in outrage. Angry discussion broke out amongst the Northern delegation.

"The methods are similar to his, but we know so little. We do not have proof. We will not turn this into a witch hunt," said Andraste, "But if proof is found, regardless of whatever deal he has made with the Southern lands, I will execute him personally. We will maintain order and respect our laws."

The Northern lords and ladies bowed their heads to Andraste as she continued on her way. She did not stop to speak with Vespasian and the

Northern officers as she passed.

"Children?" asked Sveinbiorn.

"The Emperor executed four of my siblings," answered Andraste.

"But children are sacred," said Sveinbiorn.

"Agreed," replied Andraste. She raised her eyes to his face.

"You are not grieving?" asked Sveinbiorn. He was studying her intently.

"I cannot at this time," replied Andraste.

"You are more of a demon than me," said Sveinbiorn.

"Do not judge me," responded Andraste, "And remember my earlier warning."

Andraste saw that two seats had been left open at the head table. The Queen gestured for her to approach. The King of the Island Kingdoms sat tensely at the Queen's side. Marcella and Decima eyed Sveinbiorn curiously. Aldrich continued his discussion with Decima. Andraste took her seat and Sveinbiorn sat down stiffly beside her.

"May I present Sveinbiorn Eldgrimson, an ally from the far East," said Andraste.

"I hear we are indebted to you for the liberation of our City. May I ask where you learned such sorcery?" asked the Queen.

"No," replied Sveinbiorn. Andraste smiled behind her wine goblet.

"You enforced the same spell. I thought you did not study magic," said Marcella to Andraste.

"We are self-taught," replied Sveinbiorn.

"I thought you were your mother," said the Queen.

Andraste looked to the Queen and did not know if she referred to Sveinbiorn or herself. She exchanged glances with Sveinbiorn who said nothing. Sveinbiorn turned his sea-green eyes to Decima.

"Lady Decima of the Shadow Mountains," introduced Andraste, "And Princess Marcella Tarquinius of the Southern lands."

Sveinbiorn did not respond. Platters of food were placed before them and he eyed it wearily. A servant stepped hesitantly forward to pour him a glass of wine. Sveinbiorn watched the servant's movements under half-lowered eyes. He took the jug to pour Andraste's glass himself and then set it on the table.

"Rhinauld and Brion are not you with this evening?" inquired Aldrich.

Andraste's eyes scanned the dining hall. She saw them both scowling at Sveinbiorn from the table of the Island Kingdoms. Rhiannon smiled brightly at her and looked to Sveinbiorn curiously. Brion glowered at his future bride.

"They are with our friends," replied Andraste.

"And we are not?" asked the Queen.

"We have many friends," pacified the King. He shot Andraste a look of warning. Andraste turned as she felt a small hand on her shoulder. Sveinbiorn's face softened and he even smiled.

"Aaliyah," greeted Andraste.

"Empress," responded Aaliyah. She looked curiously at Sveinbiorn. Sveinbiorn took her hand and kissed it. Aaliyah giggled.

"You are so handsome," said Aaliyah.

"Aaliyah!" exclaimed Marcella.

"What? We were all thinking it," replied the Queen.

"Mother!" said Marcella and Aldrich in unison.

"Not I," grumbled the King.

"Someday, when I am bigger, will you be my husband?" asked Aaliyah.

"Do you like big cats?" asked Sveinbiorn. Andraste laughed heartily, and even the King's mouth twitched.

"You cannot ask men to marry you," said Marcella firmly, "Now return to your table."

Aaliyah retreated reluctantly. She curtsied prettily to Sveinbiorn and then returned to her table.

"She is seven. I will find you a more suitable companion," replied Andraste. She smiled over her wine glass to Sveinbiorn.

"Such an obedient child," said Sveinbiorn, "You were never that way."

"Such is a child born of the North and the East," replied Andraste.

"You are a child of the East," corrected Sveinbiorn. He looked to the King of the Island Kingdoms.

"I was born in the North," stated Andraste.

"No, you were born in the East. I was there," said Sveinbiorn.

"Remember what I said?" asked the King.

"Yes, Aelius, I remember your warning. Do you remember mine?" asked Sveinbiorn.

All of the Caelius family watched this hostile exchange with apprehension. The Queen cleared her throat.

"How are we to address you?" asked the Queen.

"Ladies, please call me Sveinbiorn," said Sveinbiorn.

"You do not eat?" asked Aldrich.

"I prefer more rare game," replied Sveinbiorn.

Andraste shifted uncomfortably. She tried to cover her action by reaching for an oyster. Sveinbiorn abruptly swept the tray onto the floor as the conversation ceased around them. All eyes turned to Sveinbiorn who picked up an oyster, smelled it and then hurled it to the ground.

"Poison," declared Sveinbiorn.

"Are you certain?" asked Andraste.

Sveinbiorn took the orchid from her hair and placed it in her hand. It withered and died. He made a motion with his hand and ruby light encircled her hand.

"You are not in danger," said Sveinbiorn. He surveyed the table, "Did anyone else eat an oyster?"

They all shook their heads and watched Sveinbiorn carefully.

"Your sense of smell is better than mine. Can you tell where it came from? Does anyone have the scent on their clothes?" asked Andraste.

"Yes," said Sveinbiorn, "It is a distinct smell. I have only encountered it once."

"Reaper's Boutonniere?" asked Andraste.

"I do not know anything by that name. It is a small indigo flower that blooms infrequently. It is not grown in the East," replied Sveinbiorn.

"Find, but do not kill, the owner of this flower. Bring the would-be-assassin to me," ordered Andraste.

Sveinbiorn inclined his head to her. Aldrich turned to follow Sveinbiorn's progress across the room. Sveinbiorn headed straight towards the Northern delegation. Without any explanation, Sveinbiorn picked Blasius from the table by his neck and carried him across the hall to Andraste's table. Sveinbiorn threw the Northern lord to the floor in front of Aldrich. Silence fell across the hall as all eyes turned towards Sveinbiorn.

Sveinbiorn plucked a vial from the Lord's pocket and tossed it to Andraste who caught it, and lifted it to the light to ensure that Aldrich could see the contents as well. The liquid inside the vile was a brilliant indigo and even through the thick glass, a hint of a sweet fragrance wafted.

"A Northern spy," said the King. He looked to the Queen, "He tried to kill your son, and now my niece. It is your jurisdiction. The verdict belongs to you."

"What--no trial?" exclaimed Blasius, "Someone planted the poison on me!"

"You should know that if the poison on your hands is not treated, you will die within a few hours," said Sveinbiorn. Blasius paled and ceased his protests.

"It appears Blasius will die by his own hand. Take him to a cell and leave him there to perish," decreed the Queen.

"Wait," said Andraste. The guards who had seized Blasius paused.

"Why did you do it?" asked Andraste.

"The Emperor has my family. I had no choice," replied Blasius.

"You have chosen your fate but if I am able, I will help your family when I am in the North," said Andraste.

Blasius bowed deeply to Andraste. He did not raise his eyes to her as he arose. The guardsmen seized him by his arms and led him from the hall.

"Who are you?" asked Aldrich as Sveinbiorn reclaimed his seat at Andraste's side.

"Perhaps the one and only Eastern militant sorcerer," answered Andraste.

"And our relative," interjected the King as Aldrich looked from Sveinbiorn's sea-green eyes to Andraste's.

"Will you be traveling with us to the North?" asked Aldrich.

"No, he will stay here," responded Andraste, "He will remain to protect the Southern capitol which will become a place for refuge as our country-men are displaced by the war."

"You are going north?" questioned Sveinbiorn, noting the firm set of her jaw.

"I will go North with you," stated Sveinbiorn.

"If the South falls, it will slow our progress. You will stay behind and protect the Queen, Marcella, her children, and Decima. This is the purpose I summoned you for," said Andraste.

Sveinbiorn did not respond.

"In this case, I agree. Sveinbiorn should go with you-- either that, or, send Sveinbiorn to assassinate the Emperor," advised the King.

"He cannot raise a hand against the Emperor," said Andraste.

"In fact, I am obligated to protect him," said Sveinbiorn, "I once made an oath to the Empress."

"You must stay behind," said Andraste softly. Sveinbiorn did not look pleased.

"I feel safer knowing such a powerful warrior will remain to protect us. It saddens me that my foster-brother must leave us alone once more," said Decima. She lowered her eyes to the table as she spoke.

Sveinbiorn studied her and raised his eyebrows. He looked to Andraste. She shook her head disapprovingly. Andraste gingerly reached for the platter of shrimp. She hesitated and Sveinbiorn nodded to her.

"Do you still wish to leave at first light?" asked Aldrich.

"We will postpone our journey another day," answered Andraste, glancing towards Sveinbiorn.

"We should depart immediately," advised Aldrich.

"We stayed for your festival. We have prolonged our journey whenever you requested. Give me one day," replied Andraste. She met Aldrich's eyes.

"As you wish," answered Aldrich.

"Where in the East are you from?" questioned Decima. Aldrich turned his eyes to Sveinbiorn with interest.

"Sveinbiorn does not like to speak about his history," answered Andraste quickly, not giving Sveinbiorn an opportunity to reply first.

"My apologies," said Decima. She looked to Aldrich who had not taken his eyes from Sveinbiorn. The music had begun for dancing. Aldrich turned his eyes to Andraste.

"I will retire. Sveinbiorn, you will accompany me. We have much to discuss," said Andraste. Aldrich's mouth tensed in a firm line.

"Little one, you have barely eaten," said Sveinbiorn. He pushed a platter of bread, cheese and fruit towards Andraste.

"Little one? What an odd term of endearment," commented the Queen.

"He has called me such since I was a child," replied Andraste.

"Good night, Paramerion," said Aldrich.

Aldrich rose and bowed to Andraste before offering his arm to Decima who begrudgingly accepted the offered arm while her eyes rested once more on Sveinbiorn. Marcella departed as well to join her husband and children.

"You still have not forgiven the prince?" asked the Queen.

"He has not apologized," replied Andraste.

"Is he your mate?" asked Sveinbiorn.

"No, he is not my intended," replied Andraste as she blushed crimson.

"Intended? Intended for what?" questioned Sveinbiorn. Andraste shook her head at him. However, she paused as she became aware of the Queen's penetrating stare on Sveinbiorn.

"You are Victoria's firstborn," stated the Queen. Sveinbiorn grew silent and turned his eyes to Andraste.

"Yes, I know. Victoria and I had no secrets between us. Sveinbiorn, you are welcome so long as you do not harm my people or guests. We are grateful for your protection," said the Queen, "But, Andraste Valerianus, you took a great risk to break the barrier and summon such a demon, no offense meant. You must go forth with more caution. Our fate is in your hands. Do not be so rash."

"It needed to be done. My brother does not know all of our human ways. Please instruct and look after him as I would in my absence," said Andraste.

"It would be my honor," replied the Queen. Her eyes once again registered on Sveinbiorn. She saw Andraste's concerned expression.

"I will not betray him, but if he seeks my foster-daughter as a wife, he must tell her the truth of his origins," said the Queen.

"That is fair," replied Sveinbiorn, "Who is your foster-daughter?"

"Decima," replied Andraste. Sveinbiorn looked to Decima dancing with Aldrich.

"I would ask that his origins may not be made known for some time," said Andraste.

"That is fair," replied the Queen.

"Why did he call you Paramerion? Is that not a sword?" asked Sveinbiorn.

"Perhaps it is time you heard the entirety of my tale," Andraste stated hesitantly.

Sveinbiorn inclined his head. The King of the Island Kingdoms left the table. The Queen moved down to take the seat by Andraste and poured them all a glass of wine while Andraste began to spin the tale of her adventures. Sveinbiorn listened intently and asked no questions. While Andraste conveyed her drawn out saga, the Queen allowed no one to interrupt while food and wine continued to flow among the captivated listeners. It was dawn by the time Andraste finished her tale. Andraste and her two listeners had long been the only ones in the dining hall.

"We should go to bed," was all that Sveinbiorn said when she had finished.

"I will have rooms prepared," said the Queen.

"Sveinbiorn will stay with me, and then take my rooms when I leave," replied Andraste.

The Queen nodded her head. Without further ado, Andraste and Sveinbiorn returned to her chambers. Andraste prepared herself for bed before opening her door to check on Sveinbiorn who had reverted to his primal tiger form and in repose by the fire of her hearth.

"Sveinbiorn," called Andraste.

Sveinbiorn raised his head and then padded across the floor. He jumped onto the end of her bed and fell asleep. Andraste, too, slept more soundly than she had in months knowing that they were both protected.

Andraste was awoken by a chilling scream.

Sveinbiorn raised his great head from his paws and looked to Andraste. Andraste heard running towards her room. She rose quickly and grabbed her sword. Sveinbiorn padded after her.

Rhiannon was dragging a reluctant Rhinauld and Henry into the room.

"See! I told you there was a tiger in her room," said Rhiannon.

Sveinbiorn sat on his haunches and studied Rhiannon. He yawned lazily.

"Close the door," ordered Andraste.

She placed a hand on Sveinbiorn's head as he gently licked her hand in appreciation. Rhiannon's mouth dropped open.

"Of all things," laughed Henry, wiping tears from his eyes. Andraste had never seen the knight lose his composure. Henry kept laughing as he left the room.

"You are not surprised," stated Rhiannon, blushing as she looked to Rhinauld.

"I am already acquainted with the Lord of the Salt Islands," replied Sveinbiorn.

"Andra told me not to tell you," answered Rhinauld.

"There is a talking white tiger in your room!" exclaimed Rhiannon.

"Well, I suppose I could resume my human form but my natural state would be most inappropriate in the presence of females," Sveinbiorn playfully replied.

Suddenly putting two and two together, Rhiannon blushed as she eyed the bed chamber behind them and then embarrassed, looked at Andraste.

"It is not like that. He is a tiger!" blushed Andraste. She blushed even deeper.

"You must be Rhiannon. My sister has told me much about you. I hope to make your acquaintance at another time," said Sveinbiorn. He stretched his front legs into a bow.

"Sister?" cried Rhiannon.

"I am not a tiger," sighed Andraste anticipating Rhiannon's next question.

"I brought you clothes," said Rhinauld, offering the armful of clothing to Sveinbiorn who clasped them in his jaws before returning to Andraste's room.

"Many thanks," said Andraste.

Rhiannon collapsed into a fit of giggles on Andraste's sofa. Sveinbiorn remerged fully clothed in his human form. Rhiannon tried to compose herself but eyed his bare feet curiously.

"I am sorry if I frightened you," said Sveinbiorn. He bowed to Rhiannon and kissed her hand. Rhiannon blushed deeply.

"If these are the twins that mean so much to you, why do you have me protect the Caelius family?" asked Sveinbiorn.

"It is where you should be. I feel it," answered Andraste.

"Should we have Rhiannon remain here?" asked Rhinauld.

"She must see her son," replied Andraste.

"I could send for him, but the way would be too dangerous for so young a child," said Rhiannon.

"I could fetch him," offered Sveinbiorn. He saw Rhinauld's look of apprehension.

"Could you take Rhinauld or Rhiannon with you?" asked Andraste.

"Either, preferably the latter," replied Sveinbiorn.

"Remember she is engaged to Brion," said Andraste.

"A pity," responded Sveinbiorn.

There was knock on Andraste's door and Aldrich stood in the doorway.

"I heard screaming," said Aldrich, who was clearly not amused.

Rhinauld stepped in front of her and Andraste remembered she was in her night gown.

"It was only a bad dream," said Rhinauld.

"Someone claims there was a tiger in the palace?" questioned Aldrich.

"Obviously, it is not here," answered Sveinbiorn.

Aldrich surveyed the four as if they were guilty children. He bowed towards Andraste and returned to his chambers.

"We will retrieve my son tomorrow after Andraste's party leaves," said Rhiannon.

Andraste returned to her room to dress. She wore dark linen pants and a long tunic. She pulled on her well-worn leather boots and put on her Ruin sword. She tied her hair back in a ponytail as she entered the study.

"Where do you go?" asked Rhinauld as he surveyed her attire.

"I wish to practice," replied Andraste.

"I will not duel you again. You nearly impaled me yesterday," responded Rhinauld.

"But that was yesterday. Now it is today," stated Andraste.

"No," said Rhinauld firmly. Sveinbiorn entered from the veranda.

"I will duel you," said Sveinbiorn.

"I was hoping--" replied Andraste.

"I know," interrupted Sveinbiorn.

Rhinauld looked as though he would object, but Andraste was already out of the room, Sveinbiorn at her side. Rhiannon and Rhinauld followed behind. Once more they found the training yard empty. Rhinauld offered Sveinbiorn his sword.

"I do not use weapons," replied Sveinbiorn. He made no move to touch the sword. Andraste sheathed her Ruin sword.

"You will need it," predicted Sveinbiorn.

"It seems unsporting," replied Andraste.

"Demon," stated Sveinbiorn.

Andraste advanced on Sveinbiorn. He blocked her effortlessly. Before she knew it, her sword was out of her hands and across the yard. He put a finger to her throat. Andraste moved across the field to retrieve her sword. Across the field, Aldrich paused in his tracks as he walked through the opposite corridor. She saw that her Victorious were with him.

She turned her attention back to Sveinbiorn. She quickened her attack while he met her move-for-move, sidestepping most of her advances. He moved so quickly that it appeared as if she had multiple opponents. She hesitated at times not knowing which one was the real Sveinbiorn. While she paused in deliberation, he knocked her off her feet but he interceded to catch her head before she hit the ground. With great tenderness he placed her back on her feet.

Andraste stuck her sword into the ground and removed her sheath from her waist. She raised her fists towards her opponent. Sveinbiorn watched patiently and waited for her to advance. Instead of throwing a punch, Andraste kicked him straight in the jaw.

"Ha!" cried Andraste. She heard laughter from the Victorious.

Sveinbiorn raised a hand to his jaw and rotated his shoulders. His sea-green eyes laughed at her. He retaliated so quickly that she was on the ground before she realized he was advancing once again. Dazed, she looked up to find him towering over her. He offered her a hand and pulled her to her feet. He dusted her off and put an arm about her shoulders.

"Not bad for a human," conceded Sveinbiorn.

"Again?" asked Andraste. Sveinbiorn looked down at her and shook his head.

"If your powers have just been unlocked, then you must learn to control them," said Sveinbiorn.

"I will not use magic again," stated Andraste.

"In a dire situation, you may call upon your magic without even meaning to," replied Sveinbiorn, "You will be a danger to yourself."

"I do not wish to use magic again," said Andraste.

"I refer to the aforementioned," said Sveinbiorn. Andraste sighed.

Sveinbiorn removed his arm from her shoulders. He stepped to the side and drew an encircled star before him.

"Do you see how the design is even? It does not flare, it is the same thickness, and it is the same color? Good, now draw your star," said Sveinbiorn. Andraste did so as she was bid. Her star was not as uniform.

"For your power to be steady, you must obtain consistency. Try again," said Sveinbiorn. He waved his hand in the air and her original star dissipated. Andraste drew her star in the air once more.

"If it flares, then you are wasting too much energy. If it is thin, then you are running out of power or did not use enough. If it is different colors then you are in trouble. You must guide yourself by your star. If you overextend yourself, you will die," instructed Sveinbiorn.

"What were the words you said yesterday to make the tornadoes disappear?" asked Andraste.

"I will not repeat such words unless it is necessary. I will teach you no such ancient magic," replied Sveinbiorn.

"Why?" inquired Andraste.

"Such knowledge destroyed our mother. It is not for your kind," said Sveinbiorn.

"Mother was executed for dark sorcery," said Andraste. Sveinbiorn did not respond. He erased her second star.

"Center yourself and focus all of your intention into the next star," directed Sveinbiorn. Doing as she was told, Andraste redrew her star which was better than her first two but still not uniform.

"You released Brion's power and summoned me with such a star?"

asked Sveinbiorn skeptically.

"What use is such a star if I have no words to wield it?" rejoined Andraste.

"You acted without such words. You are an Anima, and with that, your instincts prompt you to do what is needed," said Sveinbiorn. He erased her star once more.

"Can you teach me how to summon the orchid?" asked Andraste.

"It has its own risk. In order to summon the orchid, I must reach my hand back into the demon lands to retrieve it," said Sveinbiorn, "We will work on direction."

He turned to look towards the archery targets. He made a star in front of himself and a beam of ruby energy shot towards the first target before erupting into flames. Sveinbiorn shut his hand and the flames dissipated.

"Let us move closer," said Sveinbiorn. However, Andraste had already drawn her star.

Sveinbiorn erased her star and eyed the targets meaningfully. Andraste moved forward. Stopping when she was twenty paces away, she drew her star; a beam of light shot from the center of her star and hit the same target. Sveinbiorn allowed her to move back ten paces. She had the same success. However, when she reached forty paces, her control loosened.

"Do not over exert yourself. Practice on your journey," said Sveinbiorn.

"Show me more magic," implored Andraste.

Sveinbiorn scooped up a rock from the training yard. It turned to gold in his hand. He passed it to Andraste to examine.

"It is not heavy," said Andraste.

Sveinbiorn took it back and effortlessly snapped it in two. The inside was still solid rock.

"More!" commanded Andraste.

"Still such a child," sighed Sveinbiorn.

Andraste's attention was diverted as a hawk flew overhead. Sveinbiorn raised his hand and the hawk landed on his outstretched hand. The hawk quieted and allowed Andraste to stroke its cheekbones. Sveinbiorn released it and the hawk returned to the sky.

"You are bleeding," stated Andraste.

"I heal quickly, so long as the wound is not from iron," replied Sveinbiorn.

He showed Andraste his hand and it was already healed. His eyes strayed as a lady approached them from across the courtyard. Andraste turned to see who distracted him.

"I am sent to inform you that the feast will begin early today as many of our guests are leaving at first light," said Decima.

"Thank you," said Andraste. Decima hastily retreated across the training yard.

"Even though the Queen spoke of marriage to her foster daughter, you should know that lady swore never to marry after her beloved was slain in the Black War," said Andraste.

"A pity," replied Sveinbiorn.

Andraste retrieved her Ruin sword and they returned to her chambers. Sveinbiorn retreated to her veranda and stretched out on one of the lounge chairs. Andraste took a long bath and dressed in a light green gown.

"Do you want to take a bath?" asked Andraste.

"I do not like water," responded Sveinbiorn.

"I was being polite. Let me rephrase: take a bath," ordered Andraste.

For the first time, Sveinbiorn truly resembled a demon given the cut-eye look he shot Andraste who only laughed at him. Reluctantly, Sveinbiorn rose and went into her bath chamber. Andraste surmised that Sveinbiorn had assumed his tiger form given the sloshing sounds of water spilling over the sides of the tub onto the stone floor beneath.

"Honestly!" Andraste laughed to herself as she heard Sveinbiorn playing in the bathtub and seemingly enjoying himself.

Andraste heard a knock on her door.

"Enter," said Andraste. Aldrich opened the door and surveyed the room.

"Are you alone?" asked Aldrich.

"Yes," replied Andraste. She heard the sound of splashing from the tub. Her eyes darted towards the bath chamber door as the sound of water splashing on the stone floor continued. Aldrich looked at her sharply.

"It is just a tiger," said Andraste.

"In your bath?" asked Aldrich. He brushed past her and opened the door to her bath chamber. Sveinbiorn, the tiger, looked at Aldrich inquisitively. Aldrich took a step back and shut the door.

"Well that explains the rumors," said Aldrich.

"Rumors?" asked Andraste. Aldrich blushed and cleared his throat.

"I was going to discuss our journey but I will leave you to-" Aldrich could not finish his sentence, "Why did you hide the tiger from me earlier?"

"To avoid this discussion," replied Andraste.

"Will the tiger be accompanying us?" asked Aldrich.

"No, he is Sveinbiorn's. He will stay to protect the city," answered Andraste.

"He is a wild animal. He could hurt the children," said Aldrich.

"He loves children," replied Andraste.

Aldrich studied her. He had lost his composure completely. He did not know what to say to her. He bowed and left the room.

"A tiger," said Aldrich as he entered his own chambers.

"It could be worse competition, my lord," replied Kasimir.

Andraste quickly shut the door to her own chambers and leaned against the door. Sveinbiorn jumped out the tub and shook himself dry. He sat in front of the fire.

"He is going to think I am mad," sighed Andraste.

"Like mother like daughter," replied Sveinbiorn. Andraste heard the voices across the hall pause their conversation.

"Just tell him," said Sveinbiorn.

"They already call me Demon of the North. What would they call us if they knew the truth?" asked Andraste.

Andraste heard a knock on her door. Sighing as she opened the heavy carved door, she found Decima outside and looking puzzled.

"Who are you talking to?" asked Decima.

"The tiger," replied Andraste.

Decima laughed aloud. Andraste stepped aside so that Decima could see inside her room. Decima let out an exclamation of surprise.

"He is quite tame. He would probably let you rub his belly," said Andraste.

"Truly?" asked Decima. She approached hesitantly. Sveinbiorn stretched out lazily.

"He is wet," said Decima.

"He just took a bath," replied Andraste. Sveinbiorn began to purr as Decima stroked him.

"What a sweetheart! I love cats. I have two at home. Obviously not tigers," said Decima regretfully, "How long have you had him?"

"He is Sveinbiorn's," replied Andraste.

"You keep his pet?" asked Decima.

"I have an affinity for tigers," responded Andraste.

"Where is his master?" questioned Decima.

"He went hunting," said Andraste.

"A pity," replied Decima. Sveinbiorn raised his head at the words. It looked as though he was smiling.

"He will be back in time for dinner," said Andraste.

"Where is he staying? No one knows what rooms he has taken," inquired Decima.

"Honestly, he slept on my veranda yesterday, and will do so tonight. He prefers to be out of doors," said Andraste, "He will take my rooms as of tomorrow."

"And you have no understanding?" asked Decima.

"Of course not! We are related," answered Andraste briskly. Sveinbiorn lifted his head and growled at Andraste. Decima withdrew her hand as the tiger gently licked it.

"On your mother's side?" asked Decima. Andraste nodded.

"You have the same eyes," said Decima, "Would you care to have a glass of wine across the hall? It would please Aldrich."

"The tiger gave him quite a scare," said Andraste. She looked unhappily towards the door.

"I imagine so," replied Decima. She gave Sveinbiorn one last caress and then rose.

Andraste followed Decima out the door. She paused to address the tiger, "Your master will return soon. Lead him cross the hall once he is ready."

"Will the tiger do your bidding?" asked Decima.

"He is not an ordinary tiger," replied Andraste.

Decima, followed by Andraste, entered Aldrich's chambers without knocking. Andraste observed that Kasimir, Egnatius, Eadbehrt, Sonje, Marcella, Brion, Rhinauld, Henry and Rhiannon were already partaking of Aldrich's wine.

"Where is our new friend?" asked Brion.

"Master or tiger?" questioned Decima.

"Both," answered Brion wearily.

"Master is hunting and tiger is delivering a message," said Decima.

Brion looked at Decima as if she had two heads.

"Eldgrimson is a peculiar fellow," stated Kasimir.

"He does not get out much," said Brion. Andraste shot him a look of warning.

"I have never seen such power," said Marcella, "I saw you training in the yard. Would he permit questions?"

"If you want to take up dueling, then yes, but do not ask him about magic," replied Andraste.

"He beat you thrice," commented Aldrich. His eyes laughed at her.

"Indeed," bristled Andraste.

"How good is he with a bow?" asked Aldrich.

"He does not use weapons," replied Andraste.

"Why would he need to?" proposed Marcella.

"I was just wondering as you once said that you would marry the man who could beat your sword and bow," said Aldrich.

"Eldgrimson is her relation on her mother's side. She cannot marry him," interjected Rhinauld. Aldrich studied Rhinauld for a moment.

"You have many relations," stated Eadbehrt.

"Don't I know," replied Andraste. She did not smile. She was relieved as Sveinbiorn entered the room and joined her side.

"Were you hunting tuna?" asked Decima as she surveyed his damp locks.

"I went swimming instead," replied Sveinbiorn. He winked at Andraste mischievously.

"The Queen has asked that I familiarize you with our ways," said Decima.

"I would be both honored and enlightened by your instruction," responded Sveinbiorn.

"You should know that men, who are not related by blood, are not permitted in a lady's chambers without a lady present or a male relative," stated Andraste.

"Well then me sleeping on your veranda is not such a scandal now is it?" asked Sveinbiorn lightly. Andraste glanced towards Decima and then back to Sveinbiorn.

"You recognize the significance of my remarks?" questioned Andraste.

"Noted, little one. I will not dishonor our house," replied Sveinbiorn not taking his eyes from Decima.

"What is the name of your tiger?" asked Decima.

"I named him after my relation, here," answered Sveinbiorn.

"You named the tiger 'Andraste'?" questioned Aldrich.

"No, Demon of the North," replied Sveinbiorn. Rhinauld and Henry both laughed heartily.

"Demon for short," said Brion.

"But he is so sweet!" cried Decima.

"I think so," responded Sveinbiorn. Brion snorted and Andraste rolled her eyes.

"We should head towards the dining hall," said Aldrich as he rose. He swept out of the room and was followed by the Southerners. Egnatius offered his arm to Sonje, who accepted it and followed after the others.

"You should offer me your arm," schooled Decima.

"Why?" asked Sveinbiorn.

"It is custom," replied Decima.

"Would you like my arm?" inquired Sveinbiorn.

"No, like this," said Andraste. She offered her arm to Rhinauld, who chortled but took her arm. Sveinbiorn offered his arm to Decima who wrapped her arm in his.

"Good," praised Decima. She directed Sveinbiorn down the hall. He looked over his shoulder to Andraste but she waved him ahead.

"You should know there will be a vigil in the temple after the socializing hour to pay respects to our fallen siblings," informed Brion.

"That is most kind," replied Andraste softly. Her merriment faded and her eyes glistened.

"Let us join the others," said Rhiannon.

Rhiannon wrapped her arm in Brion's and he conveyed her out of the room. The others followed behind. Rhinauld and Henry prattled merrily, but Andraste barely listened. She said nothing throughout the dinner. Sveinbiorn listened attentively to Decima but his eyes were on Andraste.

"Will you dance with me, Lord Eldgrimson?" asked Decima.

"No," replied Sveinbiorn. Decima's face fell and Sveinbiorn looked to Andraste. She inclined her head towards Decima.

"Call me Sveinbiorn," said Sveinbiorn. Decima smiled at Sveinbiorn and tempted to begin a conversation again. Andraste watched the pair for a while.

"You are out of sorts," stated Rhinauld.

"I must speak to my men," said Andraste. She rose and Rhinauld followed suit. He offered his arm. He led her to where Laelius was sitting as many of her men were dancing.

"Yes, Commander?" asked Laelius.

"Are we ready to depart in the morning?" asked Andraste.

"Yes, Commander," answered Laelius. His eyes, however, were on the man approaching.

"We were discussing the preparations for tomorrow's journey," Rhinauld informed Aldrich.

"We are prepared," responded Aldrich.

"Do you know the trick to get my sister to dance?" inquired Rhinauld.

Aldrich raised an eyebrow in response. Andraste stepped on Rhinauld's foot inconspicuously.

"The trick," explained Rhinauld, "is never to ask--just take her."

Rhinauld offered Andraste's hand to Aldrich who did not offer his hand in return.

"I would not intrude on your last night-" started Aldrich.

"Nonsense. I need to speak with Henry," said Rhinauld. He had not removed Andraste's offered hand. Aldrich said nothing, nor did he take her arm.

"He does not mean to dance tonight. At least not with me," concluded Andraste, "Why would the Prince of the Southern lands deign to dance with a wanton, dishonored, common exile like myself? Who knows how many men I have danced with before? The prince, after all, has his reputation to protect."

"So despite his actions and constant efforts for your protection and happiness, you have not forgotten Caelius's insults?" inquired Rhinauld lightly.

She removed her hand from Rhinauld's hold. She turned to Laelius, "I want the men ready at first light."

"You already said that," stated Laelius. Andraste's eyes narrowed in response to his impertinence.

"Well, I will find where Henry's sulking about," said Rhinauld. He returned to their table.

"Would you care to dance?" Aldrich asked her.

"It is obvious you were on your way somewhere else. My brother did not need to beg me a partner," answered Andraste.

"As you wish," replied Aldrich. He bowed to her before proceeding on his way.

"Just tell him that you like him," Laelius said over her stein.

Andraste saw Aldrich pause in his tracks. She blushed and picked a knife up from the table and began playing with it between her fingers. Aldrich moved on his way and rejoined his table.

"My days are numbered, I know," said Laelius.

"Are you drunk?" Andraste asked in disbelief. She lost her composure. She laughed whole-heartedly. She set the knife down on the table.

"No!" said Laelius rising. He stumbled, "Yes!"

Andraste signaled to Otho and Maximianus.

"Take him to his chambers immediately," ordered Andraste.

"Let us have fun with him. He never drinks," suggested Maximianus.

Andraste shot him an icy glare. She watched them proceed slowly out of the hall. They were singing a song of Otho's invention entitled, "120 Ways to Kill a Man." Each verse got progressively more gruesome.

"Empress," hissed a voice at her side.

She had not even heard Toxin's approach. She picked up the knife from the table and disguised it in her sleeve. She did not respond.

"Do not worry. I am not one of your admirers. I have not come to request a dance," said Toxin. There was not a glint of merriment in his words.

Andraste still did not respond. She gazed at him coolly, calculating his threat level.

"For the kindness you have shown my only child, and for showing us mercy when others pronounced us guilty without a second thought, I will give you a piece of advice. Stay off the Northern road, travel through the forest and never travel by night," instructed Toxin.

"Why?" asked Andraste.

Toxin turned to leave.

"Why?" Andraste commanded raising her voice. Toxin paused, "And one last piece of advice: if you think you have defeated a member of the Arisen, sever the head and burn the body."

Though Andraste willed herself to show no interest in Toxin's grizzly warning, she felt her skin crawl. She held herself calmly erect while the knife hidden in her sleeve, slid downward into her palm while she struggled with whether or not she should allow Toxin to live. As Toxin approached his daughter Hyacinth, she looked up and smiled at her father.

Andraste released the knife onto the table. Aldrich's sapphire eyes were locked on her every move. She did not stop at his table as she passed and instead went to Rhinauld and Henry, beginning an earnest conversation which Sveinbiorn struggled to ease drop on, a near impossible feat to accomplish while Decima chatted away endlessly in his other ear as she had done for the entirety of the evening.

"A warning?" Henry asked after Andraste relayed Toxin's warning.

"It is true enough. We have had to deal with the undead before. We should tell Vespasian to stay off the Northern road when he advances," advised Rhinauld.

"You are angry?" inquired Henry of Andraste.

"But not at Toxin," Rhinauld replied for her, "The prince refused to dance with her."

Henry offered his arm to her wordlessly.

"Why were we not friends before this?" Andraste asked, accepting Henry's arm.

"I have always been your friend, Empress," Henry replied, "I just have not always been able to stand you as well as I do now."

"That is cruel, Sir Henry," said Andraste, but she laughed.

The musicians had started playing a song from the Island Kingdoms. She saw that Egnatius and Sonje were retreating.

"I do not know this dance," Egnatius apologized in greeting.

"We would be delighted to show you," said Andraste.

Henry offered his free arm to Sonje who took it. Egnatius bowed to Andraste and colored as she took his arm. Egnatius glanced down the row to Aldrich's table.

"You show me great honor, Commander," said Egnatius. He took his place on the gentlemen's row and she on the ladies' side.

"Nonsense, I am honored to dance with such a noble and steadfast warrior. Besides, I love this dance and Henry is sick of me," replied Andraste.

"It is true. I only consented to dance with her out of mercy," returned Henry.

"There are many Southern lords who may be more willing dance partners," said Sonje. Her eyes darted to the Southern table.

Rhinauld and Rhiannon had joined them in the line just in time as the dance started.

"These dances are simpler then they may appear. After you learn the first sixteen counts, most of the steps repeat," said Andraste to Egnatius.

Egnatius turned the wrong way. Rhiannon reached for Egnatius' arm to help him turn in the right direction. It was Rhinauld's turn to take Andraste's hand. He winked at her wickedly, and then kissed her open palm. Her smile fell.

"Stop it," ordered Andraste. Rhinauld laughed at her.

Andraste smiled kindly as she took Egnatius's arm again, but glared at Rhinauld as she passed him once more. Andraste and Egnatius moved up the line, so now when they exchanged partners, she danced with Henry. He too kissed her open palm in greeting. She shook her head at him in disapproval.

"This is the first regular social hour you have voluntarily danced with a Southern lord?" asked Henry, "The prince is watching but not smiling. In fact, all of the Southerners are watching."

Andraste stepped on his foot purposefully. Henry made no sign of noticing.

Andraste put a hand out to guide Sonje in the right direction before retaking Egnatius's arm. They danced their steps and moved up the line. Felix took her hand with a mischievous look in his eye.

"If you kiss my hand, I swear I will beat you into this earth," whispered Andraste fiercely.

"Yes, Commander," laughed Felix, "But I am more afraid of my lord then you."

He kissed her open palm. Andraste's eyes flashed. However, it was time for her to meet Egnatius in the center for their steps. Then they were at the end of their line, so they had to stand a set out.

"You are right, it gets easier as the dance goes on," said Egnatius.

Andraste smiled at him. They reentered the set and Andraste glared at Rhinauld. He reached for her. She refused to take his arm. She danced the steps around him. He stood in place, not being able to move without disturbing the other dancers. Rhinauld laughed at her, which only made Andraste more furious. She took Egnatius' arm once more.

"I apologize. My brother is a beast," said Andraste to her partner.

"Brother?" asked Egnatius.

"We were raised together in the Salt Islands. I see him as nothing more, and a lot less at times," said Andraste.

Rhiannon giggled as she heard Andraste's response.

"That hurts, Andra," said Rhinauld.

"Not as much as it will hurt if you even think of touching me," promised Andraste over her shoulder.

Egnatius looked from Rhinauld to Andraste.

"And that goes for you to Henry. As for you Felix, all I will say, is it is going to be a long journey to the North," said Andraste. Felix grimaced.

"I changed my mind. I fear you more than Rhinauld," stated Felix.

"Do not let my lady be executed this time. I was devastated by the news," said Rhinauld. It was said in jest, but he did not smile. Andraste only glared at him. Felix looked uncomfortable.

The dance had finally ended. Egnatius bowed to Andraste. Henry reclaimed Andraste's arm, as Egnatius rejoined Sonje. Egnatius paused as he looked at the Southern table where Aldrich and his lords were seated. Aldrich summoned him. Egnatius returned Sonje to her seat and then approached the prince. However, Egnatius was unable to speak directly to Aldrich as the King of the Island Kingdoms had also stopped to speak.

Rhinauld approached Andraste on Henry's arm as they passed by the Southern table.

"Are you really angry with me?" asked Rhinauld. She glared at him in response.

"On your way, Lord of the Salt Islands," ordered the King.

Rhinauld bowed to the King stiffly and removed himself from the aisle. Henry, taking Rhinauld's cue, offered Andraste's arm to the King as lilting music for an Island Kingdoms slow dance began to play. Andraste felt all of the eyes from the Island Kingdoms watching her next move.

"Do you mean to dance, Uncle?" asked Andraste.

"I do," said the King. He took her hand and led her back towards the dance floor. He took her in his arms.

"Do you know these steps?" inquired Andraste.

"I invented these steps," responded the King. Andraste laughed pleasantly. She glanced towards the table for the Island Kingdoms.

"What was going on with that last dance?" questioned the King.

"Rhinauld," sighed Andraste. Her smile faded.

"Should I have a word with my knights?" asked the King.

"They were making a point. I told them to stop," replied Andraste.

"Oh, to be young once more," said the King, "We should find you a more worthy dancing partner. I am surprised you have not danced with any of the Northern lords. Despite his faults, Vespasian would suit you well. He cares for you."

"Do not encourage him, Uncle," replied Andraste.

"Perhaps a Southern lord? Aldrich is a fine dancer," suggested the King.

"Why are you so eager to find me a dance partner?" asked Andraste.

"I will not be around to protect you forever," replied the King. Andraste looked way as she saw the sadness in his eyes.

"I do not care for your manner of protection," responded Andraste coldly.

"Aldrich may be more suited for the job and he is not a magic user which may be more to your tastes," stated the King.

"He refused to dance with me earlier," said Andraste.

"Do you want to dance with him?" asked the King. His eyes were locked on Aldrich's table.

"No, Uncle," answered Andraste.

"That is unfortunate," said the King.

He stifled a smile as the music came to the end. Andraste curtsied to the King. He held onto her hand. Andraste paused. She looked over her shoulder and saw Aldrich approaching with purpose.

"Uncle," Andraste panicked.

"It is a dance, Andra. Besides you two danced so well together at the festival. Has so much changed?" asked the King.

"Yes. It feels like months have passed," said Andraste.

"Our time in the Southern lands has been eventful," responded the King.

Andraste did not have a chance to respond as Aldrich had reached them. The King wordlessly handed Andraste to Aldrich. Aldrich took her in his arms for a Southern waltz. The look on his face was best described as triumphant.

"I never saw the other dance performed quite like that before," said Aldrich. Andraste did not respond.

"I did not dance with you earlier because I was on my way to check on our new charge," said Aldrich. He glanced towards Hyacinth. She was dancing with Vespasian.

"Are you not going to speak to me?" asked Aldrich. Still Andraste did not respond.

"A little childish do you not think?" inquired Aldrich. The color rose even deeper in her face.

"I should have apologized sooner but you would not see me. If I had the opportunity, you would not hear me, and then you were unwell. I apologize for the words that I said to you before the battle. I am sorry for what I said. I spoke out of anger and I was out of line. I had no reason to say those things to you. I am mortified that I ever said such things to such a brave, honorable, sweet lady. And then I lost your trust once more with the rumors of the false engagement, but I have resolved that misunderstanding. I am not and nor was I ever willingly engaged to Gerlinde. I am truly sorry, my lady. Please, forgive me," said Aldrich.

"Forgiveness is not a Northern concept," replied Andraste.

"I will do anything to make it right," said Aldrich, "Tell me what to do."

"For all of your talk of me not following the Southern ways, have you tried to follow the Northern or Eastern? Stop putting me to a double standard that you will not hold yourself accountable," said Andraste.

"You are right," replied Aldrich. She was distracted as she saw Rhinauld, Henry, Felix and Vespasian watching them closely.

"I can see that my brothers are debating whether or not I need a chaperone," sighed Andraste.

"Your brothers?" repeated Aldrich, "You call them that, but-"

"Why would I let a man other than my brother be so forward?" asked Andraste. Aldrich missed a step.

"And Eldgrimson?" asked Aldrich.

"Another relation, and no, I have never danced with him," responded Andraste.

"And Vespasian?" questioned Aldrich. Andraste looked up at Aldrich in confusion.

"Stop talking," said Andraste.

Aldrich first looked offended, but then relaxed. He studied her as they danced. He could see the exhaustion in her eyes. He could feel the tension in her movements. Aldrich pulled her closer and Andraste did not resist. She followed his lead, and even smiled sadly at him as the music came to an end. He kissed her hand and released her. Andraste curtsied low to Aldrich. Rhinauld approached and bowed to them both.

"It is time, Empress," said Rhinauld.

Aldrich bowed to her and then stepped aside. Andraste swept past him and Rhinauld followed after her. They made their way to the temple.

Henry sat in the second pew and Rhinauld joined him. Brion and Rhiannon were sitting in the first pew. Brion held his head in his hands. Rhiannon had her arms wrapped around him. Andraste went to the altar and lit five candles, before sitting beside Brion. She only felt anger. She stared at the candles flickering on the altar. Sveinbiorn, in his tiger form, padded silently down the aisle and lay at Andraste's feet. She placed her hand on his head.

She heard footsteps enter behind them. She glanced behind her. She saw that all of her Victorious had entered and many of the Northern and Island delegations as well. They sat scattered in the pews behind them. They sat in silence for a few hours. Andraste heard the clock tower ring twenty-four times. Andraste turned to look behind her. She saw that many of the Southern lords and ladies had joined as well.

"Will you take Brion to his chambers?" requested Andraste.

Rhinauld and Henry rose and bowed to her. Brion composed himself and rose to go with them.

"I want to be alone. Go with him," said Andraste to Rhiannon. Sveinbiorn raised his head questioningly.

"Come, Demon," bade Rhiannon.

Sveinbiorn raised himself and padded after Rhiannon. Andraste heard the other mourners leave as well. She found herself alone in the temple. She sat for another hour. The wind blew from the open window. The candles on the altar were extinguished. Andraste felt hot tears run down her face. She wrapped her arms around her knees and cried into her skirts.

The clock tower chimed a solitary bell. Andraste forced herself to rise. She had to prepare herself for the journey. She heard footsteps on the second level. She looked up, but saw no one there. She returned to her chambers. She saw no one on her walk throughout the palace. She hesitated in front of Aldrich's doors, which were wide open. She did not see him.

"Do you need me?" Aldrich asked behind her.

She jumped at the sound of his voice. She turned to see him twenty paces behind her in the hall. He approached her slowly.

Andraste did not respond as she entered her chambers. Her hands shook as she tried to add water to the kettle. Aldrich entered the room and shut the door behind him. He took the kettle from her and filled it. He placed it on the hook in the fireplace. He returned to the table and set up the teapot. Andraste had not moved from her spot by the table. She had regained her composure.

"I will leave you now," said Aldrich.

He turned to go. Andraste reached for the back of his shirt. He froze. Her hand grasped a handful of the fabric. He did not move. She buried her face in his back. He stood for a moment. He slowly turned so that he could take her in his arms. She did not resist. He lifted her face and he kissed her tenderly. Warming to his caresses, she wrapped her arms around him. He kissed her more forcefully. She returned his kiss with equal passion. As he leaned forward to kiss her, the action pushed her back onto the table. She pulled him with her. He kissed her down her neck and to her collarbone.

"Aldrich," Andraste urged. Her hand tightened in his hair.

The kettle whistled.

Aldrich removed himself from her at once.

"Leave it," said Andraste.

"Someone will hear it and come," responded Aldrich.

He immediately took the kettle off its hook and poured water into the teapot. He returned the kettle to the hearth.

"I should not have kissed you. You are distressed. I only meant to comfort you. Please forgive me," said Aldrich. He bowed to her.

"Do not go," persuaded Andraste.

"I should not be here. It may be different in the North. Northern ladies may be allowed more freedom, but here it is a serious offense. It may not seem strange to you," started Aldrich.

"Strange?" Andraste asked. She blushed, "My prince, I have known no other."

"I will not touch you again unless you are my wife," said Aldrich. He blushed but he purposefully took a step forward. He could not divert his eyes from Andraste's.

"I never understood before, but now I do. I understand now how love can drive a man to madness. Is this how the Emperor went mad? Was he also haunted by lovely sea-green eyes?" asked Aldrich. He reached for her hand.

Andraste stepped back from Aldrich as if he had struck her. She turned her back on him and braced herself on the table.

"Leave!" ordered Andraste.

"I did not mean to offend-" protested Aldrich.

She still kept her back to him; deliberately, she poured herself a cup of tea. Andraste heard the door close followed by the muffled sound of paws padding towards her from the veranda.

"Have you no shame?" asked Andraste to the tiger.

Sveinbiorn cocked his head to one side. Andraste felt hot tears fall down her face again. She hastily brushed them aside. Sveinbiorn approached and licked her hand.

"I am fine," said Andraste. She sipped on her tea and then climbed into her bed, hoping for a few hours of sleep. Sveinbiorn slept at the foot of her bed, his tail resting on her feet.

Chapter Fifteen

When Andraste and Sveinbiorn arrived at the stables, the first light of the morning was already spreading upon them. Andraste found her horse was already saddled. The Victorious were also assembled. Rhinauld and Henry were talking to Felix. As Andraste approached her men, they surveyed Sveinbiorn with interest.

"Is this our new Captain?" asked Otho. Andraste turned to glare at him.

"He did beat you in three duels," stated Nero.

"I have no need for lackeys," replied Sveinbiorn. His sea-green eyes flashed as he studied the two men.

"You cannot take a joke?" questioned Otho.

"You would so quickly change your allegiance?" rejoined Sveinbiorn. Otho shifted uncomfortably underneath Sveinbiorn's gaze.

"It is our way. The strongest of us leads us," replied Nero.

"Andraste is the strongest of you," stated Sveinbiorn.

Andraste stepped away from her men so that she could claim her horse. Sveinbiorn followed behind her.

"Are you sure you do not want me to accompany you?" asked Sveinbiorn.

"You need to be here or the city will fall," replied Andraste.

Sveinbiorn drew a flower in the air. An orchid materialized and he presented it to Andraste.

"Keep it close to you. While it blooms, it will heal most wounds," said Sveinbiorn.

"Thank you. I will summon you if the need is dire," replied Andraste.

"Do you swear?" asked Sveinbiorn.

"I swear," affirmed Andraste.

"Then I will not come unless you call," responded Sveinbiorn.

Andraste saw Aldrich hastening down the opposite stairwell. A servant brought the prince his pack and another servant brought his horse. Rhinauld and Henry had noticed her arrival and came to her side.

"I will miss you both," admitted Andraste. She embraced Henry, who looked exceedingly embarrassed.

"And I you," said Rhinauld as he held her for a moment. He kissed her lightly on her forehead. He approached Aldrich and extended his arm, "I am entrusting my sister to your care."

Aldrich grasped Rhinauld's arm, but said nothing. He released Rhinauld's hand and then turned his attention to Sveinbiorn.

"I cannot repay you for looking after my lands and my family, but I will try," said Aldrich.

"There is no debt. I follow Andraste's orders," replied Sveinbiorn.

The two men studied each other. Aldrich slowly extended his arm. Sveinbiorn studied it and then grasped it as Rhinauld had.

"Are we waiting on Brion?" asked Andraste, surveying her assembled men in a glance.

"Rhiannon," explained Henry.

At that moment, Rhiannon and Brion came down the stairs. The lady looked as though she had been crying and Brion heartbroken. She kissed her betrothed's face once last time. Henry climbed the stairs and offered Rhiannon his arm. The lady took his arm for support. Brion took one last look at his betrothed and then hurried down the stairs to his waiting comrades.

Gnaeus embraced his father, while Laelius said something into his son's ear. Gnaeus took his place beside Rhinauld and Henry, looking mournful the Victorious.

"The relic?" asked Andraste as Rhinauld helped her mount.

"Secured in Brion's saddle bag," whispered Rhinauld.

Andraste allowed one last look to her foster siblings and Henry. Vespasian had not come to see them off.

"Depart!" ordered Andraste, before leading the way out of the city.

Aldrich was silent until they made camp that evening. He ignored Andraste completely. Andraste said little to anyone. The mood among all of them had changed. There was a sense of sadness and a deep foreboding.

In the days that followed, Andraste kept her troops off the roads, instead leading them deep into the countryside. Not until after they were far out of the Southern lands, did Aldrich acknowledge her presence and only then when he had followed Andraste who had gone to gather firewood while her men were setting up camp.

"Talk to me," said Aldrich.

"There is nothing to say," replied Andraste.

"You take on too much. Talk to me," bade Aldrich.

They stood studying each other in the silence. She lifted the load of firewood to him.

"Will you take this back?" asked Andraste.

Aldrich's face fell. Reluctantly, he approached Andraste to take the armload of firewood from her when they heard branches crack nearby. Aldrich's hands froze on the bundle he was taking from her.

"Whatever comes through those trees, do not move," commanded Andraste.

"What?" asked Aldrich.

Andraste raised a hand to cover his mouth.

The largest wolf that Aldrich had ever seen had entered the clearing. It was solid black and had glowing amber eyes, while deadly fangs protruded from its mouth. It let out a blood chilling howl which was immediately followed by the sound of paws striking the ground along with the snapping, cracking and dull thud of tree branches and fallen leaves. Aldrich instinctively moved to draw his sword but Andraste grabbed his wrist. The collected firewood fell between them.

"Trust me," whispered Andraste. She still held onto his wrist. She could feel his pulse race underneath her fingers.

They had been encircled by a pack of wolves, all equally oversized and other-worldly as their fellow.

The largest of the wolves approached them. Andraste stared into the eyes of the large wolf. It growled at her and showed its teeth menacingly. Andraste did not blink. The wolf quieted. It lowered its head and stretched out its front paws with an acquiescent yawn. It turned its golden eyes back to Andraste and past her to Aldrich. Andraste did not yield her ground. The wolf, as though considering his options, sat back on his haunches and then let out another howl before retreating in the opposite direction to the darkened border of trees, with his pack close behind.

Andraste stood as if frozen in the clearing still holding Aldrich's wrist. Her eyes followed the wolves' progress until she could no longer see or hear them.

"A bit old for hand games, do you not think, Commander?" asked Otho from overhead.

Andraste released her hold on Aldrich's wrist. Aldrich looked above them. Otho and Maximianus were both perched in trees above them. Their bows were drawn. Otho saw Aldrich's eyes locked on his bow, and he put his arrow back into his quiver.

Andraste chose not to respond but instead headed back to the encampment. Aldrich began to pick up the wood that they had dropped.

"Not even going to ask?" inquired Otho.

"He probably does not want to know," commented Maximianus.

Maximianus climbed down the tree and aided Aldrich with his task.

"Comes face to face with an Anima and does not want to know?" asked Otho.

Aldrich straightened and turned his full attention to Otho.

"See he does want to know," said Otho. He jumped down from the tree and surveyed Aldrich before continuing, "Our legends tell us the Southern people came from across the seas but in fact, we were already here. Even though our people were small in number, we were fierce and powerful. We possessed the ancient arts like the gods, powers that do not have to be studied like sorcery. We were gifted at birth with innate magical powers. Unfortunately as our people migrated and mingled over the years with your people, our abilities became diminished, eventually muted and in the end, even rare. Fortunately for us, our Commander possesses one such remaining power."

"Hope she can communicate with monsters as well as animals," commented Maximianus as he scanned the tree line, "But that is beside the point. Otho, you know the Victorious cannot talk about any of our abilities to outsiders."

"Well, did you think that I wanted to tell him something as well?" asked Otho. He glared at his comrade.

"I do not care if our Commander is fond of you, or if you are a prince. If you share our secrets, I will kill you, and your family will never find your remains," stated Otho.

"Fond of me? She hates me," responded Aldrich.

"If she hated you, you would be dead," remarked Maximianus.

Otho laughed but Aldrich had the distinct impression that Maximianus was not joking. The three warriors started to head back to the camp. Maximianus caught Aldrich's eye and recommended, "Do us all a favor, do not ask her about it."

"Well, if I had that power, I would flaunt it across the lands," declared Otho.

"If I had that power, I would have a bear eat you for lunch," claimed Maximianus. Otho laughed and Maximianus joined in.

Aldrich saw Andraste crouching by a small fire deep in discussion with Laelius. Andraste made no indication of seeing them. Aldrich joined Brion instead. Aldrich could not help but wonder what other secrets they were keeping from him.

The Victorious had no choice but to traverse the Northern road in order to proceed in the correct direction. They rode quickly at full alert, and arrived at a crossroads wherein a sign pointed in four different directions. Andraste paused to let the rest of her men catch up to her. Aldrich was the first to reach her side. Andraste turned her horse towards the Northern road.

"I would not go that way," urged a voice from the hedges.

Andraste turned her horse about so that she could face the speaker, a beggar dressed in rags. His grimy appearance made him seem older then he was.

"I would not go that way either," advised the beggar.

"Which way would you go?" asked Aldrich.

"No way," replied the beggar.

"How do you mean?" inquired Aldrich.

"This is a good place. If you were me, I would not move from here. But you are not me, so move on. This place is taken. It is mine," said the beggar.

"An insolent knave," commented Laelius.

"But his judgment is sound," said Otho.

"Why? Do you care to live in the hedges?" asked Andraste.

"I would rather stay here then travel further," replied Otho.

"It is not like you to crow like a craven," said Maximianus.

"I feel as though I will never pass this way again," responded Otho.

"Do not be a ninny. We have ridden past these crossroads a hundred times. We will do so again," barked Laelius.

Andraste urged her horse forward and proceeded at a brisk pace. She did not stop until they had reached a dilapidated estate. The main house and the surrounding buildings were in need of new roofs. The buildings were gray and looked as though they had not been painted in the eons. Some of the outer buildings leaned so precariously that a dandelion leaning against the frail walls would have been enough to make them collapse. Some of the windows were broken and shutters had fallen to the ground. Some of the structures had been burned completely to the ground as evidenced by charred planks and fallen walls.

There was a fierce storm approaching from the West. It was the middle of the afternoon, but already the skies were dark with the promise of a downpour. They could hear thunder in the distance. The horses were skittish.

"We should seek shelter," advised Laelius.

"I know this place," mentioned Andraste.

She nodded her consent and they approached the main building, which was as dilapidated as any of the other charred structures. An old woman stood proudly in the doorway and eyed them wearily.

"Good morrow, madam. We seek shelter from the storm for one night. We could pay. Could we stay in your barn?" asked Aldrich.

"How much?" the woman asked. Aldrich produced a gold coin in his hand.

"Same amount but smaller coins. If she was caught with that, she would be robbed, interrogated and/or beheaded," said Andraste.

"I know your voice," stated the woman.

The old woman turned to look at Andraste. Wordlessly the woman struggled to her knees and lowered her head.

"Commander Andraste Valerianus," addressed the woman.

Laelius quickly dismounted and helped the woman to her feet.

"We have heard rumors you would return. My name is Olga Fashingbauer. My sons, Paeter and Mikhael, fought under you at Thoran," said the woman.

"Paeter will be missed. He was a good man," replied Andraste.

"I still have the letter you wrote me. It was a good and decent thing you did- writing so many letters, so many warriors perished. The other women in the village had letters as well," stated Olga.

"It was my duty," responded Andraste.

"Duty? It was kindness and honor in a place that no longer remembers either," said Olga, "You best get in the barn before you are seen. It is rare, but there are patrols at times. Keep your money; I will not accept payment. Mikhael joined the Resistance after you were exiled. In response, the Emperor's personal guards burned our estate, but some buildings still stand."

"Is it not dangerous to remain?" asked Aldrich.

"I must be home when my son returns," replied Olga. She looked to Andraste, "You tell him his mother's proud if you see him up North."

"I will. Thank you for your hospitality," returned Andraste.

They settled themselves and their horses in the barn. Laelius stationed four men as sentries, with each man taking a different position in the hay loft.

"Do you think Olga will betray us?" Brion asked Laelius.

"If she had that intent, she would have told us to our face. You know Northern women," responded Laelius. However, as he saw Andraste's scowl, he continued, "Besides Paeter and Mikhael were both excellent men. I am sure their mother is a fine woman. If she betrayed us, she would be betraying Mikhael."

"Where is Aldrich?" asked Andraste. No one could answer her.

Andraste went to the doorway of the barn. She saw Aldrich chopping wood near the house. Olga was talking to him as he did so. She watched for a time. Once Aldrich was headed back, she found a dry place against a wall and curled up in her blankets facing the wall. The cascading rain began to tinkle against the slate roof of the barn. The only other sound was Aldrich's footsteps entering the barn.

"You made it just in time," said Brion.

"The Commander was worried," mentioned Laelius.

Aldrich glanced towards Andraste who did not move. He set his pack on the floor and then seated himself in a vacant corner. The Victorious had seated themselves throughout the barn. Hadrian softly played a mournful tune on his fife.

"Is the rain here always so cold?" asked Aldrich.

"Colder," replied Nero.

"I would have killed for rains like these when we fought in Alexius," said Maximianus.

"That is desert country?" questioned Aldrich.

"Yes. It is like you are being cooked alive. The air is humid, the heat unbearable, and the white sands are almost blinding. The winds themselves burn against your skin. I do not think it rained once the entire time we were there. The sun would finally set and you would expect a reprieve but no, it would be frigid. It was so glacial that it made me miss the warmth of Northern winter. No vegetation. No living creatures--only barren waste-land," replied Maximianus.

"It is the anus of the universe," responded Otho. The Victorious chuckled.

"That is quite a description," commented Aldrich.

"There is no reason to go there," rejoined Otho.

"Unless you are fighting off Lionden infantry," stated Laelius.

"How long were you there?" asked Aldrich.

"Near a year," answered Maximianus.

"The Commander always chose the most difficult missions. It was like she had a death wish," stated Otho.

"She picked the missions farthest away from the North that is all. We Victorious go where we are most needed," said Laelius. He eyed Otho wearily.

"I say we should have let Lionden take Alexius. There is no reason to hold such a city in such a godforsaken place," replied Otho.

"It houses one of the oldest Ruins on the continent. The city was built around the fortress," said Brion.

"Did you enter the Ruin?" asked Aldrich.

"The Commander forbade it. When we asked for a reason, she said she could not recall. It is not like her to turn away from a challenge," said Maximianus.

"We also had a horde of Lionden soldiers to contend with," stated Laelius.

"The Lionden Empire was kind enough to provide a never-ending sea of troops. There was something off about the Lionden army though," said Nero.

"How so?" asked Aldrich.

"I swear I killed the same man at least twenty times over that campaign," responded Nero.

"I had the same feeling," said Laurentius.

"Is this the part you start telling me about monsters?" asked Aldrich.

"Sometimes men are more dangerous than monsters," answered Andraste.

"So, you are awake?" questioned Brion.

"How could I sleep with your clucking?" rejoined Andraste.

"If you were not engaged in fighting at Alexius, then what were you doing?" asked Otho, eyeing Aldrich with suspicion.

"I was helping lead Resistance attacks in the Midlands," replied Aldrich.

"So while we were preserving the Empire, you were fighting to destroy it," stated Otho.

"You should rejoice, Otho. The Midlands are your homeland. You have wanted the Empire gone for years," said Laelius.

"Yes, but he wants to be the one to do it," replied Maximianus.

"I will not admit this again, but I do believe in an allegiance with the other lands. We will not be able to face Lionden alone. Not after what we combatted in Alexius," said Otho.

"Am I dreaming?" asked Andraste.

"I think you must be for Otho to issue such a statement," replied Laelius.

"Dream of something better," suggested Felix.

"The Salt Islands," suggested Valens.

"The Lord of the Salt Islands?" asked Felix.

Andraste threw an apple across the barn. It struck Felix square in the head and he fell off the hay bale he was sitting on.

"Quite a throw," said Laelius.

"Still angry?" inquired Felix. He ducked as another apple was hurled at him. He caught the third.

"Come now, when was the last time we had a roof over our heads? I was hoping for a quiet night," said Laelius.

Andraste threw the apple in her hand and caught it. She surveyed Laelius and took a bite from the apple.

"Alright, pops," said Felix. Andraste looked to her apple and then to Felix, who took a few steps farther away.

"I can still beat you in any contest any day," stated Laelius. He did not look up from his post.

"Absolutely no fighting, no duels," ordered Andraste.

"Yes, Commander," acknowledged Felix.

"I call first challenge after the completion of the mission," said Laelius.

"Noted," answered Andraste.

"No duels during a mission? So I can say whatever I want without retribution?" asked Aldrich.

"There will be delayed retribution, so you choose your words carefully, Aldrich Caelius," replied Andraste. She turned to face Aldrich.

"I have words I would say to you," said Aldrich. He rose and approached her slowly.

"You are no longer our host. I can call you out on any insults to our Commander," warned Felix.

"Acknowledged," said Aldrich. He stood facing Andraste, but she did not move.

"Speak," replied Andraste. She took another bite from her apple. She kept her eyes fixated on Aldrich.

"That is not a hound you are addressing, that is the Prince of the Southern lands," commented Brion.

"She speaks to hounds more kindly," commented Otho.

"I would speak to you privately, without a chorus," stated Aldrich.

Andraste looked pointedly at the torrential down pour and then back Aldrich. He did not budge from his position.

"You have two options. First, speak your mind. Second, hold your tongue," said Andraste.

Aldrich did not respond, so she turned to face Laelius and Felix. She took another bite from her apple. Aldrich brushed past her and went to stand in the doorway. He surveyed the rain with contempt.

"That is hostile even for you," chided Brion.

"A Southern lady would never speak so," commented Avitus.

"I know. I am the Demon of the North, and they are angels of the South," said Andraste. Laelius motioned for Felix to move away. Laelius joined Andraste's side and spoke so that only she could hear, "It is not that. My Paulina would never speak to me in such a way."

"He is not my Paulina," rejoined Andraste.

"Go speak to him," advised Laelius. He proceeded to sit next to Brion and they began to converse softly.

Andraste considered Laelius's advice and then slowly walked to the doorway. She stood on the opposite side of the opening and threw her apple core into the wood line. The raging storm throttled the building as icy blasts of air continued to shake the decayed timbers. It felt as though the entire structure would collapse at any moment. Andraste pulled her cloak tighter about her shoulders. Wordlessly Aldrich shut the barn door and secured it. He turned to survey Andraste but he said nothing. Hadrian began to play a different song on his fife. Andraste smiled in spite of herself.

"This is a song from the Island of Fortune. Do you know it?" asked Andraste.

Aldrich barely shook his head. He kept his eyes on the horses. To his surprise, Andraste began to sing softly:

"Out among the waves, underneath the stars,
I saw a man walking, along the emerald cliffs,
His hair was like a raven, dark as the night,
Not a gem in the king's coffers shone like his eyes,
He had a smile that could rival the dawn.
I rowed to shore to meet him, and he said to me,
Sigh not so, sigh no more, never sigh again,
I have been aimlessly wandering these shores,
And now, I know, all that time I was searching,
I have found you, sigh no more, I am yours.
The Eastern wind blew and kissed my cheek,
I took it as a sign and my heart rejoiced,
I took his hands and said the required words,
Forever we were bound by the gray ocean."

As her song finished, Andraste glanced to Aldrich, noting his smoldering sapphire eyes were locked upon her. Although seemingly less tense, he looked away as she approached him.

"Would you so willingly accept a stranger?" asked Aldrich.

"At first sight? Evidently not," replied Andraste.

"That is true. 188 proposals?" inquired Aldrich.

"Not one sincere," answered Andraste.

"You did not think-" started Aldrich. He stopped himself and folded his arms across his chest.

"It has been explained to me that your proposal was to correct my error and protect my honor. It was the proper response for a Southern gentleman," said Andraste. She watched her horse eat her oats intently.

"And my actions since then?" asked Aldrich.

"A benevolent host, a loyal comrade, and a formidable ally," answered Andraste.

"This is how you see me?" questioned Aldrich.

"You have thrice refused me. Such action requires you to be described thus," replied Andraste.

"Movement from the North," called Laurentius from his post in the hay loft.

Andraste tensed and her hand went automatically to her hilt.

"How many?" asked Laelius.

"Two score at least," said Laurentius.

"Troops?" asked Laelius.

"Arisen," responded Laurentius. Brion joined Laurentius at his post. He looked to Andraste and nodded confirmation.

"Olga," said Aldrich. He looked down to Andraste.

"Do they come this way?" asked Andraste. She kept her attention on Laurentius.

"No. They follow the Northern road," answered Laurentius. Aldrich hastily made his way to the hay loft to survey the Arisen troops.

"Your orders?" asked Laelius.

"We stay. We cannot be pulled out so early. We must maintain our secrecy as we make our way towards the Citadel," said Andraste.

"They will kill many innocent people," stated Laelius.

"More lives will be saved if we defeat the Emperor. We cannot risk discovery," replied Andraste. She could sense the discontent among her men. They grew silent and uneasy.

"Squadrons," said Laurentius.

"We would be overrun," said Laelius.

"From here they look like ordinary men, but how do they compare to fighting a normal man?" asked Aldrich.

"You did not get to fight them at the last battle due to your position as a healer. The Arisen soldiers are comparable to human soldiers. They move slower, but their blood and scratches have the same effect as poison. The Arisen officers propose more of a challenge. It is as if they are demons in human form," answered Laelius.

Brion had joined Andraste's side. Aldrich and Laurentius still stared intensely at the Northern road.

"Toxin's advice was sound. It is a good thing you followed it," said Brion.

"What do you mean?" asked Aldrich.

"Toxin said to stay off the Northern road and never travel by night," said Brion. He looked from Andraste to Aldrich.

"And to cut off the heads and burn the bodies, but this we already knew," added Laelius.

"I should have told the Resistance troops," said Aldrich.

"We did. I gave them such instructions. Egnatius and the Queen are well aware as is King Aelius. They are spreading the word for us in our absence," said Andraste.

"Please communicate to me all information that will affect my people in the future," said Aldrich.

Andraste scowled at Aldrich before returning to her blankets. She faced the wall once more and tried to fall asleep.

In the following days it started to feel even more frigid which did not bother the Victorious but Aldrich, who was used to the warm forgiving climate of the South, was miserable. The forest became even more dense and unruly. Due to the cloud coverage at night, Aldrich had been unable to read the stars. However, this night was particularly fine. The stars shined with purpose. The stars twinkled as if laughing at some hidden joke.

"We are not going to the Citadel," stated Aldrich.

"It is true we are going to the Citadel. I am just going to make a detour on the way," replied Andraste.

"Enlighten me," said Aldrich. His tone was deadly.

"The relic pieces need safekeeping. I am taking them to the Ice Palace," enlightened Andraste.

"You cannot touch them," stated Aldrich.

"And you cannot follow me there," retorted Andraste.

"By the gods, I will!" fumed Aldrich.

The Victorious had stopped eating their meal. The men watched the dialogue as if it were a duel.

"They will kill any man who enters there," argued Andraste coolly.

"I am a Prince of the Southern lands, who has crossed the boundary line and entered unmarked Northern territory. If I am found, I will be killed," countered Aldrich.

"I will not risk you," declared Andraste, "You are too important for the Resistance."

"It is my risk," responded Aldrich.

"Did Rhinauld visit you at the Ice Palace?" interjected Brion.

"They let him get as far as the village," admitted Andraste.

"Then we will accompany you to the village," mediated Laelius. Brion looked pleased with himself.

"He was a boy then. It was not a group of fourteen armed warriors and a sorcerer," said Andraste.

"Rhinauld got into a bit of a misunderstanding-" started Brion.

"Yes, a misunderstanding that probably has still not been forgotten," finished Andraste, the corners of her mouth twitching.

"A misunderstanding?" roared a female's voice from outside their circle, "He destroyed half the village."

The men had no time to stand. They could hear the familiar sound of arrows being drawn as they intuited that the final destination of those arrows would be their own hearts.

Andraste had already been on her feet. She slowly lowered her hood as her sea-green eyes blazed towards the direction of the voice.

"Well met, Fausta. You seem to have grown a heart in your dotage. Really? Warning us before you shoot?" ridiculed Andraste.

"Dotage?" catechized the voice, but the speaker laughed.

A woman of middle-aged years approached their camp fire, wearing full body armor which was polished as fine as any mirror in the Southern palace. As Fausta approached Andraste, who stood at attention surveying Fausta's approach, her armor took on a midnight blue-black hue in the subdued evening light.

The Victorious were poised to draw their weapons.

"I would not do that," Andraste cautioned her men.

"You look tired," nagged Fausta.

"I am tired," agreed Andraste. The older woman offered her hand to Andraste who grasped it while they embraced with their free arms.

"We hear humorous rumors from the South," alleged Fausta.

"Signifying?" questioned Andraste.

"It is said that the Goddess of Victory rode on the back of a giant white tiger into battle. They drove back the Northern forces using magic of old," said Fausta.

Andraste and Brion exchanged looks.

"We thought it was you at first but it is reported that the Goddess has raven locks and dark eyes," said Fausta.

"What sort of magic?" asked Andraste.

"The tiger created a sand wall that encompassed the city. Whatever attacked it was deflected and hurled back at the caster," responded Fausta.

"How long have they been under attack?" questioned Andraste.

"Weeks, but the Northern forces have yet to get through. Grand Sorcerer Gaius has fallen. He lost in a duel to a militant sorcerer from the East. Accordingly, the Northern forces are now laying siege," answered Fausta.

"Have there been many casualties?" asked Andraste.

"It is rumored that not a single citizen, refugee, or soldier has been harmed within the Southern capitol's walls," replied Fausta.

"That is remarkable," said Laelius. Fausta's eyes darted to the warrior nearest Andraste.

"Indeed. With the cooperation of Queen Marian, we have been using the Ice Palace transport circle to transfer refugees to the South. We are mostly sending children," said Fausta.

"It is not like the Ice Palace to evacuate," stated Andraste.

"The Arisen outnumber us. We have lost many warriors. We cannot protect these lands as we once did," admitted Fausta.

"Is there any other news from the South?" asked Aldrich.

"It is said that the militant sorcerer from the East has restored the Southern Ruins and that the Ruins are being used to house refugees from across the Empire," said Fausta.

"Is that safe?" inquired Aldrich.

"Ruins have been known to protect the innocent," answered Andraste. She turned her attention back to Fausta, "Any news from the Citadel?"

Fausta's smile faded and she did not answer Andraste's question.

Surveying the darkness wearily, Fausta ordered her troops to lower their bows and approach. A score of female warriors encircled the party. Two of their number held Priscus and Thracius captive with knives to their throats. The female captors shoved them roughly towards their comrades.

"A full unit. You are going to hunt in the forest?" inquired Andraste.

"The power of the North grows. We do not stray as far as we once did. We stay close enough to protect the village, and yet close enough to reach the Palace if needed," said Fausta. Andraste frowned.

"I have brought a gift for Mother," said Andraste.

"You may pass, but the men may not. I would have expected more of a fight from the notorious," said Fausta.

"Victorious," countered Otho. Fausta shrugged.

"I told them not to move," said Andraste, "A skirmish would have done none of us good especially after that unfortunate incident with Rhinauld."

"It is a good thing we allowed him to live. He has made quite a name for himself. Conqueror of three Ruins? Even if was with your help- that is something," said Fausta with admiration.

"Is that any way to speak of your own son?" asked Andraste, but she laughed.

There was some muttering among the Victorious, but Andraste silenced them with a look.

A younger Ice Palace warrior approached, also in the same fine armor. She wore a helmet over her dark brown hair that concealed her face. She whispered something in Fausta's ear.

"Mother is impressed by your gift. She will permit you all to pass. The men may wait at the village," informed Fausta.

"Many thanks," said Andraste.

"All that worrying for nothing," commented Otho.

"How did 'Mother' know?" asked Aldrich.

"The ruler of the Ice Palace possesses extraordinary magical powers," said Laelius, "But as to the specifics, I could not say."

"Should we blindfold them?" asked one of the warriors.

"Torture them?" suggested another.

"Feed them to the wolves?" propositioned a third.

"Girls, that is enough," ordered Fausta, "Wolves will not work on the Empress."

"But they would work on the men," commented the first warrior. She grinned wickedly.

Fausta wrapped an arm around Andraste's shoulders and the pair led the way up the hill. They rounded a bend and approached a stone road.

"Did you realize we were that close?" asked Brion to Laelius, and the older warrior shook his head. They both looked ahead to Andraste.

"Everything always happens for a reason," commented Laelius.

Seven of the female warriors took their horses and led them up along the road. The female warriors were all wearing the identical blue armor but the men could not help but notice the spots of freshly dried blood and dents in some of the armor. The remaining thirteen Ice Palace warriors followed close behind watching intently, but remaining silent.

"You have already encountered some tonight then? And so close to the village?" asked Andraste, her voice carrying on the still mountain air.

"What is some?" asked Aldrich. Brion and Laelius exchanged looks.

"The Arisen," confirmed Laelius.

Andraste and Fausta had proceeded far enough ahead that the men could no longer hear their conversation. What seemed to be a quaint village made of stone arose before them, but as they got closer, it appeared to be a city. Stone buildings rose up all along the side of the mountain, stopping within one-hundred yards of a tall palace composed of ice that glowed like a star in the darkness.

"Some village," commented Maximianus.

Fausta and Andraste were waiting for them by a fountain at the entrance of the village.

"Aldrich Caelius approach," ordered Fausta.

Aldrich did so as Fausta surveyed him mercilessly. Her glance was calculating and deadly. Aldrich felt that in that glance he had been soundly measured and found lacking.

"Mother wishes to meet the son of Marian, now Queen of the Southern lands. The rest of you will wait here," commanded Fausta.

Andraste inclined her head to her men.

Fausta did not wait to see if Aldrich followed before she turned up the road. Andraste waited for Aldrich to reach her current position. Wordlessly, they began to follow the stone road, but they lost sight of Fausta. Aldrich glanced downwards to Andraste but she was unbothered. She led the way to a tall, spindly tower and entered without ceremony. Aldrich's hand brushed against the wall of the tower and he recoiled in alarm at its coldness. He had little time for further observation as Andraste quickened their pace. Aldrich followed her into perhaps the smallest room he had ever seen. Andraste closed a grate behind him and he felt that they were being moved upwards. Andraste did not offer an explanation. She seemed agitated to have him there. They came to a stop and Andraste opened the grate, permitting Aldrich a view of a large blooming orchard despite its proximity to the Ice Palace.

"Ancient magic," stated Andraste. She granted him a smile as she saw his delight in their surroundings.

The magnificent ice doors opened before them which perplexed Aldrich as he did not see a single servant or guard maneuvering the doors. They walked into a large entryway. Two magnificent spiral ice staircases rose from the walls, leading upwards to yet another floor. Instead of mounting the stairs, Andraste walked into the foyer between the staircases with Aldrich following behind.

The halls and rooms were guarded by beautiful ice sculptures of serene goddesses in prayer and heroines fighting unseen perils. Shelves housing thousands of gilded books traversed the span of every corridor. Sheer ice panels resembling glass windows encased the books while an iridescent back light glowed softly in the background. As they passed many of the blue-armored warriors, some welcomed Andraste, but all looked at Aldrich in surprise, some in hostility. There were also many women in scholarly robes, plain clothes, and clothes from lands that Aldrich did not recognize. Finally, they arrived at the room that Andraste desired. She knocked three times on the door and waited.

"Enter," called the crackly voice from inside.

Aldrich was surprised that this room was constructed only of stone and showed no evidence of ice. In the center of the room a cheerful fire blazed, and over it a pot of what smelled like mulled wine. There were only three women present other than Fausta, who had been bent low, whispering into an elderly woman's ear.

"So I see, Andraste, you have returned and brought us a recruit," croaked the elderly woman. She laughed at her own joke.

One of the women ladled steaming red liquid into two earthen cups. She handed them to a second woman who brought them to Andraste and Aldrich. Andraste half bowed to the cup bringer and Aldrich did the same.

"You may call me Mother as do all who enter," said the elderly woman to Aldrich, who bowed ceremoniously.

"Finally, a man who knows when to remain silent," acknowledged Fausta.

"Please!" exclaimed Andraste. She blushed, embarrassed for Aldrich who chose to say nothing and stood coldly at attention.

"It was a compliment," said Fausta, amused by Andraste's reaction.

"Approach, Andraste, I want to see you better," said Mother, beckoning Andraste with one crooked finger.

Andraste reluctantly did as she was bid. Mother's bony hands grasped both of Andraste's wrists with surprising strength. Andraste winced at the contact. Noting Andraste's reaction, Aldrich took a step forward but halted when he saw the arduous look in Fausta's eyes. Mother held onto Andraste's arms for a while and then let her go.

"Mother reads memories through touch," explained Andraste.

"I am sorry you have experienced such grief since you lost us, my child. But you are much stronger now; although, you still do not possess the heart to rejoin us. That much is clear," said Mother sadly. Mother turned her gaze on Aldrich.

"The relic then? Andraste may not touch it, so I will ask you to hand it to me. Fausta, be at ease. Marian's son will not harm me," reprimanded Mother.

Fausta tensed as Aldrich took a step forward. Her fingers wrapped menacingly around the hilt of her sword. Aldrich approached slowly and offered the parcel to Mother who unwrapped it and examined it in her aged hands. Aldrich returned to Andraste's side, standing so close to her that he nearly touched her.

"Do you know what the relic is used for?" asked Andraste.

"Yes," answered Mother.

"Do you know how to keep it safe from the Emperor?" inquired Andraste.

"Yes," replied Mother.

"And my last question: do you keep an emerald dragon in one of the towers?" questioned Andraste.

"Yes," said Mother with a toothy grin, "And since you surprised me with your last question, I will give you a tidbit of praise. You were wise to send Rhinauld and Henry to look after the remaining pieces of the relic. There are two pieces here already. When Rhinauld and Henry retrieve the last remaining two, I will send for them. Stop being such a mother hen, Andraste. All of these fine men you have surrounded yourself with and still you look after them."

Andraste blushed deeply and looked at her boots.

"You will stay the night?" asked Mother. It was asked as a question, but was definitely an order.

"If it please you, Mother," replied Andraste.

"Heather, Thistle, show our guests to their rooms," ordered Mother.

"Aldrich will stay with me. I will keep him out of trouble," said Andraste. She stepped protectively in front of him.

"I would not harm a guest in our palace," cried Mother.

"Yes, but there is the palace," reminded Andraste. Mother chuckled.

"Fine, I will not take him from you," rescinded Mother.

Andraste bowed to Mother and then to the rest of the women. Fausta did not look amused. She seemed to want to kill Aldrich by the power of the look she shot him.

Andraste and Aldrich were shown down the corridor to a chamber.

"Thank you," Aldrich said to the departing women who did not acknowledge his presence. Andraste locked the door behind them.

"That was one of the strangest interviews I have ever witnessed," commented Aldrich. He offered her a smile.

"If you are allowed to address Mother, you are only permitted three questions. It is so you ask the most critical questions and waste no time," explained Andraste.

"She spared very little time with her answers," criticized Aldrich.

"If I am captured, the Emperor will not learn the relic's use or where it is being held. He will also learn that the Ice Palace houses a dragon," said Andraste, shivering.

"Is there a way to heat up this room?" asked Aldrich.

"I do not remember the enchantment. It does not matter. I was never good at enchantments," sighed Andraste.

Aldrich looked around the room. The only piece of furniture was a stone bed with a mattress and blankets. He chose to sit on the floor.

"The floor is ice. We can both sit on the bed," suggested Andraste.

"I am fine," responded Aldrich.

"You have been sleeping beside me for weeks on the road," rejoined Andraste.

"With your brother and other men present. Fifteen men who would slice off my head before I even thought of-" started Aldrich.

"So you will only sleep with me if my brother and other men are present?" teased Andraste.

Aldrich looked at her sharply. He rose and sat beside her on the bed, but was careful to not touch her. Aldrich changed the subject, "You sent Rhinauld and Henry after the other Ruin pieces?"

"Oh, that," said Andraste. Her merriment had faded. She glanced at Aldrich to see his reaction but his face was expressionless.

"I felt it was necessary," said Andraste.

"But not necessary to tell me?" inquired Aldrich.

"Do you tell me all of your decisions?" asked Andraste.

"The ones that matter," responded Aldrich.

A bell struck nine times in the distance. Andraste curled up on her side of the bed. Aldrich draped his cloak over her.

"Keep it on, you will need it," cautioned Andraste.

"I am fine," said Aldrich.

"I can feel you shivering," said Andraste. She rolled on her side to look at him. He avoided her cerulean eyes.

"Can a soldier huddle next to another soldier for warmth?" asked Andraste.

Aldrich hesitated but then positioned himself onto his side so that only their backs touched. Andraste covered him with his own cloak. She laid her back next to his.

"Why did you ask about the dragon?" questioned Aldrich.

He felt her whole body tense though she said nothing.

"Paramerion?" he asked. He sat up so that he could turn and look at her face.

"The treasure room in the Darklands reminded me of a tower I entered here as a girl," replied Andraste, "I can also sense the dragon. It calls to me."

"We do not need to fear the dragon," replied Aldrich.

"Why?" asked Andraste.

Aldrich explained the dream he had on the night that she had touched the relic.

"Why would a dragon want you to protect me?" questioned Andraste.

"Why would a dragon call you by your mother's name?" rejoined Aldrich.

Aldrich did not like the look in her eyes. He had come to recognize it. It was her look of determination and unbridled impulsiveness.

"No," said Aldrich.

"How else are we to know?" asked Andraste.

"By no means am I agreeing to go over to some tower and have a nice night chat with a dragon. What if my dream was just a dream? What if the dragon did not speak to me or would like to have us for dinner instead?" questioned Aldrich.

"Really, Aldrich, you are a Ruin conqueror. Where is your sense of adventure?" asked Andraste. She sat up in her bed, "I will go on my own."

"You will not go alone," stated Aldrich, reluctantly rising to his feet to join her.

"What is the etiquette here for night wandering?" asked Aldrich as they went out into the hall.

"You can proceed only to the strength of your ability," replied Andraste.

"What do you mean?" inquired Aldrich.

"The Ice Palace is a Ruin. Perhaps the best preserved Ruin, but a Ruin nonetheless," said Andraste.

"And the Spirit who guards it?" asked Aldrich.

"Mother," answered Andraste.

"If we are talking of Ruins, then I also assume you mean to include monsters, duels to the death, and dark magic?" questioned Aldrich with a breath of resignation.

"Yes," confirmed Andraste.

"You know what your men would say? They would mock me. I can hear Otho's voice now, 'Aldrich, you fool, you have a night alone in bed with the princess, and you choose instead to prowl a castle in the middle of the night to have a conversation with a dragon?'" said Aldrich.

"We will make a Northern man of you yet," laughed Andraste. She turned abruptly and looked at him mischievously, "And those voices in your head? They have a point."

Before he could respond, she had already darted down the hallway. He smiled as he followed her.

The rising sun assured them they had been walking for hours and yet, they continued to walk even further. The lighting in the castle was so peculiar that it made Aldrich feel disoriented; it seemed to him as though the sun and perhaps arisen and set several times.

"All of these hallways look the same to me," stated Aldrich.

"The Ice Palace is a maze. The thing is to keep walking. You do not want to open any of these doors," said Andraste. She pointed to the top corner of one such door. It was marked with and almost undistinguishable star in the upward corner.

Aldrich looked at her questioningly. She answered, "Beasts."

"But this is a school!" cried Aldrich in alarm.

"Yes, and its mission is to make its students as strong as possible to defend the Empire whether the students study warrior- or scholarly training," exhorted Andraste.

"So they allow students to wander in there?" asked Aldrich in disbelief.

"Well it only takes a couple of doors to realize not to go in the ones that are marked by the star. Usually, a warrior patrols the halls and keeps an eye on the newer students. No one has died in years," explained Andraste.

"Well, as long no one has died in years," responded Aldrich as they reached a blue and black checkered floor.

"Do not step on the black tiles from this point forward," warned Andraste. She was quickly crossing the floor in front of them. Aldrich hastened after her. The floor changed to black and white tiles.

"Now, step only on the black tiles," ordered Andraste. Aldrich followed her example. They hurried forward. The tiles turned to white and blue. Andraste hesitated.

"What now?" asked Aldrich, poised precariously on one foot.

"I do not remember which one," admitted Andraste.

She picked up a pebble and threw it at a white tile. Nothing happened. They waited. She picked up a second pebble and threw it at a blue tile. Instantly the space ahead of them was covered with a volley of arrows. They waited for the silence to resume.

"Do not step on the blues ones," ordered Andraste.

"You are enjoying yourself," criticized Aldrich as they leapt from blue to blue tile.

They left the checkered floor and entered into a tremendous library. There were tables covered with piles of opened books that were in the process of reshelving themselves. The shelves rose into a vaulted turret at least four stories tall.

"Hello, Empress," said a voice from the floor.

Aldrich leaned over the table to address the speaker and leapt back in alarm. A large griffin reading an ancient ruin text, peered over her purple spectacles in order to survey Andraste. It was such a human action that Aldrich was momentarily lost for words.

"It is good to see you, professor," greeted Andraste. The Griffin removed its spectacles and sat on its haunches.

"And you as well, Empress," replied the Griffin.

"It speaks?" asked Aldrich.

"And I heard *it* had such promise," sniffed the offended Griffin.

"You forget that outside of these walls, animals no longer speak to humans," said Andraste.

"Animals?" quibbled the Griffin.

"Pray forgive me. I was speaking so he could understand. The Professor is an Anima. She is one of the only surviving magical creatures in existence that can communicate with humans. A human that can speak to animals is also called an Anima," informed Andraste.

The Griffin seemed pacified. She ruffled her feathers back into place, but her tail flipped agitatedly on the ground.

"I am looking for a tower that houses an emerald dragon," stated Andraste.

"Make sure you do not address the dragon so inferiorly, or she may eat you for dinner. Dragons are not as magnanimous as griffins," said the Griffin archly, "But such things are common knowledge."

"Yes, of course," agreed Aldrich. Andraste shot him a look.

"Professor, do you know the tower I seek?" asked Andraste.

"Yes. But you know how things are done here," expounded the Griffin.

"I have to find it on my own or be tested," sighed Andraste.

Aldrich was starting to understand why Andraste had left the Ice Palace.

"What is your test?" asked Aldrich to the Griffin. The Griffin rose to all four paws and spread her majestic wings.

"You must answer a riddle, but if you answer wrong, you must start all the way from the orchard," replied the Griffin.

"Please, proceed," said Andraste. The Griffin did not need to be asked twice.

"Measures the passage of time,
Colored and yet a component of glass,
A mortar mixed with lime,
A single grain or a large mass," proposed the Griffin.

"Sand," replied Andraste.

"Good," said the Griffin, "You may pass. Go through the door on your left."

"Thank you, professor," said Andraste. She bowed to the Griffin.

"Are you sure you do not want to stay for more riddles? Or a chat? It has been ages. I have mulled wine and a pudding," offered the Griffin.

"Another time, professor," said Andraste over her shoulder as she ran down the hall.

Aldrich bowed to the Griffin and hastily followed after Andraste. When the door to the library shut behind him, he asked Andraste, "Is there anything else you want to tell me? Share with me? Are there any other mythical creatures lurking the corridors that I should be aware of?"

"No time now. I will tell you of my Northern education later. Perhaps instead of all that time you have spent glaring at me and being taciturn, you should have spoken to me," commented Andraste.

Aldrich grabbed her hand with such force that she fell backwards into the wall.

"Is that what you think of me?" asked Aldrich.

His face was inches from her own. He held her in place. She did not respond. She met his gaze without hesitation.

"I was giving you space. I have never met anyone like you. You will not let me be gentle towards you, so I cannot treat you like a lady of the South. You will not let me befriend you, so I cannot treat you as a friend. The only time you give me the time of the day is when imminent death approaches," alleged Aldrich.

"So you do not loath my existence?" asked Andraste. She looked up at him with her blue-green eyes and he dropped her arm.

"Of course not! But you are infuriating beyond all reason," responded Aldrich.

Aldrich headed forward down the hall with purpose and haste. He lost his momentum due to an abrupt stop. Andraste joined his side immediately.

The room before them was enshrouded in total darkness. She could not see her hand before her face, or make out Aldrich's broad shoulders, although she knew him to be only two paces in front of her. In the far distance they could see an iron door with light beaming behind a tiny window. It was but a speck of light in the darkness, like the flickering of the smallest of candle.

"Thoughts?" asked Aldrich and then quickly, "About our current predicament?"

"Phoenix?" suggested Andraste just as hastily.

Aldrich held out his hand and the large golden phoenix glided ahead, illuminating bit by bit of the room, until it disappeared behind the door.

"Did you see anything?" asked Andraste.

"No," said Aldrich, "But then, it was so fast."

Andraste moved to retake the lead, but Aldrich held his arm out to stop her while he took a step forward. Wordlessly, she followed behind him. She knew that he was right in front of her even though she could not see him. She reached out and lightly grabbed the back of his tunic. He paused and then continued. Travel was slow and cautious but eventually they reached the embossed iron door. Aldrich hesitated and Andraste pushed him gently in his lower back. He opened the door and they walked into the light.

"Mother?" asked Andraste in surprise as Mother blocked the path. Over Mother's shoulder was an open-air corridor leading to an even taller tower construed of thick sheets of ice.

"My child, you are not ready for what is behind that door," stated Mother.

"But we came all this way," protested Andraste.

"We will need the completed relic to combat the power that dwells there. Even with the shield it may not be enough to save her," cautioned Mother sadly.

"Her?" asked Aldrich.

"Andraste!" a voice called beyond the door.

"I know that voice," said Andraste in confusion.

"It is the Dragon," confirmed Aldrich.

"No, I know that voice," declared Andraste.

"You must leave now. I cannot contain her full power," warned Mother.

"Andraste!" bellowed the Dragon.

"That is my mother's voice!" yelled Andraste.

She leapt towards the door, but Aldrich restrained her in his arms.

"I do not understand," bewailed Andraste.

The Dragon was throwing itself against the ice door and breathing fire. As she hit the door, it sounded like thunder. The whole tower started shaking. Mother threw both of her hands into the air; instantly ice rose from the ground, encasing the tower in blue light. The thrashing from inside the tower stopped.

"All this time? Why did you not tell me?" cried Andraste.

"Come child," said Mother kindly.

Mother offered Andraste her hand. Andraste refused to take it. Aldrich took a step forward to stand by Andraste's side. They both stared at Mother, waiting for her explanation. Mother withdrew her offered hand.

"The Emperor was once a great man, both a warrior and a scholar but he was always too ambitious. As he read the ancient texts, he became too hungry for power. That is when the experiments began. One day while he was experimenting a curse backfired as the Empress tried to intervene and she was consumed. We tried to purge the curse with healing fire but the curse was ancient magic so our efforts also backfired. The Empress was transformed into a dragon. The transformation changed her mind as well. Sometimes she knows who she is and it is more sadness then she can bear. At other times she thinks only that she is a dragon and will not hear reason. At that stage it takes all of my power to contain her," said Mother.

"But I saw her consumed by flames at the Southern palace. I saw her die," alleged Andraste.

"Empress Victoria had already been weakened by attempting to use dark magic to release Sveinbiorn from his imprisonment. The Southern Queen attempted an ancient form of healing magic using flames to engulf Victoria but the magic was not strong enough. When Victoria could not be transformed back, we used the transport circle to bring her here," responded Mother.

"Where you imprisoned her," stated Andraste.

"We must keep the innocent safe. That is our duty. This palace is Victoria's last hope. Here we house the only texts that have the potential to save her," replied Mother.

"But why not tell me?" asked Andraste.

"You were too young. You would have killed yourself in pursuit of a cure. Worse yet, who knows what powers you could have unleashed in attempting to reverse dark magic," answered Mother.

"You have so little faith in me," said Andraste.

"What was the first thing you did when your memory was restored?" asked Mother.

"Memory was restored?" repeated Aldrich. Andraste ignored his concern.

"I released Sveinbiorn from his imprisonment," said Andraste.

"You broke the taboo. Are you prepared for the consequences?" questioned Mother.

"Sveinbiorn is and has always been our ally. He will not let anything happen to me or the South, so long as he follows my orders," said Andraste.

"And what have you promised him in return?" inquired Mother. Andraste did not respond. Aldrich studied the two women but remained silent.

"You are an Anima. You must follow the threads of life. You must maintain the web of time. If you abandon your duties, you will fall. You have the example of your mother to understand what befalls a fallen Anima," said Mother.

"I followed the threads and they led to Sveinbiorn. He was meant to be released," said Andraste.

"Threads of life? Web of time? I do not follow," interrupted Aldrich.

"Every living creature possesses a life force that can be seen as a thread of life. We are all connected. These connections produce the web of time by our interactions. When everything is balanced, time progresses as it should," said Andraste.

"Should? Do you mean fate?" asked Aldrich.

"No, we make our own fate. I mean balance is obtained," said Andraste.

"The balance of the world is in jeopardy. The dead are walking among the living. Creatures that should not exist are in this world. Furthermore, the pursuit of dark magic by the Emperor has released shadow powers into this world. The shadow powers, in turn, release dark energy, ancient magic that creates chaos and destroys," explained Mother.

"The Emperor is empowered by the shadow powers?" asked Aldrich. Mother nodded and studied him with her wise eyes.

"Could he have a cure-" started Andraste.

"Do not go down that road! Remember your duty, Andraste Valerianus!" commanded Mother. Her kind face had turned into a scowl of rage. Andraste tensed where she stood.

"Would my power be of any use? Could I save Victoria Eldgrimson?"

asked Aldrich. Andraste froze against him.

"No, son of Marian, we must have the shield to contain that power-ful curse. That is its purpose. If the curse consumes Victoria, it will be a power I will no longer be able to contain and it will destroy us all," besought Mother.

"I know you are torn, Andraste, but you must continue on your path to defeat the Emperor. Together you and Aldrich have that power. As you cannot touch the relic pieces, you would be of no use in the Ruins," comforted Mother.

"Why is that?" asked Aldrich, "Why can Andraste not touch the pieces?"

"After being so touched by a dark curse, the remnants left within her call to release the dark magic imprisoned inside the shield," presaged Mother.

Aldrich looked to Andraste who took a deep breath. She turned her attention to Mother.

"Is there anything else we should know?" inquired Andraste.

"Focus on the path to the North. Do not get distracted," replied Mother.

"That is no answer," said Aldrich.

"She cannot answer. She cannot lie," replied Andraste. She bowed to the crone.

"So you are taking your leave?" asked Mother. She touched the top of Andraste's head in parting.

"Go with my blessing," said Mother.

Mother waved her hand and a door appeared opposite of the way they had come. It opened before them. Andraste looked once to Aldrich and then headed for the door. Her cloak swept behind her in the Northern wind. Aldrich bowed to Mother before hastening after Andraste.

"Protect her!" called Mother as Aldrich towards the exit, but he was not certain. He looked towards the ice tower one last time. It could have been the Dragon.

Aldrich and Andraste emerged into the orchard.

"Paramerion," called Aldrich.

Andraste stopped and turned to look at him. Her face was stern. Whatever she was feeling, she had bottled it deep inside of herself.

"Please do not speak of this to the others," said Andraste. She forced a smile, "They already call me Demon of the North. What would they call me if they knew my mother was a dragon?"

"Paramerion," Aldrich started, but he stopped as she looked away quickly. She raised her hood and headed towards the tunnel.

"What did she mean by memory being returned?" asked Aldrich.

"You said you spoke to Rhinauld. I thought you knew," replied Andraste.

"I understood that you were abused by your uncle, but not the details. I spoke of other matters with Rhinauld, I thought you knew the particulars of our conversation," responded Aldrich.

"Rhinauld said nothing of your communications," said Andraste.

"You have seemed different of late. I thought it was because you were angry with me," said Aldrich.

"I am angry with you. I do not understand you," replied Andraste.

She kept her eyes on the road ahead of her. She quickened her pace. Aldrich fell silent as they proceeded towards the village. Upon their arrival, Aldrich made some inquiries and they were directed to a tavern.

"It is about time!" cried Otho, as they entered.

"It has not been that long," rejoined Aldrich.

"It has been two weeks," said Brion in confusion.

"Time works differently inside the palace," remarked Andraste.

"Any word from the South?" asked Aldrich.

"There have been skirmishes in all realms of the Empire as planned. There have been small losses. The Imperial Army has been mobilized and spread out to all of the resisting areas. However, there has been resistance within the Army's ranks and the North is being further divided by civil war. The Resistance forces are progressing from the South and the West by land and from the East by sea," said Laelius.

"We should get moving," avouched Andraste.

"We could both use a good meal and sleep," stated Aldrich.

Andraste did not fight him. He pulled out a chair at the table for her before sitting by her side. Brion ordered them beef stew, fresh bread and honey-ale.

"So how was it?" asked Laelius with uncharacteristic curiosity. Andraste did not respond.

"Women," said Aldrich, dismissingly.

After her hearty meal, Andraste retired to her room to bathe, ready for a restorative night's sleep. She was still in her bath as she heard footsteps run down the hall and to her door. There was a forceful knock.

Andraste rose from her bath, hastily dried off and threw on a clean tunic. The knock pounded again, more urgently. She looked through the peep hole and saw Aldrich standing before her door. She opened the door so that he could enter, and quickly closed it behind him.

"The Emperor's personal guards are here. We must leave at once-" Aldrich's voice trailed off as he inhaled the vision of Andraste standing before him in only her tunic. More sounds of footsteps charging down the hall quickly drew their attention away from Aldrich's fixation.

"We do not have time. Take off your shirt. Do not argue. They would never expect-" started Andraste.

She had already stripped him of his sword and thrown it under the bed. He wordlessly took off his shirt. She was already in the bed. They heard doors being thrown open down the hall.

"Come!" ordered Andraste.

Aldrich leapt into bed with her, making the headboard hit the wall. Andraste brought the blankets around his waist, and then pulled Aldrich to her. Aldrich hesitated. She reached for him and kissed him squarely on the mouth. The action caused her shirt to rise above her thigh. As his hand felt her bare hip, Aldrich closed his eyes. Andraste wrapped her arms around him and kissed him harder. Aldrich kissed her back.

The door to her room was opened. Again, she kissed Aldrich deeply and moved her bare leg to move him closer. He adjusted to accommodate her. She heard the door close. Aldrich pushed himself off of her. She pushed him onto his back and straddled him.

"They may come back to check," Andraste whispered.

Aldrich stared at her intently. They heard the sound of boots going down the stairwell. Aldrich removed himself and sat on the end of the bed.

"Aldrich," called Andraste.

"It is not honorable," responded Aldrich.

"I judge my honor by a different measure," stated Andraste. She rose, positioned herself behind him, and kissed his shoulder.

"No," said Aldrich, removing himself from the bed and stepping out of her reach. He elaborated, "Not until you agree to be my wife."

"Marriage? The only reason for you to insist on such a proposal is if you intend to pursue my claim to the Empire. Am I not enough as I am?" asked Andraste.

"Do you truly not understand my regard for you? Have you no consideration for my concept of honor and how I would protect yours?" questioned Aldrich.

"You have saved my life repeatedly. My life is yours. I would do anything for you," swore Andraste.

"It is not your gratitude, I desire," responded Aldrich.

"What do you desire?" asked Andraste.

"Your love," answered Aldrich.

"It is the same," replied Andraste.

"No, Andraste. It is not the same," responded Aldrich.

"Love drove my father mad. You may have anything from me, but not love. I do not love," said Andraste.

"And what you feel for your people? For your family? For Rhinauld?" asked Aldrich.

Andraste reached to the floor and threw his tunic at his exposed back. Aldrich took it from the floor, but he froze as he heard her moving. Andraste dressed quickly. Aldrich put his own shirt over his head.

"I am decent," informed Andraste.

"We should leave immediately," stated Aldrich. He still kept his back turned to her.

"No, it would cause undue attention. We will leave after the Emperor's personal guards have departed," countered Andraste.

"What about your men?" asked Aldrich.

"They are well hidden by now," responded Andraste.

Aldrich moved towards the door.

"No," ordered Andraste.

Aldrich obeyed. He reluctantly sat on a chair by her table, but he faced the fire, not her.

"You kissed me back," alleged Andraste.

"I am only human," responded Aldrich. His back was turned to her so he could not see the hurt on her face.

She sat upon the bed as they waited. Nearly two hours of uncomfortable silence passed before a tentative knock sounded on the door. Aldrich went to open it.

"They are gone. We were not discovered," informed Laelius.

Andraste picked up her pack in response. Laelius and Aldrich followed her out the door, down the stairways, through the tavern, and to the stables.

Chapter Sixteen

Aldrich and Laelius were leading the way at a brisk pace, while Brion and Andraste brought up the rear. Aldrich would not even look at Andraste, not even when she spoke to him.

"You two have quarreled again?" asked Brion as they left the main road. Andraste ignored her brother's question, but her cheeks blushed deeply.

"A lover's quarrel?" asked Maximianus over his shoulder.

"No!" yelled Andraste. Laelius turned his horse at the sound of her cry. Aldrich looked over his shoulder.

"I think the lady protests too much," commented Felix.

"It is nothing," called Brion. Aldrich and Laelius proceeded in the distance.

"That is enough from both of you," hissed Andraste.

"I have never seen the Commander so bothered," commented Otho. Felix nodded his head in agreement.

"Would you have ever thought our Commander would fall for a Southerner?" asked Maximianus.

"He is not so bad," alleged Felix.

"Silence!" ordered Andraste.

"Perhaps a song?" suggested Maximianus.

"Do not-" started Andraste. However, Felix had already started his song:

"I would give all that I possess
Just to see her face once more.
A man would I not be any less
To say it is her that I adore."

"Quiet!" ordered Andraste. Felix continued even louder than before:

"I would walk across the lands
Just to see her smile again.
I would fulfill all her demands
For my love will never wane."

Aldrich charged his horse farther ahead.

"Your lover is escaping, Commander," chastised Maximianus.

"They are under attack, you fools!" hissed Andraste. They urged their horses forward.

Aldrich had already drawn his great sword and was meeting a rider blow for blow. Laelius was meeting another horseman with his spear. Brion fired an arrow to the attacker beyond them.

"Imperial guards," confirmed Priscus.

"A trap?" asked Brion.

Aldrich was already fighting his third attacker. Aldrich struck the guard with a mighty blow. The man fell from his horse, his purple robes soaked with blood. Laelius hurled his spear at an approaching guard. By the time Andraste reached Laelius's side, Aldrich had already pursued the remaining three men into the woods. She could hear screams in the distance.

Seeing that Laelius was taking care of the last guard, she plunged into the woods after Aldrich. She followed the sounds of fighting, but then there was only silence. She hesitated before scanning the forest floor for tracks. She cautiously urged her horse forward. She stopped as she heard the sound of hooves coming towards her. Aldrich came into view.

"Are you hurt?" asked Andraste. He shook his head.

"You are covered in blood," stated Andraste.

"It is not mine," replied Aldrich. Andraste scanned him from head to toe.

"Shall we rejoin your men?" proposed Aldrich. He did not wait for a response. He passed her on the road, but avoided looking at her eyes.

"Their blades are poisoned. Are you sure you were not struck?" questioned Andraste.

"Your concern is superfluous," replied Aldrich.

"Why so unfriendly?" asked Andraste.

"Friendly would imply friendship, which we do not have. You expect unwavering loyalty and faith, but give neither. You have explained nothing regarding your memory loss, Sveinbiorn's imprisonment or even his history. Then there are the shadow powers! The list grows. You know more then you will say. How can I trust you? How can I blindly follow?" asked Aldrich.

"We go together. I do not expect you to follow," responded Andraste.

"And that is all of your reply?" inquired Aldrich.

"I will not bore you with my personal matters. As you already said, you are not my friend. In fact-- you are nothing to me," said Andraste.

She urged her horse forward to regain the lead. As they rejoined their companions, Otho opened his mouth to speak, but Andraste silenced him with a look. She seethed with wordless rage.

"Do you think they were the same guards who were at the village?" asked Maximianus.

"Too few to be the same party, but too many for scouts," answered Brion.

"So you think the woods will be riddled with Imperial guards from now on?" questioned Maximianus.

"We will go deeper into the woods," ordered Andraste, retaking the lead.

After a hard day of riding, Andraste bade her comrades to set up camp. A fog reached down from the mountains and the forest was particularly still.

"This is the last good night's sleep we may have for a while. Another two miles and we will have left the territory of the Ice Palace. No fires. Double the watch," said Andraste to her men.

She sat on her bedroll and began sharpening her daggers. Aldrich sat perfectly still and continued to his read his book.

"What are you reading?" asked Maximianus.

"It is regarding the First Republic," replied Aldrich, not looking up from his book.

"There is not enough light for reading," said Andraste.

"My eyes are fine," stated Aldrich. He continued reading. Maximianus turned his attention to Andraste.

"I do not recall. When did you arrive at the Ice Palace the first time?" asked Maximianus.

"It was shortly after my tenth summer. My uncle and Rhinauld's father thought that I could benefit from the company of women, so they sent me to be Fausta's apprentice," answered Andraste.

"Was that the best choice?" asked Otho, "No wonder you are so-"

"Choose the next word carefully," growled Felix. Otho fell silent.

"Rhiannon did not join you?" asked Aldrich. He closed his book.

"No," said Andraste. She could not shield the regret in her voice. She took a deep breath and continued, "Her father was a cruel man. He kept her close and seldom permitted her to leave the Salt Islands."

"Is it common for husbands and wives to live on different ends of the continents in the Island Kingdoms?" asked Aldrich.

"Fausta is not the wife of Rhinauld's father. She was forced to be his Muse against her will. The union resulted in my twin foster siblings. Fausta was granted her freedom, but she was required to leave her children behind. It was not a common situation," answered Andraste.

"I think those daggers are sharp enough," commented Felix.

Andraste put her weapons away.

"So you came to the Ice Palace in your tenth summer?" prodded Aldrich.

"Yes. I spent four years training there. When I reached my fourteenth year, I was summoned by the Emperor to return to the Citadel. He sent Rhinauld as his messenger. You have met Rhinauld. He did not wait at the village, which resulted in a skirmish that wrecked half the village," said Andraste.

She laughed at the memory and saw the look on Aldrich's face.

"Do not judge him so harshly. He wanted to see Fausta," admonished Andraste sadly. She fell silent.

"Why did the Emperor summon you?" inquired Aldrich.

"He gave me the choice that he gives all his daughters. I could marry or I could fight for the Empire," replied Andraste.

"At fourteen?" asked Aldrich scandalized.

"Is it not the same for the boys in your kingdom? At fourteen one can enlist in the Imperial Army," answered Andraste.

Aldrich held his tongue because he wanted her to continue.

"That is where I first met Laelius. He was one of the last surviving members of my father's people, the Valerians," said Andraste.

"You do not count all of the North as one people?" asked Aldrich.

"Before the Empire, the North possessed many clans, but no King. There were few towns or villages. My clan was composed of nomadic warriors," stated Andraste.

"What happened to them?" asked Aldrich.

"Most of our clan was wiped out in the War for Empire, by invasions, and then those who remained perished in my father's later wars," replied Andraste. Her words faded into the night as she thought about her people's past.

"So you met Laelius?" prodded Aldrich.

"Laelius was my first commanding officer. I have learned much from him. I worked my way through the ranks. We fought in the Wars in Alexius, Thoran, and Gardenia," responded Andraste.

"I was at Thoran," said Aldrich. He grimaced at the memory. The Empire had prevailed at expelling a foreign force from across the seas, but it had come at a heavy price. The Empire had not suffered such losses since the Black War.

"You were?" asked Andraste.

"In the rearguard," said Aldrich, "Where were you?"

"The vanguard with what we had assembled of the Victorious. There were only nine of us that you know at that point in time," responded Andraste.

"Ten, he knows Paulina," corrected Maximianus.

"Who were the originals?" inquired Aldrich.

"Laelius, Tobias, Otho, Maximianus, Nero, Hadrian, Valens and Felix," answered Andraste.

"How did they join?" questioned Aldrich.

"Not by choice," replied Otho.

"Speak for yourself," alleged Maximianus, "I am honored to serve the Commander."

"Maximianus hails from the North country like me. He entered the Imperial Army at fourteen and rose in the ranks. Tobias and I asked him to join us fairly early on," informed Andraste.

"And you?" asked Aldrich looking to Otho.

"My Commander gave me two options: death by her blade or join the Victorious," responded Otho.

"Otho led a rebellion in the Midlands. He is lucky that a Northern Commander spared him and his people," stated Maximianus.

"True. If it had been Varinia, I and my people would be dead," conceded Otho, "Varinia shows no hesitation. She takes lives like she is collecting apples in a basket. She wipes villages and towns off the map like in Odontown."

"Where is Odontown?" inquired Aldrich.

"Odontown does not exist anymore," answered Andraste. She did not look at Aldrich.

"Varinia often used Toxin as her henchman. Yes, I am very happy to have met this princess instead," said Otho.

"And yet, you are still here," commented Aldrich.

"I cannot return to my homeland, not after the rebellion," lamented Otho.

"He would miss us too much," retorted Maximianus.

"And the others, how did they join?" queried Aldrich.

"Nero had a choice similar to Otho's but he will tell you he benefited by his choice. Felix joined us of his own volition when our Commander asked. They knew each other in the Salt Islands. Valens sought us ought and challenged us all to duels," said Maximianus. He and Otho both laughed at the memory.

"Cato, Avitus, Thracius, Priscus, and Laurentius, were all rebels that our Commander converted to our cause," said Maximianus.

"You made these men choose between death and serving you? And you trust them?" asked Aldrich.

"I have only killed when it was absolutely necessary," stated Andraste.

"And prevented hundreds of deaths as well by your actions," admitted Otho grudgingly.

"Why do you stay?" Aldrich asked Hadrian, who had been listening to the exchange.

"No one but our Commander will change the Empire. No one else would challenge the Emperor," stated Hadrian.

"I had forgotten you were here," commented Otho, "Have you spoken since the Shadow Mountains?"

Hadrian kicked a pebble at his comrade and it hit Otho squarely in the forehead. The other men laughed.

"Who could speak with you around?" asked Maximianus.

"We should get some sleep. Our watch will be here soon enough," Andraste quieted them.

She rolled on her side. She wrapped her hood around her face to protect it from the Northern wind. Aldrich followed her example. He rolled on his opposite side, so that he did not face her and gradually fell asleep.

"You missed it, Laelius," Otho greeted the older warrior when they stopped at a stream to water their horses and refill their canteens.

"Missed what?" asked Laelius wearily.

"Commander told the prince our tale of becoming one big happy family," said Otho.

"This family needs more women," commented Valens. The men laughed.

"Quiet!" snapped Andraste.

"A little sensitive this morning?" inquired Otho.

"I heard it too. Silence," commanded Brion.

Andraste was at Brion's side. Her blade was already out and glowing red.

"Magic?" mouthed Andraste. Brion shook his head.

"Really big cat!" exclaimed Cato. Andraste turned to see where he was looking.

"That is a puma!" called Laelius.

"Not Demon," said Brion to Andraste.

"There are two," stated Valens.

"Are they not usually solitary?" asked Brion.

"They are also nocturnal," answered Laelius.

"They will still eat us for lunch," commented Otho. He had his bow drawn.

"Wait," said Andraste, "You have had all this chitchat, and they still have not attacked."

Andraste approached Laelius. He was closest to the large mountain cats.

"This is odd. I feel like they are waiting for something," said Laelius. He did not remove his eyes from the pumas.

The pumas were also watching them with their wide-set milky eyes. Their eyes were the color of a winter sky, and their fur ranged from golden to tinged with grey. They had large muscular hind legs and shorter front legs. Their paws were enormous.

"Are pumas usually that large?" asked Aldrich.

"Everything is larger in the north," answered Nero.

"Not the time," barked Laelius.

Andraste looked across the stream. She heard something approach from the western bank. It was coming directly for her. It was a puma unlike any she had ever seen. Its fur was white and its eyes were like ice. They seemed to stare right through her. It almost made no sound as it walked. Andraste felt that it wanted her to hear it approach.

"Now is a good time to use your voodoo powers, Commander," insisted Otho.

"Your powers will not work on me," said the Puma.

Her battle-tried Victorious could have been knocked over with a feather. The Puma leapt across the bank and landed a paw strike away from Andraste. It leaned forward and its nose touched Andraste's.

"Anima," greeted the Puma.

"Well met," said Andraste. She was grateful for all of her encounters with the Griffin and the other mythical creatures in the Ice Palace that had prepared her for this moment.

"The wolves said an Anima walked these woods once more," alleged the Puma.

Andraste did not flinch.

"So you have met others like me?" asked the Puma.

"None exactly like you," admitted Andraste.

She doubted the Griffin was as large as the Puma standing before her. She had met other large cats that spoke but none as magnificent as the Puma.

"Do you have other powers?" asked the Puma.

"Some of us do," responded Andraste.

"Can they defeat the ones that rise from the dead?" inquired the Puma.

"It is possible," replied Andraste.

The Puma circled her. Her horse started uncomfortably, but Andraste quieted him with her power. The Puma did not approve of her action.

"The Arisen have killed many of my warriors. We can take them down, but they keep coming. They multiply. The humans they kill join their numbers," stated the Puma.

"How many are there now?" asked Andraste.

"Eight hundred roam our hunting grounds," hissed the Puma, "Men created these monsters."

"One man created them. We travel north to defeat him," protested Andraste.

"Why would I trust your word? Men always lie," concluded the Puma.

"Do I look like a man to you?" asked Andraste. She slowly let down her hood.

"She-man, you are still a man cub," responded the Puma. However, the Puma leaned forth to sniff her once more. It looked at Andraste directly in her eyes. Andraste did not blink. The Puma backed off once more.

"The Arisen have driven you from your home?" asked Andraste.

"Yes," said the Puma. The Puma's tail twitched in irritation.

"You seek our help?" questioned Andraste.

"Yes," said the Puma. The tail twitched again.

"Lead on," ordered Andraste.

"Can we vote on this one?" Felix asked Laelius, but he was silenced by Laelius's glare.

Andraste was already proceeding into the woods after the Puma. Aldrich led his horse to follow Andraste. He was followed by Laelius and Brion and then the remaining Victorious. The Puma led them off the feeble trail and deep into the woods towards the mountain side. Andraste saw that they were heading towards caves.

"Light torches if you must. Your eyes are so inferior to ours," ordered the Puma.

Andraste nodded to her men to do so.

The Puma had them leave their horses in a cave near the entrance with a promise that no harm would come to them. They were led deep in to the caves. They passed all manners of beasts. They were led to a large cave. A giant bear, a stag, and an eagle were deep in conversation.

"So the Wolf did not lie," said the Bear as he smelled the humans approach.

"It is true?" asked the Eagle.

"Yes. I have found the Anima," purred the Puma.

"Things must be very wrong in the outside world, indeed, for an Anima to appear once more," commented the Stag.

"Silence," commanded the Bear.

"I have come for our warriors and then we will go after the Arisen," said the Puma, "The Anima and her companions are on their way north to challenge the Man-Emperor. My warriors and I will take out as many Arisen as we can to aid them in their progress."

"You still feel that all of the Arisen will not be beaten until their creator is slain?" asked the Bear. The Puma inclined her great head.

"Then we will go with you for one last battle," declared the Bear. The Puma and the Bear touched noses.

"Wait here," ordered the Puma to Andraste. The Puma padded silently down the cave into the darkness.

"What is the purpose of an Anima?" asked Maximianus.

"An Anima is a last resort of the universe trying to restore the balance. An Anima serves as a bridge for humans and creatures to communicate. There was once a time when your kind would speak with all of ours, but that time is nearly passed. There are few of our kind left who speak your tongue, and fewer still of your kind that can speak to the lesser creatures," explained the Bear. He fell silent.

No one else dared to ask a question. The silence dragged on.

"We will leave in the morning. The Arisen are strongest underneath the moon hours," said the Puma. Andraste had not even heard her return.

"You may use this cave to sleep," said the Bear. The creatures left them. The Stag even bowed to them before he left.

"Am I dreaming?" asked Felix. Valens pinched him mercilessly.

"No, then," said Felix.

They arranged themselves as comfortably as they could. Andraste was sandwiched between Aldrich and Brion. They sat on the floor with their backs against the cave wall. The silence was near unbearable.

"Why did you not return to the Ice Palace to serve? Did you have to serve in the Imperial Army?" asked Aldrich.

"I was not allowed to serve the Ice Palace," said Andraste.

"Why?" questioned Aldrich.

"She pleaded for Rhinauld's life after he invaded the Ice Palace," responded Brion when Andraste would not answer.

"And they would not let you join?" asked Aldrich.

"A warrior of the Ice Palace must be able to do whatever is asked of her. Mother's verdicts are ultimatums," replied Andraste.

"So you were forced to stay in the Imperial Army," concluded Aldrich.

"That is why Rhinauld and Andraste's deal was so perfect. If things had been different, she would have been freed from service," said Brion.

"But I became a traitor instead," lamented Andraste.

"What would you have done with your freedom?" asked Aldrich.

"Rhinauld, Henry and I were going to explore the other Ruins once Brion and Rhiannon were safely married and returned to the Salt Islands. And then, if we survived that ordeal, we would sail for the Old World," answered Andraste.

"You had no intention to be Empress?" inquired Aldrich.

"I will never be free in the North," stated Andraste.

"The Victorious have smashed heads and broken bones all across the Empire with would-be suitors," laughed Laelius.

Aldrich did not find this amusing.

"The best claim to the Empire would be through Andraste's hand. She is the only legitimate daughter of the Emperor," said Brion.

"Your half-siblings cannot inherit?" asked Aldrich.

"The North is divided in that opinion. One half support Andraste as the daughter of the Empress, and the other is divided into factions of support for the illegitimate children," explained Laelius.

"Who do you want to inherit after the Emperor?" asked Aldrich.

"Andraste," said Brion and Laelius in unison.

"Is that why you all call her Empress?" inquired Aldrich.

"We call her Empress at times because Rhinauld used to call her little Empress and it irritates her so," admitted Brion.

"You all are the monsters," muttered Andraste.

She took her head from her brother's shoulder. She felt Aldrich watching her. She did not understand the look in his eyes. She raised her knees to her chest and wrapped her arms around them. She put her head down and hoped to get some sleep.

Andraste was awakened by an enormous paw patting her boot.

"You will want to wake your men. If I do, they may die of fright," said the Puma.

The Puma padded off towards the center of the room. Andraste shook Brion awake. Laelius stirred as she did so. She looked for Aldrich. He was speaking to the Stag. She approached.

"The Stag was telling me this great joke" Aldrich started. Andraste started laughing. She could not help it.

"I am sorry," apologized Andraste. She could not stop laughing.

"I have not even told you the joke," bristled Aldrich.

Andraste composed herself and turned to look around the cave. All of her men were awake and on their feet. The Puma was not wasting any time. She was already heading out of the cave. Andraste hastened after the Puma. They were led out of the caves and into the frosty morning. The air was icily cold. Andraste could see her breath.

Their horses were waiting for them. The horses seemed unbothered by the assembled animals. Andraste saw scores of pumas, bears, and deer waiting for them. There were massive eagles circling in the sky. There were creatures that she could not even name. There were two Griffins. A large serpent that made her skin crawl as it slithered past her. On the crest of the hill was a pack of large black wolves with amber eyes. The biggest of the wolves stared at her. Andraste could have sworn that he bowed his head in acknowledgement, but he was gone as quickly as she had seen him.

The animals were moving out in groups. Andraste signaled for her men to mount their horses and they rode after them. Puma's plan was simple. Her warriors would hinder the progress of the Arisen, and Andraste's warriors would use any magic at their possession to dispose of them.

They smelled the first band of Arisen before they reached them. Andraste was glad that she had wrapped a scarf around her nose and mouth. She charged ahead at the first one she saw. He was a large brute. He was missing an eye. The other was glassy and watched her approach. His skin was gray and his long, greasy black hair blew him about him. He raised an arm to claw at her. Andraste felt Aldrich's phoenix before she saw it. It warmed her as it flew over her shoulder and struck the Arisen, and then the others behind him. The first Arisen became unanimated and fell to the ground twitching in his last moments. The same thing happened to the others before her that were touched by the phoenix. She disposed of the stragglers quickly with her Ruin sword.

"Do not let their blood touch you," called the Puma, "It will not affect my warriors, but it will affect you."

Andraste had seen such a thing occur. One of the guards on her patrol had defeated the Arisen, but the blood had touched his skin and he had transformed. She went among the corpses and quickly sliced off their heads. Aldrich rode forward to help her with the gruesome task. On one body she saw the armor of the Imperial Army. She looked away. She forced herself to count twenty-five heads, and then she and Aldrich returned to her comrades.

"Burn them," ordered Andraste.

Otho and Brion lit their arrows on fire and shot each of the corpses. The field became full of putrid smoke.

Laelius, Felix and Maximianus took the lead on the next attack.

Maximianus slashed his sword in front of him and waves of blue energy shot from his sword. The Arisen fell to their knees unable to move. Laelius and Felix moved among the corpses slicing of their heads. Once again Otho and Brion lit the corpses on fire with their arrows.

Valens and Hadrian took the next charge. Hadrian shot red lightning from his hands that slew any that approached too closely to their force, while Valens used both of his axes to chop through the Arisen. His axes glowed orange in the sunlight. Valens was careful not to get any blood on him or his comrades.

In the next wave of attackers, Thracius, Priscus, and Nero were on the front. Together they called down white lightning from the sky that wiped out the Arisen. Glaucio, Cato, Avitus, and Laurentius drove forward to remove the heads with their blades.

"Each wave brings more," commented Aldrich.

"They are drawn by the fighting," said Andraste.

The largest wave approached them yet. It was one-hundred-fifty strong.

"We will slow them down," called Puma.

Two of the packs of animals drove forward. Andraste winced at the sound of breaking bones, growling, hissing, ripping, that ensued. She took out her own bow and began shooting flaming arrows at the corpses. Aldrich's phoenix sored in front of the animal warriors, allowing them to defeat the Arisen. When his phoenix faded, Maximianus and Hadrian used their techniques to break down the Arisen.

"Do you think 300 so far?" asked Brion.

"500 to go, more or less," responded Laelius. He surveyed the condition of their men. They all knew they had a chance while the magic lasted but once that was gone it would be hopeless.

"I will take the next wave. It will give you a chance to rest," said Brion.

Andraste started to stop him, but Aldrich shook his head. Andraste remembered the lessons he had been receiving from Marcella and the Southern sorcerers.

"That has to be at least 200 hundred strong," said Otho.

"Thracius, Priscus, Nero on standby," ordered Andraste. The three men left the company to approach the front.

Brion waited for the Arisen force to get as close as possible. He held out his open palm and closed it. Every single Arisen soldier fell down. There was silence on the field. The animal warriors leapt forward ripping the soldiers to pieces. Thracius, Priscus, and Nero called down lightning on the corpses, which were enveloped in flames.

"I cannot do it again," said Brion. He looked as though he might fall from his horse. Andraste seized his reins.

"I will take him. You need your sword arm," said Aldrich. Andraste met his eyes but relented. She moved out of the way.

"What sort of magic was that?" asked Andraste.

"I have never seen the like," admitted Aldrich.

"300 left if Puma's calculations were correct," stated Laelius.

"But remember, she said that there were new ones created. The originals will be smarter and harder to destroy," warned Andraste.

"Do you think they will keep coming for us?" asked Laelius.

"I do not," answered Andraste.

They rode around the flaming field of corpses. Puma approached them.

"Do you sense more of them?" questioned Andraste.

"Not at the moment," replied Puma.

"When we can, we will need to stop. My men will need to rest and eat in order to continue the use of magic," said Andraste.

"I understand," said the Puma, "I know a place."

They rode clear of the field and the stench subsided. They kept riding.

"There will be songs about this one," said Otho lightly. However, no one was in the mood for jesting.

Puma took them to the top of a flat hill. It was spacious enough for humans, horses, and warrior creatures to stop.

"Do what you must. My warriors will protect you while you have your rest," said Puma. She retreated. Andraste moved to help Aldrich take Brion off his horse.

"Will he be okay?" asked Andraste.

"I think so," said Aldrich. He smiled at her reassuringly. Together they placed Brion on the ground. He was very pale. Andraste covered Brion with her cloak.

The others took places on the ground and started eating or tried to nap.

"Can you heal him?" asked Andraste.

"I cannot replenish magic. It seems to be exhaustion," answered Aldrich. He held out an apple to her from his bag. Andraste took it, but held it in her hands.

"You not eating is not going to help Brion," said Aldrich softly.

Andraste took a bite of the apple. Aldrich also forced rations and water on her. Andraste took them dutifully. She went to stand on the edge of the hill. She looked across the valley. It was uncommonly still. Almost everything that had once grown was now dead. The grass was brown. The trees were dead shells.

The wind blew fiercely and blew her hair about her. She walked around the top of the hill looking out as far as she could in every direction. She saw nothing that moved. She also realized that she was making her men nervous. She went and resumed her place by Brion's side. Aldrich was sitting against a rock and eating an apple. They sat for about an hour without talking.

"They come," called Puma from below.

"How many?" yelled Laelius.

"It looks like the full force," answered Puma.

Andraste rose to her feet and hurried to the sound of Puma's voice. She looked out and in the distance she could see the force approaching. Unlike the other waves of attackers, this group was organized. She could see that some of the Arisen were also different. They marched fluidly and were not as jerky as their previous attackers. Their eyes were clear, not glassy. They were better preserved. Their skin had more pallor then greyness. All of the pale Arisen wore Imperial Army armor and carried real weapons. They were surrounded by the inferior Arisen soldiers as well. The armored Arisen seemed to be ordering them through gestures. Andraste felt her blood run cold.

"How many?" yelled Laelius.

"400," answered Andraste. Her men joined her on the edge of the hill.

"We will not have time to retreat," said Puma.

"We will hold the hill. They cannot attack us all at once from here," said Andraste. She turned on her men, "We will wait for them to get as close as possible before we start attacking. When they do reach to this level, protect the magic users. Our lives depend on their survival."

"Yes, Commander," answered the Victorious in unison.

Andraste looked to Brion. He was still out cold. Puma had sent five of her own warriors to guard him. Four crouched around his sleeping body and the fifth peered out over the edge.

"What are those exactly?" asked Priscus.

Andraste looked down the hill. The Arisen were accompanied by gigantic beasts. Each creature was five times the size of a human. They looked like mixtures of all sorts of animals. They were hideous and the sounds they made were bone rattling.

"Monsters," answered Otho. No one else suggested a better opinion.

"Magical?" asked Nero.

"The ones I have come across have just been big and stupid," said Andraste.

"Finally something good," muttered Maximianus.

"Can you control them?" asked Aldrich.

"No," answered Andraste.

"The odds are about four to one. We have seen worse," urged Laelius.

"In that odds comparison, how many times have we faced things that came back to life after you killed them?" asked Felix.

"Steady. We have gotten this far. We just have to continue what we are doing," said Andraste, "We will continue with the rotation to try to conserve magical energy. Thracius, Priscus, Nero, you will be first."

"Yes, Commander," said the men.

Andraste crouched on the hill as the force approached.

Thracius, Priscus, and Nero stood in an even triangle around the hill. The Arisen and monsters divided and surrounded the hill from all sides. The Arisen soldiers started climbing up the sides of the hill. The first animal warriors were attacked. Andraste gave the signal. The skies darkened and white light lightning shot from the skies downwards on the Arisen troops. Arisen soldiers fell left and right.

Aldrich, Maximianus and Hadrian filled in the gaps between Thracius, Priscus, and Nero, and began unleashing their own powers as the lightning subsided. Aldrich's phoenix went swooping down from the east, Maximianus's blue waves from the west, and Hadrian's red lightning from the south. Otho lit his arrows on fire and shot them down onto the field of corpses.

Andraste stood beside Aldrich and waited. Each of the remaining Victorious took a post beside a magic user. It was quiet on the field. Then something unexpected happened. A volley of arrows came shooting up the hill at them.

"Shields," Andraste yelled as soon as she heard the sound. She deflected the first wave from herself and Aldrich. She heard Laelius yell out in pain as he was struck. Nero was down. Aldrich's phoenix went to Nero first and then Laelius. Andraste's attention turned back to the attackers as she heard screams of pain from below. The Arisen were proceeding up the hill and again clashing with the animal warriors.

"They are sending the full force at once. They know we cannot keep producing magic forever," stated Andraste once Aldrich's attention was back from Laelius and Nero.

She saw Glaucio take out his bow and began shooting flaming arrows at the Arisen. Many of the arrows he shot down the hill had been previously shot at them by the Arisen. Felix and Thracius laughed at his actions, but encouraged him.

"Valens to me!" called Andraste. The bulk of the Arisen force was heading up the trail to the hill. Valens joined her and she headed towards the trail head.

"Paramerion-" started Aldrich.

"Aldrich, stand in the center with Brion. You can heal my men. That is the most important task right now. Valens and I both have Ruin blades. We can fight at the front," said Andraste.

She was gone before Aldrich could protest. She did see that Aldrich did as she asked. From the center he could see their comrades better and be less of a target himself.

Another volley of arrows rained up from the hill. However, the wind seemed to be on their side this time. Most of the arrows never even made it up the hill. A few of the Arisen soldiers were starting to proceed past the animal warriors. Andraste sliced the head off the first one that approached her. Valens quickly disposed of the second. The other Victorious were busy keeping the climbing Arisen from reaching the summit of the hill.

Again and again the Arisen would fall, and resume climbing the hill with desperation. Andraste stopped counting how many she battled and cut down. Her blade flashed red all around her. Andraste saw Aldrich's phoenix fly out of the corner of her eyes towards the opposite end of the hill. She wondered which of her men was down.

Three Arisen soldiers attacked Valens at once and she ran to his aid. Slicing off the head of the largest attacker, she turned to catch another one coming up the hill.

The first Arisen officer approached. His eyes burned with amaranthine flames. He watched Andraste. He calculated. Andraste charged. However, Hadrian's red bolt of lightning struck the Arisen officer first, who fell to his knees. Andraste sliced his head off immediately.

White lightning struck from the sky in every direction, more powerful than the first time. The animal warriors were starting to be overrun. The white lightning gave time for many of the animal warriors to escape up the hill and regain their footing. Aldrich's phoenix swept down the hill to protect the animal warriors that were farthest away. It was crowded on top of the hill, but they stood their ground. The animal warriors fought at the front with Andraste and Valens. Puma went shooting down the hill barreling into the first monster with all of her might. Some of her puma warriors followed behind and together brought down a second monster. Andraste saw that the monster bled red, not black like the Arisen.

Ten Arisen officers had made it up the hill. Their armor gleamed in the sunlight. Their eyes burned violet fire. Their attention seemed to be focused on her. They acted at once, all approaching with inhuman speed. Behind them came a wave of the Arisen soldiers.

Andraste felt her heart race as she realized there was no more white or red lightning, or blue waves. Her magic users had exhausted their powers. However, they had drawn their weapons and were fighting valiantly. They guarded the unconscious form of Brion.

Valens and Andraste were back to back fighting. Aldrich's phoenix attacked four of the officers and then he was there himself. The ten officers lay at their feet, but the Arisen soldiers were upon them. Two great bears jumped at the soldiers and grappled with them. They went over the edge. Andraste and Valens charged forward to aid them, sword and axes swinging before them. Aldrich sent his phoenix out to heal Avitus, who had been struck by an arrow.

The Arisen kept swarming up the hill. Andraste turned to check on her men, and then she saw the Arisen officer behind Aldrich. The Arisen officer struck with his blade before Andraste could call out. Aldrich went down.

Andraste charged to Aldrich's aid. She knew that she would not be fast enough. The Arisen officer raised his blade again. Andraste raised her blade. She knew she was too far away, but she brought her sword down as if she could strike. She screamed. Andraste felt something inside of her awaken. Her body pulsated with unknown power.

As her blade moved through the air, a ruby-scaled dragon rose from her blade. It was the largest spirit animal that she had ever seen. It rose through the air breathing red fire at the Arisen and monsters. When its fire touched her men or the animal warriors, it seemed only to strengthen them.

She reached Aldrich's side. He was already getting to his feet. He was shaken, but it looked like he had only been stunned. She raised a hand to his wound and gold light emerged from her fingers. Aldrich spoke to her, but she did not understand. Andraste heard her men cheering as the last of their attackers fell to the fire breathing dragon.

The world went woozy. She did not know how to stop the dragon. It rained hot fiery hell upon the hill. The fire lit all of the Arisen corpses and made them disappear. She could not make it stop. Aldrich caught her as she fell. Andraste saw Brion had arisen. He raised his hand and the spirit dragon disappeared. Brion fell to his knee. For Andraste, the world went black.

"Her pulse is very weak," said Aldrich. Brion struggled to Aldrich's side. Andraste was barely breathing.

Brion made a circle in the air and made the five pointed star as he had seen Andraste do. A faint blue star emerged in the air. He cut his hand, and dropped the knife on the ground. He threw droplets of blood into the shape. The air shimmered.

"What are you doing?" cried Aldrich.

"Sveinbiorn Eldgrimson, Sveinbiorn Eldgrimson, Sveinbiorn Eldgrimson," bade Brion.

"That is dark magic," said Nero.

Nothing happened. Brion waited. He tried again. Brion calculated their chances, and then picked the knife from the ground. Ever so lightly he cut Andraste's hand and raised her palm to the center of the blue star.

"Sveinbiorn Eldgrimson, Sveinbiorn Eldgrimson, Sveinbiorn Eldgrimson," commanded Brion.

"You have no right to call me," answered Sveinbiorn.

"She is dying," said Brion.

The air shimmered before them and Sveinbiorn appeared. He dropped to one knee and surveyed Andraste.

"She is beyond my care. I know somewhere that is near here," said Sveinbiorn.

He transformed into his full-sized tiger form. The Victorious recoiled. Aldrich did not remove his hands from Andraste.

"Demon!" cried Nero. He stepped back in alarm.

"Put her on my back," ordered Sveinbiorn. Brion tried to raise himself to his feet, but he did not have the strength. Aldrich hesitated.

"If you love her, you will put her on my back, and come without question. I cannot do it alone. She will die, if we do not make haste," said Sveinbiorn.

Aldrich took Andraste in his arms without a second thought. Sveinbiorn lowered himself to the ground so that Aldrich could climb on his back. Aldrich held Andraste tightly to him and with the other arm held onto Sveinbiorn's neck.

"Find shelter. We will return to you when she is healed," said Sveinbiorn. Without another word, the demon leapt into the air, and within seconds, their comrades were out of sight.

Sveinbiorn ran through the air as if he was on the ground. It did not seem to matter to him that the ground was hundreds of feet below. Aldrich was a courageous man, but as he looked downwards, he began to lose his nerve. He looked to Andraste instead. He kept his gaze on her face until they began their descent. They had reached tall mountains with icy peaks. The winds blew fiercely and chilled him to the bone.

Sveinbiorn's paws hit the ground. Aldrich saw that they had reached a passageway between two mountains.

"You must enter there. I cannot follow. The enchantments still hold and ward off demons. You will be safe enough. Go down the passage until you find the pools. Put her in them. The waters will cleanse and restore her to health. Make haste, Aldrich Caelius," ordered Sveinbiorn.

Sveinbiorn lowered to the ground, so that Aldrich could slide off his back. Aldrich did not look behind him as headed into the dark passageway. However, as he entered through the doorway, tiny blue lights began to emerge on the cave walls. They guided his way down a winding passageway and steep stairs that led to emerald pools. A second carved stone staircase led into the emerald waters.

Aldrich slowly proceeded down the stairs into the pool. The water was pleasantly warm. Steam rose from the surface. The pool was deeper than he had expected. He stepped deeper into the pool, careful to keep Andraste's head above water. He watched her carefully. Her breathing was beginning to stabilize and her color to return. She even stirred in his arms. His own heart stopped pounding and returned to its normal rhythm. He looked up to the ceiling and saw that the history of the Republic was depicted in tiles around the dome. He began to feel drowsy.

"Return," ordered Sveinbiorn. Even though the demon was many miles above the surface, it felt as though the demon was standing right next to him.

Aldrich shook himself. Hastily he removed them from the pool. However, the waters were so inviting.

"Aldrich Caelius," commanded Sveinbiorn.

Aldrich forced himself to exit the pool. He slowly made the climb up the stairs and down the passageway to the outside world.

Sveinbiorn looked relieved to see him. The tiger's tail stopped flicking.

"Come get the things I acquired," bade Sveinbiorn.

Aldrich gently laid Andraste down in the warmth of the cave. He proceeded towards the doorway and began to feel the unforgiving winds of the North. He approached cautiously and found that in his absence the demon had obtained thick Northern clothing, blankets, furs, and rations for Andraste and himself. He picked up the items and Sveinbiorn ignored him.

"Little one," called Sveinbiorn. His tone changed drastically when he addressed Andraste. Andraste slowly raised her head towards his voice.

"You need to change. Then you can sleep as long as you like. I will watch over you," promised Sveinbiorn.

Aldrich handed her the change of clothes and turned his back.

"My men?" asked Andraste.

"All accounted for," replied Aldrich.

"Sveinbiorn how-" started Andraste.

"We will talk later, change and sleep, little one," said Sveinbiorn.

Andraste did as she was told. She was all too grateful for the fur lined boots and coat that Sveinbiorn had brought for her. However, after she was changed, she sat on the cave floor. By the time Aldrich had wrapped the blankets around her, she was fast asleep. Aldrich changed quickly. He checked on Andraste and then approached halfway up the passageway.

Sveinbiorn sat as close to the doorway as he could. His great head rested on his front paws, but he raised it as Aldrich approached.

"She sleeps. She would not have survived without your aid," said Aldrich. Sveinbiorn did not make a response.

"What is this place?" asked Aldrich.

"A great time ago before your world began, this was a sacred place of healing. Although, those who frequented these waters are now mostly gone from this world," replied Sveinbiorn.

"How did you know of it?" inquired Aldrich.

"Such places are known to my kind," said Sveinbiorn.

"Your kind?" questioned Aldrich.

"Demons," answered Sveinbiorn. The tiger's great eyes were filled with self-loathing as he issued the word.

"She does not see you as such," said Aldrich.

"My sister is more kind then the majority of her race. Truly, I think if I am half-demon, she is half-angel," replied Sveinbiorn.

"Sister?" repeated Aldrich, "Then the Emperor is a demon?"

"We share the same human mother," stated Sveinbiorn.

"She keeps many secrets," said Aldrich.

"She trusts you more than most. She will tell you all in time. Our uncle meddled with her memories. She has seen more than most humans can bear," responded Sveinbiorn.

"Is that why her nightmares are so disorienting?" asked Aldrich. Sveinbiorn nodded his great head.

"What can be done?" asked Aldrich.

"Forgive her," replied Sveinbiorn, "There are things that she had not told you because she does not remember. You will have to discover them together."

"Why do you and Mother not tell us everything?" asked Aldrich.

"It is a request from our uncle," responded Sveinbiorn.

"Why would a demon and a Ruin Spirit pay a human such respect?" questioned Aldrich.

"Our uncle is not what he seems. However, it is his right to explain everything to Andraste after the war is won," said Sveinbiorn. He lowered his great head to his paws, signaling that the conversation was over.

Aldrich quietly returned down the hall to check on his patient. Andraste slept soundly, she did not even readjust as he sat down beside her. The rejuvenating powers of the waters also carried him into a deep slumber.

He awoke at dawn to hear Sveinbiorn pacing restlessly at the front of the cave. Aldrich picked up the rucksack and swung it over his shoulder. He picked up Andraste, wrapped in all of the blankets, and headed towards the mouth of the cave.

"I have found the Victorious. They have taken refuge at the Summit. They are anxious to have their Commander returned to them," said Sveinbiorn.

"Let us go," replied Aldrich.

Sveinbiorn lowered to the ground, so that Aldrich could climb on. Once Andraste was secured, Sveinbiorn once more ran through the sky towards the rising sun.

Chapter Seventeen

Andraste woke and found herself in a feather bed under thick fur blankets. There was a red canopy above her and a fire blazing in a fireplace. The walls were made of stone.

"Easy," said Brion. He put a hand on her shoulder to push her gently back down into her pillows.

"Where are we?" asked Andraste.

"The Summit," replied Brion. Andraste frowned.

"I have been out for a week?" questioned Andraste.

"Yes," answered Brion.

"If any of us are recognized, we will all die," stated Andraste.

"There was no choice. You were beyond my or Aldrich's care. That use of magic was extraordinary," said Brion.

"What was it?" inquired Andraste.

She felt as though her head would break in two.

"Spirit dragon," answered Brion.

"Is everyone alright?" questioned Andraste.

"Our men are all accounted for. The animal warriors lost some, but it would have been a lot worse if Aldrich had not been there. Puma and the other Anima send you their thanks," answered Brion.

"And Aldrich?" inquired Andraste.

"He is fine," replied Brion, "He has been by your side most of the time, but it was his turn to sleep."

"I had the strangest dream," said Andraste.

"Sveinbiorn was here. I do not know all of the details. Once you were back with me, he departed to attend his duties in the South. You owe him your life," said Brion.

"We have duties as well. We need to leave at once," affirmed Andraste.

"We are actually relatively safe here. If you will stop arguing, I will tell you what has transpired in the North during our absence," stated Brion.

Andraste held her tongue.

"When you were exiled, acts of rebellion started all across the North. As you know these acts of rebellion turned into Civil War, which has escalated. The rebellions in the North have led to rebellions all across the Empire. As the North is divided, the Imperial Army cannot combat all of the areas. The Southern Resistance is approaching at a rapid pace. The Summit has joined the Northern Resistance. We are currently guests of Lady Moira. Personally, I think she is smitten by Aldrich and his southern charm," said Brion.

"Do we know where the Emperor is?" asked Andraste.

"He has barricaded himself in the Citadel," answered Brion, "That is enough news for now. I will let the others know you are finally awake. They have all been worried."

Andraste pulled the covers up around her. Her head ached exceedingly.

"Take this and eat this," ordered Brion.

He handed her a pill and a plate of food. Andraste consumed both. The pain in her head began to subside. Brion left the room. Andraste picked up a brush from the bed side table and brushed the tangles out of her hair. She paused as she heard a knock on her door. Aldrich stood in the doorway. She put the brush down quickly.

"Are you well?" he asked.

"I am fine," replied Andraste.

"May I bring you anything?" offered Aldrich.

"I require nothing," said Andraste.

He stood awkwardly in the doorway. Andraste thought of the Southern rule of not being alone without a chaperone. He stared at the ceilings tiles, and she realized he was thinking the same thing.

"You were struck during the battle. Are you-" Andraste started.

"You healed me," answered Aldrich.

"I see," responded Andraste. Aldrich shifted uncomfortably.

"If I am not your friend, then why did you come to check on me?" asked Andraste.

"You are still troubled by our quarrel in the woods? I am sorry I ever spouted such nonsense. For a while now I have regarded you as-" started Aldrich.

Aldrich heard the sound of several Victorious coming down the hall. He bowed to Andraste and hastily left the room. She watched his retreat in confusion.

"Already came to visit you did he?" asked Otho as he watched the prince retreating down the hall.

"Careful," growled Laelius.

"And why should he not? He has traveled with us, hosted us, brought us our families, protected us, healed our brothers, and fought with us," said Maximianus.

"Have a little crush do we?" asked Otho.

Otho was rewarded with a punch in the gut from Maximianus. Andraste laughed at them.

"Remember how fast Aldrich moved when Sveinbiorn said if you love her, you will come?" asked Maximianus. The men turned to look at Andraste. She blushed seven shades of pink to red.

"He had a debt to repay. That is all," said Andraste.

"Would you jump on a demon tiger and fly into the sky to the unknown in order to repay a debt?" asked Otho to Maximianus. The large warrior shook his head.

"That is enough," said Laelius.

The Victorious proceeded to tell Andraste the same news that Brion had already told her. Brion interceded after an hour and made them leave so that she could rest. Once she was rested, she went to pay a visit to their hostess. She was directed to the library where she found Aldrich reading to Lady Moira.

Andraste paused to listen to his voice. His deep voice was ideal for reading aloud. He was reading an excerpt from an astronomy text.

"Commander, at last you are awake. I welcome you to the Summit," greeted Moira. Aldrich closed the book.

"I will not interrupt you. I just came to thank you for your hospitality," said Andraste, directing her words to Moira.

"Nonsense. You and your company have defeated 900 Arisen. By the time bards compose their ballads, I am sure it will be 9,000. Although 900 is plenty enough! By the gods! Your men have been very limited regarding the details. Especially this Southern prince- I cannot get anything out of him," cried Moira.

"It is nothing we want to remember," said Andraste softly.

"Are you feeling better?" asked Aldrich.

"Yes," answered Andraste.

"Do you need to sit?" questioned Aldrich. He rose and offered her his chair.

"No, thank you. I need to walk about a bit," replied Andraste.

Aldrich put the book on the chair. He offered her his arm.

"Our customs are different in the North. Here when a man offers a woman his arm, it means they have an understanding," stated Andraste.

"You do not look well," protested Aldrich. He had not removed his offered arm.

"Take his arm, my Empress. I will not tell a soul," promised Moira.

Andraste took his offered arm and was glad to lean on him. She did feel dizzy.

"I will return her to her brother," said Aldrich.

He bowed his head to Moira. She seemed as if to protest, but Aldrich was already leading Andraste down the hall.

"Thank the gods, you entered. I thought I was going to have to read to her all day. That woman can turn anything into an innuendo," said Aldrich when they were down the hall.

He released her arm. Andraste let his arm go in surprise. He looked at her curiously.

"Are all Northern women so forward?" asked Aldrich.

Andraste blushed. She looked away. Aldrich still studied her. He seemed amused by her discomfort.

"Astronomy lessons?" asked Andraste.

"It seemed the most innocent thing in the library," explained Aldrich. Andraste giggled and Aldrich glanced down at her.

"I would like to learn more about the stars when this business is over," admitted Andraste.

"You should return to the Southern capital and see the observatory," suggested Aldrich. Andraste smiled at the thought, but it quickly faded.

"Are you strong enough to ride?" asked Aldrich.

"I am fine," lied Andraste.

Aldrich's sapphire eyes studied her. Wordlessly, he offered her his arm again. Andraste did not take it. She grasped her hands behind her back.

"I am fine," she repeated, trying to sound more convincing as she started down the hall.

"Cannot a warrior lean on another warrior?" asked Aldrich. He smiled.

Andraste paused. She took his arm and leaned into him. When she glanced up at his face, he was smiling. They walked around the courtyard, which had been turned into a garden. Her face fell as she saw a group of men walking down the path towards them. They wore full Imperial Armor and their red capes swept behind them imposingly.

"Who are they?" asked Aldrich.

Andraste did not answer, but she dropped his arm and her hand went to her hilt. The act did not go unnoticed by the approaching men. They stopped several paces away.

"Easy, Commander, we just came to pay our respects," said the tallest of the soldiers.

"Mikhael?" asked Andraste.

The soldier stepped forward and grasped Andraste's arm in his right, and embraced her with his left in the Northern fashion. He eyed Aldrich suspiciously.

"Southerner?" asked Mikhael.

"He is with me," answered Andraste.

"I can see that," responded Mikhael.

"Or you are with him?" commented one of the guardsmen. Mikhael silenced the guard with a look.

"Aldrich this is Mikhael. He and his brother fought under my command at Thoran. He used to be my second-in-command when I lead my squadrons," introduced Andraste.

"I joined the rebellion after your exile," Mikhael said sheepishly and then he added, "A large part of the Army defected at that point."

"You still wear Imperial armor?" asked Andraste.

"We still serve the Empire," answered one of the soldiers.

Andraste scanned the faces of his fellow soldiers. There were some that she knew and others that she did not. She grasped hands with each of them. Mikhael extended his hand to Aldrich, and the other soldiers followed his example. Aldrich seemed to relax.

"Is it true about Matthias and Tobias?" inquired Mikhael.

"Matthias was murdered by Varinia, and Tobias lost in a duel to me that Varinia had ordered," confirmed Andraste. She kept her voice even and looked each of the guardsmen in the eye.

"At least the other four squadrons could return to the North. It would have been a slaughter," said one of the soldiers.

"Any word on Varinia's whereabouts?" asked Andraste.

"No, but she is being hunted by your brother, Titus," replied a soldier.

"Did you know he is here?" asked Mikhael.

"For how long?" inquired Andraste uncertainly.

"About a month. He is leading the Northern Resistance," said Mikhael, "Anyway, my unit is about to be deployed. I just wanted to pay my respects. Give my best to Laelius."

"Olga let us stay at her farm. She said to let you know that she is proud," said Andraste, so only Mikhael could hear.

They grasped hands again and embraced with their other arms. Then the tall soldier turned and walked away.

"Mikhael," called Andraste.

"Yes, Commander," said Mikhael. He turned smartly to address her.

"Fortune favors the brave," Andraste said in farewell.

Mikhael saluted her as did the other soldiers. Andraste returned the salute. She watched the soldiers depart the garden.

"Empress? Commander? Princess? It must be very confusing being you," commented Aldrich.

"I am Paramerion," said Andraste.

"Where do you think they are headed?" asked Aldrich.

"Perhaps the Citadel," suggested Andraste, "We should leave in the morning."

"Worried someone else will defeat the Emperor?" teased Aldrich.

"I am worried he will kill them all," replied Andraste. Aldrich's smiled faded.

"I am going to speak with Titus," announced Andraste.

Aldrich moved to follow her.

"Titus is not like Brion. He fought in the Black Wars. He will kill a Southerner on sight. I know it is not enjoyable, and you will suffer cruelly, but the safest place for you is with Lady Moira," alleged Andraste.

Aldrich grimaced.

"Let me send one of the Victorious with you. You are not well," said Aldrich.

"I am fine," stated Andraste.

Her strength had returned to her as she watched her countrymen depart. She realized once more that she did not have time to waste. Aldrich bowed to her and left without another word.

Andraste followed the path where she had seen Mikhael and the soldiers depart. It led out of the castle and to a sea of red tents. Andraste's breath caught in her throat. She had not seen so many Imperial troops gathered in one place since Thoran. She composed herself and walked towards the center of the encampment. Many soldiers stopped and stared, many saluted, and many greeted her as Empress. Others came out of tents or from training areas as they heard the name Andraste Valerianus.

As she reached the largest of the tents in the center encampment, a man came out to greet her. Her brother was colossal. He was all muscle. He took after his mother's people and had blonde hair and blue gray eyes. He had grown a full beard. He did not look pleased to see her.

"Sister, have you finally come to witness the war you started?" asked Titus.

"If not me, then one of my siblings would have," answered Andraste. She concealed her surprise as Titus smiled.

"True," said Titus. He towered over her. Andraste looked up at him, unflinching.

"Your adventures have reached us in the North. You have done the Empire proud," Titus said finally. He extended her his arm. She grasped it. She saw new scars across his arm. Her hand lingered on them.

"I am well enough," said Titus.

He beckoned her to follow him into the tent. He held the tent flap open for her. He poured her a glass of wine and then sat in a chair. Andraste sat in another.

"Have you come to join us?" asked Titus as he sipped from his own wine glass.

"You know what I must do," stated Andraste.

"Then you do mean to kill father?" inquired Titus.

"Yes," confirmed Andraste.

"You are the craziest of us all. You have failed once already. Why did you come?" questioned Titus.

"I came for advice," admitted Andraste.

"Really?" Titus seemed surprised. He set down his glass, and then he asked, "Well then, little sister, what do you want to ask?"

"Do you think the Emperor is beyond saving?" asked Andraste.

"If you have to ask that, then you are not the one to go," responded Titus.

"You know he cursed me?" inquired Andraste. Titus nodded.

"When I was cursed, it made me begin to wonder if he had been cursed. Is a curse what changed him? Do you not remember? The father of our childhood is so very different from the man he is now. What if there was a way to bring him back?" questioned Andraste.

"Andraste, you are no school girl. You are a battle-tried warrior. Probably the fiercest warrior of our age, and it gives me no pleasure to admit it. You must kill him when you have the chance. Any doubt on your part and you will die. If you die, then all of our brothers and sisters will die. We have already lost six. Our men and our people will die, and the Empire will fall. You know this to be true," said Titus.

"I just had to ask," rejoined Andraste.

"Why did you not ask Brion?" asked Titus.

"You loved our father once. Brion never has. He would not understand," said Andraste softly. She took a sip from her wine.

"Well then a toast to the father we once knew," replied Titus. He held up his glass and Andraste hit it with her own glass.

"Where are you headed?" inquired Andraste.

"Come to spy for the Southern Resistance?" asked Titus.

"The 'Southern' Resistance is composed of the South, the West, the North and even men from the Island Kingdoms. It would better be named the Imperial Resistance," replied Andraste defensively.

"I am teasing. The Emperor's forces are walled up in the Citadel. We are laying siege. Every few days, I rotate the front lines with reinforcements. We can wait him out," alleged Titus.

"You think he will surrender?" asked Andraste.

"No, but we knew you were coming from the *Imperial* Resistance," replied Titus.

"So you are going to let me do your dirty work," concluded Andraste.

"I do not have your power or the Victorious. Most of the sorcerers remained loyal to the Emperor. We are at a distinct disadvantage," admitted Titus.

"I understand," said Andraste.

Titus studied her for a moment. He set down his glass of wine and rose.

"I had something saved for you. I thought we would meet at some point," said Titus.

He rummaged in the back of the tent and produced her Imperial Armor. It had been repaired, buffed and shone like new. Andraste was touched by his gesture.

"Thank you," she said gruffly.

"As much as I hate to admit it, you are the one who will win this battle. No one else had the courage to confront the Emperor. It has been for you that the Army defected. It has been your name that even commoners have come to our cause. There is no one else in the North who will keep it united and end this civil war once the Emperor is slain," stated Titus.

"Once this is over, I have no intention of being Empress," vowed Andraste.

"You may not have a choice. If you are elected at the Northern Council-" started Titus.

"You have just as much right as I. It is my opinion that it will be between you and Varinia. I will not support her. She may be even more heartless then the Emperor," said Andraste.

"If I meet with her before the Northern Council, I will end her. Only then will Matthias be avenged," swore Titus.

Titus threw her a bundle. Andraste examined it. He had also had one of her uniforms snuck out of the palace. Andraste went behind the screen to change into her uniform. When she emerged, Titus helped her secure her armor. Titus glanced at the phoenix mark on her shoulder.

"The curse?" asked Titus.

"We found a magic in the Ruins that cleansed it," replied Andraste.

"We?" questioned Titus.

"Aldrich Caelius, leader of the Imperial Resistance and future King of the Southern lands," answered Andraste.

"Is it wise to trust a Southerner with our future? Our people's future?" inquired Titus.

"I owe him my life. If not for him, I would not be standing here," replied Andraste.

They heard cheering come from outside. The troops were chanting Victorious.

"Never alone for long, are you," stated Titus.

Andraste smiled. Once within her armor, she felt like herself again. She felt stronger, more confident. She rose and went out into the sunlight. All of her Victorious, Brion and Aldrich had ridden into the camp. She saw their horses were fully packed and ready for their journey.

"Farewell, sister, remember what we spoke of," said Titus. He held out his hand to her. She took it and stood on her tiptoes to kiss his cheek.

"What was that for?" Titus asked in surprise.

"In case we do not meet again, brother," replied Andraste. She turned to reach her horse.

"If I had known you would become a genteel lady, we would have sent you to the south years ago," Titus called after her.

"Yes, but if that were the case, her swordsmanship might be lacking," commented Laelius.

Andraste laughed, but it faded as Titus's eyes rested on Aldrich. Aldrich held her horse's reins. He eyed Titus warily.

"You must be Aldrich Caelius," said Titus. His eyes were as cold as steel. Andraste and the Victorious froze. There were whispers throughout the crowd.

"I remember you from Thoran. It was a well-fought battle," conceded Titus.

Andraste wondered what had taken place at Thoran that she had not witnessed.

Aldrich held Titus's gaze until Titus looked away. Andraste mounted her horse and Aldrich passed her the reins. Brion was too angry to even acknowledge her. He gazed with blatant hatred at Titus.

"We ride," commanded Andraste.

She urged her horse forward and the Victorious thundered after her amid the applauding and cheering of her countrymen.

Andraste was flabbergasted as they rode. As they left the Summit, every village they came to was burned and every field a battleground. Unmarked graves lined the side of the road. The roads, which were usually pristine, were full of holes and debris.

In the time that she had been gone, she hardly even recognized her country. Brion and her Victorious felt the same effect. They were quiet, and even Otho did not make jokes. Aldrich said nothing and asked no questions, sensing their apprehension and sorrow.

Andraste set her bedroll next to Aldrich's when they set up camp.

"Tell me about Thoran," requested Andraste. She knew the Victorious were listening.

"You were there," responded Aldrich.

"No, but I want to know about your- the Southern troops' efforts," entreated Andraste.

"We fought well," replied Aldrich.

"You will never be part of the Victorious unless you can tell a good story," informed Avitus.

"Half of Otho's deeds are made up," added Maximianus. There was some feeble laughter from the men.

"Well," said Aldrich and he realized he had a captive audience, "As I mentioned before, we were in the rearguard since Southern troops are not allowed to fight alongside the Northern."

"Too cowardly," jibed Nero.

Andraste silenced Nero with an icy stare.

"The Northern line began to fall," said Aldrich.

"Of course it did- that was Titus's position," alleged Brion.

"That must have been when we had boarded the ships," commented Valens.

"Do you want me to tell this tale or not?" asked Aldrich irritably. The men fell silent.

"We disobeyed the ultimatum. I gave the order to push forward. We left our position to go to the aid of the Northerners. We fought together and pushed the invaders back and then we pursued," said Aldrich.

"You are really bad at telling stories," stated Otho.

"That is quite a feat, you should embellish your deeds," commented Maximianus.

"I remember now hearing about the Southern valor," said Laelius.

"You still do not remember?" Brion asked Andraste.

"Well that is because of what happened after the battle. Do you recall?" asked Felix. He grinned wickedly.

"What?" inquired Brion.

"Andraste and Rhinauld went on a three week binge celebrating? The drinking games? The cross-dressing incident?" asked Otho. Even Laelius lost his composure at the memory.

"Cross-dressing incident?" repeated Aldrich.

"The Emperor ordered Andraste and Rhinauld to return to the Citadel for a ball. Some King had made a prestigious offer for Andraste's hand. So dutifully Andraste and Rhinauld came, but Andraste came dressed as

Rhinauld, and Rhinauld came dressed as Andraste," howled Laelius.

"Not our finest moment," admitted Andraste.

"The King would not accept either of the princesses," laughed Felix.

Aldrich laughed along with the Victorious. Laelius wiped tears from his eyes.

"The Emperor never commanded Andraste to appear at another ball," said Otho.

"That is when you and Rhinauld convinced the Emperor to enter into your agreement about joining houses," said Laelius, "Thank goodness it is Rhiannon and Brion marrying. God help us from any spawn the two of you would produce."

"Can you not still marry Rhinauld?" questioned Aldrich.

"In the Island Kingdoms siblings cannot marry into another family twice. It is regarded as incest," answered Laelius.

"Is it not the same in the South?" asked Brion.

"It is unusual, but there is no taboo," said Aldrich. He glanced at Andraste.

"But Rhinauld would not marry Andraste, even if she did like him," said Otho.

"Because of Henry, of course," said Brion.

"Henry? Because he hates Andraste?" asked Aldrich. He raised his eyebrows.

"No, because of Henry," insinuated Brion. Aldrich did not follow.

"Rhinauld is a lover of men," specified Laelius. Aldrich was too stunned by the revelation to respond.

"Now that you have been inducted into the Victorious, you will find my brave warriors gossip more than any sewing circle. But keep it down now, my hens, I am trying to sleep," yawned Andraste.

The Victorious talked into the night, but they kept their voices low. They told many stories of the past and of lost comrades. Andraste tucked her hood around her face to ward off the chill of the night. Winter was fast approaching and the air was painfully cold. She felt Aldrich lay down beside her on his blankets. She watched him in the darkness.

"Come here for warmth. I will not challenge your honor. Look, the others will do it as well," whispered Andraste.

For once Aldrich did not fight her. She let him under her covers and he placed his blankets on top of them. She pulled the blankets over her head and he followed her example.

"It is warmer already," relented Aldrich. She lay on her side so that her back touched his. She felt him roll on his other side.

"Andraste," began Aldrich.

"I do not want to fight. Not tonight," Andraste said sleepily.

"I am not fighting," protested Aldrich.

"Uh-huh," said Andraste. As he laughed, she felt his breath against her neck.

"Andraste," Aldrich began again.

"Go to sleep," she whispered. Aldrich watched her. She was already asleep. Aldrich did not sleep at all that night.

They had reached the Citadel. They heard it before they saw it. They could hear pounding and smashing.

"Battering rams?" asked Maximianus.

"Yes," verified Laelius as he listened.

They could see flashes of green and purple light through the tree tops.

"Sorcery," confirmed Brion before he was asked.

"Let us not go that way," suggested Otho.

"Is there another way?" asked Aldrich.

"Yes," replied Andraste.

"The labyrinth?" asked Brion. Andraste nodded.

They rode away from the light and around the frozen lake. They came to large burial mounds. Small purple flowers bloomed from the graves in abundance.

"Tombs of the Fallen from the War for Empire," explained Laelius to Aldrich.

"My uncle is buried here," said Aldrich.

Andraste looked to Aldrich in surprise. There was so much that she did not know about him.

"Keep moving," Brion called from the lead.

They wound their way through the tombs and approached a Mausoleum. It was carved out of orange marble. Statues of the gods lined the outside.

"My mother's tomb," said Andraste. She was careful to not look at Aldrich. They both knew that it was empty.

"We will leave the horses behind. No one will find them there," ordered Andraste.

The men did so and took all the weapons that they could carry. Andraste wordlessly led them into the Mausoleum. In the center of the room was a large fountain full of water lilies and a statue of a goddess shooting an arrow at the mosaic moon on the ceiling. Behind it was a large engraved-stone scene of pictures depicting the Empress' life. A large tomb inlaid with jewels stood between the stone engravings and the fountain.

"It is lovely," admired Aldrich.

It was not what he had expected from the cruelest man known to live in the Empire. Andraste paid no heed. She had mixed feelings about this place now that she knew the truth. As a child, she had thought she could feel her mother's presence within its walls and had used it as a sanctuary, but it no longer held the same tranquility.

Andraste removed a torch from the wall and a passage opened showing stairs down into the earth. She lit the torch and the men lit others. They proceeded into the opening. As they rounded the bend, they heard the door close behind them. They went deep underground and passed many tombs. After their recent battle with the Arisen soldiers, they all felt unsettled. They did not speak.

Andraste moved quickly. She knew that once they were discovered their progress would be halted by the Emperor's sorcerers. However, they were not stopped, and it did not seem as if they had triggered any alarms. This made Andraste uneasy.

"It sounds as though the army has succeeded in entering the Citadel," commented Maximianus. They paused. They could hear sounds of cheering and stampeding above them. However, the cheering quickly turned to sounds of alarm and terror.

"Make haste!" urged Andraste.

She started racing toward the end of the tunnel. There were two goddess statues guarding the passage. Andraste took the arrow from one's bow and place it in the other's quiver. The passage opened, leading to a stairwell that led above ground. They emerged into a deserted corridor of the Citadel.

"Do you think it odd there were no traps?" Brion asked her.

"Who else would come this way? According to the curse, I should be dead by now," answered Andraste. Brion winced.

They passed in to an open hallway and stopped. The Imperial Army had entered the keep, but their own fallen brethren were transforming into Arisen soldiers.

"Go," Andraste ordered Brion, "Take the others. Aldrich, you are with me."

Brion did not argue with her. The Victorious hastened to aid the Imperial Army. Andraste prayed to all of the gods as she ran. Her spirits soared as she saw red lightning and blue waves hurtling towards the row of sorcerers.

Five soldiers in the purple robes of the Emperor's personal guards caught sight of them and charged down the hall towards them. Aldrich leapt in front of her to meet them and quickly dispatched them. Andraste hurried forward. Again they met more of the personal guards and fought them off.

They entered the throne room. Andraste's heart pounded in her chest. She readjusted the Ruin sword in her hand. It was deserted except for one man.

The Emperor sat on his throne. He looked as though he had aged a hundred years. His eyes seemed to have lost all of their light. They were glassy and cold. At first she thought he did not recognize her, but then he began to laugh coldly.

"So you live," stated the Emperor.

He rose. His sword was already in hand. He approached her slowly, dragging the blade on the floor. It made an unpleasant scratching sound that made her skin crawl. He was a skeleton of a man. His face was hollow.

"How does the curse treat you?" asked the Emperor.

"I have time yet," declared Andraste.

"I have no time to waste on you," stated the Emperor.

His ghastly appearance was deceiving. The Emperor still fought her with the same speed and intensity. His strikes were purposeful and full of power. Again and again he came at her. However, Andraste saw her opening and took it. She disarmed the Emperor as she had done on that fateful day. His sword flew across the room and hit the wall.

"No matter," laughed the Emperor.

The Emperor held out his hand towards her. The amethyst orb appeared in his palm. However, Aldrich's phoenix flew in front of her and dissolved the purple orb instantly.

"Not just a spectator?" the Emperor asked forgetting Andraste for a moment.

The Emperor raised his right hand towards Aldrich and his left hand to her. If Aldrich did not shield himself, he could protect Andraste. Wordlessly, Aldrich raised his hand in her direction.

Andraste lunged at the Emperor before he could summon his power. Aldrich lunged at the same time. The Emperor's attention was divided in twain. He hesitated as he saw the phoenix approach him. Simultaneously, the ruby dragon emerged from Andraste's sword and breathed fire at the Emperor. Andraste sliced off the Emperor's head with one mighty strike as he lunged at her. She turned to Aldrich. The spirit dragon disappeared.

"I am fine," Aldrich said. He was surveying the corpse, "Is he one of the Arisen?"

"You think my father has been dead all of this time?" asked Andraste in horror.

"Look away," ordered Aldrich.

Andraste turned her back. By the warm amber light she knew that the spirit phoenix was devouring the corpse with its flames. She felt tears stream down her face. Aldrich approached her. She turned away from him and tried to dry her tears.

"Cannot a soldier mourn his comrade's loss?" Aldrich asked simply.

Andraste let him put an arm around her and he pulled her to his chest. The sword dropped from her hand and hit the ground. The sound echoed across the great chamber.

They could hear massive cheering in the courtyard. The rest of the Arisen had fallen with the defeat of the Emperor. Aldrich released her as they heard running towards the chamber. Andraste rubbed her sleeve across her eyes. Brion was the first to enter followed by the Victorious. They surveyed the scene.

Brion approached Andraste and put a hand on her shoulder. Laelius followed his example. The others did as well. She realized there were two missing.

"Otho? Maximianus?" inquired Andraste.

"They fell, Empress," said Laelius. Andraste winced.

"Take me to them," she ordered.

Aldrich picked up her fallen sword and handed it to her. Wordlessly, she sheathed it.

"Empress," said Laelius gently.

"You know our ways," reprimanded Andraste. Her eyes were dry and cold.

Laelius led the way. The crowd of soldiers parted in order to let her pass. Laelius led her to where their comrades rested. Their cloaks covered their wounds. Their eyes had been closed and their arms folded on their chest. Andraste felt as though she may lose control of herself again. She took a deep breath and said instead, "Shields."

Wordlessly, the Victorious laid their shields on the ground in two groups. Laelius and Brion stood on either side of Andraste. Valens, Thracius, Priscus, Laurentius, and Nero lifted Otho onto their shields, which were lifted to their shoulders. Hadrian, Glaucio, Felix, Cato, Avitus, and Aldrich lifted Maximianus on to their shoulders.

Andraste led the way out of the Citadel through the rubble of the fallen wall that the Imperial Army had smashed. She led the way to the Tombs of the Fallen from the War of Empire. As they passed the soldiers, they removed their helmets and saluted. She saw other soldiers mourning over their own fallen comrades.

At the end of the row of tombs, Brion opened his hand and the earth opened on two sides. The Victorious laid their fallen comrades in the ground with their swords in their hands. They each said goodbye. Laelius and Andraste went together. Tears fell from the eyes of the older swordsman as he said goodbye to each warrior. Andraste's tears joined his own. They stepped out of the tomb. Brion waved his hand and the earth gently began to cover the remains of the men that they had cherished.

Andraste turned and saw a sea of Imperial soldiers standing in solidarity. Andraste looked past them and once more saw the bodies of the fallen soldiers behind her.

"Bury your fallen with honor and dignity. Remember their valor by telling of their deeds. Never forget what we have lost and why we have all fought together on this day. It is this friendship, this honor, this courage that will be the foundation for the new Empire," proclaimed Andraste.

The soldiers saluted her as did her Victorious behind her. Andraste proceeded down the mound and began to aid the Imperial soldiers in burying their dead. They buried many soldiers and officers that she had known. Their losses were staggering. Over and over the required words were sung. It was as if it was being sung as a round.

As the afternoon approached, she saw Titus arrive with the rest of his forces. Titus spoke to soldiers as he passed, but when he caught sight of her, he approached with purpose.

"Will you help me bury our father?" asked Andraste.

Titus stopped whatever he was about to say. Instead he nodded. Andraste looked to Brion and he came also. By her look Brion knew it was not a request. Aldrich saw that none of the Victorious moved, so he stayed put as well. The three heirs of Valerianus disappeared into the Citadel.

"They have returned," Laelius remarked to Aldrich.

It was just past twilight. The Victorious had been given rooms in the Citadel. Brion was in front and Andraste and Titus were bickering behind him.

"You cannot leave at this time. It would not be wise. You must stake your claim. If you do not accept it, civil war will continue," Titus was saying.

"You know the tradition. All of the Northern clans will have to meet before the Ice Palace to declare their support for their candidate. I am going to the Ice Palace now. There is something I must do," declared Andraste.

"You must stay and raise support," contradicted Titus.

"What words could I say that would speak louder than my actions?" cried Andraste.

Titus fell silent.

"I must go," stated Andraste.

"What could be more important?" asked Titus.

Andraste refused to speak. Titus and Andraste stood glaring at each other.

"Northern gathering?" asked Aldrich to Laelius.

"The King of the Northern tribes has always been selected through voting. Each of the clans will get to nominate and pick one of the heirs as its candidate," explained Laelius.

"What if they tie?" asked Aldrich.

"Then they debate, and revote until someone wins," answered Laelius.

"Andraste should stay," confirmed Brion as he heard their conversation.

"She must go," said Aldrich.

"You know what is at the Ice Palace?" asked Brion. He looked deeply hurt.

"If the Empress lived, would it change the proceedings?" asked Aldrich after a pause. Brion's jaw opened and he did not close it.

"Yes, but she has been dead for years," said Laelius. He considered Aldrich's question and then looked as amazed as Brion.

"Hypothetically, if the Empress had been cursed by the Emperor for twenty years, would she be freed from said curse if the Emperor died?" proposed Aldrich.

"I understand," asked Laelius, "Should I assemble the men?"

"No, she will want to go alone," answered Aldrich.

Brion put himself firmly between Andraste and Titus.

"We have all suffered heavy losses today. We need time to recover. Andraste will see you in thirty days at the Ice Palace," Brion told Titus.

Brion took Andraste by the arm and led her speechless towards Aldrich.

"Shall I get the horses?" asked Aldrich.

"No need," said Brion. Brion led them to one of the towers. The floor was lined with silver ancient ruins text.

"Aldrich, I know you must want to go to your family, but will you come with me one last time?" besought Andraste. She did not look at him.

"Yes," replied Aldrich simply.

"Stand in the center of the middle circle," directed Brion.

"What is this?" asked Aldrich.

"It is a transport circle. They used to be common, but many were destroyed in the wars," answered Andraste.

Brion spoke into a crystal ball. They could not decipher what he was saying. However, it turned cloudy with pinkish smoke and he must have received a satisfactory reply.

"Good luck," called Brion.

Before Andraste or Aldrich could respond, there was a flash of blinding light and they were transported to the orchard in front of the Ice Palace. Aldrich looked down to their feet and found they were standing on another transport circle.

"Why did we not do that in the first place?" asked Aldrich.

"We did not know if the portal was open. If you try to cross to a closed portal you can get imprisoned between. You cannot go forward and you cannot go back to where you came from. If you are not rescued within an hour, you will be entombed forever," stated Andraste.

They looked towards the Ice Palace and heard a commotion. Fires raged from inside the Ice Palace. Andraste grabbed Aldrich by the hand and they ran into the Ice Palace together. The doors opened automatically for them and seemed to direct them straight to the catastrophe.

"Did Rhinauld send you?" asked Mother.

"We have not seen him," replied Andraste in alarm.

"The portal must have been closed," said Fausta.

"Send a retrieval team for the portal immediately," Mother ordered Fausta who hurried on her way. She did not even spare time to glare at Aldrich as she passed.

"The Emperor is dead?" asked Mother.

"Yes," confirmed Andraste.

"That explains the sudden fluctuation in power levels. The dark magic he released has come here where it is tethered by your mother's life force," said Mother.

"What do we do?" asked Andraste.

"Aldrich take up the shield," ordered Mother. Aldrich did so.

"Andraste, I must warn you. There is a strong chance that we may free her soul but not be able to bring her back," presaged Mother.

"I am prepared," said Andraste.

"Aldrich direct your spirit phoenix through the shield. It will be stronger than before," directed Mother, "Andraste, if that is not enough, you will have to use your sword. I am opening the doors."

Slowly the doors to the tower opened, the emerald dragon came tearing out of its cage, its great wings flapping as it tried to take to the sky. Mother held the dragon in place with her magic. Aldrich's phoenix went flying through the shield and emerged almost as large as the dragon. It dove at the dragon. Purple smoke and lightning bombarded the shield. Aldrich fought to hold onto the shield. He lost his footing and went down to one knee.

Andraste abandoned her position and ran to him. She put one hand on his shoulder for support, and with the other she struck her sword to the shield. Her spirit dragon was summoned and attacked the emerald dragon. The emerald dragon was shrinking and became shrouded in a cloud of purple smoke, which was then consumed by the shield, until only a woman stood before them. She wore emerald robes and had luminous, sea-green eyes. Her hair, although showing signs of gray, was the color of Andraste's. Andraste's mother began to fade before their eyes.

"Something is wrong," exclaimed Andraste in agony.

"Yes," confirmed Mother.

"We will meet again someday, my daughter," said Victoria.

She tried to approach Andraste, but the phoenix would not let her approach. It was Andraste's own dragon that consumed Victoria in flames.

"It is as it should be. I cannot return to this world and remain as I once was," consoled Victoria. Andraste tried to reach for the extended hand.

"No, you must not!" yelled Mother. Mother sent her own power towards Victoria.

Andraste hastily made a circle with a five pointed star. It flared with ruby light.

"Sveinbiorn Eldgrimson, Sveinbiorn Eldgrimson, Sveinbiorn Eldgrimson!" summoned Andraste. Her brother was at her side at once. He surveyed the scene before him.

"Svein," said Victoria sadly. She reached for Sveinbiorn. However, she was met with a force field.

"Help her!" demanded Andraste.

"Do not let her follow," commanded Sveinbiorn. He stared at Aldrich.

Sveinbiorn opened a portal. Andraste did not recognize the lands behind the portal. The fields were violet and full of silver flowers, while the skies were scarlet and boasted two golden moons. Sveinbiorn gestured for Victoria to follow.

Victoria looked to Mother and then to Andraste. Mother shifted her power towards Sveinbiorn. Andraste tried to throw herself between them. Aldrich dropped the shield and tackled Andraste to the ground. Her sword clattered to the floor. His phoenix disappeared and the amethyst smoke intensified. Victoria reappeared momentarily in the flesh. However, her eyes were amethyst orbs, not their regular sea-green color.

"No!" commanded Mother.

Mother's full power struck Victoria and once again she dematerialized, but Sveinbiorn shielded the shade. Mother's power struck Sveinbiorn, but the portal closed behind them. A resounding bang and surge of energy flared in the courtyard. Aldrich shielded Andraste with his body and kept her pinned to the ground for as long as he could. After Andraste fought free of Aldrich's grasp, her mother and brother were gone and the courtyard was silent.

"How could you?" yelled Andraste.

She beat her hands into Aldrich's chest against his armor. She hit him until her knuckles bled. He did not defend himself or stop her. He waited until she tired. She collapsed to the floor.

"What did the Shade tell us at the Ruins?" asked Aldrich.

Andraste said nothing.

"What did the Shade tell you?" commanded Mother.

"We cannot bring back the dead without falling ourselves," said Andraste finally.

"Is that what happened to the Emperor?" asked Aldrich.

"Yes," answered Mother.

"Where did they go?" cried Andraste.

"They are not in this world. You cannot follow," replied Mother.

Aldrich held a hand to Andraste to help her rise. She would not look at him. He did not withdraw his offered hand.

"I apologize," said Andraste. He did not respond. She took his offered hand and he pulled her to her feet.

"Did I condemn Sveinbiorn to death when I asked for his help?" asked Andraste.

"There are many worlds besides ours and the Netherworld," replied Mother.

"Can they return?" questioned Andraste.

"I know not," answered Mother.

Fausta appeared at Mother's side.

"Rhinauld, Henry and Gnaeus made it through once Brion sent you two here. It was quite a surprise for Brion," said Fausta. However, her amusement faded as she saw Andraste's face.

"Our guests can use one of our cottages in the village until the Election," said Mother.

Fausta bowed to Mother before beckoning them to follow her. Fausta settled Andraste and Aldrich in a guest cottage and then took her leave. Andraste went into her room and closed the door without saying a word to Aldrich.

Chapter Eighteen

B rion, the remaining Victorious, Rhinauld, and Henry arrived four weeks later. They had chosen to stay in the North in order to mourn their comrades, to help with the rebuilding, and to aid Titus in building support for Andraste. Brion had not been able to find Andraste, but he found Aldrich in their shared cottage.

"How is she?" asked Brion after introductions and once he heard Aldrich's retelling of events.

"She has not spoken to me since the encounter with Victoria. She is either riding with the Ice Palace warriors or at the Ice Palace library," said Aldrich.

"What is she researching?" asked Brion curiously.

"From what has been left out, I have deduced nothing. The books are in a language that I have never seen before," replied Aldrich.

"And still you stayed?" inquired Brion.

"I will wait to hear the outcome of the Election before I return to the South," answered Aldrich.

Brion looked at a pile of books on the table.

"This is the language of the Island Kingdoms, Andraste's mother's people," stated Brion. He looked at the titles and raised his eyebrows.

"What are they?" asked Aldrich.

"These are the histories of the founding of the continent and the institution of the Republic," concluded Brion. He picked up one decrepit volume and opened a page. He commented, "I have not seen this one before. It is regarding the land beyond the seas."

Brion closed the volume and returned his attention to Aldrich.

"She is preparing for her possible election. I know it means a great deal that you remained, even if she does not say so," said Brion.

"I think she blames me for what happened," replied Aldrich.

"You kept her from harm. That is what it is important," responded Brion, "And you said yourself, she apologized. She knows she was in the wrong. Her pride is wounded. Additionally, she also just lost her parents and brother. She has never adapted to loss. She does not accept comfort from anyone except Rhinauld."

The conversation was terminated as they were joined by the Victorious, Rhinauld and Henry for dinner, but there was no sign of Andraste.

"They would not admit me into the Ice Palace," lamented Rhinauld.

"Not going to fight your way in again?" asked Henry.

"Oh, to be fifteen again," replied Rhinauld. The other men laughed.

"I could not live through that again," muttered Laelius.

They continued their meal in good cheer. The company waited until midnight for Andraste appear, but she never did, so they retired themselves in order to be prepared for the Election the following day.

Brion returned from greeting the Northern delegations. He entered the cottage and took a seat by Aldrich and Laelius. Aldrich closed his book.

"They have announced the three finalists," announced Brion.

"Is it as we suspected?" asked Laelius.

"Yes, it is Andraste, Titus, and Varinia. However, Titus withdrew his name. He and Andraste have some sort of understanding. Apparently, they were speaking into the early hours of the morning. The factions will vote again this night," stated Brion.

"Any sign of her?" asked Aldrich.

"She is sleeping," answered Brion. Aldrich had never even heard her come in.

"If Andraste becomes Empress are you going to continue your war for independence?" asked Laelius.

Aldrich and Laelius surveyed each other.

"Whether Andraste or Varinia are elected, I will offer the same terms as I proposed to the Emperor. I will propose a military allegiance in times of foreign invasion and open trade between our kingdoms," said Aldrich.

"You realize Andraste does not believe in the dismantling of the Empire?" asked Brion.

"I have no wish to fight her, but I will in order to secure the freedom and liberty of my people," returned Aldrich, "I have wished to discuss this with her, but she will not see me."

"So you stay for your duties, not for her?" questioned Laelius.

"I have the utmost respect and admiration for her, but if she will not see me, I can be nothing to her," replied Aldrich.

"And if she chose you to be Emperor?" asked Brion.

"You mean marriage?" questioned Aldrich.

"Yes," affirmed Brion, "The union of the North and South through marriage."

"She has twice refused my proposals. I will not ask again," stated Aldrich.

"It may be the most peaceful solution," replied Laelius, "It would cause you both pain to war against each other. She has suffered enough."

"She has spent her life fighting for her own freedom and having her own right to choose. I will not take that from her. I will not marry her to avoid war. I know her well enough to believe that we will find a solution without a marriage of convenience," answered Aldrich.

Laelius and Brion exchanged looks.

"Why are you asking me these questions? Does she want me to propose again?" asked Aldrich.

"I do not know what she wants. She will not see me either," replied Laelius.

"What is she planning?" asked Aldrich. He looked to Brion.

"Even I can never say what she will choose to do. In the Shadow Mountains, she took my notes regarding the formation of the Republic. By the notes she has written and the other materials gathered, she is studying the Republic," concluded Brion.

"But why the Republic?" asked Aldrich.

"I only have suspicions," replied Brion.

"Which are?" inquired Laelius.

"I refuse to speculate," said Brion. His response was unpleasing to Laelius and Aldrich. Brion picked up a book from the table and began to read.

"If Varinia is elected, will you allow her to return to the Southern lands?" asked Laelius.

"If that is her wish. Your men and their families are also welcome to remain," replied Aldrich.

"Thank you. I fear that if Varinia is elected, my Commander will not be safe if she remains in the North," replied Laelius.

"Men of leisure are we?" asked Rhinauld as he entered with Henry and Gnaeus.

"What would you have us be doing?" questioned Laelius.

"We are riding with the Ice Palace Warriors to finish off the last of the Emperor's experiments. Do you want to join us?" asked Rhinauld.

"I will go," answered Aldrich. Laelius rose as well.

"I will wait here in case Andraste needs me," replied Brion.

Aldrich left with the Northern warriors. Brion returned his attention to his book.

As the sun was setting, Andraste appeared from her room in Northern style robes. They were the deep ruby color of the Empire. They had wide sleeves and sweeping skirts. The robes were tied behind her with a black sash. She wore her Ruin sword. Her hair was braided in the Northern fashion and put up off her neck. She also wore her Commander's cape.

"Have they summoned us?" asked Andraste.

At that moment there was a knock on the door. Brion rose and spoke to the soldier waiting.

"Perfect timing," said Brion.

Andraste did not look amused. She headed towards the door. She looked composed, determined, and regal. She left the cottage and Brion trailed after her. They headed up the mountain towards the Ice Palace.

"Our friends have returned from their hunt," said Brion.

Andraste paused long enough for them to catch up. She said nothing to Aldrich. She acknowledged the new arrivals and turned to continue the way up the mountain. She was followed behind by Brion, who was joined by Titus as they passed his lodgings. Her Victorious flanked her sides. They were followed behind by Rhinauld, Henry and Aldrich. They were watched and cheered by the people lining the streets. The crowd moved out of the way so that they could pass.

As they emerged in to the orchard of the Ice Palace, they were met by throngs of people. Each delegation had the flag of their territory flying above them. Lords and ladies dressed in their finest mingled underneath fruit trees full of blossoms. Some of the petals were carried across the orchard on the wind. Imperial Army officers dressed in their full armor stood at full attention. The atmosphere was festive. However, it quieted as Andraste and her followers passed. Andraste saw that Mother and Varinia were waiting for her at the gates of the Ice Palace.

Varinia was dressed in Imperial Army armor. Her dark brown hair was tied back in a ponytail and her steel gray eyes were cold and angry. Varinia watched her half-sister approach with undisguised loathing. Andraste met Varinia's gaze without flinching. She stood beside Mother and turned to face the crowd.

Mother cleared her throat and the crowd fell silent.

"As one Emperor falls, another rises. It has come time to choose a new leader as is right and fitting with our ways and traditions. I would like all to remember that this choice is indisputable, and to go against this verdict will be seen as an act of treason punishable by death," declared Mother.

"All hail Andraste Valerianus, Commander of the Imperial Army and Empress!" proclaimed Mother.

There was a deafening roar of applause that lasted for several minutes. Andraste said something to Varinia, who snapped back, but the words were lost to the crowd. Andraste scanned the crowd with her sea-green eyes. She stepped in front of Mother and held her hand for silence.

"I am honored by your choice. I have trusted many of you for your counsel over the past weeks. I have spoken with our Commanders of my future plans and obtained their consent. I have discussed the legality of my ideas with our Council of Sorcerers and the Council of Scholars. They have approved this change for our Empire.

Throughout my exile and banishment, I have contemplated our shared fate. It is our shared fate. I hold the power to strengthen or ruin us all.

One person should not be entrusted with the fate of hundreds of thousands. It is not balanced for one person to hold the fate of so many without being questioned. How many have died because of one man's will?

Two people are better because they can negotiate and keep each other in balance. But what do we do if even our better half cannot keep us from falling?

The ancient texts portray the histories of our lands and the formation of the First Republic. I have seen these texts illustrated on four Ruins, so I know them to be authentic and true. Each of the texts depicts the First Republic being formed by the people for the people. Never before, until the recent age, has our civilization been in the total control of one individual. Our civilization was built together by people throughout the lands. In order to obtain the peace of old, we must work together.

To reach this goal, I proclaim that a Republic will be instituted once more. Each kingdom, people, realm will be represented by a representative of their election, similar to what we have done today. The Republic will rule by majority vote. The decisions that affect us all will be in the hands of the representatives. Once the Assembly of the Republic has been founded, I will cease to be Empress. From that moment there will never be an Emperor or Empress ever again.

As for the rule and protection of the Northern lands, I abdicate to my brother, Titus Valerianus," proclaimed Andraste.

There was a stunned silence throughout the assembled, even by the select few who knew it was coming. People began to speak excitedly to one another. Andraste said something to her shocked sister and then turned to leave back the way she had come. As she did so the Imperial Army and her Victorious saluted her. The others that were assembled bowed or curtsied.

Andraste returned to the cottage as quickly as she could. She was joined by her companions.

"Never saw that coming," admitted Rhinauld. Andraste ignored him.

"And not a word to any of us," alleged Felix.

"I had much to do," protested Andraste.

"It is a lot of work to dissolve an Empire," commented Aldrich dryly.

"I could not speak to you. Any of your aid or counsel would have been seen as the South meddling with our affairs. I could have no one say that I was persuaded by you," said Andraste.

"Empress, no one would ever accuse you of being persuaded by anyone. Least of all me," said Aldrich.

"What did you say to Varinia?" asked Brion quickly.

"I urged her to join the ranks of the Ice Palace. She would find happiness there, but she has chosen a different path," sighed Andraste.

"You expect the civil war to continue?" questioned Laelius.

"If she lifts a finger, Titus will have her executed and the rebellion will die out with her," answered Andraste.

"What will you do now, Empress?" asked Laelius.

"I have arranged with Titus that he will continue to rule the North. To assure him of my lack of interference, I plan to travel to the South with Brion to witness his marriage to Lady Rhiannon. We are all to meet in the capitol of the Southern lands," replied Andraste.

"Really? The capitol of the Southern lands?" questioned Rhinauld with a mischievous look in his eye.

"It is Rhiannon's choice. She wanted to meet Brion there, so that she could see him sooner. They will be able to return to the Salt Islands together," replied Andraste, "Why do you find that amusing?"

"No reason," said Rhinauld. He and Henry both turned to Aldrich.

"Will you travel with us, Prince Aldrich? We are all heading the same way," suggested Henry.

"I will go with you," confirmed Aldrich.

"It will be a more pleasant journey than before. There will be celebrations and parades all the way there," commented Rhinauld.

"A much different journey," Andraste replied, but it was evident her mind was elsewhere.

"Take the escort. You are Empress until the Assembly is founded. In order to promote stability and power, you must be seen as the Empress," urged Titus.

"I will only travel with my Victorious and Aldrich. I will be protected enough. We fought 900 Arisen with fifteen warriors. I am not worried by thieves or small armies," replied Andraste.

"My Empress, that is foolish," stated Rhinauld.

"Fine. I will permit Henry and you to come as well," answered Andraste.

"I will accept that compromise," replied Rhinauld.

"Take your squadrons," ordered Titus.

"I will not be seen taking Imperial troops into the Southern lands. Aldrich will see it as hostile," said Andraste, "We have a fragile peace to protect. I will not damage our goodwill or relations with the South. Not when we have achieved the possibility of lasting peace."

"Send for Aldrich and see what he has to say," suggested Laelius.

"I will speak to him myself. I will not send for him like a dog," replied Andraste.

"You are Empress," stated Titus.

"Yes, I am," said Andraste. She stared at Titus until he looked away.

"I last saw him going towards the Tower. The Ice Palace is permitting him to see their observatory," informed Laelius.

Andraste glared at all three men and swept out of the room. She made her way to the observatory. Her blue robes rustled against the stone floor as she passed. She found Aldrich outside on the balcony. The observatory was deserted.

"How do you find our Northern stars?" asked Andraste.

"Do you own the stars as well as all of the land? They shine just as brightly in the south," replied Aldrich. When he turned to face her he was smiling, but it faded as he saw her frustration.

"What is it?" asked Aldrich.

"It seems that now that I am Empress, everyone fights more than usual. Everyone contradicts me. Everyone has something to say," said Andraste.

"A ruler must listen," replied Aldrich.

"I was never meant to rule," answered Andraste.

She joined him at the railing and looked out across the sky. She shivered as her hand touched the railing.

"Do you want to go in?" asked Aldrich.

"No. Someone will find me," replied Andraste.

He took off his fur-lined cape and wrapped it around her shoulders. He paused as he fastened it.

"I have a request from my Commanders, and you will not like it," said Andraste.

"Try me," replied Aldrich. He leaned against the railing and surveyed her with his sapphire eyes.

"Tomorrow when we leave for the Southern capitol, the Commanders will not permit me to travel with just the Victorious, Rhinauld, Henry and you. They say I must take my squadrons," replied Andraste.

"I would assume as much. You are Empress," stated Aldrich.

"But I traveled for months with just you and my Victorious," said Andraste.

"So you were not worried about my reaction? You just want to travel with your comrades? Things will never be the same. We cannot return to the way things were," alleged Aldrich.

"I just want to sleep beneath the stars. I do not care for the pomp and circumstance that will follow with a formal party," said Andraste.

"You forget that an Assembly has not yet been formed. Until it is, the delegates will flock to your Court," replied Aldrich.

"Should I stay in the North? Not attend the wedding?" asked Andraste. She looked crestfallen.

"As the Citadel is destroyed, may I offer the Chambers of Justice in the Southern capitol? Once the delegates meet, they can designate a permanent place. It would be a fitting beginning as my homeland was where the original Republic met," suggested Aldrich.

"You have been reading the histories?" asked Andraste. She smiled up at him.

"Yes," replied Aldrich.

"Will you fight the formation of the Republic? Will you fight me?" questioned Andraste. Her smile faded.

"No. The Republic is the solution. We will have the military and economic strength of the Empire, but freedom and equality will be preserved. You were right," replied Aldrich.

Andraste relaxed. She lifted her eyes to the skies. Aldrich had not removed his eyes from her. Andraste rested her hand next to his on the railing.

"But do you not think the stars shine more brightly in the North?" insisted Andraste.

"Yes," admitted Aldrich, "The North does possess unusual beauties."

Andraste blushed and kept her eyes on the sky.

"I do have one question regarding the North," said Aldrich.

"Oh?" asked Andraste.

"Why has there not been a tea ceremony? I thought they were common in the North?" asked Aldrich.

"If we were in the Citadel, I would host one. The Ice Palace does have tea ceremonies, but men are not permitted. I think Fausta may poison our warriors, if she were to host such a gathering," answered Andraste.

"The Northern lords said that in their lands, ladies often play or dance at night," said Aldrich.

"The Ice Palace does not permit exhibitions," replied Andraste.

"That is a shame for you dance and play the shamisen," responded Aldrich.

"If we were to stay here longer, or make court in the Citadel, you would see. However, I wish to return to the South, and then the Island Kingdoms. I do not plan to return to the North," said Andraste.

Aldrich's smile faded as he saw her determined look on the horizon.

"What are you going to do after the institution of the Republic?" asked Aldrich.

"Empress, forgive the intrusion. A delegate from the Midlands has arrived," said Fausta from the doorway.

"Shall we meet the delegate together?" asked Andraste.

Aldrich gestured for her to proceed before him. Fausta rendered her usual glare and then proceeded to ignore him. Andraste fell silent. She did not speak as they returned to the village and to the Imperial camp at its base. She returned to the meeting tent.

Her Commanders congregated to the left side of the tent, the delegates in the middle, and her Victorious to the right side of the tent. Titus and Aldrich returned glares to each other. Aldrich went to stand beside the

Victorious. Andraste took her seat. She was approached by a small woman with dark eyes.

"I am Octavia Rossi, Lady of the Midlands. I have come to take my place as a delegate," said the woman. She curtsied to Andraste, but would not meet her eyes.

"You are Otho's sister?" asked Andraste.

"Yes, Empress," replied Octavia.

"He spoke of you often. We welcome you, and look forward to working with you," said Andraste.

"If I may, Empress-" asked Octavia.

"Please speak freely," said Andraste.

"Our independence has always been what Otho desired. I wondered at his choice when he chose to stay with you, and not return to our cause, but now I see. On behalf of my family and my people, I thank you," said Octavia.

Andraste did not respond. She could not respond. Octavia curtsied again and left the tent. The other delegates followed her into the night. Aldrich remained with the Victorious.

"Is there any word on Varinia's whereabouts?" asked Andraste.

"Only silence, Empress," replied Titus. He remained where he was.

"What other business?" asked Andraste as she surveyed the remaining Commanders. Brion joined Titus's side.

"You are often with the Southern prince. There is talk amongst the Northern court," said Titus.

"I have seen him as one of my Victorious for months," responded Andraste.

"It could ruin your bid for the Republic," replied Titus.

"The Republic is not in danger," answered Andraste.

"Send him away. He is your weakness," stated Titus, "And now all of the Northern court knows it."

"And all of the Southern court," stated Brion.

"I have never seen Aldrich Caelius as my enemy. I have rarely seen such courage, selflessness or honor. It is for this reason that I asked the prince of the Southern lands to join the Victorious. The Victorious was formed to serve and protect the Empire. The Victorious will serve the Republic in times of need as well. I do not see this possible without Aldrich Caelius. The defeat of the Emperor would not have been possible without his efforts," stated Andraste.

"But as you said he is the prince of the Southern lands," replied Titus.

"Cato and Avitus also hail from the Southern lands. This has never presented a problem," replied Andraste.

"The Victorious have never voted Aldrich into their ranks," stated Titus.

"My lords, we have been busy preserving your future," replied Andraste. Her eyes flashed.

"I will return to the Southern lands. I will not risk the future of the Republic," said Aldrich. He bowed to Andraste.

Laelius approached the center of the room. He bowed to Andraste.

"Yes, Laelius," addressed Andraste.

"I propose that we accept Aldrich Caelius into the Victorious," recommended Laelius.

"As do I," said Felix.

"And I," said Nero. Further consent was announced by the remaining Victorious. All of the eyes turned to Andraste.

"As do I," announced Andraste. She rose and stared at Aldrich, "As the vote is unanimous, as our rules require, I offer you a place among the Victorious. The choice is yours, Aldrich Caelius. If you so choose to join us, then the vow will be administered by Laelius. The vow is to our cause, not me."

"I am honored," accepted Aldrich.

Andraste stared at Titus without blinking as Laelius turned to face Aldrich. Titus was flushed with anger as he watched the administration of the oath.

"Do you solemnly swear to protect the Republic from all enemies foreign and domestic? And that you do so freely and of your own volition?" asked Laelius.

"I do," answered Aldrich.

"Do you promise to protect those who are weaker then yourself, and never take advantage of the powerless?" asked Laelius.

"I do," replied Aldrich.

"Do you vow to protect your fellow Victorious at all times, and stand beside us as our brother?" asked Laelius.

"I do," responded Aldrich.

Laelius extended his hand to Aldrich, who grasped it. Laelius embraced him with his free arm in the Northern style. The other Victorious came forth to grasp hands. Andraste rose and approached Aldrich. She grasped his hand in the Northern style. She removed her own war fan and extended it to Aldrich.

"The Victorious, as you know, are free to choose any weapons that they choose. Many prefer the weapons from their homelands. However, we all carry identical war fans. Keep it on you at all times, so all may know that you are one of us," said Andraste.

Aldrich took the fan from her and saluted her. He then joined the Victorious. Andraste turned her attention to Titus.

"Commanders, I will remind you that you rule the North. You do not rule me. You do not choose my friends or allies. I spent years fighting for the freedom of the people of our Empire. You will not take away my freedom or any other's. Those days are over.

The Republic will not be governed by the North alone. As I stated at the Election, the Republic will be ruled by all of its peoples. As my Victorious are assembled from warriors across the lands, I know that we can work together. I know that we can fight together. We do not have to fight each other," said Andraste.

"Yes, Empress," said Titus. He bowed to Andraste. However, neither he nor the Northern Commanders budged.

"A marriage or union between yourself and Aldrich Caelius before the institution of the Republic would not be prudent. It could renew civil war in the North and spread rebellions throughout the Empire," stated Titus.

Andraste laughed in his face.

"My Empress, what is so humorous?" inquired Titus.

"I can assure you, my lords, that Aldrich Caelius has no plans to marry me," answered Andraste. She glanced up at Aldrich, but he was not smiling. Her laughter faded. Titus looked to Aldrich for affirmation.

"My Empress will not marry before the institution of the Republic. However, after its foundation and once she is released from her position, I will support her right to marry whoever she chooses. As the Empress stated, you do not rule her, and you have no right to take away her freedom or limit her choice," alleged Aldrich.

"You will allow him to speak for you?" asked Titus.

"Are you angry that he spoke my opinion, or that you did not speak for me?" retorted Andraste. Titus colored.

"This subject is closed. We will not speak of it again," commanded Andraste.

Titus bowed to her and swept out of the tent. He was followed by the Northern Commanders. Brion turned to leave.

"Brion," ordered Andraste.

"Yes, Empress," said Brion as he turned to face her.

"If I reach an understanding with anyone, I will inform you. The next time you and Titus want to discuss my love life publically, do not," commanded Andraste.

"Yes, Empress," answered Brion. He bowed to her before leaving the tent.

"What if they know about the pledge?" asked Laelius.

"Aldrich did not return the pledge. There is no understanding," said Andraste.

Aldrich looked in confusion from Andraste to Laelius.

"Rhinauld were you listening?" asked Andraste. Rhinauld appeared from the shadows.

"Yes, Andra," replied Rhinauld.

"I require your services," said Andraste.

"Services?" asked Aldrich.

"You have not noticed?" asked Felix.

"Rhinauld serves as my escort at public events. He serves as my protector, and he serves as a foundation for gossip," said Andraste, "Perhaps this will keep the Northern lords at bay as it has done in the past."

"Your flirtations are consciously done?" asked Aldrich. He did not approve.

"It is harmless," replied Andraste. Aldrich glared at Rhinauld.

"It is a mutual agreement. If I escort Andraste, then I do not have to deal with the unwanted attentions of ladies either," explained Rhinauld.

"You will get used to it," said Henry.

"I doubt it," replied Aldrich.

"It is not my wish, but I cannot keep you at my side as I did before. You know what is at stake," said Andraste.

"As you wish," replied Aldrich. His mouth was set in firm disapproval.

"While we remain in the North, I would like you to stay with the Victorious for your protection. The Northern lords would not try anything while you are with them," said Andraste, "Rhinauld, Henry, you will remain with me."

"Yes, Empress," consented Rhinauld. He took his place at her side.

"The rest of you are dismissed," said Andraste. The Victorious left the tent.

"You should not have laughed at Titus's proposal," said Rhinauld.

"Aldrich has refused me three times. Is that not a sound enough refusal?" asked Andraste.

"Three times?" asked Rhinauld, "Rhiannon said you gave the pledge at the Southern capitol. You have asked two more times?"

"I am not discussing this anymore," replied Andraste.

"Are you sure he knows the Northern pledge? There is nothing similar in the South," stated Henry.

"You think he does not know what I offered?" asked Andraste. Henry and Rhinauld exchanged looks.

"What did you do the other two times?" inquired Rhinauld.

"It was obvious, even for a Southerner," replied Andraste.

"What did you do?" asked Rhinauld in horror.

"Go to dinner," ordered Andraste, "Do not ask him."

"Do you think he is a lover of men?" questioned Rhinauld to Henry.

"Then he would be glaring at Andraste and not you," replied Henry.

Chapter Nineteen

I t took nearly a month for the travelers to reach the Southern capitol. Every castle they passed on their way wanted to host them, and every village, township, or city had a celebration. They were exhausted by the time they reached their destination. Andraste saw Aldrich as little as possible. Aldrich spent most of his time with the Victorious.

Aldrich was beside himself to be returned to his homeland. It seemed as though every man, woman, and child had turned out to welcome them. Flowers were thrown upon them as they rode through the city and towards the palace. They were greeted on the steps of the palace by the Queen and her court, the King of the Island Kingdoms, his entourage, Lady Rhiannon, the Lady of the Shadow Mountains, and other leaders of the Imperial resistance.

Rhiannon practically flew down the steps to embrace Brion. He swept her up in his arms. He would not relinquish her to her brother or Henry and that pleased the lady exceedingly.

Aldrich crossed the steps to embrace his mother and sisters. He was welcomed, embraced, and greeted by the Southern court. Andraste and the Victorious were received warmly by the Southern Resistance. Andraste approached the King of the Island Kingdoms. He pecked her roughly on the cheek.

"I would have given my kingdom to see the faces of the Northern lords when you said you were dissolving the Empire," laughed the King. His face turned somber, "But are you sure it is what you want, Andra?"

"I am my father's child. I cannot guarantee a different fate. It is better that I am never tested," affirmed Andraste.

"I see your mind is determined and you have already proclaimed it. But, remember, you are your mother's child as well, never forget that," said the King.

"It is done," stated Andraste.

"What will you do now?" asked the King.

"My plans are not certain," admitted Andraste.

"There is always a home for you in the Island Kingdoms," offered the King.

"I would like to see them again someday," replied Andraste.

The King fell silent as the Queen approached them.

"I have your rooms prepared, Empress," informed the Queen. She curtsied low to Andraste. She continued, "Will you rest before the feasting?"

"If your Majesty will forgive me, my men and I will spend the evening with the families of Otho and Maximianus. I have much to tell them," said Andraste softly.

"I understand," approved the Queen, "We are all sorry for their loss. They will be missed."

Andraste retreated down the steps and she was followed by the remaining Victorious. They made their way to their families' quarters. There was much rejoicing and many tears shed. There were grasping of hands and many embraces. They met in a common area between the houses, feasted, and talked through the night. After midnight, Aldrich joined them and he was welcomed. It was near dawn when Andraste and Aldrich returned to the palace. As they walked back to the palace, he did not offer her his arm.

"You have been resettled in rooms near the Queen. I will have a servant take you there," said Aldrich.

Andraste's smile faded. The servant curtsied to Andraste, and she wordlessly followed the servant to her new chambers. The rooms were double the size of her previous rooms. They were pastel sea colors. Everything was dainty and ladylike. Andraste sighed. She took a long bath and then climbed into bed. She would have liked to sleep until noon, but she was awoken only a few hours later.

"Come, get ready! There is to be a tournament," said Rhiannon.

Andraste raised her head quickly from her pillow.

"Please recall that in the South, ladies are forbidden from participating," decreed Rhiannon.

Andraste put her head back down on her pillow and closed her eyes. Rhiannon shook her awake. Andraste opened her eyes again and rested on her traveling clothes.

"Your bath is ready," said Rhiannon. She left the room.

Andraste surveyed the sapphire silks that Rhiannon had set for her. She looked again to her traveling clothes and Ruin sword. She did not have much time. She leapt out of bed and dressed hurriedly in her travel clothes and leather armor. She tied her hair back in a ponytail, and pulled on her boots. She grabbed her charcoal Victorious cloak and sword. She could hear Rhiannon approaching. Andraste leapt onto her veranda and slid down the column to the ground below.

"Andraste!" yelled Rhiannon.

Andraste secured her hood and smiling to herself, she made her way towards the tournament fields.

As she approached, she saw that the field beyond the city's walls was full of tents showing the colors of noble houses from across the Empire. It had a festival atmosphere. She made her way towards the field and saw that each corner housed one of the main regions of the Empire. She made her way towards the scarlet Northern tents. She saw her Victorious, Northern officers, and lords beginning to warm up. Although it was early in the day, she saw many were already drinking.

"Heiyoh!" called Laelius as he saw her making her way through the crowd. She grasped his arm as she approached.

"Incognito?" asked Felix.

"They wanted to confine me to the dais," said Andraste.

"The Ruin sword will be a dead give way," stated Valens.

"Will you fight?" asked Laelius.

"We cannot let the Southerners win, now can we?" asked Andraste. She scanned the assembled warriors.

"Aldrich fights with the South," said Felix.

"He is our host," commented Laelius.

"He has been studying the dais intently," said Felix, "I imagine he is looking for his lady."

"What is to be the method?" asked Andraste ignoring Felix.

"They draw names for a challenge. If your name is drawn, you can challenge any warrior by knocking another warrior's shield," answered Laelius.

"Also a giveaway," said Valens.

"We thought it would be interesting if we just put up a black shield. That way the challenger will not know which of the Victorious he will face," said Laelius. He glanced at Andraste.

"I could kiss you," said Andraste.

"That might also give you away," commented Valens.

"What is the penalty for a woman fighting in the Southern tournament?" asked Thracius in concern.

"Shame, disgrace, I may never obtain a husband," answered Andraste.

"And you will be banned from the ball," said Laelius.

"So it is a win-win situation," concluded Thracius. Andraste laughed heartily.

"Rhinauld approaches," warned Laelius.

Andraste quickly sat between Thracius and Priscus on a bench. Thracius poured her a stein of golden Southern beer. Priscus began loudly to tell a story about hunting three-headed dogs.

"Lord Rhinauld," greeted Laelius. He inclined his head towards the lord.

"Rhiannon and the Queen are furious, something about standard etiquette, and ladies needing to set examples," sighed Rhinauld, "Tell your Commander to stay away as long as she can if she is able."

"No ladies present," Laelius informed Rhinauld.

"He is a rotten liar," said Andraste as she watched Rhinauld walk towards the Island Kingdoms' encampment.

"Northern men do not lie," stated Laelius.

"Should I be offended?" asked Andraste. Laelius and the Victorious laughed. They heard trumpets sound.

"It looks like the Queen is starting the tournament in your place," said Felix.

Laelius handed Andraste a sword from their communal arsenal. Andraste left her Ruin sword in the Victorious tent.

"Are sure someone will not steal it?" asked Felix.

"No one other than Aldrich or me can wield it," replied Andraste, "It is a Ruin sword."

"We missed the Queen's words," commented Laelius. They approached the field.

"The Southern lords wasted no time. We have our first challenger," said Valens.

"Who is it?" asked Andraste.

"Not one we have met. You should go. You will most likely fool those who have not yet met you," said Laelius.

"Poor fool," said Felix as he surveyed her opponent.

The Victorious cheered her as she took her place on the field. Andraste saw other duels beginning to take place across the field. She turned her eyes to her opponent. He was dressed in canary yellow and his crest was a red sun. He saluted her and Andraste returned the gesture. He advanced and moved to strike. Andraste had him defeated in three moves. He stood gaping at her. The Southern lords guffawed from their camp. Aldrich's attention had left the dais and he was studying her. Andraste quickly returned to the Victorious, who surrounded and blocked her from view.

Andraste noted that as a warrior was beaten, his shield was removed from the front of the dais. The Victorious also fought wearing their hoods. They had many challengers, so it was not long before Andraste was up to fight again. She saw this time it was Egnatius. She saluted him as she approached, and he returned the gesture.

"Who do I have the honor-" started Egnatius.

Andraste was advancing before he had time to finish. The Southern captain was talented, but no match for her. She quickly sent his sword flying towards the Southern camp. She heard Southern lords jumping out of the way and swearing, much to the amusement of the Victorious.

"I yield," said Egnatius as Andraste raised her sword to his throat. She saluted him with her sword and turned back towards the Northern camp. However, she was intercepted by a Western lord.

"I am Lucretius of the Reed Plains. I would challenge you directly, but you all use the shame shield," said the lord.

Andraste saluted him with her sword in acceptance. She waited for the lord to advance. He carried axes like the Western lords. He faked his first attack, but Andraste leapt out of the way. He came again. Andraste blocked his axes and countered swiftly with her own attack. He was driven back. She pursued him across the field. He changed his direction and came again. Andraste saw an opening and she landed her sword on his exposed side. The Western lord swore. He bowed to her and returned to the Western camp.

"Soon we will be the only ones left," commented Laelius, "And Aldrich. Do we fight him if he challenges us?"

"Victorious are always permitted to duel during times of peace," replied Andraste.

Gnaeus grinned mischievously at Andraste. He approached the shields.

"Rascal," swore Laelius, but he looked proudly at his son. Gnaeus struck the Victorious shield. They heard laughter from the Southern camp.

"Heiyoh!" called the other Victorious. They all roused themselves as Gnaeus approached.

"Who is it to be?" called Felix. Gnaeus pointed his sword at Andraste.

Andraste scrutinized Gnaeus as he approached her. He was no longer the boy that they had instructed. He was a grown man and proven warrior. However, he was still made uncomfortable by her study. Andraste approached Gnaeus and returned his salute. She waited for his attack. He did not move. They stood watching each other on the field.

Andraste attacked first. She moved quickly across the training yard. She kept her hands near her hilt. Gnaeus raised his sword and lunged at her. Quicker than he could react, she raised her war fan and caught his sword between the metal stays. She closed the fan and disarmed Gnaeus. She could hear laughing from the Victorious. She handed Gnaeus back his sword. Gnaeus bowed to her as he took it.

"You were too hasty, Gnaeus. You must be careful," said Andraste.

"Yes, Commander," replied Gnaeus.

Andraste surveyed the field, noting that in the corner near the Southern camp Aldrich had just won his last duel.

"Will you challenge us all?" Laelius called to the prince.

"No. I see it is a Victorious victory all around," replied Aldrich.

Andraste turned her attention to the shields as she saw the King of the Island Kingdoms approach the dais. He surveyed the shields before him.

"He is dressed to fight," said Laelius. He did not smile.

"He does not see the shield he seeks," said Andraste. She also did not smile.

"Andraste Eldgrimson!" bellowed the King.

Andraste handed Laelius the borrowed sword, and took up her Ruin sword from the tent. She balanced it on her shoulders as she walked. She approached the dais. She removed her hood, as she was half-way through the field.

"Aelius Eldgrimson," greeted Andraste. She waited for the anticipated tongue lashing, and lowered her eyes. She looked up to find her uncle only calculating her with his sea green eyes.

"I challenge you," said the King once Andraste looked to him.

"Aelius!" yelled the Queen in fury. The King shook his head back and laughed heartily.

"I accept," replied Andraste.

"Southern traditions-" started the Queen.

"Damn your Southern traditions. An Eldgrimson never turns away from a fight!" returned the King. He clamped a hand on Andraste's shoulder.

"As I have respected your ways, you will respect mine. This is a command from your Empress. I am first and foremost, a soldier. I will fight today and any day I please, as have my people before me," announced Andraste.

Andraste saluted the stands with her sword and then turned towards the field. The King still had his hand clamped on her shoulder.

"No holding back," said the King.

"Agreed," replied Andraste.

The stands were buzzing with excitement. During his youth, her uncle had never been beaten in a tournament. He would never fight an opponent that he had already beaten.

He pulled a Ruin sword from underneath his cape that was the mirror image of her own. Its red blade glowed in the sun light. Andraste studied it curiously. There was even more excitement building in the stands. The King gestured for her to advance. But before she could reach his spot, he had disappeared. He moved as fast as Sveinbiorn. It was as if she was fighting multiple combatants. She could ward off his blows, but she could not advance.

She felt a blow to her calf and she went down to one knee. She heard disbelief from the Northern camp. However, she raised her sword and swung with all of her might. She caught the King by surprise and hit him straight in the chest. He doubled over winded and Andraste put her blade to his throat.

"Do you yield?" asked Andraste.

"Never," swore the King.

Andraste removed her blade from his throat, and threw back her head and laughed. She used her sword to support herself. Her eyes darted to the ground and then back to her uncle. He had caught his breath and straightened. He was watching her intently with his sea-green eyes.

"How is your leg?" asked the King.

"I cannot move," admitted Andraste. The King looked to the Southern camp. Andraste shook her head, "I will manage."

"Is it broken?" questioned the King.

"No," replied Andraste. She slowly put her weight down on her injured leg. She fell to the ground. She saw Aldrich leap over the railing and start from the Southern camp at a tremendous speed. She used her sword to pull herself up.

"I just need to walk it off," said Andraste.

"Good girl," approved the King.

Andraste sheathed her sword and raised her head high. She took a step forward and then another. Aldrich paused as he reached the King's side.

"Just carry her. It will be next year by the time she makes it off the field," recommended the King.

"It is nothing," said Andraste. She took another feeble step.

"Cannot a warrior aid another warrior?" asked Aldrich.

He did not wait for her reply. He picked her up effortlessly in his arms. Already the golden light was building between them. Andraste blushed as she heard the cat calling from the Victorious. The King of the Island Kingdoms silenced them with a look and then approached the Victorious menacingly.

"Do not take me to the dais! Not the dais! Not the dais!" ordered Andraste into Aldrich's shoulder.

"Rhiannon is signaling us," commented Aldrich.

"Not the dais! Your mother will say I told you so, and then I will not be permitted to fight tomorrow," said Andraste.

"The Southern lords have questions regarding your fighting style," replied Aldrich.

Andraste raised her head and saw that Aldrich was taking her to the Southern camp. Andraste looked up at Aldrich. He said, "I do have to be near you in order to heal you, and my place is with the Southern camp."

"Your place is with the Victorious," said Andraste.

"I want the Southern lords to get to know you," responded Aldrich.

Two lords moved from the bench as Aldrich approached. Aldrich gently set her down and began to undo her leg armor. He looked up at her mischievously.

"Not a word," said Andraste.

"Get your mind out of the gutter. I was thinking about the Darklands, when the dragon injured your ankle," said Aldrich.

"Dragon?" asked one of the Southern lords.

"It hurt like hell," admitted Andraste.

"And now?" asked Aldrich.

"It is nothing. I am fine," replied Andraste. Aldrich gently examined her calf. It was already the color of summer grapes. Andraste quickly covered her leg.

"No wonder you could not stand. I knew it was bad since you went down a second time," said Aldrich.

He propped pillows against her back and then sat beside her. He lifted her leg on top of him and placed his hands on her calf. She placed her cape over her legs.

"That looks even more devious," advised Aldrich.

"Just use the phoenix," blushed Andraste.

"Yes, but then you will leave. I have not been able to spend real time with you in days. This way you have reason to remain," said Aldrich softly so only she could hear.

"You like it best when I am defenseless and in pain?" asked Andraste.

"You once said you liked it best when I was poisoned," rejoined Aldrich.

"You were much more pleasant," replied Andraste, "Much less serious. Not a single lecture on reform or the faults of the North."

She heard laughter from the Southern lords.

"What is the next event?" asked Andraste.

"Are you not supposed to be running this?" inquired Aldrich.

"I did not know there was to be a tournament until this morning. You know I am always the last to know," rejoined Andraste.

"Archery," answered Egnatius.

Andraste tested her leg. Aldrich firmly held her leg in place.

"Since you were injured, you are disqualified from the next round," said Aldrich.

"You are cheating! Not true!" cried Andraste.

"It is the rules, Empress," said Egnatius.

"But now you can cheer for our prince," suggested Eadbehrt.

"If the Empress cannot shoot, then I will not," said Aldrich.

"Afraid I will beat you?" asked Andraste.

"Yes," replied Aldrich.

She felt Aldrich's hand move up her calf and rest above her knee. She swung her leg down and stood quickly. She nearly lost her balance in the effort. Aldrich wrapped an arm around her waist to steady her.

"Many thanks. As I cannot compete, I have to see a man about a horse," said Andraste.

"That is the best excuse you can come up with?" asked Rhiannon. Andraste tensed as her foster-sister approached. The lords parted and bowed low to Rhiannon.

"Vespasian is expecting me," said Andraste.

"Still trying to buy Boreas?" asked Rhiannon.

"Yes. That is why Vespasian is avoiding me," replied Andraste.

"And he will not disobey an Imperial command. Power corrupts," sighed Rhiannon.

"He suggested a ride on the beach," said Andraste.

"He is competing in the archery round," informed Rhiannon.

"Then you should compete, so he will be beaten, and we can go riding," said Andraste.

"Your ladyship is an archer?" asked Egnatius. The lords studied Rhiannon.

"We are looking at the best archer from the Island Kingdoms," replied Andraste.

"I do not compete in tournaments," said Rhiannon firmly. Her eyes shifted pointedly to the dais.

"Heiyoh!" called Vespasian. He rode Boreas up to the Southern railing and stopped.

"Not going to compete?" asked Rhiannon.

"No, the Empress has been disqualified. There would be no point," said Vespasian.

"I would still beat you," said Andraste.

"One of these days, you will meet someone better and you will have to mind your tongue," advised Vespasian, but he smiled at her. Andraste's eyes went to Boreas.

"Watch her. She will rob you blind," advised Rhiannon.

"It is the way of your people, I know. I too was raised in the Island Kingdoms," said Vespasian.

"How many children did your father foster?" asked Aldrich.

"Just four: Henry, Felix, Andraste, and Vespasian," replied Rhiannon.

"You are all so close," said Aldrich. He surveyed Vespasian coolly. Vespasian returned the stare just as dispassionately.

"Poor motherless children all," said Rhiannon.

"That is not true. We had you," responded Andraste.

"Poor mother I was, if my daughter is the Demon of the North," sighed Rhiannon. Andraste glared at her sister and headed towards the Southern railing. Aldrich moved to lend her his arm, but Andraste waved him away.

She turned her eyes to Vespasian.

"Give me a lift to the stable?" asked Andraste.

"Is your leg that bad?" questioned Vespasian, "Or are you still after my horse?"

Andraste only smiled as she slowly maneuvered to the railing. Boreas licked her hand as she reached for him. Vespasian reached and swung her up behind him. Aldrich glowered at the Northern Commander.

"Hold on," advised Vespasian.

"No-" started Rhiannon, but Vespasian was already flying down the field. They could hear the sound of Andraste's laughter.

"It is a horse to covet," agreed Egnatius as he watched Boreas and his riders gallop out of view.

"Lady Rhiannon," said Aldrich. Rhiannon turned her attention to Aldrich.

"Will Commander Vespasian be fighting in the tournament tomorrow?" asked Aldrich.

"I believe so, Prince Aldrich. Shall I tell him to expect your challenge?" inquired Rhiannon.

"If you would be so kind," replied Aldrich. He bowed low to Rhiannon.

"Where did you disappear to yesterday?" asked Rhiannon. Andraste opened her eyes and found Rhiannon's emerald eyes narrowed and studying her.

"By the gods! What is the hour?" inquired Andraste.

"Near noon. It is time for the jousting," answered Rhiannon, "Where were you? I know you were not with Vespasian because he came to the feast."

"I went to the temple," said Andraste. Rhiannon snorted and surveyed her.

"I swear," said Andraste, "And then I came here and slept."

"You need to be more considerate to our hosts," said Rhiannon.

"I doubt either the Queen or Aldrich missed me," replied Andraste.

"You are Empress, Andra. Everyone notices when you are not present," sighed Rhiannon.

"It is a temporary position," rejoined Andraste.

"Come get ready. I already drew you a bath, and no escaping. I have a guard posted below," said Rhiannon.

"Really?" asked Andraste. She rose and went to the veranda.

"Not in your nightgown!" hissed Rhiannon.

"Who is it? Rhinauld?" asked Andraste as she picked a rose from the bush and leaned over the railing offering it to the guard.

"Sorry to disappoint, Empress," greeted Aldrich. He took the flower from her and tucked it into his armor.

"I apologize for my sister so inconveniencing you," said Andraste quickly. She blushed and stepped back from the railing so that he could not see her. Rhiannon giggled from within her chamber.

"I look forward to seeing you at the tournament. The Queen has reserved a place for you," said Aldrich.

"That is most kind," replied Andraste. She retreated into her chambers and glowered at Rhiannon.

"I did warn you," said Rhiannon, "Now get ready. We have not much time."

Andraste got up dutifully and prepared herself for the day's events. As the day was already warm, Rhiannon had selected a sapphire Southern-style gown for Andraste. Rhiannon pulled Andraste's hair back in the Southern style, and placed a rose in Andraste's hair. Trumpets sounded in the distance. Andraste did not smile once despite Rhiannon's best efforts.

"Usually you love tournaments," said Rhiannon.

"I have seen enough fighting for my lifetime," responded Andraste.

"Your spirits are unusually low," observed Rhiannon, "No word from Sveinbiorn?"

Andraste shook her head. Rhiannon wrapped Andraste's arm in her own as they proceeded down the corridor.

"Today it is jousting. It is said that the Southern prince is the best jouster in all of the Empire," said Rhiannon. She eyed her sister mischievously, "You should also know he is yet to accept a lady's token; although, he has been presented with many."

"A token?" asked Andraste.

"A handkerchief, a glove, something for luck," responded Rhiannon, "Your rose might due."

"None of those things would bring him luck," replied Andraste. She frowned as she considered the motion and Rhiannon sighed.

As they walked into the stands, Rhiannon released Andraste's arm and fell a few paces behind. The assembled lords and ladies rose for Andraste as she passed. Andraste inclined her head and proceeded to the dais. She did not stop to address Aldrich or his opponent; although, she felt Aldrich's eyes follow her across the field. The Queen rose and curtsied to Andraste. The King of the Island Kingdoms raised his glass to his niece.

"Not jousting, Uncle?" asked Andraste.

"As you cannot, I will not," replied Aelius. He poured Andraste a glass of wine.

"I thought a tournament may lift your spirits. My son says you have been melancholy," said the Queen.

"Put a lance in her hand and you will see her laugh soon enough," replied Aelius.

"It would not be seemly," advised Rhiannon.

Andraste sighed and she took her seat. Once she was seated, the others took their seats. Andraste surveyed Aldrich's opponent and shook her head. Rhinauld was shifting his lance in his hand. He saluted her once he had her attention.

"Whose handkerchief?" asked Andraste. The Queen's eyes narrowed.

"Mine. I had to save him from the Southern ladies," replied Rhiannon.

"And you? Who wears your handkerchief?" asked Aelius.

"I can have no favorite, not until I am released as Empress," answered Andraste.

"And, yet, you wear the colors of the Southern prince," stated Aelius.

Andraste glanced to Rhiannon, who would not look her in the eye.

"An oversight," replied Andraste.

She rose as the two combatants rose and approached the dais. They both saluted her and then rode to their sides of the field. Andraste remained standing. Her heart began to pound as she saw Aldrich charge. He was an excellent horseman, and she admired his bearing and form as he held the lance. It was if it was an extension of his arm. He unhorsed Rhinauld in his first attempt. Rhinauld's lance was splintered and thrown across the field. True to his character, Rhinauld only laughed and pulled himself to his feet.

"A token of luck, you say?" asked Andraste.

"Do not be cruel," replied Rhiannon. Her concern lessened as she saw Rhinauld bow to the dais.

Aldrich circled back to make sure that Rhinauld was unharmed. Rhinauld said something to the prince and they both laughed. The prince bent down to grasp Rhinauld's hand. Rhinauld came to the dais, and Andraste retook her seat.

"I would have expected a better show from a knight from the Island Kingdoms," growled the King.

"Yes, but now I can be with Andra for the rest of the day," replied Rhinauld.

"Since you are acting the part, you may be my fool," allowed Andraste.

"With pleasure, Empress," said Rhinauld. He sat at her feet and looked up at her, "Did you see how fast he moved? I have never seen his equal."

"We admired his skill," answered Andraste, "I wonder what he will make of Henry."

"Henry is the best lancer from the Island Kingdoms," explained Rhiannon to the Queen.

"We will have to wait for the rest of the tournament to progress. Do you want to see the Southern lances? They are heavier than ours," said Rhinauld.

"I do," replied Andraste. Rhinauld rose, he bowed to Andraste and then headed towards Aldrich's camp.

"You cannot leave the dais," instructed Rhiannon as Andraste rose.

"I will bring you one," said Rhinauld. He bowed once more to Andraste.

Eadbehrt rode forth and touched his lance to Egnatius's shield. Egnatius mounted his horse and prepared himself.

"South versus South. This should be interesting," said the Queen.

"Who challenged who in the first round?" asked Andraste.

"Rhinauld challenged Aldrich," answered the King. He smiled at her over his wine glass, "It appears as North and East are trying to prevent Aldrich from challenging Vespasian. Do you know why?"

Andraste heard cheering as Egnatius started to charge Eadbehrt. Eadbehrt was late starting his own horse. Egnatius hit Eadbehrt with such speed that the Southern lord was thrown over his horse and down the field. Egnatius saluted the dais and then returned to the Southern encampment. Andraste smiled as she saw Vespasian take the field. She rose once more to view the field. Vespasian tapped his lance to Kasimir's shield.

"I hope Vespasian knocks Kasimir soundly off his horse!" said Rhiannon.

"Really? Why?" asked Andraste. She was surprised by the venom in Rhiannon's tone.

"Kasimir said that Vespasian had no more right to command a legion than a plumber to dream of being a king. He also said that the Northern knights might as well not attend the tournament as they would all be pummeled into the earth," informed Rhiannon.

Vespasian raised his lance to Andraste in salutation. Andraste beckoned for the Northern Commander to approach. She heard murmuring in the stands. Vespasian rode his horse over. Andraste descended the stairs and approached to stroke Boreas's neck. Vespasian dismounted and took off his helmet. He bowed low to Andraste.

"I have heard what this Southern lord said. I will not do you the dishonor of asking to take your place. However, if you lose this challenge, I will be more then displeased," declared Andraste so that the stands could hear.

"Yes, Empress," said Vespasian.

"As I have no token to give you, instead take this kiss," said Andraste. She stood on her tiptoes to kiss Vespasian's cheek. He grinned and quickly bowed to Andraste.

"Now pummel him into the earth," commanded Andraste. She heard cheering from the Northern lords and ladies.

"As you command, it will be done," vowed Vespasian. He bowed once more to Andraste and quickly mounted his horse. He spurred Boreas to his starting position.

"No favorites?" asked the King as Andraste retook her seat.

"This is a matter of Northern pride, and as I cannot fight, I must encourage our best," said Andraste. Rhiannon looked at her in disapproval. Andraste said, "You did say something for luck."

"I will be clearer in the future, Empress," replied Rhiannon.

Vespasian was near three-thirds down the field before Kasimir's horse even started. Boreas galloped as fast as the Northern wind. The two opponents missed each other on the first pass. Vespasian turned around quickly and charged Kasimir again. He hit the Southern knight squarely in the shoulder. Andraste heard the sound of crunching bone. Kasimir cried out and was knocked to the ground. Rhiannon winced and looked way.

Vespasian dismounted quickly to aid the injured lord. Aldrich and Egnatius were already crossing the field. Aldrich held out his hand and the spirit phoenix spread from his palm and healed Kasimir. Kasimir rotated his shoulder. He stood and then extended his hand to Vespasian in the Northern style. There was cheering from the crowd. Vespasian said something to Kasimir, who crimsoned and then approached the dais.

"I hear my words insulted you, Empress. I humbly apologize for any offense," said Kasimir. He remained bowed.

"Choose your words more carefully next time, Lord Kasimir, or I will have Vespasian unhorse you again," said Andraste.

"Or do it herself," commented the King.

"Do you mean to joust?" asked Kasimir. The Queen looked more than alarmed.

"Afraid?" questioned Vespasian, "My Empress taught me to joust."

"That is true. I had forgotten. We were but children then," said Rhiannon. She smiled at the memory.

"I will not joust today, please tell your prince not to worry," sighed Andraste.

"Any other words for my prince?" asked Kasimir.

"No," replied Andraste.

Kasimir bowed to her once more before returning to the Southern camp. Vespasian bowed once more to Andraste and returned to the Northern camp.

"I admire your self-control, niece. I know it is difficult to not be on the field or with your men," said the King. He poured her a second glass of wine.

"Aldrich would defeat me," admitted Andraste quietly. She was surprised by the sound of the Queen's laughter. The King laughed as well her. The next matches proceeded and Andraste feigned interest.

"Uncle, do you have something you wish to discuss with me?" asked Andraste as she sipped her wine.

"I know your meaning, but enjoy the next few days. Does your soul not need to recover from the events of the last year? Enjoy the peace while it lasts," said the King softly, so that only she could hear.

"You expect me to accept that you tampered with my memories in order to convey a significant message in case you perished; but now that our enemy is vanquished, you will not speak of it?" asked Andraste.

"Our enemy is not yet vanquished. Enjoy these days while you can. Do not distract the others from the jousting. They too deserve some merriment after these dark times," answered the King. Andraste returned her attention to Rhiannon.

"Where is Rhinauld?" asked Rhiannon in annoyance.

"He must have forgotten his assignment," frowned Andraste.

"It looks as though there will be an interlude: a show of horsemanship," interjected the Queen.

Three, small silver rings were being hung at the top of the shield display. They danced and sparkled on the Southern wind.

"The rings," replied Andraste wistfully. She stood and went to the edge of the dais.

"The crowd has dissipated some for the afternoon meal. Ladies, it is cruel to not let her partake. Our line has always been warriors. What good is being Empress, if she cannot do anything that brings her pleasure?" asked the King. He watched his niece fondly.

The Queen inclined her head slightly in approval.

"Only the rings, no jousting," relented Rhiannon.

Andraste turned her eyesight to the Northern camp. She caught Vespasian's eyes. He released Boreas and Andraste whistled. The horse jumped over the tourney and came to Andraste's side. Andraste jumped from the dais onto the stallion in a fluid movement.

"Decorum!" called Rhiannon.

Andraste did not care. She raced across the field towards the Northern camp. She heard cheering from the Northern camp and the Island Kingdoms. Henry left his station to come watch her. As she rode by the Northern camp, Laelius threw her a lance. She caught it and turned on the first ring. She approached and threw her lance threw the first ring. She circled back and Laelius threw her the next lance. She threw it from where she was and it went through the second ring. Laelius threw her a third lance, and she went for the last ring. It was higher than the others. It began to spin more rapidly as the wind increased.

"Heiyoh!" called Gnaeus in warning.

Andraste reared her horse in alarm. She turned sharply to see a lance pass her side and through the third ring. Aldrich was farther back then she had been. She turned her horse towards the prince. As she passed, she threw her lance back to Laelius.

"What about the other two rings?" asked Andraste as she approached Aldrich.

"Good afternoon, Empress," replied Aldrich. His eyes lowered to her exposed leg. Andraste quickly adjusted her robes.

"And if I make all three rings, will I also be your champion? Will I also get a kiss?" asked Aldrich.

"Yes. Unless I also make the third ring, then you will have to spend the day in the dais as my lady in waiting," replied Andraste.

Aldrich smiled at her as he signaled his squire, who brought him a second lance. Aldrich turned his horse around and gathered momentum. His lance went through the ring easily. He rode back for a third lance, and threw it from even farther away. It went through the third ring and the crowd cheered.

Andraste frowned as she turned her attention to the Northern camp. Laelius threw her the third lance again, and the Victorious rose to cheer her. She turned to go to the starting line and saw Aldrich waiting for her. He watched her intently. He studied every movement. His study made her feel self-conscious. She slowed her pace.

"What?" asked Andraste as she approached.

"Did I not tell you how beautiful you were today?" asked Aldrich. He lowered his eyes. Andraste felt her heart begin to race. Andraste dropped her lance.

"That is a defeat," said Aldrich triumphantly. Andraste glared at Aldrich in anger.

"I must return Boreas to Vespasian," said Andraste.

"Andraste are you forgetting something?" asked Aldrich.

He brought his horse alongside of hers, and reached for her. His fingertips brushed across her waist and held her. He leaned towards her and stole a kiss before Andraste could protest. There was cheering from the Southern lords. Aldrich looked to the Southern encampment and laughed until he saw Andraste's icy stare. He removed his hand and surveyed her.

"May I say the Caelius blue suits you?" asked Aldrich.

"This gown was not my choice, but kissing Vespasian was," answered Andraste. She turned her horse and headed back towards the Northern camp.

"What happened? In thirteen years, I have never seen you drop a lance in tournament," said Laelius.

"He said I was beautiful," admitted Andraste. The Victorious began to laugh uncontrollably.

"He finally beat you in a challenge," laughed Laelius.

"Is that why he kissed you?" asked Rhinauld. He surveyed the prince, who had returned to the Southern camp.

"There you are half-wit. You were supposed to bring me a Southern lance," said Andraste.

"Do you still want to see one?" asked Rhinauld. Andraste shook her head emphatically, "I have had enough of this tournament."

Vespasian laughed at her words. Andraste smiled at her friend.

"See how the prince glares at Vespasian. It looks like you are no longer the number one enemy, Rhinauld," commented Laelius.

"We will play his mind games," commanded Andraste.

Vespasian came and encircled his arms around her waist to help her dismount. He held her longer than necessary. He bent down to whisper in her ear, "Like this?"

There was some catcalling from the Victorious. Rhinauld laughed at the pair.

"That's enough, beauty. Go return to the dais," ordered Laelius.

"No, I will stay with my Victorious. I can see the jousts better from here," said Andraste.

"You cannot joust. Rhiannon will punish us both," stated Rhinauld.

"I do not need to joust. I have a champion," replied Andraste. She pulled a handkerchief from her sleeve and dramatically bestowed it on Vespasian, who took it and tucked it into his armor.

"I will carry it by my heart, Empress," said Vespasian. He bowed once more to Andraste.

"Easy now, the Southern prince could actually pummel you into the earth," warned Laelius.

Vespasian removed his cape, so that Andraste could sit on the ground. Andraste arranged her skirts about her. Vespasian took a seat at her side and whispered into her ear as they awaited the next joust. Andraste looked up as she saw Aldrich approach the shields. He struck Vespasian's shield with such force that it flew from its hook.

"If I am killed in this tournament, know it was for your amusement," said Vespasian. He eyed Aldrich coolly.

"Vespasian has a point," stated Laelius.

"Aldrich kissed me!" cried Andraste furiously.

"So much for Southern chivalry," said Rhinauld.

"You did lose the duel. I heard your wager," stated Laelius.

Vespasian mounted his horse and saluted Andraste. He measured Aldrich in a calculating gaze. However, as soon as Vespasian was at the starting position, Aldrich charged. It was nothing like his first round. Aldrich rode with such speed and power that Andraste was mesmerized. The crowd barely had time to cheer before the opponents met at the half-way point.

Their lances bounced off of each other's armor and splintered. Laelius quickly hurled Vespasian a second lance. Aldrich was already rearmed and upon an unarmed Vespasian. Vespasian dodged the attack and caught the second lance. He was not quick enough. Aldrich hit him soundly on the third attack. Vespasian was thrown from his horse. He rose quickly, shaking his head. He moved diagonally. He made his way back to the Northern camp.

"Are you injured?" asked Andraste.

"Only my pride, Empress," replied Vespasian. He bowed to Andraste, but was wobbly on his feet. Laelius and Vitus moved to steady him.

"Sit," commanded Andraste.

Vespasian sat beside her and then fell backwards onto the grass. She moved his head onto her lap so she could examine his temple. Her hair fell over her shoulder as she did so.

"It was quite a blow," admitted Vespasian.

Andraste giggled. She raised a hand to her mouth to stop the sound. She blushed prettily. All of the Northern lords and officers stopped what they were doing and began to laugh.

"Did you just giggle?" asked Vespasian. He opened one eye to study her.

"Witnessed," replied Laelius. All of the Victorious laughed and Andraste laughed as well.

"Then it was worth it. Andraste Valerianus, Pillar of the East, Commander of the Imperial Army, our esteemed Empress, giggling like a girl," said Vespasian. He shook his head and closed his eyes.

"I am a girl," stated Andraste.

"You may have a concussion," advised Rhinauld.

"Let us get you into the shade," suggested Andraste. Laelius and Vitus helped move Vespasian into the Northern tent. Andraste followed behind.

"Do we have any Northern knights left?" asked Andraste.

"No, but the Island Kingdoms fare little better. The only remaining knight is Henry. The Western knight just lost. That leaves Aldrich and one more Southern knight. Aldrich will duel the victor," informed Gnaeus.

"I will tend to Vespasian," said Andraste.

"Rice wine?" asked Laelius as she entered the Northern tent.

"It is Andra," commented Rhinauld, already offering her a glass.

"Vesp?" inquired Andraste.

"I am here," answered Vespasian. Andraste saw that Hyacinth was tending to the knight. She spoke gently to him. Andraste exchanged looks with Laelius.

"They plan to announce their understanding at the Moon Festival," said Vitus.

"I should not have kissed him or made such a display. I apologize," said Andraste.

"It was for the North. It gave me great pleasure to see that Southern knight knocked off his horse," said Hyacinth from across the room. She smiled at Andraste shyly.

"How are your studies?" asked Andraste.

"I have learned a great deal, Empress," answered Hyacinth.

They heard cheering from the field.

"It sounds like the Southern corner," sighed Laelius.

"Aldrich must have won," commented Rhinauld. His eyes looked to Andraste, "It is your duty to congratulate the victor."

"As Vesp is in good hands, I will return to the dais," said Andraste. She smiled to Hyacinth, but the maiden was busy tending her intended.

Andraste returned to the dais to find an extremely irritated Queen and Rhiannon.

"You missed the last jousts," said the King.

"Who won?" asked Andraste.

"Aldrich," replied the Queen proudly.

"How is Vesp? Were his wounds serious?" asked Rhiannon. Andraste shook her head.

"Does he need tending?" asked the Queen.

"Hyacinth is with him," replied Andraste.

"I should have told you," said Rhiannon.

"You should have," stated Andraste.

Andraste turned to determine the cause of the Queen rising to her feet. Aldrich was still on horseback, and was riding in front of the Southern stands searching the crowd. He carried a crown of roses woven together on the tip of his lance.

"As you were not here, we already gave him the prize," said the Queen.

"He will pick the Queen of the Tournament, and she will be obligated to give him a kiss," said Rhiannon.

"Although you have already done that once today," said the King.

"Not voluntarily," replied Andraste.

"You lost a bet?" asked Rhiannon. The Queen shook her head in disapproval.

"Gerlinde?" asked the King in surprise as Aldrich made his choice.

"He is angry with me," answered Andraste. She kept her back turned. She heard the crowd applaud as Gerlinde kissed Aldrich.

"It is strange he did not pick Decima," frowned the Queen.

"She is not here," said Rhiannon sadly, "She spends most of her time in the temple these days."

"Perhaps we can convince her to attend the ball," said the Queen. The silence between them lengthened.

"Am I free to go?" asked Andraste.

"Yes, the tournament is concluded for today," replied the King. Andraste turned to leave and passed Aldrich on the stairs.

"I did not see you return," stated Aldrich.

"Congratulations," replied Andraste. She stepped back quickly.

"How is the Northern Commander? Is he hurt?" inquired Aldrich.

"He is well tended by our young charge," replied the Queen.

"Not by you?" questioned Aldrich.

"As you see," replied Andraste.

"The tournament Queen approaches," advised the King. He rose and offered Andraste his arm. Andraste took it, but turned to address Aldrich before she descended the stairs, "Enjoy your evening, Prince Aldrich."

She descended the stairs on the King's arm. Gerlinde glared at her but made room for Andraste and the King to pass. She curtsied ever so slightly.

"You are not going to attend the ball?" asked the King.

"No. I have no desire to dance," replied Andraste.

"Aldrich is throwing the tournaments and balls for you. We are all aware of your sadness. Do not forget we also have cause to rejoice," said the King.

"Uncle, I feel as though I could cry for a hundred years. I look for faces that are no longer here, and will never be here again. I see empty seats and expect my comrades to walk through the door, and then I remember that they will not come again. I try summoning Sveinbiorn twice a day and he does not answer. It is more than I can bear," responded Andraste.

The King kissed her forehead. He wrapped her arm tightly in his.

"I too look for my daughters. It will get better in time, Andra. As for now, we must cherish the living," said the King.

"Yes, Uncle," responded Andraste.

"But as for this evening, I will make your excuses," said the King, "Will you return to your chambers?"

"No, I will ride," replied Andraste, "I wish to see the Southern Ruin once more."

"Do you want Rhinauld or Henry to accompany you?" asked the King.

"I wish to be alone. I have not been alone since the Ice Palace," replied Andraste.

"As you wish," said the King. He left her at the stables and then continued to the dining hall. Andraste went to find her horse, but she was not in her stall.

"She is being reshoed," informed Aldrich. He was leading Boreas by his reins. Andraste looked to the stallion.

"We were playing for keeps," said Aldrich. Andraste frowned as she went to stroke Boreas's neck.

"He is for you," stated Aldrich. Andraste stepped back in surprise as she blushed. Aldrich offered her the reins.

"Would you be angry if I were to regift them Boreas after their announcement?" asked Andraste.

"Them?" questioned Aldrich.

"Vespasian and Hyacinth will announce their understanding at the Moon Festival," replied Andraste.

"But I thought," started Aldrich.

"Vespasian is five years my junior. I have always considered him one of my younger brothers. He does not look his age. In fact, we lied about his age so that he could join the Imperial Army with us," said Andraste, "So he is actually the youngest Commander in the Imperial Army's history."

"Yet another Northern deception," said Aldrich with a smile. He studied Andraste and the offered her his cape, "I will leave you. Forgive me, I heard part of your conversation with your uncle, and I know you desire to be alone. But take my cape; it will be getting colder as the sun sets."

"I imagine the victor of the tournament must return to the feast," alleged Andraste.

"My duties are fulfilled for this evening," replied Aldrich.

"Gerlinde will be sorely disappointed," said Andraste.

"She can console Kasimir. His pride is sorely injured," responded Aldrich. Andraste smiled up at him.

"Do you want to ride with me?" asked Andraste.

"I must rest my horse. He is weary from the day's events," replied Aldrich.

"It would be a shame to not ride Boreas when you have the chance. He could carry us both. It is a common enough custom in the North as you saw by our journey. I have seen some of your Southern court try the custom as well," said Andraste.

She did not look at Aldrich as she wrapped his cape about her shoulders.

"Is this your wish?" asked Aldrich.

"Yes, but not a command. It is your choice, my lord," replied Andraste.

Aldrich put his hands about her waist and lifted her to the saddle. He mounted behind her and pulled her to him so that she was secure.

"Do not worry. There was no one in the courtyard when I arrived, and it will be dark when we return," said Aldrich.

"I am not ashamed of you or our conduct," replied Andraste.

"But you fear Titus's threats," stated Aldrich. Andraste laid her head on his shoulder.

"I wish those damned delegates would arrive, so that you would be released," said Aldrich fiercely. He started Boreas onto the road at a tremendous speed.

"Why?" asked Andraste.

"So I could pursue you with all of the resources at my disposal," answered Aldrich.

"Am I to be hunted, my prince?" asked Andraste. Aldrich smiled in spite of himself.

"Do you not remember what Laelius told you in the beginning? If you hunt one of the Victorious, you will find yourself the hunted," admonished Andraste.

"Yes, but now, I am also Victorious," responded Aldrich.

They reached the beach as the sun began to set, and Aldrich slowed to a cantor.

"I was discourteous earlier. You surprised me by your request," said Andraste.

"Rhinauld forewarned me that you were a sore loser," replied Aldrich.

"I should have known it was one of his plots. Besides you cheated!" exclaimed Andraste.

"My apologies, Empress. I will note that complimenting you is noted as cheating," responded Aldrich.

"For all of your gallantries, you are an insolent rascal," said Andraste.

"I have been called worse," rejoined Aldrich. Andraste took a deep breath.

"What is it?" asked Aldrich.

"You distracted me once more. My point is that I owe you a kiss, as you kissed me earlier. I did not kiss you. I must fulfill our wager," said Andraste. She felt Aldrich tense against her. She lifted her lips to Aldrich and kissed him sweetly. Aldrich's grip around her tightened as he kissed her back.

"Andraste, by the gods, I only have but so much self-control!" exclaimed Aldrich as he pulled himself away from her. Boreas snorted and shook his mane.

"Such a Southern response," replied Andraste. She glanced up at Aldrich and found him blushing. Her hand brushed his thigh as she turned to look ahead once more.

"Do not worry, my prince. I will not kiss you again until you ask me to," promised Andraste.

"So you would if I asked?" inquired Aldrich. It was Andraste's turn to blush. She kept her eyes fixed on the horizon.

"We should return to the palace," said Aldrich.

"No, let us stay on the beach and watch the stars," said Andraste.

"We will be missed," stated Aldrich.

"Are we not entitled to one night? After all we have done for the Republic?" asked Andraste.

"I have done very little, but you, Empress, may do as you please," replied Aldrich. Andraste leaned into him, and when she looked up he was smiling.

Chapter Twenty

Despite her best efforts to relinquish control of the Empire, she still found herself to be essential in planning of the Republic. As kingdoms, cities and tribes picked their own delegates, the delegates flocked to join her court. The delegation would start quarreling in the morning and continue into the evening. This had necessitated her second proclamation: no discussing delegate business during dinner. After all, she was only human, and she feared that she would strike down one of the delegates. The worse part about the Assembly was that the only times she saw Aldrich was in the Assembly chambers across the room, or briefly at dinner when they were surrounded by crowds.

"You are needed at Assembly," greeted Rhiannon. She prodded Andraste in her side.

"No," protested Andraste.

"Empress," warned Rhiannon.

"What is on the docket?" asked Andraste.

"What to do in times of war," said Rhiannon.

"Kill them, kill them all," said Andraste sleepily. Her head sank back into the pillow.

"The delegates or the hypothetical invaders?" asked Rhiannon.

"You pick," said Andraste succumbing to sleep.

Rhiannon seized her pillow and pulled with all her might. Andraste fell onto the floor in an undignified heap. Rhiannon laughed heartedly, but she helped Andraste to her feet. Andraste was now wide awake. Rhiannon helped Andraste get ready and pinned her hair in the Southern fashion. It was already hot, so Andraste wore a light, short-sleeved, mauve colored gown.

"Come to the sewing room when you are let out for the day. Marcella and Decima will come as well to help me with wedding preparations," bade Rhiannon.

"So bossy," sighed Andraste.

Andraste left her chambers and headed towards the Chambers of Justice. She was distracted by the sound of swordplay from the training yard. She saw that a crowd of men were watching a duel. Andraste spotted Rhinauld and Henry and went to their side.

"Who does Aldrich duel?" asked Andraste as she surveyed the combatants.

"That is the Duke of the Reed Plains, a western territory. He is actually quite a swordsman," answered Henry.

"But no match for Aldrich," alleged Rhinauld.

"Why do they duel?" inquired Andraste.

"Our host declared that none could pursue your hand without first beating him in a duel," smiled Rhinauld.

"He has been at it since dawn," said Henry. Andraste frowned. She took a step forward.

"Do not distract him," warned Rhinauld.

"I fight my own battles," stated Andraste.

"Really? For the past year, Aldrich has fought at your side," replied Rhinauld.

Andraste winced as the Duke landed a blow on Aldrich's temple. Aldrich continued without the slightest hesitation.

"You do not have to watch," said Henry. He blocked Andraste's view with his broad shoulders.

"Commander never winces at my injuries," commented Felix.

"That is because she has dealt most of them," replied Rhinauld.

"Well at least she has never shot me," returned Felix. He and Rhinauld laughed, but realized that Andraste was not paying either of them any attention.

Andraste side-stepped Henry, so that she could view the duel. Her eyes were locked on Aldrich's combatting form. Aldrich disarmed his opponent in a fluent gesture. Aldrich was cheered by the Southern lords and the Victorious.

"That is a signature Andraste move, if I ever saw one," commented Laelius.

The Duke accepted his defeat with dignity. He bowed to Aldrich. Aldrich bowed to the Duke.

"Do you think Aldrich would beat me?" asked Andraste. She studied the prince.

"Afraid you would lose?" inquired Rhinauld.

"Do not accept any duels," advised Henry.

"I have never refused a challenge. I will not start now," said Andraste.

"But would you accept the outcome of the wager?" questioned Laelius.

Aldrich moved to rejoin the Southern lords. He was still unware of Andraste's presence.

"I was told that in the South, a lady chooses her suitor, a gentleman does not duel for her," said Andraste.

Aldrich turned at the sound of her voice and bowed to her before approaching.

"Empress, I would never be so forward. I fight only for your right to choose, not to be chosen," replied Aldrich.

"My prince, let me tend you. I see you have been injured," said Gerlinde crossing the training yard.

"It is nothing," replied Aldrich. As Aldrich turned to address Gerlinde, Andraste saw a gash on Aldrich's temple. Gerlinde was not to be deterred. She had reached Aldrich's side and lifted a handkerchief to Aldrich's brow.

"That is not necessary," said Andraste.

She reached a hand to Aldrich's face and gold light emitted from her fingertips. She kept her fingers just out of touching distance. Aldrich froze her with his sapphire eyes. She stood until the light faded from her fingertips. She lowered her hand and surveyed the gash. There was not even a scar.

"That is a neat trick," said Gerlinde. Aldrich's eyes turned to Gerlinde. Andraste wordlessly turned to leave.

"You are needed at the Assembly," said Aldrich softly.

"We are both needed," replied Andraste. They stood staring at each other in the training field.

"Well get on then," called Rhinauld.

Gerlinde curtsied to Aldrich and retreated towards the Southern lords. Aldrich and Andraste proceeded towards the Chambers of Justice. Aldrich did not offer Andraste his arm.

"How long do you plan on staying?" asked Aldrich, and then he added, "You are welcome to stay as long as you please."

"I will stay until the Assembly is fully-seated," replied Andraste.

"So soon?" frowned Aldrich.

"I will not impose on you long," assured Andraste.

"It is no imposition," insisted Aldrich.

"I plan to sail to the Old World," stated Andraste.

"Whatever for?" asked Aldrich.

"Where is your sense of adventure, Ruin conqueror?" inquired Andraste.

"Overwhelmed by my sense of duty," retorted Aldrich.

"You will not go with me, then?" questioned Andraste.

"No, Empress, I cannot go with you," answered Aldrich, "Why do you not stay?"

"I will not be a part of this new world. I cannot fit in here. There are those who will want to use me to pursue the superiority of the North, and those from other lands that will never trust me," claimed Andraste sadly.

"You are loved here. The people love you. Do you not see it?" questioned Aldrich.

"That is not reason enough for me to stay," replied Andraste.

"You will not stay to fight the Lionden Arisen with me?" asked Aldrich.

"I do not wish to fight anymore," responded Andraste.

"We will be weakened by your absence," said Aldrich.

They had reached the Chambers of Justice, which were being used for the first Assembly of the Republic.

"Why must I come today?" asked Andraste.

"They wish to show you great honor," responded Aldrich.

He could say no more as the doors opened before them. The delegates rose as Andraste entered. Aldrich seated her at the center of the room next to Decima, who had been elected Speaker. The delegates once more were seated. Aldrich took his seat.

"We will now vote to have this issue resolved. In times of foreign invasion, a Commander will be elected to lead the Imperial Forces against the invaders. The title of this Commander will be known as Paramerion," said Decima.

Andraste felt the heat rise to her face. The motion was carried. Once more the delegates rose to recognize her. Sensing Andraste's embarrassment, Decima continued to the next motion. The morning proceeded without hitch.

Andraste scanned the room. There were still only three seats left open. Once they were filled, she would be free to depart for the Old World. She was surprised at how much the thought saddened her. Her eyes swept across the room and landed on Rhinauld.

"Pay attention," mouthed Rhinauld silently. She glared at him, but straightened in her chair and listened to a Northern lord drone onwards in a flat monotone regarding taxes. She lasted a full ten minutes before her mind turned to possible awaiting adventures across the seas.

The doors to the Chambers of Justice swung open, and Laelius practically flew down the hallway to Andraste.

"Sveinbiorn has returned," whispered Laelius in her ear. Andraste rose to her feet hastily.

"If you will excuse me," announced Andraste. Her robes swished against the floor as she sped down the aisle. Laelius quickly followed after her.

"He is in his chambers. The Queen kept them for him in case he returned. He does not look well, Empress," said Laelius.

"Is he injured?" asked Andraste.

"I know not. He said only one word upon arrival and then collapsed," replied Laelius.

"What was it?" questioned Andraste.

"Andraste," answered Laelius.

Nero and Laurentius were stationed outside of Sveinbiorn's

chamber doors.

"What are you doing?" inquired Andraste.

"The prince ordered that Sveinbiorn be watched were he to return. I thought it would displease you less if the guards were our own," said Laelius.

Andraste flushed angrily.

"The prince could have banned Sveinbiorn from his lands. He does know the true nature of Lord Eldgrimson," cautioned Laelius.

"Sveinbiorn has done nothing to hurt any of us. He has saved the prince's kingdom repeatedly!" retaliated Andraste.

Sveinbiorn was sprawled out on the scarlet sofa in front of the fireplace. He raised his sea-green eyes at the sound of Andraste's voice. Andraste threw herself onto his chest. Sveinbiorn wrapped an arm around her though it seemed to cause him great pain.

"Are you injured? What do you need? What can I do?" asked Andraste.

"I will sleep while," answered Sveinbiorn.

His weight sagged against her. Andraste caught him and rested his head in her lap. There were new indigo markings across his arm that she could not understand. It looked like a form of Ruins that she could not read. They resonated against her fingers when she touched them, and a red light began to materialize. She withdrew her touch. She examined the rest of his body gently, but found no wounds. She felt his pulse. It was steady. It was reassuringly constant.

"Should I send for a healer, Commander?" asked Laelius.

"I found no wounds. You are dismissed," replied Andraste.

"Yes, Commander," said Laelius. He bowed to her and turned to go.

"Laelius," called Andraste.

"Yes?" asked Laelius.

"Thank you for informing me so quickly," said Andraste. Laelius bowed once more and left the room, shutting the doors behind him.

"Any news?" asked the King.

"No, he still sleeps like the dead," sighed Andraste.

"Demons may sleep for long periods after great battles. I would not be too concerned. You should come to dinner. You are missed in the dining hall," said the King.

"I will wait until he awakes. I do not want him to awaken alone," responded Andraste.

"You misunderstand. He could sleep for weeks," stated the King.

"I will at least stay with him until morning," replied Andraste.

"May I send Decima? She suffers cruelly," asked the King.

"Of course," said Andraste.

The King left the room and she heard him stop in front of Aldrich's chambers. Thracius opened the door for Decima to enter and then shut it soundlessly behind her. Decima looked at Andraste for answers.

"My uncle says he may sleep for weeks," stated Andraste.

"I will not trouble you," said Decima.

"You are welcome to stay. I am sure he will rest better if you are near," said Andraste.

Decima blushed and slowly sat down in the large arm chair near the fireplace.

"Where do you think he went?" asked Decima. Andraste shook her head. She could give no answer.

"And he returned alone?" inquired Decima. Andraste scarcely nodded. She looked down at her sleeping brother.

"I am sorry," said Decima.

"Anything else happen at Assembly?" asked Andraste.

"The delegates droned endlessly regarding taxes. Nothing was carried. Aldrich delivered some elegant remarks, but he was not brief," replied Decima.

Andraste did not respond.

"Did you know Aldrich tried to stop by earlier? The Victorious would not let him," said Decima.

Andraste only stared at Decima in response.

"Aldrich does not know Lord Eldgrimson as we do. Once he does, he will see there is no need. The prince does not mean to be cruel. He feels it is his duty to keep his people safe. He is being cautious, nothing more," stated Decima.

"My brother, this *demon*, has saved this city twice. He is a hero. He has saved my life, which allowed me to defeat the Emperor. We are indebted to him. He should not be treated so," replied Andraste.

Decima studied Andraste and decided to change the subject.

"How is Brion? I have not seen him since his return from the North," asked Decima.

"He is well. He is keeps to himself these days. He is mainly in the library. He is staying out of Rhiannon's way," responded Andraste with a small smile.

"The day approaches," said Decima.

"It is kind of the Queen to permit the ceremony here. It must cause her great inconvenience," said Andraste.

"The Queen lives for events. Besides Rhiannon is a favorite at court," replied Decima.

"Rhiannon is a favorite wherever she goes," acknowledged Andraste. The silence lengthened between them. Decima rose slowly.

"I must attend to my other duties. Will you let me know if there are any changes?" asked Decima. She curtsied to Andraste.

"Yes, of course," answered Andraste. Decima left the room and Andraste was left alone with her sleeping patient and her thoughts.

Once the morning session of the Assembly ended, Andraste escaped as fast as she could. Her intention was to check on Sveinbiorn. However, she was lured by the sound of Northern music coming from the dance hall. She went into the hall and found a number of Southern lords and ladies learning a Northern dance.

Kasimir and Eadbehrt saw her enter. They bowed and then approached.

"We are learning some of the Northern dances," informed Eadbehrt.

"I can see that," replied Andraste.

"Prince Aldrich was supposed to join us after the assembly. Have you seen him?" asked Kasimir.

"He was present at Assembly," answered Andraste. She moved to continue on her way.

"This afternoon there is to be a hunt. Will you join us, Empress?" invited Eadbehrt.

"There is a problem with wild boars in the Southern province. We could use your lance," added Kasimir.

Andraste shook her head and started from the hall.

"Empress, will you show the way with me?" asked Gnaeus coming to her side, "These dances are harder to show then I imagined."

"Ask Maximianus, he knows the dances the best," answered Andraste.

Gnaeus's face fell. Andraste felt the heat rush to her face as she realized her blunder, but worse her heart sunk into her chest and she once again felt her loss. She blinked back tears.

"He was the best of us," agreed Gnaeus. He did not meet her eyes.

"If you will excuse me," said Andraste hastily. She brushed a tear from her face as she turned. Kasimir and Eadbehrt stepped out of her way as she fled from the hall. She headed towards Sveinbiorn's chambers, but she was intercepted by Decima.

"No change," said Decima. She curtsied slightly to Andraste and continued her way.

Andraste altered her course and returned to her own chambers. She shut the door tightly behind her and leaned against it for support. She closed her eyes tightly to restrict the imminent cascade of tears. She took a few deep breaths to steady herself.

She slowly opened her eyes, and her attention registered on her shamisen. It was one of the few items that she had taken from her rooms at the Citadel. It had belonged to her mother. She picked it up in her arms like an old friend and seated herself out on her veranda, looking out over the ocean. The ocean was cerulean at this time of day. The waves gently lapped at the shore, and a gentle breeze blew from the South.

Andraste plucked a Northern ballad absently as she watched the tide come in. She heard a knock on her door, but she chose to ignore it. Instead, she played a more melancholy tune that better suited her mood. She sang softly.

"A great while ago I met a lass,
As beautiful as the first day of spring.
I swore to make her my wife,

But before I could, the drums called.
The nobles waged another war
That took us from our lands.
Years we fought great battles
And when I finally returned,
My lass had passed away,
Never knowing of my love,
Or how her face kept me alive,
Through those hellish days,
Or of my hopes and dreams
To always be at her side.
I laid flowers on her grave,
And, then and there, told her my vows.
May my love reach her in heaven
As I am left behind on earth."

"Andra, no wonder reports of you being melancholy are circulating through the palace," said Rhinauld from the doorway.

"I did not permit you to enter," replied Andraste. She continued to play the shamisen.

"When have I ever waited for permission?" asked Rhinauld. He leaned against the doorframe and surveyed her with his emerald eyes.

"Come, there is to be a hunt. It would improve your spirits," entreated Rhinauld.

"Not today," objected Andraste.

"Aldrich will be leading the hunt," said Rhinauld.

"Gerlinde is more pleasing than I. She will be better company," stated Andraste.

"Yes, but less good with a spear, I wager," responded Rhinauld.

Andraste smiled slightly. He walked across her veranda to the gate connecting to the Queen's veranda. Rhinauld went through the gate.

"Are you awake, Caelius? The hunt is about to leave," said Rhinauld. Andraste's smile faded.

"Proceed. I will remain behind," answered Aldrich.

"We cannot hunt without our host," stated Rhinauld.

"We do not have such a tradition in the South. My duties cause me to remain here," said Aldrich.

"Meaning your nap time? I will allow it as you fought many duels for my sister as of late. Play the prince another lullaby, Andra. Perhaps something with more cheer? Come, Caelius, you will hear better from this side of the gate," suggested Rhinauld.

Andraste shot Rhinauld a hostile look.

"I will not intrude on the Empress," said Aldrich.

"But you will eavesdrop on her playing? I do not blame you. She is very talented, and rarely performs for strangers," said Rhinauld, "But she may play for you, if you ask her. If you do not ask, then she will hide inside and play with her maps."

"I would have the Empress do as she pleases. I too know the value of an idle hour," replied Aldrich.

"Then it is up to you, Andra. Invite the prince or do not invite the prince. It is your decision. I am off to the hunt," said Rhinauld.

"Off to the hunt? You already caught us rather well," responded Andraste. She heard Aldrich's laughter from the other side of the gate.

Rhinauld rumpled her hair as he passed, and then he was gone. She heard the door to her chamber close behind him. She repositioned herself on a bench nearest the rose bushes between her and the Queen's veranda. She began to play softly. She chose a Southern tune that she had heard Decima play once before, and then songs from the Northern lands.

"You did not go on the hunt, my son?" asked the Queen from her chambers. She stopped to listen to Andraste playing, "Is that you, Empress? Why do you not join us for dinner? There will not be a meal in the great hall as the hunting party will picnic, and many of the ladies who remained are dining in the sewing room."

"The sewing room!" swore Andraste. She rose hastily. She saw that Aldrich was reclining on a lounge chair. Upon seeing her, he rose hastily.

"Rhinauld already told Rhiannon that you could not make it today. Rhiannon understood," said the Queen, "Come and eat with us."

"Yes, your Majesty," said Andraste.

Aldrich walked across the veranda and opened the gate, so that Andraste could enter on to the Queen's veranda.

"How is your brother?" inquired Aldrich.

"He is well guarded, which is even a further mismanagement of manpower as he still sleeps," replied Andraste. Aldrich frowned as he studied Andraste, but he made no response.

"It as if it were a magical slumber," replied the Queen. Andraste turned her eyes to the Queen.

"If you were in my position, would you not do the same?" asked Aldrich. Andraste held his gaze and raised her head proudly.

"I went to see him this morning. None of our healing magic had any effect," said the Queen.

"I thank you for your pains," said Andraste. The Queen smiled at her sadly, and then went into her chambers to speak to a servant.

Aldrich still waited for her response. Andraste's eyes darted to his temple and remembered his wound from the previous morning.

"How is your head?" asked Andraste. Aldrich seemed taken back. He put a hand to his temple.

"I had forgotten. It does not pain me at all," said Aldrich, "I did not thank you-"

"Thanks would be unnecessary as you fought for me- my choice," corrected Andraste.

"More duels at dawn?" asked the Queen as she returned. She smiled at Aldrich and then looked to Andraste.

"There were more this morning," said Aldrich. He turned his attention to Andraste, "Please come in."

Andraste swept through the gate. She followed Aldrich to the Queen's table. It had already been set for three. Andraste set her shamisen against the rose bush.

"I enjoyed hearing you play," said the Queen.

"I am sorry. I did not mean to bother you," blushed Andraste.

"You play very well. Although, I distinctly remember you once telling me that you did not play an instrument," alleged the Queen.

"Mother," said Aldrich.

"It is no matter, but I am curious. Do you secretly draw or paint?" asked the Queen.

"I have painted in the Northern style. My father taught me when I was younger," said Andraste softly.

"He was a great painter," agreed the Queen, "Most of the paintings in the Citadel were done by your father."

"They were burned after my mother's death. My father found them painful to look at," said Andraste. She looked towards her wine glass as Aldrich was watching her carefully.

"I am sorry for that," said the Queen, "and for your losses."

"Thank you," replied Andraste automatically.

"I had never heard the first song you sang. It was quite beautiful. Where does it come from?" asked Aldrich.

"Tobias wrote a poem, and I put it to music," said Andraste.

"It was lovely. Morbid for my tastes, but very beautiful," said the Queen. Aldrich looked apologetically at Andraste and refilled her wine goblet.

"Kasimir said you had a boar problem?" asked Andraste.

"They have been left undisturbed for too long. There numbers have grown and they are destroying farmland," replied Aldrich.

"Do you hunt often?" inquired Andraste.

"I prefer fishing, crabbing, or digging for oysters," responded Aldrich.

"As it is warm, we will just have a simple salad with grilled salmon and fresh bread," said the Queen as the platters were brought out.

"That sounds perfect," said Andraste.

"It is the best type of meal for this time of year," stated the Queen.

"Do you think the hunt will be late?" asked Andraste.

"There will not be dancing or the social hour tonight," replied Aldrich.

"You both must be relieved," said the Queen.

"Kasimir and Eadbehrt were learning Northern dances," said Andraste.

"For Rhiannon and Brion's wedding," explained the Queen.

"Did you join them?" asked Andraste.

"It was my intention. However, I was delayed. I heard the most beautiful music, which kept me from leaving the Queen's veranda," answered Aldrich.

"Just like one of the sirens from Rhinauld's adventures," stated the Queen.

"I hope I am not as lethal," said Andraste.

"Probably more so, but the sirens do not carry Ruin blades," replied Aldrich.

"Laelius, Rhinauld, and Henry think you are a match for me now. They think that you will beat me," said Andraste.

"No swordplay at the dinner table!" ordered the Queen.

"A duel? I thought we had made progress. I was daring to hope that my Empress would instruct me in the Northern dances," said Aldrich.

"Teach you the Northern dances?" asked Andraste. She looked puzzled at Aldrich. He looked way and shifted uncomfortably.

"As you wish. I would not refuse a request from my host, when you have been so generous," said Andraste, "Why do you look so confounded?"

"I did not think that you would agree," answered Aldrich.

"Do you think that I am such a beast?" asked Andraste.

"No!" exclaimed Aldrich.

"Were you teasing? Do you not want to learn the Northern dances?" inquired Andraste.

"You mistake my son's meaning. He has only seen your strength and courage. He has seen the fearless Northern warrior. He is not used to your gentle side. Why would you hide such talents and poise?" asked the Queen.

"Talents?" repeated Andraste. She looked perplexed from the Queen to Aldrich. She continued, "I do not possess as many talents or courtly airs as many of the noble ladies. The Southern ladies are much more accomplished then I."

"I doubt that embroidering pillows or drawing portraits would have done you much good at Thoran or Gardenia," replied Aldrich.

"You are very talented, my child. You will make some man an ideal partner someday," said the Queen. She smiled kindly at Andraste and patted her hand.

"Someday . . . if the remaining three Assembly seats are filled, and I am released as Empress," sighed Andraste.

"And after you explore and conquer the Old World?" inquired Aldrich.

"Maybe I will find myself a husband in the Old World," answered Andraste. Aldrich's smile faded.

"Do you think there are still peoples in the Old World?" asked the Queen.

"No, probably just monkeys and parrots," replied Andraste.

"Do you not wish to see the Old World as well?" inquired the Queen. She turned to her son.

"I do, but my duty is to my people," answered Aldrich.

"After I married your father, the Dowager Queen ruled in our stead for near two years as we toured the Empire," said the Queen. She smiled fondly at the memory. Aldrich looked to Andraste and then to his mother.

"What time would suit you for your dancing lessons?" asked Andraste.

"Why not now?" inquired Aldrich.

"Music?" questioned Andraste.

"I know a few simple tunes that your mother taught me," suggested the Queen.

Aldrich rose and offered Andraste his hand before she could refuse. She slapped his hand away, and offered her hand to him.

"If we must hold hands, then my hand rests lightly over yours. We also keep a good arm lengths distance between us. You do not tuck my arm as in the Southern style. In the Northern court that would be seen as inappropriate as we have no understanding," said Andraste. Aldrich adapted to her instructions.

The Queen started playing the shamisen. Her remarks had been an understatement, as she was a master musician. Andraste paused to listen to her play. She dropped Aldrich's hand.

"Raise your right palm, but do not touch mine. Good, now circle right. Your right, not my right," said Andraste. She then dropped her right palm and raised her left palm to Aldrich. Aldrich mirrored her actions. She turned the opposite direction and Aldrich followed.

"We walk forward, and you ever so lightly take my hand. Then I will lift my hand to the lady before me, and we will turn in a circle. The men stand to the side. When I come back to center, you will meet me. You will lift me by my waist and turn in a circle," said Andraste. She acted out the ladies' part, and Aldrich met her in the center. He picked her up lightly and turned in a circle. He put her down gently.

"We raise palms again and turn in a circle. Then we would switch partners and proceed," said Andraste.

"So soon?" asked Aldrich.

"The Northern dances are all social dances. We have no dance such as the waltz. The Island Kingdoms has couple dances, but they are not played often," said Andraste.

"Will you show me again?" asked Aldrich.

Andraste raised her right palm towards Aldrich. He raised his right palm towards her.

"Slowly," directed Andraste.

Aldrich slowed his pace. He raised his left palm and they circled each other. Aldrich lightly offered her his hand, so that she could place hers on top. They proceeded five paces. Andraste danced with an imaginary partner and returned to Aldrich, who was watching her carefully. He smiled at her warmly before lifting her and turning her in a circle. He raised his right palm to her and Andraste met his actions. They turned in a circle.

"Good," approved Andraste.

"Again?" asked Aldrich. They went through the steps again.

"You already knew this dance," stated Andraste.

"I have seen it on our travels, but I have not danced it myself," replied Aldrich.

"Perhaps a different dance?" asked Andraste.

"A message, your Majesty," said a page from the doorway. Aldrich took the message from the boy. He unrolled it and turned his eyes to the Queen.

"The prince of the Lionden Empire will join us in two days, if you have no objection," said Aldrich.

"Lionden?" asked Andraste.

"We cannot refuse. It has been years since they have sent an ambassador," stated the Queen.

"But why now?" questioned Aldrich. He frowned. His eyes turned to Andraste.

"And such short notice," disapproved the Queen.

"They did not send an ambassador after we were addressed by the Parnesian court. They must have known. And now after the Emperor has fallen, they approach," pondered Aldrich.

"Perhaps to pay their respects to the new Empress?" proposed the Queen.

"I will leave you to your preparations," said Andraste.

"It is nothing," said Aldrich quickly.

"I have taken so much of your time already. I apologize. There is something I must do," said Andraste.

She hastily retreated through the gate to her veranda. She returned to her chambers and quickly headed towards Sveinbiorn's rooms. Cato and Avitus let her pass without interruption.

"Uncle?" asked Andraste. She was surprised to find her uncle seated in a chair, watching over her brother.

"You have heard the news?" asked Aelius.

"The heir from the Lionden Empire comes?" asked Andraste.

"Yes. Sveinbiorn's second condition was the life of the Lionden Emperor," stated Aelius.

"That is why I have come," replied Andraste.

"What will you do?" inquired Aelius.

"I will bind him to this room in case he wakes before I can speak with him. The Emperor's son is not the Emperor. Sveinbiorn's hatred may not see the difference," said Andraste.

"Why does he hunger for Lionden blood?" questioned Aelius.

"It has something to do with his father," answered Andraste.

Aelius's eyes widened in horror.

"What is it?" asked Andraste.

"The last thing Sveinbiorn said to me was that the barrier had been broken before. It was why you were able to summon him so easily," replied Aelius.

"What demon could be that strong?" asked Andraste.

"Sveinbiorn's father, the Demon King," responded Aelius.

"Why would the demon not have acted? Surely we would have noticed such actions," stated Andraste.

"Unless he left our Empire and went across the seas," said Aelius.

"Do you think the Demon King has allied himself with Lionden?" questioned Andraste.

"I fear this more then I feared your father," replied Aelius.

"The Lionden have always attacked. They do not negotiate. Why send an ambassador now?" asked Andraste.

"Perhaps their Emperor is dead?" suggested Aelius.

"We would have heard of it," replied Andraste.

"Either way you are right to confine Sveinbiorn to this room until we know what is needed. We do not want another war," said Aelius, "But remember, niece. He may be your brother, but you also made a pact with a demon. You cannot take back your promise. The consequences would be dire."

"I intend to keep my word. I promised him the Lionden Emperor. Mother hated him as well. My memory is hazy. I cannot recall," said Andraste.

"Do not try so hard. It will all come back in time," said Aelius, "How do you plan on binding him?"

Andraste took her dagger from her boot and cut off a few strands of her hair.

"Old magic," approved Aelius.

Andraste drew a circle in the air and then her star. She placed the strands of hair in the center.

"Bind," ordered Andraste.

The strands of hair turned into a silver light. It shot through the air and wrapped around Sveinbiorn's wrist. He stirred in his slumber but did not wake. The silver light shimmered and then turned into a woven band around his wrist.

"He will not be able to remove it or leave this room until I release him," said Andraste.

"Why did you not do it before?" asked Aelius.

"There was no reason before," replied Andraste. She frowned at her uncle.

"Now that our business is accomplished, you should know that Rhiannon was looking for you," said Aelius.

He rose from his chair. He opened the door for Andraste.

Andraste headed towards her chambers. Rhiannon was sitting on her sofa, waiting for her.

"I am sorry," said Andraste.

"It is no matter. I also needed a few moments to myself. You were with the prince?" asked Rhiannon.

"Yes," replied Andraste. She heard the door open behind her from the veranda.

"You forgot this," said Aldrich. He presented the shamisen and leaned it against the wall. He bowed to the ladies and quickly left.

"Playing?" questioned Rhiannon as she eyed the shamisen.

"Yes," answered Andraste.

"And not a weapon in sight, that at least is an improvement," said Rhiannon.

"The Queen and the prince are excellent hosts. It is nothing more," responded Andraste.

"The prince did not go on the hunt?" asked Rhiannon. Andraste shook her head.

"He did not go on the hunt that he initiated. Nor did he attend the Northern dance classes that he insisted his lords take in preparation for the wedding. It is said he spent the whole Assembly staring at the Empress, and then was nowhere to be found for the rest of the afternoon. Nor was the Empress," said Rhiannon.

"When you say it like that, of course, it sounds devious. I spent the afternoon on my veranda. He was on the Queen's veranda. The Queen invited me to join them for dinner," sighed Andraste.

"Most excellent host. He took you to have a private dinner with his mother," said Rhiannon. She eyed her foster-sister.

"Where is Brion? I have seen little of him since the Ice Palace," asked Andraste.

"I have seen him just as much," responded Rhiannon. She frowned.

"I am sure it is nothing. You have been so busy with the wedding preparations," said Andraste.

"He does not seem like himself," admitted Rhiannon.

"Our journey was difficult, and the election was taxing," replied Andraste.

"I know," admitted Rhiannon, but she still frowned, "He no longer studies with the Southern sorcerers. In fact, he was quite rude to them."

"From what I saw in the North, he no longer needs their instruction," stated Andraste.

"But he is never rude. Something is not right," said Rhiannon.

"I am sure everything will be fine by the wedding. I will make us a pot of tea, and you can tell me what I can do to help with the wedding preparations," said Andraste.

"Thank you, Andra," replied Rhiannon. She smiled slightly but still seemed uncertain.

Andraste set the kettle above the fire before busying herself with preparing the tea.

Chapter Twenty-One

Aldrich came to her side after the Assembly ended for the morning session.

"Would you care to walk in the gardens, Empress?" invited Aldrich.

"Yes, but I promised Rhiannon I would join her in the sewing room. The ladies of the court are working on her wedding dress," replied Andraste.

"You sew?" asked Aldrich bemused.

"Of course!" exclaimed Andraste.

"Well then I will not keep you," said Aldrich. He bowed to her.

"My lord-" Andraste started as Aldrich turned to leave. He stopped and turned his sapphire eyes on her.

"I do not know where the sewing room is," confessed Andraste.

"Allow me to show you, Empress," said Aldrich. He offered her his arm. She took it.

"Three days until the wedding," Aldrich commented as they walked down the hall.

"What?" asked Andraste.

"Brion and Rhiannon's wedding," expounded Aldrich.

"Yes, of course," said Andraste quickly.

"Are you alright?" inquired Aldrich.

"Fine," replied Andraste. She kept her eyes on the corridor.

"Are you sure?" questioned Aldrich.

"Fine," repeated Andraste, "How are you?"

"I cannot complain," answered Aldrich. He was perplexed. He had never seen Andraste so flustered.

"Where will they go for their honeymoon?" asked Aldrich.

"What is a honeymoon?" inquired Andraste.

"Not a Northern tradition? In the South after a couple weds, they travel for a time," responded Aldrich.

"Oh," said Andraste, "I suppose they will go to the Island Kingdoms."

Aldrich fell silent. Andraste glanced up to him.

"What?" asked Aldrich.

"Nothing," answered Andraste quickly.

They entered the sewing room. The ladies stood and curtsied to the prince. His sister and his mother ignored him completely.

"Ladies," Aldrich greeted the room and hastily retreated as he saw their numbers.

Andraste took her place beside Rhiannon, who was deep in conversation with Marcella. They stopped and both smiled at Andraste as she approached.

"This is a needle," Rhiannon said mischievously as she dropped it in Andraste's hand. Andraste sighed but otherwise accepted the teasing well.

"It was kind of the prince to show you the way," said Rhiannon.

"He wanted to go for a walk in the gardens, but I told him I had promised you," replied Andraste.

"Andraste, I love you, but you are such an idiot," sighed Rhiannon.

"He was just being polite, like always," protested Andraste. Rhiannon and Marcella exchanged glances.

"You see what I mean. It is exactly what I have been telling you," conspired Rhiannon to Marcella.

"Does that mean I can go walk in the gardens?" asked Andraste.

"No," said Rhiannon and Marcella together.

They put her to work sewing tiny pearls onto the hem of Rhiannon's wedding dress. Marcella introduced the Southern ladies to Andraste. The Queen approached their table.

"What interesting stitches, Empress," commented the Queen.

"Seriously!" Andraste exclaimed in feigned agitation. The Queen laughed and patted Andraste's shoulder.

"What was your courtship like, Marcella?" asked Rhiannon.

"The fastest courtship I ever saw," answered the Queen.

"They were married almost as soon as they laid eyes on each other," added Gerlinde.

"There was no nonsense. No pretense. Gregor was honest about his feelings and to the point. It saved a lot of time," said Marcella. She blushed at the memories.

"Henry, retreat! Their discussion regards courtship. We should come back another time," Rhinauld said in the doorway.

"What do you want, brother?" asked Rhiannon looking up from her work.

Rhinauld sauntered in, but Henry stood close to the door.

"I was coming to talk to my sister about etiquette," answered Rhinauld. Rhiannon rose and blushed.

"My other sister," stated Rhinauld.

"By the gods! For a few days at least I am Empress! Show some respect," ordered Andraste.

"We are your family. You know we respect you," appeased Rhiannon.

"I had a funny conversation with a prince, and I just wanted to know what it was regarding," said Rhinauld. He lounged in the seat nearest Andraste.

"It was perfectly acceptable. We only spoke about Rhiannon's wedding and honeymoon," replied Andraste in confusion.

"Oh? Really? That is interesting, but not the conversation I was referring," responded Rhinauld.

"I do not know to what you refer," replied Andraste honestly.

"I hear your forming an expedition to sail to the Old World. You invite the Prince of the Southern lands, but you do not invite your brothers? Henry and I are beside ourselves. Gnaeus's feelings were also hurt," alleged Rhinauld.

Henry looked entirely composed.

"You are such a baby," said Andraste, "You know you can come."

"The Old World?" asked Rhiannon. Her face fell. Her luminous, emerald eyes welled with tears.

"After the wedding," Andraste and Rhinauld said quickly.

"Both of you? But I just got you back!" exclaimed Rhiannon.

"Rhinauld! You are a beast!" cried Andraste.

"First, I am a baby, and now I am a beast," said Rhinauld. Rhiannon composed herself.

"A bear cub is still a bear," replied Andraste.

"You are missing the point of this conversation, Rhiannon," stated Rhinauld.

"Why did you ask the prince to go with you?" asked Rhiannon. Rhinauld winked at his twin.

"He is a good traveler and a fierce warrior," stated Andraste.

"Okay. That could describe a third of the Republic," said Rhinauld.

"Tell me what you want me to say, so that I can say it, and you can leave us," demanded Andraste.

"Just thought you needed to rethink that conversation," said Rhinauld holding up his hands in defeat. He rose to leave.

"Is there anyone else who would like to humiliate me?" Andraste called, "Court is now in session."

Henry opened his mouth to say something, but Rhinauld pushed him out the door to renewed laughter by the ladies.

"And in case you were wondering, we encountered the prince on his way to his rooms. He was going to change and then go to the stables. His intention was to go for an afternoon ride as the Assembly has let out early," informed Rhinauld.

"You know my hem really cannot take any more of your stitches," said Rhiannon.

Marcella inspected Andraste's work and agreed with Rhiannon, "Yes, you really ought to go. There is no use for you here."

"You are both too cruel," said Andraste, but she was already at the door by the time she finished.

Andraste made her way down to the stables. As she was on the stairs, she saw that Aldrich was saddling his horse as Rhinauld had foretold. She paused. He seemed to be in great haste. Andraste requested her horse. Aldrich mounted, but as he saw Boreas brought into the courtyard he hesitated. He looked over his shoulder and seeing her on the stairs, rode his horse over.

"I will not keep you. It is obvious you are in haste. Please proceed. I was going on an afternoon ride. I desire to see the coast," said Andraste.

"It is true I am making haste, but only because I want to leave before I am summoned to another inane meeting or task for my sister. I was headed in that direction. Would you let me accompany you?" requested Aldrich.

"I really do not want to intrude," blushed Andraste.

"As I see it, I am intruding on your ride. Will you let me accompany you?" offered Aldrich.

Andraste consented. She proceeded down the stairs and stroked his horse's neck.

"How was the afternoon session?" inquired Andraste.

"Thank the gods, brief," replied Aldrich.

Andraste saw that Boreas was saddled, so she quickly mounted before Aldrich could assist her.

"Shall we go? I will follow you," said Andraste.

Aldrich urged his horse out of the courtyard and on to the road. Once they were out of the city, Andraste urged her horse forward and rode by his side. They rode past a small fishing village and onto the beach. The sands were pearly white and the waters clear. Andraste saw dolphins jumping in the distance. They reached a cove and Aldrich slowed to a trot and then a gentle stop. Andraste matched his movements. Aldrich dismounted and then approached her before she could object. He wrapped his arms around her waist and placed her on the ground.

"It is so beautiful here," said Andraste. Aldrich hesitated in his place. He did not remove his hands form her waist.

"Do you not prefer the North or the Island Kingdoms? I hear the beaches of the Island Kingdoms rival our own lands in beauty," said Aldrich.

"No. They are different. In the Island Kingdoms the beauty is wild and untamed but the sands are coarse and the winds more fierce. But here, it is like you are looking at a painting. It is so still, so peaceful. The sands are like pearls and the waters like tourmaline," said Andraste.

"Tourmaline? Is that your favorite?" Aldrich asked, looking at her necklace.

"Rhinauld gave me this. I typically do not wear baubles," said Andraste. Aldrich released her.

"Are there oysters here?" Andraste asked as Aldrich walked towards the ocean.

"Yes," replied Aldrich.

"How do you harvest oysters?" inquired Andraste.

"You have never dug for oysters? Is that not done in the Island Kingdoms?" asked Aldrich.

"I did not have an oyster until I dined in the Southern Kingdoms," replied Andraste.

"And yet you are so fond of them?" questioned Aldrich.

"How would you know that?" rejoined Andraste.

"It is all you eat at supper," said Aldrich.

"Have you been inventorying my supper?" asked Andraste.

"Why do you think you keep getting oysters?" replied Aldrich.

"But how are they caught?" repeated Andraste.

"I will demonstrate," answered Aldrich.

He took off his boots and rolled his pants up towards his knees. He took off his tunic and threw it over his horse's saddle. Andraste admired his broad shoulders, and her eyes lowered to his muscular torso as he turned to face her. He picked up a large piece of driftwood from the shore and waded into the clear waters. He was some distance away from her. The waters only came up to his knees.

"Is it so shallow?" called Andraste.

"Yes," answered the prince, but his eyes were surveying the seabed.

Aldrich used the piece of driftwood to ply the oyster from its place. He bent down and picked up the first oyster. He returned to the beach and held it to for her inspection. The droplets of water fell on her bare skin.

"The water here is like bath water, and not salty at all," commented Andraste.

"And the Island Kingdoms?" inquired Aldrich.

"The waters are salty and cold as ice even in the summer," answered Andraste.

Aldrich returned to the waters and threw her a second oyster. She caught it and examined it. The light brown shell was large in her hands. It was coarse to her touch. Aldrich threw her a dozen that he picked from the seabed and then moved to her position.

"Empress?" asked Aldrich.

"Have you always been so handsome?" asked Andraste as she surveyed Aldrich.

"You only notice when I am half clothed," teased Aldrich.

Andraste hid her smile as she turned toward their horses. Aldrich rinsed off the oysters in the surf and then carried them to a blanket that Andraste had unrolled on the sand.

"How do you prepare them?" asked Andraste.

"These are the kings of oysters. They are best uncooked," answered Aldrich.

They sat in the sand by their pile. He picked one up and shucked it for her. He offered it to her.

"The ones in the hall are cooked," protested Andraste.

"These are better. This is the only way to eat oysters," insisted Aldrich.

Andraste looked at it critically, but she took it from the prince. She looked at him questioningly. He took it back from her and slurped it from the shell. He opened another and offered it to her. Andraste swallowed it and her eyes widened with delight.

"If only we had a bottle of that Southern wine with bubbles," said Andraste.

Aldrich smiled at her and stood. He went to his saddle bags and came back with a bottle.

"Do you always keep such wine in your saddlebags?" inquired Andraste.

"Of course," replied Aldrich as he uncorked it and offered it to her.

"And when we were in the North?" asked Andraste as she took a swig. She returned it to him as he offered her another an oyster.

"Of course not, we were on a mission," replied Aldrich. He drank from the bottle as well and opened another oyster.

"It would have been most unfriendly to not share such delights," alleged Andraste.

"Most," agreed Aldrich as he offered her another oyster.

"But I must confess, Rhinauld said you would be going on an afternoon ride, so I brought some things," acknowledged Aldrich.

"Did he?" asked Andraste. She blushed.

"What?" questioned Aldrich. He produced grapes, cheese and bread from his saddle bag.

"Rhinauld told me that you were going for an afternoon ride as well," admitted Andraste.

"So he is playing with us?" inquired Aldrich. He did not seem to mind.

"Insufferable brother of mine," swore Andraste.

"He is not that bad," admitted Aldrich. Andraste smiled.

"And what is it he calls you?" asked Aldrich.

"Andra, as do my family," said Andraste, "You may call me Andra, if you wish."

"Andra," Aldrich said lightly. His sapphire eyes registered on her. Andraste paused as she took the oyster from his hand.

They ate their way leisurely through the two dozen oysters and shared the bottle of sparkling wine between them. Aldrich produced a pearl from the newly shucked oyster. He went and rinsed it in the surf. He returned it to her for inspection. He sat closer to her then before. She could feel his warmth beside her.

"Black?" asked Andraste.

"Black pearls are common in the Southern waters," replied Aldrich.

She held it out to him. He closed her fingers over it. Andraste lowered her eyes. She could feel him studying her. Andraste felt self-conscious.

"I have never seen such shells," commented Andraste. She held up an orange shell to Aldrich.

"Never?" inquired Aldrich.

"There are not as many shells in the Island Kingdoms. Not like this," said Andraste.

"So you have not been shelling?" inquired Aldrich. He held up a sand dollar for her inspection.

They walked side beside on the beach. Andraste picking up almost every shell she saw, while Aldrich only picked her a shell that was whole and particularly beautiful. Andraste held out the front of her gown to make a pouch for all the shells that they collected.

The sun was beginning to set. The colors of the sky were so rich, and the cerulean waters began to turn into shades of violet. The horizon was so vast. As Andraste stared ahead, the golden orb sank below the blankets of violet. It was the most magnificent sunset that Andraste had ever seen. It took her breath away.

"Empress!" a voice called up the beach. She saw four of the Victorious had found them. She looked at Aldrich and sighed.

"We should return. I will get our horses," relented Aldrich.

Andraste only smiled at him as the horses approached them as if on their own accord. Aldrich placed their shells in his saddlebag. As the evening had turned cool, Aldrich draped his cape around her shoulders. He helped her mount her horse, and then he mounted his own horse. They turned back down the beach towards the awaiting party.

"Your honor guard awaits you, Empress," said Gnaeus with a slight inclination of his head.

Andraste acknowledged him with a nod. Aldrich took the place by her side as they rode past Gnaeus. The four other horsemen rode after them. They were late for dinner by the time they reached the palace. Aldrich was the first to dismount. Andraste permitted Aldrich to help her from her horse. He wrapped her arm in his as they walked towards the dining hall.

"So there is to be an expedition?" Laelius greeted her as she passed by the Victorious's table. Andraste released Aldrich's arm as she turned to address the table.

"I want you all to hear this and consider this seriously," proclaimed Andraste as she saw all of her Victorious were listening intently.

"You all have done more than most. I release you from your service. In this time of peace, I want you to return to your homelands and aid in the rebuilding. I want you to be with your wives and your children. We have struggled and fought for so long, I want you all to be happy," said Andraste.

There was a stunned silence, but it was broken as Felix rose.

"With all due respect, Empress," said Felix, "But I will settle down when you do."

Andraste laughed with her men.

"This voyage is not mandatory and we just returned. I want you each to do as your heart tells you," said Andraste.

"Weddings? Honeymoons? Sewing? Now speaking of hearts? Empress, I do not think I know you," stated Aldrich.

"What else do soldiers speak about during times of peace?" rejoined Andraste.

"Their past deeds," answered Laelius, and he was cheered by his fellows.

Andraste reached for Aldrich's arm out of habit and realized he had not yet offered it. Seeing his error he quickly wrapped her arm in his. He drew her close.

"I do not mean to keep you," said Andraste.

"It is my pleasure, Empress," responded Aldrich.

He led her to her seat between the Queen and the King of the Island Kingdoms. He bowed and walked around the table to assume his place across from her.

"The delegate from the Summit arrived," commented the King.

"Lady Moira?" asked Andraste.

Aldrich's head turned the Northern delegation. Lady Moira caught his eye and waved brazenly. Aldrich turned back around. The Queen looked at her son questioningly.

"A special admirer of your son. They share an interest in astronomy," whispered Andraste. Aldrich rolled his yes. The Queen surveyed Lady Moira again with renewed interest. The King however was bored with the conversation.

"Your Majesty, I have a request," said the King. The Queen turned her attention to him.

"As you know tomorrow is the day that the Island Kingdoms usually celebrates the Moon Festival. I would ask that you allow us to provide entertainment from our homeland for the occasion," said the King.

"We would be honored," said the Queen, and then she asked, "What sort of entertainment?"

"The ladies of my court usually arrange displays of dancing as to exhibit their talents. My niece usually condescends to dance at such Festivals, even if she prefers the Northern dances," said the King to Aldrich.

Aldrich's attention was firmly back on their table.

"But you seem to so hate dancing?" questioned the Queen.

"She enjoyed herself well enough at the Festival of the Gods," commented Rhiannon.

Andraste nearly knocked her wine glass off the table. Aldrich reached across to catch it. Their fingers touched as he passed it back to her. Andraste would not meet his eyes.

"Rhiannon, you will coordinate with the other ladies from the Island Kingdoms," ordered the King.

"Yes, your Majesty," said Rhiannon.

Andraste busied herself with her salad. Henry caught her eye.

"Do you remember when we were traveling in the East and Rhinauld gambled away all of our money and horses?" asked Henry.

"I do," answered Andraste.

"Why do you smile?" asked the Queen, horrified by Henry's question.

"Because of the way we earned money for the journey home," replied Andraste.

"Oh?" questioned the Queen.

"We danced," responded Henry. The King's laughter boomed throughout the hall.

"I had forgotten about that," said the King.

"What did you dance?" asked Aldrich.

"Andraste portrayed the Goddess of Fortune," said Henry.

"That dance is so sad," said Rhiannon, "You two would pick the most depressing of the dances. The others are so light and full of life."

"I would like to see it," said the Queen.

"Tomorrow, then, Andraste and Henry, will perform the Dance of Fortune," said the King. Andraste and Henry both sighed.

"What will you dance?" Brion asked Rhiannon.

"The Dance of Spring," answered Rhiannon.

"You dance that well," approved Brion. He regarded Rhiannon with more attention than usual. She blushed deeply under his gaze and looked to Andraste.

"It is about time for tonight's dancing to commence," commented the Queen.

"We should speak to the other ladies directly," said Andraste to Rhiannon.

"Or we could send Henry," suggested Andraste. Both women turned on him at once.

"No," disobliged the knight. Rhiannon giggled.

"Rhinauld?" asked Andraste, but he had hastily removed himself to another table.

"Just us then," said Rhiannon. She smiled in apology to Brion. Rhiannon rose to speak to the ladies and Andraste followed.

Andraste saw that Lady Moira had cornered Aldrich for a dance. He looked less than pleased and although he acquiesced his movements looked stiff.

"Does he look like that with me?" Andraste asked Rhiannon.

"No," said Rhiannon in alarm. She surveyed the dancing prince and then Andraste. Marcella approached them. She addressed Andraste, "You really should go rescue him."

"No, I am enjoying this," said Andraste, "Besides he will be saved by protocol for the rest of the evening. He cannot dance with her again even if he wanted to."

"It looks as though Gerlinde is waiting in the eves," commented Rhiannon.

"If he wants to dance with me, he will ask," said Andraste. Marcella and Rhiannon both scrutinized her.

"If I approach, he will have to dance with me. I am Empress," said Andraste.

"He will not approach you because you are Empress," stated Marcella.

Aldrich was busy explaining the protocol of dancing to Lady Moira. She pouted but stepped aside. Gerlinde approached and nearly dragged the prince to the dance floor. Aldrich stared at the Southern lords for assistance, but they only laughed at his plight.

"Perhaps Decima will rescue him," sighed Marcella.

"No hope for the prince. She is watching over Sveinbiorn," responded Rhiannon.

"How is his condition?" asked Marcella.

"He has not improved, but he has not worsened," answered Andraste. Her spirits rapidly fell.

"You cannot retire. There is an event that you must witness. It is your duty as Empress," stated Rhiannon.

"What is it?" asked Andraste.

"You will see. If you want more information, you will have to ask my brother," said Marcella.

"It is odd he would not have mentioned it this afternoon," responded Andraste.

"He has put much effort and care into it. Perhaps he wants to surprise you," said Rhiannon.

"Did he consult you?" asked Andraste.

"Indeed. He has spoken with the delegates during the journey. He also came to the sewing chamber and consulted all of the ladies," responded Marcella.

"Oh, dear. Is it about Northern customs?" inquired Andraste.

"Customs and traditions from across the Empire," responded Rhiannon, "I think he thought you would be there when he came to the sewing chamber."

"There will be one more dance and then an announcement. You should be at Aldrich's side when this occurs," said Marcella.

Andraste nodded her consent. She started across the dance floor. Aldrich caught sight of her and turned his partner's direction so that he could see Andraste's progress. As the music came to an end, he bowed to Gerlinde. He released Gerlinde's hand and approached Andraste.

"I am told that I must be with you when this dance ends," said Andraste.

"Yes. We have arranged a vigil to honor those lost in our war for independence," said Aldrich.

The music had started for a Southern waltz. Wordlessly, Aldrich offered his hand to Andraste. She placed her hand in his and he drew her into his arms, but not too close.

"Why did you not say so earlier?" asked Andraste.

"I have much to do. It must have slipped my mind," answered Aldrich. Andraste scanned the ballroom. She was being glared at any by many fine eyes.

"You have many potential partners," said Andraste.

"With Rhiannon and Brion's nuptials approaching, marriage seems to be on everyone's mind," responded Aldrich.

"Not mine," answered Andraste.

"No, I imagine you are dreaming of adventures in unexplored lands. Particularly, when you are at Assembly," said Aldrich.

"I was never meant to be in Court or on a Council. I have not the staying power," responded Andraste.

"No. You were always meant to be wandering free," said Aldrich. Andraste blushed as he studied her. She did not know how to respond.

"You have not danced with me since we were last in the Southern capitol," alleged Aldrich.

"It is a fragile peace with the North. I fear the rumors," said Andraste softly.

"Last you were here we had an arrangement since we tied our duel. You are to spend one hour with me every evening. Do you not recall?" asked Aldrich.

"Would you hold your Empress to such an outcome?" questioned Andraste.

"Absolutely! My Empress should keep her word," answered Aldrich.

"I spent hours with you on the beach," said Andraste.

"But what about all the other days?" asked Aldrich.

"So you will not be content unless I make up my lost time?" inquired Andraste.

"Yes, I think you owe me a full day," replied Aldrich.

"You are miserly," said Andraste.

"I miss you," responded Aldrich. Andraste blushed and lowered her eyes.

"Perhaps we shall have another duel to settle this," proposed Andraste.

"I am ready," replied Aldrich, "However, since I am now a member of the Victorious, if I beat you, does that mean I become the leader of the Victorious?"

"Technically, yes, but I have already disbanded the Victorious. I would not put too much thought into it. You will not win," said Andraste.

"So confident?" asked Aldrich.

"It is not confidence, it is fact," answered Andraste.

"Tomorrow at dawn?" asked Aldrich.

"As you wish," replied Andraste.

The waltz had ended. Aldrich kissed Andraste's hand, but he did not release it. He wrapped Andraste's arm in his and began their progress to the veranda.

"If you will make your way to the beach, we will begin our remembrance of those lost in the war of independence. In the North, the East, and the South, we have similar traditions of candlelight vigils. In the North, they light lanterns. In the East, they send candles in boats out to sea. In the South, we hold candles. We have prepared candles in the methods of all three regions, and created candles as well for our brethren from the Midlands and the West. After the song has been sung, we will observe an hour of silence as is tradition in the Midlands and the West," bade the Queen.

Aldrich carefully led Andraste out of the veranda, down the stairs and onto the beach. All lights in the city had been extinguished. The darkness was magical as only the stars shone overhead. Aldrich stopped so they were just touching the shoreline. Andraste gazed up at the stars above them.

"It is said in the South that when we die our souls traverse to the heavens and become a star, so that we may watch over those we left behind," said Aldrich.

"That is beautiful," said Andraste. Aldrich looked down at her and smiled. He took a candle from the basket of an attendant and offered it to her.

"We will use them to light the lanterns," explained Aldrich.

Andraste saw her Victorious and the Resistance leaders moving through the crowd with lit candles. Laelius approached her and lit her candle. When she had turned back to Aldrich, he had produced a lantern for her.

"In the North, we send off the lanterns, so that those who have gone before us will know that we remember and honor their passing," said Andraste.

"That too is beautiful," replied Aldrich.

Andraste used her candle to light Aldrich's lantern. Aldrich released it into the sky. It rose higher and higher into the heavens and was carried by an Eastern wind. It was soon joined by hundreds of lanterns. From down the shore, hundreds of small boats filled with candles and white flowers were released into the waters of the shore and carried out to the ocean.

Andraste reached for Aldrich's arm. He wrapped her arm in his. From the opposite side Andraste heard Rhiannon begin to sing:

"Although I look to the cresting gray waves from the East,
to the West across the golden grasses of the plains,
to the South upon the pearly sands of the beaches,
to the North to the tall snow-topped mountains,
Never again will I find you in these blessed lands.

And yet, because of your courage and sacrifice,
Forever free I sail the gray waters of the East,
Forever free I ride the golden plains of the West,
Forever free I walk the pearly beaches of the South,
Forever free I climb the snow-topped mountains of the North.

Because of your actions, the Republic rises.
Because you stood, we now can all stand united.
Although you are gone from my life and these lands,
I will find you forevermore in my heart,
I will see you in the freedom of the Republic."

Rhiannon's words seemed to echo into the darkness, and then there was silence. The only sound was the gentle lapping of the waves against the shore. The lanterns were but specks of light in the distance. They could have been fireflies dancing on the horizon. The tiny ships had made their way out to the ocean. Andraste's candle still burned brightly in her hand.

When the lanterns and ships were out of sight, Andraste released her hold on Aldrich's arm. She gracefully folded her robes about her and knelt in the Northern style of prayer in the pearly sands. Aldrich remained standing. He briefly put his hand to her face. She met his eyes, and then silently he left to join Marcella and the Queen.

Laelius and Gnaeus came and knelt by her sides. She grasped arms with each for a moment, but said nothing. They were joined by the remaining Victorious, except for Aldrich, who remained with the Queen. As Andraste looked to the faces of her twelve remaining Victorious, she felt relieved that so many had made it so far, but her heart ached for the two that were gone forever. So many lives had been lost, so many people that she had cared about, including her own parents, siblings, and friends. She could still lose Sveinbiorn. Andraste felt overwhelmed by a sense of despair and loss. Large, salty tears fell from her eyes onto the pearly sands. She wept until she could produce no more tears.

Andraste woke in her chamber and felt exhausted, even though the sun had risen high in the sky. She ate breakfast on her veranda and enjoyed the sunshine. The roses on her veranda were in full bloom. Since it was a Festival day, the Assembly was not scheduled to meet.

She took a cold shower. It was already exceedingly hot. She dressed in a light green gown in the Southern style. It was low-cut and only had lace straps for sleeves. She left her hair down, but secured a few tendrils of her hair with a barrette. She put on her tourmaline necklace and the black pearl in her pocket. She left her Ruin sword and daggers in her chamber.

Andraste proceeded to Aldrich's rooms. She knocked once before entering. Aldrich stopped in mid-sentence when he caught sight of her. As she had caught him off guard, he could not hide his admiring gaze. She saw that he was joined by many of the Victorious and the Southern lords.

"Good morning," said Andraste.

"Good afternoon," replied Aldrich.

"The day seems to have gotten the better of me," admitted Andraste.

"Sleeping all this while? Really, Andra. The worst excuse for missing a duel I have ever heard," said Rhinauld.

"I did not see you there. Lurking in the shadows, Rhinauld?" asked Andraste.

"Do you accept your defeat with honor?" pushed Rhinauld.

Andraste turned her eyes to Aldrich, who was watching her intently.

"I will never accept defeat," stated Andraste. She raised her head proudly. Aldrich smiled and looked briefly to Rhinauld.

"The prince wins by default. You did not show, Empress," said Henry.

"I disagree. What was to be the challenge?" asked Andraste.

"Archery," replied Aldrich.

"Archery?" repeated Andraste.

"You would challenge the second best archer in all of the North?" asked Rhinauld.

"Commander did once say that she would marry the man who could best her bow and her sword," said Laelius.

Rhinauld exchanged looks with Henry. Aldrich quickly changed the subject.

"Have you come to check on Eldgrimson?" asked Aldrich.

"No, I came to see you," replied Andraste. Aldrich seemed taken back.

"We can leave, Empress," said Eadbehrt. He rose but Andraste shook her head. She turned her full attention to Aldrich.

"I only came to thank you for including the North and the East in your vigil. It was beautifully done. I am moved by your attention to our customs," said Andraste. She lowered her eyes and shifted uncomfortably. She glanced to Aldrich and said, "That is all."

She left the room quickly and darted into Sveinbiorn's chambers. She shut the door behind her. She could hear the low sound of male voices from Aldrich's chambers.

"That was well done," approved Aelius.

"Uncle! I did not expect to find you here," said Andraste. She blushed, but then narrowed her eyes as she surveyed her uncle, "Why are you here?"

"Half-demon or not, he is still Victoria's son," said Aelius gruffly.

"Any change?" asked Andraste.

"None," replied Aelius.

"You will stay with him a while?" inquired Andraste.

"Yes. Go to the sewing chamber and join Rhiannon. She seems out of spirits," said Aelius.

"Brion has not been himself," responded Andraste.

"Wedding," replied Aelius.

Andraste smiled at her uncle before making her way to the sewing chamber. Rhiannon's face lit up at the sight of her. The Queen, Marcella, Shannon and Sonje sat working on Rhiannon's wedding dress. There were other ladies sewing quietly at other tables, including Gerlinde and Ziska.

Andraste produced the pearl that Aldrich had gifted her and produced it to Rhiannon.

"That may be the largest black pearl I have ever seen," commented Marcella.

"Aldrich found it on the beach. I am hoping to combine it to the necklace that my brother gave me. Can you recommend a talented and trustworthy jeweler?" inquired Andraste.

"Do you have a silver ring that could be melted?" asked Marcella.

"For the cause," replied Rhiannon as she produced a silver ring from her finger, "My sister does not possess any other jewelry."

"If I may?" asked Marcella.

Rhiannon handed the pearl and ring, while Andraste handed over the tourmaline necklace. Marcella closed the pendant, ring, and pearl in her hands. She recited an incantation and her hands were covered in a white light, when it faded, she opened her palm. The pearl was now set on top of the tourmaline.

"That is a convenient skill," admired Rhiannon.

"Many thanks," obliged Andraste. Marcella helped Andraste put the necklace on.

"The prince was looking for you this morning," said Rhiannon.

"Who won the duel?" asked Marcella.

"I overslept. The lords say that Aldrich won by default," answered Andraste.

"Of course that is what the lords would say. Go give him a good lashing," bade the Queen.

"He is busy," said Andraste. She looked the Queen in surprise.

"Was Brion with the lords?" asked Rhiannon. Andraste shook her head.

"He is studying in the sorcerer's tower," reported Marcella.

"Two days before the wedding and he still is looking over scrolls," sighed Rhiannon.

"There are no preparations for him to make. Let him stay out of the way," advised the Queen. She squeezed Rhiannon's hand.

"Will you duel the prince?" asked Marcella.

"No. By her look of condemnation, my sister tells me it would not be seemly if the Empress were to fight duels," said Andraste.

"Aldrich will be disappointed," said the Queen, "He has been practicing archery and learning tips from any archer he can find for weeks."

"Did he ask you?" inquired Andraste. She addressed her foster-sister, but Rhiannon shook her head.

"You are an archer?" scoffed Gerlinde from across the room.

"One of the best," answered Andraste for Rhiannon.

"It is strange the North and the East depend on their ladies for protection. Almost as funny that in all the years that the prince has sought my company, I have never once had to duel him," said Gerlinde.

"Let me be clear," said Andraste. She turned her eyes to Gerlinde, "Aldrich is mine in all possible ways. You have no claim to him."

"That remains to be seen," replied Gerlinde. However, she blushed unhappily.

"It about time you said something!" said Shannon. She grinned at Andraste.

"Ladies, let us be civil," said the Queen. However, she smiled at Andraste.

"Rhiannon, would you demonstrate your archery skills? Just ladies will be present, as I imagine the lords are hunting," said Marcella.

"I am tired of being in this room," admitted Rhiannon.

"You girls go on ahead. I will rest here a while," said the Queen. Gerlinde also remained at her place.

Marcella led the way out of the sewing chamber, chatting along the way with Shannon. Sonje and Ziska took each of Rhiannon's arms in the Southern fashion. Andraste trailed behind and admired the Southern artwork.

"Keep up, Andra," called Rhiannon.

Andraste hurried after the ladies. She entered the training yard and saw a row of freshly made targets. A Victorious arrow pierced each of the centers of the targets.

"Aldrich?" asked Andraste. Marcella nodded and Andraste smiled in spite of herself.

Marcella rummaged in the arms room and produced two bows and two quivers. She handed one set to Rhiannon and one to Andraste.

"Good. We are alone," said Rhiannon, "You go first."

Andraste knocked an arrow to her bow and pulled it taught. She hit the first target and splintered Aldrich's arrow. She proceeded to do the same to each of the targets.

"The poor prince," said Sonje.

"He would have been devastated," agreed Marcella.

Rhiannon proceeded to knock an arrow to her bow. She split Andraste's first arrow and the Southern ladies cheered. The second target she hit near the center.

"Does anyone else wish to try?" asked Rhiannon.

"I do not know how," replied Sonje.

Andraste handed Sonje the second bow and quiver. Rhiannon began to instruct Sonje and Ziska in archery. Shannon added a few pointers, while Andraste moved across the training yard and sat on a stone bench. Marcella joined her and reviewed Andraste's targets.

"This is why you did not renew the challenge?" asked Marcella.

"I do not want to beat him," replied Andraste.

"I see," said Marcella.

"What is a Southern method of courting?" asked Andraste.

"You consider dueling courting?" laughed Marcella. Andraste cheeks crimsoned.

"I usually arrange flowers for his room. Why do you not arrange flowers this afternoon and take them to him? Upon delivery, you could ask him to walk with you in the gardens," said Marcella.

"Arrange flowers?" asked Andraste.

"I will help you," answered Marcella.

"Take a grown man flowers?" questioned Andraste.

"Arranging flowers is a Southern tradition," replied Marcella.

Marcella wrapped Andraste's arm in her own and pulled her towards the gardens. Marcella instructed Andraste on the types of flowers and the best pairings. She spoke regarding the significance of certain flowers. Andraste listened obediently and made little comment. They took the flowers to Marcella's chambers to arrange.

Andraste surveyed the rooms curiously. The rooms were immaculate. Marcella disappeared momentarily into an adjoining chamber and emerged with two vases. She began setting about sorting out the flowers on the table. She gestured for Andraste to do the same.

"Where are your children?" asked Andraste.

"They are in school," replied Marcella.

"You do not instruct them yourself?" questioned Andraste.

"No, we have teachers for that," responded Marcella.

"We live so far apart in the North that there are no schools for young children," said Andraste.

"Mothers must be exhausted," commented Marcella.

"Our children are taught by both parents, relatives, and other villagers, so that the can learn as much as possible," replied Andraste.

Marcella directed Andraste in arranging her flowers. Her instructions reminded Andraste of her first drill instructor when she joined the Imperial Army. Marcella was extremely serious, no nonsense, and had little patience for mistakes. However, when they were done, even Andraste's arrangement was quite pretty.

"Aldrich should be in his rooms by now," said Marcella.

"I cannot enter if he is alone. Will you go with me?" asked Andraste.

"Of course," replied Marcella.

Andraste picked up her vase and they proceeded to Aldrich's chambers. The doors were closed. Marcella knocked once and then entered. The rooms were deserted except for a servant taking a bottle of Southern sparkling wine and a glass towards the bath chamber.

"I will just leave the flowers here," said Andraste.

She started to put the flowers on the entry table. However, she heard the unmistakable sound of Moira's laughter from the bath chamber. Andraste missed the table and the vase fell to the floor. It broke into a hundred tiny pieces. The beautifully arranged flowers lay strewn across the floor.

"It must be a misunderstanding," said Marcella.

"I am sorry about your vase," responded Andraste.

Aldrich entered behind them from the hallway.

"I was looking for you," greeted Aldrich. His smile broadened as he saw the pearl added to Andraste's necklace. However, he was stopped in his tracks by Andraste's icy stare.

"Is Lady Moira in your bath chamber?" asked Marcella.

Her eyes narrowed at Aldrich. Aldrich's eyes darted back to Andraste and he shifted uncomfortably.

"Due to so many guests, the water is not working in some of the rooms. She and others have been using my bath chamber since it is filled by the hot springs. It seemed a little thing after her hospitality in the North," said Aldrich. He surveyed the broken vase on the floor.

"Could she not use someone else's chambers?" asked Marcella.

"What happened here?" inquired Aldrich. He knelt to pick up the broken vase shards.

"The Empress brought-" started Marcella.

Andraste rotated her hand angrily and the vase reassembled itself. The flowers and water returned to their previous arrangement. Some of the petals were damaged, but it was almost exactly as it was before. Andraste took the handle of the vase in her hand and lifted it from the table.

"Marcella taught me how to arrange flowers. I am taking these to Sveinbiorn. I am ready to duel you now," said Andraste.

"You are not armed," stated Aldrich.

Andraste gestured her free hand and her Ruin sword appeared in the air. She took it in her free hand.

"How can you do that without an incantation?" asked Marcella in disbelief.

"I am ready," said Andraste. She glowered at Aldrich.

"I will meet you in the training yard," replied Aldrich.

Andraste delivered the flowers to Sveinbiorn's room. He still slept undisturbed in his bed. She could hear Marcella chiding Aldrich in his chambers.

"How could you be so stupid?" asked Marcella.

"I did not think it would be so important," replied Aldrich, "As I said, others have used my chambers."

"It looks very bad, indeed, even from a Northern perspective. She arranged those flowers for you, even though she thought it a stupid practice. She is trying to abide by our ways. It would be decent if you did as well," reprimanded Marcella.

"Those were for me?" asked Aldrich.

"She was right not to give them to you," stated Marcella.

Andraste heard them begin to proceed down the hall. She waited until she could no longer hear their voices before leaving Sveinbiorn's rooms. She saw Aldrich studying the targets in the training yard. Marcella was still giving him a tongue lashing. Rhiannon, Sonje and Ziska were still at their archery practice. However, they stopped as Marcella's voice rose. Aldrich said nothing in response.

Andraste unsheathed her sword and threw the sheath to the ground. Aldrich turned at the sound. He reached for his own blade.

"Do you not want to change?" asked Marcella. Andraste approached with purpose.

"Step aside," advised Aldrich. Marcella quickly joined Rhiannon.

Andraste was already upon Aldrich and driving him back towards the training yard wall.

"Are you sure you would not prefer a walk in the gardens?" asked Aldrich.

Andraste swept her sword in wide arch and he leapt backwards.

"That is why I was coming to find you. It seems as though we had the same intention," alleged Aldrich.

Andraste did not hesitate. She became more aggressive in her attack. Aldrich met her blow before blow, but still he was driven backwards. Andraste did not hold back. However, she saw the purple aura begin to grow around her Ruin sword. She took a few steps back from Aldrich in order to calm herself. He watched her movements carefully and then advanced. Andraste disarmed him in a fluid gesture and then raised her sword tip to his throat.

"I yield," said Aldrich. He angrily dropped his sword to the ground.

Andraste lowered her sword and then knelt to retrieve her sheath. She turned glowering towards Aldrich, "Our previous arrangement is nullified. As you have already found a more willing companion, I advise you spend your time with her. You waste your time with me."

"Andra," said Aldrich. He took a step forward. Andraste did not meet his eyes.

"You must look to your future. I will be leaving as soon as I am able," said Andraste.

She turned on her heel and swept out of the training yard, her green skirts sweeping behind her. Rhiannon handed the bow and quiver to Ziska and ran after Andraste.

"Andra!" cried Rhiannon.

Andraste did not slow her pace. She headed towards the stables and made her way to Boreas's stall. She opened the gate and he came out to greet her. She did not wait to saddle him. He bent so that she could mount, and then she rode out of the stable. She allowed Boreas to gallop as fast as he desired as they made their way out of the city and onto the beach. She rode until her thoughts began to slow and her anger to subside.

As the sun began to set, she directed her horse to return to the palace. Boreas ran just as hard as before. As Andraste entered the palace gates, she saw Rhiannon watching the Southern road from the battlements. Andraste returned Boreas to his stall and began to brush him.

"The prince did not find you?" asked Rhiannon breathless. Andraste did not reply.

"He rode after you. He may have executed poor judgment, but he was also being a good host," said Rhiannon. Andraste glared at her foster sister.

"You and Henry have not practiced at all?" asked Rhiannon.

"Practiced what?" asked Andraste.

"The Dance of Fortune," answered Rhiannon

"No. It will be fine," responded Andraste.

"You should dress and bathe," stated Rhiannon.

Andraste surveyed her appearance. She looked positively wild with her tangled hair and unkempt dress. She nodded her consent and exited the stables. As they climbed the stairs towards the palace, she saw Aldrich ride into the courtyard.

"Andra, that is the man you love whether you will admit it or not. Go to him," urged Rhiannon.

"It is not meant to be. I cannot have him now as I am Empress as it would disrupt the balance of power. When I am released from my duties, I must go east. Something draws me there. He has chosen to remain behind. There is no point," replied Andraste. She did not spare a second glance towards Aldrich.

Rhiannon surveyed her foster sister sadly. She wrapped her arm in Andraste's in the Southern fashion. She could feel Andraste's tension. Rhiannon did not utter a further word as they reached Andraste's chambers. Andraste quickly bathed and brushed her hair. When she reemerged, Rhiannon laid out dark gray robes on the bed.

"It is in the Northern style," said Rhiannon.

She produced her own robes which were in the fashion of the Salt Islands. They changed in Andraste's bedchamber. Rhiannon braided Andraste's hair in the Northern style. There was a knock on the door and then Rhinauld entered. He carried two small, long red boxes and deposited them on Andraste's vanity.

"Before you refuse them, break them, or otherwise defile these gifts from our host, know that you will need two such items for the dance you are about to perform," said Rhinauld. He set the two boxes on Andraste's vanity and left the room quickly.

Andraste's eyes narrowed, but she opened the first box and found a beautiful scarlet Northern fan in the box. Rhiannon made no comment. Andraste opened the second box, and found a duplicate fan, but it was charcoal. Andraste gingerly picked up the first fan in her hand and examined it. She flicked it with her wrist and it opened beautifully, making a pleasant cascading sound. She smiled in spite of herself.

"It is a handsome gift," commented Rhiannon.

"You cannot help yourself: can you?" asked Andraste. Rhiannon laughed softly.

"You will need them for the dance. You should forgive the prince. It is not like you found him in the bath with Moira," stated Rhiannon. Andraste blushed deeply at the thought and her eyes flashed.

"Do you think-" started Andraste.

"No!" swore Rhiannon.

"My comments from earlier are still valid," said Andraste. However, she tucked the fans behind her in her sash.

"True," acknowledged Rhiannon. She hid her smile to herself, as they made their way to the dining hall. According to the custom of the Island Kingdoms, the dances would come before the feasting.

Two rows of the great tables had been pushed together to form a stage down the middle of the dining hall. Andraste saw the priest bellowing the tradition of the day and giving thanks. When he concluded, it was Rhiannon's turn to start off the dancing. Music started playing and Andraste saw her sister leap onto the center table to the Southerner's amazement. Rhiannon danced a quick stepping dance from the Salt Islands. Two of the ladies from the Island Kingdoms joined her and danced behind her. It was a lively dance and Rhiannon looked full of happiness. When her dance concluded, Brion took her hand, kissed it and then lifted her down from the table.

Andraste saw Henry at the far side of the table. He nodded his head to her, but did not approach. Andraste watched the other ladies' dances, and was proud of her countrywomen and their traditions. The lamps in the hall went out all at once.

"And then approached the Goddess of Fortune," announced the King.

One of the lamps was relit. As Andraste approached and stepped up onto to bench, another lamp turned on. Every time she took a step a lamp turned on. She stepped onto the table. The music changed to a mournful, haunting melody.

Andraste took one step to the left and raised her right arm slowly and turned underneath her arm. She then turned slowly in the opposite direction. She reached behind her and produced a fan from her sash. She kept it closed. She raised it above her head and pointed towards the ceiling. She rotated it in her wrist slowly. She gently lowered to her to her knees. She lowered her head and looked to the ground. She opened the fan before her with a flick of her wrist. She reached before her and slowly waved the fan a side motion. She rose and gracefully turned. She raised the fan in her right hand and kept her left hand close to her side. She raised the fan and rotated her free hand. She tossed it in her hand and opened it upside down. She raised her free hand above her head.

"The wildest and hardest to please of all the Goddesses," continued the King.

Andraste produced a second fan from the back of her sash. The music quickened. Andraste stepped side to side and did a partial turn. She folded one fan against her shoulder and opened the other. She raised the open fan above her head and then opened the other, but held it behind her back. As she lowered the first fan, she raised the other above her head. She then brought both fans before her as her arms crossed. She held them both out to her sides and rose onto her toes. She stepped to the side and kicked her leg out.

"But Fortune favors the brave," said the King.

Henry soundlessly leapt onto the table and did a handless cartwheel down the table. Andraste closed both of her fans and turned her head towards him. She slowly knelt to her knees. He made a big show of her attention, which made the audience laugh. He somersaulted several times and knelt on one knee before Andraste. He offered her his hand. Andraste tucked the fans back into her sash and gingerly took his offered hand.

"Fortune can empower a warrior," said the King.

Henry was immediately on his feet and pulling her up to him. She gracefully extended her leg. He lifted her slowly and they turned in a circle. He gently placed her back on the ground.

"Good fortune can make a warrior arrogant," said the King.

Henry turned his back on her. Andraste put her hands around his neck; he stepped forward out of her grasp. Andraste held her poise reaching for him.

"The warrior can lose Fortune's favor by such arrogance," said the King.

Andraste rotated on one leg, and began to slowly dance down the table away from Henry. She took out a fan again and rotated it in her hand.

"And without the will of the gods, the warrior will fall," said the King.

Henry slowly rotated down to the table. Andraste paused in her progress and leapt down the table to Henry. She dropped the fan on the floor.

She caught him and helped him fall to the ground. She cradled his head in her lap and let her hair fall over his face. As she did so, all Andraste could think of was Tobias dying in her arms.

The music stopped. Andraste blinked quickly as her eye glistened.

There was thunderous applause. Henry opened his eyes. He sat up. They helped each other to their feet. Andraste picked up the fallen fan and tucked it in her sash. They both bowed to the audience on all sides.

Henry jumped off the table beside Rhinauld. Both men held out their hands to her to help her down. The music commenced. Andraste scanned the dining hall.

"Aldrich could not keep his eyes off you, even with the delegate from the Summit talking his ear off. The Queen assigned him as her escort," said Rhinauld.

"There is a buffet on the veranda," replied Henry. He gestured for Andraste to proceed. The two men followed behind her.

"You missed Vespasian and Hyacinth make their announcement," commented Rhinauld, "Have you decided to not gift them Boreas?"

"You always expect the worst of me," said Andraste.

They made their plates and stood against the balcony eating. Andraste spotted Aldrich and Moira. The Northern lady did look stunning in her Southern attire. Aldrich was introducing her to any Southern lord he came across. However, his eyes were locked on Andraste.

"Did you know the heir of the Lionden Empire has arrived?" asked Henry.

"Yes, that is why Aldrich is not escorting Andra," replied Rhinauld with a frown.

"Escorted by a total stranger?" Andraste questioned uncertainly.

"Like you could not take him down with your little pinky," snorted Rhinauld.

"We know nothing about him," cautioned Andraste.

"That is why we are by your side, Empress," replied Henry. He glanced to the sides and Andraste realized her Victorious were all present on the veranda. Andraste was not pleased. Her dissatisfaction intensified as Moira leaned into Aldrich's arm.

"I feel it would be prudent for me to introduce myself," said a voice behind them, "I am Samuel of the Lionden Empire."

Andraste, Rhinauld and Henry turned. The man that stood before them was appealing to them all. He had wavy blonde hair and green eyes. He was tall and muscular. On his bare chest, Andraste could see faint battle scars. Rhinauld hastily introduced them all to the prince. However, the prince stared at Andraste with undisguised interest; he scarcely acknowledged Rhinauld or Henry. Andraste took one of her fans from her sash and hid her face behind it.

"So you are the Empress who wants to give away her empire?" asked Samuel.

"Restore it to the rightful owners," reprimanded Andraste. She raised her beryl eyes above the fan to the Lionden prince.

"Who are?" inquired Samuel. His full attention was centered on her.

"The people," answered Andraste. She turned her attention to Rhinauld, but the prince was not to be ignored.

"What makes you think the Empire will survive after you abdicate?" questioned Samuel.

"Obviously, you do not know the people of my Empire," defended Andraste.

Samuel stood five feet away from her, but she felt like he was much closer. She did not like the way he watched her. She had his complete, undivided attention and she did not want it. She began to fan herself.

"No, offense is meant, Empress. I was only curious. My apologies," said Samuel. He inclined his head towards her in the slightest of bows.

"And how fares your Empire, Prince Samuel?" inquired Andraste.

"I cannot complain," replied Samuel.

"Really? We have heard rumors that your lands had fallen to a horde of undead soldiers," alleged Andraste. She closed the fan for emphasis.

"You must have spoken to a Parnesian. They are all liars. You should be more discerning. I have no such problem in my lands," replied Samuel. He turned his green eyes to Andraste in annoyance but he forced a smile. She raised her fan and began to fan herself again.

"Is that so?" asked Andraste. She looked to Rhinauld and Henry behind the fan. They did not believe Samuel's words either.

"As we have just met, I will not ask you to dance. Perhaps another time?" proposed Samuel.

"Perhaps," conceded Andraste. Samuel returned to the dancing hall.

"No charm whatsoever," commented Rhinauld. Henry agreed with him.

"Not a fan of the heir to the Lionden Empire?" asked Aldrich coming to their side.

"You seem relieved-- or is that because Moira is no longer with you?" asked Henry.

Aldrich did not respond. His gaze lingered on Andraste. He smiled as his eyes lingered on the pearl on her necklace.

"So you heard the conversation?" questioned Rhinauld.

"I believe the whole veranda heard. We may make a courtier of you yet. It was well done, Andra," said Aldrich lightly. Rhinauld and Henry exchanged glances as Aldrich used her familiar name.

"The fan was most useful," commented Rhinauld.

"Why do you think he is here?" asked Andraste. She kept her attention on Aldrich.

"I do not know his reasons. I got very little out of him either," answered Aldrich.

"Do you think he is looking for our weaknesses?" asked Andraste.

"Already in battle mode? Easy Empress, it is a festival," cautioned Rhinauld. They were beginning to attract more attention from the lords and ladies on the veranda.

"What is that dome in the distance?" asked Henry loudly. Aldrich turned to see where Henry pointed.

"That is the observatory," replied Aldrich.

"I would love to see it," said Andraste.

"Tonight?" asked Aldrich.

"Why would I want to see it during the day?" asked Andraste.

"My duty keeps me here," responded Aldrich. His eyes searched the crowd behind her. Andraste's smile faded. She turned to leave.

"Tomorrow night?" entreated Aldrich.

"It will be Rhiannon's wedding," replied Andraste.

"Of course," said Aldrich, "About earlier."

"It is your business," said Andraste.

"Am I not yours in every possible way? Gerlinde says those were your words to the ladies in the sewing chambers," stated Aldrich. His eyes sparkled as he watched her reaction.

"I may have spoken to soon," answered Andraste. She blushed deeply and it intensified under Rhinauld and Henry's study. She quickly hid her face behind her fan.

Moira had reappeared. She took Aldrich's arm in her own and said to Andraste, "I do enjoy these Southern customs, do not you?"

Andraste did not respond. She turned to leave and Rhinauld and Henry followed.

"She has always been so proud-" Moira was telling Aldrich.

Andraste hurried down the corridor. Rhinauld caught her by the wrist and held her.

"Do not flee. The night is still young," promised Rhinauld.

"I am tired and the next days will be long," responded Andraste. Rhinauld released her.

"Remember you are to brunch with the Queen and the ladies of the Island Kingdoms in the morning," said Rhinauld. He bowed to her and she returned to her chambers.

Although on time, Andraste found that she was the last of the ladies to arrive at the Queen's chambers. The Queen was hosting the bridal party's brunch on her personal veranda. It was truly lovely with a view of the sea and hundreds of roses climbing the railing. The ladies were eating decadent pastries and sipping on sparkling wine. Rhiannon was introducing the Queen, Marcella, Decima and Moira to a game that they had played as girls.

"It is a flirting game of sorts. A lady of the Island Kingdoms may not declare her feelings until a lord has made a proposal," explained Shannon.

"So her friend might ask her: if you were Rhinauld's wife, how many children would you have?" inquired Rhiannon to Shannon.

"At least five," responded Shannon.

"And what if you were Rhinauld's wife?" Rhiannon turned to Andraste.

"One, out of duty," replied Andraste and the ladies laughed. Andraste turned on Rhiannon, "And how many children would you have, if you were Brion's wife?"

"As many as the gods will," blushed Rhiannon.

"A good answer," approved the Queen.

"What if you were Prince Samuel's wife?" asked Shannon.

"Six," said Moira. The ladies laughed. Shannon turned to Andraste.

"None," swore Andraste.

"But he is so handsome!" exclaimed Rhiannon.

"He looked at me like I was a sheep and he a wolf," explained Andraste.

"I had the same feeling," agreed Decima.

"But at least he looked at you," commented Moira.

"And if you were Prince Aldrich's wife?" inquired Rhiannon.

"Seven. They say he is a great warrior," responded Shannon.

"Nine," said Moira.

"Thirteen," said Andraste.

"Spoken like women who have never had to bear a child," commented Marcella.

"Thirteen!" exclaimed the Queen, "That is a definite answer. Why so high a number?"

"Thirteen is the largest family from one mother that I have ever encountered, and if we are judging by his feats as a warrior. . ." expounded Andraste.

"Then why did you allot only one to Rhinauld?" cried Rhiannon.

"Because when he looks at me, I am an ostrich and he is an elephant," answered Andraste. All of the ladies laughed heartily.

"Besides what would I do with a husband who is prettier than I am? Dress him up in my gowns?" asked Andraste.

"It has been done before," replied Rhiannon. The ladies roared with laughter.

"But thirteen, Empress? I have my hands full with three children," laughed Marcella.

"I would have more," said a voice from the veranda below.

"Gregor, if you bare the next ones yourself, I am for it," Marcella answered her husband. There was a chorus of male laughter from the veranda below.

"Whose rooms are below?" asked Rhiannon with a blush.

"My son's," answered the Queen with a twinkle in her eye.

"Do you think they heard our conversation?" inquired Rhiannon.

"Yes, sweet sister, and you made your future husband very proud of your answers," replied Rhinauld, "But, Empress, you have wounded me."

Shannon went to the edge of the balcony and shook a pastry at the men below. She chastised them, "Serves you right. None of you had the decency to let us know you were listening."

"You are right, my lady. A hundred apologies, but as for the Empress, I offer no condolences," said Rhinauld. He bowed to the offended lady.

"So easily offended, my brother?" asked Rhiannon. Rhinauld laughed at his sister.

"And if I was your wife, Lord of the Salt Islands, how many children would we have?" teased Shannon.

"I am good with five," answered Rhinauld. He called into the rooms below.

"And if you were my wife?" asked Felix.

"As many as the gods will," replied Shannon. She blushed and hid behind Rhiannon's shoulder. Felix moved so that he could follow her progress.

"Aldrich, if you were the Empress' consort, how many children would you have?" questioned Rhinauld.

"He will say fourteen to outdo, Andraste," remarked Marcella.

"He will say seven like our own family," predicted the Queen.

"No, he will say such things are not talked about," said Andraste. They waited. Rhinauld repeated his question to the approaching prince.

"Such things are not talked about," replied Aldrich. The ladies dissolved into a chorus of laughter.

"We should have taken bets," lamented Andraste.

"Really! An Empress taking bets," disapproved the Queen.

"Just like a Queen telling dirty jokes," retorted Andraste. The Queen laughed. They quieted as they heard Rhinauld say to Aldrich, "That is a shame. When Andraste was asked the same question, she replied thirteen."

"Thirteen?" repeated Aldrich. And then, "Are they above us?"

"Yes," said Gregor. Aldrich must have come out onto his own veranda for they heard him clearly call, "Good morning, ladies."

The ladies in turn approached the railing. Rhiannon raised her glass returned the greeting, "Good morning, Aldrich."

"Are you all well?" asked Aldrich.

"Yes, thank you. Are we not all well, Andra?" asked Rhiannon. Andraste was obligated to step forward.

"Yes, sister," agreed Andraste. She raised her glass to Aldrich in greeting.

"Thirteen?" questioned Aldrich.

"Out of context that does seem a little high," said Andraste thoughtfully. She played with her necklace. The ladies giggled.

"What was the context?" inquired Aldrich. His eyes went to the pearl.

"Your eavesdroppers will have to fill you in. We must help Rhiannon prepare for the wedding," answered Andraste. She stepped out of sight.

"We have time–" started Rhiannon.

"Do you want Brion to see you?" asked Andraste.

Rhiannon stepped away quickly from the railing. The ladies retreated indoors so they could begin preparing Rhiannon for the wedding. There was a knock on the door and a page entered. He whispered something into the Queen's ear.

"The last two delegates have arrived," announced the Queen after the page had left.

"Who are they?" asked Decima.

"Chief Orthos representing the Hill tribes in the West, and Lady Fausta, representing the Ice Palace," answered the Queen.

Rhiannon's face fell. She had not been in the same room as her mother since she was toddler. However, years of court life had led Rhiannon to recover quickly and she forced a smile.

"Will your voyage depart immediately?" Marcella asked Andraste. Her expedition had now become common knowledge throughout the court. Rhiannon's eyes glistened as she looked to Andraste for her response.

"I will wait to be released by the Assembly. It will take a week to make the preparations for the voyage, but let us not dwell on it. This is Rhiannon and Brion's day," said Andraste. She squeezed Rhiannon's hand. The ladies returned their full attention to preparing Rhiannon and keeping her in smiles.

Chapter Twenty-Two

The wedding ceremony had no sooner concluded, and Andraste left Rhiannon and Brion, when Prince Samuel approached her. Andraste took a second look at him. She had to admit he was the most handsome man she had ever seen.

"Empress, would you honor me with a dance?" invited Samuel.

Andraste could not think of an excuse without insulting the Lionden Empire. He offered his hand to her in the Northern fashion, and she placed her own hand lightly on top of his. He led her to the dance floor.

"You know our dances well," said Andraste as they started dancing. It was like dancing with her dance instructor. The prince's movements were flawless.

"Thank you," replied the prince. He expertly twirled her.

"I enjoyed watching your Northern dance last night," the prince admitted.

"Thank you," responded Andraste.

They were nearer the musicians, so she could no longer hear what he said. Samuel relented on his attempts to make conversation.

Aldrich, Rhinauld, and Henry were watching her closely from one of the feast tables. Lady Moira sat a few seats down on the opposite side of the table with Marcella and Decima. Lady Moira said:

"No, we do not make declarations of love like you Southerners do. You are always describing what you love. You say it to one another so frequently that I wonder if there is any meaning left in the word.

In the North, we have a pledge that must be initiated by a woman with her full will and consent. The words are: 'Your worries are my worries. Your battles are my battles. I will stand by you for all of my days. I will witness your life. I will look to you and follow. You will never be alone, for I will be at your side. Together we will forever be.' Then the man would have a response, but I do not recall the exact words."

"What was that pledge?" Aldrich asked to Rhinauld.

Rhinauld repeated it. Aldrich put his face in his hands in an uncharacteristic lack of discomposure.

"Andraste said it to you?" questioned Rhinauld. His eyes twinkled.

"Yes, when we first returned to the Southern lands, but it was when she offered to be my Muse. I thought she wanted to be my mistress, so I objected," responded Aldrich.

"And she refused your offer of marriage," concluded Rhinauld.

"Marriage is not a solid construct in the North. In many places, the exchange of those pledges is enough to bind a couple for life. It is not like the South where you have the priest hierarchy and the lavish ceremonies. The pledge serves as the recognition of a voluntary commitment between a man and a woman," commented Henry.

"All this time I thought that she had refused me, and she proposed to me!" sighed Aldrich.

"It is Andraste. She would propose to a man," commented Henry.

Aldrich was watching Andraste dance with the Lionden prince. He tensed as Samuel's hand brushed against Andraste's waist as he turned her.

"Do not worry, she cannot stand him," said Rhinauld.

"How do you tell?" asked Aldrich.

"She has her court face on. She is composed. She has not smiled or laughed once. She loves to laugh. I wager if he was not the heir to the Lionden Empire, she would not be anywhere near him," alleged Rhinauld.

"But he is the heir to the Lionden Empire," pointed out Henry.

Aldrich looked miserable. The music had stopped. Samuel bowed slightly. Andraste curtsied just as slightly.

"I understand it would be bad form for me to dance with you again this evening. Perhaps tomorrow?" invited Samuel.

"Perhaps," answered Andraste.

He kissed the top of her hand before he released it.

"Your dogs watch you closely," commented Samuel as his eyes glanced to Rhinauld, Henry, and Aldrich.

"My men are fiercely protective," responded Andraste. Her eyes flashed.

"Two are your foster brothers, yes? And the prince of the Southern lands?" questioned Samuel.

"He is not my foster brother," replied Andraste.

"And he is what to you?" asked Samuel.

"That is a bold question," responded Andraste.

"So then no understanding exists between you?" prodded Samuel.

Andraste did not respond. She left Samuel on the dance floor. Samuel rejoined his own people. She felt his eyes follow her across the hall. She quickened her pace.

"See, my Empress approaches like an imminent storm. Definitely not a woman in love," Rhinauld commented to Aldrich.

"Are you ill?" Andraste asked when she reached them.

"The prince lost a fierce gamble, but I am sure he will rectify his loss," responded Henry.

"What did you lose? I could win it back," offered Andraste. Aldrich flushed crimson.

"What do you think of the Lionden prince?" asked Rhinauld.

"Impertinent, smug, narcissistic," replied Andraste.

"Did he offend you?" asked Henry. His joking was aside.

"He wanted to know if I had an existing understanding with anyone," responded Andraste.

"Such things are not talked about in the North or East," Rhinauld said to Aldrich, "Only once an understanding is reached is it announced."

"I may have done something wrong," Andraste said quietly. She lowered her eyes.

"Brace yourself," Rhinauld advised Aldrich and Henry.

"I did not confirm or deny I had an understanding with you. I thought he would leave me alone if he thought-" Andraste started. Aldrich rose.

"If it keeps his hands off you, I am all for it. In fact, let us propel this charade," said Aldrich. He put a hand on her waist and pulled her to him.

He commanded, "Dance with me."

She lowered her eyes. Aldrich led her to the dance floor and pulled her close as they danced to a slow waltz. She heard whispers from the feasting tables. She ignored them. She smiled her most winning smile at Aldrich, but he was not appeased.

"Still think he means war?" asked Aldrich. His eyes were dark and angry. The music had resumed.

"I have no clue," answered Andraste, "Please do not be angry with me. It is Rhiannon's special day. Can we not enjoy it? I will clarify to the Lionden heir-"

"I am not angry with you," interrupted Aldrich. He stared angrily at the direction of the Lionden delegation.

"Are you going to show me the observatory?" Andraste asked instead.

"Yes," said Aldrich. His spirits seemed to improve, "When do you want to go?"

"After this dance," prompted Andraste, "We will have to be quick to make our escape."

Aldrich was already maneuvering them to the far entrance. As the music stopped, they stepped onto the veranda and disappeared into the night. Aldrich practically pulled her down the veranda steps and on to the beach. Andraste lost her footing in the sand, but Aldrich steadied her. He wrapped her arm protectively in his. However, he did not speak to her until they reached the deserted observatory.

"Do you mean to leave in a week?" questioned Aldrich.

"So you have spoken to Marcella," answered Andraste.

Aldrich did not reply.

"Yes, I will finally be free," confirmed Andraste.

Aldrich seemed conflicted.

"What is it?" Andraste asked in concern. She put her second hand on his arm and looked up to him expectantly.

"What troubles you? Cannot a soldier tell another soldier his concerns?" asked Andraste. Aldrich studied her for a moment.

"I swore I would not ask again. I know how much your freedom means to you. I know how much you have sacrificed and this expedition is your dream. But I cannot let you go without knowing. Not after your brothers explained the significance of the pledge you made to me when you first came to the Southern lands," said Aldrich.

Andraste froze. Aldrich felt her tension and released her arm.

"I cannot go through this life without you. I love you. I want to be the father of all thirteen of your hypothetical children. I do not want to be a day without you ever again. I feel as though I am going mad when I am allowed only one hour with you a day. I would not survive years without you. I have grown accustomed to your ways, your face. Your face is my favorite in the entire world. I miss waking and seeing your face in the morning. If you cannot love, I will accept that. I do not know the words to the Northern pledge, but tell me what you want me to say and I will say it. Whatever you want, whatever you need, I will provide it. Just be mine, and I will be yours," stated Aldrich.

Andraste thought about all of the things that she could have said. Her heart was racing and her thoughts flew around in her head. Due to her silence, Aldrich took a step back from her.

Instead of speaking, she put a hand to his face, and then pulled him down to her. She kissed him deeply. At first he was surprised, but then his arms wrapped around her. He was kissing her back. Twice he tried to withdraw and speak, and twice she drew him back to her. She was pinned against the wall by his body. It was almost more happiness then she could bear. She released him.

"I will marry you. Now that our battle is won, and I understand how much marriage means to you," replied Andraste, "And for the honor of our thirteen hypothetical children."

Aldrich reached for her again and held her. He kissed her gently on her forehead.

"You can name the date. If you want to complete the expedition first-" started Aldrich.

"Tomorrow," interrupted Andraste. She pressed herself into him.

"So soon?" asked Aldrich with a grin.

"I will be released from the Empire tomorrow morning by the Assembly, so I will be free to marry you before dinner," answered Andraste.

Aldrich laughed softly.

"Well if your schedule will permit it," replied Aldrich. Andraste flushed but he pulled her to him hard, "I am teasing. I am as eager as you.'

Andraste removed herself from him and moved towards the telescope. It took her a moment to regain her composure. Aldrich followed her movements a few steps behind.

"Are you sure you will not go with me on the expedition-" started Andraste.

"Of course, I will go with you! I will not permit my beautiful wife to leave me behind," said Aldrich, "My mother did say that after she and my father married, they traveled the Empire for two years while the Dowager Queen reigned."

"Aldrich!" cried Andraste. She nearly tackled him with the force of her kisses.

"Are you sure you do not want to wait for Sveinbiorn to awaken?" asked Aldrich.

"We do not know when that will be," replied Andraste sadly. She looked up at Aldrich, "Are you looking for ways to not marry me?"

"Of course not, but I want you to be happy. I know how much your brother means to you," said Aldrich.

Andraste stood on her tiptoes that she could gently kiss the prince. He brushed a piece of hair behind her ear and rested his hand on the curve of her cheek.

"We should return to the festival," relented Aldrich. However, he did not release her.

"Uh-huh," agreed Andraste, not moving.

"It is but one more evening," promised Aldrich.

He released her and straightened his own clothing. The action reminded Andraste to do the same. She looked up and found him watching her. He smiled at her and offered her his arm. Andraste took it, but she tucked her fan into his belt.

"So then you officially accept my offer?" asked Aldrich. Andraste raised herself to her tiptoes to kiss him.

"Andra," warned Aldrich. She withdrew with a smile.

Aldrich removed his war fan and offered it to her. She tucked in the back of her sash. As she returned her hand forward, Aldrich caught it and kissed it. They returned arm in arm to the dining hall. Andraste did not dance with any other that night.

Andraste was the first to enter the Chamber of Justice in the morning. Decima was the second. She was still rubbing the sleep out of her eyes. She looked at Andraste in surprise. Aldrich was the third to enter. Decima shot a glance from one to the other.

"Good morning," said Andraste.

"Good morning, Empress," greeted Aldrich.

Aldrich stopped by her chair. Kasimir called to him from across the room, and Aldrich looked away from her briefly.

"My mother and your uncle expect us for lunch on her veranda. Our siblings and select friends will be joining us as well," said Aldrich.

"I look forward to it," responded Andraste.

Aldrich bowed to her and returned to the Southern section to address Kasimir.

Andraste sat in agony as she waited for all of the delegates to file in. She tapped her fingers impatiently on her chair. She saw that the Queen had joined Aldrich at his desk. There were a large number of non-delegates present, including Prince Samuel of the Lionden Empire. He scrutinized her with his gaze. Andraste turned her attention back to Aldrich, who was watching her carefully.

The last delegate had finally arrived.

"If you would all take your seats," ordered Decima.

Decima waited long enough for the delegates to do so and for the chatter to subside.

"As all of the delegates have been named, sworn in, and are now present, we have come this morning to fulfill the edict of Empress Andraste Eldgrimson Valerianus. As the Assembly is fully assembled and the Republic instituted, it is now time to release the Empress," announced Decima. She turned to Andraste. Andraste rose.

"Is this still your wish, Empress?" inquired Decima.

"It is," confirmed Andraste.

"Do you release all power and rights to the title?" questioned Decima.

"I do," affirmed Andraste. There was a murmur of disbelief circling through the delegates.

"Then this Assembly does hereby relieve you of your position. We do declare that from this day forth there will never be another Emperor and Empress to rule this Republic. All governance shall be through the vote and consensus of this Assembly," declared Decima.

Decima waited for the chatter to subside in the Assembly. When silence had been resumed, she surveyed all of the delegates.

"We shall now vote as to the acceptance of this transfer of power. Please raise your right hand if you are in agreement," said Decima.

Andraste looked around the room as hands slowly raised.

"Good, then this matter is concluded. Paramerion, you are welcome to leave," said Decima. She offered her hand to Andraste in parting and Andraste took it.

Andraste cast a sideways look to Aldrich as she passed. The delegates were still standing for her. Andraste hurried out of the Chambers of Justice. The Queen followed her out of the Assembly. Andraste heard the doors closed behind her, and she inhaled deeply. The Queen offered her arm to Andraste, and they walked together as the Southern ladies did.

"It is quite a day for you. I have no objection to my son marrying you. No one could stop either of you. However, I want you to both be happy. Do you not want to wait for a full ceremony like Brion and Rhiannon?" asked the Queen.

"I am tired of being the center of attention. I just wish to marry Aldrich as soon as possible," replied Andraste.

"Marcella and Gregor were the same way. They were also married on my veranda with only a few friends and relatives," said the Queen. She smiled at Andraste.

"You realize that when you marry my son, you will also become queen," informed the Queen.

"Aldrich had mentioned it. However, we still plan on proceeding with the expedition for at least a year," said Andraste hesitantly.

"Aldrich had mentioned that to me as well. He says that you wish for me to rule in his absence. Is this true?" asked the Queen.

"Yes," confirmed Andraste.

"Then it will be so until you return," said the Queen. The Queen looked out across the sea and then turned her sapphire eyes to Andraste, "Now that is settled. Perhaps a drink while we wait for the others to join us?"

The Queen and Andraste were sipping sparkling wine as they heard voices coming down the hall. They paused in their conversation. Aldrich joined her side immediately and raised her hand to his lips. His smile was contagious. She blushed and studied her toes.

"We have an announcement," said the Queen to her assembled guests. The chatter dissipated.

"Aldrich and Andraste have announced their engagement, and their decision to be married this day," proclaimed the Queen. The sounds of approval were loud and exclamations numerous.

"Any reason for the haste?" asked Felix. Laelius elbowed him soundly in the ribs.

"No," answered Aldrich. The King crossed the veranda in a rapid pace.

"One question before we continue," said the King, "Have either of you been drinking? Do you enter this decision with coherent thought and commitment?"

"Who cares? My court cannot take much more of their courtship," sighed the Queen.

"I enter into this union with all of my heart and consent," answered Andraste.

"As do I," said Aldrich. He placed his arm around her waist.

The King of the Island Kingdoms seemed pacified.

"This is the ring your father gave me to on our wedding day," said the Queen. She produced a woven golden band from her finger. She gave it to her son.

"Place it on Andraste's finger," directed the King. Aldrich did so.

"Aldrich, do you take this woman to be your wife?" asked the King.

"I do," stated Aldrich with pride. He put the ring on her finger.

The King took a gold ring off his own hand and presented it to Andraste, and he said, "Place this ring on Aldrich's finger."

Andraste did so. Aldrich held her hands in his.

"Andraste, do you take this man to be your husband?" asked the King.

"I do," declared Andraste.

"Then before the gods may you be forever joined and never parted. May you respect, protect, and care for each other for all of your days. There is no bond more sacred then that between husband and wife. By your own oaths and witnesses may you be bound by the promises you have made. Aldrich, you may kiss your wife," said the King gravely.

Aldrich kissed her gently to cheering and congratulations.

"Is that all?" asked the Queen, "My ceremony lasted two hours."

"If you wanted a priest, you should have asked a priest," alleged the King.

"Really, Aelius!" reprimanded the Queen. She directed her guests to the veranda where a feast had been laid out before them. All ate soundly, drank deeply, and proceeded to be merry. Aldrich waited the appropriate amount of time before rising. He offered his arm to Andraste and pulled her to her feet.

"We will retire," said Aldrich.

Andraste blushed deeply, but made no protest.

"Alright, my dears," replied the Queen.

She kissed her son on his cheek and then kissed Andraste as well. Andraste played with the ring on her finger. Aldrich took her hand and kissed her ring. He wrapped her arm in his and wordlessly led her to his chambers. Once they reached the door to his chamber, he picked her up in his arms and carried her across the threshold. He kicked the door to his bedroom behind him. He laid her gently on the bed.

"What are you thinking?" asked Andraste.

"I am going to take you every way I can think of, and then do it again," promised Aldrich as he kissed her neck.

"Aldrich!" cried Andraste.

"I can say such things to my wife," replied Aldrich, and he silenced her protest with his kiss.

"Good morning," Aldrich said as Andraste opened her eyes.

Aldrich had her wrapped in his arms. Their legs were entangled.

"Have you been watching me for long?" Andraste asked. He nuzzled her neck.

There was a knock on his door.

"Come back in an hour," ordered Aldrich. He lifted the sheet to look at her and he yelled, "Come back in two hours."

"You are needed at the Assembly. It will meet at noon," said the voice. It was not one Andraste recognized.

"Fine," answered Aldrich. However, he had not taken his eyes off Andraste. He said lazily, "We have a little time then."

"My husband is insatiable," said Andraste. She blushed as she thought of the previous night's activities.

"My Queen?" he paused as he kissed her, "Have you seen my wife?"

He looked down at her in admiration and kissed her again. They whiled away the next few hours in pleasurable exchanges and whispered sweet nothings.

"Aldrich," Andraste whispered in his ear, pulling him back to her.

"You will be the end of me," groaned Aldrich.

The clock on the mantle chimed the hour. A knock sounded on the door again.

"I know," called Aldrich. He kissed Andraste and got out of bed.

Andraste wrapped a blanket around herself. She went into the bath chamber and waded into the waters. She submerged herself in the waters. Aldrich shortly joined her and she nestled in to him.

"We do not have time," said Aldrich. However, his eyes studied her in appreciation, nor did he remove himself from her.

"My clothes are in the other chambers," said Andraste.

"You do not need any," said Aldrich.

He kissed her nose. She giggled in response. He got out of the pool, and water dripped off his muscles to Andraste's appreciative gaze.

"My Queen, are you ogling me?" asked Aldrich.

Andraste blushed and looked away quickly. Aldrich laughed and wrapped a towel around his waist. She heard him go into the bedroom and the outer chamber. Andraste relaxed in the pool.

Aldrich remerged completely dressed. Andraste felt self-conscious. She went into the deeper part of the pool so that only her head emerged. Aldrich smiled at her and stood at the edge of the pool with a fresh towel in his hand.

"You will have to get out sometime," said Aldrich.

"Just leave it," responded Andraste.

Aldrich laughed but obliged her. He went back into his chamber. Andraste exited the bath and dried herself off. She wrapped the towel around herself. She opened Aldrich's closet and took out one of his shirts. She put it over her head. It was practically a dress on her. As Andraste walked into the bedchamber, she heard Aldrich speaking with someone in the outer chambers. Aldrich returned to tell her, "The Assembly is waiting on me. I will return as soon as I can."

He eyed her in his shirt and grinned. He pulled her to him and kissed her.

"Do you want to attend the Assembly with me?" invited Aldrich.

"I will be waiting here," responded Andraste. Aldrich left reluctantly.

Andraste waited a moment before poking her head out of the bed-chamber to make sure she was alone. Aldrich had shut the front door behind him. Andraste walked around his sitting room and then went into his study.

Aldrich had many fine books that interested her. She took a dusty volume from the shelf and went to sit on his veranda. Unlike her rooms and the Queen's, Aldrich's veranda was covered. Andraste saw that breakfast platters had been set out for them with the Southern sparkling wine.

Andraste poured herself a glass and lounged in one of the chairs. It was bitter then the other wines she had tasted. She ate a bit of pastry. It tasted a little strange to her. She put it down and tried another. It also seemed off. She was suddenly overwhelmed with exhaustion and decided to take a nap on one of the lounge chairs.

Andraste woke to the sound of seagulls, and the tossing of waves against the side of boat. She was in a dingy state room on a musty, decrepit sofa. She was reminded of waking on the boat after she had been cursed. Andraste felt a sinking feeling in her stomach. It worsened as she did not see her Ruin sword. Had Aldrich surprised her? Were they leaving on their expedition? However, she was not dressed in proper attire. She was still only wearing Aldrich's shirt. Surely he would not have brought her somewhere in such a state?

She went to the door and looked out through the window. It was the strangest deck she had ever seen. It was not the style of the Northern ships or the Island Kingdoms as she was used to. The sails were triangular opposed to the dragon wings of the Northern Ships, nor were they full and coarse like the Island Kingdoms ships. The ship design was totally foreign to her.

She did not see a soul on deck. As she opened the door and stepped out onto the deck, she saw a lone, tall, cloaked figure at the helm. His broad shoulders were covered by a velvet cloak. His face was concealed by a hood.

Andraste climbed the stairs. The wind was strong and unforgiving. She paused to look out over the gray and stormy sea. The Southern capitol was nowhere in sight. She could not see land in any direction.

She approached the man at the helm.

"Aldrich?" asked Andraste.

The man turned to her. He surveyed her with emerald, compassionless eyes. He was not her husband. It was Samuel of the Lionden Empire.

CPSIA information can be obtained
at www.ICGtesting.com
Printed in the USA
FFOW02n2032010715
14824FF

9 781478 759416